SHORT STORIES
for Students

Advisors

Erik France: Adjunct Instructor of English, Macomb Community College, Warren, Michigan. B.A. and M.S.L.S. from University of North Carolina, Chapel Hill; Ph.D. from Temple University.

Kate Hamill: Grade 12 English Teacher, Catonsville High School, Catonsville, Maryland.

Joseph McGeary: English Teacher, Germantown Friends School, Philadelphia, Pennsylvania. Ph.D. in English from Duke University.

Timothy Showalter: English Department Chair, Franklin High School, Reisterstown, Maryland. Certified teacher by the Maryland State Department of Education. Member of the National Council of Teachers of English.

Amy Spade Silverman: English Department Chair, Kehillah Jewish High School, Palo Alto, California. Member of National Council of Teachers of English (NCTE), Teachers and Writers, and NCTE Opinion Panel. Exam Reader, Advanced Placement Literature and Composition. Poet, published in *North American Review, Nimrod,* and *Michigan Quarterly Review,* among other publications.

Jody Stefansson: Director of Boswell Library and Study Center and Upper School Learning Specialist, Polytechnic School, Pasadena, California. Board member, Children's Literature Council of Southern California. Member of American Library Association, Association of Independent School Librarians, and Association of Educational Therapists.

Laura Jean Waters: Certified School Library Media Specialist, Wilton High School, Wilton, Connecticut. B.A. from Fordham University; M.A. from Fairfield University.

SHORT STORIES *for Students*

Presenting Analysis, Context, and Criticism on
Commonly Studied Short Stories

VOLUME 29

Sara Constantakis, Project Editor

Foreword by Thomas E. Barden

GALE
CENGAGE Learning

Detroit • New York • San Francisco • New Haven, Conn • Waterville, Maine • London

Short Stories for Students, Volume 29

Project Editor: Sara Constantakis

Rights Acquisition and Management: Jermaine Bobbitt, Sari Gordon, Tracie Richardson, Robyn Young

Composition: Evi Abou-El-Seoud

Manufacturing: Drew Kalasky

Imaging: John Watkins

Product Design: Pamela A. E. Galbreath, Jennifer Wahi

Content Conversion: Katrina Coach

Product Manager: Meggin Condino

© 2010 Gale, Cengage Learning

ALL RIGHTS RESERVED. No part of this work covered by the copyright herein may be reproduced, transmitted, stored, or used in any form or by any means graphic, electronic, or mechanical, including but not limited to photocopying, recording, scanning, digitizing, taping, Web distribution, information networks, or information storage and retrieval systems, except as permitted under Section 107 or 108 of the 1976 United States Copyright Act, without the prior written permission of the publisher.

Since this page cannot legibly accommodate all copyright notices, the acknowledgments constitute an extension of the copyright notice.

For product information and technology assistance, contact us at
Gale Customer Support, 1-800-877-4253.
For permission to use material from this text or product,
submit all requests online at www.cengage.com/permissions.
Further permissions questions can be emailed to
permissionrequest@cengage.com

While every effort has been made to ensure the reliability of the information presented in this publication, Gale, a part of Cengage Learning, does not guarantee the accuracy of the data contained herein. Gale accepts no payment for listing; and inclusion in the publication of any organization, agency, institution, publication, service, or individual does not imply endorsement of the editors or publisher. Errors brought to the attention of the publisher and verified to the satisfaction of the publisher will be corrected in future editions.

Gale
27500 Drake Rd.
Farmington Hills, MI, 48331-3535

ISBN-13: 978-1-4144-4212-9
ISBN-10: 1-4144-4212-2

ISSN 1092-7735

This title is also available as an e-book.
ISBN-13: 978-1-4144-4960-9
ISBN-10: 1-4144-4960-7
Contact your Gale, a part of Cengage Learning sales representative for ordering information.

Printed in the United States of America
1 2 3 4 5 6 7 12 14 13 11 10

Table of Contents

ADVISORS ii

WHY STUDY LITERATURE AT ALL?
(by Thomas E. Barden) ix

INTRODUCTION xi

LITERARY CHRONOLOGY xv

ACKNOWLEDGMENTS xvii

CONTRIBUTORS xix

AUNTY MISERY *(by Judith Ortiz Cofer)* . . . 1
   Author Biography 2
   Plot Summary. 2
   Characters 3
   Themes 5
   Style 7
   Historical Context 8
   Critical Overview. 9
   Criticism. 10
   Sources 21
   Further Reading 21

B. WORDSWORTH *(by V. S. Naipaul)* . . . 22
   Author Biography 23
   Plot Summary. 24
   Characters 24
   Themes 25
   Style 27

Table of Contents

  Historical Context 28
  Critical Overview 30
  Criticism 31
  Sources 42
  Further Reading 42

THE CENSORS *(by Luisa Valenzuela)* 44
  Author Biography 45
  Plot Summary 45
  Characters 46
  Themes 47
  Style 50
  Historical Context 50
  Critical Overview 53
  Criticism 53
  Sources 66
  Further Reading 66

CONTENTS OF THE DEAD MAN'S POCKET
(by Jack Finney) 67
  Author Biography 68
  Plot Summary 69
  Characters 70
  Themes 71
  Style 73
  Historical Context 74
  Critical Overview 75
  Criticism 76
  Sources 81
  Further Reading 81

DOG STAR *(by Arthur C. Clarke)* 82
  Author Biography 83
  Plot Summary 83
  Characters 85
  Themes 87
  Style 89
  Historical Context 90
  Critical Overview 91
  Criticism 93
  Sources 99
  Further Reading 100

THE DOLL'S HOUSE *(by Katherine Mansfield)* 101
  Author Biography 102
  Plot Summary 102
  Characters 104
  Themes 106
  Style 108
  Historical Context 109
  Critical Overview 110
  Criticism 111
  Sources 123
  Further Reading 123

FORTY-FIVE A MONTH *(by R. K. Narayan)* . 124
  Author Biography 125
  Plot Summary 125
  Characters 126
  Themes 127
  Style 130
  Historical Context 131
  Critical Overview 132
  Criticism 133
  Sources 144
  Further Reading 145

THE GRASSHOPPER AND THE BELL CRICKET
(by Yasunari Kawabata) 146
  Author Biography 147
  Plot Summary 149
  Characters 150
  Themes 150
  Style 151
  Historical Context 153
  Critical Overview 155
  Criticism 156
  Sources 169
  Further Reading 170

HA'PENNY *(by Alan Paton)* 171
  Author Biography 172
  Plot Summary 172
  Characters 174
  Themes 176
  Style 177
  Historical Context 178
  Critical Overview 180
  Criticism 181
  Sources 186
  Further Reading 186

THE PIT AND THE PENDULUM
(by Edgar Allan Poe) 188
  Author Biography 189
  Plot Summary 189
  Characters 192
  Themes 192
  Style 194
  Historical Context 196
  Critical Overview 197
  Criticism 199
  Sources 209
  Further Reading 210

A PROBLEM *(by Anton Chekhov)* 211
  Author Biography 212
  Plot Summary 213
  Characters 214

Themes	216
Style	217
Historical Context	218
Critical Overview.	219
Criticism.	220
Sources	229
Further Reading	229

SUZY AND LEAH *(by Jane Yolen)* 230
- Author Biography 231
- Plot Summary. 231
- Characters 233
- Themes 234
- Style 237
- Historical Context 237
- Critical Overview. 239
- Criticism. 240
- Sources 252
- Further Reading 252

THANK YOU, MA'M *(by Langston Hughes)*. . 253
- Author Biography 254
- Plot Summary. 255
- Characters 256
- Themes 257
- Style 259
- Historical Context 260
- Critical Overview. 262
- Criticism. 263
- Sources 270
- Further Reading 271

WHERE HAVE YOU GONE CHARMING BILLY?
(by Tim O'Brien). 272
- Author Biography 273
- Plot Summary. 274
- Characters 274
- Themes 275
- Style 277
- Historical Context 279
- Critical Overview. 281
- Criticism. 281
- Sources 295
- Further Reading 295

GLOSSARY OF LITERARY TERMS. . . . 297

CUMULATIVE AUTHOR/TITLE INDEX . . 309

CUMULATIVE NATIONALITY/ETHNICITY INDEX. 319

SUBJECT/THEME INDEX 327

Why Study Literature At All?

Short Stories for Students is designed to provide readers with information and discussion about a wide range of important contemporary and historical works of short fiction, and it does that job very well. However, I want to use this guest foreword to address a question that it does *not* take up. It is a fundamental question that is often ignored in high school and college English classes as well as research texts, and one that causes frustration among students at all levels, namely why study literature at all? Isn't it enough to read a story, enjoy it, and go about one's business? My answer (to be expected from a literary professional, I suppose) is no. It is not enough. It is a start; but it is not enough. Here's why.

First, literature is the only part of the educational curriculum that deals directly with the actual world of lived experience. The philosopher Edmund Husserl used the apt German term *die Lebenswelt*, "the living world," to denote this realm. All the other content areas of the modern American educational system avoid the subjective, present reality of everyday life. Science (both the natural and the social varieties) objectifies, the fine arts create and/or perform, history reconstructs. Only literary study persists in posing those questions we all asked before our schooling taught us to give up on them. Only literature gives credibility to personal perceptions, feelings, dreams, and the "stream of consciousness" that is our inner voice. Literature wonders about infinity, wonders why God permits evil, wonders what will happen to us after we die. Literature admits that we get our hearts broken, that people sometimes cheat and get away with it, that the world is a strange and probably incomprehensible place. Literature, in other words, takes on all the big and small issues of what it means to be human. So my first answer is that of the humanist we should read literature and study it and take it seriously because it enriches us as human beings. We develop our moral imagination, our capacity to sympathize with other people, and our ability to understand our existence through the experience of fiction.

My second answer is more practical. By studying literature we can learn how to explore and analyze texts. Fiction may be about *die Lebenswelt*, but it is a construct of words put together in a certain order by an artist using the medium of language. By examining and studying those constructions, we can learn about language as a medium. We can become more sophisticated about word associations and connotations, about the manipulation of symbols, and about style and atmosphere. We can grasp how ambiguous language is and how important context and texture is to meaning. In our first encounter with a work of literature, of course, we are not supposed to catch all of these things. We are spellbound, just as the writer wanted us to be. It is as serious students of the writer's art that we begin to see how the tricks are done.

Seeing the tricks, which is another way of saying "developing analytical and close reading skills," is important above and beyond its intrinsic literary educational value. These skills transfer to other fields and enhance critical thinking of any kind. Understanding how language is used to construct texts is powerful knowledge. It makes engineers better problem solvers, lawyers better advocates and courtroom practitioners, politicians better rhetoricians, marketing and advertising agents better sellers, and citizens more aware consumers as well as better participants in democracy. This last point is especially important, because rhetorical skill works both ways when we learn how language is manipulated in the making of texts the result is that we become less susceptible when language is used to manipulate us.

My third reason is related to the second. When we begin to see literature as created artifacts of language, we become more sensitive to good writing in general. We get a stronger sense of the importance of individual words, even the sounds of words and word combinations. We begin to understand Mark Twain's delicious proverb "The difference between the right word and the almost right word is the difference between lightning and a lightning bug." Getting beyond the "enjoyment only" stage of literature gets us closer to becoming makers of word art ourselves. I am not saying that studying fiction will turn every student into a Faulkner or a Shakespeare. But it will make us more adaptable and effective writers, even if our art form ends up being the office memo or the corporate annual report.

Studying short stories, then, can help students become better readers, better writers, and even better human beings. But I want to close with a warning. If your study and exploration of the craft, history, context, symbolism, or anything else about a story starts to rob it of the magic you felt when you first read it, it is time to stop. Take a break, study another subject, shoot some hoops, or go for a run. Love of reading is too important to be ruined by school. The early twentieth century writer Willa Cather, in her novel *My Antonia*, has her narrator Jack Burden tell a story that he and Antonia heard from two old Russian immigrants when they were teenagers. These immigrants, Pavel and Peter, told about an incident from their youth back in Russia that the narrator could recall in vivid detail thirty years later. It was a harrowing story of a wedding party starting home in sleds and being chased by starving wolves. Hundreds of wolves attacked the group's sleds one by one as they sped across the snow trying to reach their village. In a horrible revelation, the old Russians revealed that the groom eventually threw his own bride to the wolves to save himself. There was even a hint that one of the old immigrants might have been the groom mentioned in the story. Cather has her narrator conclude with his feelings about the story. "We did not tell Pavel's secret to anyone, but guarded it jealously as if the wolves of the Ukraine had gathered that night long ago, and the wedding party had been sacrificed, just to give us a painful and peculiar pleasure." That feeling, that painful and peculiar pleasure, is the most important thing about literature. Study and research should enhance that feeling and never be allowed to overwhelm it.

Thomas E. Barden
Professor of English and Director
of Graduate English Studies,
The University of Toledo

Introduction

Purpose of the Book

The purpose of *Short Stories for Students* (*SSfS*) is to provide readers with a guide to understanding, enjoying, and studying short stories by giving them easy access to information about the work. Part of Gale's "For Students" Literature line, *SSfS* is specifically designed to meet the curricular needs of high school and undergraduate college students and their teachers, as well as the interests of general readers and researchers considering specific short fiction. While each volume contains entries on "classic" stories frequently studied in classrooms, there are also entries containing hard-to-find information on contemporary stories, including works by multicultural, international, and women writers.

The information covered in each entry includes an introduction to the story and the story's author; a plot summary, to help readers unravel and understand the events in the work; descriptions of important characters, including explanation of a given character's role in the narrative as well as discussion about that character's relationship to other characters in the story; analysis of important themes in the story; and an explanation of important literary techniques and movements as they are demonstrated in the work.

In addition to this material, which helps the readers analyze the story itself, students are also provided with important information on the literary and historical background informing each work. This includes a historical context essay, a box comparing the time or place the story was written to modern Western culture, a critical overview essay, and excerpts from critical essays on the story or author. A unique feature of *SSfS* is a specially commissioned critical essay on each story, targeted toward the student reader.

To further help today's student in studying and enjoying each story, information on audiobooks and other media adaptations is provided (if available), as well as reading suggestions for works of fiction and nonfiction on similar themes and topics. Classroom aids include ideas for research papers and lists of critical and reference sources that provide additional material on the work.

Selection Criteria

The titles for each volume of *SSfS* were selected by surveying numerous sources on teaching literature and analyzing course curricula for various school districts. Some of the sources surveyed include: literature anthologies, *Reading Lists for College-Bound Students: The Books Most Recommended by America's Top Colleges*; Teaching the Short Story: A Guide to Using Stories from around the World, by the National Council of Teachers of English (NCTE); and "A Study of High School Literature Anthologies," conducted by Arthur Applebee at the Center for the Learning and Teaching of Literature and sponsored by the National Endowment for the Arts and the Office of Educational Research and Improvement.

Input was also solicited from our advisory board, as well as educators from various areas. From these discussions, it was determined that each volume should have a mix of "classic" stories (those works commonly taught in literature classes) and contemporary stories for which information is often hard to find. Because of the interest in expanding the canon of literature, an emphasis was also placed on including works by international, multicultural, and women authors. Our advisory board members—educational professionals—helped pare down the list for each volume. Works not selected for the present volume were noted as possibilities for future volumes. As always, the editor welcomes suggestions for titles to be included in future volumes.

How Each Entry Is Organized

Each entry, or chapter, in *SSfS* focuses on one story. Each entry heading lists the title of the story, the author's name, and the date of the story's publication. The following elements are contained in each entry:

Introduction: a brief overview of the story which provides information about its first appearance, its literary standing, any controversies surrounding the work, and major conflicts or themes within the work.

Author Biography: this section includes basic facts about the author's life, and focuses on events and times in the author's life that may have inspired the story in question.

Plot Summary: a description of the events in the story. Lengthy summaries are broken down with subheads.

Characters: an alphabetical listing of the characters who appear in the story. Each character name is followed by a brief to an extensive description of the character's role in the story, as well as discussion of the character's actions, relationships, and possible motivation.

Characters are listed alphabetically by last name. If a character is unnamed—for instance, the narrator in "The Eatonville Anthology"—the character is listed as "The Narrator" and alphabetized as "Narrator." If a character's first name is the only one given, the name will appear alphabetically by that name.

Themes: a thorough overview of how the topics, themes, and issues are addressed within the story. Each theme discussed appears in a separate subhead.

Style: this section addresses important style elements of the story, such as setting, point of view, and narration; important literary devices used, such as imagery, foreshadowing, symbolism; and, if applicable, genres to which the work might have belonged, such as Gothicism or Romanticism. Literary terms are explained within the entry, but can also be found in the Glossary.

Historical Context: this section outlines the social, political, and cultural climate in which the author lived and the work was created. This section may include descriptions of related historical events, pertinent aspects of daily life in the culture, and the artistic and literary sensibilities of the time in which the work was written. If the story is historical in nature, information regarding the time in which the story is set is also included. Long sections are broken down with helpful subheads.

Critical Overview: this section provides background on the critical reputation of the author and the story, including bannings or any other public controversies surrounding the work. For older works, this section may include a history of how the story was first received and how perceptions of it may have changed over the years; for more recent works, direct quotes from early reviews may also be included.

Criticism: an essay commissioned by *SSfS* which specifically deals with the story and is written specifically for the student audience, as well as excerpts from previously published criticism on the work (if available).

Sources: an alphabetical list of critical material used in compiling the entry, with bibliographical information.

Further Reading: an alphabetical list of other critical sources which may prove useful for the student. Includes full bibliographical information and a brief annotation.

In addition, each entry contains the following highlighted sections, set apart from the main text as sidebars:

Media Adaptations: if available, a list of audiobooks and important film and television adaptations of the story, including source information. The list also includes stage adaptations, musical adaptations, etc.

Topics for Further Study: a list of potential study questions or research topics dealing with the story. This section includes questions related to other disciplines the student may be studying, such as American history, world history, science, math, government, business, geography, economics, psychology, etc.

Compare and Contrast: an "at-a-glance" comparison of the cultural and historical differences between the author's time and culture and late twentieth century or early twenty-first century Western culture. This box includes pertinent parallels between the major scientific, political, and cultural movements of the time or place the story was written, the time or place the story was set (if a historical work), and modern Western culture. Works written after 1990 may not have this box.

What Do I Read Next?: a list of works that might give a reader points of entry into a classic work (e.g., YA or multicultural titles) and/or complement the featured story or serve as a contrast to it. This includes works by the same author and others, works from various genres, YA works, and works from various cultures and eras.

Other Features

SSfS includes "Why Study Literature At All?," a foreword by Thomas E. Barden, Professor of English and Director of Graduate English Studies at the University of Toledo. This essay provides a number of very fundamental reasons for studying literature and, therefore, reasons why a book such as *SSfS*, designed to facilitate the study of literture, is useful.

A Cumulative Author/Title Index lists the authors and titles covered in each volume of the *SSfS* series.

A Cumulative Nationality/Ethnicity Index breaks down the authors and titles covered in each volume of the *SSfS* series by nationality and ethnicity.

A Subject/Theme Index, specific to each volume, provides easy reference for users who may be studying a particular subject or theme rather than a single work. Significant subjects from events to broad themes are included.

Each entry may include illustrations, including photo of the author, stills from film adaptations (if available), maps, and/or photos of key historical events.

Citing Short Stories for Students

When writing papers, students who quote directly from any volume of *SSfS* may use the following general forms to document their source. These examples are based on MLA style; teachers may request that students adhere to a different style, thus, the following examples may be adapted as needed.

When citing text from *SSfS* that is not attributed to a particular author (for example, the Themes, Style, Historical Context sections, etc.), the following format may be used:

> "The Celebrated Jumping Frog of Calavaras County." *Short Stories for Students*. Ed. Kathleen Wilson. Vol. 1. Detroit: Gale, 1997. 19–20.

When quoting the specially commissioned essay from *SSfS* (usually the first essay under the Criticism subhead), the following format may be used:

> Korb, Rena. Critical Essay on "Children of the Sea." *Short Stories for Students*. Ed. Kathleen Wilson. Vol. 1. Detroit: Gale, 1997. 39–42.

When quoting a journal or newspaper essay that is reprinted in a volume of *SSfS*, the following form may be used:

> Schmidt, Paul. "The Deadpan on Simon Wheeler." *Southwest Review* 41.3 (Summer, 1956): 270–77. Excerpted and reprinted in *Short Stories for Students*. Vol. 1. Ed. Kathleen Wilson. Detroit: Gale, 1997. 29–31.

When quoting material from a book that is reprinted in a volume of *SSfS*, the following form may be used:

> Bell-Villada, Gene H. "The Master of Short Forms." *García Márquez: The Man and His Work*. University of North Carolina Press, 1990. 119–36. Excerpted and reprinted in *Short Stories for Students*. Vol. 1. Ed. Kathleen Wilson. Detroit: Gale, 1997. 89–90.

We Welcome Your Suggestions

The editorial staff of *Short Stories for Students* welcomes your comments and ideas. Readers who wish to suggest short stories to appear in future volumes, or who have other suggestions, are cordially invited to contact the editor. You may contact the editor via E-mail at: **ForStudents Editors@cengage.com.** Or write to the editor at:

Editor, *Short Stories for Students*
Gale
27500 Drake Road
Farmington Hills, MI 48331-3535

Literary Chronology

1809: Edgar Allan Poe is born on January 19 in Boston, Massachusetts.

1843: Edgar Allan Poe's short story "The Pit and the Pendulum" is published in the collection *The Gift: A Christmas and New Year's Present for 1843*.

1849: Edgar Allan Poe dies on October 7 in Baltimore, Maryland.

1860: Anton Chekhov is born January 17 in Taganrog, Russia.

c. 1888: Anton Chekhov's short story "A Problem" is published in Russia. It is published in English in 1917, in the collection *The Party and Other Stories*.

1888: Katherine Mansfield is born Katherine Mansfield Beauchamp on October 14 in Wellington, New Zealand.

1899: Yasunari Kawabata is born on June 11 in Osaka, Japan.

1902: Langston Hughes is born James Langston Hughes on February 1 in Joplin, Missouri.

1903: Alan Paton is born on January 11 in Pietermaritzburg, South Africa.

1906: R. K. Narayan is born on October 10 in Madras, India.

1911: Jack Finney is born on October 2 in Milwaukee, Wisconsin.

1904: Anton Chekhov dies of tuberculosis on July 2 in Badenweiler, Germany.

1917: Arthur C. Clarke is born on November 16 in Minehead, Somerset, England.

1922: Katherine Mansfield's short story "The Doll's House" is published in *Athenaeum*.

1923: Katherine Mansfield dies of tuberculosis on January 9 in Paris, France.

1924: Yasunari Kawabata's short story "Batta to Suzumushi" ("The Grasshopper and the Bell Cricket") is published in Japan. It is published in English in 1988, in the collection *Palm-of-the-Hand Stories*.

1932: V. S. Naipaul is born on August 17 in Chaguanas, Trinidad.

1938: Luisa Valenzuela is born on November 26 in Buenos Aires, Argentina.

1939: Jane Yolen is born on February 11 in New York, New York.

1943: R. K. Narayan's short story "Forty-Five a Month" is published in the collection *Dodu and Other Stories*.

1946: Tim O'Brien is born on October 1 in Austin, Minnesota.

1952: Judith Ortiz Cofer is born Judith Ortiz on February 24 in Hormigueros, Puerto Rico.

1956: Jack Finney's short story "Contents of the Dead Man's Pockets" is published in *Collier's* magazine.

1959: V. S. Naipaul's short story "B. Wordsworth" is published as part of the novel *Miguel Street*.

1961: Alan Paton's short story "Ha'penny" is published in the collection *Tales from a Troubled Land.*

1962: Arthur C. Clarke's short story "Dogstar" is published in the pulp magazine *Galaxy Science Fiction.*

1963: Langston Hughes's short story "Thank You Ma'm" is published in the collection *Something in Common and Other Stories.*

1967: Langston Hughes dies of prostate surgery complications on May 22 in New York, New York.

1968: Yasunari Kawabata is the first Japanese writer to be awarded the Nobel Prize for Literature.

1972: Yasunari Kawabata dies of self-inflicted gassing on April 16 in Zushi, Japan.

1975: Tim O'Brien's short story "Where Have You Gone Charming Billy?" is published in *Redbook* magazine.

1988: Alan Paton dies on April 12 in Durban, Natal, South Africa.

1988: Judith Ortiz Cofer's short story "Aunty Misery" is published in the collection *Pig Iron, No. 15: Third World.*

1988: Luisa Valenzuela's short story "The Censors" is published in the collection *Open Door Stories.*

1993: Jane Yolen's short story "Suzy and Leah" is published in *American Girl* magazine.

1995: Jack Finney dies of pneumonia on November 14 in Greenbrae, California.

2001: R. K. Narayan dies on May 13 in Chennai, India.

2008: Arthur C. Clarke dies of complications of post-polio syndrome on March 19 in Sri Lanka.

Acknowledgments

The editors wish to thank the copyright holders of the excerpted criticism included in this volume and the permissions managers of many book and magazine publishing companies for assisting us in securing reproduction rights. We are also grateful to the staffs of the Detroit Public Library, the Library of Congress, the University of Detroit Mercy Library, Wayne State University Purdy/Kresge Library Complex, and the University of Michigan Libraries for making their resources available to us. Following is a list of the copyright holders who have granted us permission to reproduce material in this volume of *SSfS*. Every effort has been made to trace copyright, but if omissions have been made, please let us know.

COPYRIGHTED EXCERPTS IN *SSfS*, VOLUME 29, WERE REPRODUCED FROM THE FOLLOWING PERIODICALS:

Américas, v. 47, January-February, 1995. Copyright © 1995 *Américas*. Reproduced by permission of *Américas*, a bimonthly magazine published by the General Secretariat of the Organization of American States in English and Spanish.—*Ariel*, v. 15, January 1, 1984 for "Narayan's Sense of Audience" by Harsharan S Ahluwalia. Copyright © 1984 The Board of Governors, The University of Calgary, Calgary, Alberta. Reproduced by permission of the publisher and the author.—*Bilingual Review*, v. 17, May-August, 1992. Copyright © 1992 by Bilingual Press/Editorial Bilingüe, Arizona State University, Tempe, AZ. All rights reserved. Reproduced by permission.—*Boston Globe*, October 8, 2002 for "Storytelling is a Labor of True Love for Author Yolen" by Stephanie Loer. Copyright © 2002 Globe Newspaper Company. Reproduced by permission of the author.—*Carolina Quarterly*, v. 58, spring, 2007. Copyright © 2007 by The University of North Carolina Press. Reproduced by permission.—*Children's Literature Association Quarterly*, v. 1, summer, 1976. © 1976 Children's Literature Association. Reproduced by permission.—*Christian Science Monitor*, April 13, 1988; November 4, 1996. Copyright © 1988, 1996 The Christian Science Publishing Society. All rights reserved. Both reproduced by permission from *Christian Science Monitor* (www.csmonitor.com).—*Cleveland Jewish News*, v. 79, March 30, 2001. Copyright 2001 *Cleveland Jewish News*. Reproduced by permission.—*College English*, v. 27, December, 1965. Copyright © 1965 by the National Council of Teachers of English. —*The Courier Mail*, July 26, 2008. Copyright © Queensland Newspapers. Reproduced by permission.—*English Journal*, v. 71, November, 1982; v. 87, March, 1998. Copyright © 1982, 1998 by the National Council of Teachers of English. —*Explicator*, v. 57, spring, 1999; v. 60, spring, 2002. Copyright © 1999, 2002 by Helen Dwight Reid Educational Foundation. Both reproduced with permission of the Helen Dwight Reid Educational Foundation, published by Heldref Publications, 1319 18th Street, NW, Washington, DC 20036-1802.—*Globe and Mail* (Canada), October 30, 1982. Copyright © 1982 Globe Interactive, a division of Bell Globemedia Publishing, Inc. Reproduced by permission.—*Horn Book Magazine*, v. 67, July-August, 1991. Copyright 1991 by The

Horn Book, Inc., Boston, MA, www.hbook.com. All rights reserved. Reproduced by permission.—*Hudson Review*, v. LV, No. 3 (Autumn, 2002.) Copyright © 2002 by The Hudson Review, Inc. Reprinted by permission.—*International Fiction Review*, v. 29, January, 2002. Copyright © 2002 International Fiction Association. Reproduced by permission.—*Japan Times*, December 1, 1999. Copyright © *The Japan Times*. All rights reserved. Reproduced by permission.—*Journal of American & Comparative Cultures*, v. 25, fall, 2002. Copyright © 2002 Basil Blackwell Ltd. Reproduced by permission of Blackwell Publishers.—*Journal of Commonwealth Literature*, July, 1968. Copyright © 1968 by Sage Publications. Reprinted by permission of SAGE.—*Journal of New Zealand Literature*, 2004. Copyright © 2004 University of Waikato. Reproduced by permission.—*Lion and the Unicorn*, v. 21, 1997. Copyright © 1997 The Johns Hopkins University Press. Reproduced by permission.—*MELUS*, v. 18, fall, 1993. Copyright *MELUS: The Society for the Study of Multi-Ethnic Literature of the United States*, 1993. Reproduced by permission.—*Michigan Chronicle*, February 23, 2000. Copyright © 2000 *Michigan Chronicle*. Reproduced by permission.—*Neophilologus*, v. 71, April, 1987 for "Chekhov and the Modern Short Story in English" by David W. Martin. Reproduced by permission of the author.—*Ploughshares*, v. 21, winter, 1995 for "About Tim O'Brien" by Don Lee. Copyright © 1995 Ploughshares, Inc. Reproduced by permission of the author.—*Review of Contemporary Fiction*, v. 9, spring, 1989. Copyright © 1989 *The Review of Contemporary Fiction*. Reproduced by permission.—*Skeptic*, v. 14, 2008. Copyright © 1992–2008 *Skeptic* and its contributors. Reproduced by permission.—*South Atlantic Quarterly*, summer, 1974. Copyright, 1974, Duke University Press. All rights reserved. Used by permission of the publisher.—*Spectator*, v. 287, 2001. Copyright © 2001 by *The Spectator*. Reproduced by permission of *The Spectator*.—*Studies in Short Fiction*, v. 28, spring, 1991. Copyright © 1991 by *Studies in Short Fiction*. Reproduced by permission.—*Sun Reporter*, v. 55, no. 14, April 2, 1998; v. 55, no. 15, April 9, 1998. Copyright © *Sun Reporter* April 2, 1998, April 9, 1998. Both reproduced by permission.—*Texas Studies in Literature and Language*, v. 50, Issue 3, pp. 268-284 for "Pit, Pendulums, and Penitentiaries: Reframing the Detained Subject" by Jason Haslam. Copyright © 2008 by the University of Texas Press. All rights reserved. Reproduced by permission of the publisher and the author.—*Wall Street Journal*, January 15, 2009. Copyright © 2009 Dow Jones & Company, Inc. All rights reserved. Reprinted with permission from *The Wall Street Journal*.—*Washington Post*, September 21, 1997 for "Kawabata Country" by J. Thomas Rimer. Copyright © 1997 *The Washington Post*. Translated by J. Martin Holman. Reproduced by permission of the author.—*Western Humanities Review*, v. 50, winter-spring, 1997 for "The Mansfield Moment" by Robert L. Caserio. Reproduced by permission of the author.—*World Literature Today*, v. 55, summer, 1981; v. 57, spring, 1983; v. 69, autumn, 1995. Copyright © 1981, 1983, 1995 by *World Literature Today*. All reproduced by permission of the publisher.—*Worldandischool.com*, v. 20, December, 2005. Copyright 2005 News World Communications, Inc. Reproduced by permission.—*Writer*, v. 116, 2003 for "Writers Who Make a Difference" by Elfrieda Abbe and Kevin Keefe, Ronald Kovach, Jeff Reich, and Philip Martin; v. 117, September, 2004 for "A Few Words of Advice from... Anton Chekhov" by Bob Blaisdell. Both reproduced by permission of the respective authors.

COPYRIGHTED EXCERPTS IN *SSfS*, VOLUME 29, WERE REPRODUCED FROM THE FOLLOWING BOOKS:

Fullbrook, Kate. From "Late Fiction," in *Katherine Mansfield*. Edited by Sue Roe. Indiana University Press, 1986. Copyright © 1986 by Kate Fullbrook. All rights reserved. Reproduced by permission.—Hankin, C. A. From *Katherine Mansfield and Her Confessional Stories*. St. Martin's Press, 1983. Copyright © C. A. Hankin 1983. All rights reserved. Reproduced with permission of Palgrave Macmillan.—Harris-Fain, Darren. From *Understanding Contemporary American Science Fiction*. University of South Carolina Press, 2005. Copyright © 2005 University of South Carolina. Reproduced by permission.—King, Bruce. From *V.S. Naipaul*. Palgrave Macmillan, 2003. Copyright © Bruce King 2003. All rights reserved. Reproduced with permission of Palgrave Macmillan.—Kobler, J. F. From *Katherine Mansfield: A Study of the Short Fiction*. Twayne Publishers, 1990. Copyright © 1990 by G. K. Hall & Co. Reproduced by permission of Gale, a part of Cengage Learning.—Ocasio, Rafael. From *Literature of Latin America*. Greenwood Press, 2004. Copyright © 2004 by Rafael Ocasio. All rights reserved. Reproduced by permission of ABC-CLIO, LLC, Santa Barbara, CA.—Seabrook, Jack. From *Stealing Through Time on the Writings of Jack Finney*. McFarland & Company, 2006. Copyright © 2006 Jack Seabrook. All rights reserved. Reproduced by permission of McFarland & Company, Inc., Box 611, Jefferson NC 28640. www.mcfarlandpub.com.

Contributors

Bryan Aubrey: Aubrey holds a Ph.D. in English. Entry on "B. Wordsworth." Original essay on "B. Wordsworth."

Catherine Dominic: Dominic is a novelist and a freelance writer and editor. Entries on "The Censors" and "Forty-Five a Month." Original essays on "The Censors" and "Forty-Five a Month."

Charlotte Freeman: Freeman is a freelance writer and editor who holds a Ph.D. in English. Entry on "Where Have You Gone Charming Billy?" Original essay on "Where Have You Gone Charming Billy?"

Joyce Hart: Hart is a published writer and creative writing teacher. Entries on "Ha'penny" and "Suzy and Leah." Original essays on "Ha'penny" and "Suzy and Leah."

Diane Andrews Henningfeld: Henningfeld is an emerita professor of literature who writes literary criticism and reviews. Entry on "Contents of the Dead Man's Pocket." Original essay on "Contents of the Dead Man's Pocket."

David Kelly: Kelly is a writer who teaches creative writing and literature at Oakton Community College in Illinois. Entry on "The Doll's House." Original essay on "The Doll's House."

Kathy Wilson Peacock: Peacock is a nonfiction writer who specializes in literature and history. Entry on "The Pit and the Pendulum." Original essay on "The Pit and the Pendulum."

Bradley A. Skeen: Skeen is a professor of classics. Entries on "Dog Star" and "Thank You, Ma'm." Original essays on "Dog Star" and "Thank You, Ma'm."

Leah Tieger: Tieger is a freelance writer and editor. Entries on "Aunty Misery" and "A Problem." Original essays on "Aunty Misery" and "A Problem."

Rebecca Valentine: Valentine is a freelance writer who holds a B.A. in English with minors in philosophy and professional communications. Entry on "The Grasshopper and the Bell Cricket." Original essay on "The Grasshopper and the Bell Cricket."

Aunty Misery

JUDITH ORTIZ COFER

1988

Judith Ortiz Cofer's short story "Aunty Misery" tells the tale of a mean, lonely, old woman who zealously guards her pear tree from the neighborhood children. In the course of this seemingly innocent tale, the eponymous hero is granted one wish, a wish that results in Aunty Misery simultaneously protecting her pears and ultimately cheating Death. The brief story has all of the elements of a fable, a story featuring an anthropomorphized figure (Death, in this instance) and a succinct moral. Notably, fables can be fairy tales or folklore. Ortiz Cofer's "Aunty Misery" is a retold Puerto Rican folktale. As such, the story has a rich cultural history steeped in the oral tradition (stories typically predating the written word, or without a known author, that are handed down orally through the generations). In addition, the story explores the nature of Death (mortality and immortality), while also touching on themes of loneliness and even the nature of charity. Certainly, the story is a deceptively simple folktale that contains a wealth of deeper meaning. For this reason, the story has been widely anthologized, particularly in classroom texts directed toward middle school students.

While the exact original publication information for "Aunty Misery" is unknown, the earliest identified publication occurred in 1988, when the story was featured in *Pig Iron, No. 15: Third World*, an anthology of fiction and poetry by multiple authors. A more recent version of the story can be found in the 2003 book *Choices: 17*

Stories of Challenge and Choice, with Units for Mastering Language Arts Skills.

AUTHOR BIOGRAPHY

Ortiz Cofer was born Judith Ortiz on February 24, 1952, in Hormigueros, Puerto Rico. Her father joined the U.S. Navy soon after she was born, and thus the family moved to the United States in 1954. The family settled in Paterson, New Jersey (part of the New York City metropolitan area), but often traveled back and forth to Puerto Rico. Ortiz Cofer was raised in both countries, experiencing a bicultural and bilingual childhood. As a young adult, Ortiz Cofer attended Augusta College, earning a bachelor of arts degree in English there in 1974. While a student, she married Charles John Cofer, a businessman, on November 13, 1971. The couple has one daughter, Tanya. Ortiz Cofer received her master of arts degree in English from Florida Atlantic University in 1977. From there, she began a career as an English teacher, working for the University of Miami and the Georgia Center for Continuing Education, among other institutions. As of 2009, Ortiz Cofer was a faculty member at the University of Georgia, a post she has held since 1992. Ortiz Cofer has also served as a visiting writer at several colleges, including the University of Minnesota, Duluth, and the University of Michigan.

Ortiz Cofer's first publications, all poetry chapbooks, began to appear in the 1980s. The first, *Latin Women Pray*, was released in 1980. It was followed a year later by both *The Native Dancer* and *Among the Ancestors*. Given this prolific output, it is no surprise that Ortiz Cofer was named John Atherton Scholar in Poetry in 1982. Additional poetry books followed, as did short stories such as "Aunty Misery," which appeared in *Pig Iron, No. 15: Third World* in 1988. The following year, Ortiz Cofer received mainstream recognition with the release of her first novel, *The Line of the Sun*. The book was a popular and critical success, and it was nominated for the 1989 Pulitzer Prize. As of 2009, the volume remained in print and was still widely read. Other books that followed in the 1990s include the prose and poetry collection *The Latin Deli* (1993) and the short story collection *An Island Like You: Stories of the Barrio* (1995). Another notable publication that appeared in 1990 is *Silent Dancing: A Partial Remembrance of a Puerto Rican Childhood*. The memoir directly addresses Ortiz Cofer's bicultural heritage, and it was honored with a Pushcart Prize for nonfiction. In addition, Ortiz Cofer was also awarded an O. Henry Prize in 1994.

Later publications by Ortiz Cofer tend more toward prose and personal essays, as well as work specifically written for young adult readers. In 1998, she published *The Year of Our Revolution*, a collection of stories and poetry. Two years later, she wrote *Woman in Front of the Sun: On Becoming a Writer*, a collection of personal essays on writing. The book was followed in 2003 by the novel *The Meaning of Consuelo* and in 2004 by the young-adult novel *Call Me María*, which portrays a teenage protagonist who moves from Puerto Rico to the United States. In 2005, Ortiz Cofer authored the poetry collection *A Love Story Beginning in Spanish*. Ortiz Cofer is hailed as an author who captures the Puerto Rican American experience and her works often address this topic.

PLOT SUMMARY

"Aunty Misery" begins with these words: "This is a story." This self-conscious opening seems redundant; readers are aware they are reading a story and hardly need to be reminded of that. However, the statement is effective in that it serves to elevate the fictional quality of the tale that ensues. No claim as to the story's factuality is made; quite the opposite. The story itself is about a very, very old woman who lives all by herself in a tiny hut. Her life is not as bleak as it sounds, as there is a lovely pear tree growing right outside her door. The old woman loves the tree and spends all of her time tending to it. The pear tree is even described as keeping the old woman "company." It is as if the tree is her friend (her only friend, for that matter).

The old woman is plagued by the children in her neighborhood. They steal the fruit from her pear tree and drive her insane with their antics. The children climb into the tree and shake its branches in order to harvest its fruit. Then they run off with almost more than they can carry. Adding insult to injury, the children shout mean epithets at the old woman. They make fun of her and call her Aunty Misery. Notably, while the narrator refers to the main character as an old woman, once the children refer to her as Aunty Misery, the narrator follows suit. The nickname also transforms the old woman from a person into a thing

(Misery). Thus, the nickname's power to depersonalize and dehumanize is also revealed.

A traveler, referred to in the story as a pilgrim, passes by Aunty Misery's hut to ask for shelter for the night. Aunty Misery trusts the traveler because he has an "honest face." She invites him in and cooks for him and makes him a bed by the fireplace. The next morning, as the traveler is leaving, he tells Aunty Misery that he would like to thank her for all that she has done for him. He intends to do so by fulfilling one wish. Aunty Misery replies, "There is only one thing that I desire." Even without hearing what it is, the pilgrim agrees to grant the wish. Here, the narrator points out that the traveler is actually a powerful sorcerer dressed in a disguise.

Aunty Misery tells the sorcerer that she wants anyone who climbs her pear tree to get caught in its boughs. She says that they must remain trapped there until she gives them their freedom. The sorcerer tells Aunty Misery that he has granted her wish, and he touches the pear tree as he leaves her hut. When the children return to tease Aunty Misery and steal more of her pears, the old woman stays in her hut and spies on them from her window. Many children get stuck in the tree, and they beg to be let down. Aunty Misery allows them to cry and entreat her for a long while. She finally grants them their freedom, but only after they promise never to insult her or steal from her again.

Time goes by and Aunty Misery is no longer molested by the neighborhood children. She and "her tree grew bent and gnarled with age" as the years pass. Eventually, another traveler stops at Aunty Misery's hut. He looks tired and worn out, so Aunty Misery asks him what he needs. The man tells her that he is Death and that he has come for her. His voice is described as "dry and hoarse, as if he had swallowed a desert."

Aunty Misery agrees to go with Death, but "thinking fast," she asks Death if she can bring some of the pears from her tree with her as a keepsake of the joy they have given her. Yet, Aunty Misery points out that she is old and frail and too weak to climb the tree. She remarks that the best fruit is on the highest branches. So, she asks Death to climb the tree and retrieve the pears for her. Death agrees and heaves a sigh that is "like wind through a catacomb" (an underground burial site). But, like the children before him, Death gets stuck in the tree and cannot free himself. Aunty Misery has tricked Death, and even though he yells at her and bellows with rage, she will not release him.

Several years go by while Death is trapped in the tree. No one in the world has died. People whose livelihoods depend on Death are suffering, so they "began to protest loudly." People do not go to the doctor anymore because they know they cannot die. No one buys medicine from the pharmacists for the same reason. The narrator also explains that "medicines are, like magic potions, bought to prevent or postpone the inevitable." Undertakers are all, obviously, unemployed. Old people who have tired of living are unable to die and go "to the next world to rest from the miseries of this one." Aunty Misery cannot die and is stuck in this world. But the only way to escape misery is to die. At the same time, (Aunty) Misery is keeping others from escaping misery.

Aunty Misery does understand the turmoil she has caused, and she does not want "to be unfair." So, she agrees to free Death from her pear tree as long as he promises never to come for her. Death consents, "and that is why so long as the world is the world, Aunty Misery will always live."

CHARACTERS

Aunty Misery

Aunty Misery is the main character of the story; the eponymous hero, or more accurately, anti-hero. Regardless of her lack of endearing charms, the story revolves around her. Notably, Aunty Misery is not an actual name, but a nickname, one that describes the character and her attributes. In fact, the nickname serves to underscore and highlight the character's role as a miserable old woman. However, this cannot truly be the case, as Aunty Misery's charity toward the stranger hints at a more worthy and sympathetic personality than the one ostensibly portrayed. For instance, Aunty Misery lives alone, but she is not described as lonely. She is happy caring for her beloved pear tree, which keeps her "company."

The only annoyance in her life is the children who insult her and steal from her tree. Although her resentment does make Aunty Misery appear to be something of a miser, her softer nature is revealed in her charity toward the pilgrim. She feeds him and gives him shelter and a bed by the fire. Aunty Misery asks for nothing in return for this kindness. But, when the pilgrim offers to show his gratitude by granting a wish, Aunty Misery knows exactly what to ask for. And, though she does leave the children stuck in her pear tree for some time, she ultimately lets them go as long as they agree to leave her alone. This act seems to show that Aunty Misery does not have a vindictive nature. She only wants to be allowed to live her life in peace.

Aunty Misery's charitable nature is again revealed when she sees Death disguised as a traveler. He looks so tired that she asks how she can help him. Her sympathy to the plight of doctors, pharmacists, and undertakers is also admirable. Her feeling for the elderly who have tired of life is also of note. All of these characters need Death to be freed from the tree, and in consideration of this, Aunty Misery finds a way to become immortal while still fulfilling the needs of others.

Death

Death is the catalyst that drives the story and its conclusion. Death is a noun personified—a thing made human or given human attributes. He appears in the form of a tired and worn-out traveler. Since Aunty Misery has already had a good experience aiding tired pilgrims, she offers to help him. But, when Death reveals his true identity, Aunty Misery tricks him into picking pears for her, thus imprisoning him in her tree. In this manner, Aunty Misery is able to cheat Death. Although Death plays a brief, albeit significant, role in the plot, he is the most described character. In fact, the story is predominantly lacking in descriptive language. Only Death presents an exception to that rule. When Death speaks, his voice is described as being "dry and hoarse, as if he had swallowed a desert." When he sighs it sounds "like wind through a catacomb."

Death's character is also revealed to be kind and considerate as well as honorable. When Aunty Misery asks to be allowed to bring pears with her to the next life as a keepsake, Death generously grants her request. He even goes so far as to pick the fruit for her. Death's honorable nature is revealed further when he agrees never to come for Aunty Misery after he is released from her tree.

Doctors

The doctors in the world complain about the state of affairs; namely, that Death is trapped in a tree and that no one can die. Because people have become immortal, they do not go to see the doctors. They have no need to have their ailments treated because there are no consequences if they do not. This leaves the doctors unable to make a living.

Narrator

Though the narrator is not an actual character in the story, the narrator's personality does occasionally assert itself. For instance, at the opening of "Aunty Misery," the narrator notes, "This is a story." The statement not only reminds the reader of the fictional nature of the tale that follows but also makes the reader extremely conscious of the narrator's presence. The adoption of the children's nickname for the old woman also seems to hint at the narrator's personality. The narrator changes from dispassionately calling the old woman an old woman to being influenced by the children's description.

Neighborhood Children

The neighborhood children pester and plague Aunty Misery. They tease her and insult her and steal the pears from her beloved tree. They abscond with more than they need, taking armloads of fruit, which indicates their greed and selfishness. They are the only blight on Aunty Misery's otherwise peaceful existence. The children are also responsible for naming Aunty Misery and pigeonholing her personality according to her most negative traits. However, this nickname more accurately reflects the children's perception of her than it does the old woman's true nature. It also reflects their desire to hurt her.

After the children become stuck in Aunty Misery's tree, they are allowed to sit in the tree for some time. This punishment leads them to beg and plead, and also to respect their promise to leave Aunty Misery alone from then on.

Old People

In the story, the old people of the world wish to die but are unable to do so after Aunty Misery traps Death in her tree. The old people are tired of life, and they want to be able to go "to the next world to rest from the miseries of this one." Aunty Misery is not one of these people, as she clearly wishes to live forever. Nevertheless, she is sympathetic to their plight. In addition, the use of the word "miseries" has a dual meaning. Aunty Misery cannot die and is stuck in this world. But the only way to escape misery is to die. At the same time, (Aunty) Misery is keeping others from escaping misery.

Pear Tree

The pear tree plays the role of a character in "Aunty Misery." It is beautiful and its fruit is desirable. The pear tree is Aunty Misery's only friend. She spends all of her time tending to it, and it is also described as keeping her "company." As the years go by, the tree ages alongside the old woman. It becomes as bent and twisted with age as she is. The pear tree is enchanted by a magical spell, and thus it becomes a prison to all who climb its branches. First it traps the neighborhood children; next, it serves as a cage for Death for several years.

Pharmacists

The pharmacists of the world are unable to make a living while Death is trapped in Aunty Misery's pear tree. They whine to Aunty Misery. No on can die and so they do not want to buy medicine. The narrator also explains that "medicines are, like magic potions, bought to prevent or postpone the inevitable." This comment is remarkable in that it is the only hint of social commentary in the story.

Pilgrim

The pilgrim is a traveler who stops at Aunty Misery's hut and asks for shelter for the night. Generally, pilgrims are traveling for religious purposes, but whether or not this is the case is not clear in the story. The traveler is described as having an "honest" face. However, this is not exactly true since he is actually a magician traveling in disguise. Nevertheless, Aunty Misery makes him dinner and a bed by the fire. Her charity is given out of kindness and without expectation of reward. But it does indeed pay off when the pilgrim offers to grant a wish for her. This offer is without moral guidelines or judgment, as he says that it will be granted no matter what it is. This could be potentially dangerous, and in a sense it is. The ultimate (unintended) consequence is that no one can die. The traveler is not portrayed as saying a spell, but he does touch the tree on his way out of Aunty Misery's hut. This touch apparently casts the spell that the old woman has requested. Given the traveler's incognito behavior, the only way that the reader even knows that the pilgrim is a sorcerer is because the narrator says so.

Sorcerer

See Pilgrim

Undertakers

The undertakers, like the doctors and the pharmacists, are out of work because Death is trapped in Aunty Misery's pear tree. After several years have gone by without any deaths, they finally go to the old woman and complain about the situation.

THEMES

Death

The main theme in "Aunty Misery" is the importance of death in the world. This significance is shown not only in the consequences of Death's entrapment in the pear tree but also textually. Indeed, death is personified and becomes a character that drives the climax and denouement (end) of the story. He is also the most described character in the story; he appears in the form of a tired and worn-out traveler. Although the descriptive language in the story is relatively sparse, descriptions of Death are lengthy and vivid. When Death speaks, his voice is "dry and hoarse, as if he had swallowed a desert." When he sighs it sounds "like wind through a catacomb." These uncharacteristic descriptions hint at Death's significance.

Death's importance is also evident in the havoc caused in the wake of his absence. Doctors, undertakers, and pharmacists are unable to make a living. The old cannot die. They cannot pass on to another world and rest from the "miseries" of this one. Here, Death's importance as a transformational phenomenon is noted. Death is the means through which people travel from one world to the other. He also provides the aged with a well-deserved rest and respite from the hardships of this world. Therefore, it becomes clear that Death is not only needed but wanted. This latter aspect can also be seen in the kindness he shows to Aunty Misery. He tells her he has come for her, agrees to let her bring her pears with her, and even picks them for her. Death, then, is portrayed as a benevolent force in the world.

Mortality

Mortality is a variant on the theme of death. Its value is noted slightly in the undertakers', pharmacists', and doctors' inability to make a living without it. More importantly, the value of mortality is stated fully when the old cannot die and

TOPICS FOR FURTHER STUDY

- A popular fairy tale that features another lonely, mean, old woman is "Hansel and Gretel." In an essay, compare and contrast this tale to "Aunty Misery." How and why are the outcomes of each story different? In addition, explore the implications of how the aged women are portrayed in each story.

- Many of Ortiz Cofer's works explore the intersection of two cultures; that is, the quintessential migrant experience that has shaped United States history. Tape interviews with members of your community who are immigrants and ask them about the hardships and rewards of being a member of two (or more) cultures. Compile your findings in an oral presentation for your class.

- "Aunty Misery" presents some interesting images, such as that of Death trapped in a pear tree. Create a visual representation of this or other images from the story. Use any medium you wish and present your artwork to the class.

- Use the Internet to research Puerto Rico and Puerto Rican folktales. What other tales can you find, and what do they communicate about Puerto Rican culture? After conducting your research, create a lesson plan on Puerto Rico and its folklore. What topics would you highlight if you were teaching a class on the subject?

- Write a fable that features Death as a character. Be sure to include a recognizable moral in your tale. At the end, explain in a short essay how your tale added to your understanding of "Aunty Misery."

- Read Ortiz Cofer's 2004 young-adult novel *Call Me María*. The story features María, a teenage girl who struggles with her family's move from Puerto Rico to the United States. Pay attention to the authorial voice. Is it different from or similar to the voice in "Aunty Misery"? Give a class presentation in which you explain your conclusions. Be sure to cite examples from both texts.

---

are thus unable to go "to the next world to rest from the miseries of this one."

Immortality

Immortality is another variant on the theme of death. Its troublesome nature is revealed in juxtaposition to the value of mortality. It is additionally embodied by Aunty Misery's character. The old woman earns immortality by tricking Death and extracting a promise from him that he will never come for her. However, her life before Death's appearance was stagnant and will presumably remain so. This stagnation is a sly hint at the cost of immortality. The other consequence is indicated in the story's last line. It is implied that Aunty Misery is misery personified, "and that is why so long as the world is the world, Aunty Misery will always live."

Misery

Given the implication that Aunty Misery is the personification of misery itself, the story becomes a myth or parable that seeks to explain why misery exists and why it is an inextricable aspect of life in this world. However, while the old woman is perceived as miserable by the neighborhood children (and, presumably, by the narrator), she herself does not seem miserable at all. She happily tends to her pear tree and lives her life in peace. The only thing that brings her misery is the neighborhood children, and that problem is solved early on in the story. Aunty Misery's happiness also seems to be indicated in her bid for immortality. Where the other aged people of the world wish to die in order to escape their "miseries," Aunty Misery has no such desire.

Cemetery early on a frosty morning *(Image copyright Peter Elvidge, 2009. Used under license from Shutterstock.com)*

Loneliness

Loneliness is a subtle theme in the story. Although Aunty Misery lives alone and her only friend is a pear tree, she never appears to feel lonely. Her solitary existence, however, is disconcerting to those around her, and that is why the children taunt her.

Charity

Charity, and its rewards, are a more evident theme in "Aunty Misery." Although Aunty Misery is perceived by those around her as a miserable and miserly old woman, in reality, she is caring, giving, and kind. This is shown on several occasions in the story. For example, her charity toward the pilgrim proves her to be a sympathetic personality. Not only does she give the pilgrim the shelter he requests, she also feeds him and makes him a bed in the warmest part of the house. She does so, also, without expectation of reward or payment. But charity, as the story shows, does have its rewards when freely given (this is also one of the story's morals). Aunty Misery's charitable nature is seen again when she grants the children their freedom in exchange for their agreement to leave her alone, a rather fair and just request. She also offers aid to Death when he appears as a weary traveler, and she agrees to free him so that the undertakers of the world can make a living. Ultimately, Aunty Misery's most ostensible act of charity (feeding and housing the pilgrim) inadvertently results in her achieving immortality.

STYLE

Personification

Simply put, personification is a literary device that grants personality to inanimate objects or natural phenomena. This is also known as anthropomorphizing, or granting human qualities to non-human objects. Personification occurs in the story predominantly through Death's appearance as a tired old man. Death, a natural phenomenon, is literally personified, transformed into a character that sighs and is able to pick fruit from a tree. All of the descriptive language devoted to Death is a form of personification. If Aunty Misery is indeed intended to symbolize misery and its presence in the world, then she is also a salient example of personification. In addition, the pear tree in the story is personified when it is described as keeping Aunty Misery "company."

Descriptive Language

Descriptive language in "Aunty Misery" is of note mainly because of its remarkable absence. The story has no specificity. It takes place in an unknown time and there are no clues indicating in what period in history the narrative may be set. The same is true of the story's location. Aunty Misery is not described, nor are the neighborhood children. Most of the characters in the story are inanimate objects or generic groups of people (pharmacists, undertakers, doctors). The rare instances of descriptive language are reserved for the pear tree, which is beautiful, but grows twisted with age. The sorcerer in disguise has an "honest" look. Death, of course, receives the most descriptive treatment. This is no surprise given that he is a major figure in the story.

Hero/Antihero

Aunty Misery is the main character and protagonist of the story. But Aunty Misery's role as a hero is questionable. She could arguably be described as an antihero, a literary figure whose values and or actions are antithetical (opposed) to heroism. While Aunty Misery lives a solitary life, this is not necessarily a transgression in and of itself. However, her isolation is partly why the neighborhood children pester her. She could also choose to share her pears, but instead guards them zealously, ultimately transforming her fruit-bearing tree into a prison to which only she holds the keys. On the other hand, Aunty Misery is kind and charitable. Although too selfish to die, she does release Death back into the world in consideration for others.

Third-Person Limited Point of View

"Aunty Misery" is told from a third-person limited point of view. This narrative device features an unknown narrator who is often (but not always) objective. More notably, the narrator is only able to portray the inner thoughts and emotions of one character. (If portraying the thoughts of more than one character, the narrator would be referred to as omniscient.) Aside from the one character that the narrator has insight into, other characters in the story can only be described on an external level, that is, portrayed via their actions or statements. In the story, Aunty Misery is the only character whose inner thoughts and feelings are known. Given that she is the main character, this is fairly fitting. Instances that portray Aunty Misery's inner workings occur when the narrator notes that she "saw" that the pilgrim looked honest. Another example is when by "thinking fast" she comes up with a way to cheat Death. Aunty Misery is also shown as understanding the plight of others who depend on Death. It is additionally noted that she does not want to be "unfair" to them.

HISTORICAL CONTEXT

Puerto Rican Folktales

Puerto Rican culture is a mixture of Taino (native inhabitants of the Caribbean Islands), Spanish, and African influences. As such, the folktales from this country reflect this mixed heritage. Few purely Taino myths have survived, as the islands (including Puerto Rico) were colonized by Spain in the fifteenth century. (Christopher Columbus "discovered" the island on November 19, 1493.) Tainos did not have a written language, and most died off in the sixteenth century following the country's colonization. Yet Spanish settlers did record Taino stories, all of which were part of an oral tradition (tales passed down through the generations via the spoken word). In 1505, friar Ramón Pané was commissioned by Columbus to document the Taino culture. In addition to writing of their lifestyle, Panée, who lived on Hispaniola for four years, recorded their creation myths (stories that explained their origination as well as the origination of the world), stories of how the Sun and Moon came to exist, and myths and beliefs regarding the afterlife.

Because the Taino population was decimated by the diseases carried by Spanish settlers, the Spaniards imported African slaves to aid in the establishment of the colony. Thus, in the late sixteenth century, African and Taino culture began to intermingle. Slaves also lived by an oral tradition; they were illiterate and uneducated, and so their stories were told aloud rather than written down. As Doris M. Vazquez notes in *Folktales*, "Stories from this group of people reflected their struggles and often futile attempts to be free." Yet, because of their low social status, slaves retained little of their own culture and were quickly assimilated into Spanish culture.

COMPARE & CONTRAST

- **1980s:** While Ortiz Cofer is not overtly feminist, much of her work portrays strong female protagonists and their struggles. Women's rights at this time are defined by second-wave feminism. This movement focuses predominantly on discrimination against women, particularly in regards to social equality and wage disparity.

  Today: No coherent movement in feminism has asserted itself since the establishment of third-wave feminism (a new wave of the feminist movement that seeks to avoid the strict definitions of the earlier movements) during the 1990s. The social, cultural, and political impact women have made in the twentieth century is nevertheless undeniable.

- **1980s:** Puerto Ricans living in New York City are referred to as Nuyoricans. The term also describes their literature and art. The Nuyorican Poets Cafe, an art collective at the center of the Nuyorican artistic movement, is founded in 1973. In the 1980s, the collective continues to grow in popularity.

  Today: Although the Nuyorican Poets Cafe reached the height of its influence in the 1990s, it continues to host and promote Nuyorican artists, writers, and performers. The group has been established in the same building in New York City since 1980.

- **1980s:** The literature of the day highlights female and minority writers. Hispanic American writers are particularly popular. Ortiz Cofer's work is a salient example of this phenomenon, as is the work of Mexican American author Sandra Cisneros.

  Today: The cultural emphasis in literature today predominantly falls on writers of Asian descent. Vikram Chandra and Jhumpa Lahiri are two such examples. Works by Caribbean writers, such as Edwidge Danticat, are also popular.

This rapid assimilation, coupled with the near extinction of the Taino people and the little that survives from their society, has resulted in a Puerto Rican folk tradition largely dominated by Spanish culture. Thus, Vazquez finds that "the folk tales that are told in Puerto Rico today reflect basically Spanish themes with island adaptations and very little Taino or African participation." She adds, "The tales, in general, have undergone changes in numbers, names, or settings which are more tropical or similar to Puerto Rico."

Puerto Rican Immigration and Migration to the United States

When Puerto Rico was a Spanish colony, Puerto Ricans who moved to the United States were immigrants. The first such group of immigrants arrived around the 1850s. But, after the Spanish-American War (April 1898–August 1898), Puerto Rico became a territory of the United States. Thus, Puerto Ricans who moved to the United States after 1898 were considered Puerto Rican citizens who were required to possess passports in order to travel. In 1917, the Jones-Shafroth Act was passed in the United States. This act defined Puerto Ricans as citizens of the United States. Because of this, they were able to travel and move freely between both countries. As such, Puerto Ricans living in the United States were no longer immigrants but migrants. The peak of that migration, known as the "The Great Migration," began in 1946 and lasted throughout the 1950s as businesses began to encourage the migration of Puerto Ricans to fill a demand for cheap labor. (Ortiz Cofer and her family moved to the United States in 1954.) The vast majority of this migration was centered in and around New York City.

CRITICAL OVERVIEW

Although no criticism specific to "Aunty Misery" exists, its critical success is evident in its enduring

Boy climbing tree (Image copyright Rachel L. Sellers, 2009. Used under license from Shutterstock.com)

popularity. Indeed, the story is widely anthologized and is a core part of middle-grade curriculums across the United States. Despite the lack of specific criticism, Ortiz Cofer's work in general has been widely reviewed. In fact, many critical comments about Ortiz Cofer's work would certainly seem to encompass the story at hand. For instance, "Cofer makes a difference by expanding our definition of American culture and by helping young writers from diverse backgrounds express their experiences," notes Elfrieda Abbe in the *Writer*. Certainly, this would seem to be accomplished by Ortiz Cofer's retelling of Puerto Rican folktales in English. The story does indeed create a cultural bridge of sorts.

Further discussing the ways in which Ortiz Cofer's work straddles her two cultures, *MELUS* critic Carmen Faymonville remarks that "Ortiz Cofer views both Puerto Rico and the United States as 'transnational' home space by resisting the ideological imperative of dichotomies and by refusing imposed social strictures of monolingual identity." Exploring this aspect of the author's work further, Faymonville states, "Ortiz Cofer, I argue, discovers a complex way to make sense of migrant identity by not exclusively rooting the 'self' in any one home or country. Her stance can best be described as transnational, neither assimilationist nor necessarily oppositional." In addition, the critic concludes, "Certainly, Ortiz Cofer would acknowledge that both nationally exclusive and more hybrid models of national identity still exist and that transnational identifications are not available to all." Similarly, the retold, modernized, and internationalized folktale resists such easy classification.

CRITICISM

Leah Tieger

Tieger is a freelance writer and editor. In the following essay, she explains the elements that define "Aunty Misery" as a folktale. In addition, she explores the story's themes regarding death and misery.

Ortiz Cofer's "Aunty Misery" is a retold Puerto Rican folktale that appears to explain the existence of misery in the world. The story also asserts the value of death. While the tale is Puerto Rican in origin, there is nothing in its content that indicates this. The themes in the story are universal, transcending not only culture but even time and place. For example, the story's setting is never so much as hinted at, and it is written in such a way that it could take place anywhere. The same is true of the story's inherent historical context; there are no clues as to when the story takes place, and it really could be set in almost any time period. There are no machines or modern technology referenced. But, on the other hand, there is no mention made of using the manual techniques that were relied upon before the advent of technology. This universality is a hallmark of folktales, many of which seek to explain the existence of natural phenomena through anecdote (a short, often humorous explanatory story) or metaphor (employing one item or event to represent another). These universal themes are communicated more effectively in a nonspecific context.

Folktales additionally feature the personification of natural phenomena, as is certainly the case here. Death, of course, is the most salient example. He appears to Aunty Misery as a tired traveler. His voice is "dry and hoarse, as if he had swallowed a

WHAT DO I READ NEXT?

- Old women appear in numerous folktales and fairy tales, and they alternately take on the figure of villain or hero, fool or wise elder. For a deeper understanding of this archetypal figure in mythology, read Clarissa Pinkola Estes's 1999 book *The Dangerous Old Woman: Myths and Stories of the Wise Old Woman Archetype*.

- Sandra Cisneros's 1983 *The House on Mango Street* is an oft-studied collection of vignettes particularly suited to young adult readers. The book contains supernatural elements akin to those found in fairy tales, and it also is an example of Latin American literature that addresses the nature of bicultural experience.

- Catharine R. Bomhold and Terri E. Elder's 2008 book *Twice Upon a Time: A Guide to Fractured, Altered, and Retold Folk and Fairy Tales* is part of the Libraries Unlimited Children's and Young Adult Literature Reference series. The book is a nonfiction reference reader for young adults interested in an academic exploration of fairy tales. The volume is divided into thematic units and includes further study activities sure to spark valuable classroom discussion.

- For a deeper exploration of Puerto Rican folktales read *The Three Wishes: A Collection of Puerto Rican Folktales*, which was released in 1969 and compiled and translated by Ricardo E. Alegria. Despite being published more than forty years ago, the volume contains all of Puerto Rico's best-known fables and is thus a comprehensive collection.

- To learn more about Ortiz Cofer, read her 1990 memoir *Silent Dancing: A Partial Remembrance of a Puerto Rican Childhood*. In the book, Ortiz Cofer details her early life and struggles to assimilate into two disparate cultures. The volume provides a great deal of insight into Ortiz Cofer's prose and poetry.

- For a series of legends that seek to explain Puerto Rican history from creation to modern times read *Stories from Puerto Rico* by Robert Muckley and Adela Martinez-Santiago. Published in 1999, the volume is written in both English and Spanish and includes tales addressing the indigenous cultures of Puerto Rico.

- The 2002 collection *Abu Jmeel's Daughter & Other Stories: Arab Folk Tales from Palestine and Lebanon*, by Jamal Sleem Nuweihed, Salma Khadra Jayyusi, and C. Tingley, is part of the Interlink Books International Folk Tales Series. The volume provides another look at how folktales can both shape and reflect disparate cultures. Twenty-seven Arab folk stories are included in the volume.

- A more academic history of Puerto Rico can be found in the 2007 book *Puerto Rico in the American Century: A History since 1898*. The volume, written by Cesar J. Ayala and Rafael Bernabe, explores the history of Puerto Rico from the time it became a territory of the United States.

- Another critical examination of women in fairy tales is the revised 2001 book *The Feminine in Fairy Tales*. Written by Marie-Louise von Franz, the volume explores how women are portrayed in such popular fairy tales as "Snow White and Rose Red," "Rumpelstiltskin," and "Sleeping Beauty."

- Myths are the ancient precursors of fairy tales, and the classic definitive collection of Greek myth is Edith Hamilton's *Mythology*. First published in 1942, the book has remained a mainstay on high school and college curricula.

desert." When he sighs it sounds "like wind through a catacomb." These descriptive similes are all examples of personification. They are also the only extended descriptive examples in the story. This alerts the reader to Death's importance as a major figure in "Aunty Misery." This also reinforces the idea that the story's main theme pertains to the importance of death. Some of the story's longest passages are devoted to the discussion of the doctors and undertakers who cannot make a living. It is also notable that the story's only instance of social commentary appears in this context. When the pharmacists complain of their inability to do their jobs, the narrator comments that "medicines are, like magic potions, bought to prevent or postpone the inevitable." Thus, the narrator seems to be indicating that the "inevitable" is death and that there is little point in attempting to avoid it. Ironically, the story's main character does exactly that.

Another striking passage underscoring this theme shows not only that death is important but also that it can be a benevolent force. This is shown when the narrator observes that the elderly people in the world wish to die; they want to be able to go "to the next world to rest from the miseries of this one." That death is not an end but a means of passage is also asserted in this statement. The elderly do not wish for oblivion but to go "to the next world." Death's benevolence is indicated not only in this statement, but also in his personified form. He matter-of-factly informs Aunty Misery of his identity and intention. He agrees to her requests to bring souvenirs from this world (her pears) into the next. In fact, Death not only grants this request but is even persuaded to retrieve the fruit for Aunty Misery out of consideration for her age and frailty.

Certainly, much can be learned about the nature of death in the story, but can anything be learned about the nature of misery? In other words, can "Aunty Misery" be read as an explanation for the never-ending existence of misery in the world? First of all, Aunty Misery is not personified as Death is. All of the descriptions pertaining to him indicate his inherent nature. This is not true of the story's protagonist. She is never described in any way that indicates that she is miserable or that she is the physical embodiment of misery. Quite the opposite appears to be the case. For instance, when the story opens, Aunty Misery is referred to as an old woman. It is only after the neighborhood children nickname her that she becomes Aunty Misery. In addition, while Aunty Misery is certainly miserly in her covetousness toward her own pear tree, her reaction to the children's thievery is hardly inappropriate.

Indeed, Aunty Misery's true nature hardly seems miserable at all. She lives alone but is not lonely. Quite the contrary, she seems to enjoy her solitary nature. When one thinks of the old adage that "misery loves company," the possibility that the old woman is a personification of misery becomes even more preposterous (unlikely). It would also seem that the personification of misery would not exhibit any worthy traits. Yet, Aunty Misery does show herself to be a kind, caring, considerate, and compassionate woman. She provides exemplary charity to the sorcerer in disguise. Not only does she offer him the shelter he requests but she also feeds him and makes him a bed in the warmest spot in the house. She does all of this without expectation of payment or reward. That Aunty Misery does receive a reward seems to speak for the underlying moral that charity is its own reward, or that good deeds are rewarded.

Aunty Misery also wants nothing more than to live her life in peace; she does not spread unhappiness or discord in her midst (as one might expect of the personification of misery). The punishment she doles out to the children is neither vindictive nor unjust. When the elderly who wish to die are unable to do so, Aunty Misery feels for their plight. When the doctors, pharmacists, and undertakers are destitute because of Aunty Misery's actions, she shows sympathy for them. She does not want "to be unfair." Certainly, this trait seems antithetical (opposite) to the idea that Aunty Misery is misery personified. Rather than increase or maintain the misery she has caused, Aunty Misery reduces it by agreeing to free Death. Though she does so in exchange for immortality, Aunty Misery can hardly be faulted for this. And, while the narrator concludes the story by stating that "so long as the world is the world, Aunty Misery will always live," the language pointedly avoids drawing any parallels between world suffering and Aunty Misery's existence.

Source: Leah Tieger, Critical Essay on "Aunty Misery," in *Short Stories for Students*, Gale, Cengage Learning, 2010.

Stern, finger-pointing granny (Image copyright Elena Ray, 2009. Used under license from Shutterstock.com)

Elfrieda Abbe, Kevin Keefe, Ronald Kovach, Jeff Reich, and Philip Martin

In the following excerpt, Cofer's contributions to the writing world, as evidenced by her winning a The Writer *Award, are discussed.*

The Writer Awards honor the achievements of writers who have made significant contributions to the field of writing. Through their work, teaching or other activities, these individuals have helped and influenced other writers, brought about changes in the publishing field that benefit all writers, increased awareness of issues that concern writers, or used their writing to help communities or humanitarian causes.

For the 2002 awards, a panel of six judges reviewed more than 300 nominations sent to *The Writer* by writers, editors, agents and others. This year's judges included editorial staff members from *The Writer* and *The Writer Books*.

The following award winners exemplify the many ways in which writers can make a difference as they inform, inspire and motivate us with their work....

JUDITH ORTIZ COFER: BREAKING THE MOLD

Puerto Rican-born author Judith Ortiz Cofer has emerged as a distinctive and respected voice in American literature. "She is a leader, fully engaged in making and expanding cultural definitions of gender, ethnicity, language, community and domestic experience," says Hilda Raz, editor-in-chief of *Prairie Schooner*.

Cofer makes a difference by expanding our definition of American culture and by helping young writers from diverse backgrounds express their experiences. The Writer Award recognizes her for these contributions.

Her work appears in literary journals such as the *Kenyon Review*, *The Georgia Review* and *Prairie Schooner*. She is anthologized in *The Pushcart Prize*, *O. Henry Prize Stories* and *The Best American Essays*. Her reflection on writing, *Woman in Front of the Sun*, was released last fall.

Cofer's work has won numerous awards, including the PEN/Martha Albrand Special Citation in nonfiction for her book of autobiographical essays, *Silent Dancing: A Partial Remembrance of a Puerto Rican Childhood*. The American Library Association named *An Island Like You: Stories of the Barrio* a best book of the year for 1995–96.

One of her most widely read essays, "Don't Misread My Signals," is assigned in high schools across the country. Written for *Glamour* in 1992, it counters the pervasive stereotype of the Puerto Rican woman as a "hot tamale," one that she has contended with all her life. Her response has been not to fight it but to replace it with "a more interesting set of realities." She writes: "I travel around the United States reading from my books of poetry and my novel. With the stories I tell, the dreams and fears I examine in my work, I try to get my audience past the particulars of my skin color, my accent or my clothes."

Cofer, a professor of English and creative writing at the University of Georgia, also teaches writing workshops and speaks at universities, high schools, libraries and community centers. Her lectures frequently focus on diversity in American art and culture.

"Growing up in Patterson, N.J., I didn't have any literary models," says Cofer, who was born in Hormigueros, Puerto Rico, and immigrated to the mainland with her family in 1954.

"I didn't come across a single Latino author," she says of her education. "It's been an incredible journey for me to discover that my need to write also qualified me as a model of sorts for a new generation."

But, she adds, "I don't sit down in the morning and think of myself as a role model. I sit down to write my stories and my poems, which are a necessity to me as an artist. It's not a sociological mission that guides me but a narrative impulse. I set out to tell stories about my family and the world as I know it."

She encourages her students to see the people around them. "There are people in the world who are considered beneath notice. I would like for there not to be invisible people. Good writing teaches you that everyone has an inner life. From the president of the United States to the woman who comes in and empties the trash can in the classroom.

"My hope is that the students will take this knowledge into the real world and when they meet someone who looks different, they will assume that person might be interesting, might be worth knowing...."

Source: Elfrieda Abbe, Kevin Keefe, Ronald Kovach, Jeff Reich, and Philip Martin, "Writers Who Make a Difference," in *Writer*, Vol. 116, No. 1, January 2003, pp. 21–6.

Edna Acost-Belen

In the following excerpt, Acost-Belen examines with Cofer the challenges of trying to straddle Puerto Rican and American cultures in her writing.

The last few decades have witnessed literary historians and critics in the United States engaged in the formidable task of redefining the American literary experience to recognize the presence and integrate the multiple voices of vital but neglected minority cultures. Specific issues regarding the reconceptualization and opening of the traditional canon, critical approaches, curriculum content and pedagogical practices, the place of writings in languages other than English, and the intellectual and political implications of selecting certain works above others, characterize the ongoing debate and search for explanatory models to account for the distinctive cultural experiences of minority groups, and for a more faithful definition of what constitutes the total cultural practice of the United States. Within

> I FEEL THAT THERE IS THIS INVISIBLE UMBILICAL CORD CONNECTING US AND IN MY CASE, IT BECAME A LITERARY UMBILICAL CORD. I FEEL THAT THE LIFE OF MY IMAGINATION BEGAN WITH THE WOMEN OF MY FAMILY."

this process, feminist criticism, minority discourse theory, and the writings of women of color occupy a prominent and unique place insofar as they allow for a more multifaceted approach to understanding the dialectics of oppression and the articulation of various layers of marginality and subordination found in the cultural production of these groups.

The writings of Latina authors represent an excellent illustration of how issues of gender, race, culture, and class become intertwined, expanding the terms in which marginalized groups construe their identity in relation to the U.S. mainstream society. For ethnic/racial minorities, coming of age in America implies facing the internalization of stigmatized self-images based on racial and cultural differentiations that are ingrained in the fabric of the American mainstream. With a long history of racial segregation and discrimination, U.S. society is still striving to reconcile with its true multicultural character and the need to properly acknowledge the multiple presence and contributions of immigrant groups that have come and continue to arrive at its shores. Coming from cultures in which women are burdened by patriarchal traditions that struggle to perpetuate themselves in the face of the many pressures and changes implied in the immigrant experience, minority women writers juggle with the tensions arising from these cultural dualisms, from the compounding layer of gender subordination found within the same cultures they are trying to validate, and from the collective socioeconomic and racial survival struggles of their own groups within the context of U.S. society. This emerging consciousness of the multiple forms of oppression confronting women characterizes the work of Latina writers in recent decades and entails a process not entirely exempt from contradictions. While women writers attempt to demythify the cultural roles, values, and icons manufactured by a patriarchal ideology and subvert limiting cultural beliefs about family, sexuality, and moral behavior, they are also trying to reaffirm their marginalized cultural heritage as part of the wider ethnic revitalization movement among U.S. minorities.

As Latina writers are beginning to find increasing visibility and a wider audience, Judith Ortiz Cofer joins them in telling her visions about straddling between the Puerto Rican culture of her parents and ancestors and a U.S. culture often blinded by its own prejudices and undiscerning capacity to acknowledge its own pluralistic nature. The author was born in 1952 in the small town of Hormigueros, Puerto Rico, a semi-urban municipality in which the religious fervor of being the custodians of the sanctuary of the famous Virgen de Monserrate, visited by thousands of devoted pilgrims every year, is mixed with the spontaneous, irreverent, passionate, and contradictory moralities of a small town. Growing up in the same town myself gives me a privileged advantage in capturing the resonance of a much too familiar world left behind and now being reclaimed and invoked from a distance by an engrossing literary imagination.

Both a prose fiction writer and poet, Ortiz Cofer's literary production has continuously expanded since she published her first chapbook, *Peregrina*, in 1985 and won the Riverstone International Poetry Competition. More recently, her critically acclaimed novel *The Line of the Sun* (1989) was nominated for the Pulitzer Prize. She is currently writing another novel with the working title of *Star of the Caribbean* and has a forthcoming book of prose and poetry, *The Latin Deli* (see Selected Bibliography). Ortiz Cofer combines her craft as a creative writer with other professional activities on the lecture circuit and teaching at various U.S. universities.

In this interview the author discusses the autobiographical background of her fictional works, her own cultural and personal struggles, what her work represents at an individual and collective level, and the publication perils and heightened visibility of Latino writers.

Interviewer: Among many minority writers in the United States, including Latinos, autobiography is a preferred genre. The "bildungsroman," that is, the novels of formation or of coming of age have become an essential part of this literature. So, why did you want to write a novel such as The Line of the Sun, *a narrative that seems to be so personal?*

Ortiz Cofer: Mainly because I felt that it was important to me to make my life as a bilingual person and a Puerto Rican woman the subject of a lengthy work. The reason I use so much autobiographical material in the novel is not so much that I think my life is important. I feel it is sort of an obligation. As a Puerto Rican immigrant my key experience was growing up bilingual and bicultural. Therefore I felt a need to share that with others, before I could go on. Perhaps you can call it a rite of passage or something similar. But I felt that I had to get that straight in my mind. In writing *The Line of the Sun,* I was recreating my past in a way that I could understand it myself. It was a kind of training for myself both as a thinking person and a writer to get my life straight. This is not to say that all of what I wrote is autobiographical, but it has this impetus. For example, I never lived in a tenement called "El Building." But an "El Building" was central to the Puerto Rican life of Paterson, New Jersey, so in order to better understand my life there I had to write about it. Does that make sense to you?

Interviewer: So you went from your individual experience to the collective by becoming the voice of the Puerto Rican community and other Latinos in Paterson?

Ortiz Cofer: Well, yes and no because "El Building" represented to me the Puerto Rican experience in the United States. However, I do not know any other Puerto Rican who grew up as a Navy child in Paterson. That was unique to me. I guess that the answer is yes, in that I departed from my very particular experience, which molded my world view. My father being in the Navy put me at the center of my family's life since my mother did not know much English. Therefore I became the translator, the interpreter, the decision maker, very early in my life. In addition to my immigrant Puerto Rican experience, I was also a Navy child. Yes, I went from that very unique individual experience, to being a Puerto Rican girl, to being part of a Puerto Rican community.

Interviewer: In analyzing minority literature, critics tend to stress the social and political nature of these writings in denouncing the discrimination and inequalities of U.S. society. Where are the politics in your own writing? I remember reading in the preface to your Silent Dancing, *that you prefer to* tracer politica viviendo la vida *[to make politics by living life]. With all the cultural tensions and socioeconomic hardships faced by Puerto Ricans and other Latinos in the United States, how do you think that your writings will contribute to* adelantar la causa *[advance the cause]?*

Ortiz Cofer: I feel very strongly that I am contributing in the only way I know how to contribute. If I were a musician and cared for my country, I would write music that exemplified that. I would not be a soldier, I would be a musician. I am a writer, I am not a political activist. When I wrote about those lives lived in poverty, those lives lived in naivete and fear in Paterson, what I was doing was presenting a picture of the difficulties of Puerto Rican life in that city. I was not standing on a soapbox and saying, it's damn hard being a Puerto Rican girl in Paterson, New Jersey. Because that is boring, that is preaching, and that is sermonizing. And I am not political in that way. If I have any talent at all, it lies in the fact that I can tell a story. I have always told my classes that the best teachers know that the parable is the best way to teach. Christ could have stood on the mountain and talked about philosophy and bored people to death. Instead he talked about the prodigal son and the specific things that touched people through the imagination. Not to go on about a subject which I am passionate about, but I feel that every time I write a story where a woman is strong or a woman is victimized, that I am making a statement about being a woman. And every time I write a story where Puerto Ricans live their hard lives in the United States, I am saying, look, this is what is happening to all of us. I am giving you a mental picture of it, not a sermon. So that is the way in which I am political....

Interviewer: Puerto Ricans from the Island tend to look at Puerto Rican writers in the United States, particularly those who write in English, as people who do not make an effort to get closer to their culture and language because they do not write in Spanish. And of course this is a wrong assumption. What I am interested in is knowing to what extent you have considered the possibility of writing in Spanish and what role, if any, does Spanish play in your writing?

Ortiz Cofer: I really resent the prevalent attitude that if you really care about the Island you have to write in Spanish. It is not my fault that 95% of my education was in English in American schools. My parents brought me to this country and during the periods I was in Puerto Rico I went to El Colegio San Jose, a private school where the teachers were American nuns, so I could use my English. I went to the *escuela publica* (public school) for about six months; that is my total time in a school in Hormigueros. So, how can I write well in Spanish when Spanish is my second language?? When I say it is my second language it means that English is the language of my schooling. However, my home language was Spanish; I spoke only in Spanish with my mother; I dream in Spanish. I know because my husband tells me I say things in Spanish when I am asleep. I think this may sound romantic, but I think of Spanish as my subconscious language, my cultural language, my birth language. But I cannot write in Spanish because much of the grammar is alien to me. I would be making ridiculous elementary mistakes. I cannot write a poem in Spanish since I have lost my intimacy with the language and you have to be very fluent in a language to create metaphors. I can compare anything with anything in English but ask me to compare a rose to something in Spanish and I would probably say tomato soup because its the first red thing that I can think of. I feel very close to my heritage. Even if I cannot be geographically in the place where I was born, I consider myself a Puerto Rican the same way that anybody living on the Island is a Puerto Rican and if I could, I would write in Spanish.

Interviewer: Even though, technically, you write in English, there is some degree of codeswitching into Spanish in your narratives. This is a common pattern in Latino literature. In poetry, for example, some critics have argued that this "interlingual" ability enhances artistic expression and communicative skills. That is, the connotative and denotative range of words in both languages is expanded. You told me on another occasion that one of the problems you faced while trying to publish your first book is that most of the publishers you approached thought it had too much Spanish in it. What functions do you think this "interlingual" phenomenon, this mixing of languages, serve in your own writing?

Ortiz Cofer: In my creative work, which often originates in a memory of my childhood (during which, as you know, I shuttled from the Island to the mainland on a regular basis), I try to connect with the experience through language. In my case, the two languages are necessary to recreate or recall a particular image since bilingualism is an intrinsic part of my personal experience. English is the main language of my education;

Spanish—of my imagination and creativity. I do not write in English as a political act but as a necessity. I had no choice in the matter of where I was living or attending school as a child; and I do not state this defensively, but as a fact of my life. Spanish was the language I heard at home, which my mother taught me to read and write in order to communicate with my family and other individuals who made up my world as a child. It is from the personal experience (combined with imagination, of course) that I draw for my creative work. Spanish is therefore my link to my formative years. I use Spanish words and phrases almost as an incantation to lead me back to the images I need.

I have recently been asked to justify writing in English since I consider myself a Puerto Rican. I find this accusation, in view of the circumstances I just explained, a bit illogical. If I had been taken to Italy as a child by my Puerto Rican parents, I would probably be writing now in Italian about being a Puerto Rican woman. Language matters, but no one that I know refuses to read Dante in English or Spanish. I am not comparing myself to Dante, or Beatrice for that matter, it is just that my native language and my Puerto Rican heritage are the "stuff of life" in my work. English is the vehicle for my artistic expression. I think my poem, "El Olvido" (which literally means to sink into oblivion), expresses my views better than anything I can say....

Interviewer: In your preface to Silent Dancing *you acknowledge Virginia Woolf as a literary mentor of sorts, in your act of reclaiming your memories of childhood. Woolf's belief that "a woman writing thinks back to her mothers" seems to have inspired this personal narrative. How do you find Woolf's words to apply to your own experience as a woman writer?*

Ortiz Cofer: I feel what Virginia Woolf's words do is connect all of us women, not just Latinas, but Anglo women and all women as well, to the fact that women ordinarily live in a women's world, whether we want it or not, because our generation tended more to separate men and women. Once the boys could walk they were basically in a boy's world. The women spent time with the other women. When I came home from school in Puerto Rico it was to my mother, my aunts, and my grandmother. The boys were out in *el parque* [the park] playing or in *el pueblo*. So I feel that we become a different culture in a way through our mothers. So what Woolf meant was that even though her mother died while she was a young girl, her very first memory was of her mother. The smells of her mother. The first thing she remembers is a pattern on a dress when she laid down her head on her mother's lap. That is her very first memory. I feel that there is this invisible umbilical cord connecting us and in my case, it became a literary umbilical cord. I feel that the life of my imagination began with the women of my family.

Interviewer: When and why did you decide to become a writer?

Ortiz Cofer: I always knew that I needed a creative outlet. When I was a little girl I used to dream about being a dancer or a musician. Our lives prevented that because we were never in one place long enough for me to take lessons of any kind. But I always kept little journals, little notebooks. I used to make up games for my brother and me where I would transform myself into different characters. I would say that the writing has its roots there. However, I did not think of writing for publication until after graduate school. The main reason for that was that I always thought my main vocation was becoming a teacher. I was always preparing myself to be in a classroom. When I was in graduate school I started writing poems and that did it. I did not dare show them to anybody because I thought they were so much more inferior than what I was reading in my classes. Everything changed when I met Betty Owen, my first department chair, who was very encouraging. We were having lunch and she asked me: "Why don't you write some of these stories that you tell me? Why don't you write some poems?" I told her that actually I had written a few poems and after much cajoling from her I finally showed them to her, and she told me that with a few changes the poems could be mailed out for publication. I was totally astonished. Among them was "Latin Women Pray," one of the first poems I wrote as sort of a joke to myself. She told me to send it out and showed me potential publication sources. I did not know there were so many journals out there publishing poetry. I sent it to the *New Mexico Humanities Review* because it seemed to me that they would be interested in something Hispanic and I was right. They published it. That is how I got hooked. I would write poems, Betty would critique them, and then I would send them out. That was in 1977 or '78. I had only published something in a college journal before that. My official career as a writer began with this woman reassuring me that my work was publishable. I had no sense of that before when I was just writing for myself.

Interviewer: Most Latino writers in the United States have gotten their first works published by one of the small bilingual presses, such as Arte Publico Press and the Bilingual Review Press, and that has been the case with your books Reaching for the Mainland, Terms of Survival, *and* Silent Dancing. *What are the reasons that led you to make that choice?*

Ortiz Cofer: It was a number of things. When I started sending out my manuscripts, and you may have noticed that I published most of my early poems in mainstream journals but when it came to publishing a full-length book, I initially would send it to some of the bigger publishers and university presses and all I got was this collection of beautiful rejection letters stating basically that "we really like your work but it has so much Spanish in it and the material is so exotic that we do not think that we have a public for it." At the beginning, it was hard to accept that they were willing to publish my poems individually, but when it came to publishing a book that entailed a larger investment of money, my work became too exotic....

Interviewer: What has been your experience with the bilingual presses in terms of the publication process and the promotion of your work.

Ortiz Cofer: My experience has not been entirely positive. I told you about the delay in publishing my first poetry book. I have not seen many advertisements for it or much promotion. At the time I thought this was what happened to all poetry books. Since then, I know it is common practice for most publishers to do some sort of advertising. I have to assume that the bilingual presses have a limited budget. I am grateful that these presses are so willing to take the risk with unknown writers. With *Terms of Survival,* I think Arte Publico did a very nice production job. And I think that Arte Publico did more advertising for *Terms of Survival* than I got for *Reaching for the Mainland.* But with poetry in this country you always expect very little. My experience with the first edition of *Silent Dancing* was also rather disappointing insofar as many of the essays had already been published in very good literary journals and I had high expectations for the book. One of the essays was featured in *The Georgia Review* women's issue that also included works by Eudora Welty and Joyce Carol Oates, who chose it for *The Best American Essays 1991.* Another won a Pushcart Prize, which is very prestigious. But, when the essays came out as a collection I felt that the production was not up to par. I found many errors in the book. Once again, I have to relegate that to the budgetary constraints faced by the small presses. Frankly, it is very disappointing to work on a book for as long as I worked on *Silent Dancing* and have it come out not looking as good as it should. Most of these problems, however, were corrected in the second edition and I have to credit the press for this effort. The small presses serve a big function; their work is very important; but the author should be allowed to have more control of the production. I think the small presses have to improve their proofreading and advertisement, so that they can become more competitive with university and other commercial presses. This is my pet peeve; maybe you have also heard it from other authors. We consider our books our babies and do not want them damaged at birth.

Interviewer: You write both poetry and fiction. Do you have a preference between these two genres?

Ortiz Cofer: No. I think poetry has made me more disciplined. It taught me how to write, because to write a poem takes so much skill. It requires a lot of self-discipline since poetry contains the essence of language. Every word weighs a ton. Every word counts. You cannot write a sloppy poem and get it published. I know from my experience that most of the literary journals that I submitted my work to receive over 20,000 manuscripts a year. It is a very competitive field. So you get weeded out early as a poet. Poetry taught me about economizing in language and about the power of language. So I will never stop writing poetry. When I get up in the morning I work on a poem, first. That fine-tunes my language ability. If I work on a poem and then switch to the novel, I am not going to have any flabby or loose language. I am transferring that need to economize to a different genre. That's why you may see some resemblance between my poetry and the novel....

Source: Edna Acost-Belen, "A *MELUS* Interview: Judith Ortiz Cofer," in *MELUS*, Vol. 18, No. 3, Fall 1993, pp. 83–98.

Rafael Ocasio and Rita Ganey

In the following excerpt, Ocasio asks Cofer about the influences of women and Puerto Rico on her writing.

> "I'M DISTANCING MYSELF TO SEE WHAT IT WAS LIKE TO BE A PUERTO RICAN WOMAN IN THE 1930'S AND 1940'S RATHER THAN A PUERTO RICAN GIRL IN THE 1960'S. I AM STILL USING EVERYTHING I HEARD MY AUNTS AND MY MOTHER SAY."

... RO: It is obvious that women, specifically your grandmother, are influences in your work.

JOC: A lot of my stories have to do with the fact that my grandmother, who is slightly suspicious of books, is a woman connected to her work, her children, her family, and has not had the opportunity or the time to be educated. She loves storytelling, though. If she can teach something by telling a story, she'll do it. My book of essays, *Silent Dancing*, is dedicated to that very strong narrative impulse. Most of the stories in my work date back to the times when I would sit around at my grandmother's house and listen to the women telling their stories.

RO: How did you make the transition from poetry to prose writing?

JOC: I don't feel that I've made a transition. I've added a genre. I've never stopped writing poetry. What the public mainly sees between books is my poems. The poem is an immediate source for telling a story. I found a few years ago that I got an immense amount of satisfaction from telling a story. I knew that there were certain characters I wanted to create and let them act. I chose my black sheep Angel Guzman, who is a real person and who was a real black sheep of my family. In my childhood, I had heard only stories that my mother thought a small child should hear about Guzman. I let my imagination run wild. The novel developed out of my strong sense that I could tell a story and that the natural form for it should be a novel.

RO: You once mentioned that you felt like Malinche when you announced your intentions of writing a novel.

JOC: The United States is a place of specialization. You're supposed to stick to your little corner of literature. In Latin America and Europe, writers are writers. Octavio Paz writes plays, he writes essays, he writes anything he wants, and nobody finds that suspicious. If a poet in the United States writes a novel, people say, "What for, the money?" It is true that prose makes more money than poetry. That was not my motivation, because I never believed that anything I wrote would bring me money. Some of my very dedicated friends in poetry thought that I was going to abandon poetry to become a novelist. Writing is writing. If one morning I get up and have an urge to write an essay, that's just as legitimate as writing a poem. Because of my poetry friends' original reaction, I felt like I was betraying some kind of trust. You do not have to be like a nun practicing only poetry. I feel that I have the right to experiment with any form I choose.

RO: Let's talk more specifically about your novel. The Spanish tone which permeates your English prose resembles the criollismo techniques as it presents universal values through original Latin American motifs. Would you comment on that particular style or do you feel that there is a special affinity with American and Spanish American, including Puerto Rican writers?

JOC: I intended to make the language relate to the theme. I was writing about rural Puerto Ricans, leading their lives in connections to each other and the land. I felt that idiomatic American English would defeat that purpose, because Spanish is lyrical. These people were thinking and speaking in Spanish, but I was writing my novel in English. I wrote as if it were being translated at the moment of writing. It preserved the flavor of the Spanish, because Spanish is syntactically different from English. It is also more poetic in its expression. My poems that deal with Puerto Rico are syntactically different than my poems that deal with my life in the United States. The tone is a direct result of the different syntactical construction I used in order to make it seem credible and feasible that these people were actually Spanish speakers and thinkers, not Americans impersonating Puerto Ricans.

RO: A characteristic many people have pointed out in the literature written by Puerto Ricans in New York is the highly autobiographical quality of it. Would you say that element is a particular characteristic of minority literature?

JOC: I am not an expert in minority literatures, but I have read some Jewish novels and works by other ethnic minorities. Autobiography plays a large part, but it's really a logical process. It's not that it's boring, but most everybody knows what it's like to be professional in middle-class America. Not many people know what it's like to be a Puerto Rican woman growing up in the 1960s. Why should I reach out and invent something, when my own life provides me with interesting material that is not readily available to the public? I thought to use my life first, because it was there. Like Mount Rushmore, you know. In the novel I am currently working on, I'm departing somewhat from that. The protagonist is a woman who lived three decades before I was born. She's a dancer, which I'm not. I'm distancing myself to see what it was like to be a Puerto Rican woman in the 1930s and 1940s rather than a Puerto Rican girl in the 1960s. I am still using everything I heard my aunts and my mother say. I'm using life, but I'm not using my life. I would say it is a logical thing to do. If a Black man wants to write a novel, I would say that his first choice would be to tell about being a Black man in America, rather than an Irish man in New York City, because that's politically meaningless to him. The minority writer has to take a political stand. Our lives are political.

RO: One element that really struck me when I was reading The Line of the Sun *was how you play with the boundaries of autobiography and fiction. I was really interested to see that your Marisol becomes a writer herself.*

JOC: I wrote a preface using Virginia Woolf to say that memory is ninety percent fiction. As a writer, I feel absolutely at liberty to cross over boundaries. My technique is to start with something that I know very well, like my Uncle Guzman. People loved him in spite of the fact that he was a rascal. I started with that which was absolutely true. Then I started imagining him in situations that had never actually happened. I think literature has a truth that has nothing to do with the dictionary definition of truth. I think there's factuality and there's truth. I can say to you, "My father was in the Cuban missile crisis," and tell you the dates, but that is not as meaningful as the fact that we lost contact with him for six months and thought he was dead. The truth is what I felt about my father disappearing, not that he was actually on a ship in Cuba at that time. Truth is what I can make people feel. I have tried to be accurate with history. If I'm going to talk about the Cuban missile crisis, I talk about it as a historical event that took place in particular years. The thoughts and the feelings of the people involved are mine to make up. The only license that the poet has is to make truth what she wants it to be, as long as you can convince someone else that it's important.

RO: What do you think will be the reaction of the Puerto Rican scholar and reader to your novel? What will be the reaction of the American scholar and reader?

JOC: Interestingly enough, I've gotten mainly the reaction of the American readers to my novel. That has been an interesting phenomenon to me because it was published by the University of Georgia Press, which had never published a novel before, certainly a novel like mine. They sent it to American reviewers all over the place. It has been reviewed very little by Hispanic scholars. I don't know if they're ignoring it, or if it just hasn't come into their hands. It has been reviewed very widely by Americans. I've been stunned that ninety-nine percent of the reviews have been extremely positive in what they say the message is. "We can read a book that's not just aimed at Puerto Rican audiences." They can read the book in their language and get the flavor and the sense of the Puerto Rican idiom. I feel good about having written something that will teach people how Puerto Ricans think and talk. I want Puerto Ricans to read my novel, but they're not going to learn as much as the Americans who may have Puerto Rican neighbors and not know what makes them different. I was at a conference in Paris where different writers were being discussed. A publisher said, "We don't know where to put Judith Cofer." Judith Cofer is writing in standard English, and she lives in Georgia. Until recently, I was somewhere in limbo. I'm not a mainstream North American writer, but I publish in mainstream North American journals. I'm not an island writer. All I know is that I'm a writer, period, writing about the one thing that defines me as a human being—my biculturalism. It's just now being taken seriously by the Hispanic critics. A wonderful review of my novel came out in *The San Juan Star* in English and then in *El Nuevo Dia*. Several of the bookstores immediately ordered my book. There were several people on the island very interested in what I'm doing. The reviewer for *El Nuevo Dia* said she was relieved that somebody was writing about Puerto Ricans in standard English, because there are many misconceptions held by Americans that are promulgated by some of the

Nuyorican writers who write in a language that is only understood by bilingual people....

Source: Rafael Ocasio and Rita Ganey, "Speaking in Puerto Rican: An Interview with Judith Ortiz Cofer," in *Bilingual Review*, Vol. 17, No. 2, May–August 1992, pp. 143–47.

SOURCES

Abbe, Elfrieda, Kevin Keefe, Ronald Kovach, Jeff Reich, and Philip Martin, "Writers Who Make a Difference," in *Writer*, Vol. 116, No. 1, January 2003, pp. 21–26.

"About Us," in *Nuyorican Poets Cafe*, http://www.nuyorican.org/AboutUs/AboutUs.html (accessed September 18, 2009).

Acosta-Belen, Edna, "Judith Ortiz Cofer," in *The New Georgia Encyclopedia*, October 5, 2006, http://www.georgiaencyclopedia.org/nge/Article.jsp?id=h-488 (accessed September 18, 2009).

Arana, Marie, "We Are a Nation of Many Voices," in *Multicultural Literature in the United States Today*, February 5, 2009, http://www.america.gov/st/diversity-english/2009/February/20090210140048mlenuhret0.4137842.html (accessed September 18, 2009).

Faymonville, Carmen, "New Transnational Identities in Judith Ortiz Cofer's Autobiographical Fiction," in *MELUS*, Vol. 26, No. 2, Summer 2001, pp. 129–31.

Freedman, Estelle, *No Turning Back: The History of Feminism and the Future of Women*, Ballantine, 2002.

Ortiz Cofer, Judith, "Aunty Misery," in *Choices: 17 Stories of Challenge and Choice, with Units for Mastering Language Arts Skills*, compiled by Burton Goodman, McGraw-Hill, 2003, pp. 187–88.

———, *Silent Dancing: A Partial Remembrance of a Puerto Rican Childhood*, Arte Publico Press, 1990.

Perez y Gonzalez, Maria E., *Puerto Ricans in the United States: The New Americans*, Greenwood Press, 2000.

Vazquez, Doris M., "Puerto Rican Folktales," in *Folktales*, Vol. 2, Yale-New Haven Teachers Institute, 1993, http://www.yale.edu/ynhti/curriculum/units/1993/2/93.02.12.x.html (accessed September 18, 2009).

FURTHER READING

Algarin, Miguel, and Bob Holman, eds., *Aloud: Voices from the Nuyorican Poets Cafe*, Holt, 1994.
> The Nuyorican Poets Cafe, a famous New York City art collective, is known for sponsoring writing-based performance events that are typically multicultural in scope. This collection of pieces performed there sheds light on a style of literature that owes its inception to the Puerto Rican immigrant community.

Aliotta, Jerome J., and Sandra Stotsky, *The Puerto Rican Americans*, Chelsea House, 1995.
> Part of Chelsea House's The Immigrant Experience series, this volume examines Puerto Rican history and culture as well as Puerto Ricans' place in American history and culture.

Andersen, Hans Christian, *Hans Christian Andersen: The Complete Fairy Tales and Stories*, translated by Erik Christian Haugaard, Anchor, 1983.
> Andersen is the author of hundreds of classic fairy tales, and this comprehensive edition features 156 of them. Notes accompany each story with commentary and historical context.

Anselmo, Angela, and Alma Rubal-Lopez, *On Becoming Nuyoricans*, Morehouse, 2004.
> Part of the Counterpoints: Studies in the Postmodern Theory of Education series, this book portrays two Puerto Rican sisters who are raised in New York during the 1950s and 1960s. They, and other Puerto Ricans like them, are often called Nuyoricans.

Rivera, Nelson, *Visual Artists and the Puerto Rican Performing Arts, 1950–1990: The Works of Jack and Irene Delano, Antonio Martorell, Jaime Suarez, and Oscar Mestey-Villamil*, Peter Lang, 1997.
> For a deeper understanding of Puerto Rican culture, this book will introduce readers to leading contemporary artists from Puerto Rico. Both visual arts and the performing arts are explored in this volume.

Urciuoli, Bonnie, *Exposing Prejudice: Puerto Rican Experiences of Language, Race, and Class*, Westview Press, 1996.
> This book also looks at the Puerto Rican immigrant experience, albeit from a more psychological standpoint. Part of the Institutional Structures of Feeling series, the volume focuses particularly on ethnographic studies of Puerto Ricans living in the metropolitan New York area.

B. Wordsworth

V. S. NAIPAUL

1959

"B. Wordsworth" is a short story by V. S. Naipaul that was first published as part of the novel *Miguel Street* in 1959. The book, which is a collection of interrelated stories, is available in a Vintage edition published in 2002.

Naipaul is one of the most widely read and respected writers in the world, and this story was one of the first he wrote. Of Indian descent, he grew up in Trinidad, spending some of his childhood in Port of Spain, the capital city. Trinidad was a British colony at the time. In the fictional stories in *Miguel Street*, Naipaul draws on his memories of the people he grew up with, who were also Trinidadian of Indian ancestry. "B. Wordsworth" is therefore set in Trinidad in the 1940s. Naipaul would have been about ten years old at the time, and the story is told by an unnamed boy of about that age. The boy encounters and becomes friends with an older man named B. Wordsworth who likes to think of himself as a poet, and is so named after the great English poet, William Wordsworth.

"B. Wordsworth" is a story of friendship between a fatherless boy and a sympathetic adult. It reveals much about life in the poorer areas of Port of Spain during this period, and it also raises the question of what it means to be or try to become a poet. The story is an accessible example of Naipaul's early work and also an introduction to West Indian literature, which first began to make an impact beyond its borders in the 1950s.

V.S. Naipaul *(Indranil Mukherjee / AFP / Getty Image)*

AUTHOR BIOGRAPHY

A Nobel Prize-winner and the author of numerous novels and nonfiction books, Vidiadhar Surajprasad Naipaul was born in Chaguanas, Trinidad, on August 17, 1932, to parents of Indian ancestry. His father was a journalist. In Naipaul's early years, the family moved around a lot, but in 1938, they settled in Port of Spain for several years. Naipaul recalled this as a peaceful time during his mostly unsettled childhood, and it was his observations of the street life in the poor areas of the city that eventually made up the substance of his novel *Miguel Street* (1959). However, Naipaul disliked the limitations of life on a small Caribbean island, and in 1950, he was able to escape, with the help of a scholarship, to study English literature at University College at Oxford University in England. He already knew that he wanted to be a writer, but it was not until he started writing about the people in the community in which he grew up in Trinidad that he found his subject matter. He wrote *Miguel Street*, which includes the story "B. Wordsworth," in the mid-1950s, but he decided not to publish it until later. His first published novel was *The Mystic Masseur* in 1957, followed by *The Suffrage of Elvira* (1958). All three novels are set in Trinidad. *Miguel Street* received the Somerset Maugham Award in 1961, the same year Naipaul's fourth novel was published. This was *A House for Mr. Biswas*, which many consider to be his finest work. It is also set in Trinidad, and the protagonist is based on Naipaul's father.

Meanwhile, Naipaul had returned to Trinidad for visits in 1956 and from 1960 to 1961. The fruits of his second visit included his first nonfiction work, *The Middle Passage: Impressions of Five Societies—British, French, and Dutch—in the West Indies and South America* (1962), an account of the history of the West Indies. Naipaul spent a year in India in 1962 and published his impressions of the country in *An Area of Darkness* in 1964. In his fifth novel, *Mr. Stone and the Knights Companion* (1963), he broke new ground, setting the novel in England with English characters. The novel received a British literary award, the Hawthornden Prize. His next novel, *The Mimic Men* (1967), won the W. H. Smith Literary Award. Another nonfiction work followed, *The Loss of El Dorado* (1969), a history of Trinidad.

In the 1970s, now settled in Wiltshire, England, Naipaul produced some of his finest work, including the short story collection *In a Free State* (1971), which won Britain's prestigious Booker Prize. The novel *Guerrillas* (1975) established Naipaul's reputation in the United States, a reputation solidified by the publication of *A Bend in the River* (1979), set in Africa. In 1978–1979, Naipaul was in the United States, teaching at Wesleyan University in Connecticut.

Naipaul continued to publish regularly throughout the 1980s and 1990s. *Among the Believers: An Islamic Journey* (1981) resulted from the study of contemporary Islam that he made on visits to Iran and other Muslim countries in 1979. *Finding the Center* (1984), consisting of two personal narratives, was followed by the autobiographical novel *The Enigma of Arrival* (1987) which became a bestseller. Notable publications in the 1990s include *India: A Million Mutinies Now* (1990), *A Way in the World* (1994), and *Beyond Belief: Islamic Excursions among the Converted Peoples* (1998).

In 2001, Naipaul was awarded the Nobel Prize in Literature. He published the novel *Half a Life* the same year, and his fourteenth novel, *Magic Seeds*, appeared in 2004. He has been nominated for the 2009 Man Booker International Prize.

Naipaul married Patricia Ann Hale in 1955. After her death in 1996, he married Nadira Khannum Alvi.

PLOT SUMMARY

"B. Wordsworth" is set in Miguel Street, a poor area in Port of Spain, Trinidad, during the early 1940s. It is narrated by an unnamed young boy who lives there with his family. He is used to seeing beggars come to the house seeking food. But one afternoon someone rather different turns up. After the boy has returned from school, a strange but well-spoken man arrives and asks if he may watch the bees in the palm trees that stand in the yard. The boy's mother says it will be all right if the boy keeps a watch on the stranger. The man and the boy spend about an hour watching the bees. It transpires that the man is a poet and his name is B. Wordsworth. The B is short for Black. He claims to be the greatest poet in the world. B. Wordsworth asks the boy about his mother, and then pulls a poem out of his pocket. He says the poem is about mothers and that he will sell it to the boy for four cents. The boy's mother refuses to buy it and says the man must leave. B. Wordsworth confides in the boy that he has not yet sold a single copy, but he likes to wander around watching things.

A week later the boy meets the poet again at the corner of Miguel Street. The poet says he has a mango tree in his yard and invites the boy to come and eat some of the mangoes. The boy goes to the poet's hut on Alberto Street and eats about six mangoes. When he returns home, his mother beats him for being gone without permission. He goes back to B. Wordsworth, and the two of them take a walk together. At the racecourse, they lie down and look up at the night sky. B. Wordsworth tells the boy the names of the stars.

The boy and the poet become friends. B. Wordsworth tells the boy not to tell anyone about him, and the boy agrees. He enjoys visiting the man, and he asks him why his yard is unkempt. B. Wordsworth tells him a story about a young couple who were in love and married. They were both poets. The wife became pregnant, but she and the baby died. The sad husband never cultivated their garden again.

They continue to take walks together and visit local points of interest. They go to cafés for ice cream. The boy enjoys these trips.

One day, B. Wordsworth announces that he is going to tell the boy a secret. He says he is writing the greatest poem in the world. He has been working on it for five years, writing one line a month. At that rate, he says, it will take him twenty-two years to complete it. He hopes the poem will help humanity.

As the days go by, they continue to walk together and sometimes watch the ships come into the harbor. But B. Wordsworth never confides in the boy any more lines from his poem.

One day, the boy asks his friend how he makes a living, and the poet replies that he sings calypso (a type of music that originated in the Caribbean), and that raises enough. The boy asks him if he will be rich when he finishes his poem, but the poet does not reply. Another day, when the boy visits B. Wordsworth in his hut, the poet looks old and weak. He confesses that he is not having much success writing his poem. The boy thinks the man is dying, and he begins to cry. The poet tries to comfort him. He says he will tell the boy another secret if he agrees to go away and never come back to see him again. The boy agrees. Then B. Wordsworth confides the secret: the story he told about the young couple and the wife who died was not true; also, all his talk about poetry and the greatest poem in the world is not true either. The boy runs home crying.

A year later, the boy goes again to Alberto Street, but he finds that the poet's hut has been pulled down, replaced by a large building. The trees in the yard have been cut down. There is nothing there to show that B. Wordsworth ever existed.

CHARACTERS

The Narrator

The unnamed narrator is a young boy who is being raised by his mother in a house on Miguel Street. His father is dead. (This is revealed in "Love, Love, Love, Alone," one of the other stories in *Miguel Street*). The boy's age is not given, but he is no younger than eight and probably no older than nine or ten. He is still young enough to need his mother's permission to leave the house, and she beats him severely when he displeases her. He is a perceptive, inquisitive boy, and he readily accepts the friendship offered by B. Wordsworth because he learns a lot through the old man, such as the names of the constellations. Growing up fatherless, the boy needs a man in his life. However, as a young boy, he is still naïve enough to believe everything B. Wordsworth tells him, and he does not question that B. Wordsworth will write the greatest poem in the world. He thinks the poem will make the poet rich. The boy gets very attached to B. Wordsworth and is upset when the old man breaks off the relationship and confesses that the stories he told were not true.

The Narrator's Mother

The narrator's mother is a widow who is raising her son on her own. She is not described in any detail but she is certainly not short on discipline. She whips her son with a switch for not telling her where he was going, and he is accustomed to receiving beatings from her. She is poor but not as poor as some in the neighborhood, and she is willing to give either food or small amounts of money to beggars who come to the house.

B. Wordsworth

B. Wordsworth is a man of about sixty. He is small and neatly dressed, speaks grammatical English, and lives in a one-room hut with a yard that has mango, coconut, and plum trees in it. The narrator meets him when B. Wordsworth comes into the yard and asks to watch the bees in the palm trees. He does this for an hour. He likes to sit and just observe nature. He calls himself a poet, and his last name is the same as that of William Wordsworth (1770–1850), the great English Romantic poet. It is unstated whether this is B. Wordsworth's inherited last name or whether he chose it himself because he wanted to identify himself with the great poet, whom he calls his brother. The B in his name stands for Black, suggesting that he is the black Wordsworth. B. Wordsworth, however, lacks a realistic understanding of his own abilities. He is writing what he says will be the greatest poem in the world, a poem that will speak to all humanity, but he only manages to write one line of it. The truth is that such a poem is beyond his very modest powers. Although he has managed to write at least one poem, about mothers, he cannot find anyone who is willing to buy it. The meager living he makes comes not from poetry but from singing calypso songs.

B. Wordsworth also likes to nourish romantic notions of his own past. The story he tells the boy about the young wife and unborn child who died is supposed to be about himself and to explain why he lets his yard grow untended. The wife loved the garden and after she died the man said he would never touch anything in it. Later, B. Wordsworth tells the boy the story is not true. He may have made it up because he does not want to admit that he is too lazy to trim the yard, or it may be that he just likes stories.

B. Wordsworth might be seen as living an unproductive, pointless life, comforted by illusions, but in fact he is a positive influence on the boy. He teaches him how to observe nature and for a while makes his life exciting, full of trips to local places of interest. He teaches him to look with wonder upon the world. But B. Wordsworth's tragedy is that he never makes the impact on the world that he wants to. In fact, after he dies, it is as if he never existed. No one but the boy remembers him.

THEMES

Friendship

The young boy and B. Wordsworth form an unusual but genuine friendship. Each one contributes something to it. The boy finds B. Wordsworth a very interesting character. He has probably never met anyone quite like him. He listens to the poet's fanciful words without cynicism or judgment, and he learns a lot from him. Since the boy's father is dead, B. Wordsworth for a while fills a gap in his life. His horizons expand as a result of the friendship of the old man, and the world became a most exciting place. He becomes emotionally attached to B. Wordsworth and cries when their relationship comes to an end. For B. Wordsworth, perhaps the boy is a surrogate son or grandson. He certainly gains a lot from their relationship. He is no doubt delighted to have found someone who takes him seriously and listens to him, since he likes to speak of what he knows and the values he lives by. Probably no one else listens to him. So each fills a need for the other.

Poetry

B. Wordsworth tells his young friend much about poetry and the poet. A poet must be in touch with nature; he must observe the world closely in an unhurried way. The poet is perceptive and can see what others cannot, about people, places, and life itself. He also feels compassion for all living

TOPICS FOR FURTHER STUDY

- Write a short story or sketch that features several characters based on people who live on your street. In the dialogue, try to capture the way the people actually speak, as Naipaul does in "B. Wordsworth." As an alternative, write a story in which one character tries to base himself on someone famous—a movie star, perhaps, or a popular singer.
- Make a drawing or painting that illustrates a scene in "B. Wordsworth." Then write a paragraph that explains your visual description of the scene.
- With several other students, adapt "B. Wordsworth" and create a dramatic performance based on the story. Split the boy narrator's role among two students. One should read the narrative passages; the other should read the dialogue. Other students can take the roles of the mother and B. Wordsworth. Videotape your performance, add music for effect, and lead a discussion afterward about the story.
- Read the rest of the short stories in *Miguel Street*. Write an essay in which you select two characters in addition to B. Wordsworth and compare what all three characters have in common. Are they successful? Happy? Do they work hard, doing what they love, or are they misfits in some way?
- Read some of the seventeen stories in the young-adult anthology *Rites of Passage: Stories about Growing Up by Black Writers from Around the World*, edited by Tonya Bolden (Hyperion Press, 1995). Write an essay in which you examine the pivotal events in one of these stories and what the main character learns from them. Then compare those events to what the narrator in "B. Wordsworth" learns from his friendship with B. Wordsworth. What, for example, has the narrator learned about life by the end of the story?

things. B. Wordsworth tells the boy he "can watch a small flower like the morning glory and cry," and he adds, "when you're a poet you can cry for everything." B. Wordsworth has adopted what he thinks is the correct manner for the poet, and the boy makes this observation about his friend: "He did everything as though he were doing it for the first time in his life. He did everything as though he were doing some church rite." The poet, then, looks at familiar things as if they are unfamiliar, and he has an attitude of reverence for life. The poet's task is to reflect on his experiences and write about them in a way that makes them meaningful for everyone, not just himself. Thus B. Wordsworth wants to write a poem that "will sing to all humanity."

Failure

B. Wordsworth has large ambitions but little in the way of achievement. He has conceived a goal—to become a great poet—that exceeds whatever small talent he may have. He appears to have done nothing much else in life, and his life might be seen as aimless. He convinces himself that he is writing a great poem, although he knows in his heart (as his later confession to the boy shows) that this is not true. He says that once, when he was twenty years old, "I felt the power within myself," but that power, whatever it was, never produced anything. He must know that it has gone now and will never return. Seen in this light, his determination to link himself to the great poet William Wordsworth is a comic exaggeration.

Instead of doing something productive, B. Wordsworth sits around watching nature, dreaming his life away. The reality of his situation, behind the illusions he cultivates, is poignantly revealed in the incident when the policeman who has found him and the boy lying on the ground looking up at the stars asks him what he is doing there. B. Wordsworth responds, "I have been asking myself the same question for forty years." This might be seen as a humorous response that also emphasizes the inquiring nature of the poet's mind, but it also reveals, perhaps inadvertently, the uncertainty and lack of direction that has characterized B. Wordsworth's life. The truth is that B. Wordsworth's life is a failure. He has achieved nothing in his life, which is a story of unrealized potential. In truth, he is a sad, lonely old man, and when he dies he is soon forgotten. It is as if he never existed.

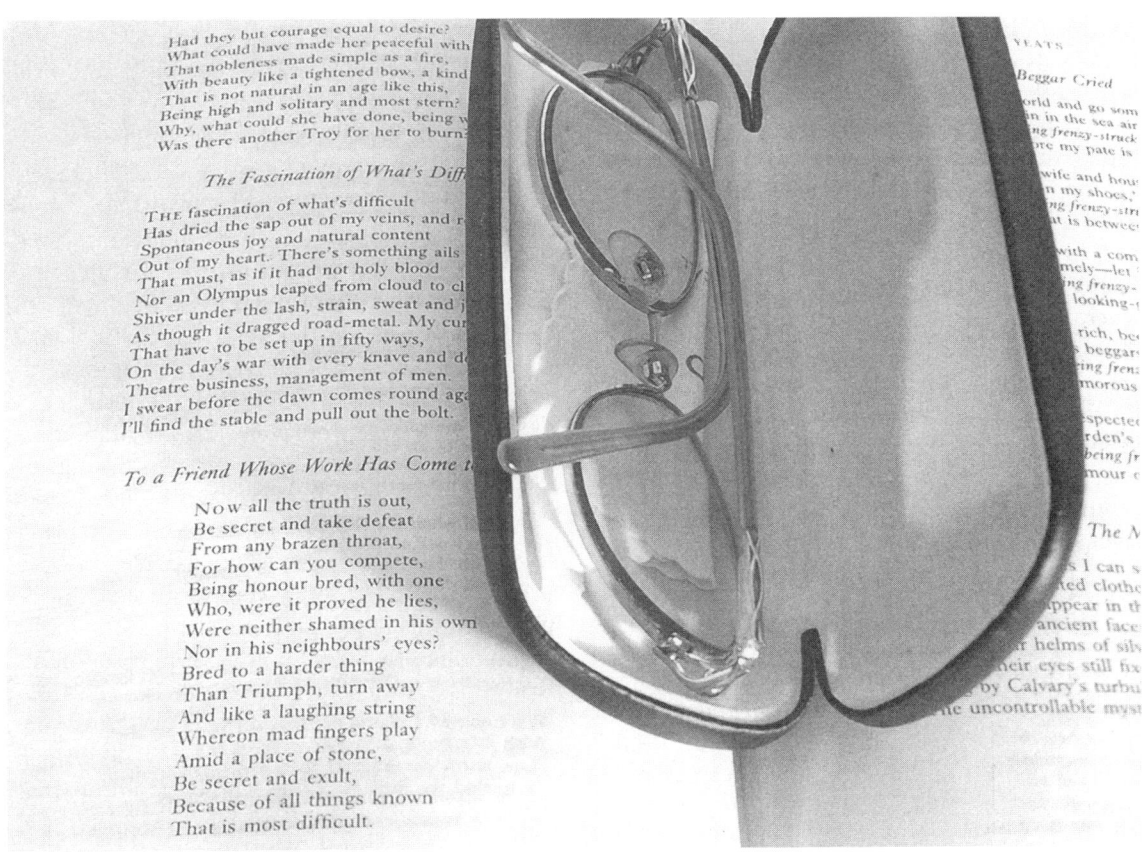

Reading glasses for poetry (Image copyright Peter Baxter, 2009. Used under license from Shutterstock.com)

STYLE

Dialect

Of the three characters given dialogue in the story, two of them speak a local dialect that might be called non-standard English. When B. Wordsworth first comes to the narrator's house, the boy calls to his mother, "Ma, it have a man outside here. He say he want to watch the bees." In the second sentence, the second-person form of the verb "to say" is used, instead of the grammatically correct third-person form, which would be "he says."

A bit later, the boy asks B. Wordsworth about his occupation: "What you does do, mister?" The inverted word order is noticeable ("you does" rather than "does you,") as well as the use of the third-person form of the verb "to do" ("does") rather than the grammatically correct second-person, "do" (since he is addressing the man directly as "you"). This is the exact reverse of the previous example, in which the second-person rather than third-person form is used.

The boy's mother speaks in the same way. She says, for example, "You think you is a man now and could go all over the place?" The grammatically correct form of the sentence would be, "You think you are a man now and can go all over the place?"

The examples here are not to suggest that the way these people speak is "wrong"; they just show that the author is capturing the local idioms and making the story authentic, since that is likely the way people who lived in the poorer areas of Port of Spain spoke at that time.

In contrast to the other two characters, B. Wordsworth speaks in perfectly grammatical sentences. He has obviously learned carefully how to speak in this way. "His English was so good, it didn't sound natural," the narrator says. The contrast between B. Wordsworth and the way the others speak is another way of showing that B. Wordsworth does not really fit in his environment. He is clearly different from most people there. This is in keeping with his self-image of being a poet destined for greatness.

Symbolism

B. Wordsworth models himself after William Wordsworth, who is known as a nature poet. B. Wordsworth's identification with nature rather than with the human world can be seen in the environment he creates for himself. Although he lives in Alberto Street, which is part of the town, it does not seem like it to the young narrator. Not only is the yard green with several trees, but also "the place looked wild, as though it wasn't in the city at all. You couldn't see all the big concrete houses in the street." B. Wordsworth's environment is therefore in keeping with his perception of his vocation as a poet of nature, among other things. The natural environment is a symbol of his choice in life, to be close to nature.

A year after the boy has stopped seeing B. Wordsworth, he returns to Alberto Street but finds it much changed. B. Wordsworth's hut has been demolished, "and a big, two-storied building had taken its place." The trees are also gone, and "there was brick and concrete everywhere." While B. Wordsworth was alive, there was a small portion of the town that seemed to be in harmony with him, but after he dies even that vanishes. The brick and mortar that replace the old hut and yard are a symbol of the march of progress that may improve the material conditions of people's lives but perhaps also exclude something positive that B. Wordsworth, for all his failure and illusions, stood for. It is as if there is no longer a place for the romanticism that the boy associated with B. Wordsworth and absorbed from him. It has given way to the hard world of practicalities.

HISTORICAL CONTEXT

Trinidad in the 1930s and 1940s

Trinidad, where the story is set, and where Naipaul lived until he was eighteen, was colonized by Spain in the sixteenth and seventeenth centuries, and Spanish control continued until 1797, when the island was captured by Great Britain, which then assumed control. In the 1840s, the British began recruiting laborers from India to work on the cocoa and sugar plantations. These workers were virtual slaves during the three- to five-year period of their indenture. However, many of them, once they had completed their indenture, established plantations themselves and prospered in their new country. Naipaul himself is the grandson of an indentured Hindu laborer who left India for Trinidad. Most of the characters in Naipaul's novel *Miguel Street*, including the narrator, are also of Indian heritage.

During the time the story is set, in the early 1940s, Trinidad was still under British rule. People like B. Wordsworth, a poor, underemployed calypso singer who has few prospects in life, were common during this time in Port of Spain, one of the biggest cities in this impoverished colonial society. Economic conditions in Trinidad, as well as in Tobago, a neighboring island that in 1888 had been incorporated with Trinidad into a single British colony, had worsened during the 1930s. Large numbers of workers suffered from malnutrition and disease, and the infant mortality rate was very high. Many people, in both urban and rural areas, were destitute. Unemployment was also high following layoffs on the plantations after 1929, and housing was poor. Bridget Brereton, in her book, *A History of Modern Trinidad, 1783–1962*, reports on the verdict of the Forster Commission, set up by the British government in 1937 to examine the unrest that swept through the island in 1937. Brereton writes, "Some of the worst examples of worker housing were in Port of Spain, where the Commission saw barracks 'indescribable in their lack of elementary needs of decency'." In 1937, there were riots and strikes all over Trinidad, including Port of Spain. The unrest, which is mentioned in "The Coward," one of the stories in *Miguel Street*, provided the impetus for the emergence of a trade union movement in Trinidad and Tobago. This was a major development on the islands from 1937 to 1950.

During World War II, the British government agreed to allow the United States to lease land on which to construct air and naval bases on Trinidad. These construction projects provided thousands of Trinidadians with jobs and paid them much higher wages than they had received before. The Americans also undertook public works, such as road building, and were admired by the local population for their "competence, their modern personnel practices and their aura of easy money," writes Brereton. In *Miguel Street*, there are several references to the money the Americans brought to the island during the war. The following passage appears in "The Coward": "The Americans were crawling all over Port of Spain in those days.... Children didn't take long to find out that they were easy

COMPARE & CONTRAST

- **1940s:** In 1946, the first elections in which all adults are allowed to vote take place in Trinidad and Tobago. Voters elect a legislative council.

    1950s: The formation of the West Indian Independence Party in 1952 and the People's Democratic Party in 1952 begins an era of party politics in Trinidad and Tobago. There is a growing push for independence from Britain. The general election in 1956 is won by the People's National Movement (PNM), led by Eric Williams, and the PNM, which is particularly strong in Port of Spain, forms a government that lasts from 1956 to 1961. The colony gains its independence from Britain in 1962.

    Today: Trinidad and Tobago is an independent republic and has been since 1976. It is a parliamentary democracy.

- **1940s:** In 1943, during World War II, oil accounts for 80 percent of all exports from Trinidad and Tobago. The oil industry employs 15,000 workers. However, the majority of workers in Trinidad are employed in agriculture.

    1950s: In 1954, the Soldado marine oil field is discovered, and production begins in 1955.

    Today: Petroleum and natural gas production are major factors in Trinidad and Tobago's prosperous economy. They account for 40 percent of the Gross Domestic Product and 80 percent of exports.

- **1940s:** Port of Spain is known for its calypso singers. The calypso was developed in this region at the turn of the century. Two types of calypso flourish during this period: the oratorical calypso, with complex words and sentences sung in English, and the ballad calypso, which tells a story in simpler language. The presence of American servicemen in Trinidad during World War II leads to calypso becoming internationally known and very popular in the United States and Europe. The steel band is invented in Port of Spain in the 1930s and 1940s.

    1950s: The most famous calypso singer is Sparrow. Sparrow is a supporter of the People's National Movement and writes songs in support of black nationalism. Calypso becomes a vehicle for social protest.

    Today: Calypso and steel band music performances form an important part of the annual carnival season in Trinidad, which runs from Christmas to Lent (the period leading up to Easter).

---

people, always ready to give with both hands." In that story, the narrator (the same boy who narrates "B. Wordsworth") encounters an American soldier and tries to beg some chewing gum from him, without success. He thinks the man is drunk. In "Caution," the local people are sad when the war ends and the Americans begin to leave. According to Brereton, the American presence in Trinidad during World War II transformed the way the local people saw themselves: "The 'American occupation' demolished the myth of white superiority; Trinidadians saw white Americans perform hard manual labour and laughed at the antics of drunken 'bad behaviour' sailors. The automatic deference to a white face became a thing of the past."

The West Indian Novel

According to Robert D. Hamner, in *V. S. Naipaul*, the West Indian novel, by which he means mainly the literature of Jamaica, Trinidad and Tobago, and Barbados, can be said to have begun in the 1950s. Hamner cites Edgar Mittelholzer's *A Morning in the Office* (1950), Samuel Selvon's *A Brighter Sun* (1952), and Roger Mais's *The Hills Were Joyful Together* (1953) as being

Bananas for sale at a local market in India (Image copyright Jeremy Richards, 2009. Used under license from Shutterstock.com)

among the pioneering novels. Another such novel was John Hearne's *Voices under the Window* (1954). The pace of this new literature increased during the late 1950s and 1960s. Naipaul's four novels set in the Caribbean were published during this period. *The Mystic Masseur* (1957) describes the rise of a Trinidadian healer, writer, and entrepreneur who becomes a successful politician during the last stages of colonial rule in the 1950s; *The Suffrage of Elvira* (1958) deals with Trinidadian electoral politics. The other two novels are *Miguel Street* (1959) and *A House for Mr. Biswas* (1961). Hamner quotes George Lamming, a West Indian poet and novelist who stated in 1960, "We have seen in our lifetime an activity called writing, in the form of the novel, come to fruition without any previous native tradition to draw upon." Lamming was originally from Barbados. He lived in Port of Spain, Trinidad, from 1946 to 1950, and then, like Naipaul, emigrated to England. His books include *The Emigrants* (1954) and *Of Age and Innocence* (1958). Another Trinidadian writer of this period who also emigrated to England in the 1950s was Michael Anthony. His first novel was *The Games Were Coming* (1963).

CRITICAL OVERVIEW

The humor and pathos of *Miguel Street*, the collection of stories in which "B. Wordsworth" appears, has long been admired by readers and critics, who have also appreciated the skill with which Naipaul accurately renders the street life of these impoverished Trinidadian citizens. Among the early reviewers, Charles Poore, in the *New York Times*, describes *Miguel Street* as "a beguiling book about growing up in the West Indies. The sketches are written lightly, so that tragedy is understated and comedy is overstated, yet the ring of truth always prevails." The book has continued to attract attention from the many critics who have discussed Naipaul's work. In a comment about all the stories that certainly applies to "B. Wordsworth," Bruce King, in *V. S. Naipaul*, notes the following:

> Incongruity between pretence and reality is characteristic of Miguel Street. Gestures, words and ideas do not have the same meaning in an impoverished colonial society as elsewhere. What appears self-expressive turns out to be a lie, masks for failure.

A number of critics comment directly on "B. Wordsworth." In *V. S. Naipaul: A Critical Introduction*, Landeg White offers the following view of B. Wordsworth:

> His pose is not ridiculous for his sense of wonder is genuine and his excitement over simple actions communicates itself to the narrator. But there is no poetry in Miguel Street... and the dreams by which he has lived are only dreams.

White does not admire the ending of the story, however, in which the narrator writes, after he returns to Alberto Street and finds B. Wordsworth's home demolished, "It was just as though B. Wordsworth had never existed." White regards this ending as "embarrassing... surely the most mawkish thing Naipaul has ever published." In White's view, Naipaul was led into this misstep by his sympathy for B. Wordsworth and his consequent need to "impose a special lonely insight on the child."

For Richard Kelly, in *V. S. Naipaul*, B. Wordsworth "resembles Lewis Carroll's White Knight in his gentle madness.... His energy and imagination make the dull island come alive." (The White Knight is a character in Carroll's fantasy novel *Through the Looking Glass*.) However, Manjut Inder Singh, in *V. S. Naipaul*, takes a different view. He sees in the character B. Wordsworth "creative sterility and lack of invention.... His metropolitan fantasy is an ideal which can bring no fulfillment, just like others born in lower echelons cannot hope to achieve anything." For Suman Gupta, in *V. S. Naipaul*, B. Wordsworth is typical of the kind of character Naipaul creates in Miguel Street: "These are characters who are out of touch with the realities of their place and time, and of themselves. They invariably construct themselves and their ambitions in ways which are somehow impossible in Miguel Street."

CRITICISM

Bryan Aubrey

Aubrey holds a Ph.D. in English. In this essay he discusses "B. Wordsworth" in terms of what it means to be a poet.

Is B. Wordsworth, the character who appears in Naipaul's short story of that name, a real poet or is he a fake, a dreamer? His name, which is presumably not the name he inherited but one he adopted for himself to fit his self-image, clearly shows how he wants others to

> "HE IS TOO MUCH IN DEBT TO A CULTURE IMPOSED ON HIM FROM WITHOUT, WHICH IS AT LEAST PART OF THE REASON HE CAN WRITE NO MORE THAN ONE LINE OF HIS PROJECTED MASTERPIECE. HE DOES NOT KNOW WHAT TO WRITE *ABOUT* OR *HOW* TO WRITE IT."

think of him. The B in his name, he tells the young narrator, stands for Black, and Black Wordsworth says he is the brother of "White Wordsworth," by which he means William Wordsworth (1770–1850), one of the leading English poets of the Romantic movement. B. Wordsworth obviously feels an emotional and spiritual kinship with the great English poet. "We share one heart," he says. That one sentence suggests that B. Wordsworth does indeed have some affinity with the man he has chosen as a model because it is close to a phrase that Wordsworth himself wrote in his poem "The Old Cumberland Beggar," which was published in the 1800 edition of Wordsworth's famous *Lyrical Ballads*. The narrator in the poem praises those who give to those in need, because "we have all of us one human heart." B. Wordsworth also resembles William Wordsworth in his ambition to write a long poem that will "sing to all humanity." Wordsworth's *The Prelude* (1850) is an autobiographical poem in which he tells the story of the development of his own mind. He hoped the poem would have universal appeal and would inspire others to understand the vast capacity of the human mind, especially in its interactions with nature.

Another thing that B. Wordsworth has in common with his role model is that they both like to observe nature in a passive kind of way. In Wordsworth's poem, "Expostulation and Reply," two friends have a friendly discussion in which one man complains that the other sits alone for hours doing nothing except observing nature, to which the other replies that just sitting in nature in a state of "wise passiveness" is preferable to his friend's habit of poring over books. In the companion poem, "The Tables Turned," the same speaker tells his friend to put down his

WHAT DO I READ NEXT?

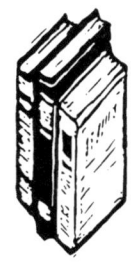

- Naipaul's *A House for Mr. Biswas* (1961) is the last of the four novels Naipaul set in Trinidad, and many critics and readers regard it as his finest work. The main character is Mohun Biswas, who is born in a mud hut and whose main ambition in life is to own his own house so that he can provide a place for his family. Although he dies at the age of forty-six, Mr. Biswas (whose character is based on Naipaul's memories of his father) achieves his dream. The novel is a serious one, but it also contains some of Naipaul's best comic writing.

- *Cannery Row* (1945), a novel by John Steinbeck, is set in Monterey, California. The novel presents the lives of several eccentric characters, all of whom live on the same street, which is lined with sardine canning factories (hence the name Cannery Row). With its humor and underlying pathos, this novel has always been one of Steinbeck's most popular. A modern edition was published by Penguin in 1993.

- *Winesburg, Ohio* is a collection of twenty-two interrelated short stories by Sherwood Anderson, first published in 1919. The stories revolve around the protagonist, George Willard, and the inhabitants of the fictional town of Winesburg in Ohio, most of whom live drab, disappointing lives. A number of critics have likened *Winesburg, Ohio* to Naipaul's *Miguel Street*, although the protagonist of Anderson's novel is a far more developed character than Naipaul's boy narrator. A modern edition of *Winesburg, Ohio* was published by Bantam Classics in 1995.

- *The House on Mango Street* (1984) is a coming-of-age novel by Mexican American writer Sandra Cisneros. The novel was the first of Cisneros's books to achieve prominence. It tells the story of a young girl growing up in the Chicano area of Chicago. With its array of colorful if not always admirable characters who all live on the same street, it resembles Naipaul's *Miguel Street*.

- *A Small Place* (2000), by Jamaica Kincaid, is an essay that explores the history of Antigua, where the author grew up. The small Caribbean island, which achieved its independence from Britain in 1981, is first presented through the eyes of an American tourist, but then the author examines colonialism and its troubled legacy.

- George Lamming's *In the Castle of My Skin* (1991) is an autobiographical novel by one of the most accomplished West Indian writers. It is set in Barbados, seen through the eyes of a young boy, in the 1930s. The turbulent events of that decade set the stage for the independence movement in Barbados. The novel has been praised for its poetic and imaginative qualities.

- *Growing Up Filipino: Stories for Young Adults* (2003), edited by Cecilia Manguerra Brainard, contains twenty-nine short stories by Filipino American writers about their experiences growing up and their thoughts about their cultural heritage and their integration into mainstream American society. The book is organized into five sections: Family, Angst, Friendship, Love, and Home. Each author provides an introduction to his or her story.

---

books, go out in nature and "bring with you a heart / That watches and receives." B. Wordsworth tries to emulate this. He likes to just sit and watch things. When the narrator first meets him, they both sit for an hour watching the bees in the palm trees in the narrator's yard.

B. Wordsworth says, "That's what I do, I just watch." He says he can watch ants, as well as other insects, for days. He does not offer any explanation of why he does this, but since he thinks of himself as a poet, it is likely that he watches so he can quietly absorb into himself different aspects of nature and understand how other creatures behave. One is reminded of the story about one of the great twentieth-century poets, Rainer Maria Rilke. When Rilke was working as secretary to the artist Rodin, he was in a barren period as far as writing poetry was concerned. Rodin told him to go to the zoo and look at an animal until he really saw it. He suggested that learning to see just one animal might well occupy the poet for two or three weeks. One of the results of Rilke's attempt to learn how to see was his poem "The Panther," in which he tries to describe the world of a caged panther from the panther's point of view. (The story is told by Robert Bly in his edition of Rilke's poems, *Selected Poems of Rainer Maria Rilke*.)

In addition to his cultivation of a "wise passiveness" when in the presence of nature, Wordsworth is known as a poet of deep feeling. He even defined poetry as the "spontaneous overflow of powerful feelings." Following his mentor, B. Wordsworth also likes to think of himself as a man of feeling. After he tells the boy that Wordsworth is his "brother," he says, "I can watch a small flower like the morning glory and cry." He probably thinks this is a suitably Wordsworthian sentiment. Perhaps he has on his mind the concluding lines of Wordsworth's "Ode: Intimations of Immortality":

> Thanks to the human heart by which we live,
> Thanks to its tenderness, its joys, and fears,
> To me the meanest flower that blows can give
> Thoughts that do often lie too deep for tears.

According to B. Wordsworth, "when you're a poet you can cry for everything." He believes that the poet must feel compassion for everything in creation. Perhaps he is simply moved by the beauty of nature, aware that such beauty is often fragile and will soon vanish, like the morning glory. He may also be aware, like Wordsworth, of the tragedies of human life. It was the real Wordsworth who, in *Lyrical Ballads*, expressed compassion for those who are outcasts, on the margins of society, such as beggars, vagrants, the insane, and the mentally retarded, and in "Lines written a few miles above Tintern Abbey," he wrote of listening to "The still, sad music of humanity." This is the kind of poet B. Wordsworth wants to be—a man who feels the sorrows of the world and can speak consoling words to others.

One thing the astute young narrator notices about B. Wordsworth is that "he did everything as though he were doing it for the first time in his life." This is an interesting comment. It suggests that B. Wordsworth does indeed have the kind of gift that is extremely useful to anyone who wants to be a poet. It seems that he has retained a kind of wonder about life. He does not allow himself merely to repeat actions out of habit or have his perceptions dulled by routine. Everything is always new, and this is part of the feeling that poetry can create in the reader. Much poetry is concerned with enabling people to see things in a fresh way. A familiar object, for example, might be presented in terms of a sharp metaphor or simile that enables a reader to see it completely differently than he or she has done before. It was not Wordsworth but another English Romantic poet, Percy Bysshe Shelley, who gave expression to this idea. In *A Defence of Poetry*, Shelley writes that poetry "strips the veil of familiarity from the world, and lays bare the naked and sleeping beauty which is the spirit of its forms." He continues, stating that poetry "creates anew the universe after it has been annihilated in our minds by the recurrence of impressions blunted by reiteration."

Perhaps one of the most powerful passages in "B. Wordsworth" is the incident in which B. Wordsworth and the narrator lie down at night looking up at the stars. B. Wordsworth tells the boy to think about how far away the stars are. The boy does so, and something splendid happens: "I felt like nothing, and at the same time I had never felt so big and great in all my life. I forgot all my anger and all my tears and all the blows." (He is referring to the beating he received from his mother.) B. Wordsworth has succeeded in conveying to this young boy a feeling with which many of the Romantic poets were familiar, that of losing oneself in the vastness of nature and becoming one with it. Lord Byron, for example, wrote in stanza 72 of Canto III of *Childe Harold's Pilgrimage*, "I live not in myself, but I become / Portion of that around me," and he refers to mountains, oceans, the sky, and the stars. The experience Byron describes is exactly what the young boy in the story feels, and it is to B. Wordsworth's credit that he acts as a teacher, encouraging in the boy something of the response a poet might indeed have to the grandeur of nature and the universe.

Based on all this, it would seem that B. Wordsworth has many of the qualities that make up the poet. He has cultivated a poetic sensibility that has communicated something genuine and beautiful to his young friend. But is he really a poet? There is, of course, a problem with this: B. Wordsworth does not actually manage to write any poems. Certainly, he has large ambitions in that direction, but the "greatest poem in the world" that he boasts he is in the process of writing turns out to be a myth, the product of his own imagination, his need to believe that he is a poet with a grand task to accomplish. The reality is far less grand and much sadder, and it is here that the story touches on issues that are beyond the control of B. Wordsworth. He is an example of a man with talents and ambitions that are unsuited to the time and place in which he lives. At the most basic level, the slums of Port of Spain in the 1940s are not a promising environment for a would-be poet. But the issue goes deeper than that. In *V. S. Naipaul*, Suman Gupta points out the irony of the fact that B. Wordsworth, a black man in Trinidad, chooses as his poetic model a white man who lived in England, the colonial power. Gupta goes on to note, in connection with Miguel Street as a whole, as well as Naipaul's other early fiction set in Trinidad, "Lack of authenticity... is what Naipaul finds in Trinidad: individuals who entertain aspirations which make little sense in Trinidad, a culture which treasures texts and ideas which are patently out of place." This is B. Wordsworth's situation exactly, and it highlights the problem of the writer in a colonial society. His identity is shaped by an alien culture. Before he can write, he must first discover his true identity—in B. Wordsworth's case as a black man in Trinidad—and also his subject matter. Just what is he going to write about? It is not for nothing that B. Wordsworth is presented as speaking perfect, grammatical English, unlike most of the other people in Miguel Street. The narrator's observation that "his English was so good, it didn't sound natural" has great significance. B. Wordsworth himself is not "natural." He is too much in debt to a culture imposed on him from without, which is at least part of the reason he can write no more than one line of his projected masterpiece. He does not know what to write *about* or *how* to write it. Naipaul himself is an illustration of this very difficulty. When he left Trinidad for England in 1950, his favorite authors included Charles Dickens, the Brontë sisters, and Joseph Conrad, all British writers. The only model available to him as a writer was that of the British novel. But Naipaul was not British; he was from Trinidad, and it was not until he decided to write of what he knew at first hand—the people he knew growing up in Trinidad—that he found his subject matter. His writing became authentic. Even if he had discovered that secret while still living in Trinidad, it would not have helped him much, since as Bruce King notes in *V. S. Naipaul*, there were no opportunities at that time for writers within Trinidad: "As it lacked any local literary market, any local publishers interested in local writing, and any local readership, the writers were expatriates living and publishing in London." B. Wordsworth's best hope of becoming a real poet, then, appears to be to hop on a plane to England. But where will a man who spends his time wandering around Port of Spain, gazing at bees and ants, and whose only income is from singing calypsos during the calypso season, be able to pull off such a feat? "It is the poet's tragedy," he says, speaking more wisely than he knows.

Source: Bryan Aubrey, Critical Essay on "B. Wordsworth," in *Short Stories for Students*, Gale, Cengage Learning, 2010.

Bruce King
In the following excerpt, King discusses the comedy of Miguel Street *and the influences behind it.*

While Naipaul's first three books of fiction are extraordinarily popular because of their comedy, implicit are such themes as the way impoverished, hopeless lives and the chaotic mixing of cultures result in fantasy, brutality, violence and corruption. The three books are also social history showing the start of protest politics during the late 1930s and how Trinidad began to change during and after the Second World War. The infusion of American money and the beginnings of local self-government created new possibilities where few existed before; but such social change is treated amusingly, without the analytical perspective found in later novels.

The origins of *Miguel Street* (1959), a volume of linked short stories, can be found in 'Prologue to an Autobiography' (1982) where Naipaul recalls thirty years earlier, in a room of the BBC in London, writing the first sentence of 'Bogart' from his memories of Trinidad. It was one of those gifts from the muse that writers need to get started:

> The first sentence was true. The second was invention. But together—to me, the writer—

> "UNLIKE SUCH BOOKS THERE IS IN *MIGUEL STREET* LITTLE SENTIMENTALITY FOR PARADISE LOST, NONE OF THE EXPATRIATE'S USUAL YEARNING FOR THE PROTECTION OF FAMILY, TRIBE, FRIENDS, UNQUESTIONED CUSTOMS AND OBLIGATIONS."

they had done something extraordinary. Though they had left out everything—the setting, the historical time, the racial and social complexities of the people concerned—they had suggested it all; they had created the world of the street. And together, as sentences, words, they had set up a rhythm, a speed, which dictated all that was to follow. (*Finding the Centre*, p. 19)

The antiphonal refrain, 'What's happening there, Bogart?', 'What's happening there, Hat?', brought to the surface memories of people and the life he had known in Port of Spain and soon a small world, full of its own life and ways, having its own unique manners and morals, was sketched in. Naipaul's subject was an impoverished area of Port of Spain with its cultural diversity, fantasies, chaotic and changing standards, its fashions and imitation of style, its mistaken notions of masculinity and mistreatment of women, its self-defeating excuses, its limitations and the improbability of achievement from those living in such an environment.

The tales reflect a time when Naipaul's family had moved from the enclosed Indian world of the countryside to the more ethnically varied Port of Spain. Miguel Street is a racially mixed community predominantly black, brown and Indian but with some Spanish, Portuguese and 'whites'. Although to the boy who narrates the stories the men lounging on the streets represent community standards, the people seem in transit and houses rapidly change owners. Miguel Street is not exactly a slum as its inhabitants look down on those areas where the people are dirtier, poorer or rougher. Style is important to the men as it is a way of asserting visibility in an impoverished colonial society which offers few opportunities for riches, fame or achievement. Style may be a matter of imitating a current movie star like Bogart, noticeable eccentric behaviour, mystification about the past, or an apparently careless disregard for social conventions (Laura has eight children by seven fathers). Status may be gained by having, like Eddoes, a night job as a garbage man, allowing freedom from work during the day and the display of a uniform along with the pickings of the trash of the wealthy in other parts of Port of Spain. Style is the underdog's way of being unique, a way to assert identity, a mask for failure.

Many of the stories evolve from the boy's admiration of the pretences of those around him to a revelation of failure. B. Wordsworth claims to be writing a great poem and tells of a tragic love affair, but he is an unemployed calypso singer who has never written poetry; his romantic love story is a lie. Popo busies himself with carpentry, supposedly making some ideal Thing Without a Name, but he makes nothing; the furnishings of his house are found to be stolen. In many stories the entrance or exit of a woman from a man's life leads to some major change in behaviour and the central character is arrested by the police. In Miguel Street nothing is made, no business succeeds, no art work is finished, no love or marriage lasts.

Miguel Street differs from Steinbeck's *Cannery Row* and Joyce's *Dubliners* in its social comedy and seeming lightness of tone, the impression of business and activity. Bogart may be 'the most bored man I know' and the boy when he grows up and leaves school may turn to drinking and whoring because 'What else anybody can do here except drink?' but the narration does not romanticize, sentimentalize or protest; rather there is a Trinidadian world of the carnivalesque in the public displays of imitated and assumed character. Everyone appears to be play acting in public, creating small dramas. There is a tolerance, even an appreciation, of eccentric self-display.

Incongruity between pretence and reality is characteristic of Miguel Street. Gestures, words and ideas do not have the same meaning in an impoverished colonial society as elsewhere. What appears self-expressive turns out to be masks for failure and is the result of Trinidad being a colonial backwater, a place without the means to enable a better life. Even leaving is difficult. There is worse poverty elsewhere in the West Indies as is shown by the Grenadians coming to Trinidad. Qualifications for better jobs can only be gained by taking British examinations. In a colony which then had no university and few secondary schools, further education means going abroad, and that requires money or one of the few government scholarships. It also means a break with the past and facing an alien world without the support of family, friends and excuses. When the narrator does leave at the conclusion he is 'looking only at my shadow before me, a dancing dwarf on the tarmac'.

'Man-man,' an often anthologized story from *Miguel Street*, shows that Naipaul had already devised the methods and structures he would often use in his books. An analysis will be useful towards understanding what is consistent as his fiction evolves. Like many of Naipaul's narratives, 'Man-man' is based on fact; there was a well-known person like him in Port of Spain. The selectivity of presentation means that there is a subtext of implied explanations to be inferred; the larger significances are understated. Naipaul binds together the narrative and the prose by repetition of sounds, words, phrases, sentence patterns, images, parallel and analogous events. What seems simple and easy, almost natural story telling, will be found to be highly crafted towards continuity, movement and the symbolic. While the prose is economical, straightforward, rapid in movement and clear in its presentation, its sound patterns are richly textured, creating a sense of organic flow. There are, for instance, the 'm' sounds in the first paragraph: Miguel, Man-man, mad, him, am mad, many, much, madder, Man-man. The second paragraph picks up the 'm's': He didn't look mad. He was a man of medium height. The continuity and movement are built from repetitions and variations. The method of organization of sound and connectives is a model for the story and the book, which move rapidly while being tightly woven and organized.

Like many of the novels Naipaul will write 'Man-man' is organized by two contrasting halves. In the first half there are a number of seemingly discontinuous episodes, which reveal character, circumstances, desires and context, but which suggest a lack of direction, an aimless shuffling around, and which end in a failure requiring a new start. The second half shows the character driven by some new prospect, rises in excitement, develops and expands the possibilities, has continuity, but instead of a climax there is a burst bubble, a rapid descent. Within this scheme there are other clearly articulated sections, especially in the first half; the second half is more continuous as the story gathers together its themes for what at first appears a new start....

The structure of *Miguel Street* as a book is similar to that of 'Man-man.' The various stories are linked subsections of a larger story concerning the narrator and his relationship to Hat, which comes to a conclusion in the next-to-last story of the volume and which is followed by the narrator's disillusionment and departure for England. The first half of the book has two sections. 'Bogart' to 'The Coward' are tales of failure which follow a pattern of amusing fantasy followed by deflation. Each central character is a mockery of some ideal: Popo is a philosopher, Morgan is a comedian. There is often a clear break, loss of wife, temporary disappearance or loss of direction by the main character, then a change as the story becomes more serious, reality is found to be more dangerous and violent than it first appeared, often the police come and the fantasy collapses; the character is defeated or found to be a fake. As the volume proceeds the stories become more complex, as humiliations are shown to be the basis of the eccentricities which produce local heroes, heroes who are fraudulent and dangerous....

The early stories portray a world of men without purpose. While the men treat their women as inferiors, their world is held together by women; the failure of the men is typified by their relation to, or lack of, women. This is anticipated in Bogart with his humiliation at not being able to have children and his deserting his wives to: 'Be a man, among we men.' These men are illustrations of the weakness of the West Indian male, his inability and unwillingness to be responsible for a family and a woman. It is the women who are strong. Morgan tries to act like a patriarch, but wanting the approval of other men he carries on supposedly comic public trials of his children and when this backfires he gets drunk and bellows: 'You people think I am not a man, eh? My father had eight children. I his son. I have ten. I better than all of you put together.' Morgan tries to prove his manliness by an affair with Teresa Blake, is caught by his wife and publicly humiliated: 'Mrs Morgan was holding up Morgan by his waist. He was practically naked, and he looked so thin, he was like a boy with an old man's face.' In reading these stories and *Biswas* it might be remembered that the duties of a Brahmin include education and having a house and family.

The stories in *Miguel Street* usually take place in public. Naipaul has commented that in the West Indies life is public, unlike in England where life takes place indoors behind shut doors and curtained windows. But the Trinidadian camaraderie of the street is seen as hollow, something the boy outgrows as he learns it is a world of failure, of talk rather than achievement. The characters are adrift, aimless, culturally, socially, politically, economically and ethically impoverished, without realizable ideals. Thus the humiliations, eccentricity, play-acting, brutality and failure.

After 'Titus Hoyt' there is a deepening of emotion, the characters become more complex or there is a recognition of tragedy. Laura may be heroic as the archetypical West Indian matriarch, having children by different men, surviving on her wits and what she can get from her men, but when her own unmarried daughter has a child and starts to repeat the cycle of West Indian womanhood she feels it would be better for her daughters to die than to be like herself. Contrasted to the women of Miguel Street is Mrs. Hereira who descends from the rich secure white world, leaving her almost perfect husband, for a drunk who violently beats her. A story concerning the relationship of sexual desire to sadism, masochism and love, it also anticipates Naipaul's later novels, such as *Guerrillas*, where well-off whites, bored with their security, look for emotional excitement by playing at being unconventional and idealistic, expecting that when life becomes dangerous they can return to the safe world from which they came. Mrs. Hereira is a forerunner of Jane in *Guerrillas* and Yvette in *Bend*. Romantic love is a luxury of the rich white. The boy's mother, an Indian, says: 'If somebody did marry you off when you was fifteen, we wouldnta been hearing all this nonsense, you hear. Making all this damn fuss about your heart and love and all that rubbish.' Naipaul's novels differ from most European and American fiction in portraying romantic love and sexual freedom as destructive, a dereliction of one's real duties. The perspective is Indian rather than European.

Indian attitudes are often playfully present in the stories. Uncle Bhakcu, 'The Mechanical Genius,' reads the *Ramayana* every day and succeeds as a pundit, although a West Indian one crawling under cars trying to be a Western mechanic while 'Hindus waited for him to attend to their souls.' In 'His Chosen Calling' Eddoes, from a low Hindu caste, is a sweeper and proud of his inheritance. British social comedy is tinged by Hindu notions of caste and fate.

Some stories have allusions to or quotations from the calypsos. Originally from Trinidad, the calypso is brutal in its comments on topical events. The difference between the calypso and the newer Soca (a mixture of calypso and black American soul music) is that the former gives priority to the words and is satiric, the latter to music and is for dancing. While Naipaul's use of the calypso adds to the colour and realism of his stories, it also shows the likely Trinidadian response in contrast to the innocence of the boy narrator; the calypso represents the harsh actualities of the society in contrast to the humanism and sympathy for characters inherent to the conventions of European fiction. Naipaul has often written with approval of the direct honesty of Trinidadian discussion of such matters as race when he was younger. Like the Calypsonian he observes and comments without sentimental illusions.

The calypsos are also social history and are used, along with references to films, cricket matches and well-known events to create a record of Trinidad for a decade from the late 1930s until after the war. Approximately twelve years pass; the boy narrator is eight years old at the start and over eighteen at the conclusion. At the start Trinidad is a colony dependent on England, then the war brings the Americans with their money, new kinds of social relations, attitudes, jobs; next come elections and talk of independence. There are two frames of reference: history as seen locally and local history in relationship to the wider world. Such use of an outside, European historical frame of reference was common to many works of fiction of the late colonial and early independence period when writers had both to put local society on the literary map and to relate its chronology to what foreign readers would know. Later writers would no longer feel that such a broad perspective was necessary. They had become more confident that readers were interested in fiction told from a Trinidadian, Indian or African angle; the former colonies had become less marginal to modern history. When Titus Hoyt takes the unwilling boys to Fort George and tells them that the fort was built in 1803 when the French were planning to invade Trinidad, and 'we was fighting Napoleon', the boys are stunned as: 'We had never realized that anyone considered us so important.'

The stories allude to a time when Trinidad was important for its plantations, a former economy which is recalled by the remains of decaying buildings. There is a history here, a possible, 'usable past', when Trinidad was a significant place in the Empire and part of world trade and worth fighting over in contrast to the impoverished, neglected Trinidad of the 1930s and 1940s in which the outside world seems distant and incomprehensible to Bolo and others.

Miguel Street consists of memories of a lost childhood homeland. Nostalgia is the usual subject matter of the first book of an expatriate colonial writer. Unlike such books there is in *Miguel Street* little sentimentality for paradise lost, none of the expatriate's usual yearning for the protection of family, tribe, friends, unquestioned customs and obligations. Naipaul may have felt such emotions, and from his comments in 'Prologue to an Autobiography' and *The Enigma of Arrival*, there is reason to think that Trinidad remains emotionally 'home' in contrast to the alienation of exile, but the short stories are astringent in their ironies. They are his *Dubliners* and *A Portrait of the Artist as a Young Man*. They show why it was necessary to leave and remain away from home.

The developing perspective of the boy narrator as he grows up shows his understanding that a period of his life has ended, the secure world he knew has fragmented; Hat, his adult mentor (the substitute father figure in the stories), has aged, become crazed for a woman, been jailed and broken. If the narrator does not leave Trinidad he will become another failure like those he admired. Even the Americans have departed, packed up their base and left, taking with them the money, attitudes and new opportunities which became available during the war years. Under the comedy is criticism of 'home' and its acceptance of its fate and habits of accepting defeat. Bolo, in 'Caution,' fails so often at everything he does that when he wins some money on the sweepstake he refuses to believe it, as it would destroy his sense of being a victim; he tears up the ticket and withdraws into himself. It is easier to blame the imperial powers or racial discrimination or Trinidadian corruption than to accept past foolishness and failures of character....

Source: Bruce King, "Miguel Street, the Mystic Masseur, and The Suffrage of Elvira," in *V. S. Naipaul*, 2nd ed., Palgrave Macmillan, 2003, pp. 23–40.

Bruce Bawer

In the following excerpt, Bawer explains how Naipaul "honors the human" in his writing.

Last December, on the day after being presented with the Nobel Prize for Literature, V. S. Naipaul sat down in Stockholm for a televised conversation with three fellow literary laureates, Günter Grass, Nadine Gordimer, and Seamus Heaney, and with Per Wästberg, a member of the Swedish Academy. One might have expected that the topic under discussion would be writing and literature, but the Nobelists soon turned to politics. Naipaul, alone in resisting this direction, protested that he is not political: he just writes about people. "Perhaps that's too frivolous," he suggested slyly. Gordimer, perhaps failing to understand that there was more than a little irony in the air, and that in Naipaul's view writing about people, far from being frivolous, is in fact precisely what a serious writer does, was quick to challenge his self-characterization, insisting: "Your very existence as a boy living under colonial rule in Trinidad was political!"

This was, needless to say, meant as praise. To many members of the literary (and academic) establishment, after all, colonialism is the paramount literary theme and political issue of our time, and to be a child growing up in a colonial setting is to fill a strictly defined role in a familiar morality play. It is to be a victim, and thus a figure of virtue—and thus, of course, political. And to be political is to be serious. (In such circles, indeed, politics is the ultimate seriousness.) For Naipaul, contrarily, who *was* that boy in Trinidad (he was born in Chaguanas, a village of 1500 that his father sardonically called "the peasants' paradise"), and who would certainly place colonialism at the head of his own list of literary themes, to be truly serious is to transcend the merely political. To be serious is to notice and remember the specifics, the contradictions, the ambiguities—to honor the whole human person rather than to reduce him or her to a one-dimensional symbol of virtuous victimhood or (for that matter) anything else. It is to tell the truth about the world, however much that truth may confound ideology, rather than (as Naipaul himself put it in his Nobel Prize speech) to turn "living issues into abstractions."

Naipaul, born in 1932, has honored the human from the very beginning—though at the beginning, to be sure, he did it largely with humor....

Three more volumes of Trinidad fiction followed. After *The Suffrage of Elvira* (1958), another satirical yarn, and *Miguel Street* (1959), a linked sequence of Chekhovian character sketches, Naipaul published the most splendid book of his entire career: *A House for Mr. Biswas* (1961)....

Source: Bruce Bawer, "Civilization and V. S. Naipaul," in *Hudson Review*, Vol. 55, No. 3, Autumn 2002, pp. 371–84.

Ervin Beck

In the following essay, Beck describes Naipaul's calypso-influenced, Trinidadian form of writing.

V. S. Naipaul's novel *The Mimic Men* (1967) is probably the best known and most complex handling of the postcolonial literary trope of "mimicry" (Ashcroft, Griffiths, and Tiffin) in Caribbean literature. The short story about Black Wordsworth in *Miguel Street* (1959), the first book Naipaul actually wrote (c. 1955), is also his first explicit handling of the problem of literary mimicry—that is, the colonized subject responding to the English literary canon thrust upon him by colonial education and an imposed foreign culture. "B. Wordsworth" not only depicts the condition that Naipaul personally reacted to in his own experience, but in the context of the whole of *Miguel Street* it also shows how Naipaul overcame the problem of British precedent and indigenized English fiction writing by using a calypso-influenced, Trinidadian form.

The most obvious mimicry in the story, of course, is the name of the Port-of-Spain poet "Black Wordsworth," which cannot be his christened name but is the result of his self-naming. The man is so colonized that he abandons his native Trinidadian identity and chooses that of the pre-eminent English poet transmitted by empire, William Wordsworth.

The name "Black" also indicates that the poet has accepted the racist definition of himself given him by his colonizers.

Black Wordsworth imitates his namesake in many ways. He discovered his calling as a poet at the age of twenty years, when he "felt the power within myself." William Wordsworth, too, began writing poetry at twenty as a response to his tour of the Alps in 1790. Black Wordsworth's life in Port-of-Spain also mimics William Wordsworth's. He deliberately fits himself into the Wordsworthian tradition of "nature poet" by choosing to live in an urban compound entirely given over to vegetation—his own wild place. "White Wordsworth was my brother. We share one heart," he says.

The autobiographical narrative that he summarizes for his young disciple, the narrator, replicates that of Wordsworth's speaker in the Lucy poems: young love turned tragic by the death of the beloved. We do not have enough evidence to know whether Black Wordsworth's death-doomed love was an actual experience, but in light of other Wordsworthian elements in Black Wordsworth's self-creation, it may be more imagined than real.

As a would-be poet, Black Wordsworth shows that he has been most profoundly influenced by Wordsworth's lyric masterpiece "Ode on Intimations of Immortality from Early Childhood," which has been canonized as "the great ode" in English. Black Wordsworth's ambition to equal William Wordsworth by writing the greatest poem in the English language, and to do so by writing one line a month, is realized in the single line that he has been able to compose: "The past is deep." If one had to condense William Wordsworth's "Ode" to four words, "The past is deep" would not be a bad summary, because the poem is grounded in the Platonic notion of the soul's immortality, hence its eternal (deep) past. We learn by that single line that Black Wordsworth is so entirely overwhelmed by Wordsworth's achievement that even in his most creative moments, he cannot go beyond his master.

However, when Black Wordsworth tells the narrator that he can "watch a small flower like the morning glory and cry," he reveals that he has profoundly misunderstood the work of his master. When at the end of the "Ode" William Wordsworth says he is finally able to conjure up "thoughts that lie too deep for tears," he means, of course, that he has matured into adulthood—out of mere sensory experience—and become able to transcend the emotions of loss through the cultivation of his intellect and "philosophic mind." In finding mere tears at the end of his poet's quest, and also in writing poems about "mothers," Black Wordsworth reveals that he is essentially a sentimental poet.

Both conditions—a poet's immature fixation on the physical environment and a colonized subject's fixation on the colonizer's canonical culture—explain the creative paralysis in Black Wordsworth's life. Black Wordsworth therefore represents the colonized poet that Naipaul the writer knew he had to avoid becoming. In real life, the author moved to England, as the narrator also does at the end of *Miguel Street.*

Some hints in the story suggest that Black Wordsworth could have avoided colonialist mimicry, too. After all, despite his failure to sell his Wordsworthian poems, he did earn his small living by writing and selling calypsoes: "I sing calypsoes in the calypso season," he tells the narrator. Had he specialized in the calypso genre, he might have become indigenously creative and earned both money and a name for himself in his community

Naipaul shows his mastery of creative mimicry insofar as his story replicates a kind of European realism, but in a calypso-like form. Snatches of lines from calypsoes appear in other stories in *Miguel Street,* namely "The Thing Without a Name," "The Pyrotechnist," "The Maternal Instinct," "The Blue Cart," "Love, Love, Love Alone," "Caution," "Until the Soldiers Came," and "Hat." But, more important, each short story itself is calypso-like in being a gossipy, satiric sketch of a socially aberrant character. Naipaul's book illustrates the more recent value placed on mimicry in postcolonial thought, as in the work of theorist Homi Bhabha, who sees mimicry as always imperfect and therefore creative in its own mongrelized way.

Source: Ervin Beck, "Naipaul's 'B. Wordsworth,'" in *Explicator*, Vol. 60, No. 3, Spring 2002, pp. 175–76.

Philip Hensher
In the following excerpt, Hensher explains the effect of Naipaul's travels on his artistic trajectory.

... The key to Naipaul's artistic trajectory, I think, lies in the series of extraordinary polemical travel books he started to write in the 1960s. Beginning with *The Middle Passage* in 1962, Naipaul travelled through the relics of colonialism in the New World, and returned to the India of his ancestors in *An Area of Darkness* and two subsequent books. His two studies of Islamic civilisation, *Among the Believers* and *Beyond Belief,* came later; like all these studies, they seem to be driven by a furious, confident conviction, and not at all by tact. The blazing certainty which allows Naipaul to take on a gigantic cultural fact like caste takes the breath away, and in the end they are thrilling whether or not they command assent. For what it's worth, I find a lot more to agree with in the Indian books than in Naipaul's studies of Islam, but he has written nothing more exciting than *Among the Believers.* The vividness of the encounters, the force of the polemic and, always, the beauty of the writing are compelling, and propel the reader through what can seem an all-encompassing unfairness.

They are superb books on their own terms, but viewed in the context of Naipaul's career, it is tempting to think that he undertook the grand enterprise, which began by investigating the roots of his own complex culture, in a spirit of self-improvement. Such an investigation of the great movements of cultures and empires which converge on this particular individual would draw Naipaul across the world, and the project had a gigantic impact on Naipaul's fiction. The emphasis changed distinctly between Naipaul's first novels and the extraordinary sequence which began in the 1970s. His first novels are rooted in his personal history, and explore the extraordinary position of a family doubly deracinated, an Indian view of Trinidad in the last days of empire, dreaming of London. Rich as this ambiguous cultural experience was, Naipaul might have started to reflect by the early 1960s that the individual personal experience was not a sufficient basis for his ambitions. He could perfectly well have continued in the sumptuous vein of *The Mystic Masseur* and *A House for Mr Biswas* all his career, and he would still have been a wonderful novelist. Instead, he sent himself out into the world, and the steadily expanding horizon beneath his contemplation is depicted in a series of masterpieces, of an intellectual scope and grandeur not seen in English since Conrad.

That is emphatically not to denigrate the first Caribbean novels. They have a delirious hilarity—the dazzling pay-off of *The Mystic Masseur* infallibly provokes a bark of laughter, and the raucous tale of 'the Mechanical Genius' in *Miguel Street* has the same blissful sense of escalating outrage as the best of Waugh. The powerful charm of the manner, too, in which the driest and most sophisticated of narrators eyes chaotic lives isn't the least of the attractions of *A House for Mr Biswas.* But, looking back, what is chiefly striking is the mastery of architecture, the innovative and complex structures, and an underlying seriousness in the treatment of big themes. *Miguel Street,* for instance, is a complete delight, and goes down like a gin fizz at sunset, but its daring is unmistakable. Brilliant, for instance, to structure the novel unconsecutively and without any clear chronology, so that characters pop up 20 pages after their deaths are reported; how unobtrusively it conveys the message that nothing, really, will ever change here. The fervent tone of the conclusion, as the narrator departs for England for good, might seem curious in so delicate and merry a comedy; that it is entirely natural shows how serious the attention to cultures has been throughout. In *A House for Mr Biswas,* that grand and tragic exploration of a bad writer's life in the most elevated terms, he showed how rich the multiple conflicts of cultures, languages and discourses could prove. In the end, *A House for Mr Biswas* is not just a desperate and heartrending individual tragedy, but a suggestive parable about deracination; Biswas is not at home in his place, in the literature he aspires to, in his skin. . . .

Source: Philip Hensher, "A Perfectly Targeted Prize," in *Spectator*, Vol. 287, No. 9037, October 20, 2001, pp. 44–45.

John L. Brown

In the following excerpt, Brown praises Naipaul's skill as a novelist, focusing on his dark vision of the world.

V. S. Naipaul has traveled far since his Trinidad beginnings. He was born there in 1932, a third-generation West Indian of Hindu ancestry. His father, a reporter with literary ambitions, encouraged his son to study and write. Even as a very young man Naipaul was determined to get away from the narrow, neocolonial world of his birth. At eighteen he left for England, took an Oxford degree, worked for the BBC, began to write. With his early stories of West Indian life he received immediate recognition from British critics as the most talented of contemporary Caribbean writers. He was covered with prestigious English literary prizes, four of them in a little more than ten years. Lately he has begun to pick them up in the United States as well, winning in 1980 the Bennett Award, given to a "writer of literary achievement" who is considered to "have received insufficient attention"—which, to tell the truth, is not really Naipaul's case. In the opinion of some of his disgruntled West Indian colleagues he became a prize exhibit of the London intellectual establishment, living proof of the generous recognition of colonial talents in the capital. He has often been accused, in judgments motivated, it would seem, more by envy than by justice, of "looking down his long Oxonian nose" at the trivialities, the pretensions and the provincialism of the West Indies. One Trinidadian official indeed informed me that "Naipaul is certainly not our favorite native son"—something of an understatement. Naipaul seemed to have adapted swiftly to English life. He married a young English woman, acquired a prose style hailed as masterly. His eye was unerring in observing English scenes, as he demonstrated in *The Mimic Men* and in *Mr Stone and the Knights Companion.* . . .

But remarkable as Naipaul's travel books may be, he is essentially a novelist, and it is as a novelist that his achievement must be evaluated. In the field of fiction he is certainly no innovator. He has mastered the craft of traditional narrative and shows little interest in technical experiment. He is closer to Dickens or Balzac than he is to Joyce or *le nouveau roman*; his concern is to tell a story and also to discuss ideas. He would never subscribe to Flaubert's ideal to "write a book about nothing." *Miguel Street*—the first of his Trinidad stories to be written, although it was published in 1959, after *The Mystic Masseur* and *The Suffrage of Elvira*—consists of a series of sketches about a lower-class neighborhood in Port of Spain. There is the vivacious Laura, mother of eight children by as many fathers, "whose shouts and curses were the richest things I ever heard. She like Shakespeare when it comes to using words." There we also encounter B. Wordsworth, the poet who had never written poetry but who lived it; Man-man, who thought he was the Messiah and who sent out invitations for his crucifixion; Eddoes, "one of the aristocrats of the street" because he drove the garbage truck and only had to work mornings.

Miguel Street differs from most West Indian writing about the poor in that it expresses no overt social protest, but rather a humorous delight in these colorful characters, apparently happy in spite of their poverty. These vignettes, with their mix of sentimentality and irony (and perhaps with a dash of condescension as well), are always charming and occasionally even somewhat coy. The leading character of *The Mystic Masseur* (1957), Ganesh, already appears in *Miguel Street* no longer as a pundit in a dhoti but as a rising politician in "an expensive looking lounge suit." Pundit Ganesh Ramsurmmari, after having failed in a series of undertakings, finally gains a reputation as a learned man and a mystic. He then embarks on a political career, is elected to the Trinidad Legislative Council, becomes more and more British and finally assumes the name of G. Ramsay Muir, M. B. E. . . .

After *Biswas* the novelist's vision of the world grows darker. He will never be able to find his way back to the innocence of *Miguel Street.* . . .

Source: John L. Brown, "V. S. Naipaul: A Wager on the Triumph of Darkness," in *World Literature Today*, Vol. 57, No. 2, Spring 1983, pp. 223–27.

Harriet Blodgett

In the following excerpt, Blodgett discusses how the characters from the stories of Miguel Street *are simple but live in settings that are universal.*

... The narrator of his *Miguel Street* (1959) is describing all Naipaul's novels when he says, we "saw our street as a world, where everybody was quite different from everybody else." Naipaul's five novels are peopled by quite singular characters who dwell on a street with universal boundaries. He transmutes the vagaries and quotidian confusions of modern antiheroes into energetic, universalized fiction in the precisely phrased, deftly ironic novels—*The Mystic Masseur* (1957), *The Suffrage of Elvira* (1958), *A House of Mr Biswas* (1961), *Mr Stone and the Knights Companion* (1963), and *The Mimic Men* (1967)—which have earned him his impressive list of awards and honors....

Granted the particularity of Naipaul's Caribbean descriptions and the vitality of his dialect, seeing him only as a skillful local colorist or regional sociologist underestimates him. Naipaul's novels are about contemporary man and how he manages to survive and sometimes almost flourish. His books are not confined within their local settings nor, for all their explicitly precise detail, are they tied to literal realism: he finds metaphor more expressive. The local settings are convenient to his ideational purposes. As a society "continually growing and changing, never settling into any pattern"..., Trinidad invites themes of instability and flux, and as a colonial and emergent nation it provides a good setting for problems of dependency and freedom. The narrator of *Mimic Men* aptly says, "It has happened in twenty countries."... The dominant pressures in Naipaul's fictional world derive from man's precarious existence. He has not only to contend with psychic conflict and cultural fragmentation but to exist in a hard world within an indifferent universe.... At their best, Naipaul's characters are resilient, managing to transcend nonentity by their stubbornness. Naipaul may not willingly suffer people's pretensions, deceptions, and illogicalities, but he can admire their refusal to be the counters of fate or circumstance....

Source: Harriet Blodgett, "Beyond Trinidad: Five Novels by V. S. Naipaul," in *South Atlantic Quarterly*, Summer 1974, pp. 388–403.

SOURCES

Brereton, Bridget, *A History of Modern Trinidad, 1783–1962*, Heinemann, 1981, pp. 178, 192.

Lord Byron, *Childe Harold's Pilgrimage*, in *Lord Byron: Selected Poems*, edited with a preface by Susan J. Wolfson and Peter J. Manning, Penguin, 1996, p. 440.

Gupta, Suman, *V. S. Naipaul*, Northcote House, 1999, pp. 5, 17.

Hamner, Robert D., *V. S. Naipaul*, Twayne World Authors Series, No. 258, Twayne Publishers, 1973, p. 17.

Kelly, Richard, *V. S. Naipaul*, Continuum, 1989, p. 22.

King, Bruce, *V. S. Naipaul*, St. Martin's Press, 1993, pp. 13, 19.

Naipaul, V. S., "B. Wordsworth," in *Miguel Street*, Heinemann, 1974, pp. 56–65.

Poore, Charles, "Miguel Street," in *New York Times*, May 5, 1960, http://www.nytimes.com/books/98/06/07/specials/naipaul-miguel.html?_r=1&scp=1&sq=miguel%20street&st=cse (accessed September 8, 2009).

Rilke, Rainer Maria, *Selected Poems of Rainer Maria Rilke*, translated from the German and with commentary by Robert Bly, Harper & Row, 1981.

Shelley, Percy Bysshe, "A Defence of Poetry," in *Shelley's Poetry and Prose*, selected and edited by Donald H. Reiman and Sharon B. Powers, W. W. Norton, 1977, pp. 505–506.

Singh, Manjut Inder, *V. S. Naipaul*, Rawat Publications, 1998, p. 95.

"Trinidad and Tobago," in *CIA: The World Factbook*, https://www.cia.gov/library/publications/the-world-factbook/geos/td.html (accessed September 14, 2009).

White, Landeg, *V. S. Naipaul: A Critical Introduction*, Harper & Row, 1975, pp. 48, 53.

Wordsworth, William, "Ode: Intimations of Immortality from Recollections of Early Childhood," in *The Norton Anthology of English Literature*, 4th ed., edited by M. H. Abrams, Norton, 1979, p. 218.

———, *Lyrical Ballads: Wordsworth and Coleridge*, edited with introduction, notes and appendices by R. L. Brett and A. R. Jones, Methuen, 1968, pp. 104, 106, 116, 209, 266.

FURTHER READING

Dooley, Gillian, *V. S. Naipaul, Man and Writer*, University of South Carolina Press, 2006.
 This is a survey of Naipaul's life and work. Dooley writes in a clear style, without scholarly jargon, as she assesses a half-century of Naipaul's writing. She connects his life with his work and traces the evolution of his style.

French, Patrick, *The World Is What It Is: The Authorized Biography of V. S. Naipaul*, Alfred A. Knopf, 2008.

In this biography, French presents a portrait of Naipaul that reviewers have called unflattering to the writer, but few have complained that it is inaccurate. As the authorized biographer, French was permitted access to all Naipaul's papers, and he does try to be sympathetic to a man who is widely seen as a difficult personality.

Jussawalla, Feroza, ed., *Conversations with V. S. Naipaul*, University Press of Mississippi, 1997.

This is a collection of twenty-two interviews Naipaul has given over a period of thirty-six years.

Rogozinski, Jan, *A Brief History of the Caribbean: From the Arawak and Carib to the Present*, rev. ed., Plume, 2000.

This is a 432-page history of the Caribbean, from the arrival of Columbus in the Bahamas in 1492 to the end of the twentieth century.

The Censors

LUISA VALENZUELA

1988

Luisa Valenzuela, an Argentine novelist and short story writer, published the short story "The Censors" in English in 1988, and later, in a bilingual Spanish/English short story collection, in 1992. A well-known and highly acclaimed author in her own country, Valenzuela began to gain critical attention in the United States in the 1980s. Her story "The Censors" focuses on the efforts of the main character, Juan, to infiltrate the government censorship office in order to intercept his own letter to his beloved Mariana so that the letter can be successfully sent without harm coming to either Mariana or himself. As Juan moves through the ranks of the censorship office, he becomes increasingly devoted to his work, and when he finally comes across his own letter, he censors it with enthusiasm, as he would any other letter. He is subsequently executed. Like many of Valenzuela's works, "The Censors" is reflective of the turbulent political atmosphere in Argentina during the 1970s and 1980s. The story features themes of government oppression on the political level and psychological transformation on the personal level. The duality of this structure is characteristic of Valenzuela's fiction, in which political and personal realities are explored in tandem

Valenzuela's "The Censors" first appeared in English in the 1988 short story collection *Open Door Stories*, published by North Point Press. A bilingual edition of the story was published in 1992, by Curbstone Press, in the collection *The Censors*.

Luisa Valenzuela (© Jerry Bauer. Reproduced by permission.)

AUTHOR BIOGRAPHY

Valenzuela was born in Buenos Aires, Argentina, on November 26, 1938. Her mother was a respected writer who guided Valenzuela's early interest in writing and literature. When Valenzuela was twenty years old, she traveled to France and married a French merchant marine sailor, Theodore Marjak. Settling in Normandy, France, the couple had a daughter, Anna Lisa, but divorced six years later. In the early 1960s, Valenzuela moved to Paris, where she wrote for Radio Television Française and gathered material for her first novel, *Hay que sonreír* (1966; later translated as *Clara* and published in English in the volume *Clara: Thirteen Short Stories and a Novel*, in 1976). In 1964, Valenzuela returned to Argentina, where she worked as a journalist. In this capacity, Valenzuela traveled throughout South America. Having received a Fulbright scholarship to participate in the esteemed University of Iowa International Writing Program, Valenzuela traveled to the United States for the first time in 1969. In 1972, her travels took her to Barcelona, Spain, where she lived and worked for over a year. Valenzuela returned to Argentina in 1974, the year in which Argentine president Juan Perón died and his wife Isabel Perón became the president of Argentina (Isabel Perón had been serving as her husband's vice president until the time of his death). Amidst the political turmoil in Argentina, which intensified following a 1976 military coup, Valenzuela returned to the United States. She served as writer in residence at Columbia University in 1978. This marked the beginning of Valenzuela's increasing involvement in New York City. In 1985, she held the position of writer in residence at New York University, and she then served as a faculty member in the university's creative writing department for several years. From 1978 through 1990, Valenzuela divided her time between New York City, Buenos Aires, and Tepoztlán in Mexico. In 1990, she returned to Buenos Aires, where she continues to write in Spanish and to be published both in Spanish and in English translation.

PLOT SUMMARY

As Valenzuela's "The Censors" opens, the narrator relates that Juan, the main character, has recently received the address of a woman, Mariana, with whom Juan appears to have had a relationship. Mariana now lives in Paris, France, and Juan is certain, having been given Mariana's address from "a confidential source," that Mariana still cares for him. He immediately writes her a letter, one that soon begins to torment him, as he tries to recall what, precisely, he has written and sent off to Mariana. Although he seems certain that the letter he has written is completely benign, Juan begins to second-guess himself. He reflects on how the people employed at the censorship offices examine and smell and handle each letter as they attempt to "read between the lines." Juan understands the extent to which each letter is circulated throughout the enormous bureaucracy, and he doubts that many of the letters actually make it to their intended recipients. Months and even years can pass before the letters are sent on their way. During the examination process, Juan believes, the liberties enjoyed by both the letter's sender and its intended receiver may be jeopardized. He fears their lives may even be in danger while the contents of the letter are being investigated by the censors. Juan begins to worry that harm may befall Mariana as a result of his attempting to reach her through his letter. He believes that Mariana, who probably now thinks she is safe in Paris, could be kidnapped by the secret operatives of the censorship office.

Compelled by his desire to protect Mariana, Juan devises a plan to get a job at the censorship office and attempt to intercept his own letter. Juan is hired immediately; he observes that no one bothers to check references, because so many censors are needed. The reader is informed that the censorship offices would not overlook "ulterior motives," of individuals who apply for censorship jobs only to protect their own interests. However, they are lenient when hiring, as the new censors are likely to identify many suspicious pieces of mail in the process of intercepting their own. In short, the narrator suggests to the reader that Juan is not fooling the censorship office, but he is hired nonetheless.

Gradually, Juan settles into his work for the post office division of the censorship office, and he is happy to know he is doing everything he can to find his letter to Mariana. After Juan is transferred to the division where envelopes are screened for evidence of explosives, a fellow worker is injured by an explosion. One worker attempts to organize a strike in order to force the management into paying higher wages for such risky work. Not only does Juan not join the strike, he reports the organizer and is subsequently promoted to the division where envelopes are examined for evidence of poisons. Eventually, he is promoted to a division in which he reads the letters and analyzes their content. He still holds out the hope of finding his letter to Mariana. As Juan becomes increasingly absorbed in his work, however, his goal of finding his own letter begins to fade from his mind. Juan is surprised by the various methods people employ to send covert messages within their personal correspondence. In apparently innocuous messages, Juan sees evidence of people conniving to organize a rebellion against the government.

Juan is so attentive to possible threats against the government encoded in private letters that he is again promoted. The narrator observes that it is unclear whether this promotion makes Juan happy. He no longer reviews many letters, as so few make it through to this level. He reads and studies them diligently, returning home by the end of the day exhausted but pleased to have "done his duty." His mother frets over him, telling him that young women have called looking for him. She sometimes leaves him wine, which he refuses to drink, as he does not wish to impair his senses in any way. He now views his work as "patriotic" and accepts the sacrifices that are necessary on his part in order to perform his job properly. Just as he feels he has discovered his true purpose in the censorship division, his letter to Mariana reaches him for censorship. He censors it as vigorously as he has many other letters. He is executed the next morning. The reasons for his execution are not explicitly stated, although the narrator describes Juan as "one more victim of his devotion to his work." This suggests that Juan is executed because, as a censor, he has identified subversive material in his own letter. Although he knows he had no ill intentions toward his government when he wrote the letter, Juan treats his own letter with as much suspicion as any other. Therefore, after he has censored it and hands it off to his superiors, he is found to be guilty of having dangerous intentions and is subsequently executed.

CHARACTERS

Juan

Juan is the main character in Valenzuela's "The Censors." He enthusiastically writes a letter to Mariana, a woman with whom, it appears, he has been romantically involved. Juan is convinced that Mariana is still interested in him, and having received her address (the reader is not informed of the source of this information), he proceeds to write to her. The narrator describes his composition as not only a letter but "*the* letter" (emphasis in original). Having sent the letter, Juan considers what he has done, what the implications may be of having sent this letter to Mariana. Juan is aware of two things: first, that his letter is utterly innocent, and second, that the government's censors have a reputation for overzealousness in the performance of their job duties. When Juan considers that it may take years before his letter is deemed acceptable to send on to its intended recipient and that, despite the harmless nature of his missive to Mariana, she might be placed in danger by it— might even be kidnapped by the "Censor's Secret Command"—Juan is compelled to act to protect her. Once he has secured a position at the censorship office, Juan begins to undergo a significant transformation. Prior to his employment at the censorship office, when Juan notes that the censors do not leave any comma unchecked, his reflections suggest that he possesses some disdain for the actions of the censors. He seems to find their examination of the mail unnecessarily thorough and the censors themselves dangerous, as their opinions regarding the content of the mail could result in harm coming to senders and receivers of letters. For some time, Juan works hard and is promoted as a result of his attentiveness in censoring letters and because he informs his superiors of a plot by workers to go on strike. However, he seems to still have Mariana and her safety in mind; he still hopes to find his letter to her. Before long, however, Juan begins to see things differently. As he continues to examine people's letters, his experience is described in terms that suggest that he is becoming more concerned with the possible deceptive intentions of the people sending letters than he is with Mariana's safety. "These were horrible days," the narrator says, "when he was shocked by the subtle and conniving ways employed by people to pass on subversive messages." This sense of shock changes Juan. He grows suspicious of the most innocent-sounding phrases in letters, convinced that many people are attempting to plot against their own government. By the time Juan finally comes across his own letter to Mariana, he is convinced of the deceptive intentions of the letter writer, even though that person is himself. Through his fanatical censorship of his own letter, Juan seals his own fate. His censoring of his own letter convinces his superiors that he poses a threat to the government, and Juan is executed. By the end of the story, Juan has been psychologically transformed. He becomes the very thing he feared at the story's beginning—an overzealous censor—and through this change he endangers his own life.

Juan's Mother

Juan's mother does not appear in the story but is mentioned near the end, after Juan has been promoted and appears to be wholly dedicated to his job. The narrator informs the reader that Juan's mother is the only person who notices the changes in Juan's behavior. She frets over him, leaving him wine and messages that young women want to meet him at the bar. Her efforts are in vain, as she is unable to distract Juan from his sense of purpose at the censorship office.

Mariana

Mariana is the woman in whom it is presumed that Juan is romantically interested. She has moved to Paris and does not appear in the story, but Juan has somehow come into possession of her address and is convinced "that she hadn't forgotten him." Juan's concern for Mariana's safety is what motivates him to get a job at the censorship office and to try and retrieve his letter. Juan expresses his fears that the censors often interpret even innocent letters as threatening. The implication is that the censorship office might use the censored letters to punish individuals for subversive intentions. Juan fears that Mariana could even be kidnapped as a result of his writing to her. By the end of the story, Juan has all but forgotten about Mariana. He censors his own letter to her without regard for his safety or hers.

Narrator

The narrator is the unnamed persona relating Juan's story to the reader. In this story, the narrator offers commentary on Juan and his decisions and foreshadows events to come. For example, in the opening paragraph, the narrator discusses Juan's carelessness and reminds the reader that happiness is "a feeling you can't trust," suggesting that Juan's happiness at receiving Mariana's address will have negative effects. Juan's happiness, the reader is warned, will "get the better of him." The reader does not learn how this comes to pass until the story nears completion. The narrator also informs the reader of things about which Juan has no knowledge. For example, the reader is told that Juan's mother would tell him that young women had called looking for him, "though it wasn't always true."

THEMES

Paranoia

Without knowing the context within which "The Censors" was written, it would be easy to view Juan's actions and perceptions in the story as paranoid. However, many of his fears, when considered within the framework of the repressive Argentine government that Valenzuela lived through in the 1970s and into the 1980s, may have been justified. Immediately after sending his letter, Juan begins to rethink everything he has written, wondering what might be misinterpreted by the censors. He knows how thoroughly they examine each letter, studying it as a physical object (Juan talks about how they smell and feel each letter) and as a message with questionable

TOPICS FOR FURTHER STUDY

- Valenzuela's fiction is heavily influenced by the political events of Argentina's recent past. Using online sources and works such as Luis Alberto Romero's *A History of Argentina in the Twentieth Century* (published by Pennsylvania State University Press in 2002), compile a timeline summarizing key events in the political history of Argentina from the 1970s to the present. The report should focus on political leaders, revolutionary movements, and the impact of economic crises on the nation's leadership. To present your report, create a written document or an electronic presentation such as a Web page or PowerPoint presentation. Be sure to cite the sources you use.

- In "The Censor," Valenzuela explores the way the intense censorship of personal mail generates fear that is well justified when one considers the actual dangers people faced, as well as a pervasive sense of paranoia. Consider the way censorship, in recent years, has been an issue in the United States and remains an issue today. Investigate which individuals or organizations (such as, perhaps, parents, school boards, and branches of local, state, or federal government) would be operating as censors and what types of materials (for example, music lyrics, literature, or reports in the media) might be the targets of censorship. What types of penalties are incurred if censored items are deemed unacceptable in some way? Reflect on your personal feelings about censorship and about what facts your investigation revealed. Write a persuasive essay in which you incorporate your findings and use the data to attempt to convince the reader of the validity of your opinion regarding censorship.

- Valenzuela's "The Censors" reveals the fear experienced by individuals living under the rule of a repressive government. Julia Alvarez's young-adult novel *Before We Were Free*, published in 2004 by Laurel Leaf, explores a similar situation from the perspective of a twelve-year-old girl living in the Dominican Republic under the dictatorship of Rafael Trujillo. In the story, secret police search private homes, and family members mysteriously disappear. Form a book group and read Alvarez's novel. In your group's discussion, examine the similarities between Alvarez's novel and Valenzuela's short story. Talk about the impact of government policies on families, and what it would be like to live under such an oppressive regime. What dangers do the children and young adults in these situations face? With your group, create a presentation in which you describe to the class the plot, characters, and themes of the book, as well as its similarities to Valenzuela's story.

- In "The Censors," Valenzuela depicts very little of Argentine culture. Juan's mother leaves food and wine for her son, but Juan's existence is focused on his work as a censor. Research the culture of Argentina. What are the traditional foods, customs, and forms of entertainment historically enjoyed by Argentine citizens? By yourself or in a small group, create a multisensory presentation on Argentine culture for the class. Consider preparing traditional foods, playing samples of music, and showing videos of traditional dances or celebrations. An oral report, either delivered live or recorded, should accompany your presentation.

---

content. Anything out of place, such as a stain, and even the punctuation the letter writer used, Juan observes, is investigated. The result of such examinations, Juan concludes, is that both the sender of the letter and the person to whom it is addressed are in jeopardy and may remain so for years, as it may take that long for a letter to be thoroughly scrutinized by all levels of the censorship office. Even when one has a general grasp of the historical Argentine political situation, it

Mail is censored in "The Censors." (Image copyright Stian Iversen, 2009. Used under license from Shutterstock.com)

seems hard for modern readers in a free country to comprehend that a misplaced comma could be seen as evidence of a plot to undermine the government and could lead to the execution of anyone associated with the letter containing the offending punctuation mark. This, however, appears to be what Juan is suggesting. Moved by this intense fear of the harm that might befall Mariana, himself, or both of them, Juan seeks to intercept the letter by getting a job in the censorship office. In this way, Valenzuela demonstrates the ways in which the fears inspired by the censors create a sense of paranoia in Juan. He is moved by his fear to take actions most people would consider extreme; he essentially enters enemy territory in order to protect himself and Mariana.

When Juan takes the job of censor, he becomes the likely source of paranoia for anyone who has recently sent a letter. He is now investigating those stains and commas himself. Juan begins to suspect most of the letters he encounters as having evidence of subversive intentions. In innocent, harmless comments that letter writers make about the weather or the cost of products, Juan finds evidence of rebellion. As Juan becomes what he has feared, his own paranoia is redirected. Rather than fearing that everything he wrote would be suspected by the government of being seditious (that is, something that incites people to rebel against the government), he now suspects that everything anyone writes in a letter poses a threat to the government. So blinded is Juan by his paranoia as a censor, he is even suspicious of himself. He censors his own letter, an act that leads to his execution.

In "The Censors," Valenzuela is exploring this relationship between paranoia and censorship. She shows how the genuine fears that government censorship inspires in people lead those people to be suspicious of everything and everyone.

Love

Valenzuela's treatment of the theme of love in "The Censors" is subtle. The word itself does not appear in the story, yet it is a powerful force. Love is the source of Juan's happiness when the story opens—he has just found out Mariana's address. He seems thrilled to learn that Mariana has not forgotten about him since she moved to Paris. Out of love for Mariana, Juan eagerly writes a letter, and because he loves her, Juan feels driven to protect her by getting a job at the censorship office. Juan feels compelled to intercept the letter, fearing he might have inadvertently caused Mariana harm by sending it. Motivated by love, Juan turns to deception to protect Mariana. He secures a job with the censorship office under false pretenses; he intends to intercept his letter to Mariana in order to save her from harm. He decides to "sabotage the machinery." In the end, Juan is transformed by the machinery—by the bureaucracy that is the censorship office—and saves no one.

Valenzuela offers us another portrait of love in "The Censors" through the character of Juan's mother. Juan's mother is extremely concerned about her son. The narrator informs us, too, that she tells Juan that a young woman (Lola) has called for him and is waiting for him at the bar with her friends. Significantly, the narrator points out that what Juan's mother tells him is not always the truth. Juan's mother lies in order to try and save him, to "get him back on the right track." Valenzuela presents us with two characters, Juan and his mother, who lie with good intentions. They deceive for the sake of love.

STYLE

Irony

Valenzuela uses irony throughout "The Censors." Irony is a literary technique in which an author conveys to the reader that there is a discrepancy between what appears to be true in the story and what is actually true. Often the characters in the story are not aware of this discrepancy. In "The Censors," Juan is not aware of the transformation he has undergone, from a person aware of the dangers posed by overzealous censors, who see threats where none exist, to a person who takes his job—to identify subversive intention—somewhat too seriously, to the point that he sees threats where none exist. Juan's lack of awareness leads ultimately to his death, for he sees subversive content in his own innocent letter. The narrator comments on this situation at the end of the story by describing Juan as "one more victim of his devotion to his work." This statement too, is ironic, in that a person who is devoted to his work typically does not die as a result of this devotion. Another example of irony in the story is the fact that Juan has gotten the job at the censorship office to protect himself and Mariana from the danger possibly posed by the letter he has sent, and yet at the censorship office he exposes himself to danger on a daily basis, handling letters that possibly contain explosives and poison.

Omniscient Narrator

In "The Censors," Valenzuela employs an omniscient third-person narrator. Third-person narration is a storytelling technique in which the narration is conducted by a person outside the story's action. An omniscient narrator, unlike one whose point of view is limited to particular characters, comments at will on the characters or events in the story. Valenzuela's story begins with the narrator exclaiming, "Poor Juan!" The reader is thus introduced to the narrator as a storyteller with an opinion about the characters and events in the story, and to Juan, as a person with whom we should feel some sympathy. The narrator informs the reader that Juan is a victim; he is tricked into thinking that finding the address of his former love interest is something that will bring him happiness, when in fact it is "really one of fate's dirty tricks." The narrator also shares information with the reader that other characters in the story do not possess, such as the fact that Juan's mother occasionally lies to him and that the censorship offices are not always strict in their hiring practices. Valenzuela uses this style effectively, as the omniscient narrator allows Valenzuela the opportunity to be overtly ironic. In addition, the all-knowing narrator conveys a sense of authority that is similar to that wielded by the censor. The narrator shares the information deemed acceptable for the reader to read, while omitting certain information from the reader as well; the reader, for example, never learns the fate of Mariana.

HISTORICAL CONTEXT

Government Oppression in Argentina in the 1970s and 1980s

Valenzuela's "The Censors" was written in the aftermath of a period of great turmoil in Argentina's history. Juan Perón was a popular president in Argentina when he was first elected and during the early years of this administration

COMPARE & CONTRAST

- **1980s:** After enduring a long period of violence and instability in the wake of the military coup that ousted President Isabel Perón, the government of Argentina, which is now led by President Alfonsín, faces a severe economic crisis. President Raúl Alfonsín is elected in 1983 and serves through 1989.

   Today: Argentine president Cristina Fernández de Kirchner is sworn into office in 2007. While Argentina's economy has suffered recurring crises throughout the twentieth century, the early years of the twenty-first century are a period of some growth. When President Fernández de Kirchner takes office, however, the world is experiencing an economic downturn, and Argentina suffers as well. The government raises taxes and nationalizes private pension funds in order to stave off further declines.

- **1980s:** Amidst the restoration of the government from military rule to democracy and the efforts of the government to save Argentina from economic collapse, unemployment rates skyrocket. During the late 1980s, unemployment rates remain at about 16 to 17 percent of the labor force.

   Today: Along with gradual improvements in the economy made in the twenty-first century, unemployment declines to under percent by September 2008, according to the CIA *World Factbook*, although it begins to rise again in 2009.

- **1980s:** The post-boom movement in Latin American literature features a general reaction to, and rejection of, the earlier boom period of Latin American literature. Post-boom writers often reject the experimentalism of boom writers and instead embrace and explore political and social realism in their works.

   Today: As post-boom writers have now been writing for many years and are still publishing, many no longer are as fervent in their reaction to the principles of the boom period. Some, such as Gabriel Garcia Márquez, have used magical realism in their works, incorporating elements of fantasy or magic in an otherwise realistic work. Márquez and other writers may also focus on stories in which the personal history of the characters is of primary importance. Other up-and-coming writers, such as Pola Oloixarac, examine social and political issues in their writing. Oloixarac, in a work published in Argentina in 2009 but not yet translated into English (*Las Teorías Salvajes*, or "Savage Theories"), focuses on the discrimination against women in Argentina.

(1946–1952). A supporter of unions and the working class, Perón also granted women the right to vote. Part of his popularity was attributed to the personal and political popularity of his wife Eva Perón, or Evita as she was known. Eva died in 1952. Juan Perón was, however, known for the violent repression of his opponents. Although he was re-elected in 1952, his government was overtaken by military generals, and in 1955, he resigned. The economy worsened, and the government was led by a succession of military and civilian rulers. Many Argentines remained loyal to Perón and prayed he would return to power, which he did in 1973. His second wife, Isabel, served as his vice president, and took over the rule of Argentina when Perón died in 1974. Isabel Perón's real name was Maria Estela Martinez; a former dancer, she was known by her stage name. Isabel Perón's government was increasingly influenced by an advisor, Jose Lopez Rega, who had strong antiliberal, anticommunist, and antilabor union views. Assassinations of leaders of such groups were ordered under Lopez Rega's command. As

Scales of justice (Image copyright JustASC, 2009. Used under license from Shutterstock.com)

tensions in the country mounted, Isabel Perón allowed armed forces whatever power they deemed necessary to subdue any rebellion against her government. In 1976, military forces seized control of the government and ousted her. The period from 1976 through 1983 was one of extreme violence, as rebel guerilla forces challenged the government's military forces. Civilians who spoke out against the military government or supported either the Peróns or liberal organizations were killed or mysteriously disappeared. A war with British forces over a group of islands known as the Malvinas helped to bring about the end of this military rule. The government, which had never succeeded in gaining popular support and had now lost an embarrassing skirmish with the British, allowed elections to take place in 1983. Newly elected President Raul Alfonsín took office in 1984 and attempted to restore democracy to Argentina. The new president faced many obstacles, including the facts that military leaders remained a powerful force in the government and that a severe economic crisis loomed.

Post-Boom Spanish Fiction

A literary movement in the 1960s and 1970s among Latin American writers, known as the Latin American boom or Spanish boom (as they published their works in the Spanish language) featured works of experimental fiction. These writers questioned the nature of reality and explored questions related to the human condition in nontraditional ways. Realism was rejected. The works might contain fantastic or supernatural elements, or they might present the story's events in a nonlinear or nonchronological fashion. Post-boom writers are those, such as Valenzuela, writing a generation after the boom writers. The post-boom is sometimes described as a reaction against the boom principles. Post-boom fiction tends to embrace realism as a storytelling method. The details of daily life enhance the fiction, and stories are typically conveyed chronologically. Often, political and social realism is the focus, with post-boom writers exploring the turbulent social and political problems that plagued many Latin American countries in the 1970s and 1980s. Donald L. Shaw, in his evaluation of this type of writing in *The Post-Boom in Spanish American Fiction*, describes the post-boom "as a movement in which fiction tends to reestablish a closer connection with the here and now of Spanish America." Shaw describes the way elements of some of Valenzuela's fiction, such as her focus on the individual and his or her private reality and on the significance of language, are reflective of the complex nature of the boom period itself. That is, Valenzuela treats reality as a personal matter and does not always overtly explore the larger political and social reality. In this way, Valenzuela presents a subjective portrait of reality, and one that is reflective of the questioning nature of boom fiction.

CRITICAL OVERVIEW

Like the work of many authors who do not write in English, Valenzuela's fiction often generates more criticism in its original language than in English. Relatively little has been written in English about Valenzuela's short fiction in general, compared with the criticism of her novels, and even less about "The Censors" in particular. Donald L. Shaw examines Valenzuela's place in the post-boom literary movement of Latin American or Spanish-language literature. In his study, *The Post-Boom in Spanish American Fiction*, Shaw discusses the elements of post-boom fiction and describes the way Valenzuela's writing contains elements of both the boom period and the post-boom period. He writes that Valenzuela's work reaches "toward a positive 'order,' toward an explicable world in which ideals of love, justice, beauty, reason, and human solidarity exist and are meaningful." Nevertheless, Shaw goes on to say, Valenzuela is deeply suspicious "that that is not how things are."

Other critics more directly explore the source of Valenzuela's suspicions by studying the impact of political events in Argentina on her works. In *Reading the Feminine Voice in Latin American Women's Fiction: From Teresa de la Parra to Elena Poniatowska and Luisa Valenzuela*, María Teresa Medeiros-Lichem maintains that the language Valenzuela uses in her fiction is generated in part by the "ineluctable urge to speak out fears, to decipher the horror caused by human cruelty under the political repression in Argentina in the late 1970s and early 1980s." In an interview with Sharon Magnarelli published in *Reflections/Refractions: Reading Luisa Valenzuela*, Valenzuela discusses the relationship between terrors of the political situation in Argentina and her views on censorship. Within her critical examination of Valenzuela's writings, Magnarelli observes that Valenzuela is "one of Latin America's most frequently acclaimed and highly esteemed writers." Valenzuela's work, Magnarelli writes, "examines life, reality, and our sociopolitical structures from different vantage points and in a variety of contexts in order to suggest new definitions or even a plurality of interpretations for situations not necessarily recognized as problematic." In other words, Valenzuela explores issues from various viewpoints, attempting to demonstrate that perceptions of reality shift depending on one's perspective. Such an assessment may be applied to "The Censor." When Juan's perspective changes, his perception of reality is altered. The reader is consequently forced to question the issue of censorship from a variety of angles. The fact that Valenzuela does not answer all the reader's questions in "The Censor" (What happened to Mariana? How, exactly, did Juan's censoring of his letter lead to his execution? To what extent does Juan accurately convey the threat posed by the censorship office?) appears to be typical of Valenzuela's fiction. As Magnarelli observes, Valenzuela's "prose rarely offers solutions to the problems it posits, for that is not her intent."

CRITICISM

Catherine Dominic

Dominic is a novelist and a freelance writer and editor. In the following essay, she explores the ways in which Valenzuela uses the character of Juan in "The Censors" in order to explore the complexities of censorship and the various forms it takes.

In an interview with Magnarelli in *Reflections/Refractions: Reading Luisa Valenzuela*, Luisa Valenzuela discusses her views on censorship, describing the different ways censorship can affect individuals. In particular, Valenzuela points out that one type of censorship occurs when an individual "will often refuse to read what he fears might hurt him, what might raise his consciousness or make him think beyond what he wants to hear." Valenzuela goes on to

WHAT DO I READ NEXT?

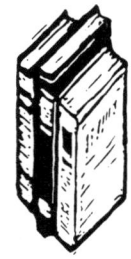

- Valenzuela's *Symmetries* is an acclaimed collection of stories in which Valenzuela experiments with the short story form. This collection was originally published in 1993 in Spanish as *Simetrías*, and it was made available in English in a 1998 edition by Serpent's Tail.

- Valenzuela's novel *Black Novel with Argentines* was first published in English in 1992 and is available in a more recent edition published by Latin American Literary Review Press in 2002. The work was originally published in Spanish in 1990 as *Novela Negra con Argentinos*. It is a thriller set in New York featuring exiled Argentines.

- Isabel Allende, another prominent female Latin American author, published her first young-adult novel, *City of the Beasts*, in 2002, through HarperCollins. The book features a fifteen-year-old American boy and the twelve-year-old daughter of an Amazon jungle guide, whom the American meets on a trip to the Amazon that he takes with his journalist grandmother. In addition to exploring the friendship that develops between the two children from different cultures, the work has environmental themes. It is the first in a series.

- Lawrence Thornton's *Imagining Argentina*, first published in 1987 and available in a 1991 edition by Bantam, is a novel exploring the turbulent modern history of Argentina. The work is set in Buenos Aires, where Valenzuela has lived much of her life, during the oppressive military rule Argentina endured after the death of Juan Perón and the deposition (overthrow) of Isabel Perón.

- *The Little School: Tales of Disappearance and Survival in Argentina* by Alicia Partnoy, with a preface by author Julia Alvarez, is Partnoy's memoir. She was one of the Argentines who disappeared during the years of military government oppression, and in her book Partnoy reveals how she survived the concentration camp in which she had been imprisoned. The work, published in 1998, is available through Cleis Press.

- *Censorship: The Knot That Binds Power and Knowledge*, by Sue Curry Jansen, was published by Oxford University Press in 1991. It explores the history of modern censorship, exploring its variant forms worldwide.

- Travis Holland addresses censorship in the Soviet Union under the dictatorship of Joseph Stalin in his 2007 novel *The Archivist's Story*. This dark novel addresses some of the same cross-purposes of a reluctant government censor as does "The Censors."

---

identify the further ramifications of this way of thinking, stating that "to avoid the pain of confronting a reality that is not at all pleasant (people are disappearing or tortured or dead), one just refuses to recognize or acknowledge that reality." Valenzuela speaks from personal experience. She is quoted elsewhere (as cited in Shaw's *The Post-Boom in Spanish American Fiction*) as stating that, in Argentina in the 1970s, "some writers suddenly disappeared; many were threatened by the paramilitary forces. Publishers' offices were bombed and thousands of books were destroyed." The anxiety that Juan conveys in "The Censors" regarding the harm that might come to him or Mariana as a result of his letter is rooted in the oppression that Valenzuela witnessed her fellow Argentines experiencing for many years. Valenzuela uses the character of Juan to personify (that is, to embody certain ideas) the different methods of censorship. Juan censors others in marking up and deleting portions of their letters; he censors himself in the same way, marking up his own letter. Juan censors himself in the subtle, subversive way Valenzuela describes, by refusing to see reality and acknowledge that people's lives are becoming

> "JUAN CENSORS HIMSELF IN THE SUBTLE, SUBVERSIVE WAY VALENZUELA DESCRIBES, BY REFUSING TO SEE REALITY AND ACKNOWLEDGE THAT PEOPLE'S LIVES ARE BECOMING ENDANGERED AS A RESULT OF HIS ACTIONS AND THOSE OF ALL THE CENSORS."

endangered as a result of his actions and those of all the censors.

Throughout the short story "The Censors," Juan enacts the role of the censor in a number of ways. As the story opens, Juan establishes the dangers posed by the censors. He describes the way the censors may take years to process a letter and send it on its way; sender and recipient may be dead before the letter reaches its destination. Both sender and recipient, Juan points out, are in danger. He expresses his fear that Mariana could be kidnapped, even in Paris, by the secret operatives employed by the censorship office. As soon as Juan obtains a position with the censorship office, he no longer seems concerned with the fact that anyone who has sent or been sent a letter is in danger. Initially, Juan seems focused on obtaining his letter to Mariana, but his focus soon wanes. When Juan is finally in a position to read and analyze the content of letters, his "noble mission blur[s] in his mind," and his attitude toward the censors begins to shift. Juan begins to focus not on retrieving his letter but on the deception used by the people who have written the letters. He expresses his surprise that people would scheme in such a manner. This is described as a "horrible" time for Juan. He is stunned to discover how "conniving" people can be. In apparently innocuous phrases about the weather or the prices of goods, Juan now sees covert plans to stage a revolt against the government. Juan has become consumed by his role as a censor. He is psychologically transformed. The transition takes place over an undisclosed amount of time. But in this time frame, the Juan who was once fearful of being thought to have subversive intentions comes to see such subversion in everyone else. His paranoia has been transferred from the government to those he believes are trying to dismantle the government. Living in a culture of fear both prior to and during his time in the censorship office has altered Juan's perceptions.

The narrator informs the reader that Juan is not interested in the wine his mother leaves for him or the girls who his mother tells him have called. Juan goes home after work, eats his dinner, and retires for the evening, devoted to his purpose. He has become one of the people he feared when the story opened. Having already linked the activities of the censors—their habits of studying every stain and stray mark on the page—with the state of imminent danger in which letter writers and letter receivers exist, Juan has now become the force of oppression, the source of danger to others. Not only does he actively censor the writings of others but he has also begun to censor himself in one of the ways Valenzuela describes. Juan refuses to acknowledge the truth; he no longer expresses his awareness that his actions, the actions of all the censors, jeopardize people's lives. Rather, Juan becomes ever more zealous in his role as censor.

Juan now censors more letters than most of the other censors at the office; his basket of censored letters is "the best fed," as well as "the most cunning," a phrase that suggests that Juan is as conniving in his attempts to point an accusatory finger at the letter writers as he suspects the writers of being themselves. This phrase further implies that Juan is less concerned with the truth of the letters' content than he is with impugning the intentions of the individuals sending and receiving letters. By the end of "The Censors," Juan thoroughly represents the self-censor Valenzuela has described, the individual who refuses to confront reality. So blinded is Juan to the truth of what he has become, that when his own letter to Mariana reaches his hands, "he censored it without regret." Juan censors himself in the sense that he alters the original sentiments he sought to express to Mariana, just as he has revised and deleted the writings of countless of other individuals who have attempted to send letters. In this way, Juan alters the truth of his self-expression and the expression of others. Such a transformation of reality for political purposes is among the tragedies enacted by Juan's censorship. Furthermore, by refusing to acknowledge that physical harm is the likely result of censoring, Juan signs his own death warrant when he censors his letter to Mariana. He gives no thought to the consequences of his actions. One such consequence is his own execution the following morning. The reader is left not knowing what might become of Mariana, but from what Juan has suggested earlier in the story, it appears likely that her life is also in jeopardy.

As Valenzuela demonstrates through the character of Juan, censorship may take a variety of forms, but in all its iterations, at its core, censorship represents a denial of truth. Significantly, when the censor alters or eliminates truth, nothing is created to take its place. No ideology remains save that of control and oppression. Juan once mentions his ability to detect "the wavering hand of someone secretly scheming to overthrow the Government." His enthusiasm lies in his skill at ferreting out what he believes is deception, but Juan never speaks about having anything to believe in after he loses his belief in his need to protect Mariana. His "noble purpose" has indeed been "blurred." Juan is not full of political fervor. He speaks only of what he is against, not what he is for or what he works in service of. This vacuum that is left in the wake of the censoring and the subsequent executions is itself a thing to be lamented. Valenzuela suggests through "The Censors" that the destruction of personal and creative expression by a repressive government results in a void. The end of "The Censors" leaves such a void: Juan is dead, and Mariana's fate is unknown. The government aims to destroy truth and distort reality through the activities of the censors. Valenzuela's work leaves its own void, as the reader is left ponder what remains—what is left to believe in—in the world Valenzuela has described.

Source: Catherine Dominic, Critical Essay on "The Censors," in *Short Stories for Students*, Gale, Cengage Learning, 2010.

Rafael Ocasio
In the following excerpt, Ocasio explains how Valenzuela's works explore the negative side of humanity.

...Short story writer and novelist, Luisa Valenzuela stands out among the internationally famous women writers from Argentina. Her works are complex explorations of the dark side of the human psyche. Learned in Argentine history, Valenzuela offers a sound view of national cultural patterns, particularly of issues that pertain to national politics. Of special literary interest is her exploration of Argentina's military background, including the dynamics behind the practice of torture and the country's massive censorship under military dictatorships. She writes from a feminist perspective; her approach to Argentine history includes a detailed analysis of gender-bound obstacles, often stemming from the strongly chauvinistic military past....

Valenzuela was back in Argentina in 1974, at a time of high political uncertainty. General Juan Perón, elected president in 1973, seemed to have lost his support among powerful military circles, which had allowed general elections after their dictatorship. Perón's death in office left a shaky government in the hands of his wife and vice president, Isabel de Perón, who was deposed in a military coup in 1976. Valenzuela experienced this period, which became the inspiration for her short story collection *Aquí pasan cosas raras* (1976, *Strange Things Happen Here*, 1979).

> THE CENSORSHIP THAT HAD BEEN INITIATED FOR PRINTED PUBLICATIONS, SUCH AS NEWSPAPERS AND BOOKS, EXTENDED EVEN TO REGULAR CONVERSATION WITH FRIENDS IN THE PRIVACY OF ONE'S HOME. HOW AN INSTITUTION CAN HAVE SUCH AN OVERWHELMING CONTROL OVER THE PEOPLE IS VALENZUELA'S CONCERN IN 'THE CENSORS.'"

Valenzuela's stand against military dictatorship at the time is evident. She edited *Crisis*, a magazine with a strong political outlook, a national voice of political discontent. Valenzuela's *Strange Things Happen Here* gives testimony to the earliest of the military's abuses. She testified that in 1976 she nearly fell victim to military wrath; shortly after she had left for a trip to the United States, the police came to her home with an arrest warrant.

She left Argentina in voluntary exile in 1979. Shortly before her departure, Valenzuela had become part of a complex network of activists who were successful in smuggling out of Argentina official documentation on the military campaign, the Dirty War, which had led to the disappearance and deaths of political activists. These *desaparecidos,* or "disappeared ones," and the convoluted, repressive military infrastructure became important subjects in Valenzuela's best-known novel, *Cola de lagartija* (1983, *The Lizard's Tail*, 1983). This novel dwells on the cult of "The Dead Woman," a cryptic allusion to Eva Perón, Juan Perón's first lady during his first presidency (1946–1955).

Valenzuela lived in New York City from 1979 to 1989, where she taught Latin American literature and offered seminars for writers at Columbia University and at New York University. She was a Guggenheim fellow in 1983. While in New York, she continued writing for newspapers, such as the *New York Times*.

Valenzuela has lived in her native Argentina since 1989. She continues to have an active role in the literary documentation of the Dirty War and often comments on her experiences of living under a military regime and the psychological trauma to the national psyche:

> There was no freedom left; you couldn't do anything. We couldn't collaborate. It was impossible because the repression was furious and penetrated everything. And you never knew where the next blow was coming from. At first it was open, and you could always see it coming. But then came the paramilitary groups, the parapolice, the gangs hired to incite violence, and I didn't think I'd be able to write anymore if I stayed. I felt asphyxiated. Besides, something very strange happened. People began to acknowledge and justify the situation, saying it was a dirty war. You couldn't talk to anyone. If you said someone had disappeared, they'd tell you the person must have done something. (García Pinto 208)

Her novel *Realidad nacional desde la cama* (1990, *Bedside Manners,* 1995) offers a surrealist approach to the experiences of a Latin American woman who is visiting her native country, which remains nameless, after living in exile for many years. The traumatic experiences of military persecution are greater than just the physical damage.

Like Julio Cortázar, another Argentine writer and her literary mentor, Valenzuela sets out to explore the psychological mechanisms behind the dictatorship in Argentina following the military coup of 1976. Human rights violations of thousands of *desaparecidos,* their torture and, in many cases, deaths while in concentration camps or inside military facilities, are still matters of controversy in Argentine political circles. Valenzuela's short story "The Censors" is not an eyewitness account of these crimes. Instead, in a simple and straightforward story, she explores the military censorship that allowed cover-up of illegal activities by their own staff.

Valenzuela's short story describes how military censorship went beyond the power of official censors. It had a negative psychological effect on civilians, who often became their own most severe censors. The censorship that had been initiated for printed publications, such as newspapers and books, extended even to regular conversation with friends in the privacy of one's home. How an institution can have such an overwhelming control over the people is Valenzuela's concern in "The Censors."

"The Censors" is extremely concise. There is only one protagonist, a colorless character named Juan. As the story begins, Juan finds the address of Mariana, a friend who has just moved to Paris. Such a mundane event leads to a series of unusual situations. An omniscient narrator informs the reader that the knowledge of

Mariana's address came from unstated and mysterious circumstances that must be kept anonymous because highly confidential sources are involved. Juan believes that Mariana's address is her message to him that she loves him, so he immediately writes her a letter.

The narrator also serves as the eyewitness to changes in Juan's behavior after he writes the letter. According to the narrator, the letter marks the beginning of Juan's downfall. This is a dark comment about a presumed love letter to an absent love.

After mailing the letter, Juan experiences changes in his personality. He cannot concentrate at work and spends countless sleepless nights. He obsesses over "the letter," which is described as "irreproachable, harmless." Soon the reader realizes that Juan is not worried about a negative reaction from Mariana (presumably to his romantic letter), but about a complex process of censorship by professional censors at the post office.

In her exploration of the psychological mechanisms behind censorship, Valenzuela chooses to write in the genre of the absurd. This is evident in the narrator's exaggerated description of the process of censorship as Juan imagines it: "He knows that they examine, sniff, feel, and read between the lines of each and every letter, and check its tiniest comma and accidental stain." Juan makes a sudden decision: he will become a censor in order to intercept his own letter.

Juan's becoming a postal censor is central to Valenzuela's study of the psychological effects of living under a totalitarian censorship. His tasks as a devoted and efficient censor are described within the aesthetics of the absurd. Techniques related to the absurd present incredible events that appear innocuous to a disturbed character. Juan becomes a man with an obsession: he has to intercept his letter before another censor does. The task itself is presented as an impossible deed.

The process of the censors' reading correspondence is, indeed, absurd. For example, after a letter is mailed, the censoring can take months and, in complex cases, years. In those extreme cases, as the sender and the receiver patiently wait, their lives are at stake because the authorities view all letters as potential subversive texts. From the censors' absurd points of view, statements such as "the weather's unsettled" or "prices continue to soar" are a message in code to overthrow the government. What type of government and what country Valenzuela leaves unsaid. This is part of her own censorship, for she seems to be reproducing in her story the censorship that she has experienced.

The government in "The Censors" appears to be operated by the military, as indicated in departmentalized sections of the Post Office's Censorship Division. In a highly bureaucratic system, Juan starts working in Section K, an area where envelopes are screened for explosives. The job is dangerous, as he soon realizes when an envelope explodes and a fellow worker loses his right hand. In another section, other censors inspect the envelopes for poisonous dust. These sections reveal the military's obsession with obstructing the guerrilla activities of subversive groups.

Soon Juan is transferred to another division, after having warned the postal administration that disgruntled workers were planning a strike. This event explains why Juan, surprisingly, begins to agree with his superiors. His reasons for betraying his fellow workers remain unexplored. Was Juan aiming for a fast-track promotion so that he might gain access to other sections where his letter might be? Or was Juan purposely helping to identify enemies of the system? These are questions that remain unanswered, and they are at the core of the story's message.

At the end of the story, Juan has become the best of the censors. He has forgotten the real reason behind working as a censor, as the narrator critically points out: "Soon his work became so absorbing that his noble mission blurred in his mind." He finds his letter to Mariana, which he coldly censors "without regret," despite knowing that he will be executed, "one more victim of his devotion to his work."

The story has a specific political message. Juan's zealous behavior, reflected in his voluntary confession of subversive activity, is a direct product of the totalitarian regime of this unnamed country. One can argue that the absurdity in Juan's behavior is not his ultimate sacrifice as the best censor of the hated Post Office's Censorship Division but the process that leads him to become a censor in the first place. The narrator points out that, like Juan, many others had become censors in order to find personal letters. They were allowed to become censors because the authorities doubted that they would be able to find them. At any rate, these individuals were the best censors because they had a dual quest: to find their letters and to prove to their superiors that there was no motive in their impeccable performance other than a desire to serve the system well.

As the story ends, the reader realizes that the narrator's comments are part of an official report on Juan's performance as a censor. The narrator becomes identified with "they," whom the reader must assume are Juan's supervisors—the ultimate censors. Symbolically, their power over the civilian population includes their ability to know the people's concealed motives and their intimate thoughts. Juan is not punished because he attempted to rescue his letter, but because he dared to break down the system: "Well, you've got to beat them to the punch, do what every one tries to do: sabotage the machinery, throw sand in its gears, that is to say get to the bottom of the problem to try to stop it." Although this appears to be a direct quote from Juan, the reader may interpret it as the censors' transcription of information on Juan provided by an acquaintance of his. The power of the censors is, therefore, reinforced as almost endless.

It can be argued that in "The Censors" Valenzuela wrote a story from the perspective of a writer fearing censorship. Juan's absurd task, reading letters with a keen eye, becomes a metaphor for the restrictions imposed on writers. Juan is also a character who experiences a significant existential crisis. This is visible in his sudden transformation from an activist against a totalitarian regime into the most conscientious of the censors. The comment is political and goes to the core of complex psychological reactions to life under a dictatorial government.

Source: Rafael Ocasio, "Women Writers: New Perspectives on Latin America," in *Literature of Latin America*, Greenwood Press, 2004, pp. 181–86.

Caleb Bach

In the following excerpt, Bach provides an overview of the impact that violence and war had on Valenzuela's writing.

Argentine writer *Luisa Valenzuela* has defined her country's origins in terms both violent and lyrical. In a 1983 essay penned for the *New York Times,* she referred to the discovery of the Rio de la Plata by Juan Diaz de Solis in 1516: "Poetry was already lurking: on board with Solis was Martin del Barco Centenera, who wrote an ode titled *The Argentina,* . . . a misnomer since there was practically no *argentum,* no silver, there. . . . It was written while the first settlers, surrounded by Indians, were forced to eat their dead. That is why I believe we are descendants of

> **DURING THE LATE SEVENTIES VALENZUELA'S WRITING WAS STRONGLY SHAPED BY EVENTS IN HER HOMELAND, A MILITARY GOVERNMENT COMMITTED TO THE 'DIRTY WAR,' WHICH INVOLVED PERSECUTION, TORTURE, AND THE DISAPPEARANCES OF THOUSANDS OF PERSONS."**

poets and cannibals." At the time, Valenzuela's essay was celebratory and quite specific: "With the return of democracy, the poets' time has come." Still, it reflected an abiding concern that has occupied her during much of her career: why this penchant for self-destruction from a human spirit that also can find expression through peaceful dreaming with words?

In Valenzuela's case, to claim direct descent from poets is accurate. Through her mother, Luisa Mercedes Levinson, a well-known author of novels and haunting, ironic short stories, she came to know many other prominent members of Argentina's literary community. "I grew up with all these writers: Jorge Luis Borges, Ernesto Sábato. They came to our home. That's one thing that probably led me to write. My mother collaborated with Borges on one story ("La hermana de Eloisa"). As a child I thought writing was dreary, drab, but they loved it. They could be quite obnoxious but funny. That impressed me that writing was more lively than one would think."

As a teenager Valenzuela placed her first articles with the youth magazine *Quince Abriles*. Instead of attending the university, she went straight into journalism on a full-time basis, working for several Buenos Aires newspapers and magazines (*La Nación, El Mundo, El Hogar*). At age eighteen she published her first short story, "Ciudad ajena" ["The City of the Unknown"], a tale suffused with the themes of death, eroticism, and dreams that would endure in much of her later work. For a time Valenzuela also worked at the Biblioteca Nacional, which was directed by Borges and his deputy, José Edmundo Clemente. Valenzuela recalls that she wrote press releases for lectures sponsored by the library. "God knows what I wrote. I didn't even type well. But I was very proud because I knew I was in the presence of someone important. Borges was always pulling some book off the shelf and explaining. He could still see a little bit. The way he related to books was very beautiful." . . .

At age twenty, headstrong and impulsive, Valenzuela left home and headed for France. "Yes, I've been prone to radical shifts in my life," she ruefully admits, "and French sailors!" In rapid succession she married Theodore Marjak, who was in the French merchant marine, resettled in Normandy, and gave birth to her daughter, Anna Lisa. "But I got seasick," she says with a smile, and so the marriage ended in divorce six years later. . . .

Abrupt, even perverse twists in the way a story evolves and culminates characterize many Valenzuela plot lines. This quality may have its roots in her early childhood when her older sister told her bizarre stories with scary endings. Valenzuela was a finicky eater, and when a shocking tale would cause her to open her mouth in astonishment, her sister would be able to get a spoonful of food in. "But I loved them. It wasn't a sort of torture. I loved the horrible stories." Does Valenzuela do that a bit as a writer? "Yes. I like fear. I don't write for little children. At least I try not to. It is one of my pleasures of writing. Suddenly the whole thing comes about in an unexpected way."

In 1964, Valenzuela's wanderings took her back to her homeland where again she worked as a journalist for *La Nación* while completing a screenplay for *Hay que sonreir*. (It later won an award from Argentina's Institución Nacional de Cinematografía.) But she continued to travel throughout Europe and in the United States—always "a tumbleweed, blowing up against a fence somewhere . . . looking for the almost mythic Here-Place, the center of my metaphor" (her words from a 1983 autobiographic sketch). Travel would prove to be the machine behind much of her writing, as if distance made her see things better ("separation sharpens the aim," she has said).

"I have been a traveler all my life," Valenzuela explains. "Even when not on the move I've dreamed of traveling by inventing excursions and adventures, even if it's just around the block. I wanted to be an explorer. I'm a Sagittarius, so that probably has something to do with it." Valenzuela also believes that real home dwells within the person. "I don't know what missing [home] is. When I'm away I'm absolutely there. I'm energized by unpredictability, things coming apart both in my writing and my life. It's uncomfortable, but it makes me go. The moment I feel secure, I get out of the situation."

In 1969 it was wanderlust and a Fulbright grant that took Valenzuela to the United States as a participant in the International Writers Program at the University of Iowa. She disliked Iowa City, "which was neither city nor countryside," but in the solitude of this alien setting and the company of "many other neurotic writers" she wrote her second novel, *El gato eficaz* ["The Efficient Cat"]. The feline creature in the title proves to be a "cat-o-nine deaths," a kind of composite of many of the world's evils that accompany a female narrator through a series of strange adventures at once eschatological, violent, erotic, and humorous. Valenzuela abandoned the linear narrative of *Hay que sonreir* and opted for a more daring, subversive, and (as one critic said) "fragmented, respectful disrespect" for language: run-on words, invented terms (like *telecoito,* or long-distance lovemaking), and even words that transform themselves or disintegrate before the reader's eyes (smite me, *imíteme, imitáteme*), much like characters in the novel itself. Outlandish puns and word play, parodies of social taboos, newspaper clippings, diary entries, legal abstracts, operating instructions—all come together in this highly energized yet deeply disturbing novel, which disassembles literature and demythologizes traditional behavior.

As to the role of humor in her writing, Valenzuela responds with a quiet grin: "Humor is serious business, very serious. Because I don't believe there is any life without humor. Of course, not everything is laughable. It's just that it gives you the other face of the same thing. Otherwise you see things unilaterally. The humor that is not always laughing so directly at things also allows you to see more obscure parts. I wouldn't even be looking at certain things if I didn't take a humorous slant to get into it. Sometimes they criticize me seriously. They say, 'You break the climate by making a joke in the middle of this horror,' which I do a lot. Humor is the mortar of life . . . motor of life!"

During the late seventies Valenzuela's writing was strongly shaped by events in her homeland, a military government committed to the "dirty war," which involved persecution, torture, and the disappearances of thousands of persons.

Como en la guerra [*He Who Searches*], her third novel, employed some of the same kaleidoscopic techniques found in *El gato eficaz* but also mirrored the author's residency first in Barcelona and Mexico and her return to Buenos Aires. As she later wrote in the preface to *Open Door* (a 1988 English-language collection of some of her favorite short stories: "in 1975, upon returning to my city after a long absence . . . it wasn't mine any longer. Buenos Aires belonged then to violence and state terrorism, and I could only sit in cafés and brood. Till I decided a book of short stories could be written in a month, at those same café tables, overhearing scraps of scared conversation, seeping in the general paranoia." And thus *Aquí pasan cosas raras* [*Strange Things Happen Here*] was born, a collection of highly imaginative tales populated with misfits and perverts, Valenzuela's barely disguised portraits of oppressors compensating for their own sense of impotence or inadequacy. In "A Story About Greenery," a thistle manages to prosper despite a municipal edict prohibiting foliage in public places and in the story "Los mejor calzados" ["The Best Shod"], a city takes pride in its beggars who wear nice shoes. (They have been confiscated from the bodies of those who were tortured and executed.)

The oppressive "atmosphere of self-censorship—should I write indecipherably so that nobody could read over my shoulder?" (as she later remembered asking herself)—compelled Valenzuela to find a new place of residence. Thanks to a timely invitation to be a writer-in-residence at Columbia University, she opted for New York City. In 1981 she was named a fellow at the New York Institute for the Humanities, a prestigious multidisciplinary research facility, and the following year she was awarded a Guggenheim Fellowship. Throughout the 1980s Valenzuela conducted many stimulating seminars at Columbia while also teaching writing courses at New York University....

In 1988, while writing *Novela negra con argentinos* [*Black Novel (with Argentines)*], Valenzuela decided to leave New York City, which had been her base of operations for nearly ten years. "It was a question of language. I was so invaded by the English language. I was worried because I was dreaming and talking to myself in English. I always wrote in Spanish but if I stayed any longer, I would have to start writing in English." Chillingly faithful to the modern-day reality of many a big city, *Novela negra* features two Argentine writers living a New York existence defined by the basest of circumstances (mindless killings, sexual perversion, foul cynicism at every turn). "My feeling when I was writing was why do I write these horrible things about New York when I really love this city. Then I concluded it was my farewell, my goodbye to New York. I saw the worst part because I was trying to disengage myself."

For the moment, this vagabond storyteller has returned to her homeland and defined her "Here-Place" as an apartment in a quiet, secluded part of the Belgrano district of Buenos Aires. She has continued to travel for conferences, as a lecturer, and to give workshops, but she has still found time to continue writing. In 1990 she issued a polemic on the situation in Argentina entitled *Realidad nacional desde la cama* ["National Reality from the Bed"]. In 1993, Editorial Sudamericana issued a new collection of her short stories, *Simetrías* ["Symmetries"], among them some fairy tales revised for adults, ghost stories, and personalized accounts set in Venice, Bali, and California's Big Sur.

It had been Valenzuela's intention to do a historical novel based upon the life of Juana Azurduy, a heroine of the nineteenth-century wars of independence from Spain who possessed courageous assertiveness remarkable for those times. "I went to Sucre, Bolivia, in July, 1993, and worked in the archives at the Casa de Libertad. I was there for the anniversary of Azurduy, and so they asked me to speak. They even brought out the urn with her ashes, which I held. It was very moving. But then, after nothing had been published on her here, suddenly a book came out by Paco O'Donnell [former Argentine ambassador to Bolivia] and so . . . well, I had been speaking too much and not doing it. You have to do things!"

If Valenzuela is hard on herself (and she always is), it is because she feels strongly that one must live what one believes. She demands of herself and those around her the very best kind of thinking—inspired aspirations—and therefore is distressed by the cultural banality so common the world over. "Here in Argentina, our 'postmodernist' government is more interested in bigger shopping centers than better theaters. Buenos Aires used to be more profound. One could sit in a café and talk, and now few can even afford to buy a cup of coffee." Could the tragedy of Argentina's recent past at least be perceived as a catalyst for serious work? "I don't believe that sort of thing. Not at all," Valenzuela states emphatically. "There's no such thing as a placid situation... because there's human soul that necessarily is not placid. They used to say to me in the United States: 'You are lucky because you have all these terrible things to fight against and that makes you create.' I thought that a terrible idea. A writer always has to find that force and do things without having to fight because of horrible things you're going through."

Perhaps it is inappropriate to describe Valenzuela's life on the edge with a linear chronology; after, she favors circular, spiral, or even concentric configurations for the passage of events and as to those events themselves, she prefers to describe them with ambiguity. That is to say, her books are not for the "*desocupado lector*," or lazy, uninvolved reader, as her biographer, Sharon Magnarelli, has pointed out. But it also should be noted that she does not intentionally confuse her audience: Her prose is crystalline, and her choice of words precise. It is rather that, like the true teacher, she prefers to trigger self-education by posing questions, not by serving up simplistic solutions. Her goal is to provoke thoughtfulness, dislodge the apathetic from their comfortable yet fallacious, worn-out assumptions, and see with acuity the disturbing reality within which we live. "I write about heresies: when religion ends up falling over the wall which is fascinating, especially dogmatic religions. They are so dogmatic they have to collapse and turn into good things. I also write about power. Now I am asking myself what is love all about. Since I don't have hints of an answer, I might be writing something about it because, as I said, I like to write about that which I don't know."

During our conversation the phone rang, and Valenzuela learned that a close friend's son had just died in a motorcycle accident. Visibly pained by the call, later she nonetheless reflected: "We walk on the edge of death, and there is a certain excitement, it is interesting. It's horrible to say that. But there is strength there too. There's this precarious business but to die has its own strength, validity. He had the right to buy a motorcycle and kill himself. This is not committing suicide. This is some sort of following a destiny that belonged to him. I have no right to deprive him of it. It has a strength that one has to honor. I don't know whether I said it very well, but I have a very strong feeling about that. He did *his* life."

Source: Caleb Bach, "Metaphors and Magic Unmask the Soul," in *Américas*, Vol. 47, No. 1, January–February 1995, pp. 22–7.

Fernando Ainsa

In the following excerpt, Ainsa describes how fear is symbolized in Valenzuela's work.

Child psychiatrists utilize a test called "The Land of Fear," developed on a principle using short phrases and drawings, which allows them to measure anxiety in children. The test is arranged into four categories: aggression, insecurity, abandonment, and death. The symbols that embody this "land of fear" are of a cosmic nature (natural disasters such as earthquakes, fires, floods, and volcanic eruptions) and represent a terrifying bestiary (dragons, monsters, wolves, and other malevolent animals) as well as violent or wicked beings (hangmen, devils, witches, torturers, skeletons, ghosts, and apparitions). The landscape of this realm is made up of dismal forests, cemeteries, impenetrable castles, dark dungeons, and a vast arsenal of instruments of torture. Coffins and masks are objects of daily life. Children have no difficulty in identifying with this "land," where, beyond their personal anguish, they recognize the symbols and images that represent what is regarded as the iconography of traditional fear.

This childhood land of fear may be, nevertheless, the faint reflection or dramatic foreboding of a real country where individual fear has turned into collective panic. A land shrouded in secretive silence, with latent and deep-seated fears, wrapped in complicit cowardices, one directed by parodic autocrats and ruled by a system that is legitimized by its own terror, founded with torturers capable of falling in love with their victims or of crying over their victims' bodies, and with homes that are transformed into prisons—a land, sadly, where the borders of anxiety and anguish dissipate into an uncertain urban landscape that could well be Buenos Aires or New York.

This subtle transition from individual fear (forged from archetypal childhood fears, vacillating, ambiguously, between fear and cowardice) to collective terror, lived out like a nightmare, perhaps best sums up the allegory of fear which serves as the theme and leitmotif of Luisa

> WEARINESS WITHOUT APPARENT CAUSE, A FEELING OF FAILURE, AND AN INABILITY TO REACT GIVE RISE TO THIS VAGUELY DEFINED FEAR, ALTHOUGH IRONICALLY, THE CENSOR WHO TRIES TO 'SPARE' MARIANA OF 'ANXIETIES' IN THE SHORT STORY ['THE CENSORS'] SUCCUMBS TO HIS OWN PREOCCUPATION."

Valenzuela's work. It is to this inquiry, the exploration of this "land of fear"—as literally evident as it is skillfully and ironically invoked—that the following pages are dedicated.

FROM NATURAL FEAR TO "IMAGINATIVE" FEAR

Fear, one must recall, is one of the fundamental human emotions. Omnipresent and subtle, its varied expressions have spanned centuries, manifesting themselves as much in the fear of the unknown as in reactions to danger, as much in individual visions as in collective fear (if not panic). Every civilization is the product of "a protracted struggle against fear" (G. Ferrero), since fear is born with man in the darkest ages of his history. In any case, fear "is in us" (George Delpierre), for "all men are afraid" (Jean-Paul Sartre). Nevertheless, if fright or anxiety can be diffuse, fear is always determined by some cause and obeys and reflects a concrete and immediate situation. Fear has a precise object which confers its specificity and identifies a situation that must be confronted. Fear is manifest in those "moments of greatest awe" ("momentos de máximo asombro"), surprise, or coincidence, that "sudden fear" ("de golpe se asusta" [AP (Aquí pasan cosas raras), 12]), that "sheer cowardice" ("cobardía pura"), or that sensation by which "Pedro's legs shake because it's too much of a coincidence" (ST [Strange Things Happen Here], 5; "a Pedro le tiemblan las piernas por demasiada coincidencia"), to which Valenzuela alludes in her short stories.

One is always "afraid of something." When one is afraid, one believes one knows what one is afraid of and acts according to that cause, generally, concealing it out of so much shame at confessing that one is afraid. It is not unusual, therefore, that there should be as many fears as there are objects of fear, including the fear of being afraid. Nevertheless, thanks to this *objectification*, one can externalize danger, identifying it so that one may better fend against it, whether by submission, flight, or direct confrontation. In this regard, Valenzuela suggests:

> Huir no siempre es cobardía, a veces se requiere un gran coraje para apoyar un pie después del otro e ir hacia adelante. Nadie huye de espaldas como debiera huirse, por lo tanto nadie sabe lo que es la retirada, el innoble placer del retroceso, disparar hacia atrás en el tiempo para no tener que enfrentar lo que se ignora.
>
> (GE [El gato eficaz], 37)
>
> (Fleeing is not always cowardly; at times it requires great courage to put one foot before the other and go forward. No one flees with one's back turned, as one should flee; therefore no one knows what retreat is, that ignoble pleasure of withdrawing, leaping back in time to keep from having to face what is unknown.)

This includes the idea of getting used to living with fear, a protective device that Bella, the protagonist of *Cuarta versión* (Eng. *Fourth Version*), assumes when "slowly she forgot the dangers" (OW [Other Weapons], 46; "poco a poco fue olvidando los peligros" [CA [Cambio de armas], 48]), or that Chiquita, the protagonist of "De noche soy tu caballo" (Eng. "I'm Your Horse at Night"), adopts in choosing to drown herself in happiness, "trying to keep calm" ("tratando de no inquietarse"). Theirs is a daily fear that turns to indifference in cities like New York.

> Este *cool* neoyorquino, de dónde le habrá crecido a ella. Qué contagiosas son las ciudades, se comenta, heme aquí ahora asumiendo esta información como si tal cosa, con aire indiferente, tragándome mi horror, mi espanto.
>
> (CA, 71–72)
>
> (Where did she get her New York cool? Cities are so contagious, she thinks. Here I am now, taking in all this information without batting an eyelash, looking indifferent, swallowing the horror, the shock.)
>
> (OW, 67)

Such is a fear that can, moreover, arouse itself or "nourish itself," as Valenzuela explains in *Donde viven las águilas* (1983; Eng. *Up Among the Eagles*).

> ...voy como al descuido alimentando mi miedo, algo callado y propio. Ellos me ven pasar con el palo sobre los hombros y los dos

baldes que cuelgan del palo, acarreando agua, y me gustaría saber que nada sospechan de mi miedo. Es un miedo doble faz, bifronte, pero nada hermano de aquel que me impidió bajar una vez que hube escalado la montaña. Este no es un miedo simple, éste refleja otros miedos y se vuelve voraz.

(*DV* [*Donde viven las águilas*], 21)

(... almost nonchalantly nourishing my fear. They watch me go by carrying water, the pole across my shoulders and the two pails dangling from it, and I would like to think they do not suspect my fear. This fear has two faces, not at all like the one that kept me from returning after I had climbed the mountain. No, this is not a simple fear; it reflects others, and becomes voracious.)

(*C* [*The Censors*], 255)

In all cases, fear of the dark, fear of great depths, fear of heights, fear of great speeds or of instability, childhood fears whose recurrence is triggered by any fright with which they are associated (fear of being alone, of getting lost, nighttime fears), and the inevitable fear of death are accepted as *natural fears*. All render deep primordial emotions that are layered in the depths of humankind through generations, for they are collective ancient fabulations that are particularly open to superstitious or magical interpretations. All are vital feelings and emotions that are linked to intense, imaginary situations: the fear of being violated, the fear of punishment, the fear or anxious desire of a violent act. The acute and profound fear of death, the fear of something (dying) that no one can avoid—as J. C. Barker reminds us—since no one escapes death, although this mysterious experience that is "so special, uniquely inexplicable, this fear of something that will never be known," can never be related to others (Paul Tillich). This Valenzuela herself notes in describing that "day-to-day part of me that fears suffering and death, the part that is astonished—the part, perhaps, that is alive out of cowardice" ("parte cotidiana de mi misma que teme al sufrimiento y a la muerte. La parte que se asombra, quizá la que más vive por cobarde" [*GE*, 37]), since fear can also disguise itself as "prudence": "It wasn't that I was afraid; I was just being prudent, as they say: threatening cliffs, beyond imagination—impossible even to consider returning" (*C*, 221; "No fue miedo, fue prudencia como dice la gente: precisamente demasiado hoscos nunca imaginados, imposibles de enfrentar en un descenso" [*DV*, 19]).

If in some cases objective dangers can justify fear, it is the process of the *subjectivization of risk* that brings about a transformation of the nature of such dangers and alters their intensity, according to the degree of the anxiety or emotivity of the subject. It is this subtle passage from fear *in* darkness to fear *of* darkness—of which Jean Delumeau speaks—that marks a qualitative difference between animal fear in facing danger and man's capacity "to imagine," to dream fear. As Bachelard has emphasized, "The dream can be more intense than experience," whereby the dreamer becomes trapped in the deception of his own dream and of the ghosts he creates. That same imagination which lies at the root of creative, artistic, and scientific activity intensifies, exaggerates, and favors what Victor Hugo poetically summarized thus: "Voici le moment ou flottent dans l'aire / tous ces bruits confus que l'ombre exagere" (Here the moment in which floats through the air / all the confused noises exaggerated by shadows).

Fear qualitatively produced, thanks to its imaginative complement, is a fear one lives much like "a situation," a condition that extends from an initial suggestion to a slower development and, subsequently, more important duration, carrying with it not only the emotional, physiological reaction from the initial sudden fear but also giving shape to real mental representations by precipitating the heightened stimulation of the imagination. Moreover, because the imagination dreads the void, it invents what it does not know, even though it might lose itself in the consequences of its representations. These are the "demands of the mysterious" and of the enigmatic, as Roger Caillois would have it, that create the exaggeration which fear and the supernatural invite.

THE SWEET FRIEND FEAR
Luisa Valenzuela plays with both recourses. An "imaginative" fear is "objectively" established in her portrayal of such cities as Buenos Aires in *Aquí pasan cosas raras* (1975; Eng. *Strange Things Happen Here*, 1979) and *Realidad nacional desde la cama* (1990; Eng. *Bedside Manners*, 1994) or New York, "the city that offered me all that is other: the perception of shallow fears" ("la que me dio todo lo otro: la percepción de los miedos a flor de piel"), in *El gato eficaz* (1972) and in *Novela negra con argentinos* (1990; Eng. *Black Novel [with Argentines]*, 1992).

In Buenos Aires, where so many "strange things are happening," to be afraid can presuppose that one cannot know "if something is true or a lie" and that one can feel surrounded by "some sort of" trap or by "dark motives." Just as seemingly "out of place" is the kind of fear one suspects is "imaginary," inasmuch as Buenos Aires cannot permit itself—cannot permit one—the luxury of a "conscious hallucination," although one might add that "we who have known him for some time can be sure his fear has nothing to do with the imaginative" (*OD*, 19; "nosotros que venimos tratando desde hace un rato podemos asegurar que su miedo nada tiene de imaginativo" [*DV*, 65]). On the contrary, fear in New York "is a sweet friend fear that's good for the gut, a fear that subsumes me by forcing a trembling from within—a fear that I miss, I need" ("es un dulce miedo amigo bueno para las tripas, miedo cercándome a mí misma forzándose a temblar para adentro. Miedo que echo de menos, que me falta" [*GE*, 15]).

Nevertheless, if fear generally has an object and a cause, anxiety is, on the contrary, a feeling of undefined insecurity, a permanent uneasiness that confuses behavior. Weariness without apparent cause, a feeling of failure, and an inability to react give rise to this vaguely defined fear, although ironically, the censor who tries to "spare" Mariana of "anxieties" in the short story *"Los censores"* (*DV*; Eng. *"The Censors"*) succumbs to his own preoccupation.

Beyond anxiety lies anguish. Anguish is born from one's perspective and from the anticipation of danger, even when such danger is unknown. In this latent predisposition of the individual, the threat feels indefinite, uncontrollable, like an empty form anticipating its contents. The indefinite wait in the face of an indeterminate danger condemns one to an exhausting yet painful, disorienting state of individual behavior, a permanent feeling of drowning....

Source: Fernando Ainsa, "Journey to Luisa Valenzuela's Land of Fear," in *World Literature Today*, Vol. 69, No. 4, Autumn 1995, pp. 683–90.

Brooke K. Horvath

In the following review, Horvath discusses the themes of violence, power relations, and community in Valenzuela's short stories.

According to Evelyn Picon Garfield, Luisa Valenzuela "has become the most translated contemporary woman author from Latin America"— and for good reason, as readers of this journal's special issue on Valenzuela (Fall 1986) are well aware. The popularity and importance of her work reside both in the themes she dramatizes and in the means she employs to effect this drama, and if Valenzuela reminds one at times of García Márquez or Lydia Cabrera, Donald Barthelme or Paul Bowles, her fiction nonetheless achieves a distinctive voice that allows her to address issues she has clearly made her own.

As Valenzuela's first story collection since *Up among the Eagles* (*Donde viven las águilas*) appeared in Spanish in 1983, *Open Door* provides both something new for American readers and a selection of the author's best earlier short fiction. The book opens with the fourteen stories comprising the '83 collection, gathered together for the first time in translation, and follows with eleven selections from *Strange Things Happen Here* and seven stories from *Clara* (or *Los Heréticos*). As Valenzuela remarks in her Preface, "For the time being, here are my favorite stories from the three collections. But I must hurry, now, and write others: it is the only way I know of jamming a foot in the door so it won't slam in our faces."

Readers familiar with Valenzuela's work will recognize in *Open Door* the author's characteristic heterogeneity of subject matter, artistic method, and thematic concerns. Shamanistic figures, folkloristic superstitions and ritual magic, cultic beliefs and indigenous legends jostle urban settings, café life, state-of-the-art state terrorism, and the amorous doings of vacationing bourgeoisie to yield modern political parables and twice-told (albeit revamped) myths, small comedies of manners and mocking parodies of middle-class conventionality, ironic illuminations of religious realities and secular tales of physical and/or psychological terror. Similarly, traditional narrative techniques combine with a postmodern experimentation (fragmented narration, magical realism, randomness, and linguistic pranksterism) in the service of themes that are as timeless as the search for truth, community, or control over nature's mysteries, and as topical as sexual and political persecution in present-day Argentina or the nature of power relations within and among contemporary social classes. Here, in short, are stories that explore the boundaries of what is currently thought possible in fiction while reminding us of what must be demanded from fiction in our time.

As one moves through this collection, changes in focus are evident. The newest selections are the most artistically adventuresome and, according to their author, speak to "my love for Latin America and my passion for reinventing its myths." Stories gathered from *Strange Things* look most unswervingly at a Buenos Aires given over to violence and government-sanctioned illegalities, whereas those of her first volume "walk in writing the tightrope between religious fanaticism and heresy." Yet different as these stories may be one from another, they all reveal Valenzuela's dislike of "dogmas and certainties" and share her sense of urgency, of knowing something that desperately needs saying. All witness to her efforts to jam that foot in the door, the door of her title, which is also the name, so we are told, "of the most traditional, least threatening lunatic asylum in Argentina."

Source: Brooke K. Horvath, "A review of *Open Door*," in *Review of Contemporary Fiction*, Vol. 9, No. 1, Spring 1989, pp. 243–44.

SOURCES

Bach, Caleb, "Metaphors and Magic Unmask the Soul," in *Americas*, January 1, 1995, pp. 22–27.

Central Intelligence Agency, "Argentina Economy 2009," in *CIA World Factbook*, 2009, http://www.theodora.com/wfbcurrent/argentina/argentina_economy.html (accessed September 20, 2009).

Fox, Geoffrey, "The Emergence of 'El Pueblo,'" "Unresolved Conflicts: The Turbulent Years, 1955–1973," and "What is the 'True Argentine?': Unity and Diversity in National Character," in *The Land and People of Argentina*, J. B. Lippincott, 1990, pp. 111–25, 126–48, 149–74.

Frenkel, Roberto, and Jaime Ros, "Unemployment, Macroeconomic Policy, and Labor Market Flexibility: Argentina and Mexico in the 1990s," in *Kellogg Institute Working Papers*, Working Paper No. 309, February 2004, pp. 1–34.

Magnarelli, Sharon, "From *Hay Que Sonreír* to *Cambio de Armas*" and "Censorship and the Female Writer—An Interview/Dialogue with Luisa Valenzuela," in *Reflections/Refractions: Reading Luisa Valenzuela*, Peter Lang, 1988, pp. 1–14, 203–20.

Medeiros-Lichem, María Teresa, "Luisa Valenzuela: 'La Mala Palabra,'" in *Reading the Feminine Voice in Latin American Women's Fiction: From Teresa de la Parra to Elena Poniatowska and Luisa Valenzuela*, Peter Lang, 2002, pp. 167–202.

Reyes-Tatinclaux, Leticia, "Luisa Valenzuela," in *Dictionary of Literary Biography*, Vol. 113, *Modern Latin-American Fiction Writers, First Series*, Gale Research, 1992, pp. 303–12.

Shaw, Donald L., "The Post-Boom," and "Luisa Valenzuela," in *The Post-Boom in Spanish American Fiction*, State University of New York Press, 1998, pp. 3–24, 95–118.

Valente, Marcela, "Argentina: Women Writers Who Break the Mould," in *Inter Press Service News Agency*, July 11, 2009, http://ipsnews.net/news.asp?idnews=47623 (accessed September 20, 2009).

Valenzuela, Luisa, "The Censors," in *The Censors*, translated by David Unger, Curbstone Press, 1992, pp. 24–31.

FURTHER READING

Barnitz, Jacqueline, *Twentieth-Century Art of Latin America*, University of Texas Press, 2001.

> Barnitz's survey of the contemporary art of Latin America includes numerous photographs, explanations of various artistic movements, and extensive discussion of the impact of cultural, historical, and political events on trends in twentieth-century Latin American art.

Levine, Laurence, and Kathleen Quinn, *Inside Argentina from Perón to Menem: 1950–2000 from an American Point of View*, Edwin House Publishing, 2001.

> Levine, a former president of the United States-Argentine Chamber of Commerce as well as a lawyer for Argentine Airlines, explores, with the help of Quinn, the political workings that contributed to the violence between the Argentine military forces and guerilla resistance during the post-Perón years, discussing the events leading up to this period of unrest and the economic impact of this civil war in the years that followed.

Varona-Lacey, Gladys, ed., *Contemporary Latin American Literature: Original Selections from the Literary Giants for Intermediate and Advanced Students*, McGraw-Hill, 2001.

> Varona-Lacey presents a collection of writings by the most notable Latin American authors of the last hundred years, including the work of Noble Prize winners Pablo Neruda and Gabriel Garcia Márquez.

Wilson, Jason, *Buenos Aires: A Cultural History*, Interlink Books, 1999.

> Wilson explores the modern culture of the capital city of Argentina, discussing modern Argentine writers from Buenos Aires and the influence that European literature had on them. He also explores the traditional and modern forms of music and dance of the city, the importance of soccer to Argentina in general and Buenos Aries in particular, the cult surrounding Juan Perón's first wife Eva, and the political events that have had an impact on every aspect of daily life in post-Perón Argentina.

Contents of the Dead Man's Pocket

JACK FINNEY

1956

Readers and critics usually know Jack Finney for novels such as *The Body Snatchers* and *Time and Again*. Finney was also an expert short story writer. Like Stephen King (who readily names Finney as a major influence on his writing), Finney is a master of storytelling and suspense, creating tales that often include an ironic ending.

"Contents of the Dead Man's Pocket" is one of Finney's best. First appearing in *Collier's* magazine on October 26, 1956, the story was later included as the final tale of Finney's critically praised 1957 collection *The Third Level*. Although the collection is no longer in print, it is readily available in libraries and used book stores; in addition, "Contents of the Dead Man's Pocket" has been widely anthologized in literature textbooks, including *Glencoe Literature: The Reader's Choice: Course 5*, published by McGraw-Hill/Glencoe in 2006.

"Contents of the Dead Man's Pocket" tells the story of Tom Benecke, a young and ambitious Madison Avenue advertising executive. When a slip of paper containing notes for an important project blows out his window, Benecke foolishly steps out onto an eleventh story window ledge to retrieve it. When he nearly loses his life, he has an epiphany, and rethinks the values that have led him to endanger his life for his ambition.

Finney's use of active verbs and sensory images makes the story highly suspenseful, and

Jack Finney (Kim Komenich / Time Life Pictures / Getty Images)

his plot offers an excellent model of the classic short story structure. A surprise ending, laced with irony, demonstrates Finney's skillful handling of the genre.

AUTHOR BIOGRAPHY

Walter Braden Finney, better known as Jack Finney, was born in Milwaukee, Wisconsin, in 1911. His name at birth was John Finney; however, when his father died soon after his birth, the child was renamed Walter Braden. Despite this, Finney continued to be known as Jack throughout his entire life.

Finney grew up in Forest Park, just outside of Chicago, and attended Proviso Township High School. Graduating in 1929, Finney graduated from Knox College in Galesburg, Illinois, in 1934. He was an active student, participating on the swim team, ROTC, and the student newspaper.

Finney entered the work force as an ad agency copywriter, working for twelve years in Chicago and New York. He was working for the Dancer-Fitzgerald-Sample advertising agency in New York in 1946 when he sold his first story to *Ellery Queen's Mystery Magazine*. The story, "The Widow's Walk," was published in July 1947, and won an award from the magazine.

Finney's first work to appear in publication was the short story "Manhattan Idyl," which appeared in *Collier's* on April 5, 1947. He quickly placed many more stories in mainstream publications such as *Ladies' Home Journal* and *Good Housekeeping*, winning numerous awards for his efforts along the way.

By 1953, Finney was producing longer works; his first was serialized by *Good Housekeeping* in 1953 and appeared as the novel *5 Against the House* in 1954. In 1955, Finney published a science fiction novel *The Body Snatchers*; this novel and the film based on the novel, *Invasion of the Body Snatchers*, directed by Don Siegel and released by Allied Artists in 1956, made Finney's career. On the basis of his royalties from this work he was able to leave his work as a copywriter and devote himself to writing full-time.

In 1956, "Contents of the Dead Man's Pocket" appeared in *Collier's*. The next year, Finney included this story as the final entry in his well-received short-story collection, *The Third Level*. Many of the stories in this volume thematically addressed time: time travel, or in the case of "Contents of the Dead Man's Pocket," the malleable nature of time during a crisis.

Some of Finney's fame as a writer rested on the adaptability of his stories to film and television. In addition to *The Body Snatchers*, many other novels and short stories appeared as films or television shows. Jon L. Breen, in his 2008 book *A Shot Rang Out: Selected Mystery Criticism*, notes that while Finney wrote "with one eye on the possibility of screen adaptation," he was never "a hack who pandered to his audience."

Although Finney published his last short story in 1965, he continued to write for the rest of his life, producing a number of popular novels. Among these, the illustrated novel *Time and Again*, published in 1970, became his best-known work and inspired an Off Broadway musical adaptation in 2001. The novel also won the Grand Prix de l'Imaginaire when it was translated into French in 1994.

Finney's last novel was, fittingly for a man so dedicated to the theme of time, *From Time to Time*, published in 1995. He died of pneumonia on November 14, 1995, in Greenbrae, California.

PLOT SUMMARY

"Contents of the Dead Man's Pocket" is the story of Tom Benecke, a young advertising executive in New York City who risks his life to retrieve a scrap of paper that has flown out the window. This action results in a change in Tom's attitude toward work and his values in life.

As the story opens, Tom is working at home on a project he wants to present to his supervisors the next day. The apartment is small; he works in the living room, not in a dedicated home office, and the hallway connecting the bedroom and living room is described both as "short" and "little." In addition, the apartment is hot. The apartment is located high over Lexington Avenue on the eleventh floor of the building. In a crucial plot move, Tom decides to open the window.

Tom's wife is in their bedroom, getting ready to go out to see a film. Tom feels guilty that he is not going with her; the work he is doing is not essential, but it is something that he wants to do, something he believes will further his career in advertising and might earn him a raise. Clare, Tom's wife, tells him that he works too hard and too much, although she does not seem at all angry or upset that she will be going to the movies alone. When Tom kisses Clare goodbye, he is tempted to go with her. At the same time, he wants to finish his project for presentation.

As he stands at the apartment door watching his wife go down the hall, a breeze from the hallway comes into the apartment. Just as Tom closes the door behind him, he sees the yellow sheet of paper with all of his notes that has been sitting on his desk go flying out the window.

Tom is panicked. The yellow sheet of paper contains all of his research notes, which have taken hours and hours of time in the library and in supermarkets as he observed shopper behavior. Without the sheet of paper, he will have to redo all of his work. He imagines this will take several months, much too long for his project to have any impact with his supervisors.

MEDIA ADAPTATIONS

- Stephen King wrote a short story called "The Ledge," in homage to Finney's story "Contents of the Dead Man's Pocket." "The Ledge" was dramatized as part of the 1985 film *Cat's Eye*, produced by the Dino De Laurentiis Company, directed by Lewis Teague, and starring Drew Barrymore and James Wood.

When he looks out the window, he sees the paper resting on an outside window ledge, about five yards from his window, caught in a corner. Tom at first believes he will have to abandon the paper, but then he thinks about how he might retrieve it. Nothing in the apartment is long enough to reach the paper, so once again he imagines that the paper is gone forever. However, as soon as he thinks this, he also thinks how this project, along with others he has done, "would gradually mark him out from the score of other young men in his company." He believes that these projects represent "the beginning of the long, long climb to where he was determined to be, at the very top." As soon as he has these thoughts, he knows that he must go out on the ledge to retrieve the paper.

Once he is out on the ledge, however, what seemed like a relatively easy task when he was in the apartment turns into a life-threatening gesture. He begins to make his way to the paper, but once he has it in hand, he is frozen with the fear of falling. He screams for help, but none is forthcoming. For several pages, Finney establishes the utter terror of being on a ledge eleven stories up in horrifying detail.

Finally, Tom begins inching his way back to his apartment. The image of the inside security of the living room contrasts with the danger of the outside ledge in Tom's mind, but he knows he must not dwell on this. Just when the reader believes that Tom's situation cannot get any worse, it does.

Tom blindly feels his way to his apartment, but suddenly reaches the edge of the building and nearly falls. But as he tries to right himself, he inadvertently closes the window to his apartment. His situation now is dire. He tries to break the glass in the window, but the rebound as his hand bounces off the glass nearly sends him toppling backward. He imagines waiting for Clare to return to let him in, but then realizes that the whole long trip to retrieve the paper has only taken eight minutes, and that Clare will not return for at least four hours, by which time he'll be dead on the pavement below.

He attempts to attract attention from passersby below and from people in the apartments opposite by lighting papers with a match and launching them burning out into the night air. Nothing helps. Suddenly, he realizes that he has no identification on him, only the yellow sheet of paper with notes that are comprehensible only to him. No one would understand who he was or why he had been out on the ledge if were to fall. The contents of his pocket would reveal nothing.

This revelation strikes him hard, and he realizes that, should he die, he would do so after wasting his life with his ambition and work. He decides that he must risk everything to return to the life promised by the other side of the glass, the interior of his apartment. But he knows he will only have one attempt at breaking through the window with his fist; if he is unsuccessful, he will surely fall to his death.

He balls his hand into a fist, thinks of his wife, musters all his strength, and breaks his hand through the window as he calls out his wife's name. That he calls out to her at a life-and-death moment is a signal that his entire frame of reference has changed as a result of being out on the ledge: success at his job is not nearly as important as having a happy life with the woman he loves. He is elated when his hand breaks through the window, and he climbs into the living room.

Rather than sitting down to work, he demonstrates his new-found set of values by quickly preparing to go out and find his wife. As he opens the door, the yellow piece of paper now resting on the desk, is picked up by the wind, and "unimpeded by the glassless window, sail[s] out into the night and out of his life." Tom's response is to laugh heartily, and leave.

CHARACTERS

Clare Benecke

Clare is Tom Benecke's wife. She appears only briefly in the story as she is preparing to go out to watch a movie for the evening. Clare is pretty and thin with light brown hair. Finney makes her almost a blonde, but stops just short, suggesting perhaps that although she is as beautiful as the blonde ideal of the day, she is also a good wife who does not normally go out on her own in the evening. Clare is also portrayed as a very nice person as well, and her outward appearance reflects her inner kindness. She is understanding of Tom's decision to work and does not try to provoke guilt in him for not going out with her. She does not reappear in the story after leaving the apartment, although it is her departure that sets in motion the rest of the story. In addition, it is the thought of Clare that allows Tom to plunge back into the apartment at the last possible moment.

Tom Benecke

Tom Benecke is the protagonist of the story, and the narration is from his point of view. He is tall, dark, and lean, rather than thin, implying a wiry strength. Tom has been working on a project during all of his free hours, demonstrating that he is both ambitious and directed. In addition, it is likely that he is very talented at his job in advertising in that he seems to understand the kind of research he must do in order to back up any claims he wants to make for his project.

Tom seems torn between his love for his wife and his need to achieve great things at his job as the story opens. He feels guilt for not going out with her and instead choosing to stay at home to finish up the presentation he wants to make to his boss in the morning. The project is one he has set for himself, not one that has been assigned; this fact emphasizes the fact that Tom is a go-getter and a self-starter, someone who not only wants to climb to the top of his profession but also has the talent to do so.

It is Tom's ambition that leads him out onto the ledge when the paper with all his notes unexpectedly flies out the window. In addition, the decision to go after the paper demonstrates that he is a risk taker, someone who quickly weighs the risk-to-benefit ratio and acts. Unfortunately, in the case of this story, he comes very close to having calculated wrongly. Indeed, although he must take risks in his profession and live with the consequences, he has not previously been up against a life-and-death decision. His problem in this story is that he does not recognize that his decision to go out the window creates exactly that, a life-and-death situation.

Tom also is a courageous man, despite feeling fear while out on the ledge. When the consequences of his hasty decision become clear, he takes action, although he is frightened. After a momentary paralysis brought on by looking down at the street, he nevertheless continues to try to get back inside his apartment.

Finney further demonstrates that Tom is an intelligent man. Once in the difficult situation, he attempts a variety of actions to solve his problem, carefully moving from the least dangerous to the most. He also is intelligent enough to realize that he has been wasting his life; although the decision to go out on the ledge is clearly an immediate life-and-death decision, his ongoing decision to work rather than enjoy time with his wife is a longer-term life-and-death decision. When Tom is faced with death, he realizes that what he wants more than anything is a life with his wife.

By the end of the story, Tom is a wiser man than he was when the story opened. His epiphany opens the door for him to lead a more balanced and sane life, one that includes important human relationships, not just work.

THEMES

Values (Philosophy)

In "Contents of the Dead Man's Pocket," Finney explores modern values. The main character, Tom, is a young, hard-working, conscientious advertising executive. He wants to distinguish himself in his field and rise to the top of all the young men who are working in his company. Tom thinks about the project he is working on, along with other projects he has developed independently, as the way to make this happen: "They were the way to change from a name on the payroll to a name in the minds of the company officials."

Further, when his wife Clare tells him that he works too hard and too much, he replies, "You won't mind though, will you, when the money comes rolling in and I'm known as the Boy Wizard of Wholesale Groceries?" This suggests that Tom sees success, both in terms of money and reputation, as a direct result of his own hard work and effort. He seems to be saying that if he works hard enough, he will be able to provide for himself and Clare the kind of lifestyle he thinks that they both want.

However, when Tom goes out on the ledge to get the piece of paper containing all of his project notes, he is literally risking his life for financial and professional success. His prospects, he believes, have flown out the window with the piece of paper, and so he chooses to endanger his future by going after them.

Once outside, with no way to get back into his apartment, he suddenly realizes that what he wants more than anything is a secure life with his wife. He also realizes that if he were to fall, with nothing in his pockets except the piece of yellow paper, he would have lived a meaningless life. Thus, the title of the story points to this thematic concern. Symbolically, because Tom's values are misplaced, when he is out on the ledge, he thinks of himself as a dead man with nearly empty pockets. When he is able to break through and reenter his home, his change of values allows him to truly begin living his life, a life that includes meaning, love, and happy relationships with other people.

Alienation

Alienation is a common theme in many twentieth-century stories. In general, the term means isolation or disconnection from a group or society. In psychology, the term alienation means loss of identity and a state of depersonalization. In "Contents of the Dead Man's Pocket," Finney is not concerned so much with Tom Benecke as an alienated character but rather with the alienating tendencies of modern life.

In the first place, Tom and his wife live on the eleventh floor of an apartment building in one of the largest cities in the world. They have no connection to the natural world but rather are surrounded by human-made artifacts. Although they are surrounded by people, there is a suggestion in this story that Tom has few or no real relationships with others. Indeed, the story suggests that human relationships are difficult in the modern world.

To set up the dichotomy between alienation and belonging, Finney places Tom out on a ledge looking down at the city. He is separated from the security and sense of connection his life offers him by a pane of glass he cannot immediately break through. While he is out on the ledge, Tom is totally alienated and cut off, not only from his former life but from the city around him.

TOPICS FOR FURTHER STUDY

- With a small group of peers, watch several episodes of the original series of *The Twilight Zone*, available at http://www.cbs.com/classics/the_twilight_zone/video/video.php. Take note of the style and content of the episodes. Using the viewed episodes as a model, write a screenplay for "Contents of the Dead Man's Pocket," videotape the production, and present it to your classmates.

- Write a short story about a time when you felt great fear but were able to overcome it. Be sure to be specific with your details, and use as many sensory images as you can to give your story suspense. What did you learn from having to overcome fear?

- In the 1950s, advertising grew dramatically with the rapid rise of the television industry. Research advertising in the 1950s, using the Internet, digital archives available through library databases, and images, either from hard copies of magazines in libraries or by using images available online. Prepare a PowerPoint presentation using advertising images from the 1950s and discuss what these images reveal about the decade. How does a knowledge of the decade deepen your understanding of the story?

- Author Stephen King published *Night Shift* in 1978, a collection of short stories including one called "The Ledge." Because King has cited Finney as one of his greatest influences, most critics agree that King wrote this story with a nod to "Contents of the Dead Man's Pocket." Read King's story, and write an essay comparing and contrasting the two stories. Which do you believe is the better story and why? Support your opinion with examples from both short stories.

- Examine "Contents of the Dead Man's Pocket" closely, making a list of verbs used by Finney. How often does he use state-of-being (linking) verbs? How often does he use action verbs? How does this affect the suspense of the story? Write a scene of at least five hundred words in which your main character is in great danger, and see if you can do so using no more than five (and preferably fewer) state-of-being verbs. Now, write the same scene, substituting state-of-being verbs for your active verbs. Ask a few of your peers to read your two stories and evaluate which one is the most interesting and suspenseful. Report back to your class on the use of verbs in writing fiction.

- Many of Finney's short stories and books are about time travel. Read the novel *Kindred* (1979), by African American science fiction writer Octavia Butler. How does Butler use time travel to explore slavery? Why does she use time travel rather than simply setting the story in the past? Write a review of the book in which you discuss the role of time travel as a means of social commentary.

- Read the young-adult novel *Touching Spirit Bear* by Ben Mikaelsen, a story that involves a life-and-death situation in which the main character revises his values. How does Mikaelsen hold the reader's interest throughout the story? Write a review of this book, noting the author's style, the setting, and the theme of values.

For example, when he looks down from the ledge, Tom sees "moving black dots of people." These people have no identity nor connection with Tom; they are no more than dots. Likewise, when Tom cries out for help, no one responds, and he remembers "how habitually, here in New York, he himself heard and ignored shouts in the night." Further, when he looks into his own living room through the glass, it is as if he understands how his concentration on his work has led him to be alienated from the life he is currently living. Finally, he has the realization that there are individual people

Blank notepad and paper clip (Image copyright Cardiae, 2009. Used under license from Shutterstock.com)

living in all of the apartments around him, but completely alienated one from another: "No more than twenty-odd yards from his back were scores of people, and if just one of them would walk idly to his window and glance out...."

The repeated images of isolation and loneliness, made real by the extreme situation, emphasize the thematic concern of the story. It becomes a cautionary tale of how easily modern life can alienate an individual. In addition, the story provides an education for Tom, who comes to understand the danger of isolation and the necessity of connection. When he successfully reenters his apartment, it is as a changed man, someone who will actively fight against the alienating forces of modern society.

STYLE

Plot

"Contents of the Dead Man's Pocket" offers an excellent example of plotting in a short story. Ross Murfin and Supryia M. Ray in *The Bedford Glossary of Critical and Literary Terms* define plot as the "arrangement and interrelation of events in a narrative work, chosen and designed to engage the reader's attention...(or even to arouse suspense or anxiety) while also providing a framework for the exposition of the author's... theme." Murfin and Ray go on to distinguish plot from story in that story is simply a "narrative of events ordered chronologically, not selectively."

In "Contents of the Dead Man's Pocket," Finney begins his plot with exposition, that is, details about the setting and the main character. Within the first page, readers know that Tom is ambitious, lives in New York, is young and handsome, has a beautiful wife, and that he chooses to stay home to work rather than go out to the movies. This exposition, selectively chosen, down to the detail of the apartment being hot and Tom feeling guilty, sets up the rest of the plot.

After the initial expository phase, the catalyst occurs. A catalyst is a plot device that moves the story forward and introduces the rising action that will ultimately lead to the climax, falling action, and resolution of the story. In this case, the piece of paper flies out of the window, serving as a catalyst. Now Tom must reach a decision: should he go out on the ledge to retrieve the paper or stay inside? The conflict in this case is between Tom and himself, between his common sense and his ambition, and represents yet another plot device. The conflict pushes the action forward, causing suspense and anxiety within the reader.

When Tom reaches a decision to go out on the ledge, the action continues to rise. The reader wonders if Tom will survive this event or fall to his death. Each selected detail Finney provides contributes to the upward arc of the story.

Typically in a short story, the action rises to its highest point at the climax, another plot device. The climax is the moment in a story of greatest intensity, a turning point when the outcome is unclear. In the case of "Contents of the Dead Man's Pocket," the climax occurs when Tom smashes his fist through the window while calling out Clare's name. The reader knows that there is an equal chance that Tom will be successful or that he will fall to his death, the mark of a good climactic scene.

After the climax, the action in a short story falls rapidly to the resolution. Sometimes called the denouement, the resolution completes the story: usually, conflicts are resolved, and the reader has a sense as to what might happen after the story. In "Contents of the Dead Man's Pocket," the resolution is Tom's decision to grab his coat and go find his wife. It demonstrates that he has learned the lesson the story had to teach him. Finney, of course, the master of the surprise ending, lets the paper fly out of the window again. When Tom laughs at this event, the reader knows that his inner conflict has been resolved, and the plot concludes.

Epiphany

The word epiphany comes from a Greek word meaning "showing forth." In literary criticism, the term has been used figuratively. Irish writer James Joyce first used the term to describe a moment in a story when a character has a sudden revelation or insight about an event, or object, or situation. In the case of "Contents of the Dead Man's Pocket," Tom's epiphany occurs when he realizes that he has nothing in his pockets except for the yellow piece of paper filled with his incomprehensible notes. This leads him to the knowledge that if he falls, no one will know who he is, nor anything about his life. His life will seem as empty and unintelligible as his pockets. This, in turn, leads him to the larger truth: he has been living a wasted life.

The moment of epiphany in a short story can be a great catalyst for change on the part of the protagonist. Surely, in this story, Tom's life will be markedly different after his reentry to his apartment.

HISTORICAL CONTEXT

The Cold War

The explosions of the atomic bombs at Hiroshima and Nagasaki, Japan, brought World War II to an end, and the rapid growth of the Soviet Union's military power and ambition cast a pall over the Western world, including the United States, in the post-war years. The Cold War is a term used to describe the tensions, both political and ideological, between the United States and the Soviet Union between 1945 and 1990. This tension created fear in both nations as both countries stood ready to escalate to nuclear war.

A direct result of the Cold War on the population of the United States was a sense of dread and anxiety, brought about by the awareness that the world could end in a flash, with little or no warning. Russian dictator Nikita Khrushchev's famous 1956 speech did nothing to alleviate these fears. As reported in the November 26, 1956 issue of *Time* magazine, Khrushchev declared, "About the capitalist states, it doesn't depend on you whether or not we exist.... Whether you like it or not, history is on our side. We will bury you!"

Khrushchev's speech and other events of the year, including hostilities between Egypt and Israel and the Soviet invasion of Hungary, led people to wonder if the end of the world was near. This questioning led people to seriously question their values and goals. Some people became alienated and disengaged from life itself; others sought to find ways to make their lives meaningful. Writing in the midst of this milieu, it is little wonder that Finney pictured his protagonist alone on a ledge, trying desperately to return to a time and place where he has been secure.

Advertising

After World War II, there was considerable worry among U. S. economists about how to sustain the economy that had been fueled for nearly a decade by demands of the war, first as the U. S. helped England and France, and later as the nation became an active participant in the war. With the war over, the demands for products and services might drop precipitously, just at the same time thousands of men were returning home in need of jobs. However, as Alfred E. Eckes and Thomas W. Zeiler wrote in *Globalization and the American Century*, "Some had worried that demobilization would bring a renewal of the Depression, but this concern proved unfounded. American consumers had a pent-up demand for consumer goods—especially automobiles, televisions, washing machines, and houses."

In the early 1950s, the television industry was just beginning. Television programming, paid for with advertising dollars, further spurred the growth of the consumer society. As more and more homes obtained televisions, more and more people were exposed to advertisers trying to persuade viewers to buy products. In an ongoing cycle, advertisers urged people to buy televisions, television programming was paid for through advertising revenues, and television commercials embedded in the programming created the desire for the viewer to buy more goods, including televisions.

COMPARE & CONTRAST

- **1950s:** The computer industry is in its infancy, although by 1958, American companies are producing one billion dollars' worth of computers a year. Individuals, however, still rely on paper and pen to take notes.

  Today: The United States boasts a huge computer industry, and personal computers have found their way into most American homes. Young people, in particular, use their computers for nearly all writing assignments.

- **1950s:** In an effort to spur consumer spending, the first credit cards are introduced. The first credit card is the Diners Club card.

  Today: Credit cards are a way of life for most people, leading some to incur huge credit card debt as they habitually spend more on consumer goods than they earn.

- **1950s:** The United States and the Soviet Union are engaged in the Cold War, a time of increased tensions between the two nations as they each struggle to expand geopolitical and ideological control of the world.

  Today: The Soviet Union no longer exists as a nation, and the United States's status as the remaining superpower is being challenged by China.

- **1950s:** Escapist fiction and films, often in the genres of science fiction, mystery, and suspense, attract audiences and distract them from the dangers of the world.

  Today: Science fiction resurges as a popular form of entertainment, while mysteries and suspense stories continue to retain great popularity among readers and viewers.

- **1950s:** Television becomes a central part of American life, encouraging and reinforcing the values of a consumer society.

  Today: The advent of digital media and DVR means that fewer people are watching commercials on television, leading advertisers to look for other ways to persuade people to buy consumer goods.

For many Americans, success became measured by how much money one could earn and how many goods one could buy with that money. Grasping for material success is what motivates Finney's protagonist to go out on the ledge to risk his life for a scrap of paper in "Contents of the Dead Man's Pocket." Significantly, young Tom Benecke learns that security, meaning, and life itself are not consumer goods, and cannot be purchased for any amount of money.

CRITICAL OVERVIEW

By the time Finney wrote "Contents of the Dead Man's Pocket," his work was becoming increasingly better known through his publication in the "slick" magazines of the day, including *Collier's*, *Ladies' Home Journal*, and *Good Housekeeping*. In addition, his two novels published by that date, *5 Against the House* and *The Body Snatchers*, were popular successes.

In 1957, when Finney published his short story collection *The Third Level*, the volume including "Contents of the Dead Man's Pocket," he was greeted with considerable critical and popular response. Michael Beard, writing in the *Dictionary of Literary Biography*, reports that the "critical reception from the science-fiction establishment was almost unanimously positive." Beard further notes that famed science fiction writer and critic Damon Knight praised *The Third Level* when it was selected as the best short story collection of 1958 in the publication *Infinity Science Fiction*.

Likewise, Finney critic and biographer Jack Seabrook notes in his book *Stealing Time: On the Writings of Jack Finney* that the contemporary

> "WHILE OUT ON THE LEDGE, TOM HAS AN EPIPHANY: THE HOURS HE HAS SPENT WORKING RATHER THAN BUILDING A MEANINGFUL LIFE FILLED WITH HUMAN RELATIONSHIPS HAVE DRAINED HIS LIFE OF VALUE."

Red brick apartment with fire escapes (Image copyright Bateman Photo, 2009. Used under license from Shutterstock.com)

reviews of *The Third Level* were "mostly favorable." Seabrook also argues that the stories of *The Third Level* "secured for [Finney] an honored place in the ranks of twentieth-century writers of fantasy."

Other writers found Finney's work in this collection to be exceptional. Stephen King, for example, writing in *Steven King's Danse Macabre* called *The Third Level* a "benchmark collection of short stories." He further credits Finney with being highly influential on *The Twilight Zone* television series, which premiered just a year after the publication of *The Third Level*. King asserts that "Finney actually defined the boundaries of [Rod] Serling's *Twilight Zone*." Further, King writes, "it was Finney's concept that made Serling's concept possible." King compares Finney's stories to "those startling Magritte paintings where railroad trains are roaring out of the fireplaces or those Dali paintings where clocks are lying limply over branches of trees."

In the 2008 collection of essays *A Shot Rang Out: Selected Mystery Criticism*, Jon L. Breen argues that, thematically, the stories of *The Third Level* and Finney's later collection *I Love Galesburg in the Springtime*, address "the nostalgia for a past better and happier than the present." This theme, growing out of the historical context of the 1950s, surely underpins not only Finney' short stories in general but also "Contents of the Dead Man's Pocket" specifically.

CRITICISM

Diane Andrews Henningfeld

Henningfeld is an emerita professor of literature who writes literary criticism and reviews. In the following essay, she addresses the theme of time in "Contents of the Dead Man's Pocket," placing the story within the context of Finney's body of work and the twentieth-century understanding of time.

Much of Finney's body of work addresses the thematic concern of time. Indeed, *The Third Level*, the volume that includes "Contents of the Dead Man's Pocket," has many stories about time and time travel. The opening story, "The Third Level," for example, concerns a man who finds a third level at Grand Central Station, one that leads directly from the present day to 1894. In addition, Finney's most popular novel, *Time and Again*, is about a man who becomes part of a secret government project to travel to the past.

There are many reasons why Finney turns so often to the subject of time. In the first place, during the 1950s when he began his career and when the stories of *The Third Level* were written, people were both fascinated and horrified by the implications of scientists and theorists who demonstrated that time is relative. Yet even before

WHAT DO I READ NEXT?

- *A Century of Great Suspense Stories*, edited by Jeffery Deaver and published in 2003, offers young adults a wide range of classic mystery and suspense fiction.
- African American science fiction writer Octavia Butler's 1979 novel *Kindred* is a suspenseful exploration of slavery using time travel as a plot device.
- Hugh Monroe, better known as Saki, was an early twentieth-century master of the surprise ending. *The Collected Short Stories of Saki* (1999) is an excellent introduction to this writer's work.
- Jack London's short story "To Build a Fire" has many elements similar to "Contents of the Dead Man's Pocket." The story is available in the book *The Best Short Stories of Jack London* (1986).
- Finney's novel *Time and Again* (1970) is perhaps the writer's best work. The illustrated novel is about a secret government time travel project, sending the main character back in time to historic old New York.
- Stephen King acknowledges Finney as an inspiration. King's collection of short stories *Night Shift* (1978) is a good place to look for similarities between the two writers.
- *Adland: A Global History of Advertising* (2007) by Mark Tungate includes a close look at Madison Avenue in the 1950s, the probable location of Tom Benecke's advertising agency.
- Ray Bradbury's classic *Dandelion Wine*, written in 1957, is an excellent example of the work of another writer whose career parallels that of Finney.
- Paul Harrison's short young-adult non-fiction book *The Cold War: How Did It Happen?* (2005) provides a quick overview of the period in which Finney wrote "Contents of the Dead Man's Pocket."
- *Twilight Zone* was a popular television series of the late 1950s featuring stories similar to those found in *The Third Level. Twilight Zone: 19 Original Stories on the 50th Anniversary*, published in 2009 and edited by Carol Serling (the wife of the television series's host, Rod Serling) is an excellent sampling of stories.

Einstein's groundbreaking 1905 publication of the theory of special relativity, psychologists and other theorists had begun contemplating the troubling nature of time.

One such writer was the French philosopher Henry Bergson. As Peter Childs explains in his book *Modernism*, Bergson distinguished two different kinds of time, chronological time and duration. According to Childs, "Bergson thought that 'reality' was characterized by the different experience of time in the mind from the linear, regular beats of clock-time which measures all experience of time by the same gradation." Bergson called the psychological time "duration," and clock time "chronology." The main point of the argument is that there are instances when a person experiences time to be moving much more quickly, or alternately, much more slowly, than the clock indicates.

The second reason Finney seems so interested in exploring time in his fiction can also be explained by the historical context. By the mid-1950s, the general public understood that nuclear weapons, unleashed for the first time in 1945, could wreak horrible damage on the planet. Indeed, in the midst of the Cold War, with both the United States and the Soviet Union rapidly building their nuclear arsenal, it became very clear that one or both nations could blow up the entire world several times over.

Some people built fallout shelters in their back yards with the mistaken belief that this would someone save them from annihilation, but most people realized that such effort was folly. If a nuclear conflagration began, few would survive the initial attacks, and even fewer the devastation of the planet. The knowledge affected people differently: some lived wildly as if there were no tomorrow, others longed for a simpler past, and some chose to re-examine their values to begin building more meaningful lives. It became a question of how one used one's time.

Now, obviously, "Contents of the Dead Man's Pocket" does not address time in terms of time travel. Finney's concern with time in this story is much more subtle, yet it is also clear that he considers Bergson's concept of duration in crafting the plot of the story, as well as the intersection of time and values in establishing the message of the story.

In the opening scene of "Contents of the Dead Man's Pocket" there does not seem to be any compression or expansion of time. That is, Clare seems to be getting ready to go out at a normal rate, and Tom's thoughts about whether he should go to the movies with her also seem to take place at a fairly steady rate. From the time the paper flies out of the window, however, time does not move at a regular rate but increasingly slows down as the action rises.

Tom's decision to go out on the ledge is largely decided by a comparison of the time it took him to assemble the data on the paper and the time he believes it will take him to retrieve it. First he totes up the days and hours he believes that he has spent on the research until he is convinced that the paper represents "countless hours of work." Next, he imagines how long it will take him to go out the window and return with the paper: "To simply go out and get his paper was an easy task—he could be back here with it in less than two minutes—and he knew he wasn't deceiving himself." What Tom *is* deceiving himself about, however, is the difference between chronological time and duration. Once out on the ledge, he quickly perceives this error.

Finney accomplishes the contrast by slowing down time dramatically for Tom, by using words such as minutes, then seconds, then moments, then instants, and recounting each of Tom's steps in agonizing detail. Whereas the opening scene was accomplished in just two pages, the remaining story takes about another seventeen pages. Yet, it is likely that the first scene and the remainder of the story in terms of chronological time are about equal. Tom recognizes the difference between duration and chronological time when he glances at his watch while on the ledge: "Clare had been gone eight minutes. It wasn't possible, but only eight minutes ago he had kissed his wife good-by. She wasn't even at the theater yet!"

According to Childs, Bergson argued that "duration encompasses those times in a life which are significant to an individual, and which are necessarily different for each individual." Thus, for Clare, walking down the street to watch a movie, time moves quickly. For Tom, on the other hand, time stretches and becomes immense, as he is experiencing perhaps the most significant experience of his life.

Additionally, Finney addresses the connection between values and time in this story. One of the most telling ways a person reveals his or her values is by how he or she chooses to use time. People devote the most time to the things they value, whether they recognize it nor not. While, in this story, Tom would assert that he certainly values his wife Clare more than his work, his actions do not bear this out. Rather, it seems apparent that Tom's ambition has blinded him to his own values. When he chooses to stay home and work rather than accompany Clare to the movies, he is demonstrating what has worth for him.

Likewise, as noted, when Tom weighs the hours of work he has spent on the piece of paper, it is clear that the paper is very, very valuable to Tom, so valuable, in fact, that he risks his life to retrieve it. Once Finney moves the scene of the story to the ledge, outside in the dark, he emphasizes the isolation and loneliness of contemporary life. Tom cries for help, but no one pays attention, just as Tom remembers he has done himself when he has heard a cry in the past. When Tom looks at the surrounding apartment windows, he sees people going about their lives, but he is unable to connect with them.

While out on the ledge, Tom has an epiphany: the hours he has spent working rather than building a meaningful life filled with human relationships have drained his life of value. If he were to die, no one would even know who he is.

When he chooses to risk everything to regain entry into his apartment, it is as if Tom has resolved to spend his time differently in the future, doing the things that he most values.

His ability to laugh at the last moment, when he loses the paper once more, signals a complete change in his attitude toward time and his life.

It is tempting to read the end of the story biographically, as Jack Seabrook notes in *Stealing through Time: On the Writings of Jack Finney*. He suggests that Tom's embrace of a new life is "parallel to Jack Finney's decision in the late 1940s to leave behind his life as advertising man in New York City and move to California to devote his time to writing." Whether this is the case or not, it is significant that when readers last see Tom, he is laughing honestly and heartily. He has shaken off the isolation of modern life, and the false values of wealth and ambition. He is ready to embrace life, in all its glory.

Source: Diane Andrews Henningfeld, Critical Essay on "Contents of the Dead Man's Pocket" in *Short Stories for Students*, Gale, Cengage Learning, 2010.

Jack Seabrook

In the following excerpt, Seabrook discusses "Contents of the Dead Man's Pocket" and the meaning behind the story.

... Finney's next published work was the novella, "The House of Numbers," which will be discussed in the next chapter. His third story to see print in 1956 was the outstanding suspense tale, "Contents of the Dead Man's Pocket," which appeared in the October 26, 1956 issue of *Collier's*. This was to be Jack Finney's last story in *Collier's*, where his first published work had appeared in 1947. The magazine, which had been founded in 1888 and had reached a circulation of 2,500,000 during World War Two, had begun to decrease in popularity after the war and ceased publishing on December 16, 1956, less than two months after "Contents of the Dead Man's Pocket" was published ("Collier's Weekly" and "Crowell-Collier").

Unlike "Second Chance," "Contents of the Dead Man's Pocket" is narrated by a third person, omniscient narrator, who tells the story of Tom Benecke, a resident of an apartment on the eleventh floor of a building in New York City. His wife Clare leaves to go to the movies by herself as he stays home to type a memo for his job. A sheet of paper suddenly flies out the window and sticks onto the wall by the ledge outside. On the sheet is all of the research that Tom has done to support "his idea for a new grocery-store display method"; Tom thinks, "of all the papers on his desk, why did it have to be this one in particular!"

Suspense begins to build as Tom climbs out onto the narrow ledge to retrieve the sheet of paper. He slides along, eleven stories above Lexington Avenue, panics when he looks down, and nearly falls, his body swaying "outward to the knife edge of balance." After being frozen with fear, he begins to edge back along the ledge to his apartment window, but in the process of breaking another near fall he accidentally shuts the window.

Unable to break the glass and terrified by the knowledge that his wife will not be home for hours, he tries to send signals by dropping first flaming letters and then coins to the street below, but his attempts go unnoticed on the busy streets of New York. Finally, the only thing left in his pockets is the sheet of paper he had climbed out on the ledge to retrieve. He thinks of falling to his death and "[a]ll they'd find in his pockets would be the yellow sheet. *Contents of the dead man's pockets,* he thought, *one sheet of paper bearing penciled notations—incomprehensible.*"

Tom thus comes to realize that he has put his life in jeopardy for something worthless. He laments his wasted life, regretting all of the nights he stayed home working while his wife went out and all of the hours he'd spent alone. He resolves to make one final attempt to break the glass, knowing that if he fails the strength of the blow will cause him to fall to his death. As he puts his all into the blow, he speaks his wife's name and feels himself falling through the broken window into the safety of his apartment.

He puts the sheet of paper on his desk and opens the front door "to go find his wife." Blown by a draft from the hallway, the sheet flies out of the window again, but this time, "Tom Benecke burst into laughter and then closed the door behind him." The door that closes at the end of "Contents of the Dead Man's Pocket" is clearly both a literal and a figurative one, representing the end of a wasted life and the beginning of one that promises to have more meaning. One can read into this a parallel to Jack Finney's decision in the late 1940s to leave behind his life as an advertising man in New York City and move to California to devote his time to writing.

Stephen King allegedly wrote his story "The Ledge" as an homage to Finney's "Contents of the Dead Man's Pocket" (Newman 197–98), and the latter stands as one of Jack Finney's most suspenseful short stories.

Jack Finney also published a one-act play in 1956 entitled *Telephone Roulette,* which is discussed in chapter seventeen.

Three short stories were published in *Good Housekeeping* in 1957; two were romantic comedies and none were chosen to be reprinted in either of Jack Finney's subsequent short story collections....

Between 1947 and 1957, Jack Finney published thirty-eight short stories, two serialized novels that were later expanded into book form, and a novella. It was clearly time for some of his best stories to be collected in book form and, in 1957, his first collection of short stories, *The Third Level,* was published. It collected eleven stories that had been published before and added "A Dash of Spring," for which no prior publication source has been found.

The stories chosen for this collection were "The Third Level," "Such Interesting Neighbors," "I'm Scared," "Cousin Len's Wonderful Adjective Cellar," "Of Missing Persons," "Something in a Cloud," "There Is a Tide," "Behind the News," "Quit Zoomin' Those Hands Through the Air," "A Dash of Spring," "Second Chance," and "Contents of the Dead Man's Pocket." The back cover copy on the 1959 paperback edition of *The Third Level* sets forth the collection's theme: "Their subject is time... But time on a new level, a diverting, sometimes frightening level, where the Past, the Present, and the Future are all joined...." While not exactly true of all of the stories in *The Third Level,* this blurb shows that time travel tales were becoming a hallmark of Jack Finney's fiction....

Source: Jack Seabrook, "More Short Stories and the Third Level," in *Stealing Through Time on the Writings of Jack Finney,* McFarland & Company, 2006, pp. 45–8.

Darren Harris-Fain

In the following excerpt, Harris-Fain examines science fiction writers and time travel.

... Three award-winning works by Sturgeon, Niven, and Leiber all came from genre writers, that is to say, authors who identified themselves, primarily through the magazines and publishers to whom they marketed their work, as science fiction and/or fantasy writers. But there are authors who sometimes write science fiction and yet are not considered science fiction writers. They write in a variety of genres, perhaps, or they emerge from the mainstream with a work that is undeniably science fiction, even if the publisher does not market it as such or the author acknowledge it as such. Thus Jack Finney, who in 1955 published *The Body Snatchers,* a story better known in its film incarnations, in 1970 published what many consider one of the finest time-travel stories ever written, *Time and Again.*

In many ways, *Time and Again* looks backward twice. Not only does the story take the protagonist from the 1970s to the 1880s, but how he gets there is reminiscent of an earlier tradition of time-travel stories. Before H. G. Wells's novel *The Time Machine* (1895), which posited scientific theories about the fourth dimension and used a mechanical device to enable the Time Traveler to explore the future, time-travel stories were less concerned with the actual process of temporal travel. For instance, in Mark Twain's *Connecticut Yankee in King Arthur's Court* (1889), the eponymous hero finds himself in medieval England following a blow to the head. Finney, following Wells and numerous others in the intervening decades of such stories, is more scrupulous and, like Wells, throws in some theoretical speculations about the nature of time, but in essence his protagonist, part of a government experiment, simply manages to find himself nearly a century in the past by researching the period, being placed in a setting that duplicated the conditions of late-nineteenth-century New York City, and then wishing himself there.

What is remarkable about Finney's *Time and Again* is not so much the mode of time travel as the results. While the plot is not terribly original, involving political intrigue, some action and adventure, and of course a love story, and while the concept of the character from another time coming to terms with a different time was hardly original by this point in the history of science fiction, the presentation of the setting more than makes up for these facts. Finney presents readers with an 1880s New York that is so vividly realized and depicted that they feel, along with the protagonist, that they truly are there. In fact, *Time and Again* is more a historical novel than a work of science fiction, and in this sense it is comparable to another time-travel novel of the 1970s, Octavia E. Butler's *Kindred* (discussed in chapter 3). Yet part of what makes *Time and Again* so effective is the fact that it is not simply a historical novel in which the characters accept their world as routine. Through the eyes of his time traveler, Finney shows this lost world to be almost as strange and alien as any setting in more conventional works of science fiction....

Source: Darren Harris-Fain, "After the New Wave, 1970–1976," in *Understanding Contemporary American Science Fiction*, University of South Carolina Press, 2005, pp. 19–63.

SOURCES

Beard, Michael, "Jack Finney," in *Dictionary of Literary Biography*, Vol. 8, *Twentieth Century American Science-Fiction Writers*, edited by David Cowart, Gale Research, 1981, pp. 182–85.

Breen, Jon L., *A Shot Rang Out: Selected Mystery Criticism*, Ramble House, 2008, pp. 29–41.

Childs, Peter, *Modernism*, Routledge, 2000, pp. 48–50.

Eckes, Alfred E., and Thomas W. Zeiler, *Globalization and the American Century*, Cambridge University Press, 2003, p. 152.

Finney, Jack, "Contents of the Dead Man's Pocket," in *The Third Level*, Rinehart, 1957, pp. 170–88.

"Foreign News: We Will Bury You!," in *Time*, November 26, 1956, http://www.time.com/time/magazine/article/0,9171,867329,00.html (accessed September 5, 2009).

King, Stephen, *Stephen King's Danse Macabre*, Berkley Books, 1981, pp. 245–46.

Murfin, Ross, and Supryia M. Ray, *The Bedford Glossary of Critical and Literary Terms*, 2nd ed., Bedford/St. Martin's, 2003, pp. 347–48.

Seabrook, Jack, *Stealing through Time: On the Writings of Jack Finney*, McFarland, 2006, pp. 3–10, 21, 41–49.

Simpson, Philip L., "Cold War Novels and Movies," in *Americans at War: Society, Culture, and the Homefront: 1946–Present*, Vol. 4, edited by John Phillips Resch, Macmillan, 2005, pp. 39–42.

FURTHER READING

Clareson, Thomas D., *Understanding Contemporary Science Fiction: The Formative Period: 1926–1970*, University of South Carolina Press, 1990.

> While this book does not mention Finney directly, it spends considerable time situating science fiction and many of Finney's fellow writers within the historical context of the 1950s.

Finney, Jack, *From Time to Time*, Touchstone, 1995.

> This novel is a sequel to the 1970 *Time and Again*, and is Finney's final work.

Finney, Jack, *Invasion of the Body Snatchers*, Touchstone, 1998.

> This book is a new edition of Finney's classic 1955 novel *The Body Snatchers*, the story of alien invasion and human triumph.

King, Stephen, *On Writing: A Memoir of the Craft*, Scribner, 2000.

> The famous horror writer discusses his own writing and the art of storytelling in this book, which is an excellent introduction for students on the craft of writing.

Yapp, Nick, *1950s: Getty Images*, Langenscheidt Publishing Group, 2008.

> This book offers a collection of photographs taken during the 1950s as well as a useful introduction, providing the student with a visual overview of the decade.

Dog Star

ARTHUR C. CLARKE

1962

Sir Arthur C. Clarke is universally acknowledged as a grand master among science fiction writers. His place in the development and growth of the genre is almost unparalleled, but even more important is his use of the science fiction genre to communicate to a general audience the possibilities of human technical achievement. Clarke was well placed to undertake this work, having served in the radar branch of the Royal Air Force during World War II. Around that time Clarke became the first to consider the possibility of geosynchronous satellites to support a worldwide telecommunications network. Having earned a degree in engineering immediately after the war, he became president of the British Interplanetary Society and directed basic research on space travel—a precursor of the American space program. Throughout the 1950s and 1960s Clarke wrote popular books about space flight and speculated about the exploration of the solar system. This period culminated in his collaboration with Stanley Kubrick on the landmark 1968 film *2001: A Space Odyssey*.

Clarke's story "Dog Star" was originally published in 1962 in the pulp magazine *Galaxy Science Fiction* under the title "Moondog." It was reprinted in 1967 in his collection *The Nine Billion Names of God: The Best Short Stories of Arthur C. Clarke* and has been frequently anthologized. "Dog Star" shares the focus of much of Clarke's early work: to show how technology would radically alter the lives of the World War II generation.

Arthur C. Clarke (AP Images)

AUTHOR BIOGRAPHY

Clarke was born on November 16, 1917, in Minehead, Somerset, England. He grew up pursuing astronomy as a hobby and reading the then-popular science fiction pulp magazines. During World War II, Clarke served as an instructor in the new radar technology program for Royal Air Force personnel. During the war he considered the fact that a satellite orbiting Earth at a distance of 23,336 miles (now called the Clarke orbit in his honor) would have an orbital period equal to one day and thus remain stationary over the same position on Earth. While this was well known, it occurred to Clarke that if three satellites evenly positioned around Earth were put into this orbit, they would be able to see each other as well as one third of the surface of Earth and thus could instantly transmit radio signals from one area of Earth to another. This idea serves as the basis for the modern network of communications satellites necessary for the infrastructure of television, international telephony, satellite radio, and GPS systems. After the war, Clarke published his idea in the article "Can Rocket Stations Give Worldwide Radio Coverage?" in the October 1945 issue of the radio journal *Wireless World*.

After his discharge from the Royal Air Force, Clarke received a bachelor's degree in mathematics and physics at King's College, London. From 1947 to 1950 and again in 1953 Clarke served as chairman of the British Interplanetary Society, a nonprofit organization devoted to promoting space flight. It was responsible for the first detailed plan for a moon flight, roughly matching the parameters of the Apollo program.

Clarke produced a large number of science fiction novels including *Childhood's End* (1953) and *Rendezvous with Rama* (1972), short stories "I remember Babylon" (1960) and "The Star" (1955), and nonfiction books promoting space flight, including *Interplanetary Flight* (1950) and *The Exploration of Space* (1951). In 1962 he published his short story "Dog Star" in the science fiction pulp magazine *Galaxy*. Clarke's best-known work is his collaboration with Stanley Kubrick on the novel and screenplay for the 1968 film *2001: A Space Odyssey*. Clarke also served as the host of a number of television series, including *Arthur C. Clarke's Mysterious World*, which explored the differences between science and pseudoscience.

Clarke was also interested in the exploration of the oceans. In 1953 he settled permanently to Sri Lanka, where he could scuba dive and explore coral reefs the year round. This interest is reflected in his novel *The Deep Range* (1954). Sri Lanka also served as the setting of his novel *The Fountains of Paradise* (1978), which promoted the idea of a space elevator. Clarke died on March 19, 2008, from complications resulting from post-polio syndrome.

PLOT SUMMARY

"Dog Star" is told by a first-person narrator who never reveals his name. There are two levels of representation in what he says. He must be imagined as relating this story both to an audience of his own contemporaries in the future, who share his knowledge of everyday reality, as well as to the reading audience of 1962, who view everything he says as new and extraordinary. At the beginning of the story, the narrator dreams of hearing his old dog Laika barking to be let out. When he awakens, he is devastated by feelings of loss over separation from his dog. He mentions that she is 250,000 miles away, which is the first clue that he is on the moon. The dog is also five years away, meaning—as is revealed later in the story—he left her on Earth five years ago, shortly after which she died. He then starts to undergo a life-or-death crisis, but exactly what that involves he postpones to tell the story of Laika instead.

The narrator reveals that he found Laika when she was but a puppy, abandoned on the side of the road, where he spotted her while driving from the observatory, where he is employed as an astronomer, to Mount Palomar. He mentions that he advertised in the local Pasadena newspapers to try to find her owner (without success). This inevitably suggests that he works at the Mount Wilson observatory in Pasadena, California, which is about ninety miles from Palomar. The narrator also mentions that his car was a "new '92 Vik," suggesting that this part of the story takes place in 1992 or 1993.

The narrator has little interest in keeping a pet for himself and originally intended to entrust the dog to the janitor at Palomar. Nevertheless he is overcome with affection and pity for the dog and decides to keep it. He then describes in some detail the difficulties in house-breaking the puppy, and expresses his eventual admiration of the fact that the dog can come into the observatory with him and is content to sit quietly and not cause any disturbance while he works. The narrator's senior colleague, Dr. Anderson, suggests naming the dog Laika after the first dog sent into orbit by the Soviet Union. She is beloved by the entire observatory staff. As Laika grows up, it becomes clear she is a nearly pure-bred Alsatian (a euphemism for German shepherd, introduced into English during World War I because of anti-German popular sentiment).

Laika's affection for the narrator only increases and became more demonstrative. He takes her everywhere except on overseas trips to professional conferences. She accompanies him on a trip to Berkeley, where he is attending a seminar and staying as a houseguest with a faculty couple from the University of California, who are none too pleased to have a large dog invade their house. During her first night there, Laika begins whining and barking to be let out, so the narrator gets up to attend to her, wishing that his hosts not be awakened by the noise. While they are outside a terrible earthquake strikes, the most powerful since the Great San Francisco quake of 1906, which levels the house and kills his hosts. The narrator refuses to be evacuated until the Red Cross agrees to take Laika as well. Clarke, writing in the early 1960s, intended these events as predictions of the kinds of things that were likely to happen. Although the scientific study of earthquakes was in its infancy in the 1960s, it was clear that San Francisco would suffer other major earthquakes; in fact, the Loma Prieta earthquake of 1989 is the type of thing Clarke meant to suggest, although that seismic event was not as powerful or destructive as either the 1906 quake or Clarke's fictional quake.

The narrator presents as fact the idea that Laika has somehow sensed the earthquake was coming and acted purposefully to save his life. After that he grows even closer to the dog. Nevertheless, the narrator soon receives a job offer to become assistant director at the new Farside Observatory being established on the moon. This represents an important technical development since astronomy performed outside Earth's atmosphere will mark a tremendous advance over the way it has been practiced heretofore. As he says, "In a few months, I could hope to solve problems I had been working on for years. Beyond the atmosphere, I would be like a blind man who had suddenly been given sight." Naturally he cannot take Laika with him. Despite everything Laika has come to mean to him, he hardly hesitates before accepting the offer and handing Laika over to Dr. Anderson and his wife.

The narrator describes his trip to the moon in some detail, both to make it clear that it is more or less routine, closer in nature to an airline flight than the cutting-edge effort being put forth in the 1960s space race when Clarke was writing. At the same time, he mentions enough unusual circumstances to make it worth telling to his contemporary audience. The principal difficulty is radiation from a recent solar flare. Once on the moon, he resolves to set aside any guilt he feels about abandoning Laika—which was no different from her original owners, who had abandoned her by the side of the road—so that it would not interfere with his work. About a month later, he receives news that Laika has died, evidently of grief over their separation, but he only plunges all the more deeply into his work: "Though I never forgot Laika, in a little while the memory ceased to hurt."

Only now does the narrator return to the crisis point five years later with which he began the story. Because he has been awakened while dreaming of Laika, he realizes that the Farside Observatory is being shaken by a seismic tremor and is able to sound a general alarm and get into his own pressure suit, saving the lives of all but two of his colleagues.

The narrator rejects any supernatural explanation for the events he has described. He suggests that the keener senses of dogs are able to detect earthquakes sooner than human beings. His own unconscious memories of the first earthquake managed to alert him to the danger from the second before his fellow astronomers on the moon realized what was happening: "Though in a sense one could say that Laika woke me on both occasions, there is no mystery about it, no miraculous warning across the gulf that neither man nor dog can ever bridge." Clarke creates a seemingly sentimental story of supernaturalism only to reject any such possibility. Even if the narrator wishes he could indulge in such a fantasy, he recognizes it as a human failing rather than a scientific possibility.

CHARACTERS

Acquaintances

When the narrator of "Dog Star" has occasion to visit the University of California at Berkeley, he stays with academic colleagues, who are not happy to have a large dog like Laika in their house. The narrator tries to pacify them by suggesting that she will deter burglars: "'We don't have any in Berkeley,' they answered rather coldly." These are the only lines spoken in the story by any character except the narrator. Even here Clarke does not differentiate between them. They respond as if they were members of a Greek chorus speaking in unison. The narrator cannot be bothered to differentiate between them. A few hours later they are killed in an earthquake.

Dr. Anderson

Dr. Anderson is the only human being in the story whose name the reader learns. He is a senior astronomer who works in the same observatory as the narrator. He is the one who suggests the name Laika for the puppy the narrator adopts. Perhaps he is meant to be old enough to remember the sensation made by the launch into orbit of the original Laika. In any case, he suggests it as an appropriate name for an astronomer's dog. When the narrator leaves for the moon, Anderson and his wife take Laika: "The old physicist and his wife had always been fond of her, and I am afraid that they considered me indifferent and heartless—when the truth was just the opposite." However, they merely witness Laika's decline since the dog is dead within a month of her master's departure.

Narrator

The main character of "Dog Star" is the story's narrator. His name is never revealed. He (as is characteristic of narrators) fails to introduce himself to his audience. Nothing is directly conveyed of his life except that he is a brilliant young astronomer, most likely an American. Although his character is reasonably well drawn, it is nevertheless difficult to discern since it is remarkably similar to many of Clarke's other heroes. The narrator is chiefly notable for his utter lack of ordinary human feeling. One reason for this is that science fiction writers generally work in a quite different way from mainstream authors. Instead of developing a story from character, the science fiction setting itself becomes the main idea and, as it were, the main character of the story. The well-known science fiction author Philip K. Dick says that in science fiction a short story is about an idea, whereas a novel is about character, with the understanding that the main character is the artificial, imaginary world created for the narrative, whether it is a fantasy world like Tolkien's Middle Earth or, as for Clarke, the future. This can hardly be said to be truer of any author than it is of Clarke. The narrator and every other character in "Dog Star" are firmly subordinated to the presentation of Clarke's world of the future.

From an emotional point of view, "Dog Star" concerns the narrator's relationship with his dog. While such relationships are common and can encompass very strong emotions, the narrator himself finds it singular and overwhelming. Reflecting on it years after Laika's death, he finds that the cessation of the relationship filled him with "fear of loneliness, and fear of madness," with a feeling of "transcendental sadness" that was "desolating." Yet he abandoned Laika quite voluntarily when it became necessary to take a position on the moon to advance his career: "After all, she was only a dog. In a dozen years she would be dead, while I should be reaching the peak of my profession." The dual attitudes the narrator displays toward Laika seem difficult to reconcile. The narrator further complicates matters by saying of his abandonment of her, "No sane man would have hesitated over the matter; yet I did hesitate, and if by now you do not understand why, no further words of mine can help." In fact, anyone who loved his dog would hesitate, even if he eventually made a pragmatic decision. With the sole exception of his feeling for Laika, the narrator is nothing if not pragmatic. He cannot conceive of hesitating for an emotional reason as being anything but extraordinary and beyond human understanding. For him, his relationship with his dog is the only intense, affective relationship in his life and seems like a sublime mystery that others cannot share or comprehend. The intensity and, as he thinks, the uniqueness of his feelings create a sense of superiority over those who he believes cannot understand. But he is unable to empathize with his prospective colleagues at the Farside Observatory, many of whom will be separated not from their dogs but from their spouses and children.

The narrator seems to have completely rejected his own emotional life in favor of developing his intellect and his professional position. By his own admission, he has "made very few friends among human beings." Indeed, he seems very detached from everyone around him. Other people are not important enough to name: they are the janitor or university acquaintances. In fact, his acquaintances in Berkeley are the only people in the story, other than the narrator himself, who are allowed to speak directly. But even their single statement, which is obviously spoken only by one of them, is attributed to them collectively, as if their individual identities do not matter. They are killed in an earthquake while he survives. The narrator calls them his friends but their deaths do not seem to affect him in any way. Rather, he is only concerned with the safety of his dog. In the same way, the narrator mentions no human he is sorry to leave behind when he travels to the moon. The narrator's closest human relationship is probably with his superior at the observatory; the narrator can most easily function within the student-teacher relationship he must have excelled at in school. Dr. Anderson not only has the distinction of being the only named human character in the story but also has the additional distinction of having earned a doctorate, which is reflected in his title. This defines the relationship and keeps it from becoming a genuine friendship. The narrator realizes that even Anderson considers him "indifferent and heartless." The narrator denies that this is true precisely because of what he feels about Laika, but the fact that this perception nevertheless exists demonstrates how completely unsuccessful he is at human relationships. Any astronomer would give up his dog and a great deal more for the chance to work full time at the most important observatory in the world (perhaps in the solar system). Anderson thinks the narrator is heartless not because he is willing to leave his dog behind for the new job but most likely because he finds him generally unconcerned about his fellow human beings.

As desperately important to the narrator as his relationship with Laika is, even this is sustained entirely by the dog's emotion. While the dog is enthusiastic and demonstrative in her special affection for the narrator, he has no idea how to reciprocate. Even naming the dog is too affective an act for the narrator; he leaves it to Dr. Anderson. The narrator admits, "I have never liked dogs, or indeed any animals." Even when he picks up Laika as a puppy abandoned by the roadside, he does not want to touch her and wishes he had worn gloves, as if he might be contaminated by direct contact. Rather than risk damage to the upholstery of his new car, he locks the puppy in the trunk. He does not allow himself to feel outrage at her former owner over the cruelty of the dog's abandonment, reasoning that "since I shall never know the facts, I may be jumping to false conclusions." Only a mind coldly devoted to logic would worry about the small possibility that Laika was abandoned for any reason other than to dispose of her.

The narrator of "Dog Star" has completely denied his own inner life in favor of an intellectual, professional, technocratic facade. As a consequence, his outpouring of repressed emotion into his relationship with his dog becomes too overwhelming for him. It is perhaps a relief that he is eventually able to leave her behind on another planet. Certainly after the separation he did not think of her. He does not even dream of her before the dream at the climax of the story that he believes saved his life. But even this dream he rationalizes away rather than accept the possibility of a redefined, redemptive relationship with Laika.

Laika

Laika is the title character of "Dog Star." The title is not, in fact, that closely applicable to her, but Clarke seems to have wanted some word that had both canine and astronomical associations. He first thought of calling the story "Moondog" before settling on "Dog Star." A young puppy abandoned by her former owners, she is left on the side of the road in the Pasadena hills and is picked up by the unnamed narrator. She is the only character that is physically described:

> She was a beautiful animal, about ninety-five per cent Alsatian.... Apart from two dark patches over the eyes, most of her body was a smoky

gray, and her coat was soft as silk. When her ears were pricked up, she looked incredibly intelligent and alert; sometimes I would be discussing spectral types or stellar evolution with my colleagues, and it would be hard to believe that she was not following the conversation.

Laika develops a special affection for her rescuer, becoming ecstatic whenever they are reunited. In fact, they are seldom apart since Laika is permitted to go anywhere in the observatory, even into the workrooms for the telescopes themselves. She is especially liked by the senior astronomer, Dr. Anderson, who suggests her name (after the first dog to be launched into space) and eventually adopts her when the narrator has to abandon her.

Once Laika accompanies the narrator on a trip to Berkeley, California. During the night she makes a big fuss to get out of the house. When she and the narrator are outside, a massive earthquake strikes, destroying the house and killing everyone inside. The narrator believes that her canine senses somehow alerts her to the danger in time to get out. After that incident he is even more inseparable from his dog. However, when he is offered an opportunity to advance his career by taking a post at the new Farside Observatory on the moon, he does so, leaving her in the care of Dr. Anderson and his wife. She dies within a month. Thereafter, although he scarcely thinks of her during the day, he dreams of her one night and awakens just in time to realize that the Farside Observatory on the moon is being destroyed by a seismic tremor. The narrator finally eulogizes Laika as "brimming with an unselfish, undemanding love."

THEMES

Parapsychology

Clarke was not interested in paranormal phenomena per se. That is, he did not automatically believe in the claims of the supernatural. What interested Clarke was a class of items that seem to represent valid pieces of evidence that have not yet been fully accounted for by rationalist, materialist, or scientific explanation. In rhetorical terms, this is called paradoxography, a category that is true but seems false. More directly relevant to Clarke is the term "Forteana," named after Charles Fort, author of *The Book of the Damned* (1919) and other similar collections of this kind of material, which Clarke read in his youth. Fort

TOPICS FOR FURTHER STUDY

- "Dog Star" and Jack London's "To Build a Fire" both concern the relationship between a man and a dog during a crisis involving survival. How are the stories different? How are they similar? What themes do they have in common? Write an essay comparing the two stories.

- Robert A. Heinlein's 1958 young-adult novel *Have Space Suit—Will Travel* also involves a trip to the moon. In a class presentation, describe the different approaches to the theme adopted by Clarke and Heinlein.

- Make a PowerPoint presentation comparing the space-faring capabilities described in Clarke's "Dog Star" with those currently in use or in development. Topics may include NASA's plans to return to the moon or manned travel to Mars. Use illustrations found on the Internet, which might include photographs of possible locations for the Farside Observatory mentioned in the story, sites near the moon's south pole that NASA intends to explore for signs of ice, and illustrations of the Constellation system of rockets and space vehicles currently being developed by NASA together with images of space vehicles used for lunar travel in science fiction illustrations from the 1960s (for example, from the film *2001: A Space Odyssey*.

- Create an audiovisual presentation about Clarke's commitment to Sri Lanka, using as sources biographies of Clarke plus his nonfiction books and essays set there.

believed that there were many verifiable facts about the natural world that science could not yet explain but that scientists purposely ignored—even suppressed—so as not to have to alter their dogmatic theories. In fact, this is the opposite of the way scientists work. Their constant aim is not to prove but rather to disprove established theories and gain recognition and career advancement in direct proportion to the degree of change they can bring about in scientific thought. Since Fort's time, this has been clarified by Thomas Kuhn in *The Structure of Scientific Revolutions* and Arthur Koestler in *The Sleepwalkers*. While scientific orthodoxy is a valid concept to a greater degree than might seem likely, young scientists nevertheless make their careers by criticizing and overturning existing orthodoxies. The paradigm of scientific methodology allows new ideas to be accepted rapidly and widely once they are proven. New discoveries are frequently made accidently (for example, while working along an entirely different line of research).

In "Dog Star" Clarke introduces two paradoxographical ideas, namely, that animals can predict earthquakes and that dreams can similarly predict earthquakes. The narrator of Clarke's story inevitably espouses the strictest scientific rationalism: "It is hardly necessary for me to say that I do not believe in the supernatural." He nevertheless accepts as fact that his dog Laika was able to predict an earthquake, which was confirmed by additional instances: "In the second San Francisco earthquake, Laika was not the only dog to sense approaching disaster; many such cases were reported." However, he attributes the prediction to natural causes, as he does his own prediction of the quake on the moon: "And on Farside, my own memories must have given me that heightened awareness, when my never-sleeping subconscious detected the first faint vibration from within the Moon." The mechanism in the first case is to be understood as also operative in the second. It is often suggested that dogs can sense some minor tremor or other event leading up to an earthquake by using their nonhuman senses.

Clarke delighted in these kinds of unexplained facts and devoted a good portion of his career to promoting them. He acted as the host of three television series that did nothing but catalog such information: *Arthur C. Clarke's Mysterious World* (1980), *Arthur C. Clarke's World of Strange Powers* (1985), and *Arthur C. Clarke's Mysterious Universe* (1994). For instance, he suggested that if there were a large, apelike creature (not a single individual but rather a breeding population of at least hundreds if not thousands of individuals), like the so-called Bigfoot, living in close proximity to millions of people in the Pacific Northwest in forests thick with hunters, campers, and hikers, then there would be some physical evidence. If a living specimen could not be produced, then bones or other remains would be available. However, in many other cases Clarke appeared to believe that the phenomenon was unexplained, if not inexplicable, and did not offer commonly accepted explanations for them. The idea that dogs can predict earthquakes is a similar case. Even supposing that a dog's superhuman hearing could feel a tremor too slight for even the most sensitive seismic equipment to detect, how could a dog that had never experienced an earthquake—and had no reason to think that houses are subject to collapse—deduce from this that the house it is in is about to come crashing down? Is it not far more likely that a human being whose life was saved by a dog barking to be let out (for the usual reason) would make a meaningful connection in his own consciousness—when that event happened to be followed by a devastating earthquake—between the two events, which were only accidentally connected in time? Clarke is correct in believing that the truth of the matter can never be known since the phenomenon cannot be tested experimentally. He is actually on firmer ground when he describes the narrator of "Dog Star" dreaming about the quake a few seconds before it occurs, since one function of dreams is to keep the dreamer asleep. Facts from the perceptible world that would otherwise cause one to wake up are often incorporated into dreams to delay the sleeper having to wake up to attend to them. The narrator's dream of events related to the earthquake might well have served the purpose of keeping him asleep in the face of perceptible tremors announcing a new earthquake.

Exploration

Clarke tended to view human history teleologically, that is, as if it were leading to a final, specific, predetermined goal. It was obvious to Clarke that the goal was space flight and the exploration of the solar system and beyond. Clarke pointedly describes the trip to the moon by the narrator of "Dog Star" as a voyage, a physical journey beset by perils and dangers. It is linked to the tradition of Atlantic exploration stretching back to Portugal's Prince Henry the Navigator in the fifteenth century—which ultimately brought about contact between Americans and European culture—as well as the circumnavigation of the globe. However, the narrator's purpose in undertaking his voyage is purely scientific and is aimed at discovering

Closeup of the moon *(Image copyright Brad Thompson, 2009. Used under license from Shutterstock.com)*

knowledge for its own sake. His voyage is linked even more closely to such early scientific explorers as Alexander von Humboldt and Charles Darwin, both of whom used their worldwide travels as the basis for important scientific advances.

STYLE

Science Fiction

One could easily point to some of the most important twentieth-century novels, all of which concern events that seemed similar to events likely to transpire in the future, including Aldous Huxley's *Brave New World*, George Orwell's *1984*, and Anthony Burgess's *A Clockwork Orange*. However, as Tom Shippey has pointed out in his study of the fantasy novelist J. R. R. Tolkien, none of those novels is considered science fiction by mainstream literary critics. What, then, is science fiction?

One answer, based on history, is that science fiction is a genre that first appeared in U.S. pulp magazines in the 1920s. Bearing titles such as *Astounding* or *Galaxy*, these magazines represented the most important part of Clarke's reading during his adolescence—and were where almost all of his early novels and short stories were first published. For example, "Dog Star" premiered in *Galaxy*. In that sense, Clarke is definitely a science fiction author. Moreover, he has received major awards from organizations representing science fiction writers and fans rather than mainstream literary awards, like the Booker or Nobel prizes. In fact, Clarke is usually considered one of the great science fiction writers, along with Isaac Asimov and Robert A. Heinlein.

As a genre, science fiction tends to concern itself with subjects such as space or time travel, contact with aliens, and the like. Since the majority of the readers of the science fiction pulps were boys in their teens, characters tended to be supermasculine heroes fighting evil, natural forces, or some other extraterrestrial opponent. Factors like literary style and character development were secondary. In the 1960s, in the context of the space race, science fiction seemed to overlap with popular interests. Clarke used the occasion to defend science fiction against attack by mainstream critics:

> Science Fiction is often called escapism—always in a negative sense.... Of course it's not true. Science fiction is virtually the only kind of writing that's dealing with the real problems and possibilities; it's a concerned fiction. Its's the mainstream that escapes from these things into small anxieties—away from fact, away from things that threaten or enrich our lives.

What Clarke's statement reveals is that science fiction and literary fiction are quite different from each other. Science fiction is primarily concerned with finding meaning at the highest level, namely, in the structure of the universe rather than anything comprehensible on a human scale, while literary fiction is insistent that only in creating the likeness of individual human lives can any meaning be embedded in a work of fiction. In Anthony Burgess's *A Clockwork Orange*, the reader sees the action of characters in a future whose events might seem all too predictable because of their palpable reality. In "Dog Star" the narrator feels uncomfortable and awkward and abandons human feeling in favor of pure science. Clarke thus reduces his work to a prediction of the future, one that fails to deal with " real problems and possibilities " in a meaningful way.

Skepticism

The anonymous narrator of "Dog Star" cultivates a technocratic persona. Part of this image involves assuming an identity as a skeptic, someone who only believes anything on the basis of evidence and its reasoned interpretation. This is almost inevitable for a scientist and astronomer, who must work in his professional life with a physical universe and purely mechanistic explanations, although many working scientists simultaneously maintain private religious beliefs. In the case of the narrator, skepticism is a core part of his identity. For this reason he can state, "It is hardly necessary for me to say that I do not believe in the supernatural." When confronted by the seemingly uncanny events involving his dog warning him of the two earthquakes (in person in Berkeley and through a dream on the moon), the narrator offers up what at first appear to be rational explanations. In fact, these are poorly thought out and badly reasoned rationalizations. At best the two incidents are anecdotes, not scientific evidence. His interpretations seem geared toward erecting an emotional barrier between himself and necessary human emotion.

HISTORICAL CONTEXT

Observatories

The narrator of "Dog Star" is a professional astronomer, with the story revolving around the future of astronomy. Clarke believed that once space travel became routine, older earthbound astronomical observatories would replaced by instruments located away from Earth: "The stories of Mount Wilson, Palomar, Greenwich, and the other great names were coming to an end; they would still be used for training purposes, but the research frontier must move out into space." Clarke's vision of the future certainly has some parallels in history as it has unfolded since the 1960s. Clarke mentioned the problem of astronomical observation through Earth's atmosphere, but almost as great a concern is light pollution from nearby cities, which makes physical observation difficult. The first reaction to these problems was to move new observatories up and away from cities, though not as far as space. Important new observatories since the late 1960s have been built on isolated mountain tops, both to avoid light from human habitation and to get above as much of the atmosphere as possible. Such observatory sites include volcanic mountains at Mauna Kea in Hawaii and La Palma in the Canary Islands, as well as several locations in the Andes mountains in Chile. The expansion of such sites continued unabated even after the launch of NASA's space-based telescopes. One reason this is so (which Clarke did not foresee) is the ability of recent computers to compensate for atmospheric distortions and produce images (even from Mt. Palomar, outside San Diego) that are comparable to those produced by the Hubble Space Telescope.

Soviet Space Dogs

Laika (which means "barker") in "Dog Star" is named after the Russian space dog, the first animal to make an orbital flight. Clarke had no need to mention this explicitly since in 1962 Laika was a world-famous celebrity. On November 3, 1957, Laika orbited in Soviet satellite

COMPARE & CONTRAST

- **1960s:** The manned exploration of space seems to be a limitless vista that will dominate the next phase of human history.

   Today: Many of the important discoveries of space exploration are made by unmanned missions and satellites.

- **1960s:** Space exploration is a matter of fervid popular interest, increasing through the 1950s and 1960s and peaking with the Apollo 13 moon landing in 1969.

   Today: The general public has little interest in space exploration and NASA's share of the federal budget is decreasing.

- **1960s:** Scientific knowledge makes paranormal phenomena, such as being able to predict the future based on dreams or animal behavior, seem a bizarre relic of the past that few take seriously.

   Today: Belief in such paranormal phenomenon is on the rise thanks to its promotion in the mass media.

- **1960s:** It is commonly assumed that a variety of nuclear-propulsion systems will be used in even the earliest stages of space flight.

   Today: Many promising avenues of research concerning the use of nuclear-propulsion systems for space flight have been abandoned for political and safety concerns.

Sputnik 2. Unfortunately she died a few hours into the flight due to overheating. (Until 2002, the Soviets claimed it was a planned death because of the limited amount of oxygen the small satellite could carry.) Her flight was an intentional humiliation of the United States in the space race; the mission seems to have been planned only after the United States announced it would put a chimpanzee in orbit in 1958.

The rationale for putting animals into orbit was to determine if any unforeseen conditions in space might be dangerous or fatal to human astronauts. The United States chose chimpanzees because they are the genetic species closest to human beings, while the Soviets chose dogs because they could easily be trained to undergo long periods of inactivity. In fact, the dogs were trained in much the same way as human astronauts, undergoing simulated flights and launches, as well as centrifuge training to simulate the acceleration of launch. The testing program encompassed a number of suborbital flights from 1951 to 1960, followed by a series of orbital flights from 1960 to 1966. Laika's 1957 flight was unscheduled, and of limited scientific value, because it was hastened for propaganda purposes. Dezik, a dog who participated in a 1951 Soviet suborbital flight, was adopted as a pet by one of the researchers on the program. This might have suggested the adoption of Clarke's Laika in "Dog Star." However, Clarke's own favorite dog was named Laika after the space dog.

CRITICAL OVERVIEW

"Dog Star" is an orphan among Clarke's works. Though in many ways among the most typical of his stories, it has received little or no critical attention. It plays no part in the source material for Stanley Kubrick and Clarke's *2001: A Space Odyssey*. Little is known about the circumstances surrounding the story's composition since it is neglected by Clarke's biographers. However, in his authorized biography of Clarke, Neil McAleer suggests that in 1961 (the probable date of the story's composition) Clarke's thoughts were divided between the events of the space race—with Soviet cosmonaut Yuri Gagarin becoming the first man in space on April 12—and his own financial crisis following

A dog looks for the dog star. (Image copyright William Attard McCarthy, 2009. Used under license from Shutterstock.com)

the rejection of his novel *Glide Path* by several publishers. One can see how "Dog Star," with its mood of desperation and loss, fits into that frame of mind. However, McAleer does mention that at this time Clarke kept five dogs at his home in Sri Lanka, including his favorite, Laika, suggesting that the relationship between the narrator of "Dog Star" and his fictional Laika reflects Clarke's own life.

In his essay in the critical volume on Clarke edited by Joseph Olander and Martin Greenberg, Peter Brigg suggests that Clarke writes in three modes. The first he calls the projector, in which Clarke gives a "precise scientific extrapolation that depends upon detailed scientific knowledge carefully explained to the reader to communicate Clarke's fascination with the possibilities at the frontiers of scientific thinking." Brigg quotes Clarke himself as justifying this style:

> In each case some unfamiliar (but I hope plausible and comprehensible) scientific fact is the basis of the story action, and human interest is secondary.... If it is done properly, without the information being too obtrusive or redolent of the textbook, it can still have at least the entertainment value of a good puzzle. It may not be art, but it can be enjoyable and intriguing.

Even Clarke's projector-style stories often turn on the surprise revelation at the end of a scientific fact in a manner reminiscent of a punch line. It is not surprising that Clarke often gives his work a humorous cast and produces a second style of works Briggs designates by their wit. The last of the modes Briggs sees in Clarke's work is the mystic, in which Clarke searches for a deeper meaning that transcends science. Within Brigg's typology, "Dog Star" best fits the first category (projector), although the facts it depends upon, such as the prediction of earthquakes, are not scientific but paradoxographical, neither clearly scientific nor supernatural. Though Clarke presents "Dog Star" as scientific, the ambiguity of the story and its almost cosmic sense of loss also reveal elements of the mystic category.

CRITICISM

Bradley A. Skeen

Skeen is a professor of classics. In this essay, he compares "Dog Star" with the actual space-related events of the last half century.

Clarke wrote about science and its future impact with a greater purity of intention than any of his contemporaries in the science fiction category. It would not be going too far to say that Clarke's main purpose—especially in "Dog Star"—is to instruct and inform. Clarke's readers in the 1960s were living at the beginning of a revolutionary period, although many of them may have been slow to realize it. The revolution that has unfolded since then has been referred to as the information age and the space age, among various other names, but these phrases at best reflect part of a general expansion of both technology and basic science at an ever-accelerating rate of change. Clarke's technique in "Dog Star" is to illustrate typical global events that technological and scientific change will produce within a few decades. Strictly speaking, very little happens in the story. There are indeed two seismic tremors that put the narrator's life at risk, but these hardly seem to be the point of the story. Nor does the narrator provide a detailed explanation of any startling bit of technology, as a golden-age science fiction character might have done, as if to say: this is a rocket; see the wonderful way it works. The point of the story is in all the little details that the narrator seemingly mentions in passing without explaining, which his fictitious audience, the populace of the world of the future, understands perfectly well. Clarke subtly builds up an image of the world his narrator inhabits in much the same way a more conventional author might develop character. In this way, Clarke reveals that, for him, even in a short story the main character is the created fictional world of the future. Clarke's purpose in "Dog Star" is to provide a tour of the world that will be created by the technological and scientific revolution that began after World War II and continues to this day. Clarke's intention in "Dog Star" is simply to illustrate typical events in the world that technological and scientific change will produce within a few decades.

If science fiction is a genre of ideas, it is fair to question the ideas Clarke expounds in "Dog Star." If one purpose of the story is prediction, then it is fair to test the accuracy of the predictions. To do that, some estimate of the story's absolute chronology must be made, and Clarke—by no means accidentally—has provided ample means to do so. He wanted his readers to think to themselves, "This is what the world will be like when I am old," or "This is the world that my children will live in." Clarke allows

WHAT DO I READ NEXT?

- *Other Spaces, Other Times: A Life Spent in the Future* (2009) by Robert Silverberg provides a chronicling of the science-fiction genre by an author who was named a Grand Master by the Science Fiction Writers of America.

- Clarke's 1977 volume *The View from Serendip* collects a number of his nonfiction essays and articles, including several on the history and culture of his adopted home of Sri Lanka (known as Serendip in medieval Latin and the origin of the term "serendipity," meaning accidental discovery).

- Young science fiction enthusiasts will enjoy Ray Bradbury's *The Martian Chronicles* (1950) as another master of the genre spins a series of short stories into a loose frame novel.

- Robin Anne Reid's 1997 *Arthur C. Clarke: A Critical Companion* presents a biography of the author and a general assessment of his later novels.

- For a sociological look at the effects of the space program, the essays collected by editors David Bell and Martin Parker in *Space Travel and Culture: From Apollo to Space Tourism* (2009) provide perspectives from science to pop culture.

- Read about the real Laika, the Soviet dog launched into space in 1957, in *A Ball, a Dog, and a Monkey: 1957—The Space Race Begins* (2007) by Michael D'Antonio. The author chronicles the competition between the United States and the Soviet Union to win the space race.

> CLARKE'S INTENTION IN 'DOG STAR' IS SIMPLY TO ILLUSTRATE TYPICAL EVENTS IN THE WORLD THAT TECHNOLOGICAL AND SCIENTIFIC CHANGE WILL PRODUCE WITHIN A FEW DECADES."

the story's absolute chronology to be established by providing a single absolute date, and a relative chronology to be derived from that by a few clues and assumptions. The only date that the narrator provides occurs in his description of a car he once owned as "my new '92 Vik," meaning it was a 1992 model. This means he probably found Laika as a puppy in 1992, or no more than a year off in either direction. After a few years passed, he moved to the moon and had to abandon Laika, at which time he estimated she might live another dozen years. That would mean roughly four years had passed, making it 1996. The quake that serves as the climax of the story occurs "five years later," or roughly 2001—not coincidentally the date Clarke and Kubrick chose for *2001: A Space Odyssey*. Another work of literature written at about the same time as "Dog Star" is Anthony Burgess's 1962 novel *A Clockwork Orange*, which is also set at an indefinite time in the future and similarly provides the only clue to its date in the form of a car's model year. The narrator, Alex, is the leader of a street gang. He steals a car for a joyride, "a newish Durango 95." That novel plays out over the course of about four years, so it could also encompass a date close to 2001. Clarke and Burgess would, however, seem to present opposite views of the future. Whereas Clarke presents a world of unlimited progress and technological and scientific growth, including the colonization of the moon and outer space, Burgess depicts a violent, totalitarian dystopia marked by the failure of democracy, the family, art, and civilization itself. However, they are not quite opposites. In *A Clockwork Orange*, Burgess presents exactly the same vision of space exploration as Clarke. When Alex and his gang beat up an old, homeless man for no reason except the pleasure of committing an act of violence, their victim asks, "What sort of a world is it at all? Men on the moon and men spinning round the earth like it might be midges round a lamp, and there's not no attention paid to earthly law nor order no more." While Burgess balances the possibilities of the development of human life in many different directions, Clarke has no interest in the future except for the exploration of space. Clarke's one attempt to deal with the future of humanity rather than human technology occurs in his novel *Childhood's End*, which sees humanity evolve into a single interconnected entity of pure energy able to merge with the galactic over mind (something similar, albeit less fully explained, occurs in *2001: A Space Odyssey*), which can be read as a way of avoiding the human condition in his work. Clarke seems to believe that the advance of technology and space travel will carry along human civilization. The point is addressed in "Dog Star" when Clarke's narrator spends a few days with academic colleagues in Berkeley, California. They object to having the dog Laika in the house. When her owner tries to smooth it over by suggesting that having a German shepherd in the house would deter burglars, they tell him there are no burglaries in Berkeley. As in *Childhood's End*, Clarke seems to imagine that as technology advances, crime and the human suffering it causes will diminish. In actual fact, statistics compiled by the State of California reveal that in 2001 over fourteen hundred burglaries were reported in Berkeley, or one for about every twenty-two households. Thus, as technology has advanced—in some ways even faster than Clarke imagined—social cohesion has moved in a very different direction than he envisioned.

By his own admission, Clarke's stories about the exploration of the solar system are a sort of travelogue of the future. His original aim in working with film director Stanley Kubrick was to turn some of his stories about the exploration of space into "a kind of semidocumentary about the first pioneering days of the new frontier." On September 10, 1962, the year "Dog Star" was published, Clarke gave an interview to the BBC in which he outlined an estimated future timetable for the exploration of the solar system, predicting a lunar orbit in 1967 and a moon landing in 1970, or shortly thereafter (in accord with the announced plans of the American space program). He went further out on a limb to predict a flight around Mars by 1980 and a landing there by 1990. He also predicted the future of technology in essays published in *Profiles in the Future*, also published in 1962 and updated several times.

It therefore seems reasonable to compare the predictions Clarke makes in "Dog Star" with the history of space flight as it actually unfolded between 1962 and the present, well beyond the probable date in the story (2001).

At the climax of his travelogue of the future, Clarke cannot resist mounting his paradoxographical hobbyhorse. He introduces the well-worn cliché of dogs predicting earthquakes and makes it sound scientifically plausible, for all that it is deeply irrational. He even tacks on a rationalization for dreams as predictors of the future. Indeed, these elements form the climax of "Dog Star." Clarke is responsible for promoting the belief in psychic powers in reality in *Arthur C. Clarke's Mysterious World* and his other television series. Pioneering shows like Clarke's and *In Search Of* in the 1970s spawned their own industry of paradoxographical television shows and, more recently, entire cable networks devoted to UFOs, ghosts, and psychics. This, in turn, supports the shockingly widespread belief in such pseudoscientific ideas. While scientific investigation of psychic phenomena has unequivocally shown that they have no basis in reality, exposing Clarke's greatest failure in predicting the future of scientific progress, Clarke's legacy has played a very important role in encouraging pseudoscientific belief.

Clarke imagined that the first moon landing would quickly lead to routine travel to the moon and the establishment of permanent bases there. His narrator expects to live on the moon for several years, describing his particular voyage there as one might a long plane flight, interesting for the unusual things that happened but unexciting in and of itself. In reality, after the initial reconnaissance of the Apollo program, mankind has not returned to the moon. Clarke missed this, perhaps because he did not realize the degree to which the Apollo program was part of political rivalry during the cold war rather than a natural outgrowth of technological advancement. Once the apparent victory was achieved by the United States in successfully completing the first landing, both powers lost interest in the moon. There is very little scientific reason to go to the moon.

Concerning the seismic tremor that occurs on the moon at the climax of "Dog Star," in 1962 the science of plate tectonics and the causation of earthquakes on Earth was only beginning to be understood, so Clarke can be forgiven for transporting the familiar phenomenon of an earthquake to the moon. In fact, the moon does not exhibit any plate tectonic activity, ruling out seismic tremors.

The narrator of "Dog Star" becomes the deputy director of an astronomical observatory on the far side of the moon. Clarke is absolutely right that space travel is a tremendous boon to astronomy. He acknowledges that he is doing no more than reporting the conventional wisdom of the astronomical community at the time of writing (in fact, the first proposals for a space telescope date back to the 1920s) when he says: "As far back as the nineteen-sixties it was realized that Earth was no place for astronomical observatory. Even the small pilot instruments on the Moon had far outperformed all the telescopes peering though the murk and haze of the terrestrial atmosphere." In the real history that unfolded after the 1960s, the solution was not to put a telescope on the moon but rather in low Earth orbit, a solution that was cheaper yet retained all the advantages of getting out from under the obscuring blanket of the atmosphere. This potential was realized by the launch between 1990 and 2003 of NASA's Great Observatories, the Hubble Space Telescope, the Compton Gamma Ray Observatory, the Chandra X-ray Observatory, and the Spitzer Infrared Space Telescope. While it is true that, as Clarke imagined, some additional benefit could be obtained by placing an instrument on the far side of the moon—a result of the shielding from the sun and reflected light from either Earth or the moon— the same effect could be achieved by placing a telescope in lunar orbit rather than on the surface of the moon. It is worth noting that none of these actual telescopes are manned instruments. Clarke always imagined that human beings would be needed to operate complex machinery in space. In his initial idea for communications satellites, he envisioned them as orbiting space stations with human crews. In 1962, no one could have imagined the rapid advances in computer technology that would make a human presence in space largely unnecessary. Regarding Clarke's prediction of a landing on Mars by 1990, since he envisioned a manned mission that prediction still has not come true, but there have been many landings of unmanned missions on Mars even before that date.

On the whole, Clarke seems to have been overly enthusiastic in his predictions of a human rush into space, modeled on the exploration and colonization of the Americas by European civilization. He was certainly right that the ability to travel in space has vastly increased the sum of human scientific knowledge. Outer space has not been developed to anything like the degree Clarke imagined, or to the extent actually possible, because the political driver of the space race collapsed even before the Soviet Union. The majority of voters seem to have little interest in the advancement of science—or at least for paying for it through taxation. Popular, and therefore political, apathy about space is one thing Clarke did not envision.

Source: Bradley Skeen, Critical Essay on "Dog Star," in *Short Stories for Students*, Gale, Cengage Learning, 2010.

Ian Barry

In the following article, Barry writes about Clarke's impact on the future of science fiction.

When Arthur C. Clarke died recently, the world lost not only one of its best-known visionaries, but the world of science fiction lost perhaps its best-known ambassador. So now, in an age in which science fiction seems to become a reality almost daily, is there anyone to pick up the torch and light the way into the future?

In many ways there is not a straight-forward answer to this question. The notion of what constitutes science fiction and its relationship to society in general has changed enormously since Clarke's writing was at its heyday. If, like me, you are used to thinking of his work as still somehow flying the flag for the science part of science fiction, it is surprising to learn how far ahead of his time he was and how far back some of his concepts date.

His first novel *Prelude to Space* was written in 1947—more than 60 years ago and only two years after World War II—and published in 1951. It covers the lead-up to the launch of the first craft to travel to the Moon, a multi-stage device which uses a nuclear-powered mainstage to lift a manned second stage into orbit and beyond; and this at a time when the conventional wisdom was that rocket-powered space flight was an implausible concept. The very next year he wrote a short story, "The Sentinel," which was eventually to become his best-known work, *2001: A Space Odyssey*.

Because of his science background, including work on the British radar project in the war, and the way he incorporated scientific reasoning into his stories, Clarke was considered a pioneer of "hard" science fiction writing. This insists on scientific accuracy to explain the backbone of the plot. The writers of hard SF use a proper understanding of physics, chemistry, and engineering to contain and inform their narratives.

Many of the genre's finest writers, indeed many of the 20th century's most imaginative writers, have contributed to this body of work and have expanded the range of what is scientifically possible in the mind of the general population. Even if the ideas are not yet physically achievable, we have all been prepared for the future to some extent by the work of authors such as Larry Niven, Greg Benford, Ben Bova, Kim Stanley Robinson and even Carl Sagan. Most of these international award-winners are also practising scientists in their own right.

Probably the person best-positioned to progress the visions of the future begun by Clarke is Stephen Baxter, who co-wrote four novels with him. Baxter is also a prolific producer of what is now being called speculative fiction. His best-known work is in the series of books known as the *Xeelee Sequence*, which attempts a future history of mankind for several billion years into the future. Baxter and Clarke were perfectly matched in this regard as Clarke's 1953 novel *Childhood's End* dealt with a similar theme.

A surprise contender in the ratings to keep Clarke's legacy alive is an Australian, Greg Egan. Most Australians would not have heard of him, yet he has won the sci-fi equivalent of the Man Booker prize, the Hugo Award, for his fiction and been nominated several other times. That puts him up there with better-known writers such as Isaac Asimov, J. K. Rowling, Neal Stephenson, Ursula Le Guin and, of course, multiple winner Arthur C. Clarke. Egan is a computer programmer as well as a writer and his broad-ranging interest in science, both present and future, is obvious across the range of his material. For anyone interested, his back catalogue has just been re-released by Gollancz. He is also a proponent of that art form which has all but disappeared from mainstream literature—the short story—so the collections in either *Axiomatic* or *Luminous* offer a smorgasbord of fantastic ideas.

The thing which has changed the most in the past 60 years is the actual science. There is so much more of it these days and its range and complexity has pushed its understanding beyond the capacity of nearly all of us.

We accept the benefits of advances in science and expect to have our consumer products regularly improved or expanded, but have little knowledge of how any of it is done; and certainly few of us have the knowledge or ability to think about the wider ramifications of where the future might take us. For that we need people with the skills and the imagination to translate those visions of the future for us.

Arthur C. Clarke may have left us but there are still some talented people around whose willingness to engage the future uplifts us all.

Source: Ian Barry, "Fictional Future Looking Bright Post Clarke," in *Courier Mail*, July 26, 2008, p. M22.

Gregory Benford

In the following article, Benford memorializes the life of Clarke and the impact he had on science and science fiction.

Lucky prophets become vindicated sages in their own lifetimes. Arthur C. Clarke, who died on March 19, 2008, was the luckiest of men, becoming the most famous of science fiction authors by writing of wonder when many were writing of despair.

Clarke was not unique in his optimism. He stood in a tradition of English futurists who have used fiction, non-fiction, or both to paint their visions: H. G. Wells, J. D. Bernal, Olaf Stapledon, Freeman Dyson. They held that only science makes reliable prediction possible and the prospects for human society intelligible. Clarke believed that general laws for scientific extrapolation exist in a way that they do not in politics or economics. One such law was that "when a distinguished but elderly scientist states that something is possible, he is almost certainly right. When he states that something is impossible, he is very probably wrong."

Clarke, the eldest of four children, was born on December 16, 1917 to farming parents in Minehead in the south-west English county of Somerset. Following service as a radar instructor and technician with the Royal Air Force in the Second World War, he honed his scientific acumen working as an editor for the academic journal *Physics Abstracts,* while earning a first-class degree in mathematics and physics at King's College London.

Humanity's leap into space confirmed Clarke's role as a seer of the possible. In the immediate postwar years, he was twice chairman of the British Interplanetary Society, one of the earliest organizations dedicated to promoting space exploration. Clarke stayed true to the society's motto, "From imagination to reality," when, in 1945, he proposed the use of satellites in geostationary orbits as communications relays. Clarke never patented the idea, but promoted it ceaselessly. Geostationary satellites have since revolutionized communications and weather forecasting, although Clarke's own dry assessment was that "my early disclosure may have advanced the cause of space communications by about fifteen minutes."

In *Profiles of the Future* (1962), his elegantly phrased "Inquiry into the Limits of the Possible," Clarke balanced his scientific knowledge with his creativity to explore more comprehensively what might be achieved within the bounds of scientific laws. Books on futurology date notoriously fast, yet this one has not, perhaps because Clarke was unafraid of being adventurous. And many of his predictions have come to pass: he foresaw that mobile telecommunications would mean that no one could fully escape society, even at sea or on a mountain top. He went on to describe huge electronic libraries, the breakdown of censorship and high-definition electronic screens.

Clarke favored wise hopefulness, but saw dangers as well. His 1946 essay "The Rocket and the Future of Warfare" anticipated the essentials of nuclear war waged with intercontinental ballistic missiles, and called for measures to avoid it. At the time, many were concerned at the prospect of nuclear conflict (the United States proposed international regulation of nuclear weapons, but the Soviet Union refused to be drawn in), but few had foreseen the fateful mating of the bomb and the rocket.

Whether writing fiction or non-fiction, Clarke achieved a unique rendering of the aesthetic that combines the signal qualities of scientific endeavor: intelligence, tenacity, and curiosity. His fiction has few villains, neglecting conflict and the broad spectrum of emotion. For Clarke's purposes these were pointless, even regrettable, diversions. A cool, analytical tone, springing from a pure, dispassionate statement of facts and relationships, pervades his writing. But the result is never cold, and indeed is often aphoristically witty. On religion: "I don't believe in God, but I'm very interested in her." Of space and politics: "There is hopeful symbolism in the fact that flags do not wave in a vacuum." On progress: "New ideas pass through three periods: it can't be done; it probably can be done, but it's not worth doing; I knew it was a good idea all along."

Undoubtedly Clarke's greatest success was his coauthorship, with Stanley Kubrick, of the film and novel *2001: A Space Odyssey.* The film's technological futurism, grounded in hard science, together with its iconic, mystical opening, made it a cultural benchmark and the embodiment of Clarke's assertion that "whatever other perils humanity may face in the future that lies ahead, boredom is not among them." Kubrick observed of Clarke: "He has the kind of mind of which the world can never have enough, an array of imagination, intelligence, knowledge and a quirkish curiosity, which often uncovers more than the first three qualities." Clarke later relished the story of an immigration official threatening to bar his entry to the United States until he had explained the ending of *2001*.

Clarke moved permanently to Sri Lanka in 1956 to pursue one of his life-long passions, scuba diving. He continued to dive even after he was partially confined to a wheelchair in the 1980s: he felt, he said, "perfectly operational underwater." He founded Asia's first diving shop there, and restored the business after the 2004 tsunami. Sri Lanka gave Clarke creative isolation, but he was an early citizen of the global village, traveling and later keeping in touch with friends, colleagues and fans through daily e-mails. Surrounded by tropical cuisine, he never gave up his taste for a steady diet of English food, roast beef and Yorkshire pudding being favorites.

His home in Sri Lanka contained a room he called the Ego Chamber. Amid the many awards stored there is a tribute from Apollo 11 astronaut Neil Armstrong that epitomizes Clarke's peculiar contribution to science: "To Arthur— who visualized the nuances of lunar flying before I experienced them."

Up to the last, Clarke viewed humanity's ability to further expand its realm of experience, and so survive and prosper, with signature wry confidence. As he told a convention of the European Mars Society in 2002 by video-link from Sri Lanka: "Whether we become a multi-planet species with unlimited horizons, or are forever confined to Earth, will be decided in the twenty-first century amid the vast plains, rugged canyons and lofty mountains of Mars."

Source: Gregory Benford, "Arthur C. Clarke (1917–2008): Visionary Science-Fiction Author," in *Skeptic*, Vol. 14, No. 2, 2008, pp. 11–12.

M. Candelaria

In the following excerpt, Candelaria writes about imperialism in regard to science fiction and how Clarke's stories focus on the journey to imperial metropolises.

The exploration of space, encounters with alien beings, and the establishment of interstellar human empires are some of the most recognizable tropes of science-fiction. Since most science fiction using these tropes also draws, explicitly or implicitly, on historical models of exploration, conquest, and empire-building, it must be asked whether this fiction represents a glorification of historical imperialism. Nor is this an idle question, for Edward Said's definition of imperialism clearly encompasses this type of imaginative conquest: "Imperialism means thinking about, settling on, controlling land that you do not possess, that is distant, that is lived on and owned by others" (7). While Said does not explicitly include imaginative lands in his formulation, science-fictional territories, whether intra- or extra-solar, must be included in the "distant" lands category. If "we must try to look carefully and integrally at the culture that nurtured the sentiment, rationale, and above all the imagination of empire" (12), then such an analysis must be faulty if it excludes an entire segment of imaginative production. Furthermore, a deeper analysis of Said's definitions of imperialism implies a crucial role for this type of imaginative conquest. Said stresses that imperialism allowed "decent people [to] think of the imperium as a protracted, almost metaphysical obligation to rule subordinate, inferior, or less advanced peoples" (10). Abdul JanMohamed extends this, saying that imperialist discourse seeks to create a practice that "can continue indefinitely" (81). By portraying empires of great spatial and temporal extent, science fiction creates a sequence of futures whose implicit final term is an infinite and eternal empire.

But are all science-fiction texts that utilize these tropes of interstellar exploration and conquest glorifying imperialism? And if not, how can these texts be distinguished? Looking at another definition of imperialism by Said gives us a vital clue: "Imperialism means the practice, the theory, and the attitudes of a dominating metropolitan center ruling a distant territory" (9). Since imperialism resides in the attitudes and practices of the imperial center, the imperial metropolis, gauging the attitudes of a text toward that imperial metropolis it portrays should be an effective shorthand method for determining the text's attitudes toward imperialism. This article will provide a brief definition of "imperial metropolis," then apply that definition to texts by two SF Grandmasters, Isaac Asimov and Sir Arthur C. Clarke, to demonstrate how the imperial metropolis unlocks the attitudes toward imperialism of these two authors. Then two contemporary popular SF series, *Star Wars* and *Star Trek* are analyzed to demonstrate how they follow the patterns established by the Grandmasters.

During the heyday of European imperialism, the late nineteenth and early twentieth centuries, European influence, both in the form of military strength and exported capital, extended to the far reaches of the globe. In return, goods, services, and people from these far reaches came to Europe to trade in, be educated in, or simply to gawk at the grandeur of the great imperial centers, chiefly London, Paris, and, later, New York. With the great advances in science and technology during the Industrial Era, these cities became not merely administrative centers, but also icons of advancement and sophistication. These cities ostentatiously embraced their iconic identities with industrial landmarks such as the Crystal Palace and the Eiffel Tower. The creation of these imperial centers, these imperial metropolises, also created, by implication, the imperial margin or periphery. Over the imperial period, the ideas associated with the center and the margin were ossified into almost mythic status by the theorists and practitioners of imperialism. The center became not only a place where science was practiced and applied, but became a temple of science itself. It became not merely a civilized city, but the embodiment of civilization itself. It became not merely a commercial hub, but a commercial star, holding the world in orbit with its mass of capital. Thus, the imperial metropolis came to represent—in its own eyes—all civilization, all science, all commerce, while the periphery became the embodiment of savagery, primitivism, and lawlessness.

When science fiction authors were creating and refining the genre, they built their conceptions of the future on what they knew of the past. Empires of the future were almost uniformly reflections of imperial pasts, but not all authors promote the imperial metropolis' traditional view of itself. Some invert this view with an aim at completely undermining imperialist ideologies....

In direct opposition to Asimov's goals, procedures, and ideals is Sir Arthur C. Clarke, who builds his novels not around a movement away from and subversion of, but, rather around a journey toward and the ultimate reification of the imperial metropolis. Richard D. Erlich notes in contrasting Clarke with Ursula Le Guin:

"[Clarke] has presented worlds in which transcendence is possible and can lead to true superiority: a universe in which masters may justify their status as part of the Order of Things" (122). Clarke builds this superiority into an imperial structure, with centers of sophistication and peripheries of barbarity. In *The Empire Writes Back,* Ashcroft, Griffith, and Tiffin stress the symbolic ties between standardized language and lawfulness: "the center, the metropolitan source of standard language, stands as the focus of order, while the periphery, which utilizes the variants... remains a tissue of disorder" (88). Clarke repeats this pattern, although he emphasizes science rather than language, and stresses that beings with high technology have an equally high sense of peace and order. While this pattern is evident in most of Clarke's work, I will use as examples only three of Clarke's most influential and well-known works: *Childhood's End, 2001: A Space Odyssey,* and *Rendezvous with Rama.* In all these works, Clarke emphasizes the disparity between the colonial center and the colonial margin through a journey from the margin to the center. In the imperial metropolis, people from the periphery experience uncomprehending awe, which leaves the reader with a deeply-imbedded sense of the superiority of the imperial power....

Because imperialism is not just a single idea, but a cluster of related ideas including attitudes toward science, morality, race, military power, and ultimate truth, determining a text's relationship to imperialism is an important step toward decoding that text. Identifying and understanding the imperial metropolis within the text is a shorthand method for deciphering imperialist attitudes and is therefore a concept that warrants closer scrutiny and development.

Source: M. Candelaria, "The Colonial Metropolis in the Work of Asimov and Clarke," in *Journal of American & Comparative Cultures,* Vol. 25, No. 3 and 4, Fall 2002, pp. 427–32.

SOURCES

Arthur C. Clarke's Mysterious World, DVD, directed by Charles Flynn and Peter Jones (1980; Granada, 2008).

Brigg, Peter, "Three Styles of Arthur C. Clarke: The Projector, the Wit, and the Mystic," in *Arthur C. Clarke,* edited by Joseph D. Olander and Martin Harry Greenberg, Taplinger, 1977, pp. 15–51.

Burgess, Anthony, *A Clockwork Orange,* W. W. Norton, 1962, pp.14–18.

Burgess, Colin, and Chris Dubbs, *Animals in Space: From Research Rockets to the Space Shuttle*, Springer Verlag, 2007, pp. 61–84, 143–68.

California Department of Justice, "California and FBI Crime Index, 2001," in *Criminal Justice Statistics Center*, http://stats.doj.ca.gov/cjsc_stats/prof01/01/11.pdf (accessed Sept. 13, 2009).

Clarke, Arthur C., *Childhood's End*, Ballantine, 1953.

———, *The Deep Range*, Harcourt Brace, 1957.

———, "Dog Star," in *The Nine Billion Names of God: The Best Short Stories of Arthur C. Clarke*, Harcourt Brace & World, 1967, pp. 78–84.

———, *The Exploration of Space*, Harper, 1951.

———, *The Fountains of Paradise*, Harcourt Brace, 1979.

———, *Glide Path*, Harcourt Brace, 1963.

———, *Interplanetary Flight*, Harper, 1951.

———, *The Lost Worlds of 2001*, New American Library, 1972.

———, *Profiles of the Future: An Enquiry into the Limits of the Possible*, Gollancz, 1962.

———, *Rendezvous with Rama*, Harcourt Brace, 1979.

———, *2001: A Space Odyssey*, New American Library, 1968.

Dick, Philip K., unpublished foreword to *The Preserving Machine*, in *Science Fiction Studies*, Vol. 2, Part 1, March 1975, pp. 22–23, http://www.depauw.edu/sfs/backissues/5/dick5art.htm (accessed September 22, 2009).

Fort, Charles, *The Book of the Damned*, Boni and Liveright, 1919, http://books.google.com/books?id=lW1HAAAAIAAJ&source=gbs_navlinks_s (accessed September 22, 2009).

Koestler, Arthur, *The Sleepwalkers*, Macmillan, 1968.

Kuhn, Thomas S., *The Structure of Scientific Revolutions*, University of Chicago Press, 1970.

McAleer, Neil, *Arthur C. Clarke: The Authorized Biography*, Contemporary Books, 1992, p. 181.

Schefter, James, *The Race: The Uncensored History of How America Beat Russia to the Moon*, Doubleday, 1990.

Shippey, Thomas A., *J. R. R. Tolkien: Author of the Century*, Houghton Mifflin, 2001, pp. vii–xxxv.

Welfare, Simon, and John Fairley, *Arthur C. Clarke's Mysterious World*, A & W, 1980.

FURTHER READING

Clarke, Arthur C., *Prelude to Space*, Sidgwick & Jackson, 1953.

> Clarke's first novel deals with the preparation for a two-part spacecraft—in many ways reminiscent of the space shuttle—designed for the first manned flight to the moon. Having explained all the technical problems encountered in such a voyage and the ways they might be overcome through technology available in the early 1950s, Clarke ends his narrative without actually seeing the space flight through to completion.

Heinlein, Robert, *The Man Who Sold the Moon*, Shasta, 1950.

> This frequently reprinted short novel was the first science fiction effort to realistically depict the process of scientific research, industrial development, and long-term planning involved in launching a space program capable of sending a man to the moon in the near future. It is the basis of the Academy Award-winning 1950 film *Destination Moon*.

Hollow, John, *Against the Night, the Stars: The Science Fiction of Arthur C. Clarke*, Ohio University Press, 1987.

> This is one of the few general academic treatments of Clarke. Hollow uses Clarke's writings as a chronological guide to his themes and symbolism.

Siddiqi, Asif A., *The Soviet Space Race with Apollo*, University Press of Florida, 2003.

> Originally published in 2000 under the title *Challenge to Apollo*, this is a comprehensive history of the Soviet manned space program.

The Doll's House

KATHERINE MANSFIELD
1922

Katherine Mansfield's short story "The Doll's House" shows how rigid social values and class consciousness are handed down from one generation to another. The story takes place in a suburb of Wellington, New Zealand, where the three Burnell sisters receive an extravagant doll's house from one of their parents' wealthy friends. When they start bringing other girls home from school to view this magnificent new toy, jealousies and rivalries arise, as friends compete to prove who is closer to these sudden celebrities. The poorest children at the school, the Kelvey sisters, find themselves excluded from the social circle that forms around the doll's house. Girls mock them in order to raise their own status, and Mrs. Burnell forbids her daughters to allow such low-class people into the yard. The littlest innocent Burnell, Kezia, defies her family by inviting the Kelveys over to look at the doll's house, but their visit opens them up to further abuse and humiliation.

The story is written with Mansfield's characteristic precision, with fully realized characters inhabiting a carefully rendered world. Modern readers will find very little difference between the rules of social exclusion in suburban New Zealand in the 1920s and the same situation anywhere in the world today.

"The Doll's House" is one of the last stories written by Katherine Mansfield before she died at the age of thirty-four in 1923. It was first

Katherine Mansfield (Topical Press Agency | Hulton Archive | Getty Images)

published in *Athenaeum* on February 4, 1922, and then was included in the collection *The Dove's Nest and Other Stories*, published soon after her death in 1923. It is also available in *The Collected Stories of Katherine Mansfield*, published in 2006.

AUTHOR BIOGRAPHY

Mansfield was born Kathleen Mansfield Beauchamp on October 14, 1888, in Wellington, the capital of New Zealand. Her father, Harold Beauchamp, was a clerk for an importing firm though he worked his way up over the coming years from one position to the next: he became a partner in the business in 1889, a director of the Bank of New Zealand in 1898, and the chairman of the bank in 1907. Her mother, Annie Burnell Dyer Beauchamp, was constantly ill, having been weakened by rheumatic fever when she was in her teens. She stayed at home and watched over Katherine and her five siblings, of whom only three survived childhood. In 1893, the family moved to Karori, a suburb of Wellington. Their house there, called "Chesney Wold," was the model for the house in which "The Doll's House" takes place. The family moved back to Wellington in 1898, to a large, spacious house with rolling gardens. Katherine attended Wellington Girls' High School in 1898–1899. It was during this time that her first stories were published in the *High School Reporter*. In 1900 she attended Miss Swainson's private school, where she founded a small magazine. She attended Queen's College in London from 1903 to 1906, studying cello at first but being drawn into writing. She traveled throughout Europe while at Queen's and returned to New Zealand after graduation. During this period she had several affairs with other girls she met at school.

Back in her native country, she began publishing under her pen name, Katherine Mansfield. She became pregnant by Garnet Trowell, who was the son of her former cello teacher. In 1909 she married George Bowden, a singing teacher she had known for three weeks, but left him the day after the wedding to travel with a light-opera company. She soon had a miscarriage. In 1910 she returned to London and lived briefly with Bowden before meeting John Middleton Murry, with whom she fell in love and whom she eventually married in 1918, when her divorce from Bowden became final. While in London, she and Murry edited the magazines *Rhythm* and its successor, *Blue Review*, which published her works. She also wrote reviews for *Athenaeum*, an old, established literary magazine that Murry edited. She met and socialized with many important writers of the time, including D. H. Lawrence, Lytton Strachey, George Bernard Shaw, Bertrand Russell, and Virginia Woolf, who became a close friend.

Having contracted tuberculosis in 1917, she traveled the world seeking treatments, ending up at the Institute for the Harmonious Development of Man at Avon near Fontainebleau, outside Paris, where she died of a hemorrhage on January 9, 1923.

PLOT SUMMARY

"The Doll's House" begins when an elaborate doll's house is delivered to the home of the

MEDIA ADAPTATIONS

- A seventeen-minute video adaptation of "The Doll's House" was produced and distributed by SLEP in 1968.

- Hayward Historical Film Trust of Auckland, New Zealand, produced a motion picture in 1973 titled *Katherine Mansfield's "The Doll's House" in the Author's Own Words*. Directed by Rudall Hayward, it was released on videocassette by Hayward Film Productions in 1994.

- This story is included in an unabridged audiocassette of *The Short Stories of Katherine Mansfield*, read by Rosemary Harris. Spoken Arts of Greenwich, Connecticut, released this recording in 1988.

- An audiocassette recording of *The Doll's House, and Other Stories* was released in 1999 by Pearson Education. Ann Ward did the reading.

Burnell family. It is a gift from Mrs. Hay, who has been staying with them for a while in their house out in the suburbs but has recently returned to the city. The doll's house is massive, so big that the delivery man needs the help of the Burnells' handyman to carry it into the yard. It is left in the yard because it is newly painted, and Aunt Beryl, who lives in the house, finds the smell of its paint offensive. She hopes that the odor will dissipate by the end of the summer.

The doll's house is amazing to all who see it because it accurately reproduces a real house in miniature, including such fine details as chimneys, window panes, wallpaper, umbrellas, and plates on the table. Kezia, one of the Burnell daughters, finds the lamp on the dining room table to be the most interesting aspect. The dolls that are included with the house seem too big to live in a house like this, but Kezia and the other children are enchanted with the details of the doll's house.

The three Burnell girls—Isabel, Lottie, and Kezia—are excited about their new doll's house, and they want to bring friends from school home to see it. Their mother, however, is concerned that having too many girls come through the house might create too much trouble, so she puts limitations on the visitors; only two guests can come over at a time, and they are not allowed into the house. Isabel, as the oldest Burnell, is allowed first choice of which friends to invite. The girls are anxious, but they arrive at school just in time for classes. Later, at recess, Isabel is able to gather the girls around her and describe the house to them. All of the girls gather and are impressed. They are so enthusiastic about taking their turns to go to the Burnell house that they compete to show each other who is a better friend to Isabel. Outside of the group, off to the side, stand the Kelvey sisters.

Lil and Else Kelvey come from a poor family. In general, the families where they live are wealthy, but the school district serves a wide geographical area, and families from the poor areas on the outskirts of town send their children there as well. The Kelveys' mother does laundry for some of the families of Lil and Else's schoolmates, and no one even knows where their father is, although rumors abound that he is in jail. The girls dress in hand-me-down clothes and in strange garments sewn together from things the rich households gave to their mother. Most of the poor children at the school are accepted by the students and their families, but the Kelveys are not. As the Burnell girls stand at the center of attention, choosing which girls to invite to their home to see the doll's house, the Kelvey sisters are not even considered.

Over the course of weeks, all of the girls from school except the Kelvey girls go to view the doll's house. Kezia asks her mother if she may invite the Kelveys to see it, but her mother adamantly refuses. She will not say why she will not let them come to the house, but she assumes that Kezia understands the social rules that prohibit such a visit. At school, the other children become aware of the Kelveys' social situation when they see them excluded from viewing the doll's house. At first, they talk rudely about the Kelvey sisters among themselves, but in time they are emboldened to risk offending them. To show off to the other girls, Lena Logan walks over to Lil Kelvey and asks if she plans to be a servant when she grows up, which makes the other girls laugh maliciously. Their laughing makes Lena turn even meaner, and she shouts out pointedly that the Kelveys' father is in prison. The other girls are delighted to see the Kelveys humiliated.

That afternoon, Pat, the handyman, picks up the girls in the buggy, and when they arrive home, they find that there are visitors. The older two girls run upstairs to change into their good clothes, but Kezia goes out into the yard by herself, feeling estranged from her family. When she sees the Kelvey sisters walking along the road, she climbs up on the gate and calls out to them, inviting them into the yard to take a look at the doll's house. Lil Kelvey knows that Kezia's mother has forbidden them from entering the yard, and so she is hesitant to enter, but Kezia tells her that no one will see them. Else tugs on Lil's skirt to show that she would like to see it very much.

The three girls stand before the doll's house. Kezia opens it and just as she starts to show the Kelveys the inside, her Aunt Beryl notices them from inside the house and calls out angrily, telling the Kelvey girls to leave their yard and never come back, chasing them away "as if they were chickens." She yells at Kezia and slams the doll's house shut. Scolding Kezia and shouting at the lower-class Kelvey girls makes her feel good.

The Kelvey sisters walk away from the Burnell house. Lil is humiliated by the things that Aunt Beryl has called her. After the two girls sit quietly for a brief while, Else, who has not spoken up to this point in the story, tells her sister, smiling with pride, that she did, in fact manage to catch a view of the little lamp that was the object of Kezia's attention.

CHARACTERS

Aunt Beryl

Aunt Beryl is a self-centered woman who imagines herself to be sensitive, even though she is callous about the feelings of others. When the doll's house is delivered to the Burnell home, it is Aunt Beryl who insists that it should be kept outside because she finds the fumes of its recent paint job so powerful that they make her feel sick. At the end of the story, she is in a terrible mood because a man named Willie Brent, with whom it would shame Aunt Beryl to be associated, has written to say he wants to meet with her. Brent's letter has threatened to confront Aunt Beryl publicly at her house if she does not comply, angering her. Her mood picks up when she sees the Kelvey children in the back yard. She races out into the yard and tells them to leave, and she yells at her niece Kezia, who invited them to look at the doll's house. She is proud of her rage.

Isabel Burnell

As the oldest of the Burnell daughters, Isabel is a reflection of the kind of social hierarchy that rules the society in which they live. Her age gives her privileges over her sisters. When their mother limits the number of schoolmates the girls can bring home to see the doll's house, Isabel is allowed to choose which friends to invite first. Because the other girls at school are interested in seeing the doll's house, they compete to be her friend. Their competition makes Isabel snobbish. When she hears the other children mocking the Kelvey girls, she goes along with the mockery, and this makes Lena Logan approach the Kelveys with outright cruelty, which delights Isabel and her friends.

Kezia Burnell

Kezia is the youngest of the Burnell sisters, and the one who is most inclined toward empathy and fanciful imagination. It is Kezia who finds the little lamp in the doll's house fascinating. She thinks that it makes the doll's house look as if it is lived in, even though the dolls who come with the house do not seem as if they belong. While her older sister Isabel tells the other girls at school about the doll's house, Kezia tries to interject her thoughts about the lamp, but she is ignored, unable to take any of the attention away from Isabel. Later, after all of the other girls from the school have come to view the doll's house, Kezia approaches her mother and asks if she can invite the Kelvey sisters, but her mother is adamant that they cannot be invited to the house, telling Kezia that she should know why it would be wrong. Kezia does not appear to agree with her mother's position, however. On the afternoon that the Kelvey sisters are mocked at school by Lena Logan and the rest of the girls, Kezia wanders away from the rest of the family, into the back yard. Seeing the Kelvey sisters, she invites them into the yard, through the gate, in direct defiance of her mother's command. She even overcomes their hesitation by telling them that no one will see them. Bringing them to the doll's house, Kezia crouches down and is about to share the things about it that she finds wonderful, but her aunt comes, chases the Kelveys away, and chastises Kezia. She never finds out, as readers do later, that Else Kelvey did in fact listen to her on the playground, because she was looking for the lamp that Kezia found so enchanting.

Lottie Burnell

Lottie is the middle Burnell sister, younger than Isabel and older than Kezia. She lives in Isabel's shadow, forced to wait before inviting friends home to look at the doll's house until Isabel is finished inviting all of her friends over.

Mrs. Burnell

The mother of Isabel, Lottie, and Kezia is a very class-conscious woman. She is the one who makes the rule forbidding her daughters from bringing home more than two girls at a time and refusing to let any of the girls come into the house. Lil Kelvey knows that she is not allowed to come to the Burnell house because Mrs. Burnell talked to her mother, setting down this rule. When Kezia directly asks if she can have the Kelvey girls over to look at the doll's house, Mrs. Burnell is adamant in her refusal, assuming that her daughter understands why she would be so horrified at such a prospect.

Emmie Cole

Emmie Cole is one of Isabel's friends. She is one of the two girls chosen to be the first ones allowed to come to the Burnell house to look at the doll's house.

Mrs. Hay

Mrs. Hay reflects the kind of wealthy, sophisticated people with whom the Burnell family associates. She is only mentioned in the first few lines of the story. She has been a guest at the Burnell house, and the story begins just after she has left. She sends the family the doll's house mentioned in the title, as a thank-you gift for their having hosted her.

Else Kelvey

Else is the younger Kelvey sister. She is tiny and slim, the opposite of her sister, with large eyes that are described as looking like an owl's. She follows her older sister, Lil, everywhere she goes, holding onto the hem of Lil's skirt so that she does not become lost. Else does not speak aloud, but instead she tugs on Lil's skirt, and whatever is on her mind is simply understood.

Else does not react when the other girls tease the Kelveys. She seems to have no opinions until Kezia invites the sisters into the Burnell yard to look at the doll's house; then, she is insistent about going in to look at it, even after Lil points out that Mrs. Burnell told their mother to keep Lil and Else away. At Else's insistence, Lil leads her in, but they only manage to get a quick glimpse of the inside of the doll's house before they are chased from the yard by Aunt Beryl. Having been chastised by a stranger, the two sisters sit dejected until Else speaks for the first time in the story, telling her sister that she saw the tiny lamp. Although she is quiet, she does pay attention, having heard Kezia talk about the little lamp while all of the other children paid no attention. Her declaration about seeing the lamp shows some small measure of triumph, even though Aunt Beryl has done her best to belittle Else and her sister.

Lil Kelvey

Lil is the elder of the two Kelvey sisters, the one who is aware of the burden of being low on the social hierarchy. She is large and plain looking, and her mother dresses her conspicuously, with a dress cut from material the Burnells gave her mother and a woman's hat that once belonged to the postmistress. Her little sister, Else, follows her everywhere, holding onto her skirt. The two sisters are shunned by the other children at the school, but they have a special bond, so that Lil understands Else's needs and wants even when nothing is said aloud. Lil is good natured about accepting the teasing of her classmates. When Lena Logan asks if she plans to be a servant when she grows up, Lil only smiles, though she is ashamed.

When Kezia invites Lil and her sister into the Burnell yard, Lil is conflicted. She is curious about the doll's house, but she knows that Mrs. Burnell has forbidden them from entering the yard. She goes in because her little sister urges her to do so, and almost immediately, Aunt Beryl runs from the house, chasing them away, talking to them cruelly. Later, when they are out of sight of the Burnell home, Lil sits quietly, blushing with humiliation. Her sister talks to her and is answered with silence.

Lena Logan

Of all of the girls who compete to show Isabel that they are her friends, Lena Logan is the most aggressive. When the conversation among the popular girls turns to the awfulness of the Kelvey sisters' lives, Isabel is shocked, which Lena takes as a cue to taunt them. Goaded by Jesse May, she becomes wrapped up in the attention given her. She starts by just asking an impolite question and, seeing that Lil Kelvey is embarrassed, shouts insults about their father directly at them. Her cruelty is rewarded when all of the girls jump rope euphorically, thrilled at the nerve that Lena has shown.

Jessie May
Jessie May is one of the girls who competes to be Isabel's best friend when she talks about letting her friends see the new doll's house. She is not brash enough to openly insult the unpopular Kelvey sisters, but she does bet Lena Logan that she is not brave enough to insult them to their faces, and her goading is enough to set Lena after them.

Pat
Pat is the family's handyman. He helps the deliveryman carry the doll's house into the Burnells' yard and he pries it open when it is stuck. Later in the story, he is sent to pick up the Burnell sisters at school and bring them home.

THEMES

Class Conflict
The town that is depicted in "The Doll's House" is clearly one with a range of different social classes, as Mansfield explains in the fourteenth paragraph. This explains why people of different classes are attending the same school. For examples of the different economic levels represented here, she mentions judges and doctors, storekeepers and milkmen. Readers know that the Burnell family is very wealthy from the start because their guest, Mrs. Hay, is obviously affluent enough to send an extravagant gift like this massive doll's house, while Aunt Beryl is so comfortable in her position that she takes a condescending attitude toward "sweet old Mrs. Hay" and finds fault with the handcrafted toy. When the Burnell daughters want to bring their schoolmates home to see the doll's house, Mrs. Burnell sets down rules that show her belief that the children at the school are of a lower class than her children. She will not allow them to come to tea or even to enter the house.

At the bottom of this scale is the Kelvey family. Mrs. Kelvey does laundry for other families, which was about the lowest-paying and least prestigious position there was at the turn of the twentieth century. Mr. Kelvey's whereabouts are unknown. He could be gone for some good reason, but the neighbors assume the worst and tell each other that he is in jail, which would be a powerful mark of shame for the Kelvey family.

The poor, lower-class Kelveys are not only looked down on by the Burnells, they are actively shunned. Mrs. Burnell explicitly tells her children that the Kelvey girls are not to be included with the children who are invited to see the doll's house. Later, when all of the other girls have seen it, Kezia asks again, to see if her mother has changed her mind, but Mrs. Burnell responds as if the question is ridiculous. Later, when Aunt Beryl chases the Kelvey girls out of the yard, her bad mood lightens, indicating that being rude to lower-class people is actually pleasurable to those who hold higher social status.

Conformity
One of the most powerful phenomena explored in this story is the way that people, especially children, find themselves swept by social trends into behaving terribly. The story starts with an act of kindness, when Mrs. Hay sends a gift to the Burnell children that she thinks they will enjoy. They are not allowed to enjoy the doll's house indoors because their Aunt Beryl thinks that it reeks of paint, which is a sign that she finds it to be cheap or inferior. The girls decide that they would like to show the house to their friends, but their mother puts a restriction on how many friends may visit the Burnell house at once. Because the invitations are limited, they become valuable, and the girls at the school begin competing for the affection of Isabel Burnell, who, finding herself the center of attention, encourages their competition.

The competition for Isabel's attention—to be able to become one of the first to view the doll's house—leads to cruelty, as Lena Logan, at Jessie May's urging, crosses the school yard to taunt the Kelvey sisters. Lena's behavior becomes progressively worse. First, she hides her insult inside a question, as if she is actually curious about Lil Kelvey's intentions for when she grows up. After a while, though, emboldened by the laughs from the popular girls, she shouts out an insult about the Kelveys' father with no regard for their feelings whatsoever. Her aggression creates a bond between all of the girls in Isabel's social group, who go about their play

TOPICS FOR FURTHER STUDY

- With a group of other students, hold a discussion about particularly outstanding toys that you had in childhood. Try to come up with at least one insight about the person who gave it to you and explain it to your classmates.
- How do families like the Kelveys survive in your community? Use the Internet to find job statistics to determine how much Mrs. Kelvey would make doing laundry, and where her salary falls in with the government's poverty standards. Then, search for at least three social agencies (federal, state, local, or private) that could help them financially and prepare a PowerPoint presentation on what they could do for this family of three.
- One reason critics assume that Katherine Mansfield was so conscious of class decisions was because of the way the indigenous Maori people of New Zealand were treated by Europeans. Research the Maori, and create a Venn diagram showing the similarities between them and the native people who once lived where you live now.
- The Kelveys have jam sandwiches for lunch, while the other girls eat mutton. Plan the kinds of dinners you might expect a poor family to eat today as opposed to a rich family's dinner. Research the relative nutrition content of the two meals and list them. Write a report about how nutrition relates to finance.
- In the story, Aunt Beryl is upset about the letter that she received from Willie Brent, though the narrator does not say why. Write the letter from Willie Brent to Aunt Beryl insisting that she come to meet him.
- Imagine how things would have been different if the doll's house had been given to the poor Kelveys instead of to the rich Burnells. Would they have sold it out of need? Would it have made them popular with the other girls? Rewrite the story of "The Doll's House" with this one significant change.
- Read award-winning English author Rumer Godden's young-adult novel *The Dolls' House*. In this book the dolls themselves cause the tension. Write an essay that compares the themes of both books with similar names.

---

filled with joy. Their group finds cohesion in excluding the Kelveys, with the dangerous thrill of doing something so socially offensive giving the girls something in common.

Moral Ambiguity

The central character in this story is Kezia, the youngest Burnell daughter. She is presented as the sort of wide-eyed innocent who can appreciate the doll's house as a toy. It spurs her imagination as she thinks of who might live there and what their lives might be like. To her, the imaginary world of the house is so real to Kezia that she can tell what fits in it and what does not. The lamp, she decides, is perfect for it, while the doll family that comes with the house is not at all appropriate.

Enchanted as she is with the imaginary world of the doll's house, Kezia does not understand the complexities of class consciousness. While her sister Isabel uses the doll's house to improve her social status, Kezia just thinks of it as a wonder to be shared. That is why she does not understand why her mother will not allow her to bring the Kelvey sisters into the yard to see it. When she asks if they can come over, her mother tells her that she knows why they cannot, but she does not. She does not understand social exclusion.

This unclear moral situation obviously affects Kezia, even if she does not say so. When the Burnell daughters come home to be presented to visitors, she wanders away from the family, into the yard. It is there that a rebellious streak

A doll house (Image copyright Morgan Lane Photography, 2009. Used under license from Shutterstock.com)

develops; she sees the Kelveys walking up the street and invites them in, directly contradicting her mother's orders. She tries to calm her divided loyalty by keeping the Kelveys' visit a secret, but she is found out by Aunt Beryl and scolded. In the end, though, Kezia's gesture does prove to be worthwhile, as young Else Kelvey takes some pride in having seen the lamp and is just as enchanted with it as Kezia is. There is a common bond between the youngest daughters of both families that softens the harshness of social exclusion.

STYLE

Omniscient Narrator

"The Doll's House" is told from a third-person point of view. The narrator is not a character within the story, one who would speak of herself or himself as "I" or "me," but is instead an outside observer, reporting on all of the characters as "he" or "she." Frequently, third-person narrators will limit themselves to conveying the thoughts and impressions of just one character, viewing the action of the story from a single perspective. In this story, however, the narrative perspective changes often. Readers are told what Aunt Beryl, the Burnell sisters, and the Kelvey sisters are thinking. Sometimes the narration does not go into the characters' minds, however, instead conveying what they think by offering precise, detailed descriptions of their actions.

The narrator's omniscient point of view is not entirely consistent, however. Else Kelvey is consistently referred to as "our Else." This nearly brings the narrator into the story, creating a character who has a relationship to Else and the other characters. Aside from this one linguistic twist, there are no other clues of the narrator's personality. The use of the word "our" is alone in establishing the narrator as a character, while the rest of the narration is from the omniscient point of view.

Symbolism

Mansfield uses the lamp in the doll's house as a symbol. It clearly means something to Kezia Burnell. Though that meaning is not directly explained, readers can tell from Kezia's association of the lamp with a smile and the phrase "I live here" that the lamp's significance has something to do with an unfulfilled need to belong. Like most symbols in literature, its precise meaning is open to interpretation, so that different readers will understand it differently. At the end of the story, the importance that Kezia places on the lamp is shared by Else Kelvey. Else is proud that, in spite of being treated badly by the Burnells' Aunt Beryl, she has managed to sneak a look at the lamp. The story does not say what the lamp means to Else or even hint at whether its meaning is the same for her as it is for Kezia, but Else does share Kezia's enthusiasm for it, so it clearly means something to her.

HISTORICAL CONTEXT

New Zealand History

This story takes place in Karori, which is on the outskirts of Wellington, the capital of New Zealand. At the time the action takes place, New Zealand was in its postcolonial phase. The country colonized relatively late. The first Europeans to arrive were the Dutch, in 1642, but the country remained open to sailors from around the globe, who settled there and traded freely with the indigenous Maori tribesmen. In 1840, the British signed a treaty that made the country a protectorate of the United Kingdom. A constitution granting self-government rule was ratified by the United Kingdom in 1854 and came into effect in 1856. Though independently ruled, the country maintained a strong relationship with Great Britain and relied almost entirely on it for economic trade. During the Boer War (1899–1902) and World War I (1914–1918), New Zealand fought on the side of the United Kingdom. It also has a strong relationship with Australia, which is its closest neighboring country and another member of the Commonwealth of Nations.

The unbalanced social situation presented in "The Doll's House" mirrors one of the greatest conflicts in New Zealand at the turn of the twentieth century, an issue that Mansfield wrote passionately about throughout her lifetime: the treatment of the indigenous Maoris by the Europeans who settled on their shores and laid claim to their land. New laws that were passed in the early 1890s made it easier to build on land that had been ceded to the Maori, leading to claims of ownership or of the right to purchase the land. Banks refused to lend money to Maori citizens to develop their land, giving the Europeans a financial advantage. The Maori began a unity movement, Kotahitanga, comprised of indigenous tribes that supported candidates for Parliament, giving support to several Maori political parties. Despite the struggle, the native people of New Zealand suffered under distinct social and political disadvantages, and the political system was arranged to encourage more Europeans to come to the country, which only served to further the disadvantages of the Maori. Many of European descent were aware that their fortunes were built upon the repression of the Maori, and they supported them in their struggles for social equality.

Modernism

Although Mansfield is not one of the first names to come up when the subject is discussed, her writing is considered to be a clear example of modernism, an artistic movement that began in the early decades of the twentieth century. Modernism is a complex generalization that critics use to describe a great change that occurred in the arts at that time. As with most literary movements, there is no clear consensus about when it began or ended. It is generally viewed in terms of what it is not and is defined as a rebellion against the artistic traditions of the nineteenth century. As the new century dawned, artists responded to the changes in the world around them, from industrialization to widespread electrification to the advent of the automobile to innovations in architecture that gave builders the ability to turn cities into series of tunnels, blocking out the sky. One common theme that progress brought was a sense of alienation that made artists look at people as separated from nature and, in a sense, separated from reality.

In poetry, modernism manifested itself most clearly with free verse. Writers like Ezra Pound, William Carlos Williams, and T. S. Eliot created poems that trained their readers' focus on the words rather than on the form. In fiction, writers like James Joyce and Virginia Woolf ignored traditional expectations about plot and character and tried to convey for readers a heightened sensory experience. To its detractors, modernist writing often seemed pointless as well as formless, but the new styles brought into literature through modernism affected mainstream writers from Ernest Hemingway to Hart Crane. By the 1920s, modernism was no longer a reaction against the mainstream: instead, it was the

COMPARE & CONTRAST

- **1922:** A gift of an ornate doll's house is one of the most elaborate playthings that someone could give to a child.

  Today: Children are sophisticated, as are their playthings. Electronic gaming systems and computers are more entertaining and expensive than motionless objects to some children.

- **1922:** It is not uncommon for a wealthy family like the Burnells to have unmarried aunts living with them.

  Today: Extended families under the same roof are usually a sign of economic need. It is rare that a woman who can afford her own place would not prefer to live alone.

- **1922:** A school district that mixes poor children with wealthy children is a source of disappointment to elitist parents who would like their children kept apart.

  Today: The United States has made a point of actively integrating schools, in spite of protests from parents who fear that mixing children of different races and economic status creates social chaos.

- **1922:** Many wealthy households employ servants, such as maids, butlers, housekeepers, and gardeners.

  Today: It is very rare for a family to have maids or butlers. Much domestic work is provided by paid contracted laborers, such as housecleaning and gardening contractors.

- **1922:** Children from impoverished backgrounds are openly treated differently, even by their teachers.

  Today: Prevailing attitudes have changed, so that people tend to recognize social intolerance as being mean spirited.

- **1922:** New Zealand is a distant dominion of the British Empire. The few travel books about it are written from the perspective of wealthy Europeans.

  Today: The Internet allows students anywhere in the world to read a variety of perspectives on New Zealand, or to chat with other students there about what their lives are like.

---

mainstream in art, eventually to be supplanted sometime around the 1950s by the even more theoretically abstract postmodernist movement.

CRITICAL OVERVIEW

Mansfield had a relatively short literary career, dying at the age of thirty-four, but even in her lifetime her writing was recognized for its excellence. In a review of *The Dove's Nest and Other Stories*, the collection that contained "The Doll's House" and was first published in the year she died, Raymond Mortimer praised Mansfield's ability to empathize with her characters. "Few writers have better described the unorganised flow of thoughts and feelings that continually move through the different layers of human consciousness," he wrote in the *New Statesman* in 1923, "and especially the distorting influence of egotism upon the whole individual outlook."

A few decades later, a review in the *Times Literary Supplement* in 1946 specifically mentioned "The Doll's House," along with the short stories "Prelude," "At the Bay," and "The Garden Party" as works that, "today no less than when they first appeared, present an immediacy of artistic achievement that she never surpassed." A hundred years after her birth, in 1988, Mansfield was still admired as one of the greatest writers of the short story and one of the finest writers associated with New Zealand. Witi

Ihimaera, a New Zealand writer, opened a book in homage to Mansfield with a letter to the author. "Throughout the past year," Ihimaera wrote, "many, many people from all over the world have wished to say 'thank you' for illuminating our lives and our literature. Mine is but a single token of aroha [love] and respect." To this day, Mansfield's admirers express their gratitude for the insight that she shared in her works.

CRITICISM

David Kelly

Kelly is a writer who teaches creative writing and literature at Oakton Community College in Illinois. In the following essay, he examines how Mansfield has placed the characters in "The Doll's House" in matching pairs to compare their personalities.

Mansfield's story "The Doll's House" is a work that relies on the careful balance of its elements in order to make its unstated points felt. Elements are juxtaposed against each other to highlight their similarities and differences. Mansfield does this tactfully and subtly, so that even a careful reader might not see it until the story's end. It is at the end, in the second-to-last line, that Else Kelvey, known throughout as "our Else," speaks, and it is then that things fall into place. In an instant, it becomes clear that Else is a kindred spirit with Kezia Burnell, which leads to other observations about similar relationships throughout the story.

The Burnells are really a mirror image of the Kelveys, a point that is not immediately apparent because there are three girls in one family and two in the other. It becomes clearer when one considers the middle Burnell, Lottie. She has no presence in the story; she never even speaks, but only serves to amplify Isabel's positions. Ignoring Lottie, at least for a while, leaves two Burnell sisters and two Kelvey sisters. There are also two sisters of the previous Burnell generation who have speaking roles in the story. In addition, there are girls who come two-by-two to the Burnell house. The only male presence is Pat the handyman, though in the story he does not really exert any personality; as a laborer, he functions for the Burnell household as a shovel or his handy pocket knife would function for Pat himself. He is a device for the family to use, not something to be dealt with. Mr. Kelvey,

WHAT DO I READ NEXT?

- Other adventures involving the Burnell family are related in Mansfield's stories "Prelude" and "At the Bay." Both can be found in *The Collected Stories of Katherine Mansfield*, published in 2006 by Wordsworth Classics.

- Maori writer Witi Tame Ihimaera is one of the most prominent contemporary writers in New Zealand and is a winner of the prestigious Katherine Mansfield Fellowship. His 1987 novel *The Whale Rider*, about a girl born into the Maori royal lineage, is considered a modern classic of young-adult literature. It was adapted into a critically acclaimed film. The novel is available in a 2005 edition from Heinemann Educational Publishers.

- Readers interested in Mansfield's way of thinking would be interested in reading *The Journals of Katherine Mansfield*. They were edited by Mansfield's husband, John Middleton Murry, and published by Alfred A. Knopf in 1927. Ecco Publishing issued a reprint in 1983.

- Mansfield was a great friend of the influential writer Virginia Woolf, who considered her to be the writer most like herself. Chapter 22 of Hermione Lee's 1999 biography, *Virginia Woolf*, is named "Katherine," and is about the relationship between these two great writers. The Woolf biography was published by Vintage in 1999.

- Mansfield was also a good friend of the British writer D. H. Lawrence. His short story "Daughters of the Vicar," available in the collection *Selected Short Stories*, which was published by Dover in 1993, has a similar theme of class consciousness and social climbing.

- In 2004, Canadian novelist Janice Kulyk Keefer published a novel, *Thieves*, based on Katherine Mansfield's colorful life. It depicts the chaos that surrounds the lives of Mansfield and her circle of friends, all great artists but struggling to control their lives. It was published in Canada by HarperCollins.

> **IF LIL HAS BEEN SILENCED WHEN SHE ATTEMPTED TO EDGE INTO THE GROUP AND LISTEN TO ISABEL'S DESCRIPTION OF THE HOUSE AND HUMILIATED BY LENA'S DIRECT ASSAULT ABOUT HER FATHER, SHE ENDS UP ULTIMATELY MORTIFIED BY AUNT BERYL SHOOING HER AWAY LIKE A RAT."

according to Gillian Boddy, appeared in an earlier draft of the story, driving a fish wagon but always so drunk that he is in constant danger of falling off. In the published version he is simply absent, like the father of the Burnell household.

Reading the story in terms of its dichotomies makes it easier to see how it works. The plot can be boiled down to a basic contrast between the two oldest daughters, Isabel Burnell and Lil Kelvey, as they reach the point in their lives when their social fortunes take them in opposite directions. The crux of the story, its heart, is a different matter, but its focus is on the schoolgirls making sense of the prevailing social order. The first few pages show how Isabel stumbles across the secret of social success as she goes from bragging about the lively new doll's house to pitting her schoolmates against each other for her affection. This all culminates in the yard at lunch one day when the other girls notice that Isabel might be amused by mocking Lil's poverty. Told that Lil will grow up to be a servant, Isabel's words properly express shock, but her eyes convey just the slightest hint of another meaning. Another girl picks up on the clue and goes to taunt the pathetic Lil, first with a snide question and then with outright hostility. The girls find delight in Lil's humiliation. Mansfield's wording about this leaves no doubt that a corner has been turned: they were, she says, "deeply, deeply excited, wild with joy." It is such a transformative moment that she leaves it up to readers' imaginations as she explains that the girls are driven to doing unspecified "daring things." Sexuality is not necessarily involved, but the feel of transgression and the pretense of maturity associated with it are certainly there. The girls find themselves moved up to a new social level by taunting Lil, and at the top of them all is their leader, Isabel.

And that is not even the final humiliation of Lil. This comes at the end of the story when, having been shown some degree of awkward kindness by Kezia, she is put down again. This time, it is not a gaggle of girls who are learning that cruelty can benefit them socially, but an adult, who berates Lil simply for existing. Though she does not know it, Lil could be as refined as the enchanting doll's house that started the social disruption and Aunt Beryl would *still* find herself objecting to the girl's smell. If Lil has been silenced when she attempted to edge into the group and listen to Isabel's description of the house and humiliated by Lena's direct assault about her father, she ends up ultimately mortified by Aunt Beryl shooing her away like a rat. Her mortification is so complete that her little sister Else tries to comfort her, petting the feather on her beaten old hat and pointing out that some good came from this miserable adventure after all, as she has at least seen the little lamp. In this, Else offers hope.

The story can be viewed as the divergence of Isabel and Lil, who do not start as social peers but rise and sink, respectively, so that they end up far, far apart. The story's heart, however, is clearly found in the way that their younger sisters, Kezia and Else, form an unspoken, possibly even unrecognized, bond.

Kezia is the outcast of her family. Unlike Else, she has no comfort to offer her sisters, who do not need comforting anyway. While Else stands behind Lil, holding on to the hem of her dress so that they won't be separated, Kezia tries to wheedle her way into Isabel's discourse to the schoolgirls about the new doll's house, finding her effort futile. In the story's final scene, Kezia walks off by herself as her family is inside, preparing to receive visitors. She does not feel any need to be with them, and they, apparently, find no need to go out looking for her, until Aunt Beryl, taking out her own frustrations, comes out and scolds her. There is no indication that Kezia and Else have anything in common until Else tells her sister about seeing the lamp, speaking with the same delight that warmed Kezia. Mansfield gives no indication whether interest in the lamp is passed from one to the other or just grows spontaneously in both youngest sisters; if both just happen to find the lamp enchanting, it says something about young people and their ability to be enchanted, while if Else is just repeating what she has heard, readers can be sure that, as a Kelvey, she is in for a lifetime of valuing things that are beyond her reach.

There is one more pair of sisters in this story: Aunt Beryl and the mother of the Burnell family, whose name is not given but who is identified as Linda in Mansfield's story "Prelude." Little is said about either one of them, but enough is given for readers to know that the same dynamic exists with them as well. Linda is an absolutist: she knows that she does not approve of poor people, and her disapproval is so thorough that she cannot even understand why she should have to explain it to her daughter Kezia. Beryl's emotions are more complicated. She does not accept herself as a snob without justifications, telling herself that she actually likes "dear old Mrs. Hay" but that the doll's house she sent has substandard paint, or that the Kelvey sisters just happened to have crossed her when she was having a bad afternoon. These two sisters fit the pattern, even though it is a loose fit. Linda, like Isabel and Lil, is a fatalist, understanding that things are, for better or worse, just the way they are, while Beryl is more like Else and Kezia in taking a more philosophical approach.

Like any good story, "The Doll's House" is more than the sum of its parts, and taking it apart to find relationships does not explain it, but merely points readers into the direction of understanding. It might be nice for readers if all of the sisterly relationships in this story remained consistent— if all of the younger sisters stood by to offer comfort to the older sisters, for instance, or if the older children were equally social climbers or accepting of their fate. Such clarity would make the story easier by making it less challenging, and that is precisely what would take away its magic. Mansfield has created these characters as real people, not just as emblems. They do not just represent positions, they exist. The fact that they exist in clear relationships to one another is just another testament to the author's firm controlling hand.

Source: David Kelly, Critical Essay on "The Doll's House," in *Short Stories for Students*, Gale, Cengage Learning, 2010.

J. Lawrence Mitchell

In the following excerpt, Mitchell discusses Mansfield's special attention to everyday objects, specifically the "little lamp" in "The Doll's House."

... Let us now turn to the 'little lamp,' as it appears in 'The Doll's House.' Claire Tomalin suggests that it had its genesis in one of John Middleton Murry's 'stories of staggering ineptitude' (1988:113) published in *Rhythm*. Any such borrowing seems highly unlikely, given what is known of Mansfield's *modus operandi*. In any case, the evidence that follows demonstrates the anteriority of the image in Mansfield's writings, how deeply embedded it was in her consciousness, and thus the tenuousness of Tomalin's claim. Yet the symbolism of the enigmatic lamp remains very much in question. Is it merely the object of a capricious child's affection? Is it, as Mansfield's contemporary, Gerald Bullett, would have it, 'the emblem of ecstasy, paradise, the world's desire' (1926:111)? Does it stand for 'the compensatory gift of vision' (Hankin 1983: 221)? Or does it illustrate 'the classic association of lamps and knowledge' (Fullbrook 1987:117)? However we interpret the object itself within the story, it certainly has an aesthetic role, and it is that role which concerns us primarily. The little lamp perfectly exemplifies the twofold aestheticization so characteristic of Mansfield's real-life response to the world of objects: the aestheticization of the commonplace and of the miniature. Any discussion of this neglected feature of Mansfield's fiction must therefore begin with Mansfield's 'kick-off' (her term) for the story, that is to say Else's triumphant statement at the end of 'The Doll's House:' 'I seen the little lamp.' What the despised Else [Kelvey], daughter of a washerwoman, shares with Kezia, the little girl who lives in a big house, is an aesthetic response—an intuitive grasp of the importance of the little lamp. For the other children, the doll's house itself is the main attraction; it is an object of curiosity, of course, and of envy, but ultimately no more than a toy. For Kezia, on the other hand, the doll's house re-inscribes the adult world in miniature and thereby becomes accessible to her exquisite sensibility. The very fount and source of power is the little lamp, that sacred object which derives much of its portentousness from Kezia's mysterious and inarticulable enthusiasm for it. Moreover, the ontological status of Kezia's assertion that 'the lamp was real' must be distinguished from that of earlier statements about 'real windows' and 'real bedclothes.' In the special reality of the lamp we discern—along with Kezia and Else—something of the numinous that is entirely lacking in quotidian objects such as windows and bedclothes. Dunbar (1997) makes a similar point in the service of a different argument:

ONE OF THE EARLIEST SKETCHES SHE PRODUCED TOWARDS THAT END WAS 'A RECOLLECTION OF CHILDHOOD,' WHICH LINKS THE BIRTH OF HER SISTER GWEN WITH THE ARRIVAL OF A DOLL'S HOUSE, THE GIFT OF A NEIGHBOR, MRS HEYWOOD."

'When Kezia affirms that for her the lamp is "real" she is unknowingly using the word in its old, idealistic sense' (p.174–75).

The innocent intensity of the child's vision in the story somehow seems sufficient; yet it masks an array of private associations and pivotal moments in Mansfield's life, the relevance of which has never been examined. We have to go back to 10 July 1904 to locate the first unembellished reference to the lamp, in a letter to Sylvia Payne, Mansfield's cousin, describing the view from her bedroom window in Queen's College hostel of 'the lamp in the Mews below' which she labels 'an old old comrade of mine' (*CL* I: 14). Oddly enough, the name of the mews or alley was 'Mansfield Mews,' a fact which—given the coincidence of family association—may account for young Kathleen Beauchamp's special feeling for it and which may even have been a hitherto unacknowledged factor in her selection of 'Mansfield' as a 'nom de plume.' Three years later, the same phrase has been incorporated, with writerly thrift, into one of Mansfield's early vignettes for *The Native Companion* (1 October 1907): 'Down below, in The Mews, the little lamp is singing a silent song' (cited in Stone p. 25). From its humble beginnings as a commonplace street lamp emerges the first version of the now domesticized and fully anthropomorphicized 'little lamp' with its Whistlerian luminosity. For many years this image and the attendant phrase seem to have lain dormant in Mansfield's imagination, until revivified under very different circumstances during World War One. Increasingly disillusioned with Murry's fecklessness and imagining herself in love with Francis Carco, whom she had met in Paris through Murry, Mansfield made what she later fictionalized as 'An Indiscreet Journey' into the French *Zone des Armées* to spend a few days with her own 'petit soldat.' Given the strong feelings provoked by the war, it is hard not to see Mansfield's act as, at one level, a gesture of solidarity with those who—like her brother and unlike her English lover—had heeded the call to arms. In her 'Home Diary for 1915,' towards the end of [a] long entry for 20 February, she recorded her impressions:

> We spent a queer night. The room—the room. The little lamp, the wooden ceiling, the bouquets of pink daisies that unfolded at dawn [...] There was a fire in our room and a tiny lamp on the table. The fire flickered on the white wood ceiling. It was as though we were on a boat. We talked in whispers, overcome by this discreet little lamp [...] It was so warm & delicious, lying curled in each other's arms, by the light of the tiny lamp le fils de Maeterlinck, only the clock & the fire to be heard (*Notebooks*, 1997 II: 9–12).

In this account of the four-day tryst, the little lamp is crucial to the mood of intimacy and both conceals by its discretion and reveals by its light. The evidence of the poem 'Secret Flowers,' suggests that the light of love shone from the lamp: 'Is love a light for me? A steady light, / A lamp within whose pallid pool I dream over old love-books?' This poem was first published in the *Athenaeum*, 22 July 1919. Given Vincent O'Sullivan's observation in his 1988 edition that this was "the one Athenaeum poem that Murry did not include in *Poems 1923* or *1930* (p. 92), it appears highly likely that he had come to associate the poem with Mansfield's tryst with Carco. Yet the lamp apparently remained too private a symbol to bear inclusion in the fictional version of this notably 'indiscreet' journey. The interpolated allusion in the entry to the Belgian symbolist, Maurice Maeterlinck (1862–1949), is revealing: it suggests that Mansfield somehow saw this idyllic moment in terms of Maeterlinck's fatalistic belief in man's incapacity to understand 'the mystery of his destiny' or to control 'the obscure forces that govern his life' (Braun 1964:277). No doubt she particularly had in mind Maeterlinck's use of a symbolic lamp in such plays as *The Seven Princesses* (1891), *Pelléas et Mélisande* (1892), and *The Blue Bird* (1909)....

One of the earliest sketches she produced towards that end was 'A Recollection of Childhood,' which links the birth of her sister Gwen with the arrival of a doll's house, the gift of a neighbor, Mrs Heywood. From this account, dated February 17, 1916, we first learn of the existence of a 'doll's lamp' on the bedroom table of the doll's house (*Journal* 1954:101–03). But, it should be noted, this detail is not yet represented as any more important than any other—the verandah, the balcony, the door that opened and shut, and the two chimneys: 'I had gone all through it [the doll's house] myself, from the kitchen to the dining-room, up into the bedrooms with the doll's lamp on the table, heaps and heaps of times' (*Journal* 1954:102). Ruth Mantz, who did some of the most painstaking investigation of Mansfield's early life, turned up another relevant detail in her account of the Beauchamps' life at their new home, Chesney Wold, in the country outside Wellington: 'There were only footpaths and no street lights in Karori. At home they used big lamps of the same sort as the little lamp in the doll's house' (1933 p. 102). Yet the lamp that Kezia accepts from her grandmother with all solemnity in 'Prelude,' as she makes her first entrance into her new home, is not deemed too big for the little girl to hold, even as it takes shape as a 'bright breathing thing' (p. 17). With it in her hands, Kezia's powers of perception change and, yet again, she proves herself her mother's daughter, for the parrots on the wallpaper seem to come to life and fly past her, just as the poppies on her mother's bedroom wallpaper later come alive for her. So, while the 'little lamp' of 'The Doll's House' has its immediate source in the 'doll's lamp,' and is to that extent relatively transparent as a symbol, it derives much of its hidden power from three widely disparate sets of associations identified here: Mansfield's fondly remembered schooldays at Queen's College in London from 1903 to 1906, her indiscreet journey of 1915 to France, and romanticized recollections of her childhood home in New Zealand. There may even be another strand in the conceptual history of the lamp. In August 1914, Sir Edward Grey, the British Foreign Secretary, solemnly announced that 'the lamps are going out all over Europe; we shall not see them lit again in our lifetime.' The very range of these associations allowed Mansfield to blend the 'discreet' lamp in a French *pension* with the lamp that symbolized the domestic tranquility of her family home. On another plane, this strategy allowed Mansfield to substitute for the memory of a soldier-lover in February 1915 the far more poignant memory of a soldier-brother who had been killed on 7 October 1915, so that the light of the 'little lamp' would serve to illumine the darkness of his death in her life. Between 1915 and 1921, then, the 'little lamp,' with its cluster of associations, had had time to mature into an aesthetic object which, with its personal reverberations muted—but not its emotional power—was embedded in and became the centerpiece of a story that speaks and sees only through the eyes of a sensitive little girl in far-off New Zealand.

Here we must return to Mansfield's initial reference in her journal entry of 1916—'A Recollection of Childhood'—to the lamp in the actual doll's house, which was given to the family in 1890. Why, in her grief, would she have chosen, ostensibly in memorializing her brother, to focus on an event that occurred in 1890–91, some three years before he had even been born? The answer is surely that Leslie's recent death brought to mind not just the birth of Mansfield's sister, Gwen, but her sudden and disturbing death a few months later. Biographers and critics have long been aware of a photograph showing baby Gwen in the arms of her grandmother Dyer, with the original of the doll's house behind them which was first reproduced and discussed in the Mantz biography. Mary Burgan, however, makes the case that 'Mansfield's [journal] narrative [...] is so indirect that none of the biographers seem to have noticed that the infant [in the photograph] is dead' (1994:3). That is, the grandmother is actually holding a dead child on her lap. Since there is good reason to accept this statement, 'The Doll's House' of 1921—a direct descendant from 'A Recollection of Childhood' of 1916—must be reinterpreted as a constituent part of Mansfield's 'long elegy' for her brother, along with *Prelude* and 'At the Bay.' The vase of white lilies and the 'funny little man with his head in a black bag' in 'A Recollection of Childhood' are obvious internal clues (*Journal* 1954:103) to what is happening. The idea of photographing a dead baby and hanging the picture over the fireplace, as described in this vignette, may now seem bizarre. In fact, 'photography of dead infants was a memorial ritual in late-nineteenth century New Zealand,' as Burgan notes (Note 1,178) and the practice was widespread in the United States too. John Pultz makes the point explicitly: 'In order to have visual records of dead children, parents paid photographers to photograph their bodies in their homes; sometimes parents went so far as to carry their child's body to a photographer's studio for a post-mortem portrait' (p. 33). He supports his statement with an 1850 daguerreotype of a dead child propped up in an armchair. Thus the 'little lamp' becomes more than the 'lamp of art' or the 'lamp of knowledge'—it becomes the lamp of constancy that burns in memory of the living spirit of her dead siblings: sister and brother united in death. In Pater's terms, it becomes 'a sort of material shrine or sanctuary of sentiment' (Buckler p. 226). This reading is consistent with Susan Stewart's understanding of the doll's house itself within the economy of the miniature, although she makes no reference to—and is perhaps unaware of—Mansfield's story: 'The dollhouse [...] represents a particular form of interiority, an interiority which the subject experiences as its sanctuary (fantasy)' (p. 65). This notion of sanctuary, generously interpreted, is crucial to the reading of Mansfield's doll's house here.

In the construction of the original doll's house gifted to the Beauchamp children, no detail had been spared to make it, in miniature, as 'real' as possible—from real bedclothes to real glass windows. Yet there is one relevant, albeit intriguingly anomalous, feature of the story: the dolls, observes the narrator, 'were really too big for the doll's house' and 'didn't look as though they belonged' (p. 3). The motivation for these comments is by no means clear and no adequate explanation within the framework of the story itself seems possible. Dunbar notices this detail and offers a tentative and not altogether convincing explanation....

By the time she wrote 'The Doll's House,' then, she was fictively preparing a place for herself—a sanctuary of sorts—just as she had for Leslie in *Prelude,* and she could not afford to be 'really too big,' if she were to become the doll that did belong in the doll's house. Her aesthetic of the miniature had become entwined with an aesthetic of death. And, as Michel de Certeau reminds us, 'the death that cannot be said can be written and find a language.'(1988: 195)....

I began by identifying the characteristic way in which Mansfield gave life to objects by projecting herself into them, by fetishizing them. Now it is possible to reread 'The Doll's House' with that practice in mind and to understand its importance to Mansfield as she was forced to contemplate her own death. Jonathan Trout spoke for his creator too when he fulminated against 'the shortness of life!' in 'At The Bay.' I have already argued that for Mansfield the little lamp served, among other functions, to memorialize her sister, Gwen, and her brother, Leslie—symbolism not so different from lighting a candle for someone in the Catholic Church that Mansfield once nearly joined under the influence of her 'Catholic cousins', Connie Beauchamp and Jinnie Fullerton. Now I want to take the argument one step further. Mansfield's highly developed aesthetic sense was reflected in myriad ways: in her response to what Virginia Woolf called 'solid objects', in the colours in which she dressed, even in the way she organized her environment. At times she quite self-consciously worked for an aesthetic effect in which she became an integral part, indeed the centrepiece, of a sort of *tableau vivant*. In his autobiographical novel, *The Last Romantic* (1937), William Orton, one of her former intimates, vividly recalled a visit to her rooms in Cheyne Place around 1911....

It would be perfectly consistent with the kind of self-consciousness so vividly recaptured by Orton that, in 'The Doll's House,' one of her last major stories (the sub-text of another, 'The Fly,' is also the death of a relative in the war), Mansfield would conceive of a fictional final resting place beside her siblings, 'herself accurately in the centre.' By projecting herself into the lamp, safely miniaturized, she could become both a sort of auto-icon—her own aesthetic object—and, once again, the child in the house....

Source: J. Lawrence Mitchell, "Katherine Mansfield and the Aesthetic Object," in *Journal of New Zealand Literature*, No. 22, 2004, pp. 31–54.

Robert L. Caserio

In the following excerpt, Caserio analyzes the "The Doll's House" in respect to autonomy.

...There is one late story of Mansfield's, however, "The Doll's House," which turns out to be a fable about the way in which the artist's autonomy, however hallucinatory and free-floating it might be in inspiration and in form, is compatible with the desire to make art be not autonomous, not exclusively the housing of autonomous agonized lyric moments, but a miniature copy of the great world outside of fiction. The story returns to the New Zealand children in "Prelude." They have been given a superb, fully furnished doll's house, whose lifelikeness is summed up for Kezia in "a teeny little lamp": "'You couldn't tell it from a real one.'" The children boast about their acquisition at school, and invite their friends to see the toy. But Kezia's family forbids extending the invitation to Lil and "our Else," who are daughters of a washerwoman and a convict. Kezia breaks this commandment; but when the forbidden girls are discovered on the family property contemplating the house, they are expelled with harsh snobbery by Kezia's aunt. At first the expelled sisters are overwhelmed by shame and hurt. Yet the moment of their recovery comes when "our Else" shyly and softly says to her sister, with a "rare smile," "'I seen the little lamp.'" What has happened, obviously, and what has been shown by Mansfield, is that a lifelike miniature, an almost exact artistic double of a real thing, can create such wonder and interest that it has the power to change the real world, as well as to copy it. This model, having inspired a breach in Kezia's class feeling, also consoles the class-damaged children for their hurt, by giving them the liberty to be conscious, in a new way, of what is real. Even so realistic a model or copy of the world can be made, of course, only on condition that a piece of the whole become autonomous enough to stand for the whole. But in this story the independence of art from the world and its dependence on the world seem mutually possible, and mutually transformative.

Source: Robert L. Caserio, "The Mansfield Moment," in *Western Humanities Review*, Vol. 50, No. 4, Winter–Spring 1997, pp. 344–47.

J. F. Kobler
In the following excerpt, Kobler considers the influence Mansfield's relationship with her parents had on the "The Doll's House."

In "The Doll's House," finished at the end of October 1922, Mansfield returns to the Burnells at a time that seems a few years later than that of the other stories about Kezia and her family. The story implies that they have been living in their house in the country for some time now, and Kezia, Lottie, and Isabel are all in school. There is no mention of a son; Father Stanley does not appear; Mother Linda utters but two sentences. "The Doll's House" is about the children—especially Kezia, who violates the family rules by inviting the outcast Kelvey girls to look at the wonderful dollhouse sent to the Burnell children by "dear old Mrs. Hay" (*KM*, 570), after a stay with the family. The fabulous dollhouse is the talk of the school, and the children are allowed to invite their school friends to come see it, though under terribly strict rules for children: no more than two at a time, just to look, not to stay to tea, not "to come traipsing through the house" (*KM*, 572), but to stand quietly in the courtyard admiring the little house as, the story implies, everyone should admire the Burnells and their big house.

Much scapegoating occurs in this story. The Burnells do not approve of the school to which the girls go, but there is no choice. They must go and be mixed all together, the children of a judge, a doctor, a storekeeper, even a milkman; however, "the line" is drawn at the Kelveys, whose mother is a "hardworking little washerwoman" (*KM*, 573) and whose father is thought to be in jail. The children at school learn from their parents, taunting and teasing the Kelvey girls—Lil and our Else (she is always called that) Kelvey—in sport. One of the girls hisses at the Kelveys, "Yah, yer father's in prison!" These scapegoating words "deeply, deeply" excite all the other girls, who are so released from their own fears and limitations by heaping them on the Kelveys that they skip rope faster and harder, doing more "daring things" than they have ever done before (*KM*, 575).

One day Kezia, who is said only to have "made up her mind," speaks to the Kelvey girls and invites them to look at the dollhouse. Although Mansfield writes of Kezia's hesitation in inviting them, she offers neither internal nor external reasons for Kezia's going against her mother's explicit orders. Lil, who is even more a victim of socialization than is Kezia, is afraid to accept the invitation, but our Else, who never speaks, implores with her eyes; thus, they go to look at the dollhouse. Descriptions of the Kelvey girls include their looking like "two little stray cats" and standing "still as a stone" (*KM*, 576). When Aunt Beryl discovers the invasion of her courtyard, she shoos the Kelveys out "as if they were chickens" (*KM*, 577). Later she thinks of them as rats. These images add up to the point that the adult Burnells do not even consider these little girls human. That Mansfield is depicting the psychology of scapegoating becomes even more obvious with an otherwise pointless paragraph about Aunt Beryl's feelings after she has chased the Kelveys away and shouted "bitterly" at Kezia, "Wicked, disobedient little girl." Aunt Beryl's "afternoon had been awful" because of a letter "from Willie Brent, a terrifying, threatening letter" that demands she meet him or expect a visit from him at her front door. Now, having "frightened those little rats of Kelveys and given Kezia a good scolding," Beryl's pain is lifted, the "ghastly pressure" is gone, and she can return to "the house humming" (*KM*, 577).

But our Else has the last word. The furnishing in the doll's house that Kezia loves most "frightfully" is a tiny lamp "in the middle of the dining-room table." Well out of sight of the Burnells, the Kelvey girls sit down to rest and our Else speaks her only words in the story: "I seen the little lamp" (*KM*, 577). Only Kezia in the Burnell family is capable of seeing and demonstrating the light of love—or human understanding, compassion, or whatever a reader wants to call it.

That Mansfield found her new form by going back to the emotional days of her childhood attests to the great influence of that early time on her life; her feelings of love and hate for her parents were so mixed that only by giving them different shapes and names could she come to grips with them.

Source: J. F. Kobler, "The New Zealand Stories," in *Katherine Mansfield: A Study of the Short Fiction*, Twayne Publishers, 1990, pp. 14–27.

Kate Fullbrook

In the following excerpt, Fullbrook examines class in regard to "The Doll's House."

... Kezia probably has a less important role in 'At the Bay' than in any of the Burnell stories, but she is once again at the centre of 'The Doll's House' (1921). The little girls in this story, like Nora in the play by Ibsen after which it is named, and like the little girl in 'Pearl Button', are female rebels in revolt against the sexual and social rules that are meant to divide them into hostile and permanently alienated camps. Kezia is the heroine, and the story concerns her breaking her family's injunction against allowing the 'impossible' Kelvey girls to see the Burnells' new doll's house.

Lil and Else Kelvey are the pariahs of the playground. They are poor children who are used by the school and the parents of the other girls as negative object-lessons of what, for females, is beyond the pale. The Kelveys are 'shunned by everybody'.

> They were the daughters of a spry, hard-working little washerwoman, who went about from house to house by the day. This was awful enough. But where was Mr. Kelvey? Nobody knew for certain. But everybody said he was in prison. So they were the daughters of a washerwoman and a gaolbird. Very nice company for other people's children! And they looked it. Why Mrs. Kelvey made them so conspicuous was hard to understand. The truth was they were dressed in 'bits' given to her by the people for whom she worked.

The narrative mimics the tone of the self-righteous, disapproving, genteel community (and these are women's tones, women's voices defending their class territory). Aside from the fundamental class snobbery in operation here, there is an explicit outline of what conformity to female stereotype must mean. Women must not work, they can only be fully validated on the production of a suitable male from whom they ought to derive their status, their being is closely bound up in their clothes. Self-sufficiency, hard work, and cheerful courage (supposedly valued by the same culture) are unacceptable: Mrs Kelvey and her daughters fail on every sexist point.

On a day that the outcasts have been particularly tormented in the schoolyard, Kezia violates her mother's ban on the girls. Seeing them coming down the road she is torn, in a moment reminiscent of Huck Finn's espousal of the 'nigger' Jim, between the social conscience her culture has been developing and an individual stroke of consciousness.

> Nobody was about; she began to swing on the big white gates of the courtyard. Presently, looking along the road, she saw two little dots. They grew bigger, they were coming towards her. Now she could see that one was in front and one close behind. Now she could see that they were the Kelveys. Kezia stopped swinging. She slipped off the gate as if she was going to run away. Then she hesitated. The Kelveys came nearer, and beside them walked their shadows, very long, stretching right across the road with their heads in the buttercups. Kezia clambered back on the gate; she had made up her mind; she swung out.

As in 'Pearl Button' the gate is a sign of vacillation between being shut into or moving out of convention. And again, the central character swings free. Kezia asks the Kelveys in and they have a chance to see the doll's house before Aunt Beryl shoos them off. The shadows of the girls, 'stretching right across the road with their heads in the buttercups', is what decides Kezia to make her move. The delicacy and beauty of the highly original image contrasts strongly with the clipped, factual language of crude perception that records Kezia's sighting of the girls, and the text reflects the shift from the crudity of dispassionate observation to Kezia's sympathetic recognition of the outlaw children. The shadows that merge the little girls with the beauty of the flowers simply ignore the confining man-made road and its straight lines. Kezia does the same as she obliterates the class lines of her acculturation and recognises the Kelveys as in some sense equals. And in doing so, Kezia denies the values their rejection represents.

The doll's house itself is a complex symbol that precisely suits the story. Given to the Burnell girls by Mrs. Hay ('Sweet old Mrs, Hay,' a woman whose bland, rustic, vegetable name connotes her conformity), the doll's house has to be left outside. As Beryl thinks:

> No harm could come to it; it was summer. And perhaps the smell of paint would have gone by the time it had to be taken in. For, really, the smell of paint coming from that doll's house... the smell of paint was quite enough to make anyone seriously ill...

The doll's house is completely furnished, down to 'the father and mother dolls, who ... were really too big for the doll's house', just as real people are 'too big' for the kind of married life that the doll's house metonymically represents. Even when new, the doll's house smells revolting, like the institution it imitates. And just as the Kelveys are used as a negative lesson for the Burnell girls, the doll's house is meant for positive female instruction. It is an invitation to sweet domesticity, to boast about possessions; it provides an opportunity for a complete childish parody of the approved method for women to locate their identities in their houses and in the things and people they manage to stuff into them. But the doll's house is also a fabulous toy, a playground for the wayward imagination, and it contains one item that particularly catches Kezia's fancy: a tiny lamp that almost looks as if it could be lit. Katherine Mansfield once more uses the classic association of lamps and knowledge to indicate the rebelliousness of Kezia's reaction to the house. Although the lamp is false, as is the system of values embodied by the house and summed up in the persecution of the Kelveys, it is the *idea* of the lamp that catches Kezia's attention. The linkage of Kezia and the Kelveys earlier in the story is repeated via the mediation of this image. Else nudges Lil at the very end of the story: 'she smiled her rare smile.' I seen the little lamp," she said softly. Then both were silent once more.' The image unites the girl-children, the outcast and the privileged, in their imaginations which refuse the patterns dictated by their culture and create alternative patterns of their own....

Source: Kate Fullbrook, "Late Fiction," in *Katherine Mansfield*, edited by Sue Roe, Indiana University Press, 1986, pp. 86–128.

C. A. Hankin

In the following excerpt, Hankin discusses how Mansfield used her own life experiences in writing "The Doll's House."

...Two entries in Katherine Mansfield's journal indicate that 'The Doll's House,' completed on 30 October, 1921, had its genesis at least as far back as February 1916. Then, in the aftermath of Leslie's death, Katherine was gathering together her memories of the country where she and her brother had been born. 'I begin to think of an unfinished memory which has been with me for years,' Katherine wrote. 'It is a very good story if only I can tell it right, and it is called "Lena," It plays in New Zealand and would go in the book.' While she was working on 'The Aloe' during those months in Bandol, recollections of her childhood came flooding back. One of them involved the doll's house which had been given to the Beauchamp children by a Mrs Heywood, just before the birth of the sickly baby, Gwen. Although Katherine was only two at the time she remembered that

> Meg and Tadpole had gone away... and they had gone before the new doll's house arrived, so that was why I so longed to have somebody to show it to. I had gone all through it myself, from the kitchen to the dining room, up into the bedrooms with the doll's lamp on the table, heaps and heaps of times. But there was nobody to show it to.

What was worse, 'all day, all night grandmother's arms were full, I had no lap to climb into, no pillow to rest against. All belonged to Gwen.' Even 'old Mrs McElvie came to the door', to ask about the baby. Then one day grandmother and Gwen were photographed: 'the picture was hung over the nursery fire.... The doll's house was in it—verandah, balcony and all. Gran held me up to kiss my little sister.'

Confused though Katherine's recollections of herself at the age of two may well have been, the external details of 'The Doll's House,' like those of her other New Zealand stories, are remarkably true to life. Mrs Heywood is merely changed to 'Mrs Hay,' and Vera, Charlotte and Kathleen Beauchamp become the same Isabel, Lottie and Kezia Burnell who appear in

> **THE CENTRAL INCIDENT IN THE NARRATIVE—THE INCIDENT WHICH APPEALS TO THE SURVIVING CHILD IN EVERY READER—IS THE REJECTION, INDEED THE VICTIMISATION, OF THE KELVEY CHILDREN BY THOSE MORE SOCIALLY FAVOURED."

'Prelude' and 'At the Bay.' The Mrs McElvie of Katherine's recollections is transformed into the mother of the 'Kelvey' children. Mrs MacKelvey, according to Ruth Mantz, was the well-liked village washerwoman in Karori, although her husband was not in prison but a gardener. Of the three MacKelvey children, Ruth Mantz writes, 'Lil, the eldest, was the only normal one.... "Our Else," the artistic one, was the mother's favourite.... They all looked after her.... This "pathetic little wish-bone of a child" cared only for the one thing: she loved to paint.'

There was only one primary school in Karori, which the children of rich and poor alike attended. Amongst Kathleen Beauchamp's schoolfellows were the little MacKelveys, who every day trailed to and fro past the gate of her house. Kathleen shared a desk with Lena Monaghan. Ruth Mantz quotes Katherine Mansfield's later unpleasant memory of the Monaghan children: 'To me it's just as though I'd been going home from school and the Monaghans had called after me, and you—about the size of a sixpence—had defended me and p'raps helped me to pick up my pencils and put them back in the pencil box.' According to Maude Morris, who like Katherine Mansfield was tormented as a child by the Monaghans, Lena Monaghan was the model for the spiteful Lena Logan, who cruelly taunts the Kelvey girls. The Monaghans, like the Logans in the story, even kept cows. Yet another contemporary confirms the accuracy of Katherine's portrayal of the teacher who 'had a special voice for [the Kelveys] and a special smile for the other children when Lil Kelvey came up to her desk with a bunch of dreadfully common-looking flowers.' The real-life teacher, apparently, was a snob who favoured the rich children and harassed the poor.

Thus virtually all the characters in Katherine Mansfield's most famous story of childhood injustice existed in reality. What Katherine's association of the doll's house with the birth of a rival for grandmother's love suggests is that the emotions which inform the story were also true to life. The central incident in the narrative—the incident which appeals to the surviving child in every reader—is the rejection, indeed the victimisation, of the Kelvey children by those more socially favoured. Suffering a sense of rejection since the birth of Gwen, Katherine displaced onto the washerwoman's children her own deep sense of being less attractive than her sisters, less loved by her parents and peers. In memory it was the author who longed to have someone to show the doll's house to; in the story Isabel, the dominant older sister, exults over the new possession at school. Kezia's resentment of Isabel is never openly expressed in 'The Doll's House.' But here, as in all the stories in which Katherine Mansfield depicts her childhood self along with her sisters, she is contrasted favourably with the eldest sister.

The differences in temperament and attitude between Isabel and Kezia are sharply defined in 'The Doll's House.' In this story, where the child's world is shown to be a microcosm of the adult's, the bossy eldest sister who 'was always right' is ranged alongside the heartless Aunt Beryl and the mother who forbids the washerwoman's children to see the doll's house. Imitating the adults in their snobbish ways, Isabel uses the acquisition of the elegant doll's house to court popularity at school. It is she who points out the beauties of the house and chooses 'who's to come and see it first.' Later, it is Isabel who encourages Lena Logan to bait the Kelvey children. While the Kelveys' social difference places them at the end of the pecking order, Kezia suffers from being overshadowed by her sister. At school 'nobody paid any attention' to Kezia's opinion that 'the lamp's best of all'; and at home Mother sharply dismisses her plea for the Kelveys with, 'Run away, Kezia.' Her action in inviting the outcast children to see the house is therefore one of rebellion—against the mother who would not listen, and against the sister who had 'the powers that went with being eldest.' Kezia's generous deed is also her own brief bid for a share of the gratification which the doll's house had afforded Isabel.

Rivalry among the sisters, although never emphasised by the author, underlies the thematic structure of 'The Doll's House.' Heightening the work's emotional impact are echoes of that archetypal story of childhood maltreatment,

'Hansel and Gretel.' In her 1910 'Fairy Story' Katherine had surely drawn on 'Hansel and Gretel' in her depiction of the woodcutter. Here, the 'spinach green' doll's house with its door gleaming like a 'slab of toffee' is reminiscent of the edible house which enticed Hansel and Gretel. Just as the hungry children in the fairy tale are driven away by their wicked stepmother, so Kezia is told to 'run away' by her mother, while the poorly fed Kelveys are commanded by Aunt Beryl, 'run away, children, run away at once. And don't come back again.'

As in her other mature stories, Katherine Mansfield softens the anxiety inherent in her theme. Overlaying the work's psychological meaning is the obvious moral indignation at class discrimination. But even more important in terms of the story's overall effect is the symbol of the 'little lamp.' Its beauties appreciated only by Kezia and the Kelveys, the lamp is at once a symbol of the three children's separateness—and their innate superiority. Kezia shares with the Kelveys a sense of being underprivileged. The appreciation of the washerwoman's children for the little lamp suggests that they, like her, have a compensatory gift of vision.

The lamp, with its ability to irradiate and transform the darkness, represents the imagination of the artist who has the power to transform reality, to create an ideal world 'subject to *his* laws—his "vision."' Katherine Mansfield modelled Our Else, who with her sister looks dreamily over the hay paddock at the end of the story, on the real Else MacKelvey, who in fact cared only to paint. Possession of artistic imagination, the author seems to be saying, transcends more than the hurts of reality. It transcends all social distinctions.

Source: C. A. Hankin, "More Thrilling than Love—Honesty," in *Katherine Mansfield and Her Confessional Stories*, St. Martin's Press, 1983, pp. 206–21.

Don W. Kleine

In the following excerpt, Kleine discusses Mansfield's view of childhood based on her stories, including "The Doll's House."

...Since Dickens, I wonder if any fiction writer has disclosed the opportunities of such double vision so impressively as Katherine Mansfield. Expert in the weathers, mental and circumstantial, which authenticate a child's milieu (and guiltless of the bathos and charlatanry which are often their Dickensian equivalents), she exerts at times a unique, puzzling

> "'THE DOLL'S HOUSE' IS THE MOST ALARMING OF MISS MANSFIELD'S DISPATCHES FROM CHILDHOOD'S MAGIC LAND."

power over the memory, refreshing it to remind us we forgot; fusing two worlds alien and magnetic as planets and sexes, in a perception of loss at once portended and lamented....

Miss Mansfield's legacy is surely diverse for one who died at thirty four. Yet, after all, the chief vindication of her radical, introspective instrument is to be found in the handful of her stories which capture the private life of the young to link it with the life of elders in haunting, exact images of social process, personal growth and loss, family intimacy. Based upon her New Zealand girlhood, such writings as "At the Bay," "Prelude," "The Garden Party," "The Doll's House," and "The Voyage" are acknowledged to be the core of Miss Mansfield's accomplishment. "Debts of Love," she called these masterpieces, but they are equally transfigurations of an obsessive sorrow, arbitrating distances of space and time which perplexed her from the day she left Wellington at nineteen. "A long typical boat dream [last night]. I was as usual going to N.Z." Such *Journal* entries reveal that the death of a well-loved brother in 1915 focused childhood memories. It was as if more than a brother had died, and must now be fiercely reconstituted, "perhaps not in poetry. Nor perhaps in prose. Almost certainly in a kind of *special* prose."

A chronic homesickness shrewdly polarizes past and present, lending her creative intelligence a resonance matched but fitfully in the far more numerous England and South of France stories. To be sure, if Miss Mansfield's domination of childhood and adolescence may be traced to the ambivalences of early self-exile, her private dilemma is objectified in definitions of European adulthood as well, by a dualism tensely imagined—a foreboded deprivation not of what we had but of what we should have, a sensed disparity between the promises and shattering betrayals of experience. We leave the youthful heroine of "The Garden Party" weeping gladly for the inviolable dead man who almost spoiled her afternoon. Adult analogues in pieces like "Bliss," "Life of Ma Parker," "The Daughters of the Late Colonel," "Marriage à la Mode," and "Miss Brill" are left staring amazed upon abruptly ruined lives. While Katherine Mansfield's *Journal* counsels mystic acceptance (she died seeking it in Gurdjieff's Institute near Fontainebleau), the largest portion of her work indicates implacable unforgiveness. Its light exclamatory cadence, fanciful childlike free play, brilliant irony and impersonality, hardly conceal the underlying, exasperated romantic idealism. "I adore Life," she declares in a letter to Murry's brother, "but my experience of the world is that it's pretty terrible."

In resolving this dualism by anticipating it, the New Zealand fictions do suggest the higher accomplishment. Immediacy and clarity give these a rapt, charmed ambience, as if some preternatural deceit had been performed upon our expectations; yet within an idyllic suspension, the relationships of offspring gain a pertinence uncommon in any serious fiction. Exemplary for their reconquest of a fugitive elsewhere so quaintly at large, such prodigies of recall are richly in need of exploration.

"The Doll's House" is the most alarming of Miss Mansfield's dispatches from childhood's magic land. Three small sisters are given a wonderful, life-like house for their dolls. One of them, Kezia, falls in love with a tiny lamp inside, which seems to smile at her and say "'I live here.'" Over the next few days, all her classmates are allowed to inspect the doll's house, except the washerwoman Mrs. Kelvey's daughters. This creepy pair are natural outcasts, fair game for the taunts of respectable schoolmates like Lena Logan. One day Lena's squeals prove particularly bitter; after school Kezia, sitting on a gate, sees the Kelveys pass by. In an impulse of experimental generosity, she invites them to see the doll's house. But after a moment her grown-up aunt has discovered them, and drives the two outlaws away like chickens. Once out of sight, the Kelveys sit down on a big red drain pipe along the road. Reminiscently, the younger murmurs, "'I seen the little lamp.'"

The factuality of this unhappy fable might have seemed a gratuitous slander, had it been argued by an author to whom infant folkways are knowable from the outside and at a terrific distance. It isn't, however, much of an Eden if you're in it: "Now they hovered at the edge; you couldn't stop them listening. When the little girls turned round and sneered, Lil, as usual, gave her silly, shamefaced smile, but our Else only looked." Such terrors are transcribed with the laconic circumstantiality of a police blotter. Yet when Lena glides over the playground to ask Lil if it's true she's going to be a servant when she grows up, we can hardly doubt that absent elders are looming dimly in shadow like the tall, anonymous figures of Freudian nightmare.

If schoolchildren find in a doll's house a simulacrum of the adult world, the adult world finds its image in schoolchildren. "Nudging, giggling together, the little girls pressed up close" to Kezia's sister Isabel, custodian of the amazing house. "One by one they put their arms round Isabel's waist and walked her off. They had something to whisper to her, a secret." The future is writ small in such little women, whose apprenticeship proves convincing only because its infantile basis is accurately intuited: "And sliding, gliding, dragging one foot, giggling behind her hand, Lena went over to the Kelveys...." In short, the juxtaposition of a toy's mental pleasures and the hard-hearted rites of a playground persuades us of our own mixed humanity: "'Yah, yer father's in prison!' she hissed, spitefully.... This was such a marvelous thing to have said that the little girls rushed away in a body, deeply, deeply excited, wild with joy. Some one found a long rope, and they began skipping. And never did they skip so high, run in and out so fast, or do such daring things as on that day."

The smiling lamp lives in the animistic fancy of an ignorant child, and the wide world shrinks to fit within "a perfect little house" for dolls, which encloses it as a glass ball encloses an artificial snowstorm. Real snow is general all over "The Dead"—but it is profitless to compare the small, perfect story with the large, imperfect one. Rather we might note how more formidable New Zealand writings draw a measure of power from Katherine Mansfield's exact apprehension of childhood....

That the rightness and depth of stories like "The Voyage" or "The Doll's House" presume a shrinkage of range is hardly surprising. Humanly concrete, a child's sense of life is humanly eccentric, since he lacks forms with which to attach his eerie, brilliant insights to the experience he receives with such appalling intensity. Cramped by the inexplicable resistances of a world in which there is little else for him to do but play, the deeds of his imagination often suggest the solemn audacity of a lunatic. To explore this disparate, whimsical purview, Miss Mansfield suspends it in a void created by subtracting our own climate of factuality. The void is not absolute, however, but is electrified with strategies of poetic indirection which travel into Kezia Burnell's immediate, hermetic province (as well as the hermetic domesticity of elders) to transfigure it with a fine resonance of implication....

Source: Don W. Kleine, "An Eden for Insiders: Katherine Mansfield's New Zealand," in *College English*, Vol. 27, No. 3, December 1965, pp. 201–09.

SOURCES

Boddy, Gillian, "From Notebook Draft to Published Story: 'Late Spring,' 'This Flower,'" in *Critical Essays on Katherine Mansfield*, edited by Rhonda B. Nathan, G. K. Hall, 1993, p. 106.

Ihimaera, Witi, "Dear Katherine Mansfield," in *Dear Miss Mansfield: A Tribute to Kathleen Mansfield Beauchamp*, Penguin, 1989, reprinted in *The Critical Response to Katherine Mansfield*, edited by Jan Pilditch, Greenwood Press, 1996, p. 232.

"Katherine Mansfield: 1888–1923," in *Katherine Mansfield Birthplace Te Puakitanga*, The Katherine Mansfield Birthplace Society, http://www.katherinemansfield.com/mansfield/ (accessed September 22, 2009).

Meyers, Jeffrey, *Katherine Mansfield: A Darker View*, Cooper Square Press, 2002.

Mortimer, Raymond, Review of *The Dove's Nest and Other Stories* in *New Statesman*, July 7, 1923, reprinted in *The Critical Response to Katherine Mansfield*, edited by Jan Pilditch, Greenwood Press, 1996, p. 13.

Review of *Katherine Mansfield's Stories* in *Times Literary Supplement* (London, England), March 2, 1946, reprinted in *The Critical Response to Katherine Mansfield*, edited by Jan Pilditch, Greenwood Press, 1996, p. 49.

Smith, Philippa Mein, *A Concise History of New Zealand*, Cambridge University Press, 2005.

FURTHER READING

Bennett, Andrew, "Hating Katherine Mansfield," in *Angelaki: Journal of the Theoretical Humanities*, December 2002, pp. 3–16.

    This article looks specifically at the complex relationship between Mansfield and Virginia Woolf, who considered her a friend yet also felt bitter jealousy toward her as a writer.

Dunbar, Pamela, *Radical Mansfield: Double Discourse in Katherine Mansfield's Short Stories*, St. Martin's Press, 1997.

    This book is divided into themes, such as "Isolation" and "The Self," which can be found throughout the range of Mansfield's stories, discussing examples for each.

Hankin, Cherry, "Katherine Mansfield and the Cult of Childhood," in *Katherine Mansfield: In from the Margin*, edited by Roger Robinson, Louisiana State University Press, 1994, pp. 25–35.

    Hawkins shows how Mansfield broke from Victorian traditions in providing realistic behavior of children in stories like "The Doll's House."

Kaplan, Sydney Janet, *Katherine Mansfield and the Origins of Modernist Fiction*, Cornell University Press, 1991.

    In twelve chapters, Kaplan takes apart the concept of "modernism" and looks at Mansfield's involvement in every step of its development.

New, W. H., *Reading Mansfield and Metaphors of Form*, McGill-Queen's University Press, 1999.

    New's book serves as a survey of where Mansfield's literary reputation stood at the end of the twentieth century.

Shen, Dan, "Subverting Surface and Doubling Irony: Subtexts of Mansfield's 'Revelations' and Others," in *English Studies*, April 2006, Vol. 87, Issue 2, pp. 191–209.

    This article offers a detailed account of how some of Mansfield's stories (though not specifically "The Doll's House") can be subjected to in-depth analysis.

Smith, Angela, *Katherine Mansfield: A Literary Life*, Palgrave, 2000.

    A concise overview of Mansfield's life and works including a multi-page analysis of "The Doll's House."

Forty-Five a Month

R. K. NARAYAN

1943

Indian novelist and short story writer Raspier Krishnaism (R. K.) Narayan is known for his ability to capture the details of daily life in India and for his insight into the social and cultural issues particular to Indian society. In his short story "Forty-Five a Month," Narayan presents a working-class Indian family. He vividly portrays the family's financial struggles and succinctly comments on the effects such monetary issues have on the relationships among the family members. In "Forty-Five a Month," a little girl eagerly anticipates an evening out with her father, who has promised to take her to the cinema (movie theater). The father, however, is chronically overworked. He is prepared to hand in his resignation in order to avoid being asked to work late yet again and miss the chance to fulfill his promise to his daughter. On the evening he is required to work well beyond regular hours yet again, he is also promised a raise. The father remains at work, returning home hours after the time he had arranged to pick up his daughter for the movie. He finds her asleep, dressed to go out. In this short work, Narayan depicts the torment endured by a loving father who is forced to choose between supporting his family and spending time with them, characterizing a commonplace dilemma of working-class Indian families in the 1940s. The title refers to the amount of money, in rupees (Indian currency), that the father will earn after the raise goes into effect.

Originally published in the short story collection *DOD and Other Stories* in 1943, "Forty-Five

R.K. Narayan (© Dinodia Images / Alamy)

a Month" has been included in other Narayan anthologies and is available in an expanded version of *Mallei Days*, a collection originally published in 1942 but expanded and reissued in 1982 by Viking Press.

AUTHOR BIOGRAPHY

Narayan was born Raspier Krishnaism Iyre Narayanaswami on October 10, 1906, to R. V. Krishnaism Iyre and Gnana Iyre, in Madras, India. (Madras is now known as Chennai.) Narayan spent his youth in Madras, cared for by his grandmother and maternal uncle, visiting his parents in Mysore, India, where his father worked as a teacher. After being schooled in Madras, Narayan joined his family in Mysore in 1922 to attend the school where his father was now headmaster. Narayan graduated from Maharaja College in Mysore in 1930, earning a bachelor of arts degree. He worked for a short time as a teacher but had also written several manuscripts and stories for which he sought publication by English publishers. Having little luck in getting his work noticed by English publishers, Narayan sent the manuscript for anovel to a friend who was studying at Oxford. The friend was able to get the manuscript into the hands of English novelist Graham Greene, who was instrumental in getting Narayan's work published. The novel, *Swami and Friends*, was published in 1935. With Greene's help, Narayan continued to write and be published in English.

Narayan married Rajam Iyre in 1934. They had met the previous year, when she was fifteen years old. Their only child, a daughter, was born in 1936. In 1939, Narayan's young wife died.

In 1941, Narayan became the editor of an Indian journal and subsequently founded his own publishing company, Indian Thought Publications. Several novels and short story collections, including *DOD and Other Stories* (1943), the collection that includes "Forty-Five a Month," were published in the years that immediately followed. In 1958, Narayan traveled to Berkeley, California, where he wrote one his most popular novels, *The Guide*, which was published the same year. Throughout the decades that followed, Narayan continued to travel and write, publishing the novella *Grandmother's Tale* in 1992. Narayan died in Chennai, India, on May 13, 2001.

PLOT SUMMARY

Narayan's short story "Forty-Five a Month" opens in the classroom of a little girl named Shanta. The child asks her friend whether it is five o'clock yet, explaining that her father has promised to take her to the cinema later that evening. Shanta tells her teacher that she must go home because it is five o'clock. The teacher uses the opportunity to discuss with the class how to tell time. The other children, however, can tell the proper time no better than Shanta. After explaining to Shanta that the current time is only two forty-five, the teacher tells the children to return to their seats. Shanta does so, but only for ten more minutes, at which point she approaches her teacher once again, insisting that she must go home early or her father will be angry with her. The teacher dismisses Shanta, who runs home and looks for her mother. Shanta's mother returns from the house next door, where she had been visiting with friends. When Shanta's mother asks her why she is home from school early, the girl replies with a question, asking whether her father has come home from work yet. Shanta proceeds to dress in her best clothes and tie a ribbon onto the end of her braided hair, asking her mother if she will be coming along for the evening.

Shanta's mother, who informs Shanta that she will not be going with Shanta and her father, attempts to keep Shanta from standing at the gate and looking down the street for her father. Frustrated that the hour is growing late and her father has not yet returned, Shanta questions her mother, who suggests that Shanta's father had to work late. Despite her mother's repeated requests for her to come inside, Shanta persists in waiting at the gate, until she takes it upon herself to walk to her father's office. She soon becomes lost and is helped home by a servant from one of the nearby homes.

Meanwhile, Shanta's father, Venkat Rao, recalls his impulsive decision to promise his daughter an outing to the cinema. Rao feels saddened by the fact that he has little time to spend with his daughter, who he fears spends much of her time alone, without the toys, dresses, and excursions that other children enjoy. He laments the fact that he works late every evening and spends much of his weekend at the office as well. Having promised Shanta he would take her out and that she should be ready by five o'clock, Rao proceeds to his office the morning of the appointed day, resolved to resign if his superiors attempt to force him to work late into the evening once again. At five p.m., Rao approaches his manager and asks to leave, explaining that he has pressing personal business to attend to. His manager tells Rao to get back to work, insisting that nothing should be more urgent than his job. Rao returns to his desk, observing that it is now half past five. Anticipating that he would have to remain at work for another two hours to complete the task his manager has set for him, Rao pens his resignation letter, a note filled with anger at the fact that he has had to work like a slave for almost no pay. Rao then walks to his manager's desk, and places the note, sealed in an envelope, on the manager's desk. The manager, not noticing what Rao has done, informs Rao that he is to receive a pay raise of five rupees. Rao immediately pockets the letter. When the manager questions him, Rao lies, explaining that the letter was a request for some time off. The manager interrupts, telling him that under no circumstances will Rao be allowed any leave for at least two weeks. Rao responds by saying that he understands, which is why he decided to withdraw his request. Once again returning to his desk, Rao works until nine o'clock.

At home, Rao finds his daughter asleep in her best dress; his wife explains that Shanta refused to change her clothes or eat anything and would not lie down for bed, as she was worried about wrinkling her dress. Distraught, Rao attempts to wake Shanta, saying that he could still take her to a late show. Shanta does not wake up, but she kicks her legs and cries out in irritation at having her sleep so disturbed. Rao's wife asks him not to wake Shanta, and she soothes her daughter back to sleep. Rao explains to his wife that he does not know whether he will be able to take Shanta to the cinema at all, as he has been given a raise, implying that now he will have to earn the increase by working as much as ever, if not more.

CHARACTERS

Kamala
Kamala is a young schoolgirl, a friend of Shanta's. Kamala incorrectly assures Shanta that it is five o'clock in the afternoon.

Manager
Venkat Rao's manager is Rao's direct superior. As long as Rao needs his job to support his family, he is at the mercy of his manager. The manager views work as a man's most urgent responsibility, and he suggests to Rao that his duties in the office should be viewed as his top priority. The manager also asks Rao if Rao knows how many hours he himself works. Rao does not answer, but recalls how the other clerks in the office joke that the manager's wife must beat him whenever he is at home, which is why the manager spends so much time in the office. While the manager expects much of Rao, Rao's hard work has earned him the manager's respect, as evidenced by the fact that the manager informs Rao that he has recommended to his superiors that Rao receive an increment (that is, a raise).

Mrs. Rao
Mrs. Rao is Venkat Rao's wife and Shanta Rao's mother. Her first name is not provided. The reader is introduced to Mrs. Rao when Shanta returns home from school early. Mrs. Rao questions Shanta about her sudden appearance at home, and argues with her about what Shanta selects to wear on her outing. Mrs. Rao urges Shanta to wear a long skirt and thick coat, but

Shanta selects a thin frock. Mrs. Rao's choice indicates her concern for her daughter's health and comfort. She further reveals her practical and cautious nature when she scolds Shanta for waiting in the direct sun, and then again for standing outside after it has gotten dark. When the story shifts from Shanta's point of view to Rao's, Rao recalls how his wife doubted that he would be able to keep his promise. This suggests that Mrs. Rao is familiar enough with her husband's schedule and habitual lateness at the office to doubt that he will be able to take Shanta to the cinema. When Rao returns home, late, after Shanta has been in bed for hours, Mrs. Rao tells her husband how Shanta would not change out of her dress or eat, and how the child refused to lay down, so certain was she that her father would arrive in time to take her to the cinema. Mrs. Rao then insists that her husband cease his efforts at trying to wake the child, and she comforts her daughter back to sleep.

Shanta Rao

Shanta is a young girl, the daughter of Venkat Rao and his wife. In school, she questions her friends and teacher persistently about the time, insisting that she must be home at five o'clock to go to the cinema with her father. Not only is Shanta's eagerness to spend time with her father apparent in her actions at school but her desperation to not disappoint him is evidenced as well. As she informs her teacher, Shanta is anxious to avoid having her father be angry with her for not being ready on time. Once home, Shanta refuses food or drink and gets ready for her evening out. She and her mother argue about what she will wear, as Shanta selects a thin dress, whereas her mother wants her to wear something warmer. Shanta persists in waiting outside for her father to come home. Her mother chastises her for standing out in the sun, and later, for being out as it is starting to get dark. This indication of the passage of time demonstrates Shanta's stubborn belief that her father will keep his word. She even attempts to walk to his workplace, but quickly becomes lost and is escorted home by a servant from another home. From her father's perspective, Shanta's life seems devoid of the pleasures enjoyed by other children, and it is this perception that prompted him to answer her request for a trip to the cinema in the affirmative. When Rao arrives home after nine p.m., long after Shanta has fallen asleep, Shanta's mother informs Rao that Shanta waited for him, apparently still convinced her father would be taking her to the cinema when he got home.

Venkat Rao

Venkat Rao is Shanta's father. He feels that Shanta has been denied many of life's joys, compared with other children, and he feels as though he has no time to spend with her. Certain he has neglected both his wife and his daughter, Rao tells himself that at least his wife has her own circle of friends; she cannot be as lonely and bored as Shanta. All of these thoughts make Rao resolve to stand up to his manager and insist on leaving at five o'clock to take Shanta out to the cinema. However, after Rao politely requests time off, the manager does not permit him to leave but rather scolds him for not viewing work as his most urgent priority. Rao pens a passionately angry letter to his manager and resolves to resign, but before he can do so, he is told that he will be receiving a raise, so he stays at work until nine o'clock. Upon seeing his daughter asleep, still dressed in her pretty pink dress, Rao is deeply moved and saddened. He tries desperately to explain to his wife that he might not be able to take Shanta out at all. Rao seems to fear that even more will be required of him now that his salary has been increased by five rupees, and he despairs at having even less time with his family.

Rao's anguish is clearly and repeatedly depicted. His intentions to stand up for himself and for his family life are demonstrated through his thoughts and the undelivered letter. Yet Rao only presents a polite and dutiful attitude toward his manager. His anger and anguish remain hidden from the workplace. As much as Rao wants to spend more time with his family, particularly his daughter, Rao also appears terrified to jeopardize his income. His sense of duty to provide for his family outweighs the sorrow he feels at not being able to be a meaningful part of his daughter's life.

Teacher

Shanta's teacher plays a minor role in the story. She questions Shanta when the child tells her she must leave at five o'clock. Eventually, the teacher grants Shanta permission to leave school early.

THEMES

Working Class

The family that is the subject of Narayan's "Forty-Five a Month" is a working-class family. In a working-class family, one or more members of the family earn the money the family needs for

TOPICS FOR FURTHER STUDY

- In Narayan's "Forty-Five a Month," Venkat Rao's plans to see a movie with his daughter are thwarted by his professional obligations. Despite his rebellious thoughts, Rao is submissive to his manager. Economic necessity likely forces Rao to behave in this manner and Rao is aware that his manager probably earns more than he does. Rao may also feel that his manager, because of that higher income, is of a higher class standing. Research the relationships between wealth, social class, and the Hindu caste system in India. How did such distinctions affect the daily life of Indians in the 1940s? What types of discrimination were suffered by members of lower classes and castes? Using print and online sources, prepare a PowerPoint presentation in which you share your findings. Be sure to cite all sources.

- *Climbing the Stairs*, by Padma Venkatraman, published by Putnam Juvenile in 2008, is a young-adult novel set in India during World War II. The work centers on a fifteen-year-old girl and her perceptions of India's participation in the war, the Indian fight for independence against the British, and Mohandas Gandhi's role in this revolution. *Climbing the Stairs* takes place during the same time period as Narayan's story "Forty-Five a Month," which, by contrast, makes no mention of the political events occurring then. Read *Climbing the Stairs* and examine the ways in which the political events surrounding Vidya, the main character, contribute to her sense of isolation and her sense of self. In what ways do World War II and the fight for Indian independence change Vidya and her family? Write an essay in which you explore these issues.

- Narayan's story "Forty-Five a Month" ends with the father, Venkat Rao, arriving home and realizing he may never have the time he wishes to spend with his daughter. Shanta remains asleep as Rao expresses his fears to his wife. Consider what might happen next in the story, after Shanta wakes up in the morning and realizes what has occurred. Write a short story in which you explore, from Shanta's point of view, her reaction to her father's decision to remain at work that evening and her interaction with him. What role does Shanta's mother have in your story? Would she defend Rao if her daughter expressed her disappointment? Would Shanta be understanding or angry? Might Shanta discuss what has happened with her friends at school? Remain consistent with the nature of the characters as Narayan has established them, but explore how each would react and respond to one another in the aftermath of the failed outing.

- *Echoes of the White Giraffe*, by Sook Nyul Choi, was published in 2007 by Sandpiper. In this young-adult novel set in Korea during the Korean War, Choi explores the parent-child relationship, focusing on the interaction between a teenage Korean girl (Sookan) and her mother. Although Sookan is older than Narayan's Shanta in "Forty-Five a Month," both girls have relationships with their parents that are shaped by forces beyond their control. Read Choi's novel and compare the characters of Shanta and Sookan. In what ways are they alike? What expectations do they have of their parents? What expectations do their parents have of them? How do Sookan's and Shanta's mothers attempt to guide or protect their daughters? Are they successful? Discuss these questions with a book group you have formed. Collectively agree on which aspects of your analysis you would like to present to your class and develop a format for a presentation.

A raise means more money. (Image copyright Swissmacky, 2009. Used under license from Shutterstock.com)

basic necessities. Working-class jobs are typically viewed as those that are low-paying, often require long hours, and often involve physical labor. The working class is distinguished from the middle class (or bourgeoisie, as it is often called) in that working-class individuals typically are less educated and earn just enough to secure the necessities of life, such as food, clothing, and shelter. Middle-class individuals typically earn enough to pay for necessities as well as additional luxury or convenience items, or goods or services with educational or entertainment purposes. The Rao family in "Forty-Five a Month" relies on Venkat Rao's meager income from his office job for necessities. From Rao's description of Shanta's life, the family has little extra income for toys and trips to the cinema. Rao describes how hard he works for a small amount of money. Although there is apparently enough money for Rao to consider a rare trip to the cinema, he is clearly desperate to continue drawing his meager income, and he is willing to sacrifice his relationship with his family in order to keep earning his salary. His desperation suggests the family's great need and also implies that the Raos do not, in all likelihood, have money saved on which they could live if Rao sought another job. Rao's predicament reflects Narayan's sympathy for working-class individuals. Regardless of Rao's poignant awareness of the fact that his daughter is essentially growing up without him, he feels compelled by his family's circumstances to continue working for a company that pays him so little and asks for so much in return. It is Rao's awareness of just how much he is sacrificing that makes this particular working-class story so tragic.

Parent-Child Relationships

Narayan depicts the relationship Shanta has with both of her parents in "Forty-Five a Month." Shanta's mother is chatting with the neighbors when Shanta arrives home from school early. The mother is concerned about Shanta, wondering why she could possibly be home before the usual time. A protective mother, Mrs. Rao (Narayan does not supply the mother's first name), argues with Shanta about what Shanta will wear for her evening out. She firmly urges Shanta to wear something warm, but she relents under

Shanta's equally firm insistence that she will wear a thin dress and knickers instead of the warm coat and long skirt Mrs. Rao suggests. Despite her eagerness and the argument she has just had with her mother, Shanta displays affection and concern for her mother when she asks whether she is coming along to the cinema as well. (She is not.) Mrs. Rao continues to demonstrate her protective but lenient attitude toward her daughter when she asks her to come inside (first, out of the sun, and later, before it gets dark). Both requests are met with disobedience. When Rao tells Shanta he will take her to the movies, Mrs. Rao is described as smiling in a cynical manner and advising her husband not to make "false promises to the child." Despite her skeptical attitude toward her husband, Mrs. Rao once again attempts to protect Shanta, this time from the disappointment Mrs. Rao fears is inevitable. She soothes Shanta back to sleep when Rao attempts to wake her, having arrived home late. While Mrs. Rao both indulges her daughter and also attempts to protect her, Venkat Rao is tortured by guilt at not being able to provide his daughter with the luxuries other children enjoy: "dolls, dress and outings." He fears Shanta's life is "a drab, colourless existence." Rao seems to understand that his daughter needs his time as much as the family needs his income, yet Rao does not follow through on his plan for resigning if his manager does not allow him to leave on time on the night he has promised to take Shanta to the cinema. His guilt is extreme; upon seeing Shanta asleep in her dress when he returns home after nine o'clock, Rao's "heart bled." His relationship with his daughter is characterized as much by his sense of duty to buy her the things she needs as it is by his desire to give her more and to spend time with her. Rao's guilt and grief characterize his relationship with Shanta, and these are the overriding emotions that pervade "Forty-Five a Month."

STYLE

Third-Person Multiple Point of View

Narayan's "Forty-Five a Month" is written in what is known as the third person, a method of storytelling in which the narration is conducted by a person outside the action of the story. The narrator in "Forty-Five a Month," for example, informs the reader of what Shanta is doing, but the narrator is not Shanta. In "Forty-Five a Month," the narrator tells the story in the third person, but from the limited viewpoint of two characters: first Shanta, then Venkat Rao. The viewpoint is said to be multiple, in that it involves more than one character, and it is a limited point of view in that the narrator confines the storytelling to what Shanta thinks, experiences, and observes, and then what Venkat Rao thinks, experiences, and observes. If the narrator was omniscient, or all-knowing, rather than telling the story from a limited point of view, the narrator would also comment freely on the thoughts, experiences, and observations of any or all characters in the story and on overarching issues related to the story's social or cultural context. An omniscient narrator may discuss things that none of the characters have any knowledge of. The narrator in "Forty-Five a Month" does not make such remarks. The narration is limited to Shanta's point of view and that of her father. Narayan's choice of this type of narration allows the tension between his two main characters, Shanta and Venkat, to be fully exposed and carefully explored.

Realism

Narayan's style in "Forty-Five a Month" is characteristic of many of his writings. He realistically portrays intimate family relationships within the context of urban, working-class, everyday life in an Indian community. This realism is conveyed in straightforward prose and enhanced through the many details Narayan offers. Narayan lists the lessons Shanta has been involved with in school. He describes the way she is currently occupied with cutting paper, an activity she quickly grows bored with, as evidenced by the fact that she throws her scissors down and runs to the teacher, insisting she must go home. Such details—the list of activities, the colored paper, the scissors being thrown—appear trivial but contribute to the reader's ability to visualize the scene Narayan sets. Other descriptions also convey a sense of realism and at the same time speak to the environment in which Shanta is growing up. Narayan describes the way Shanta stores precious scraps of ribbons and lumps of chalk in a cardboard soap box. The fact that such apparently worthless items are treasured is significant, as is the fact that the treasures are stored in a box that previously had such a mundane use. These details imply that the Rao family is not very well off, financially. A trip to the cinema, therefore, is indeed the prize that Shanta's actions suggest it is. Her father's comments support the idea that taking his daughter to see a movie would go a long way toward pleasing a girl who does not have a lot of other joys in her life. In fact, from Venkat Rao's point of view, his daughter is "growing up all alone and like a barbarian more or less." Narayan's simple, honest tone; the descriptive details; and the commonplace, universally appealing subject matter (a man's struggle to provide for his family) all contribute to the realism of the story.

HISTORICAL CONTEXT

Movement for Indian Independence from Britain

At the time that Narayan was writing "Forty-Five a Month," India was a colony of the British empire and was struggling to gain independence from Great Britain. This independence, declared in 1947, was not fully achieved until 1950, when India established its own constitution and declared itself a republic. During the early1940s, the efforts to establish an independent India were complicated by World War II (1939–1945). Some leaders in the Indian government urged support of the British army, whereas other factions within the country aligned themselves with the Japanese, whom the British were fighting. Many conflicts within the country—during the war and previously—were rooted in rifts between Hindus and Muslims. In 1942, the Indian National Congress sought to rally support for the movement against British imperialism by issuing a call for Indians to join what was known as the Quit India movement (Indians wanted the British to "quit," or leave, India). Countless Indians, including women in large numbers, participated in a movement often guided by principles of nonviolence and noncooperation urged by Mahatma Gandhi. Indians were instructed to peacefully resist the British governing forces. Strikes and boycotts were organized. Violence did erupt, however. Police stations and railway stations were bombed, and telegraph and rail service was disrupted. The British, under Viceroy Linlithgow (the viceroy served as the head of the British administrative rule in India), ordered a large-scale repression of the movement, including the massive deployment of troops. Many Indians were arrested, and some lost their lives. Given the number of Indians who participated and the amount of British manpower required to contain the movement, the Quit India movement was viewed as ultimately successful, despite the casualties, in preventing a long-term continuation of British rule in India following the end of World War II.

Caste and the Working Class in World War II India

Because of India's involvement in World War II, an involvement engineered by the British governing bodies in India, the economy in India was mobilized for the manufacture of goods and services needed for the war effort. However, India was forced to initially finance much of its own participation in the war. While many people were employed in the manufacture of wartime necessities, the government in India also raised taxes and printed more money, resulting in inflation and severe economic stress for many Indians, many of whom were considered working class or lower middle class. Individuals in this category had little savings and lived from paycheck to paycheck, working long hours, often for low pay. In some manufacturing and textile industries, workers organized into unions to help protect their rights; the Communist and Socialist parties had been present in India for some time and contributed to both the empowerment and the unrest of workers in various industries.

Related to the idea of class structure is the notion of caste, a term that refers to the Hindu belief in inherited social class affiliation. Members of various castes are often associated with a particular group of occupations or with wealth and land ownership. Lower castes did not possess the same rights and opportunities as those with a higher caste status. In the 1940s, political efforts were made, with the involvement of Gandhi, toward the goal of the social equalization of the castes, that is, toward nondiscrimination based on caste status. However, as John Keay observes in *India: A History*, "in pursuit of caste equality, caste identity was not being eroded but actively promoted." In other words, government attempts to level the social, educational, and professional opportunities of all Indians had the effect of drawing attention to caste rather than ignoring it, as a means of supporting social equality.

COMPARE & CONTRAST

- **1940s:** India is a colony of Great Britain. The relationship between India and Great Britain grows violent, despite the efforts of Mohandas Gandhi (who is given the title of respect "Mahatma") for peaceful resistance, as India struggles to gain its independence. India, along with Pakistan, declares independence from Great Britain in 1947.

   Today: India has been an independent republic since 1950, when its constitution was written. There remains a strong British presence in India in terms of the military and legal systems established in India, as well as in the world of sport, as the British introduced cricket to India during the colonial period. In Great Britain, there are large numbers of Indian immigrants (more than one million, according to 2007 statistics), whose beliefs, traditions, and food influence British society and culture.

- **1940s:** Many new manufacturing jobs are created because of India's involvement in World War II. The workforce of India, as a British colony, is mobilized to help in the British war effort. The complex nature of the relationship between India and Great Britain results in India financing much of the war effort initially, which leads to inflation. The prosperity that might have been possible for many working-class Indians because of the increase in manufacturing jobs is undercut by inflated prices and higher taxes.

   Today: India is not immune to the economic slump that is endured globally during the middle and later years of the first decade of the twenty-first century. The growth rate of the Indian economy slows considerably between 2008 and 2009, resulting in fewer new jobs.

- **1940s:** Prominent Indian writers (such as Narayan and Raja Rao) often write in English in order to receive critical attention and wider distribution. Indian fiction written in English embraces realism and often focuses on everyday life in villages and cities. Some writers focus on the personal hardships of individuals, while others explore more overtly the social and political struggles of India during its struggle for independence and its involvement in World War II.

   Today: Indian writers today write in English and in their native languages, such as Hindi, Urdu, or Bengali. Their writing reflects the multicultural nature of India, representing diverse genres and styles. Contemporary Indian fiction writers include Salman Rushdie and Amit Chaudhuri.

CRITICAL OVERVIEW

Narayan's short story "Forty-Five a Month" is not often discussed in great detail by critics, who often mention the story only in cursory fashion, within the context of Narayan's short fiction in general. Often the story is grouped thematically by critics and treated as an example of one exploration of a particular theme. P. S. Ramana, in *Message in Design: A Study of R. K. Narayan's Fiction*, views "Forty-Five a Month" as one of the stories in which Narayan has an opportunity to use his subject matter to explore large-scale social injustices. However, Ramana notes that Narayan seeks to expose the light, humorous aspects of the situations, instead of delving into the tragedy of injustice. Ramana also explains that Narayan views the characters in these stories of social injustice "as individuals whose sufferings are personal tragedies rather than being symptomatic of an unjust system." Kapileswar Parija, in *Short Stories of R. K. Narayan: Themes and Conventions*, includes "Forty-Five a Month" in the category of Narayan short fiction that deals with the love of a father for

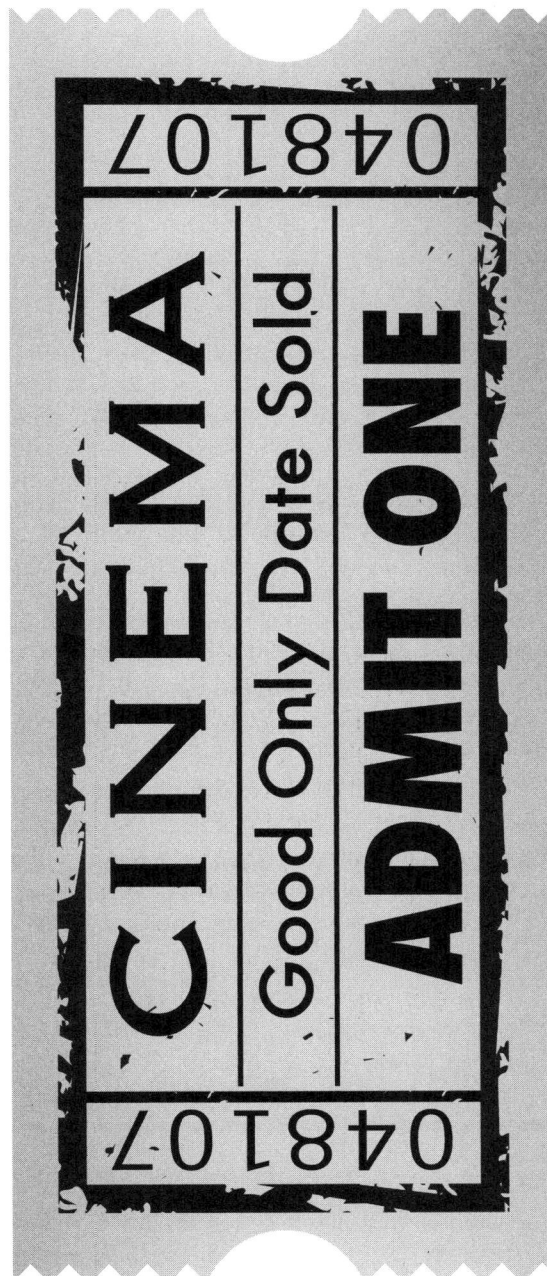

A girl wants to go to the cinema. (Image copyright belle23, 2009. Used under license from Shutterstock.com)

Narayan's poignant treatment of the character of Shanta. In general, Raizada writes, Narayan's stories involving children incorporate "ironical situations which besides being amusing and entertaining, provide a peep into the nature and character of the eager, innocent and easily credulous nature of children." The role of children in Narayan's fiction is also touched on by C. V. Venugopal, in *The Indian Short Story in English (A Survey)*. Somewhat dismissive of Narayan's treatment of young characters, Venugopal describes Shanta as a "pretty little child" who is used by Narayan in "Forty-Five a Month" to "present touching and tender moments in lower middle class life." Venugopal goes on to observe that "the world of Narayan teems with the prattling little children who win us over."

CRITICISM

Catherine Dominic

Dominic is a novelist and a freelance writer and editor. In the following essay, she explores the ways in which Narayan contrasts the characters of Shanta and Venkat Rao and their experiences, maintaining that Narayan heightens the tragedy of "Forty-Five a Month" by juxtaposing Shanta's innocence, trust, and strength with Rao's fears and weaknesses.

Narayan's short fiction in general is often viewed as an insightful exploration of Indian life, and it has been observed that while Narayan explores aspects of the human condition, he does so on a personal level and that he avoids making overt political statements. In particular, Narayan's "Forty-Five a Month" has been regarded as a work in which the author's depiction of the struggle of a father to juggle the demands of providing for his family and enjoying their company is balanced or even outshone by the author's tender and humorous portrayal of the man's daughter, Shanta. However, if Narayan's portrayal of Shanta is understood in terms of Narayan's juxtaposition of Shanta's experiences and those of her father, Venkat Rao, the daughter's characterization no longer appears as the sweet, light, comic element of the story that lifts the tale out of the realm of the depressing and tragic. Rather, Narayan juxtaposes the child's happy, innocent eagerness with the father's succumbing to the numbing necessity of his job. The relationship between the two characters emphasizes the

his children. This emotion, Parija argues, is depicted by Narayan as "one of the most beautiful experiences of life." Another critic, Harish Raizada, in *R. K. Narayan: A Critical Study of His Works*, focuses on the experience of the child rather than that of the father and, like Ramana, finds that Narayan is able to draw out light, entertaining elements in stories such as "Forty-Five a Month." Raizada praises

WHAT DO I READ NEXT?

- Narayan's *Mallei Days*, originally published in 1943, is available in an expanded edition published in 2006 by Penguin Classics. The collection of short stories is set in the fictional town of Mallei, India, loosely based on Mysore. It is among Narayan's best-known collections and inspired an Indian television series of the same name.

- *The Guide: A Novel* by R. K. Narayan was originally published in 1958 and is available in a 2006 edition from Penguin Classics. This novel, which centers on a tour guide who has just been released from prison and is mistaken for a holy man, is among Narayan's most popular. Narayan won the National Prize awarded by the Indian Literary Academy for this work. It is the highest literary honor one can achieve in India.

- *Secret Keeper*, written by Mitali Perkins and published by Delacorte Books for Young Readers in 2009, is the fictional story of a teenage girl who lives in Calcutta, India. *Secret Keeper* offers students of "Forty-Five a Month" insights into modern Indian culture and the role of children and young adults in it.

- Mahatma Gandhi was a major political force in India during Narayan's lifetime. While many of Narayan's works are not overtly political in nature, Gandhi is treated in Narayan's novel *Waiting for Mahatma* (1955).

- *Gandhi: His Life and Message for the World*, written by Louis Fischer and published by Mentor in 1982, examines Gandhi's life and discusses his teachings.

- English writer Graham Greene was instrumental in initially helping Narayan to get his fiction published. Greene's own short stories in *Complete Short Stories*, published in 2005 by Penguin Classics, allow a cross-cultural comparison of the two friends' writings.

- *Religion in India: A Historical Introduction*, by Fred Clothey, explores the various religions practiced in India, their historical development, and the impact of religion on events in India's history, such as the struggle for independence from Great Britain. The work was published by Routledge in 2007.

---

tragedy inherent the story. Narayan's delineation of the child's expectant joy in "Forty-Five a Month" tips the scales of the story toward tragic pessimism and away from the bright optimism of Shanta's youth, because the contrast between the experiences of Shanta and those of her father is so stark.

"Forty-Five a Month" is neatly divided approximately in half. The first portion of the story is told from the point of view of Shanta, a young schoolgirl, and the second portion of the story is told from the point of view of her father. As the story opens, the reader is introduced to Shanta, who impatiently waits to escape the schoolroom. The tender age of Shanta and her classmates is apparent in the opening scene, as the children are unable to tell the time. Shanta desperately wants to get home before five o'clock, as her father has promised her a trip to the cinema. Her urgency is clear in the number of times she makes reference to the time, and through her actions. She throws her scissors aside rather than laying them on the desk; she runs to the teacher rather than walking or raising her hand. When Shanta tells the teacher her father asked her to leave early, her teacher asks her what time she is supposed to leave. "Now," Shanta answers, after learning moments before that it was not yet three o'clock.

Narayan endears the child to the reader not only through her eagerness to leave but through her struggle to properly answer her teacher's

> NARAYAN'S DELINEATION OF THE CHILD'S EXPECTANT JOY IN 'FORTY-FIVE A MONTH' TIPS THE SCALES OF THE STORY TOWARD TRAGIC PESSIMISM AND AWAY FROM THE BRIGHT OPTIMISM OF SHANTA'S YOUTH, BECAUSE THE CONTRAST BETWEEN THE EXPERIENCES OF SHANTA AND THOSE OF HER FATHER IS SO STARK."

question about the time. Two paragraphs and several lines of dialogue—not a small amount of space in such a short story—are used in the humorous relating of Shanta's attempt to read the clock, as her teacher has instructed. Shanta, upon being asked to tell her teacher what time it is, examines the clock face, "laboriously" counting the numbers she sees, before telling her teacher that it is nine o'clock. The teacher instructs Shanta to look not just at the long hand but at the short one. After announcing that as the short hand is at "two and a half" that the time must be "two and a half," Shanta returns to her seat, having been informed by her teacher that the time is two forty-five.

Once the exasperated teacher has excused Shanta from class, Shanta runs home, asking her mother whether her father has returned home from work yet. Of course, he has not, but Shanta proceeds to ready herself for her evening out, refusing both her coffee and *tiffin* (lunch, or a light meal). A lengthy paragraph is expended in the relation of Shanta's readying herself for her outing. Against her mother's wishes, Shanta selects a lightweight pink dress. She ties a ribbon in her hair, powders her face, and places a vermilion (red) mark on her forehead. (This is a type of Hindu ornamentation with spiritual significance. Hinduism is a religion practiced by many people native to India.) Narayan's characterization of Shanta as incredibly earnest and eager is reinforced in the next small section of the story, when Shanta waits outside for her father until dark. Her conversation with her mother mirrors that which Shanta shared with her teacher. Like Shanta's teacher, her mother attempts to redirect the child's attention, but to no avail. Eventually, the determined Shanta takes off down the road, certain she will be able to find her father's office. She is helped home by a servant from a nearby residence. This is the last information the reader is given from Shanta's perspective. When she next appears in the story, Shanta is asleep. Narayan has demonstrated in the first half of the story Shanta's sense of joyful expectation. The child is intently focused, unable to be turned away from being prepared for her father's arrival by her teacher, her mother, the hot sun, the onset of darkness, or utter fatigue. Shanta, her mother reveals at the end of the story, would barely eat anything and refused to change out of her dress or lie down, for fear of wrinkling her clothes. Against the evidence and past experience, all of which suggest that her father will not make it home in time to take her to the cinema, Shanta believes in her father for the simple reason that he is her father and he made a promise.

In the next half of the story, Narayan depicts Venkat Rao, Shanta's father, as a man desperate to change his life. He has become tired of working all hours for little pay and sacrificing his relationship with his only child in the bargain. Rao is deeply concerned about his daughter's welfare, as evidenced by his comments about her lack of material possessions. Rao characterizes his daughter's life as dull and devoid of entertainment, friends, or pleasure. When he is asked to stay late on the evening of his date with his daughter, Rao dutifully returns to his desk, just has Shanta had returned to her seat when her teacher had told her it was not yet time to go. Rao crafts a rancorous letter in which he insists he has not been purchased "body and soul for forty rupees." He states that he would rather die with his family of starvation than continue being employed in such a manner. He curses his manager, stating his intention to haunt the manager, along with his family, should he, his wife, and his daughter all die of starvation. The letter is indicative of the intensity of Rao's rage and frustration. However, unlike his daughter, Rao does not receive permission to leave. Shanta persists until she is rewarded with the result she has sought—the approved, if irritated, dismissal by her superior. Rao, upon being told he is to be given a five-rupee increment, or raise, returns to his desk and diligently completes his work. While Shanta lives up to her end of the bargain—she is ready by five o'clock just as her father instructed—Rao breaks his promise, unable to persist as effectively as his daughter. Rao's ability to provide for his family is at stake; he is no schoolboy. However, the reader is aware of Shanta's experience, while Rao is not. Just as Shanta is not aware of the dilemma her father faces, so Rao is unaware that Shanta has lived every moment of this day focused on the prospect of an evening with her father. She has overcome her own obstacles and accomplished her goal of not letting her father down. She was ready; her father would have no reason to be angry with her, as he had told her he would be if she were not ready on time.

Rao is clearly tormented by the decision he has made. His heart breaks when he sees his daughter, asleep and still dressed to go out, when he arrives home after nine o'clock. The reader's heart breaks for Shanta, for her belief in her father, her innocent trust, has been breached. Narayan reveals Shanta's story first. The reader experiences her excitement, her impatience and anticipation. Having witnessed first-hand all the preparations and good intentions and hopefulness wrapped up in Shanta's story, the reader is then thrust into Rao's tale. His inability to stand up to his manager, to risk the loss of income and to instead be available to his daughter, appear to the reader as graver transgressions than they might have otherwise seemed, had not Shanta's story been told first.

Narayan skillfully crafts his narrative so that Shanta's tale ends right along with the demise of any power she has to control her own situation. She does her part. She is ready on time and she waits. Rao's story opens at a point when he may still shape his fate—he can stay, he can go, he can attempt to reason with his manager. Rao hesitates, though; he fumbles, accepting without a fight the powerlessness that was so forcibly thrust upon Shanta by her age and circumstances. Narayan further contrasts Shanta and Rao by depicting their very different reactions to similar instructions: daughter and father are both told to return to their seats, to keep working. Shanta cannot obey. Rao tries to resist, but he soon retreats to his desk, defeated. By contrasting the characters and their situations, Narayan heightens the story's sense of tragedy. Shanta and the reader are both let down by Rao. Treated first to a depiction of Shanta's own expectations, which are shaped by her youthful innocence, happiness, and trust, the reader's fall from expectation to reality is a harsh, painful one, and Rao's anguish becomes the reader's own. The tragedy the reader experiences is informed by both Shanta's hopes and by Rao's torment.

Source: Catherine Dominic, Critical Essay on "Forty-Five a Month," in *Short Stories for Students*, Gale, Cengage Learning, 2010.

Ramesh Avadhani

In the following excerpt, Avadhani describes the universality of Narayan's mythical town of Malgudi.

The business of the novelist, wrote Graham Greene in *A Sort of Life*, is the novel, nothing else. No other Indian writer, to my mind, fulfilled this axiom as much as R. K. Narayan. His fifteen novels and five collections of short stories are ample testimony to his passionate intent—to dish up broth after bubbling broth that has as its ingredients the foibles, struggles, and yearnings of simple souls on whom complex circumstances descend.

Narayan draws many of his characters from the Tamil Brahmins of southern India, a community that prides itself as the pinnacle in wisdom and culture gleaned from the ancient scriptures of the Ramayana, Mahabharata, and Vedas. And the irony that Narayan gently nudges us to see is that his characters have still some way to go to reach those summits!

His stories are set in the fictitious town of Malgudi, which is "almost a day's journey from Madras." Yet it appears to me that any reader in any part of the world would resonate with the thoughts, feelings, and desires of Narayan's characters. It is this universality of emotions simmering in a niche setting (Malgudi), involving a typical community (Tamil Brahmins), that makes the irresistible blend of the common with the exotic.

Simple souls, complex circumstances.

As we begin reading Narayan's novels, his protagonists (mostly male) come across as simple souls going about their lives without much fanfare or fuss. Their deportment is one of apparent contentment. Yes, they may be worried by a minor glitch in their trade or profession or a household task that hasn't yet been satisfactorily completed, but Narayan is not in a rush to offer us any clues as to what is to follow. It's the calm before the proverbial storm. A colorful character drops in or a surprising event takes place. Voila, the protagonist is transformed and, one by one, all the other characters touched by him.

From then onward, we are swept along on a roller-coaster ride through the many turbulences that are inevitable when personal desires clash with external obstacles. Sometimes, the characters, while in mid-journey, appear stranded at a dead end, but Narayan merrily invents another character or a situation or backpedals to explain what happened in another time in another place... and the journey continues....

FOUNDING FATHER

Along with Mulk Raj Anand and Raja Rao, R. K. Narayan is regarded as the founding father of Indian fiction in English. To me, what sets Narayan apart is his dexterous weaving of a magical blend of Western technique and Indian substance. He succeeds in a remarkable way in making an Indian sensibility at home in English art. While much of India considers Narayan as its greatest writer in English, it comes as a pleasant surprise that a whole legion of fans abroad consider him as the one of the three greatest writers (Huxley and Greene being the other two) in English literary fiction of the twentieth century. In fact, Graham Greene was single-handedly responsible for introducing the Indian writer to the rest of the world. Greene and Narayan shared a friendship for more than fifty years via letters and met only once in 1964, in London.

I once asked R. K. Laxman, Narayan's younger brother and cartoonist of *The Times* of India, in Bombay, as to how much money Narayan made from all his novels. This was after the million-dollar advance Vikram Seth secured for his novel, *A Suitable Boy*. "More than all the other Indian writers put together," Laxman said with a lofty chuckle.

Yet, all of the foregoing is a superficial appreciation of Narayan's fiction—the core is something else: sad comedies about the human condition. This is one of the most difficult of genres in fiction. Nimbly and deftly, with optimal amount of words and sympathetic tone in language, Narayan unravels the universal riddle of the human race—the complex fusion of sincerity and self-deception that we all practice. To write engagingly and dispassionately on such matters requires a sensibility distanced from melodrama and aloofness, a stunningly unified point of view, as well as a strong foundation in a unique social milieu in which the comedy and the pathos are intermingled—neither of them submerging the other. It requires above all, equanimity of the highest order, a temperament that even angels would envy. For that is what R. K. Narayan aspired to—to accept his own lot that so peaked and troughed all his life, without recourse to self-pity, exaggeration or sentimentality—his failure in exams, the loss of his wife Rajam after just four years of marriage, the numerous rejections of his early manuscripts, and finally, the loss of his only child, Hema, to cancer, a few years before his own death (May 13, 2001). I am sure that is what he would have liked his countless admirers to also emulate (although he never admitted it so in any of the interviews to my knowledge).

EARLY YEARS

Rasipuram Krishnaswami Narayanswami, the third of eight children, was born in 1907 in the coastal city of Madras (Chennai, where the tsunami wreaked havoc) in a Tamil Brahmin family. His maternal grandmother there raised him while the rest of the family lived in Mysore, a small town about three hours drive from Bangalore on the mainland. It was his grandmother who instilled in him a love for classical music and Indian folktales. He was educated at a Lutheran mission and two other Madras schools before his father, a school headmaster, summoned him to Mysore in 1922. A reluctant pupil, prone to daydreaming and completely at sea with arithmetic and other subjects, Narayan himself admits that he was not gifted to pursue the academic line. As if to substantiate this, he failed his University Entrance examinations twice, the first time ironically in English. This provided him with two years of nothing to do but read, muse and savor all that life unfolded about him. College was academically boring but socially absorbing. Many of his friends of the time find their way later into his novels. He graduated in 1930, took up a teacher's job, resigned after just four days, and in September of that year, on a day chosen by his grandmother, opened an exercise book and waited for inspiration to strike. Malgudi steamed into his imagination in the form of a railway platform. The rest we know.

Source: Ramesh Avadhani, "The 'Malgudi Magician': A Profile of R. K. Narayan," in *World & I*, Vol. 20, No. 12, December 2005, p. 3.

Harsharan S. Ahluwalia

In the following excerpt, Ahluwalia debates how Narayan's awareness of his audience influences his writing.

R. K. Narayan is one of those creative writers who make a living out of their writing. He has struggled very hard to establish himself, i.e., to make himself and his works acceptable to a particular audience in the English-speaking world. Narayan's awareness of his audience is matched by his acute understanding of the commercial aspect of imaginative writing. Describing the book buying situation in his home town (Mysore) in an article published in 1953 he says that among a population of two hundred and seventy-five thousand persons capable of reading and appreciating his books and financially able to buy them, only 200 copies of his novel, *The Bachelor of Arts,* had been sold. In another essay, Narayan says, "The commercial aspect of literary life is alien to our culture; and book-buying and book-keeping [*sic*] are not considered important. Our tradition is more 'Aural,' that means a story-teller is in greater demand than the story-writer. The story-teller who has studied the epics, the Ramayana and the Mahabharata, may take up any of the thousand episodes in them, create a narrative with his individual stamp on it, and hold the attention of an audience, numbering thousands, for hours, while the same man if he sat down to write his stories would hardly make a living out of his work. Being ideal listeners by tradition, our public are not ideal readers." Because of this non-commercial outlook on writing, the writer is considered above wants; he writes to please himself. On the other hand, in the West the commercial outlook on writing has never been looked down upon. Narayan would agree with Dr. Johnson: "No one except an idiot ever wrote but for money." Because of the apathy of Indians to book buying, Narayan published almost all his books first abroad and then in India. After their acceptance in the West, his novels have of late been prescribed in Indian Universities on undergraduate and postgraduate syllabuses. As a result, his sales increased in India in the sixties and the seventies. Even so it cannot be said that Narayan has become popular with Indian readers.

In this connection, certain facts throw interesting light on the relative standing of Narayan in India and the English speaking world. Between 1935 and 1952 his novels appeared first in England. Indian reprints came several years later. From 1953, he caught on in the United States when Michigan State College Press published six of his novels during a period of three years from 1953–1955. After 1955 Narayan's novels have been first published in America, then in Britain and lastly in India. To consider commercial publication of his novels in England and America alone, *The Financial Expert* was published by Noonday (six editions) and Time; *The Guide* by Signet and Penguin; *The Man-eater of Malgudi* by New English Library (Four Square); *The English Teacher* by Pyramid; *Printer of Malgudi* by Arena; *The Vendor of Sweets* by Avon; *Swami and Friends* by Fawcett and Oxford. Paperback editions of all his novels are now being reissued in America by Chicago University Press and in England by Heinemann. Some of his novels have also been translated and published in Russia, Poland, France, Israel, East and West Germany, Sweden, Norway, Finland, Holland, and Yugoslavia.

Narayan shows keen awareness of the demands put on him by the Western readers and publishers. Foreign publishers, he writes, expect an Indian writer "to say something close to the image of India that they have in mind." This problem is not faced by writers writing in Indian languages for Indian readers because both have the same values and they participate in the same range of experience. Foreign readers crave the Indian flavour and for them this flavour is exotic. Most of the articles published about India in American and British newspapers and magazines bear out this view. Narayan himself has succumbed to the temptation of producing pot-boilers such as "New Role for India's Holy Men," "Ghee is Good," and "Why Go Matha is Loved" which he wrote with an eye on the audience of *New York Times Magazine.*

Narayan's own limitations reinforced by his desire to write for the reading public in England and America have clearly demarcated the frontiers of his art. When asked in an interview how he "picked up" themes for his novels and stories, he replied "that he waits for 'some propitious moment'—an incident, a report in the papers, an eccentric he stumbles across. Any of these becomes 'a jumping off ground for a chain of ideas.'" Almost all his novels start with a situation or character which seems to come straight from life, after which the novels develop in the writing. Narayan is not the novelist who conceives the whole novel in advance. It is not to be wondered at that most of his novels are not well made.

Narayan has an eye for the absurd in Indian life. With the observation of eccentric characters in absurd situations, he is entertaining. He is a gifted caricaturist. By careful selection and exaggeration of details, the characters are made to look entertainingly grotesque....

Some of the delightful comic episodes in Narayan's novels read like short stories, others like cartoons or comic strips.... Narayan presents various shades of humour from gentle irony to parody. If his comedy has any purpose, it is the purpose of a cartoonist, i.e., not to let life become too solemn. Narayan's comic vision, which is his strength, also makes his art limited....

To conclude, Narayan's peculiar genius as a comic entertainer has helped him win a large audience in the English-speaking world. This reading public, in turn, has not allowed him to venture out into other areas of human experience. He has got along prosperously with one little spot called Malgudi to the almost complete exclusion of any concern with socio-political forces at work in the country. What need has he to look at the vast panorama that India has been and is!

Source: Harsharan S. Ahluwalia, "Narayan's Sense of Audience," in *Ariel*, Vol. 15, No. 1, January 1984, pp. 59–65.

C. N. Srinath

In the following article, Srinath considers the importance of the fictional Malgudi in Narayan's fiction.

R. K. Narayan's Malgudi has not changed much since 1935 when he wrote his first novel. It is the same pace of life, same locale, same topography, which should naturally amount to monotony; but thanks to the novelist's craftsmanship in not resorting to descriptions of the place, Malgudi is alive as a character. In novel after novel we find the familiar landmarks such as Nellappa Grove, the Lawley Extension, Kabir Road, the Albert Mission school, the spreading tamarind tree, the river Sarayu, the Mempi hills—all these are presented realistically, but what makes it a living reality in art is the ability of the author to give a mythical aura to factual details. Any attempt of the novelist to be realistic in the narrow sense in presenting the changing circumstances of the technological world would have meant ruin to Narayan's art, which thrives on familiar characters in limited surroundings, the life of a small town that refuses to grow into anonymity but like his characters strives toward self-identity. Hence the mythical realism becomes essential for Narayan to communicate the spirit of the place.

It is interesting to watch how, while Malgudi remains more or less the same, there is a gradual development in the protagonists of the novels—from Swami of the first novel to the bachelor of arts to the English teacher and the guide to the sweet-vendor "Philosopher" Jagan. It is a world

> A LIVELY INTEREST IN THE FAMILY AND DOMESTIC LIFE AND AN AVERSION TO ACADEMIC AND SCHOLARLY THINGS WHICH WE FIND IN THE AUTOBIOGRAPHY ARE ALSO TRUE OF A TYPICAL NARAYAN CHARACTER IN FICTION."

of commoners and ordinary folk, but these people possess extraordinary qualities that lend themselves to the very stuff of Narayan's comic art. Not all the characters are mild and vague about their future. We have Margayya and Raju, who hold dynamic notions of themselves, and in wanting to achieve their private goals, which are opposed to the norms of society, they fail; but their failure is an essential process of self-exploration leading to self-knowledge. Narayan achieves this without any rhetorical consciousness of the deep traditional rhythm that pulsates through the Indian scene. The way Narayan does it, one wonders if his awareness is any deeper than that of one of his own characters. It gives one a feeling of limitation, but for Narayan's art it is immensely supportable, this delicate, implicit sense of tradition in the very common men he creates. What Narayan told Ved Mehta about himself is relevant here: "To be a good writer anywhere you must have roots—both in religion and in family. I have these things." We find both religion and family have had an impact, one subtle, the other direct, on men and women in Malgudi that has found sometimes queer, sometimes meaningful manifestations in novel after novel.

If in Narayan there is no trace of intellectuality, it has never endangered the integrity of his art, for the stuff of his fiction is life as it is lived on the road, in markets and homes. The individual merges into the society without much ado, implying a philosophical acceptance. This amounts to the traditional emphasis on the community, which is the ultimate principle in governing the destiny of individuals. In a country where all the arts, literature and philosophy are geared to a realization of the values of the community, which are placed always above the individual interests, Narayan's work sounds so natural, authentic. But paradoxically, it is the same tradition which has produced extraordinary individuals whose personal aspirations ultimately nourished the community and its well-being. And the frontiers of Narayan's art are visible and concrete, which is the secret of his success and the source of his strength and his limitations as well.

Swami and Friends, Narayan's first novel, is undoubtedly one of his best works, and as a boy's classic it has very few parallels in English fiction either in India or abroad. While we are initiated into the Malgudi world for the first time, we are also introduced to the typical Narayan character, Swami, who is also Chandran of *The Bachelor of Arts*, Krishnan of *The English Teacher,* Sampath of the same title, Margayya of *The Financial Expert,* Raju of *The Guide*. It is a buzzing world of schoolboys, their mischiefs, envies, anxieties, fears, wishes and wishful thoughts. In such an atmosphere where cricket and cricket-talk permeate, Swami and his friends form a coterie: Somu, the Monitor of the class; Mani, the mighty good-for-nothing, absolutely nonchalant in the matter of studies and a terror to his teachers; Shankar, the most brilliant of the boys, who evokes much jealousy in one section of the class, which accuses him of currying the teachers' favor by washing their clothes; and Samuel, called the Pea because of his size. The group is complete when Rajam the aristocrat joins the gang. Narayan evokes male adolescent psychology through an authentic presentation of the attitude toward studies and examinations of both the bright boys and the indifferent, ever-playful lot, who come across perhaps most colorfully and vividly due to the novelist's secret predilection for them. The description of the enormous nonacademic preparation for the examination provides ample opportunity for Narayan's humor and gentle irony. Here is an inventory of the stationery items listed by Swami to be handed over to his father:

> Unruled white paper 20 sheets
> Ruled white paper 10 sheets
> Black ink 1 bottle
> Clips...12
> Pins...12

While Narayan makes fun of the misplaced enthusiasm and easy-to-afford devotion of Swami and his group, he brings out the wisdom of innocence in the boys when, for example, Swaminathan is worried about the ripeness and sweetness of mangoes that figure in an arithmetical problem. It is only an adult mind that indulges in the maze of figures and numbers to arrive at a meaningless solution. What does Swaminathan care if one gets ten mangoes for fifteen annas or ten annas for fifteen mangoes? The crucial thing is whether they are ripe and sweet at all.

The excitement and tension that prevail in a boy's world are authentically portrayed by the novelist when we see Swami's group itching to start a cricket club and wrangling over the choice of a name for it; Friends Eleven, Jumping Stars, Excelsiors, Champion Eleven and finally Malgudi Cricket Club because of its irresistible magical associations with M. C. C. Then these nonentities called "M. C. C. Malgudi" write to the sports dealers in Madras in a language and an easy confidence behind which there is neither cash nor credit prompting the dealers to honor the letter.

> Dear Sir,
>
> Please send to our team two Junior Willard bats, six balls, wickets and others quick. It is very urgent. We shall send your money afterwards. Don't fear. Please be urgent.
>
> Yours obediently,
>
> Captain Rajam
>
> (CAPTAIN)

That Narayan, who employs the comic-ironic mode when dealing with the limits of the common man's world, should see ample scope for recognition of the source of all these adult fears and anxieties, aspirations and actions in the world of boyhood here reveals both the pervading human folly and his own comic sense in probing deep into the less explored regions of human consciousness. The way Narayan presents human folly makes one begin to wonder whether by shedding it one is not depriving oneself of the "naïveté of being human," to use Walsh's phrase.

Chandran of *The Bachelor of Arts* combines the adolescent mood and temper of Swami and the maturity of Krishnan in *The English Teacher*. The episodes depicting his college life, his relationship with teachers, his extracurricular activity, his love life—all these suggest a natural development of the Swami period in man's life. *The English Teacher* is a logical development of *The Bachelor of Arts,* where we find evidence of settled life and the poise of family harmony, which unfortunately is short-lived.

The flow of the quintessential comic sense of Narayan is thwarted by the tragic death of Krishnan's wife, and artistically, in a way, the limits of the comic vision turn out to be subjective in excluding the tragic and letting it stay apart. The comic vision has a sufficiently mature accommodative sweep to include the tragic in it, but for Narayan the artistic distancing or detachment seems to be a luxury at a time of personal loss, the more so as we know the novel to be autobiographical.

Coming to *The Financial Expert,* Narayan's sixth novel, one is struck by the ingenuity of craftsmanship in projecting the rise and fall of the protagonist Margayya in five sections, corresponding to the five acts of an Elizabethan tragedy. Narayan's treatment of Margayya, monetary wizard that he is, is comic but not without a tinge of sadness. The strength of Narayan's comic art is to present even a rogue from human angle and thereby shed light on his likable weakness as well. It is just such a low-key, twinkle-in-the-eye attitude to life's little ironies that can produce both Margayya, with his mystique of wealth amassed at society's expense, and also his son Babu, who can ruin his father's career. Narayan seems to believe in the wheel of life's moving, making many adjustments with the axle, pins and ball bearings; it is this movement that is presented, without any rhetorical embellishment.

The next important novel of our study should be *The Guide,* which is perhaps the most widely discussed of Narayan's works. The book, which has all the ingredients of a commercial film (indeed it was made into one), both in the maturity of the comic vision and in the novelist's artistic sophistication shown in the treatment of his theme (a sophistication which was lacking in the earlier novels), transcends the limits of a seemingly bizarre story. The authenticity in the treatment of Raju, an ordinary tourist guide with no extraordinary qualities except a certain cunning with which he plays on the gullibility of the village folk and Rosie the dancer, shows Narayan's artistic restraint in projecting Raju as a saint. It is this restraint which makes Raju's character and Narayan's art look credible.

The growth of self-knowledge in Raju, interestingly enough, comes mainly through Rosie, though his time in jail might have contributed its share to the maturing of the erstwhile railway guide into a Swami. Similarly, though on a different plane, Ramaswamy in *The Serpent and the Rope* needs Savithri for his self-knowledge (however corrupt she may be in aping the external features of Western civilization), for she represents essential Indian womanhood. It is true that Raju does not show the same kind of awareness of which Ramaswamy is capable, but the tone that Raju employs while narrating the story of his life to Velan has an undercurrent of maturity and wisdom born of experience.

Raju achieves this maturity only toward the end and by an arduous path, however, and one sees the paradoxical element in his character from the beginning. As a guide, he can speak eloquently about a waterfall or a temple or a hilltop, though he is not really interested in it; he speaks like a connoisseur of dancing, shows a sensitive appreciation of Rosie's art and does everything to promote her, but turns out to be a mercenary manager who craves only fame; he is put in prison on a charge of forgery but leads a profitable life there, winning loyalty from fellow prisoners and respect from the superintendent; he holds forth on the philosophy of the Bhagavad Gita yet craves for a *bonda* right in the middle of the discussion. We realize that Raju does not take himself seriously while the entire village is hanging on his every word. Ironically, it is that faith the villagers have put in him that at first infuriates him but touches him too.

> Lying on his mat he brooded. He felt sick of the whole thing. When the assembly was at its thickest, could he not stand upon a high pedestal and cry, "Get out, all of you and leave me alone. I am not the man to save you. No power on earth can save you, if you are doomed."

But soon a change takes place in him, and he resolves to chase away all thoughts of food. This resolution gives him a peculiar strength, and being encouraged by the very purity of his thought and motivation, he feels like pursuing it; indeed, his character develops on these lines.

> "If by avoiding food, I should help the trees bloom and the grass grow, why not do it thoroughly?" For the first time in his life he was making an earnest effort, for the first time he was learning the thrill of full application outside money and love; for the first time he was doing a thing in which he was not personally interested.

So ultimately it is the community around him that becomes the focal point in the novel, not the tourist guide to Malgudi, Rosie's lover and patron/promoter, not even the night guide to the skies. For he is moved by the recollection of the big crowd of women and children touching his feet. Raju is no longer a private man. He has lost all his privacy and has been feeling miserable about it for many days, but now he draws strength and sustenance from the very people whom he has detested having hang around him. Raju, the imposter, impresario and ex-convict, has in spite of himself become a kind of saint. Indeed, he has transformed "a slab of stone to a throne of authority," and the novelist's feat in bringing out this remarkable change in the character amounts to a growth, a certain maturity of vision in the writer no less than in the character. That Narayan has achieved this in terms of comedy, by working out a smooth transition between the comic and the tragic, is the merit of this novel.

The Sweet-Vendor, while continuing the line of *The Guide* in presenting the ambivalent development of its protagonist, is significant in fusing the comic with the serious, and to achieve this Narayan resorts to such familiar themes of his as the father-son relationship, domestic life, Gandhism, the Indian paradox of attachment to wealth and a desire for total renunciation. Added to these in *The Sweet-Vendor* is a kind of East-West encounter, as Mali brings his girlfriend from America to assist him in his machine-story-writing adventure.

Jagan, the sweet-vendor, is presented comically as an astute businessman and a Gandhist who is simple and frugal in his habits, the author of *Nature Cure and National Diet*, a regular reciter of the Gita. If his "oddities"—such as taking only twenty drops of honey per day instead of sugar, or using margosa twigs for brushing his teeth and having only ten-watt bulbs in the house—provide ample scope for comic portrayal, we are also made to see another, more human, side: namely, his love for Mali, his remembrance of his early married life, his generosity toward Mali's wife. Narayan shows us the potential of his comic art to achieve the profound when in the end we see Jagan, who has hitherto believed in the sweetshop or Mali as his sole salvation, reach a higher level of perception and detachment by recognizing the responsibility of each individual for his own salvation.

Narayan's ever-alert eye for the comic does not spare even the epics—the Ramayana and the Mahabharata. His *Gods, Demons and Others*, an earlier work, is not really noted for any reinterpretation of myth or legend, but neither is it a mere paraphrase of the stories found in the Indian Puranas. There is an unmistakable freshness of approach and insight in the presentation of some characters. It is interesting to note that Narayan, more than any Indian novelist except Raja Rao, has been inspired to a considerable extent by the Puranas, not merely in the ingenious way one of the legends is adapted in *The Man-Eater of Malgudi*, but also in the art of storytelling. His essay "The World of the Storyteller" reveals the secrets of his own success as storyteller. The essay has a poetic appeal while it evokes an atmosphere by creating the widening circles around the focal point—namely, the storyteller. The seeming naïveté of such an approach should serve as a corrective to the high-strung intellectual of modern times who is eager to present a theory of fiction.

The choice of material by and large suggests a writer's vision, and that Narayan has chosen such characters as Narada and Ravana in his *Gods, Demons and Others*, who reappear in his *The Mahabharata* and *The Ramayana*, only defines the contours of his comic vision. The characters and situations that lend themselves to comic treatment are the very stuff of Narayan's art. Narayan has strayed outside fiction to everyday life, which is after all full of fictional possibilities. His *Dateless Diary* and *Reluctant Guru*, the latter a collection of fascinating essays on a variety of subjects such as the postman, cows and milk, and on educational policies, and his autobiography *My Days*, which brings out vividly his painful college days and their demand of much effort and preparation for examinations (Narayan was not a serious student known for any academic distinction while in college, and his term as a schoolteacher lasted only one day)—all these are recollected in a tone which is pleasantly reminiscent, and because of the novelist's preoccupations in life and fiction, one does not see anything surprising in the autobiography. A lively interest in the family and domestic life and an aversion to academic and scholarly things which we find in the autobiography are also true of a typical Narayan character in fiction.

If Narayan does not believe in any systematic and critical study of his own work, it is because he as a storyteller is in the tradition of the *bhagavatar*, the traditional Indian storyteller of his own essay "The World of the Storyteller," who expects an instant response from his audience to his stories or descriptions of a puranic character and incident. It is a live art medium which engages the attention of the public constantly; Narayan himself, a lover of Carnatic music, knows that a tradition of instantaneous, simultaneous performance and response (which is true of our music concerts) exists, and he may be happy if his work is responded to in a more or less similar manner. A writer like Narayan does a service to criticism as well in freeing it of its jargon, which is a tribute to the "naïveté" of his art.

"THE MOST IMPRESSIVE ARE THOSE THAT OPEN A WINDOW ON TO THE BLEAK, TEDIOUS LIVES OF THE WHITE-COLLAR WORKERS OF INDIA, THAT LARGE SEGMENT OF THE POPULATION WHO DRAG OUT THEIR LIVES AT FORTY OR FIFTY RUPEES A MONTH IN GOVERNMENT OR BUSINESS EMPLOYMENT."

When we take stock of Narayan's entire work, we do come across novels and short stories which really are naïve and poor, such as *Waiting for the Mahatma* or *The Painter of Signs,* but that is the price a writer has to pay for being prolific and also for having produced such fine works as *The Guide* and *The Sweet-Vendor,* which have set such a high standard, making consistency a casualty.

Source: C. N. Srinath, "R. K. Narayan's Comic Vision: Possibilities and Limitations," in *World Literature Today*, Vol. 55, No. 3, Summer 1981, pp. 416–19.

Perry D. Westbrook
In the following excerpt, Westbrook discusses the human quality in "An Astrologer's Day."

The first of R. K. Narayan's three volumes of short stories, *An Astrologer's Day and Other Stories* (1947), contains thirty pieces, all of which had previously appeared in the Madras *Hindu.* Thus they had been written for, and presumably read and enjoyed by, the readership of one of India's greatest English-language newspapers. Though this readership would include most of the British, Anglo-Indians, and Americans living in South India, it would be made up overwhelmingly of true Indians. It is an important point. Narayan is an Indian writing for Indians who happen to read English. He is not interpreting India for Westerners. In Europe and America, of course, Narayan's reputation rests upon his novels. The publication in London of *An Astrologer's Day* followed two well-received novels, *Swami and Friends* and *The English Teacher,* but long before he was a novelist with an enthusiastic Western following, Narayan was an Indian journalist loved by his fellow-countrymen.

Paradoxically, however, though Narayan's short pieces have been welcomed in the *Hindu* for over thirty years, his novels have never been popular in India; indeed, I myself have found that they are obtainable there only with the greatest difficulty. Another book-hunter reports that in the leading bookshop of Bangalore in Narayan's own Mysore State not a single book by Narayan was available. On being queried, a clerk replied that there was no demand for Narayan's works. Narayan himself has stated that in the city of Mysore, where he has lived most of his life, perhaps only 200 of the population of 275,000 have ever read any of his books. And yet Mysore justly has the reputation of being an important centre of education and culture. The fact is that Narayan's books have first been published in England, and more recently in the United States, and have only later appeared in Indian in unattractively printed paperback editions.

Any reader of Narayan is aware that his stories are cut from very much the same cloth, both in quality and in pattern, as his novels. There is no intrinsic difference to explain why in the same cities where his novels are obtainable, several thousand or more subscribers to the *Hindu* read him with gusto. It becomes even more of a puzzle when we consider that the Indian booksellers do a brisk business in British and American novels and in continental novels in English translation. The most cogent explanation seems to be that of lingering cultural colonialism on the sub-continent. Too many educated Indians simply will not accept the possibility of excellence of style in the English writing of a compatriot. In the early years of the independence of the United States much the same prejudice existed. Publishers and readers alike preferred to read books—at least in the category of *belles lettres*—imported from the 'old country'; American authors were deemed to produce something less than the authentic product.

The newspaper origins of the short stories would tend to place them in the category of reporting on Indian life and thus make them more acceptable to readers who would ignore his longer and more ambitious works. The reportorial quality is especially marked in his second collection, *Lawley Road,* in which the selections are sketches and vignettes rather than plotted stories. In *An Astrologer's Day* the tales also accurately mirror Indian life and character, but most of them appear to have been chosen for the ingenuity of their plots. The title story, 'An Astrologer's Day,' is a good example. The description of the astrologer pursuing his profession on the sidewalk provides an entirely typical glimpse of Indian street life. The astrologer himself, a fake driven into imposture by hard luck, is well drawn. The trickiness of the plot (its O. Henry quality) results from the coincidence of the astrologer's being requested, during a day's business, to forecast the fortune of a man he recognizes as one whom he had stabbed and left for dead years ago. It was this crime that had forced the astrologer to flee from his village. But the victim recovered, as he informs the astrologer, and has been devoting his life to tracking down his assailant so as to get revenge. The astrologer, who recognizes the man without himself being recognized, informs him that his enemy has died beneath the wheels of a lorry. Thus the astrologer saves himself from attack and learns, to his great relief, that he is not a murderer after all. Though such situations do credit to an author's ingenuity, they do not suit modern taste. Yet they are in a long and honoured tradition, that of Chaucer's 'The Pardoner's Tale', itself derived from the Sanskrit. As a part of ordinary life, coincidences are legitimate material from any story-teller. At any rate, more than half the tales in *An Astrologer's Day* depend on such twists for their effect. Many of them have other merits as well, such as compelling atmosphere or a memorable character, but perhaps the most justifiable of them are those which present ghosts. 'An Accident' vividly conjures up on a lonely mountain road the ghost of a man killed in an automobile accident who now devotes himself to helping other motorists in distress. 'Old Man of the Temple' evokes the mystery and desolation of one of the ruined temples along the South Indian highways. 'Old Bones' exploits the atmosphere of the more isolated of the *dak* bungalows (government-operated overnight hostels). These are skillfully told stories of pure entertainment.

But some of the stories in *The Astrologer's Day* do not depend upon coincidence or some strange circumstance. The most impressive are those that open a window on to the bleak, tedious lives of the white-collar workers of India, that large segment of the population who drag out their lives at forty or fifty rupees a month in government or business employment. Examples are 'Forty-Five a Month' and 'Fruition at Forty,' accounts of dreary, lifelong wage-slavery. In depicting such prisoned lives Narayan is at his best, even in stories freighted with 'surprise endings'. Thus in 'Out of Business' the destructive mental effects of unemployment on a former gramophone salesman are vividly presented, though the suicide that he narrowly escapes would have been a more convincing conclusion than the gratuitous turn of luck that saves him from it. More believable is the fate of Iswaran in the story of that name. Iswaran, a representative of the vast army of Indian students whose sole goal in life is the passing of government examinations, is driven by repeated failure to a suicide that even his last-minute discovery that he has finally passed with honours cannot deter his crazed will from carrying out. Most prominent in all these stunted lives is the intolerable humiliation that is part of the daily routine. The insults endured by a jewelry-shop clerk in 'All Avoidable Talk' and the clerk's feeble attempt to rebel are unparalleled even in Gogol's and Dostoevsky's fiction on similar themes. Indeed a comparison with the insulted and injured in the works of the great Russian authors is inevitable. The tutor in 'Crime and Punishment,' the twenty-ninth story in Narayan's volume, suffers true Chekhovian and Dostoevskian indignities, as does also the porter in 'The Gateman's Gift,' whose employer speaks to him exactly twice in twenty-five years of service. Blighting frustration, of course, figures in all these tales but most severely in 'The Watchman,' one of the most powerful short stories Narayan has written. Here a young girl wishes to study medicine but her poverty-stricken family try to force her into a marriage she abhors; she drowns herself at night in a temple tank—at the second attempt, as a watchman stopped her the first time. The pathos lies in the inability of even the best-intentioned person to help a fellow human being in distress. This is the ultimate frustration....

Source: Perry D. Westbrook, "The Short Stories of R. K. Narayan," in *Journal of Commonwealth Literature*, No. 5, July 1968, pp. 41–51.

SOURCES

Alam, Fakrul, "R. K. Narayan," in *Dictionary of Literary Biography*, Vol. 323, *South Asian Writers in English*, Thompson Gale, 2006, pp. 252–64.

Beatina, Mary, "Introduction: R K. Narayan in the Tradition of Indian English Literature," in *Narayan: A Study in Transcendence*, Peter Lang, 1993, pp. 1–22.

"China and India See Slower Growth," in *British Broadcasting Corporation (BBC) Radio World Service*, February 27, 2009, http://www.bbc.co.uk/worldservice/business/

2009/ 03/090302_china_india_growth.shtml (accessed September 20, 2009).

Chopra, P. N., "Second World War and Nationalist Movement," in *A Comprehensive History of India: Modern India*, Sterling Publishers, 2003, pp. 271–79.

Dear, I. C. B., and M. R. D. Foot, "India," in *The Oxford Companion to World War II*, 2001, http://www.encyclopedia.com/doc/1O129-India.html (accessed September 15, 2009).

Keay, John, "At the Stroke of the Midnight Hour: 1930–1948," and "Crossing the Tracks: 1948–," in *India: A History*, HarperCollins, 2000, pp. 484–508, 509–535.

Mason, Brian, "Immigrants Define Emerging British Relations with India, Pakistan," in *Public Broadcasting System (PBS) Online NewsHour*, August 14, 2007, http://www.pbs.org/newshour/indepth_coverage/asia/partition/britain.html (accessed September 20, 2009).

Narayan, R. K., "Forty-Five a Month," in *Mallei Days*, Viking, 1982, pp. 74–79.

Parija, Kapileswar, "Major Themes," in *Short Stories of R. K. Narayan: Themes and Conventions*, Renaissance Publications, 2001, pp. 21–61.

Pontes, Hilda, "R. K. Narayan: Man and Writer," in *R. K. Narayan*, Concept Publishing, 1983, pp. 3–36.

Raizada, Harish, "His Stories," in *R. K. Narayan: A Critical Study of His Works*, Young Asia Publications, 1969, pp. 46–83.

Ram, N., "Mallei's Creator: The Life and Art of R. K. Narayan (1906–2001)," in *Frontline*, Vol. 18, No. 11, May 26–June 8, 2001, http://www.thehindu.com/fline/fl1811/18110040.htm (accessed September 15, 2009).

Ramana, P. S., "Selection and Construction of Short Stories," in *Message in Design: A Study of R. K. Narayan's Fiction*, Harman Publishing, 1993, pp. 69–101.

Singh, Vijai P., "The Concepts and Theories of Social Stratification," in *Caste, Class, and Democracy: Changes in a Stratification System*, Schenkman Publishing, 1976, pp. 3–20.

Venugopal, C. V., "R. K. Narayan," in *The Indian Short Story in English (A Survey)*, Prakash Book Depot, 1976, pp. 75–89.

FURTHER READING

Hasan, Zoya, *Politics of Inclusion: Caste, Minority, and Representation in India*, Oxford University Press, 2009.
> Hasan studies the experiences of Indian Muslims and members of the lower castes in India, focusing on the history of the discrimination against these groups and the government's attempts at affirmative action.

Kumar, Neeraj, *Women in the Novels of R. K. Narayan*, Indian Publishers Distributors, 2004.
> Kumar, in this oft-cited study, offers a detailed critical analysis of the female characters in the novel-length works of Narayan.

Lebra, Joyce C., *The Indian National Army and Japan*, Institute of Southeast Asian Studies, 2008.
> During the time period in which Narayan's story takes place, the Japanese, who fought against the British in World War II, aided the Indian fight for independence from the British. Lebra's work examines this relationship, focusing on the military phase of the Indian independence movement and on the evolution of Japanese policy regarding Indian independence.

Rao, Raja, *Kanthapura*, George Allen & Unwin, 1938, reprinted, Oxford University Press India, 1990.
> Raja Rao was Narayan's contemporary, a fellow Indian author writing in English. This novel focuses on the way the struggle for Indian independence led by Gandhi affects a small village in southern India. The work has been counted among the most notable works of Indian fiction.

The Grasshopper and the Bell Cricket

YASUNARI KAWABATA

1924

Yasunari Kawabata was in the early stages of his writing career when he wrote "Batta to suzumushi," (The Grasshopper and the Bell Cricket) in 1924. Although he eventually gained fame and earned the Nobel Prize for Literature as a novelist, Kawabata preferred the short story genre and wrote hundreds of short stories until his death in 1972.

Translated by Lane Dunlop and published in the short story collection *Palm-of-the-Hand Stories*, "The Grasshopper and the Bell Cricket" is roughly 1,350 words long, short enough to be considered what is referred to as "flash fiction." Although brief, Kawabata chooses his words with great care and presents the reader with a vividly imagined scene rife with imagery and symbolism.

The Japanese and English languages vary greatly, and at times, meaning or intent can be lost in translation. The same can be said of American and Japanese culture. In order to understand Kawabata's meaning, it is important to understand certain aspects of Japanese culture.

The bell cricket, for example, is not just another noisy insect. In Japan, the plain little bell cricket is revered and loved for its song. Each male bell cricket sings his own unique song, made individual by wing and body vibrations. There is even a Buddhist temple named after the insect, and for centuries, people have journeyed there to meditate

Yasunari Kawabata (© *Mary Evans Picture Library*)

to the sound of the bell crickets' songs. Those songs, heard collectively, are believed to be the voice of Buddha.

AUTHOR BIOGRAPHY

Kawabata was born on June 14, 1899, in Osaka, Japan. Kawabata's father died when Kawabata was two years old. In the next seven years, his mother, sister, and grandmother died. By the age of nine, Kawabata's life had brought more sorrow than anything else, and he found solace in reading. He read widely, but favored difficult Japanese classic texts, which he credited with influencing his use of language and sense of writing style. He decided to become a writer.

His blind grandfather, with whom he lived, became bedridden. Kawabata kept a diary detailing his care of his beloved grandfather. In May 1914, Kawabata's grandfather died. People began to refer to Kawabata as the "master of funerals" for having spent so much of his short life tending to the dead. The sadness of Kawabata's experience would stay with him for life and find its way into his novels and short stories. His first important novella, *Diary of a Sixteen-Year-Old* (1925), vividly recalls his experiences at his grandfather's deathbed.

A local newspaper published some of his poems, essays, and short works of fiction. Following the sudden death of his English teacher in 1917, Kawabata wrote "Shi no hitsugi o kata ni" ("With Our Teacher's Casket on Our Shoulders"). The story appeared in the periodical *Dan'ei* that same year; it was Kawabata's first story published in a literary journal.

Kawabata was accepted into Tokyo's First High School, one of the most prestigious public schools in Japan. He disliked English literature and lacked confidence in his writing skills. He also struggled with feelings of not belonging anywhere or to anyone, a condition he referred to as "his orphan's disposition," as noted by Van C. Gessel in the *Dictionary of Literary Biography*.

Kawabata embarked on a walking tour across the Izu Peninsula in 1918 to try to clear his head. Along the way, he met a variety of people ranging from simple country folk to traveling entertainers. What resulted was one of his most highly praised stories, "Izu no odoriko" ("The Izu Dancer"), published in 1926. The trip helped restore his self-esteem, and he returned to school ready to work. At school, he helped found a literary magazine. He also published his short stories in the literary journal *Bungei Shunju*.

Although this was a time of great professional growth, Kawabata's personal life suffered when his planned marriage to a fifteen-year-old waitress fell through. Kawabata received a letter from her telling him something catastrophic had occurred and that she could never see him again. The young writer was devastated and turned once again to his work as an emotional outlet. He began writing and publishing literary critiques and reviews, an endeavor he pursued for twenty years. He gained a reputation as a fair, unbiased critic.

Kawabata graduated university in 1924 and helped launch a bold, experimental literary journal called *Bungei Jidai* (The Age of Literary Arts). The journal and its writers reacted to what they construed as the dull writings of the naturalist movement. These authors searched for new ways to express feelings and depict situations of human interaction. Reader response was positive and the writers were labeled neoperceptionists, members of the new sensationalism school. The movement itself did not last past the 1920s, but it had a remarkable influence on Kawabata. In 1924, he wrote and published "Batta to suzumushi" ("The Grasshopper and the Bell Cricket").

Despite eventually being recognized with the Nobel Prize for Literature in 1968 for his novels, he preferred short stories. Frederick Smock of *American Book Review* explains, "Kawabata believed that the very short story—the story that fits into the palm of one's hand—holds the essence of the writing art. It is to fiction what the haiku is to poetry." Throughout his career, Kawabata wrote more than 140 palm-of-the-hand stories.

Kawabata met Hideko Matsubayashi in May 1925. The couple moved in together and lived in common-law marriage until 1931, when they officially wed. They had a daughter in 1927 who died before the traditional naming ceremony, and the couple never tried to have children again (although they did adopt the daughter of a cousin in 1943). The loss caused Kawabata to distance himself further from the emotional attachment of family relationships.

Kawabata decided his career would best be served if he lived in a city. The couple moved to Tokyo in 1927, where he developed friendships with artists and performers who provided endless material for Kawabata's stories. He published his tales in 1930 as *Asakusa kurenaidan*, translated and published in the United States in 2005 as *The Scarlet Gang of Asakusa*. During this time period, Kawabata also fostered the careers of several Japanese writers.

Kawabata gave lectures on literature at the Bunka Gakuin school in Tokyo from 1930 to 1934, and in the fall of 1933, he joined the staff of another literary journal, *Bungakukai*. One of his most beloved and critically hailed novels, *Yukiguni* (*Snow Country*), was written in 1935. The novel found its genesis in a magazine article Kawabata had written, and he published the rest of the book piece by piece. Never satisfied with how the story ended, he crafted a palm-of-the-hand version of it just three months before his death. That story, too, is included in the volume *Palm-of-the-Hand Stories* (1988).

Success with *Snow Country*, published in its entirety in 1937, brought Kawabata wealth, and he purchased a second home in the resort town of Karuizawa. He and his wife lived there during the summers of World War II. The home became a haven as the Japanese military increased its control over its country through strict censorship of speech and writing. Kawabata was disillusioned and concerned at the disregard for the traditional culture he so loved. Kawabata contacted other established writers and requested book donations. With these books, he established a library called Kamakura Bunko library. After the war, it became a publishing company and reprinted affordable editions of classic Japanese texts. It was a key factor in the resurgence of interest in Japanese literature after the war.

A revised edition of *Snow Country*—the one Kawabata considered complete—was published in 1947 to much acclaim. In 1947, publication of a sixteen-volume set of Kawabata's works began, and in 1948, he was elected president of P.E.N. Japan, an association of writers. In this position, Kawabata was able to influence literary activities in Japan. He was instrumental in getting Japanese texts translated and distributed throughout the world. During his seventeen-year term, Japanese literature made monumental strides in international recognition.

In 1954, he developed an addiction to sleeping pills, and the quality of his work was affected. His writing turned toward popular fiction as he wrote serialized novels in newspapers and women's magazines. He published his final work, a volume of short stories, *Nemureru bijo* (*House of the Sleeping Beauties and Other Stories*), in 1961. Around that same time, he received the Bunka Kunsho, or Medal of Culture, the highest honor given to writers by the Japanese government.

As his physical and emotional health failed in the 1960s, Kawabata could not finish some works he had begun, but he was instrumental in establishing the Museum of Modern Japanese Literature in Tokyo. The museum opened in 1967.

Despite being the first Japanese writer to earn the Nobel Prize for Literature, Kawabata continued to suffer from depression. His condition worsened in 1970 when he received word that his brightest protégé, the author Yukio Mishima, had committed suicide. The impact of Mishima's death was so strong that, even when asked by an editor to write about the suicide months later, Kawabata could not. According to the *Dictionary of Literary Biography* entry, Kawabata explained, "I am not free for a single moment from the grief and sorrow I feel over Mishima's deplorable death." Kawabata took his own life on April 16, 1972, by placing his head inside a gas oven.

Kawabata did not leave a suicide note but there is speculation that the intensity of his grief, depression, and severe insomnia became too much for him to bear. Kawabata's funeral was sponsored by P.E.N., the Japan Writers Association, and the Museum of Modern Japanese Literature. Kawabata was buried with his favorite fountain pen, his pipe, glasses, a volume of his writings, one hundred sheets of blank writing paper, a kimono, and the purple ceremonial *hakama* (Japanese pants) he wore to accept his Nobel Prize.

PLOT SUMMARY

The opening scene of "The Grasshopper and the Bell Cricket" finds the unnamed narrator walking outside the university (equivalent to the American high school). He turns to approach the upper school, which could mean the school that was situated higher up the hill, or it could mean a school attended by young teens, perhaps the equivalent of an American middle or junior high school. Since the school has a playground, it is more likely to be a school for younger children.

Although the time of day is never specified other than to indicate "a dusky clump of bushes," the reader learns that it must be dusk, if not dark. Kawabata implies this when his narrator discovers the bright lanterns bobbing along the base of the embankment. If it were daytime, lanterns would not be needed and the colorful light shining through them would be all but invisible to the naked eye. As it is, the narrator watches in wonder at the sight of twenty children engaged in an insect chase.

Immediately from this first scene, Kawabata employs vivid imagery. The walls of the university are tile-roofed, and the fence is constructed of white board. He describes the individual colors of the children's lanterns as they bob through the dark. The first two paragraphs are constructed almost completely using sensual imagery, a literary technique Kawabata will continue to rely on throughout the story.

The scene witnessed by the narrator is so idyllic that he likens it to a fairy tale, and he explains how the children came to participate in the insect chase in progress before him. What began as one child curious to find the owner of the singing from within the bushes soon became twenty children, all eager to hunt and capture the singing grasshoppers. Although one of the children bought his red lantern (and eventually discarded it as something gaudy and tasteless), most of them carefully and lovingly constructed their own lanterns out of multicolored paper, which they cut into various designs.

These lanterns are important to the children, and what was sufficient one night was not so in the light of day. So each day, the children would thoughtfully craft a new lantern. The lanterns represent the individuality of each child, and the children put mighty effort into besting one another. "Look at my lantern! Be the most unusually beautiful!" Those lanterns, with their mystical patterns and superb craftsmanship, are what the children are using to light their insect chase.

Kawabata never specifies the ages of the children, but given the nature of the activity, the reader assumes they are young enough to still enjoy such innocent activity but old enough to have the skills to have produced such fine and intricate lanterns.

One boy—whose name we eventually learn is Fujio—stands and shouts out to his peers, "Does anyone want a grasshopper?" A number of children reply that yes, they would like the grasshopper. Even as they crowd around him, the boy repeats the question. As still more children approach him to claim the grasshopper, he asks his question a third time. Finally, one of the children who responds is a girl, and it is this particular girl whom Fujio wanted to attract.

Fujio hands the girl, Kiyoko, his insect. It turns out to be not a common grasshopper but a bell cricket. In Japan, bell crickets are beloved for their unique singing, and their song is considered by many to be the voice of Buddha.

When Kiyoko announces that the insect is actually a bell cricket, the other children are excited in an envious way. She looks at Fujio as she places the cricket in her little insect cage that hangs at her side. Fujio grasps the cage and holds it at eye level so he can peer inside. With his multicolored lantern also at eye level, he glances at Kiyoko's face.

At that point, the narrator realizes that Fujio wanted Kiyoko's attention all along, and the narrator admits to a pang of jealousy at this experience of first love. Suddenly, he sees something no one else can see because they are standing too close to Fujio and Kiyoko.

In the light of his lantern, the design of which included his name, "Fujio" shines on Kiyoko's white kimono. And in the light of Kiyoko's lantern, the design of which also included her name, "Kiyoko" shines on Fujio's waist. Neither child would ever know that this occurred, but the narrator sees it and understands the meaning: for one brief moment—perhaps more, if their lives' paths dictate it to be so—Kiyoko and Fujio belong to one another.

At that point, the narrator imparts the wisdom he has gleaned only through decades of living and loving. He advises Fujio to take pleasure in a girl's delight and to appreciate her when she believes something to be more than it is but accepts it even when the truth is revealed. The narrator then warns Fujio that even when he has the intelligence to look for a life partner who is not like all the other girls or women, he will find that most of them are common and plain, like grasshoppers. "Probably you will find a girl like a grasshopper whom you think is a bell cricket."

The narrator sees Fujio as a man, when his heart has been broken and he becomes jaded to love. At that point, the narrator says, even a bell cricket (that rare woman who is special and unique and worthy of love) will seem like a grasshopper (common and nothing special). He pities Fujio for his inability to ever know that there was one moment in time when his name was written on the breast of a girl, when she was his, and he was hers.

CHARACTERS

Children
In addition to Fujio and Kiyoko, there are eighteen children on the embankment, chasing and catching insects. Using only the light that shines from their lanterns, they hunt the insects and capture them in tiny cages.

Fujio
Fujio is the young boy who gives Kiyoko what he believes is a grasshopper but which in reality is a bell cricket. Although he has announced his find and invited the other children to come see his grasshopper, his intent was to attract Kiyoko and give her the insect as a token of his admiration.

Kiyoko
Kiyoko is the young girl who accepts from Fujio a bell cricket. She is the object of Fujio's desire. Kiyoko is representative of all the girls in the world as well as that which is good and pure.

Narrator
The unnamed narrator is an adult from whose point of view the story unfolds. Although the narrator's gender is never pointedly named, the reader can assume he is male because he ends the story by giving Fujio advice on women in what seems like a man-to-man way.

THEMES

Fate
Fate is destiny, an event or course of events that will happen in a person's lifetime. Fate is predetermined; it cannot be altered or changed from what it was always meant to be. This is an integral belief in the traditional Japanese culture and a primary theme in Kawabata's "The Grasshopper and the Bell Cricket."

The idea that fate makes itself known in subtle signs is emphasized in the final scene, in which Fujio's name shines brightly onto Kiyoko's chest at the same time her name is visible through the lantern light on Fujio's waistline. To the unaware observer, these are children engaging in a favorite activity and nothing more. But as the narrator notices the chance interplay of light and color with the children's names, he realizes what he is seeing may be neither chance nor play but the two children's fates—their futures with either partners of quality and individualism or those possessing nothing that sets them apart from the crowd.

Love
None of the themes in Kawabata's story is overtly examined; true to traditional Japanese literary style, they are merely suggested, hinted at, alluded to. Kawabata uses very simple language to depict the incredibly confusing paths love often takes. Love is a theme touched upon in the final scene of the story as the narrator witnesses Fujio and Kiyoko together, their names shining upon one another's clothing. That brief encounter gives the narrator a glimpse into the lives of Fujio and Kiyoko, and he suddenly—as evidenced by the use of an exclamation point in an otherwise tranquil scene—desires to give Fujio advice. In his

TOPICS FOR FURTHER STUDY

- Choose a partner to work with. One of you is an interviewer, one is Kawabata. Brainstorm questions to ask that will provide your audience with a strong sense of Kawabata as a writer. What kind of training did he receive? What made him want to be a writer? How did his childhood influence his work? Base the answers on research. Videotape the interview and play it for the class, or conduct it live in front of your classmates.

- Using an art-oriented computer software program, such as Corel Painter or Artweaver, draw or paint a scene from the short story. Add a short written explanation of the scene and explain your interpretation.

- Kawabata ultimately committed suicide. Research his tragic personal life and write a brief report on it. As you write the report, take into consideration not only his circumstances but Japanese culture and events that happened during his lifetime that might have influenced his decision to take his own life.

- Kawabata's story is a parable—a succinct story that illustrates a moral lesson. Parables differ from fables in that parables usually do not feature talking animals or plants, and they differ from fairy tales in that their settings include no magical elements. A parable sometimes, but not necessarily, includes a character facing a dilemma. Read Shel Silverstein's much-beloved book *The Giving Tree*. Compare it to "The Grasshopper and the Bell Cricket." How do the two stories differ? How are they similar? Compare and contrast and list your findings with a Venn diagram or T-chart.

---

mind, he warns the boy that even if he searches in the most unlikely places for a girl of substance (a bell cricket), he will most likely find girls he believes to be like bell crickets but who in reality are mere grasshoppers. After many disappointing experiences with love, Fujio will likely carry such a wounded heart that even when a genuinely interesting, intelligent, and worthy girl comes along, he will fail to recognize her.

Individualism

Individualism is a theme woven throughout "The Grasshopper and the Bell Cricket." In the scene where the narrator spies the children with their amazing, handcrafted lanterns, Kawabata juxtaposes the idea of individualism with conformity. Although there are twenty children engaging in the same activity, each child has put great effort into being different from every other child in the way he fashions his lantern. There is not one color but a rainbow of variety. There is not one common lantern shape but many. There is not one design but an endless array of designs, and each child strives not only to craft a different design, but one more intricate, more difficult, more unique than the others.

The concept of the value of individualism is also carried out in the grasshopper-versus-bell cricket scenario. Bell crickets are prized for their songs, no two of which are alike. Whereas individual grasshoppers vary little if at all, every male bell cricket sings a different song. In fact, his song is how he finds a mate. The narrator wants Fujio to understand and recognize the value of finding a mate who stands out from the rest, who is unique and special, like the bell cricket.

STYLE

Imagery

Imagery is a technique a writer uses to involve the reader in the story. He does this by appealing to the reader's senses. Kawabata uses imagery throughout his brief story, beginning with the first paragraph, in which he gives specifics. The university wall is not just a wall but a "tile-roofed wall"; the fence is constructed of "white board"; and the trees are not just trees but orange and black cherry trees.

Imagery abounds in Kawabata's passages involving the children's lanterns. He uses the phrase "bobbing cluster of beautiful varicolored lanterns, such as one might see at a festival" and then lists the individual colors. Just from this brief choice of words, the reader sees in his mind's eye exactly what the narrator is seeing as he watches those children on their insect chase. Kawabata has

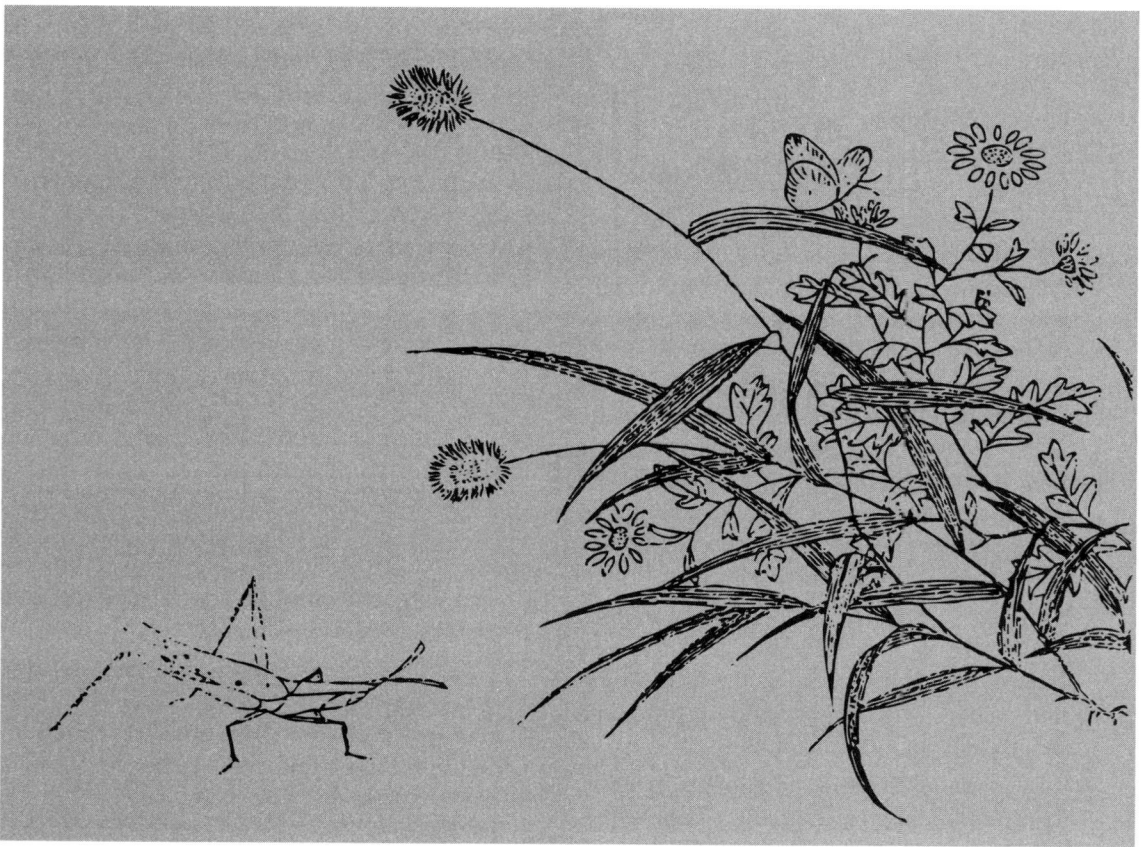

Traditional Chinese stroke painting of a grasshopper (Image copyright John Lock, 2009. Used under license from Shutterstock.com)

put the reader into the story, next to the narrator. In doing so, he makes the scene that plays out between Fujio and Kiyoko come alive, and it is as if the reader is experiencing it, not just reading about it.

Kawabata does the same when he describes in detail the way the children so carefully construct their lantern designs. His child-artists cut "lozenge leaf shapes in the cartons, colorcoding each little window a different color, with circles and diamonds, red and green...." He again relies on imagery to emphasize the importance of the scene in which Fujio and Kiyoko unknowingly shine their names onto each other. "... wasn't the name 'Fujio' clearly discernable?" Kiyoko's pattern is not projected as clearly, but could be made out "in a trembling patch of red on the boy's waist."

First-Person Point of View

Stories can be narrated from several different perspectives. First-person point of view uses the word "I" and is a technique that allows the reader to feel she is not so much reading about something but is somehow sharing in the story itself.

Kawabata's narrator is talking to his audience directly. As he sees and experiences something, so does the reader. Even though the narrator is not truly involved in the plot of "The Grasshopper and the Bell Cricket," he is on the sidelines and therefore able to get a clear perspective on what is taking place. And because he has that viewpoint, so does the reader. In this case, the first-person perspective makes the story more intimate. Think of the difference between a conversation with a friend and listening to a lecture.

Symbolism

Symbolism in this short story is apparent, but only to a reader who has an understanding of traditional Japanese culture. This very fact is why some stories that get translated into another language tend to lose some of their meaning. In some cases, there is no word for what an author has written, and so a translator must choose the word that has the most similar meaning. Depending on the choice made, the meaning of the text can change.

Kawabata's respect for traditional Japanese culture is symbolized in "The Grasshopper and the Bell Cricket" in several ways. Of the approximate 1,350 words in the story, about 375 of them are used to describe the colors and intricacies of craftsmanship that go into the construction of the children's lanterns. That is over one-fourth of the entire story. Lanterns are icons of good luck in the Japanese culture, and in traditional culture, much effort and attention went into the making of them. Even in the twenty-first century, Japanese hold lantern festivals. To devote such a large amount of space in such a brief story to this one aspect signifies its importance.

Colors hold special meaning in traditional Japanese culture. By itself, the color red is believed to protect against evil forces and demons. It is also the color worn by brides and, when combined with white, symbolizes an auspicious or happy occasion. Kiyoko's lantern light shines red as it reflects her name onto Fujio's clothing.

Fujio's name is inscribed on Kiyoko's breast in green. Originally, there was no word in the Japanese language for the color green. It simply did not exist. Around the beginning of the twentieth century, the Japanese language was in flux as new words were being added to reflect the changing culture. One of those new words was "midori," which means "green." Before the inclusion of this word, green was considered just another shade of blue. Without seeing Kawabata's original Japanese manuscript for this story, there is no way to know if he used the word *midori* or if he used the Japanese word for blue (*ao*). Either way, Lane Dunlop translated it to mean the color green. Because of its relative newness to the Japanese language, the color green does not hold symbolic meaning.

The color white symbolizes the sacred. It is used in many Japanese rituals, including weddings and funerals. It is also the background of the Japanese flag, which features a red sun (remember: red and white together signify a happy occasion). Kiyoko's kimono is white. So here we have the interplay of red, white, and green (or blue?). Kawabata uses color to symbolize the innocence and sacredness of youth as well as the potential for the possibility of happiness.

Even Kiyoko's name falls into a similar translation: "pure, clean child." She symbolizes that which is pure in the world—true love—as well as all the women Fujio will meet in his lifetime, both the grasshoppers and the bell crickets.

HISTORICAL CONTEXT

Japan in the 1920s was in a state of great transition. World War I was over, but the country would never be the same. Just as the decade was one of great societal and cultural value shifts in the United States, so it was in Japan. Western influence was infiltrating every aspect of the Japanese way of life, leaving those who favored tradition over modernity feeling uneasy and uncertain.

Art often mimics reality, and this held true of literature in 1920s Japan. In the 1910s, much of Japanese literature fell into the artistic realm of naturalism. As a literary movement, naturalism emphasized man's accidental, physiological nature over his moral or rational characteristics and qualities. Naturalism had its roots in Europe, and its writers tended to focus on social issues and themes. Japanese writers put their own spin on the school of thought, and it quickly became a movement largely composed of autobiographical fiction that revealed the excesses and confessions of its writers.

Everything was changing—language, thought, societal norms and expectations—and writers wanted alternatives. As a result, the 1920s was rife with literary movements, but none as strong as the proletarian (worker) literature movement. The movement was in its infancy and would gain momentum throughout the 1930s as Japan became a more militaristic state and divided the country into those who favored such a government and those who did not.

Strong as it was, the proletarian literary movement shared its spotlight with other literary schools of thought as Japanese writers took this transition as an opportunity to experiment with form and content. One such school was called new sensationalism; Kawabata was a key member. Kawabata defined new sensationalism as "Expressionism in epistemology and Dadaism in formal expression." In simpler terms, this means the movement emphasized expression of inner experiences using irony and cynicism. World War I left many people in a mood of disillusionment. Artists expressed their

COMPARE & CONTRAST

- **1920s:** The major literary movement of 1920s Japan is the proletarian, or pro-worker, movement. Historians generally agree this movement began with the publication of the magazine *Tane maku Hito* (The Sower) in 1921. Writers of the proletarian movement are both laborers and intellectuals who favor socialism. By the 1930s, the Japanese government will censor and ban all proletarian literature. Kawabata is considered one of the last traditional Japanese writers of the modern movement.

    Today: Japanese fiction covers a wide variety of themes and styles, so there is no primary literary movement. As has traditionally been the case where fiction is concerned, Japanese literature places emphasis on emotions over plot development and action. Of great popularity in the contemporary fiction market is Manga, which constitutes a billion-dollar industry in Japan. Manga, literally translated, means "whimsical pictures," and is a Japanese comic style that includes science fiction, mystery, action-adventure, and more.

- **1920s:** This is the era of modernization in Japan. Western culture greatly influences the concept of modernization in Japan, and its citizens are caught trying to balance tradition with modernity. Everyday items like furniture take on a new style, and the culture is all about change in form, function, and attitude. In this social climate where America's Roaring Twenties "Anything goes" attitude influences and clashes with Japan's traditional sense of tranquility and harmony, the writing style and treatment of themes by writers like Kawabata stand out for their adherence to tradition. He has no use for Westernization or modernization, despite the fact that he is a recent college graduate and among the youth who are most willing and eager to usher in change.

    Today: Japan is one of the most highly industrialized countries in the world. Unlike the 1920s, this is an era where the boundaries between tradition and modernity are clear. Writing Kawabata's clearly falls into the realm of Japanese traditional literature, though it was initially on the cusp of modernism.

- **1920s:** Japan experiences an economic recession. This, combined with the rapid rise of industrialization in the aftermath of World War I and the impeding influence of Westernization, gives an air of uncertainty to the culture. That Kawabata should write, during this time, a piece of flash fiction surrounding an event as innocent as children engaged in an insect chase illustrates the tensions of a society longing to hold on to tradition even as it lets go to embrace change.

    Today: Like children in various industrialized societies across the globe, those in Japan forsake much of the more traditional forms of play for video games, organized sports, and other activities. Traditional Japanese icons such as the lantern continue to represent the culture, but on a more formal level, as in festivals (Japanese Lantern Festival) and other special events.

---

outrage over the destruction of so much and so many through their art and reacted against the traditional, existing artistic (including literary) techniques.

Unlike the proletarian literary movement, which was based on ideological principles, or naturalism, the more traditional school of thought, which was founded on principles of natural science, new sensationalism stood on literary principles. Where proletarian literature emphasized politics and theory, new sensationalist (or neoperceptionist) literature focused on the emotional, personal, individual side of life's experiences.

Multi-colored lanterns at a country market (Image copyright Les Scholz, 2009. Used under license from Shutterstock.com)

The movement itself did not last long (approximately 1924–1930), but it had its own journal, *Bungei Jidai* (The Age of the Literary Arts). It was in this journal that Kawabata published his first significant fiction in the form of brief sketches he called "palm-of-the-hand stories." Kawabata continued to write in the new sensationalist style to the end of his life.

CRITICAL OVERVIEW

Kawabata is considered one of Japan's most accomplished writers and one of the last to write in the classical Japanese tradition. Unlike more modern Japanese writers, Kawabata did not adopt a style that could easily be understood on an international level. Instead, he embraced the concept of "less is more" and strove to make every word choice matter. In "The Month of Cherry Blossom," in *New Statesman*, writer Jason Cowley calls Kawabata a miniaturist who "compresses where others seek to inflate and enlarge." Calling him a writer who knew the value of silence, Cowley suggests that reading Kawabata is an act of collaboration between the author and the reader. "Kawabata challenges you to interpret and imagine, to colour in and shade the empty spaces of his stories."

Although Japanese readers living during Kawabata's lifetime were familiar with this traditional style, many modern readers across the globe are not. Others read to be entertained; they do not necessarily want to have to fill in those blanks or shade those empty spaces. And yet Kawabata's talent continues to be appreciated both in his homeland and beyond. In his review of *Palm-of-the-Hand Stories*, *American Book Review* writer Frederick Smock judges the book as one of "those dozen or so volumes necessary to life."

Kawabata won the Nobel Prize for Literature in 1968 based on three of his novels: *Yukiguni*, 1937 (*Snow Country*, 1957); *Sembazuru*, 1952 (*Thousand Cranes*, 1958); and *Koto*, 1962 (*The Old Capital*, 1987). And it is as a novelist that he earned his fame. Marlene A. Pilarcik, in *Modern Language Studies*, writes that the author's works are remarkable for their wistful beauty and haunting lyricism.

"They express the essence of the Japanese soul, but also draw on the universality of human experience." Perhaps that is why, almost a century after "The Grasshopper and the Bell Cricket" was written, it continues to be read and appreciated by audiences around the world.

The story did not appear in the American market until its translation in 1988. That same year, *Library Journal's* Kitty Chen Dean reviewed not only that story but the entire *Palm-of-the-Hand Stories* volume and called Kawabata a "master storyteller reminiscent of James Joyce, but with a smaller, sharper, more incisive vision."

The term lyricism arises again and again among critics, who cite it as one of Kawabata's primary strengths. Lyricism refers to a writer's ability to gently express emotion, and although Kawabata's novels are infused with lyricism, it is more obvious in the writer's short stories. In 1924, the same year "The Grasshopper and the Bell Cricket" was published, critic Kameo Chiba wrote an article in the November issue of the Japanese journal *Seiki*. In it, he credits Kawabata and his contemporaries with being "sensually alert to diction, lyricism, and rhythm that are far fresher than anything ever before expressed by any of our sensitive artists." That sensual lyricism made him both a traditionalist (in style) and a modernist (in form).

In addition to his lyricism, Kawabata's writing style reflects the author's emphasis on mood and atmosphere over plot, structure, and other features associated with the creation and analysis of fiction. This tendency is directly influenced by those European modernist techniques that led Kawabata to help found the new sensationalism literary movement.

CRITICISM

Rebecca Valentine

Valentine is a freelance writer who holds a B.A. in English with minors in philosophy and professional communications. In this essay, she argues that despite his affiliation with Japan's new sensationalism movement, Kawabata's "The Grasshopper and the Bell Cricket" is distinctly a traditional piece of literature because it is constructed using principles of Japanese aesthetics.

Although Kawabata was honored with the Nobel Prize for Literature for three of his novels,

WHAT DO I READ NEXT?

- *The Master of Go* (1972) is considered by many to be Kawabata's finest novel, although it is essentially a work of nonfiction. The book centers on an official match of Go, a traditional Japanese game similar to chess. The game began on June 26, 1938, and ended on December 4 that same year. The Japanese Go master spent three of these months in the hospital, and Kawabata was a newspaper reporter covering the event.

- Editor Donald R. Gallo's *On the Fringe: Stories* (2003) is a collection of eleven short stories written by well-known young-adult authors, including Chris Crutcher and M. E. Kerr. The Columbine High School shooting was the inspiration for this compilation, which addresses themes of self-esteem, isolation, and violence.

- *America Street: A Multicultural Anthology of Stories* is a 1993 compilation of fourteen short stories featuring teens. Editor Anne Mazer has pulled together stories exploring assimilation, the nature of family, and the struggles inherent in a multicultural society.

- Isaac Asimov and Groff Conklin have edited the collection of short stories *50 Short Science Fiction Tales* (1997). The stories, written in the 1940s and 1950s, envision a future that has already come to pass. Most of the tales range from three to five pages, though some are merely one page in length.

- Donald Keene's *Appreciations of Japanese Culture* (2003) is a reprint of a 1971 collection of twenty essays that explore various aspects of Japan's traditional culture. He addresses aesthetics, literary tradition, and war, among other topics. This book is a valuable teaching tool for any class studying Japanese culture and tradition.

- *Teens in Japan* (2007) is a concise cultural commentary on the life of teens in modern Japan. Author Sandy Donovan explores customs, societal expectations, and lifestyles of Japanese teens.

"KAWABATA WAS A TRADITIONALIST IN EVERY SENSE OF THE WORD. BY HIS OWN ADMISSION, HIS LITERARY SENSE WAS INFORMED AND DIRECTLY INFLUENCED BY THE JAPANESE CLASSICS, AND WHEN HE SAW HIS COUNTRY FORSAKING ITS HERITAGE BY BUYING INTO THE WESTERNIZATION OF ITS CULTURE, HE TOOK STEPS TO DELAY THE INEVITABLE."

he preferred working in the genre of short stories, in particular, stories so small they can fit into the palm of one's hand. These stories, which Kawabata continued to write over a span of fifty years, were not translated into English until seventeen years after the author's death. Analysis of these stories reveals a Kawabata not immediately obvious in his novels. Despite the common, modern perception that Kawabata had a stronghold on the new sensationalism literary movement in modern Japan and therefore is primarily an experimental writer, critical analysis of his palm-of-the-hand stories and "The Grasshopper and the Bell Cricket," in particular, reveals a writer dedicated to exploring his universe using the principles of traditional Japanese aesthetics.

The aesthetic principles of traditional Japanese literature—all art forms, actually—can be traced to two philosophical schools of thought: Zen Buddhism and Taoism. Kawabata revered traditional literature, particularly Murasaki Shikibu's *The Tale of Genji*, written during the Heian period (794–1185). Kawabata credits such texts with influencing his style and literary sensibilities.

Inherent in those traditional texts are the Japanese culture's aesthetic principles, the tenets that pertain to the mind and emotions in relation to the sense of beauty. Regardless of art form, these aesthetic principles never fluctuate; there are seven of them, and there will always be seven. In no particular order, those seven principles are: simplicity, tranquility, naturalness, nonattachment, profundity, sublimity, and asymmetry.

Western readers cannot appreciate to the full extent of its potential any of Kawabata's short stories without a grasp of the meaning of these seven principles and how they inform traditional Japanese art. Perhaps this is why his stories went so long without translation; undeniably, Western aesthetics, which fall into the modernist school and which eventually heavily influenced Japanese literature, are almost diametrically opposed to Japanese aesthetics. After World War I, Japanese society began turning its back on tradition in favor of Western values and beliefs. Kawabata recognized this shift, and it grieved him.

Although this is a much simplified comparison, it serves to contrast the modern school of thought with traditional Japanese aesthetics. When considering and judging the depth of beauty, be it a story, a painting, or a garden design, modernism favors logic over intuition, a sense of progress versus a cyclical nature, a sense of clarity over ambiguity. The Japanese aesthetic values the organic form—whatever it may be—over symmetry, the concept of nature above anything man-made, and the idea of living in harmony with nature rather than controlling it. These are just some examples of differences between Western (modern) and Japanese (traditional) aesthetics. They provide a launch point for understanding how traditional Japanese culture perceives the universe.

Simplicity refers to the idea of making do with the minimum, accepting as good only what is appropriate, never going overboard. In literature, this would play out in the length of a piece of writing. This is, in part, why the poetic form haiku is favored in Japan. It is written economically, following a simple format.

Tranquility is the feeling of calm and balance. This principle can be achieved by word choice as well as setting and tone.

Naturalness is the trait of organic being. In a garden, naturalness would be achieved by a design that looks as if everything just happened to grow where it appears. In literature, the writer achieves naturalness by constructing his piece so that it seems to have merely unfolded—that the story has been there all along, and the reader just managed to stumble upon it. There is no contrivance or forced formulaic structure.

Nonattachment is the idea that humans are not invested in anything of this earth. Nothing depends upon anything else; it just exists. In literature, nonattachment is what allows the reader to enjoy a story simply because it is enjoyable. It has its own worth, independent of any meaning a reader may or may not imbue it with.

Profundity is the idea of having depth and intensity. Traditional Japanese profundity is subtle; it fluctuates and shifts, depending upon the meaning found within it. Profundity makes a piece of literature timeless as well as endless in that there is no right or wrong way to read it. What one reader sees, another may not. The writer sees his job as one of suggestion rather than revelation.

Sublimity refers to the essence of an artistic work (or life experience). Stripped of all nonessential verbiage and explanation, a work can be appreciated for its innate clarity.

Asymmetry, or irregularity, is the idea that beauty is found in a balance based on lack of control. It implies a dynamic of give and take, and imperfection contributes to that beauty.

Even a basic understanding of these principles gives a reader unfamiliar with traditional Japanese aesthetics a springboard from which to jump into the writing world of Kawabata. The fact that his palm-of-the-hand stories are so incredibly brief sometimes makes them difficult to grasp because they are over before they barely begin. In his notes to *Palm-of-the-Hand Stories*, translator Lane Dunlop admits to struggling for connection with the stories. After translating three of them, he was "unable to find any others that reached me.... I mistook their subtlety for slightness, their lack of emphasis for pointlessness."

Using "The Grasshopper and the Bell Cricket" as a representative title for Kawabata's short story collection, one begins to see that the Nobel Prize winner may have written his novels to attract a wider audience, but he lived to write those stories in the hopes of keeping alive a tradition he saw quickly fading. Although Kawabata applies all seven Japanese aesthetic principles to his story, three stand out: simplicity, tranquility, and profundity.

The basic story of "The Grasshopper and the Bell Cricket" is simple. A man watches as children engage in a favorite childhood activity and, from his vantage point as an outsider looking in, turns a seemingly chance event into a life lesson. At a mere 1,350 words, Kawabata presents the story without decoration or superfluous prose. As readers, we do not know the frame of mind the narrator is in when he first encounters the children. And it does not matter. We do not know his physical traits or those of the children. And it does not matter. We do not know the exact ages of the children, or the setting beyond the fact that the activity takes place on an embankment outside a school playground. We are given no information that is not absolutely essential to the story.

The most detailed section of the story is the description of the children's lanterns and the construction process. While this may seem unnecessary, it actually is important. Because lanterns and lantern making are almost sacred aspects of the Japanese culture, the passages pertaining to the lanterns are integral to understanding Kawabata's meaning. Whether the reader is Japanese or American—or something else—he cannot finish reading those passages and not grasp the reverence bestowed upon the lanterns.

Kawabata imposed upon his story a sense of tranquility in several ways. The entire story is actually one scene, and even though that scene involves almost two dozen children running around flinging lanterns throughout the dusky air, the reader is not encouraged to believe it is chaotic or raucous. Using phrases like "coming together of children on this lonely slope" and "the candle's light seemed to emanate," Kawabata gives the reader a sense of calm. And yet there is excitement, too, as the children cry out, "It's a bell cricket! It's a bell cricket!" It is interesting to note that Kawabata does not say the children are yelling or screaming; he only indicates or suggests the excitement by the use of exclamation points. When the bell cricket is discovered, something big has happened, and the reader knows it. Even when Fujio initially announces his willingness to give away his insect, he shouts just once. After that, Kawabata describes him as calling out; he is beckoning to the other children, not bellowing. And so it is with setting as well as word choice that Kawabata infuses his story with a sense of tranquility and energizing calm.

Finally, Kawabata creates a sense of the subtly profound with his use of symbolism as well as his allusion to the future. Traditional Japanese culture tends to value allusion—the suggestion of the possibility of something—over explicitness. The narrator alludes to Fujio and Kiyoko's futures. While the reader may want to know if the two ever fall in love, Kawabata is not willing to make the reader's job of figuring that out so easy. Maybe they will, maybe they will not. Even the scene in which the two children's names are shining on one another involves imagination: is the narrator really seeing what he thinks he sees? Kawabata writes, "if it was chance or play," as if to suggest that maybe the narrator is not completely sure of what he is witnessing. And so even the here and now are merely alluded to, rather than explicitly explained.

In a sort of crossover with the aesthetic principle of naturalness, Kawabata's story really only matters because he is telling it. It may very well have been that the children participated in the insect chase using lanterns they poured their hearts and souls into to make, and Fujio might have given Kiyoko what he thought was a grasshopper but was in actuality a rare bell cricket, and none of it would have mattered because there would have been no one there to see it. The event itself is not contrived or natural; it is a common scene in traditional Japan. It would have occurred even had no one been there to witness it. This is the naturalness. But there was someone there—the narrator. And he watched and imagined. And so this simple, common event became a catalyst for one man's imaginative prediction into the future. That the grasshopper was actually a bell cricket came to hold profound meaning.

Kawabata was a traditionalist in every sense of the word. By his own admission, his literary sense was informed and directly influenced by the Japanese classics, and when he saw his country forsaking its heritage by buying into the Westernization of its culture, he took steps to delay the inevitable.

Although he experimented with the form of the novel and eventually gained international acclaim for his efforts, he found the idea of sustaining a self-contained piece of art difficult. From the 1920s until his death, Kawabata kept returning to the short story, the genre he preferred. In his critical essay "The Asymmetrical Garden: Discovering Yasunari Kawabata" in *Southwest Review*, Thom Palmer says it best: "The 'palm-sized' stories constitute the marrow of his artistic essence, and this essence is a constant refinement and exploration of the East's prototypical aesthetics and philosophical thought." For Kawabata, the novel was a grasshopper; the short story was the bell cricket.

Source: Rebecca Valentine, Critical Essay on "The Grasshopper and the Bell Cricket," in *Short Stories for Students*, Gale, Cengage Learning, 2010.

Children playing outside at dusk (Image copyright Kirsty Pargeter, 2009. Used under license from Shutterstock.com)

Peter M. Carriere

In the following article, Carriere illustrates differences between modern and geido symbolist writing styles, but states that Kawabata demonstrates both styles, as his purpose is to awaken or reinforce in the participant a sense of culture and spirit.

In his article "Alternative Modernity? Playing the Japanese Game of Culture" (1994), Andrew Feenberg suggests that Yasunari Kawabata's novel *The Master of Go* (1954) embodies the Zen Buddhist principle that playing Go in traditional Japan constituted a quest for self-realization and a path to spiritual unity—in effect, a "Tao," or "Way," the Way of Go. The goal of the contest was not victory but spiritual enlightenment: as a momentary refugee from culture, the self was reduced by subjection to rule and struggle to the nothingness of Zen, and the game became an agent of consciousness effacement, the Zen "no-mind" that is a prerequisite for spiritual unity. This insight, that immersion in Go constituted a Way in traditional Japanese culture, suggests that Kawabata's immersion in the aesthetics of religion and culture was an attempt to create an aesthetic Way in the spirit of cha-no-yu, or tea ceremony, which he described in his Nobel Prize acceptance speech of 12 December 1968 as "sad, austere, autumnal," concealing "a great richness of spirit." The object of the tea ceremony is to awaken

> "KAWABATA'S PREFERENCE FOR THE GEIDO AESTHETICS OF EARLIER WRITERS MAKES IT CLEAR THAT HE SAW LIFE IN CONTEMPORARY JAPAN AS VULGAR."

or reinforce in the participant a sense of cultural identity and spiritual connection through its ritualized aesthetics. The object of other forms of aesthetic rituals, such as the art of fiction, for instance, might do the same. Indeed, such a connection between art and religion flourished during Japan's medieval period (950–1400), when "religious and aesthetic values became virtually co-terminous in what was called geido—the 'Tao' (or Way) of aesthetics." This essay will examine the aesthetic, cultural, religious, and historical contexts out of which Kawabata's pre-war masterpiece *Snow Country* (1947) and his last novel, *Beauty and Sadness* (1961), emerged in order to show that geido was an abiding element of Kawabata's fiction.

The phrase "alternative modernity" implies that Kawabata's modernism differs from traditional understandings of the term. By definition, however, the art of modernism is subjective, recondite, esoteric, and avant-garde. Furthermore, the symbolist aesthetic often noted in Kawabata, with its emphasis on spirituality and culture, informs the works of modernism's most celebrated writers, including T. S. Eliot, James Joyce, Joseph Conrad, and W. B. Yeats. Yeats's well-known affinity for Japan originated in his symbolist perception that Japan supported a culture infused with myth, legend, and a hazy kind of spiritualism arising out of a unique blending of Shinto and Buddhism.

Because of geido's similarity to the symbolist writing of some modernists, critics often suggest that Kawabata's art tends toward the symbolic. Gwen Boardman relates that in Kawabata's rewriting of *Snow Country*, his characterizations went from "more 'realistic' and straightforward to 'lyrical' and symbolic." According to Paul St. John Mackintosh, *Snow Country* "does the native spirit good by going back to the oldest Japanese literary traditions," and yet the novel is "modern in its narrative discontinuity and almost symbolist imagery." And Kawabata's involvement with other young artists in the Shinkankaku-Ha and its publication *Bungei Jidai* (1924) was, according to Boardman, "a reaction against the naturalistic writing and the 'proletarian' literature of their time." When this same reaction in Europe takes a spiritual direction, it is labeled symbolist, though the difference is that symbolism is subjective and somewhat occult, whereas geido uses aesthetics as a Way within Buddhism, an established religion.

Western discussions of Kawabata's art imply that his fiction may be grasped either in terms of unique Japanese aesthetic categories or Western existentialism. In "Elements of Existentialism in Modern Fiction," Mita Luz de Manuel suggests that Kawabata's modernism originates in the pervasive existential personality of his characters, that he "may well have connected Buddhist 'emptiness' or 'nothingness' with the nihilism of Western philosophy." Those who interpret Kawabata through Japanese aesthetic categories usually point out that his art contains yugen (mysterious or shadowy essence), mono no aware (poignant melancholy), sabi (refined, seasoned simplicity), or wabi (a calm, clear state of mind perfected in the tea ceremony). Wabi and sabi also suggest the quiet sadness Kawabata spoke of in reference to the tea ceremony. Kawabata used all of these aesthetic labels as keys to his art in the Nobel speech (though in his English translation Edward Seidensticker used descriptive phrases rather than these esoteric terms).

Enlightening as these efforts may be, however, analyses based on Japanese aesthetics leave Western readers unsatisfied as to the real purpose of Kawabata's art. We may see mono no aware as an abiding element in *The Sound of the Mountain* (1954) or *Beauty and Sadness*, but we still want to know what purpose it serves. The fact that *Snow Country* may illustrate wabi or sabi does not tell us what these two aesthetic qualities achieve. The existential model is at odds with Kawabata's symbolist propensities as well as his Nobel speech, in which he insists that it would be a mistake to confound the nihilism of Western existentialism with the nothingness of Zen: "This is not the nothingness or emptiness of the West. It is rather the reverse, a universe of the spirit in which everything communicates freely with everything, transcending bounds, limitless" (JBM 56). Kawabata is insistent on this point and he returns to it at the close of his address: "My own works have been described as works of emptiness," he notes, "but it is not to be taken for the nihilism of the West. The spiritual foundations would seem to be quite different" (JBM 41).

A unique feature of Japan is what Steve Odin refers to as "the primacy of aesthetic value experience or artistic intuition as the distinguishing feature of Japanese culture." This primacy of aesthetics permeates even the most mundane conditions of life in Japan, to the extent that ordinary store purchases are wrapped with painstaking attention paid to their final aesthetic presentation, or food is prepared and served with a focus on its aesthetic appeal. Even behavior—bowing and sitting, for example—has aesthetic as well as social components. The dominance of aesthetics in a culture infused with the traditional spiritual mysteries of Shinto and Buddhism means that a complex layering occurs in Japanese artistic expression as aesthetics, religion, and culture merge. Hence Kawabata's fiction must be seen as an expression of what it means to be Japanese: the self living in harmony with nature, culture, and spirituality through the disciplined application of aesthetics.

In the Nobel address, which is a discussion of Japanese aesthetic principles and their meaning and importance to the writer, Kawabata alluded to significant and abiding figures from Japan's literary history in his artistic development. Writers such as Dogen (1200–1253) and Myoe (1173–1232) were not just early inspirations. Their art and the eras in which they wrote epitomize the geido aesthetics Kawabata adopted as he strove to achieve the same degree of harmony with nature, art, spirituality, and culture that he perceived in their work. Dogen suggested to Kawabata "the deep quiet of the Japanese spirit" (JBM 69), while Myoe inspired the severe beauty and austere cold of *Snow Country*.

Kawabata began his Nobel speech by quoting a poem by Dogen called "Innate Spirit," followed by one by Myoe on the winter moon. These two poems set the tenor of the rest of Kawabata's address. Both poems illustrate yugen. Dogen's poem seems like a simple, four-line expression of the four seasons: "In the spring, cherry blossoms, / in the summer the cuckoo. / In autumn the moon, and in / winter the snow, clear, cold." But Kawabata's explanation of it sheds light on the poem's embodiment of yugen, in which that which is described becomes simply the foreground to the greater essence that lies behind: "The snow, the moon, the blossoms, words expressive of the seasons as they move one into another, include in the Japanese tradition the beauty of mountains and rivers and grasses and trees, of all the myriad manifestations of nature, of human feelings as well" (JBM 68).

Myoe's poem, three short lines on the cold wind and winter moon, evokes the same ephemeral sensations. The winter moon becomes the simple foreground for "the myriad manifestations of nature, of human feelings," even spiritual feelings, since it was a session of Zen meditation that evoked the poem: "Winter moon, coming from the / clouds to keep me company, / Is the wind piercing, the snow cold?" The austere beauty of nature in winter, the cold, clear air and moonlit night, suggest that which is not part of the scene: "When we see the beauty of the snow," writes Kawabata, "it is then that we think most of those close to us, and want them to share the pleasure. The excitement of beauty calls forth strong fellow feelings, yearnings for companionship, and the word 'comrade' can be taken to mean human being" (JBM 68).

Kawabata's evaluation of later writers, those whose historical moments were closer to his own, clearly suggests that geido became for him an artistic goal. For example, Ryokan (1758–1831) was important because in his work "one feels...the emotions of old Japan and the heart of a religious faith as well" (JBM 65). To Kawabata, Ryokan suggested that Japanese artists must be guided by the aesthetic purity of the past rather than the vulgar present: "Ryokan, who shook off the modern vulgarity of his day, who was immersed in the elegance of earlier centuries...lived in the spirit of these poems....The profundity of religion and literature were not, for him, in the abstruse" (JBM 65). Behind this description of Ryokan lies Kawabata's self-portrait: the twentieth-century author rejecting the vulgarity of a decadent present through immersion in the elegance of traditional Japanese aesthetics. Speaking of his novel *A Thousand Cranes* (1959), Kawabata declared it "a negative work, an expression of doubt about and a warning against the vulgarity into which the tea ceremony has fallen" (JBM 68). In this context "tea ceremony" may be seen as a metaphor for Japanese culture.

Kawabata's preference for the geido aesthetics of earlier writers makes it clear that he saw life in contemporary Japan as vulgar. Some critics have observed that he turned away from it. Kawabata's declaration following Japan's defeat in World War II that he would never write again reinforces such observations and suggests that the author interpreted the war's outcome as a destruction of the potential of geido to merge nation, culture, and spirituality through art.

Kawabata did write again, of course, but his fiction now warned against the vulgar intrusion of Western culture into Japanese life. These warnings sometimes appear as the insertion of foreign elements into moments focused on Japanese tradition. *The Sound of the Mountain,* whose theme contrasts the animism of Japan's Shinto past with life in the fragmented and vulgar present, is set near Tokyo, where the daily routine of the protagonist, Shingo, immerses him in the conditions of life in a contemporary industrial city while his traditional house and the mountain that speaks to him provide a cultural refuge. The ambiguous animism of the mountain—evoking the traditional Japan of Myoe and Dogen—coexists with Shingo's daily business existence in modern Tokyo, where Shingo's son is having an affair with his secretary. This contemporary setting serves as a metaphor for the intrusion of foreign elements into Japanese life and contributes to the novel's mono no aware or melancholy tone.

Beauty and Sadness begins with Oki Toshio traveling to Kyoto by express train on December 29 in an undefined year, perhaps the late fifties or early sixties, in order to participate in the ceremony of the New Year's bells, whose "lingering reverberations held an awareness of the old Japan and of the flow of time." During the trip, an American couple photograph Mount Fuji as the train passes. Mount Fuji's status as a sacred mountain creates a severe contrast with the superficial act of the American tourists, who see the mountain as a mere photographic object to be venerated for its crude aesthetic rather than its sacred spiritual essence. When Oki arrives in Kyoto he does not go to a traditional ryokan, but straight to the Miyako Hotel, one of the better Western hotels in Kyoto. The discordant note sounded by Oki's preference for a non-Japanese hotel during a trip to recover the "old Japan" creates an inescapable irony and reveals a degree of ambivalence in his quest to recover tradition. Both incidents are projections of Kawabata's conservative artistic and cultural attitude and create ironic juxtapositions that serve as moral warnings against the decadence into which contemporary Japanese culture has fallen.

While the Kyoto of *Beauty and Sadness* may boast Japan's most traditional cultural environment, the novel reads less like an attempt to revisit traditional Japan than a story concerned with the tangled web of relationships between Oki, his wife, his former mistress, and the children of these relationships. In the course of the novel, Oki's son has an affair with the young protegee of Oki's former mistress and drowns in a motorboat accident on Lake Biwa. Despite the novel's traditional title which proclaims a principle of Japanese art—only that which is sad or tragic can be truly beautiful—its subject is infidelity and involves the intrigues of unrequited love, and the setting could be any modern country. Motorboat accidents, fast trains, Western-style hotels, cafes and coffee shops, even the suggestion of a lesbian relationship between Oki's former mistress and her young protegee all give the novel a contemporary feeling. *Beauty and Sadness* is an elaborate presentation of the tragic consequences of life in a tainted culture, making the novel yet another "negative work," a powerful artistic expression of the decadence of postwar life in a battered nation.

But the moment responsible for *Snow Country* was the prewar 1930s, Japan's modern Nationalist period, when the fervor for tradition and cultural unity became intense. This historical moment, in contrast with the sixties era that produced *Beauty and Sadness,* was permeated by "government efforts at national spiritual mobilization." The direct effect on art and culture of this spiritual mobilization may be seen in the translation project involving *The Manyoshu,* whose more than 4,500 poems were compiled during the eighth century. Begun in 1934, the same year that saw the publication of the first part of *Snow Country,* the project marked the first attempt by Japanese scholars to produce an English translation of *The Manyoshu.* As the introduction indicates, the project arose out of the need to assert traditional Japanese culture and the superiority of Japan's organic social structure against encroaching influences from the West: "But filial piety [and by extension devotion to culture, nation, and emperor], so sincere, intense and instinctive as shown in the Manyo poems is not likely to be duplicated by any other people and under any other social order." According to Donald Keene, the spirit of *The Manyoshu,* which was republished in 1940, was "constantly invoked by literary men" during the war years between 1941 and 1945 because certain works contained expressions of clan unity and therefore a sense of filial obligation to country and emperor. There is a spiritual condition in this appraisal, since Japan has always traced the origins of both country and emperor to its mythological past.

What immediately strikes the reader of *Snow Country* is that the story takes place in Niigata Prefecture, away from Tokyo, the city that represents in the Japanese mind all that is modern and Western in Japanese culture. "Tokyo is Japan, but Japan is not Tokyo" the saying goes, with the obvious implication that visitors wanting to know the "real" Japan must venture into rural areas. These form the setting of Kawabata's novel, which, not so coincidentally, was also the home of Ryokan, who "lived his whole life in the snow country," as Kawabata noted enthusiastically in his Nobel speech (JBM 64). The two major characters of the novel are the Tokyo visitor Shimamura and the snow-country native Komako, who says at one point in the novel, "Tokyo people are very complicated. They live in such noise and confusion that their feelings are broken to little bits." Komako's feelings are intact and vibrant, unlike those of Shimamura, the Tokyo refugee she is destined to love.

The novel's snow-country setting is a northerly region of the main island of Honshu in what is known as the reverse side of Japan, the area close to the Japan Sea that is swept by cold winds from Siberia during the winter. Whereas Tokyo embodies Japan's contemporary, industrial, Eurocentric energies, the reverse side of Japan represents the Japan of unbroken tradition, of life close to nature, life rich with aesthetic and spiritual potential far removed from the bustle of life in the twentieth century. In the Japanese mind the region evokes the shadowy cold of winter, which makes it the perfect embodiment of yugen. Less complicated by Western intrusions into the story than *The Sound of the Mountain, Beauty and Sadness, The Lake,* and some of Kawabata's short stories, *Snow Country* embodies the innate spirituality of Dogen and the severe beauty of Myoe. Begun during a time of hope, when recovery of tradition seemed possible, the novel epitomizes Kawabata's twentieth-century triumph over what he described in reference to *A Thousand Cranes* as "the vulgarities into which the tea ceremony has fallen" (JBM 68).

The novel's setting recalls Myoe's poem on the winter moon in which that which is foregrounded in the poem becomes the spartan expression of all things not seen—summer, grass, trees, and close friends and fellow human beings—forming a literary counterpart to the traditional sumie inkwash drawing. Rendered in monochrome black ink on a white or pale background, sumie drawings contain three planes: a clear foreground, a midground, and a distant background, "which fades into the mystery and depth of enveloping pictorial space." The transitions among the planes occur in "an atmospheric haze of concealing mists and vapors...further enhancing the quality of yugen in its sense as 'hidden depths.'" This spartan art evokes in the Japanese mind a rich sense of unity with those things not expressed, both cultural and spiritual, and becomes an embodiment of the opposite of itself. Taken to an extreme, this artistic concept suggests in the empty character of Shimamura precisely those things he lacks and those things missing in the austere, snowy region that serves as the novel's setting. Rather than being precisely defined and enumerated, however, that which is missing, as in the sumie drawing, must remain intuitive and ephemeral, though one would naturally expect a Japanese reading audience to agree, at least to some extent, on what is missing, since geido merges spirituality and culture.

Kawabata's use of geido as a principle of the novel's development, and the intricate layering of some of its cultural conditions, creates for readers a refined cultural ritual similar to the tea ceremony. Yukio Mishima recognized this principle in the introduction to Kawabata's collection *The House of Sleeping Beauties and Other Short Stories,* where he noted that in the works of great writers, there are those whose meaning is culturally obvious, and "we might liken them to exoteric...Buddhism. In the case of Mr. Kawabata, *Snow Country* falls in [this] category." Mishima was referring to the novel's merging of culture, religion, and aesthetics as an expected and predictable characteristic of Japanese art, especially the art of the Master intended for Japanese readers. Such readers would instantly recognize that the love affair between Shimamura and Komako is both a literary allusion to Tanabata, a festival from mythology that celebrates the story of the Oxherd and the Weaver Maid, and an expression of mono no aware, defined by Mackintosh in a reference to *Snow Country* as "the pathos of things, the sadness of their transience," a Buddhist concept at the heart of Japanese life and thought.

Symbolized by the cherry blossom, which flowers for a brief moment then fades, impermanence defines the relationship between Shimamura and Komako. Both know their affair is doomed from the start: the Japanese male visits hot springs more for momentary relief from the monotonous patterns of his organized life at home than to discover anything of lasting value or importance. Shimamura is no different, and both he and Komako know why Shimamura visits each year. Their mutual awareness that the affair is fated to flower only briefly casts over the story a feeling of recurring poignancy, or mono no aware. But the love affair becomes a foreground vehicle for the expression of deeper cultural perceptions. Paradoxically, the transitory love affair between Shimamura and Komako reinforces a sense of cultural unity, particularly in Japanese readers, who would be expected to grasp Kawabata's aesthetic motives.

Tanabata is a national festival celebrated on the seventh day of the seventh month every year. Though the myth was originally Chinese, it found its way into Japanese cultural mythology, and became such an established feature of the literary landscape of early Japan that 120 songs about it found their way into *The Manyoshu*.

The story is simple. The Oxherd star and the Weaver Maid star love each other so much that they are constantly together and neglecting their duties. So the Ruler of Heaven separates the two young stars: they will exist for eternity on opposite sides of the Heavenly River, or Milky Way, being allowed to meet one day a year, the seventh day of the seventh month. The ubiquitous references to the Milky Way in the last chapter of the novel and Shimamura's once-a-year visit to Komako's snow-country village, with his side trip to the Chijimi cloth weaving region famous for its weaver maidens, reinforce the novel's connection to this traditional myth.

The allusion to the Tanabata myth in Shimamura's side trip to Chijimi, and the connection between it and the love story of Shimamura and Komako, suggest that the world of Shimamura and Komako retains its ancient mythological roots: "the land of Chijimi [symbolically the land of weaver maidens] was very near this [Komako's] hot spring," writes Kawabata (SC 125). But Shimamura is disillusioned by Chijimi. Seeking the ancient cloth-weaving villages and weaver maids engaged in their personal weaving rituals, he finds instead villages mostly deserted, where an old woman smiles knowingly at his suggestion that the maidens of the village might occupy themselves during the winter by weaving Chijimi cloth. Shimamura remembers that his guidebook had told him that weaving cloth in the old way was impractical and too labor-intensive for modern times, and during his visit he thinks about leaving Komako. Chijimi predicts the novel's final outcome as Shimamura, disillusioned by the intrusion of the contemporary industrial present into this isolated rural environment, transfers his disillusionment to the affair with Komako. When he returns to Komako's village the end of their relationship is near. But it is not a final, existential end, for even as Shimamura's connection to Komako and her snow-country village is terminating, Shimamura is being spiritually absorbed into the region of the snow country, where "generation after generation of his ancestors had endured the long snows" (SC 128).

His absorption is so intense that it becomes a religious experience, a Way, in which, as he loses connection with Komako's material world, he finds himself drawn up into the Milky Way with the sparks of the cocoon warehouse fire that ends the novel: "The sparks spread off into the Milky Way, and Shimamura was pulled up with them. As the smoke drifted away, the Milky Way seemed to dip and flow in the opposite direction" (SC 139). Shimamura stumbles, and Kawabata ends the novel with Shimamura's head falling back and the Milky Way flowing down inside him with a roar (SC 142).

In the last few pages of the novel, references to the Milky Way occur nineteen times. While it is easy to see the symbolic connection between the love affair and the Tanabata myth, the ending seems too saturated with aesthetics, spirituality, and culture for these geido qualities to be mere coincidence. The Milky Way is often referred to in Japanese mythology as the Bridge of Heaven, the path taken to earth by the country's founding deities. Each mention of it in the novel tends to merge the Tanabata myth with the spiritual origins of Japan's mythical past. These expressions are typical: "the Milky Way came down to wrap itself around the earth" (SC 136) or, referring to Shimamura, the Milky Way "like a great aurora flowed through his body to stand at the edges of the earth" (SC 137).

"*Snow Country* is perhaps Kawabata's masterpiece," writes Seidensticker in the introduction to the novel's English translation. And it is not incidental that both the setting and the story evoke the cultural, artistic, and spiritual sensitivities of the tea ceremony and become an embodiment of the traditional Japanese aesthetic principles designated by geido. *Snow Country*'s final scenes constitute both a rejection of the vulgar and decadent present and an apotheosis of geido, of Kawabata's insistent demand for the traditional Japanese unity of spirit, culture, and self through art.

Source: Peter M. Carriere, "Writing as Tea Ceremony: Kawabata's Geido Aesthetics," in *International Fiction Review*, Vol. 29, No. 1–2, January 2002, p. 52.

Donald Richie

In the following article, Richie states that the sense of evanescence that is Kawabata is what links him strongly to his country and culture and what makes him universal.

This collection of stories, plus an essay and a dance-drama, was originally published in 1958 as *Fuji no Hatsuyuki*. It is late Kawabata—most of the major works had already appeared, the author wrote much less during these years, and he died in 1972.

That these works form a meditation on death is not surprising. Many of Kawabata's works—early and late—are just that. He called himself a master of ceremonies at funerals, and though he was referring to duties at the demise of friends, his writing was from the earliest informed by thoughts of death.

Indeed, this awareness of transience creates the Kawabata tone. In a way it makes him "Japanese," because these people are traditionally less inclined to deny the facts of life (and death) than are those of at least several other countries. It also makes him universal, because these are facts that, like it or not, we must all face.

This lends Kawabata's work a certain cohesion—this and the facts that he often finished works long after they were originally published, and that all of his writing shares a relatively narrow repertoire of themes.

Readers of a work as early as "The Diary of My Sixteenth Year" will find that one of the stories here, "Nature," might be considered a continuation. The story "Yumiura" could be seen as a late metamorphosis of "The Izu Dancer." Indeed, one Japanese critic saw it as that, stating that the aged woman turning up at the novelist's door is really the child dancer now grown old. In any event, Kawabata included both works in a collection of his favorites published shortly before he received the Nobel Prize.

A theme that is often found in Kawabata's works (as well as in the writings of many other authors) is the nature of self-awareness. The woman in "This County, That County" is surprised to discover that two entities can express themselves through her; the man in "Nature" has lived a life as a woman and Kawabata is very interested in what Thomas Rimer has called "the interplay between character, gender and self-knowledge."

In "Silence," the author visits another writer, victim of a stroke, who can no longer speak and seems "a living ghost." Interwoven into this is a "real" ghost story, one side of the theme lending body to the other. The essay "Chrysanthemum in the Rock" contains its own ghost, since the rock is eventually a grave stone and the various themes of awareness, ghosts and death are all gracefully gathered together.

Kawabata's means are famously economical. Indeed, perhaps the only way to treat the great truths he deals with is through a style this laconic. Through ellipses, thrown-away observations and intimations, Kawabata is able to suggest his meaning without explicitly stating it. One must infer when reading Kawabata, and this modest exercise means that one brings to him what is necessary for his intentions to flower.

The sense of death that hovers just about the Kawabata page would, indeed, be impossible were it directly delineated. Rather, author and reader together weave the pattern. Translating this into another language is a problem. This work has been translated into German and Russian, and I can have no opinion as to their success.

In English, Kawabata is fortunate in having had good translators—Edward Seidensticker, Howard Hibbett and now Michael Emmerich.

This sense of evanescence that is so palpable in Kawabata is what, I believe, links him so strongly to his country and its culture, and what makes him at the same time so universal. He wrote about the most important subject and his words directly reach us. After his suicide, no note was found, but one obituary remembered something he had said: "A silent death is an endless word."

Source: Donald Richie, "Kawabata and Great Truths," in *Japan Times*, December 1, 1999.

Janet Jurgella

In the following excerpt, Jurgella discusses how to use dramatic interpretation as a means to teach the classics through student skits, based on "Grasshopper and the Bell Cricket."

…So what else is new? It is inherent in English classrooms today that interpretation of literature includes dramatic activities such as readers' theater, role playing, and student-generated skits. I have three unique theatrical favorites which have worked well for me.

India's Rabindranath Tagore authored a timeless poem, "The man had no useful work." The poetic narrative questions whether humankind values a productive livelihood more than it values the individual. I've developed a "blind" performance of this poem which unfolds as the students, under my cue, perform individual parts assigned to them on a piece of paper they drew from the pot. The paper slips direct students to, for example, be the narrator, look up a word in the dictionary, read the girl's lines, answer questions about the author, draw a scene from the poem on the board, even interject their opinion after a particular line is read. After a silent ten-minute prep time, the performance begins with my asking "Where is the author Rabindranath Tagore from, and when did he live?" The student, whose slip of paper included directions to look up those facts, answers. It moves on to "Will the narrator of the poem please begin reading?" and continues as the students see their individual parts form a whole, defining words, pointing out pictures drawn on the board, reading lines to the final few students who wrap up with their prepared answer to "What does this poem say about the individual and society?"

"The Grasshopper and the Bell Cricket" by Yasunari Kawabata of Japan looks at elements of nature and true beauty through the eyes of a quietly observant narrator. A very simple dramatic activity, which I call "zoom in on nature," reinforces Kawabata's tale of epiphany. After we have read and discussed the story, small groups choose an incident of nature written on a slip of paper—anything from "a blooming flower" to "an eclipse." They have to really "zoom in" to first visualize, then perform these moments in nature. One of the most powerful of these skits was when a boy jumped up through his groupmates' circle of arms, diving and landing onto the floor with such force that the class gasped, then guessed correctly that he was the lava exploding out of a volcano.

Another simple, dramatic, yet realistic, corollary leaves students thinking—and talking—after walking out of the classroom. I have revived the classic film adaptation of Shirley Jackson's short story "The Lottery" in my world literature class. Our closing activity is staging a lottery of our own. It takes just a few minutes as the students each draw a square of paper from my "black box," hold it in their hands until the signal, then slowly unfold it to see who received the one with the black dot. (Coincidentally, last semester, the student who "lost" the lottery was the same boy who earlier had exploded through the volcano!)

Source: Janet Jurgella, "Classic Connections: Aiding Literary Comprehension through Varied Liberal Arts Alliances," in *English Journal,* Vol. 87, No. 3, March 1998, p. 18.

Thomas J. Rimer

In the following article, Holman reviews a collection of Kawabata's stories and praises the prose and themes of stories that hearken back to traditional, classic Japanese literature.

"As death approaches, memory erodes," writes Kawabata in one of the graceful and often unsettling stories contained in this new collection. These few words reveal the themes that pervade these diverse tales, but can only begin to suggest their range and subtlety.

Kawabata (1899–1972), the first Japanese writer to receive the Nobel Prize, in 1968, has long been known in the United States and Europe for such novels as *The Sound of the Mountain, Snow Country* and others that often hark back to the traditions of classical Japanese literature. He employs devices from those long poetic traditions in order to create in modern prose his remarkable effects: juxtapositions of image upon image to open up the depths of feeling lurking behind placid surface reality. These stories, most of them composed when he was a young writer, serve as a reminder that he was then fascinated by the work of the European imagists and symbolists, who often used similar techniques in order to move from fact to suggestion.

Many of the 20-odd stories that make up this collection are only a few pages in length. A number of them are justly famous in Japan, but only one, "The Dancing Girl of Izu," has received wide circulation in translation, in a slightly shortened version by the great Edward Seidensticker, first published in the 1960s and available in a variety of editions over the years. "The Dancing Girl," like many other stories included here, contains strong autobiographical elements, but these are used not for their own sake, as possible self-revelations, but as a means to suggest the difficulties of penetrating toward any kind of ultimate truth.

ACQUISITIONS DEPARTMENT

P00VJNMNB

22

Routing   *4

SORTING
Y05D04X
Shipping

152510639 canflg26 RC1

Ship To: JT 5995A00 C
ACQUITIONS DEPARTMENT
MISSISSAUGA LIBRARY SYSTE
301 BURNHAMTHORPE RD, W.
MISSISSAUGA, ONT.
L5B 3Y3

Volume: 29
Edition:
Year: 2010
Pagination:
Size:

ISBN	Qty	Sales Order
9781414442129	1	C 2129963 26

Customer P/O No
46157
Title: Short Stories for Students

Format: C (Cloth/HB)
Author:
Publisher: Gale Cengage
Fund:
Location:
Loan Type:
Coutts CN: 10722679

Order Specific Instructions

COUTTS INFORMATION SERVICES:

This conviction, so important to an understanding of Kawabata's basic artistic stance, is most clearly revealed in the second story, "Diary of My Sixteenth Year." The story contains three layers: the narrative itself, an afterword appended in 1925, and a second afterword attached still later. The material presented in the tale itself, Kawabata tells his readers in the first afterword, is taken from his teenage diary and concerns his attempts to care for his dying grandfather, by then his only close relative. The old man grows weaker as the story progresses. Kawabata tells us in the second afterword that he was to die some eight days later.

It is easy to see why he was regarded as such a precocious writer, for the description of the old man, from his incoherent mumblings to his seemingly constant need to urinate, is gripping to read, particularly when experienced through the consciousness of the young boy, who is forced to help the situation along as best he can. According to the first afterword, in his published version Kawabata added only an occasional parenthesis to the original text, in order to identify persons and places and, occasionally, to augment his memories of his own responses. In the second afterword, however, he acknowledges that "since I wrote that first Afterword as fiction, there are some parts that differ from the truth." He proceeds to make further corrections and suggestions, then makes the following statement, which goes to the core of his ambitions in this short but remarkable work:

> "I cannot simply imagine that something has 'vanished' or 'been lost' in the past just because I do not recall it. This work was not meant to resolve the puzzle of forgetfulness and memory. Neither was it intended to answer the questions of time and life. But it is certain that it offers a clue, some piece of evidence."

In resolutely seeking for such clues, Kawabata removes "Diary" from that genre of nihilistic literary game so much practiced in the West in the postwar years. For Kawabata, the fact that we cannot know is perhaps more an occasion for chagrin, for humility. "Bad as my memory is," he writes, "I have no firm belief in memory. There are times when I feel that forgetfulness is a blessing."

Other stories in the first part of this collection circle around the sense of loss that Kawabata felt as a youngster over the many deaths in his family, and how this radical loneliness marked his very conceptions of reality. No wonder, as he records in one of these stories, he was referred to as "The Master of Funerals."

The book's second section contains a number of brief stories that reveal Kawabata's ability to put a moment of poetic vision into a page or two of striking prose. These sketches, often referred to as haiku-like, reveal his penchant for the excitements of literary experimentation. Many are purely lyrical. Some reveal an acute sense of the social conditions found in interwar Japan, such as "The Money Road," which describes some remarkable events that took place after the great earthquake of 1923 virtually destroyed Tokyo, or "The Sea," which describes with understated poignancy the plight of Korean laborers in the Japanese countryside.

Given the difficulties of Kawabata's subtle and difficult language, the translator, J. Martin Holman, has generally struck an excellent balance between accuracy and the need to create a certain level of evocative possibility. Holman is to be congratulated for making available in English a number of striking works by this now-classic Japanese author. He chose well from among the various possibilities available to him.

Source: Thomas J. Rimer, "Kawabata Country," in *Washington Post*, September 21, 1997, p. X04.

Mary Jo Moran

In the following article, Moran advises that teachers should introduce students to non-Western writers such as Kawabata because he succeeds in integrating Western and Eastern techniques, producing superb fiction.

Awarded the Nobel Prize for Literature in 1968 for "contributing to spiritual bridge-spanning between East and West," Yasunari Kawabata, one of Japan's best modern writers, appeals to today's students because he understands and writes about a world afflicted with alienation.

Kawabata's life was one marked by recurrent, personal tragedy. His father died when Kawabata was only two and his mother died a year later. By the time Kawabata was sixteen, his only sister and grandparents were dead, and he spent the remainder of his adolescent years in several boarding schools. Thus, he shares the scars of alienation, one of modern society's characteristic maladies, with today's youth, and the intense loneliness he experienced during his early years is reflected in his writing.

> "HE SUGGESTS A CHARACTER OR SITUATION MUCH AS A SUMIEE PAINTER EXPRESSES THE ESSENTIAL NATURE OF HIS SUBJECT IN A FEW ABBREVIATED STROKES."

Thousand Cranes (New York: Berkley, 1965, written in 1947), treats loneliness and the fragility of human relationships with rare sensitivity. As the novel opens, the reader meets Kikuji, a young man in his late twenties who has recently lost both his parents, and who, for the present, has abandoned his heritage and traditions. However, Kikuji's resolve to ignore his roots wavers when he accepts an invitation to attend a tea ceremony where he will be formally introduced to Yukiko Inamura, the girl of the thousand cranes, by Chikako, his father's first mistress. While participating in this tea ceremony, he also meets Mrs. Ota, his father's second and last mistress, and her daughter, Fumiko.

As the novel unfolds, Kikuji, struggling to break with established traditions, has the choice of either embracing the past, its ugliness represented strikingly by Chikako who is disfigured by a large, ugly birthmark on her breast, or a future, characterized by the purity and innocence of the Inamura girl. Although Kikuji intuitively knows that no goodness or life can come from a relationship with Chikako. he can not escape her and consequently becomes enmeshed in his father's past. The venom he was so keenly aware of during the innocence of his youth becomes an integral part of him.

Thus, Kawabata strongly proposes that Kikuji becomes possessed by his father's spirit, while Fumiko, after her mother's untimely suicide, becomes possessed by her mother's spirit. Neither can escape fate, and family history is doomed to repeat itself because both Kikuji and Fumiko become romantically involved in a relationship which proves destructive to both.

Kawabata's writing is characterized by brevity. In the first ten pages of the novel, the reader not only meets the novel's major characters and becomes immediately acquainted with intertwining details of their past but is also introduced to the novel's theme, conflict, and recurring symbols. *Thousand Cranes* is rich in symbolism and imagery.

> Back in his bedroom after brushing his teeth, Kikuji saw that the maid had hung a gourd in the alcove. It contained a single morning glory....
>
> It was a plain indigo morning glory, probably wild, and most ordinary. The vine was thin, and the leaves and blossom were small.
>
> But the green and the deep blue were cool, falling over a red lacquered gourd dark with age....
>
> In a gourd that had been handed down for three centuries, a flower that would fade in a morning....
>
> There was something unsettling in the idea of a cut morning glory.

Repeated references are also made to colors, birds, flowers, and other natural phenomena.

Against the backdrop of the Japanese tea ceremony, Kawabata examines the role and importance of ritual and tradition, the transience of life, parents' influence on children, the role of fate in individual lives, and life's cycle of birth, death, and rebirth. Readers are continually reminded of their own mortality as Kawabata juxtaposes the novel's characters and the age-old tea utensils.

In *Snow Country* (New York: Berkley, 1960, written in 1937), Kawabata examines male-female relationships. Shimamura, an idle but wealthy married man from Tokyo who has inherited his money, meets two women, Komacho, a sensitive, warm geisha, and Yoko, a young girl strangely different from other hot spring natives.

The reader visits the snow country on the west coast of Japan's main island three times with Shimamura. The coldness of the setting and Shimamura's incessant awareness of others as "cold" accurately reflect his character. Through these trips, Kawabata concentrates on developing Shimamura's relationship with Komacho and his inability to love. Kawabata's power of characterization is striking as both characters become unique. Komacho's beauty and warmth draw the reader to identify and sympathize with her, but one is repelled by Shimamura's cold, indifferent self-centeredness.

Although Shimamura believes that "only women are able really to love," he cannot justify his lack of emotional response to us. His is a wasted life, symbolized by his area of specialization, the Western ballet, chosen because he has not seen the Western dance. Thus, living with his own fantasies, he can remain untouched by experience. In describing Shimamura, Kawabata states simply, "He preferred not to savor the ballet in the flesh; rather he savored the phantasms of his own dancing imagination, called up by Western books and pictures. It was like being in love with someone he had never seen."

Kawabata's female characters, as well as his understanding of the female psyche, distinguish his work. In *Snow Country*, Kawabata paints a picture of Komacho:

> The high, thin nose was usually a little lonely, a little sad, but today, with the healthy, vital flush on her cheeks, it was rather whispering: I am here too. The smooth lips seemed to reflect back a dancing light even when they were drawn into a tight bud; and when for a moment they were stretched wide, as the singing demanded, they were quick to contract again into that engaging little bud. Their charm was exactly like the charm of her body itself. Her eyes, moist and shining, made her look like a very young girl. She wore no powder, and the polish of the city geisha had over it a layer of mountain color. Her skin, suggesting the newness of a freshly peeled onion or perhaps a lily bulb, was flushed faintly, even to the throat. More than anything, it was clean.

Snow Country and *Thousand Cranes* introduce Western readers to unfamiliar aspects of Japanese culture and geography while they contrast pre- and post-World War II Japan. Kawabata succeeds in integrating Western literary techniques with Eastern spirit while achieving superb psychological fiction. In *Thousand Cranes*, while speaking to Kikuji about her mother's suicide, Fumiko says, "She died because of herself. If you say it was you who made her die, then it was I even more. If I have to blame anyone, it should be myself. But it only makes her death seem dirty, when we start feeling responsible and having regrets. Regrets and second thoughts only make the burden heavier for the one who has died."

Both novels fool the reader at a first, casual glance. They are short, the print large, the vocabulary unsophisticated. But during a more thoughtful reading one is struck by the profound meaning expressed in elegant simplicity. Kawabata's style is paradoxical, simple, yet profound, descriptive, yet suggestive.

Kawabata's style resembles that of the Japanese Sumiee painter. He suggests a character or situation much as a Sumiee painter expresses the essential nature of his subject in a few abbreviated strokes. Through language, Kawabata presents a visual image suggesting an intuitive experience beyond the confines of language. Like the artist, Kawabata depends upon a response from his reader to complete his work. He relies on our common pool of experience which awakens intuition and meaning in the mind of the reader.

While most undergraduate and graduate English programs do not include a study of non-Western literature, today's secondary English teachers are equipped with analytical reading skills. We must use those skills to teach non-Western literature if we are to prepare students to live in today's world. Like Kawabata, we must begin bridging the gap between the West and the East.

Source: Mary Jo Moran, "Recommended: Yasunari Kawabata," in *English Journal*, Vol. 71, No. 7, November 1982, pp. 75–76.

SOURCES

Chiba, Kameo, "The Birth of the Neoperceptionists," in *Seiki*, November 1924, reprinted in "Kawabata: Achievements of the Nobel Laureate [1969]," in *World Literature Today*, Vol. 63, No. 2, Spring 1989, pp. 209–12.

Cowley, Jason, "The Month of Cherry Blossom," in *New Statesman*, August 21, 2006, p. 46.

Dean, Kitty Chen, Review of *Palm-of-the-Hand Stories*, in *Library Journal*, Vol. 113, No. 3, August 1988, p. 174.

Gessel, Van C., "Yasunari Kawabata," in *Dictionary of Literary Biography*, Vol. 330, *Nobel Prize Laureates in Literature, Part 2: Faulkner–Kipling*, edited by Jeffrey Louis Decker, Thomson Gale, 2007, pp. 449–62.

Hooper, Rowan, "Animal Tracker: Bell Cricket," in *Japan Times Online*, March 25, 2004, http://search.japantimes.co.jp/cgi-bin/fe20040325at.html (accessed September 16, 2009).

Kawabata, Yasunari, "The Grasshopper and the Bell Cricket," in *Palm-of-the-Hand Stories*, translated by Lane Dunlop and J. Martin Holman, Farrar, Straus and Giroux, 2006, pp. 13–17.

"Modernity—East Asia—Urban Cosmopolitan Modernity (1920s–1930s)," in *Science Encyclopedia*, http://science.jrank.org/pages/10268/Modernity-East-Asia-Urban-Cosmopolitan-Modernity-1920s-1930s.html (accessed September 18, 2009).

Palmer, Thom, "The Asymmetrical Garden: Discovering Yasunari Kawabata," in *Southwest Review*, Vol. 74, No. 3, Summer 1989, pp. 390–402.

Parkes, Graham, "Japanese Aesthetics," in *Stanford Encyclopedia of Philosophy*, December 12, 2005, http://plato.

stanford.edu/entries/japanese-aesthetics/ (accessed September 14, 2009).

Pilarcik, Marlene A., "Dialectics and Change in Kawabata's *The Master of Go*," in *Modern Language Studies*, Vol. 16, No. 4, Fall 1986, pp. 9–21.

Raeside, James, "Yasunari Kawabata," in *Reference Guide to Short Fiction*, edited by Noelle Watson, St. James Press, 1994, pp. 287–88.

Smock, Frederick, "Small Lanterns," in *American Book Review*, Vol. 10, No. 6, January/February 1989, p. 15.

"Wabi and Sabi: The Aesthetics of Solitude," in *Hermitary: House of Solitude*, http://www.hermitary.com/solitude/wabisabi.html (accessed on September 21, 2009).

FURTHER READING

Aesop, *Aesop's Fables*, translated by Laura Gibbs, Oxford University Press, 2008.

    Aesop was supposedly a tongue-tied slave who received the power of speech through a miracle. Although these fables were first published in the late 1400s, they are still enjoyed by readers of all ages. This edition includes six hundred fables.

Akutagawa, Ryunosuke, *Rashomon and Seventeen Other Stories*, translated by Jay Rubin, Penguin Classics, 2009.

    The short stories contained in this collection explore human nature and moral ambiguity. Like Kawabata, Akutagawa's writing style is simple and spare, and his treatment of the human condition makes him one of Japan's most highly respected authors.

Kawabata, Yasunari, *Snow Country*, translated by Edward G. Seidensticker, Vintage, 1996.

    This novel found its genesis in the short story "Gleanings from Snow Country" (1972), also published in *Palm-of-the-Hand Stories*. Kawabata writes a haunting story of wasted love between a wealthy man and a mountain geisha. This is one of the three novels that earned Kawabata the Nobel Prize for Literature.

Shapard, Robert, and James Thomas, eds., *New Sudden Fiction: Short-Short Stories from America and Beyond*, W. W. Norton, 2007.

    Each of the sixty stories in this compilation is 2,000 words or less. Writers hail from around the globe and include those well known (Ian Frazier, Tobias Wolff, and Sam Shepard) as well as those new to the scene. The variety of themes and styles makes this volume ideal for use in the literature classroom.

Tanaka, Yukiko, *To Live and to Write: Selections by Japanese Women Writers 1913–1938*, Seal Press, 1987.

    Nine Japanese feminists explore the challenges and obstacles of life in pre-World War II Japan. The tension of being caught between the limitations of tradition and the demands of modernity is reflected in these stories as they touch on themes of politics, gender, poverty, and many others.

Ha'penny

ALAN PATON

1961

Drawing on his real-life experience as a principal in a reformatory school in South Africa, Alan Paton creates a heart-wrenching short story called "Ha'penny" about a young boy in search of family love. Ha'penny is a twelve-year-old boy who has spent most of his life on the streets. After being caught stealing, he is sent to the reformatory where the narrator works. In the course of conversations with the boy, the narrator hears stories from Ha'penny that he has trouble believing.

The narrator portrays himself as a compassionate man. He understands that many of the boys in the reformatory need affection and attention more than anything else. He especially enjoys working with the younger boys, who respond to a little compassion by improving their studies and staying out of trouble. However, despite the narrator's knowledge about the boys' psychological needs, he makes a grave mistake with Ha'penny. This mistake, the narrator believes, has dire consequences for Ha'penny, but the narrator cannot do anything to change those results. The best the narrator can do is to learn from his mistakes.

"Ha'penny" was published in Paton's collection of short stories, *Tales from a Troubled Land*, in 1961. There are ten short stories in this collection. Most of them focus on incidents that occur in a South African reformatory, providing readers with a background of boys' lives spent in jail.

Alan Paton (The Library of Congress)

AUTHOR BIOGRAPHY

Much of Paton's writing draws from the details of his own life experiences, which occurred in South Africa. He was born on January 11, 1903, in the city of Pietermaritzburg, which is the second largest city in the province of KwaZulu-Natal in South Africa. His parents, James (a civil servant) and Eunice, were English settlers. Paton studied science at the University of Natal and in 1922 earned a certificate in teaching.

For several years, Paton wrote poetry and fiction while teaching at local high schools and later at Pietermaritzburg College. However, his early writing dissatisfied him, and he threw much of it away. In 1928, Paton married Dorrie Lusted. They had two sons, David and Jonathan. In 1935, he gave up teaching and took the position of principal at the Diepkloof Reformatory. This change was to become an important part of the transformation in his writing.

Paton began his new position enthusiastically. Not liking what he saw at the reformatory, Paton began making great improvements in the lives of the boys who were forced to live there. He was so full of enthusiasm about transforming the reformatory that he spent his own money for visits to other reformatory institutions around the world. He adopted as many beneficial practices as he could. The changes he made at his reformatory, he believed, would better prepare the boys when their sentences were completed and they were returned to the outside world.

While he traveled, Paton also began writing again. This time, his efforts were more successful. He began the novel that would become his most famous, *Cry, the Beloved Country*, which was published in 1948. In this novel, Paton explored the relationships of black and white South Africans, a theme that would be repeated in his other works. This novel was adapted to film, first in 1951 and again in 1995. Paton proved to be a prolific writer. The long list of his publications include his second novel, *Too Late the Phalarope* (1953) and *Ah, but Your Land Is Beautiful*, which was published in 1981.

Paton was also very active in politics. He was the founder and president of the Liberal Party for fifteen years, from 1953 until 1968. This group protested the system of apartheid that was in full force in South Africa at the time. The country's apartheid government banned this party in 1968. In 1967, Paton's first wife died of emphysema. He wrote about his life with his first wife in his book *Kontakion for You Departed*, which was published in 1969. Paton was remarried the same year to Anne Hopkins.

Paton also wrote nonfiction essays, most of them with a political theme. Since 1989, an award has been handed out in Paton's name, sponsored by the Johannesburg *Sunday Times* for meritorious works of nonfiction that reflect the standards that Paton set.

Paton died on April 12, 1988, at his home in Durban, Natal, South Africa. His last novel, *Save the Beloved Country* was published posthumously in 1989.

PLOT SUMMARY

Paton's short story "Ha'penny" is set in a youth reformatory in South Africa. The narrator informs the readers that there are six hundred youths incarcerated there. Out of that number, about one hundred are between the ages of ten and fourteen. There have been discussions among

MEDIA ADAPTATIONS

- Books on Tape has a 1983 recording available of the ten short stories found in Paton's collection *Tales from a Troubled Land*, which includes the story "Ha'penny."

---

various administration officials about whether these younger boys would be better off if they were separated from the older ones, the narrator reports, since they could be easier to train and to reform. Younger boys, the narrator says, "turn instinctively towards affection, and one controls them by it, naturally and easily." If this change in organization had taken place, the narrator would have liked being the principal of the school for younger boys, as his life and his job would have been much easier, he says.

To support his claim about the younger boys' need for affection, the narrator mentions how the boys watch him at various events, such as during a football game. The boys are not obvious about their stares, but nonetheless, the narrator notices them looking at him. If he acknowledges them with a nod or some other expression, the boys then change their focus and return to paying attention to the activity that is going on. They are more content after they receive a sign of interest from him. The narrator also gets pleasure from these small interactions. Had the boys been his own children, he confesses, he would undoubtedly have spent more personal time with each boy, but even the small gestures—a slight tweaking of an ear or merely standing near the boy—are of great significance. The boys, toughened as they are by their circumstances, have learned not to show their feelings. However, the narrator can tell by the quick flash of a smile or even by a concentrated effort not to grin that the boys appreciate his efforts to single them out, even momentarily.

Sometimes, even the older boys react to these brief exchanges. They watch the narrator interact with the smaller boys and then attempt to emulate the quick, nonverbal communications with the narrator. The narrator understands that, although the gestures are seemingly insignificant in themselves, they are symbolic. The narrator believes that his small attentions to the boys signal to them that, despite the conditions at the reformatory, everything is all right. Even at times of unrest inside the walls of the school, when the normal communications between the administrators and the youths are strained, the practice of these small gestures of understanding is helpful in making the boys understand that "nothing important [has] changed."

On Sundays, the narrator takes some of the younger children for car rides, driving along the streets of nearby towns. While they ride, the narrator asks the boys questions about their families and the towns they are from. One of the boys is Ha'penny. He is always the most talkative child. Ha'penny tells long stories about his family. He says that he is from Bloemfontein and that his mother works as a maid for a white family. Ha'penny has two brothers, named Richard and Dickie, and two sisters, Anna and Mina. The narrator doubts the truth of Ha'penny's stories (he points out that in English, "Richard and Dickie are the same name"), and one day he examines the boy's personal files. He discovers that Ha'penny is an orphan who has been passed along to several foster families and was classified as a troubled youth; he was caught stealing before he was turned over to the authorities at the school.

This information prompts the narrator to look further into Ha'penny's case. Ha'penny, he discovers, writes regularly to a Mrs. Betty Maarman, but she never writes back. When the narrator questions Ha'penny about this, Ha'penny concludes that she might be sick. With his curiosity aroused, the narrator writes to the social welfare officer at Bloemfontein and asks the officer to investigate the matter.

When the narrator next takes Ha'penny out for a car ride, he questions him again about his family. Ha'penny sticks to his story, but this time, when he says his brothers' names, he refers to them as Richard and Tickie. When the narrator asks about the new pronunciation of the second brother's name, Ha'penny corrects the narrator, telling him that he had always said Tickie.

Shortly after this exchange, the narrator receives confirmation that there is a real Betty Maarman and she has four children, named Richard, Dickie, Anna, and Mina. Mrs. Maarman has told the officer that Ha'penny is definitely not her child. She does know of him, but only as a "derelict of the street." Mrs. Maarman never responded to Ha'penny's letter because in his letters he always referred to her as "mother." She wanted no part of the game he was playing.

The narrator has a completely different attitude toward Ha'penny. He sees a young boy who had such a great need for a family that he went to the trouble of making up an imaginary connection with the Maarman family. Ha'penny's record at the reformatory is "blameless," and he goes out of his way to please the people around him. This makes the narrator feel "a great duty towards him."

The narrator continues to ask the boy questions. He especially wants to know about the boy's mother. When Ha'penny speaks, he cannot say enough about the woman's kindness. "She was loving, honest, and strict," Ha'penny says. The narrator concludes that Ha'penny might have turned to the woman, just as he turned to him, in hopes she would open up her heart to him. Mrs. Maarman obviously had been unable to. She would not take him into her home, which might have relieved the boy of the loneliness of living on the streets.

The narrator informs Ha'penny that his so-called brother's name is definitely Dickie, "not Tickie." Ha'penny knows his deception has been uncovered. If the narrator knows the correct name, then he must also know the rest of the story. This causes Ha'penny's "whole brave assurance" to crack. Ha'penny has been exposed, not as a liar but as something worse: a boy without the support and love of a family. The narrator states, "I had shattered the very foundations of his pride, and his sense of human significance."

Shortly afterward, Ha'penny becomes ill with tuberculosis. The narrator writes to Mrs. Maarman, telling her everything he knows about Ha'penny. Mrs. Maarman replies that she will have nothing to do with the boy. Her reasons are based on race and social culture: she is colored and wants nothing to do with Ha'penny, who is from a Mosuto tribe (an original South African tribe). The tuberculosis quickly weakens Ha'penny, and in desperation, the narrator sends money to Mrs. Maarman, hoping to entice her to make a visit. She relents and visits the reformatory, where everyone accepts her as being Ha'penny's mother. She sits with him, talking to him about her children and saying that they are waiting for him to come home. To help encourage him back to health, she tells him of all the things they will do together when he is better.

The narrator visits Ha'penny, but he senses that he no longer belongs in Ha'penny's world. He berates himself for not having handled the situation more wisely. He should have realized the emotional need of the boy to have his imaginary family.

Ha'penny dies and is buried at the reformatory. Mrs. Maarman requests that Ha'penny be listed as her son on the marker for his burial site. She tells the narrator that she was ashamed that she did not want to bring him into her family. If she had, she believes, he would not have gotten sick, or "it would have been different."

After Mrs. Maarman leaves, the narrator reflects on his role in Ha'penny's life. In the future, he promises himself, he will act differently toward the children who have been put in his care. He will "be more prodigal" (more lavish) in his support of them.

CHARACTERS

Ha'penny

Ha'penny, though his name makes the title of Paton's short story, is not the protagonist of this story. He is, however, the main focal point. The narrator of this story concentrates his attention on Ha'penny because it is through this young boy that the narrator learns a very serious lesson.

Ha'penny is a twelve-year-old boy who is incarcerated in a reformatory for boys. He has spent most of his life on the streets and is an orphan. On a racial level, an identification process that was very much a part of the apartheid system into which he was born, he is considered a black child. His roots can be traced back to an ancient South African tribe. Since Mrs. Maarman shuns him because of his heritage, it can be assumed he is not of mixed heritage, such as Mrs. Maarman is.

Since Ha'penny has no family, he makes up an imaginary one. He has watched Mrs. Maarman and her children, and he is drawn to her. His desires are so strong that he comes to believe he is a part of her family. This need leads Ha'penny to write Mrs. Maarman letters and to talk to the narrator about her family as if he were her son and her children were his siblings. As readers (and the narrator) later find out, it is this belief of belonging, even though it is imaginary, that keeps Ha'penny alive.

When his imaginary world collapses, Ha'penny loses his desire to live. Though his wish for Mrs. Maarman to pretend to be his mother comes true, it comes too late. The most that readers can hope for is that Ha'penny dies in peace, with Mrs. Maarman at his side. In this story, Ha'penny represents some of the hardships and discriminations that black people were facing in South Africa. The emphasis, in this story, is on the youth. The narrator believes he can turn around the lives of the impoverished black youth. Through this episode in Ha'penny's life, this story exemplifies how difficult that might be.

Mrs. Betty Maarman

Mrs. Maarman is the woman that Ha'penny pretends is his mother. She refers to herself as a colored person, a classification under the apartheid system in South Africa that identifies Mrs. Maarman as being of mixed races. There is no mention of a husband, but Mrs. Maarman has four children, Richard, Dickie, Anna, and Mina. She works as a cleaning woman, and although she claims to know who Ha'penny is, she wants nothing to do with him at first. She knows that Ha'penny is a thief and does not want to have this criminal element associated with her family. Her children have never been in trouble, and she wants to keep it that way.

Whether it is the money that the narrator sends to her, the fact that Ha'penny is very sick, or the narrator's persistence, Mrs. Maarman finally gives in and comes to the reformatory to visit Ha'penny. Once she has made this commitment, she regrets having shunned the boy when he needed her help. She believes that if she had come to his rescue earlier, Ha'penny might not have come down with tuberculosis. Even if he had contracted the disease, Mrs. Maarman thinks he would not have died because he would have had a home and a family to support and love him. In the end, Mrs. Maarman gives Ha'penny all her attention and love. She tells everyone at the reformatory that she is Ha'penny's mother. She insists that Ha'penny's cemetery marker list him as a part of her family.

Narrator

The narrator is never named or identified. Readers, after learning about the author's biography, might assume that the narrator is a male who holds the position of principal of the reformatory. However, this is never stated. Readers know that the narrator has an administrative position at the reform school because he has access to the boys' records, has the authority to take them for car rides, and has a keen interest in how the boys are treated.

From the way the narrator describes the boys, readers can also deduce that the narrator is a compassionate person. He is not there merely to keep order; he cares about the boys' mental and emotional health. He searches for ways to fulfill their needs. He relates to them, at least on a peripheral level, as if they were his sons. While the boys are in his care, he studies them, watching the way they communicate with one another, and determines, from their gestures, how best to respond to them. He takes them out of the reformatory for rides through the countryside and the towns because he is thinking about their future. He knows that one day they will be returned to society and he wants them to adapt successfully.

Nothing is known about the narrator's life outside his job at the reformatory. This keeps readers in the dark about the personal side of the narrator's life, but it intensifies the narrator's focus on the lives of the boys at the reformatory, especially Ha'penny. The narrator's relationship with Ha'penny reflects the complexities of the narrator's mind. While he demonstrates his compassion and understanding, he errs in fully comprehending the fragile nature of Ha'penny's psychological state. The narrator's main concern is to help Ha'penny. In the end, though, the narrator's unmasking of the young boy's deceptions strips Ha'penny of his main defenses. The narrator moves in a direction that is diametrically opposed to what is needed for Ha'penny's health.

Although he blunders in his dealing with Ha'penny, the narrator proves, in the end, that he is wise enough to learn from his own mistakes. Though he is powerless in saving Ha'penny, he vows never to make the same blunder with another boy. The narrator also is not so involved in his own defense as to ignore the strength and courage of Mrs. Maarman, who is able to overcome her initial reluctance to care for Ha'penny. This shows that in spite of his mistake, the narrator is not a weak man. He does not catch his error in time to save Ha'penny, but he is able to accept his miscalculations, forgive himself for the consequences, and then move on.

THEMES

Loneliness

The theme of loneliness is a prominent one for the focus character in Paton's short story "Ha'penny." The twelve-year-old boy has apparently lived by himself on the streets throughout most of his youth. Though he is being housed with a group of youths in the reformatory, he feels separated from them because he has no family. Ha'penny is an orphan with no real stories to tell that confer a sense of belonging. Therefore, he makes up the stories he needs.

To help conceal his grave sense of loneliness, Ha'penny creates stories about a family. He fabricates details of an imaginary life spent with a mother and four siblings (who are based on a real family). He desperately wants to belong to someone. These stories probably began while he was living on the streets. He must have observed Mrs. Maarman and her children from the streets. His loneliness made him distressed; the only escape was to pretend to be a part of their daily experiences. Then, while in the reformatory, he shares his stories with the narrator. He hopes his stories will convince the narrator, as well as the other boys who overhear the stories, that he is not alone in the world. Also, telling these stories out loud might ingrain them more deeply in Ha'penny's mind, allowing him to pretend even more fully that they are true. It is Ha'penny's made-up stories, the narrator concludes at the end of the story, that helped the boy to relieve the pain of his loneliness and thus survive.

Regret

The most tragic moment of Paton's short story is the death of Ha'penny. However, the narrator's regret for the young boy's death is also a strikingly poignant development. The narrator, as sympathetic and compassionate as he believed he was in his relationships with the boys in his charge at the reformatory, makes a serious miscalculation with regard to Ha'penny. Although the narrator understands that the young boys in his care need affection and attention almost as much as they need physical nourishment, he neglects to understand the importance of Ha'penny's need for family, even if that family is imaginary.

The narrator appears unable to stop himself from finding the truth of Ha'penny's background. He is compelled to discover who Mrs. Maarman is and whether or not Ha'penny is a part of her family. As soon as he does discover the truth, he immediately confronts Ha'penny. The confrontation is subtle and oblique, but the harm it does is still damaging. Without his imaginary family, the young boy is thrown into the abyss of loneliness and falls mortally ill. The psychological damage caused by having to face the truth makes the boy weak.

The narrator takes full blame for the boy's deterioration. He regrets not knowing better. Although the narrator tells Mrs. Maarman that no matter what she had done, Ha'penny would have gotten sick, he also feels responsible. If he had allowed Ha'penny to continue living in his make-believe world, he might have been stronger and not succumbed to the illness.

Mrs. Maarman also suffers from regret. She devotes herself to the boy in the last days of his life as if she is repentant. She stays at his bedside and tells everyone that she is his mother, hoping this will make Ha'penny feel stronger. She even insists that he be listed as her son on the marker placed on his grave. She regrets she did not help him sooner. She thinks she should have taken in the boy when he was living on the streets. If she had, he would have been stronger and might not have gotten sick. If he still became ill, at least he would have had her love and protection.

Familial Love

In his opening remarks, the narrator discusses the needs of the boys he takes care of in the reformatory. He understands the boys' need for affection and enjoys his more compassionate exchanges with them. "Had they been my own children I would no doubt have given a greater expression to it," he says. It is with these words that Paton begins to develop the theme of familial love in this story.

The narrator understands that he is limited in what he can give to the boys in the reformatory. The needs of the boys are far greater than he can supply because their most important need is that of family love. This is a special love that imparts a sense of belonging and of unconditional acceptance. No matter what a child does, even a child who gets into trouble serious enough to send him to a reformatory, he will always be a part of his family. Even if the family denounces him, his membership remains indelible. To emphasize the comfort a troubled boy finds in familial love, Paton uses the character Ha'penny. Here is a boy without a family, but the need for familial love is so great that this boy not only creates an imaginary family but dies when his fantasy of that love is destroyed.

TOPICS FOR FURTHER STUDY

- Read Shelley Pearsall's young-adult novel *Trouble Don't Last* (2002) about the relationship between a young slave boy and an older slave man. Write an essay comparing their relationship with the relationships in "Ha'penny."

- Create a papier-mâché map of South Africa, forming the physical features of the land—mountains, shorelines, lakes, and rivers. Then, locate the areas mentioned in this story and in the author's life, such as Johannesburg, the city of Pietermaritzburg, and the province of KwaZulu-Natal. Paton worked in the Diepkloof Reformatory. Find out where this school is located and place a marker on the map. Research the geography, weather, and any environmental issues that South Africa is facing. Comment on the information you have found while you present the map to your class.

- Provide a timeline of all the major events in the history of apartheid. Provide dates for when this political system was put into effect; the largest confrontations; the political actions against apartheid; the dates of the imprisonment and/or release of some of the leading protestors, such as Nelson Mandela and Steve Beeko; and the major events at the end of apartheid. Create a PowerPoint presentation for this project and be prepared to answer questions when you show it to your class.

- Imagine that you are Ha'penny and write a letter to Mrs. Maarman. Remember that you are pretending that Mrs. Maarman is your mother. Provide details of your day, what you are studying, what you might have done with your friends, what you think about at night before you go to sleep. How would you express your emotions? Would you tell her how much you missed her and the children? Would you ask questions about what Richard, Dickie, Anna, and Mina are doing? Make it as heartfelt as possible. Read the letter to your class.

- Research youth reformatories in the United States. Do they still exist, and are they still called reformatories? Who is sentenced to reformatories and why? How many such institutions are there in the United States? How many children are incarcerated in them? Choose a specific reform school and find out what its typical programs are like. Do the inmates continue to take classes? Provide as many interesting details as possible. What was the most startling bit of information that you uncovered? Write a research paper on the topic, providing the names of sources that you have used.

- Reread the section in Paton's short story in which the narrator discusses how the younger boys need attention and affection. Note the actions that take place between the narrator and some of the boys. Then, put together a group of five of your classmates to play out the scene. One will play the role of the narrator. The other four will represent the boys in the reformatory. While you read the passage, have your fellow students act out the silent communications between the narrator and the boys. Feel free to make up your own signs of affection, such as patting one boy on the head or tousling his hair. The narrator might wink at another boy or tug on his ear. There could be a smile or a wave. Make sure the boys react to the narrator in very subtle ways, as they have learned not to allow too much of their emotions to show.

STYLE

Epiphany

In a piece of fiction, an epiphany is the realization that occurs at the moment that the main character discovers an important insight about himself or herself, about another character, or about a relationship. This realization might be of almost any type, such as religious, psychological, or political. Epiphanies in fiction are also often followed by

Looking down the road (Image copyright Tatiana Grozetskaya, 2009. Used under license from Shutterstock.com)

consequences, which are sometimes dramatic but can also be humorous. The most general definition of a fictional epiphany is an event that causes the main character to change. It can provide a powerful emotional moment for the reader as well.

In Paton's short story "Ha'penny," the narrator reaches an epiphany at the end when he understands his connection to Ha'penny's illness and subsequent death. For the narrator, this is a psychological as well as a relational epiphany. On one hand, the narrator has learned a lesson through his relationship with Ha'penny. After Ha'penny succumbs to tuberculosis, the narrator comprehends the boy's psychological need to keep his imaginary family alive. The narrator had not fully understood how fragile Ha'penny's mental state was. When he brought the truth to the surface, Ha'penny's whole world collapsed, making him lose the desire to live. The narrator then promises himself he will not make this same mistake in his relationships with other children at the reformatory.

The epiphany the narrator experiences also has psychological consequences. Though he thought he understood how to help promote the psychological health of the young inmates in his care, he discovers too late that he might have been arrogant in his assumptions. He discovers that he might not have been as smart as he thought, that his conclusions and assumptions might have been misguided. His errors have a devastating result—Ha'penny's death.

Objective Narrator

Paton tells this short story from the perspective of the narrator. This narrator is the main character through whose eyes, ears, and inner voice readers are told the story. There are no physical descriptions offered about the narrator; it is told as if the narrator were writing a diary. In this way, the narrator is presented as if he were interested only in telling the story, not being a character in that story. Rather, he sees himself as a witness. Just as a reporter for a magazine or newspaper does not insert personal information or descriptions of himself or herself into a story, so too the narrator of this story remains distant. Unlike in a newspaper story, however, the reader is placed inside the narrator's mind and not only observes what is happening but also hears what the narrator thinks and concludes concerning what is happening around him.

In using an objective narrator, the story directly conveys what the narrator experiences but not what other characters are feeling or thinking. Therefore, readers do not know what Ha'penny or Mrs. Maarman is thinking or feeling, at least not directly. Mrs. Maarman does tell the narrator about some of her feelings, but the reader is never privy to what she is thinking. Ha'penny, likewise, is seen only through what the narrator tells the readers. In a story as short as this one, the author can keep the storyline simple and brief by using just this single point of view.

HISTORICAL CONTEXT

Apartheid

Apartheid officially began in South Africa in 1948, when the National Party gained office in an election that gave the right to vote only to white people. With the passing of the apartheid laws in the same year, racial segregation and discrimination became part of the institution of government. It was through these laws that, among other things, mixed-race marriages were prohibited and certain jobs were specifically classified as being only for white people. By 1950, the apartheid government had passed the Population Registration Act, which defined groups of people according to their appearance and heritage. These classifications were white, black, Asian, and colored. In 1951, the Bantu Authorities Act was

COMPARE & CONTRAST

- **1960s:** A large group of blacks in the town of Sharpeville, South Africa, revolts against the discrimination caused by apartheid. The police respond, killing 69 people and wounding 187. Nelson Mandela is also imprisoned during this time because he has been working against apartheid.

    Today: South Africa, now with a freely elected republic with black majority rule, is enjoying economic success as the most developed and most modern country in Africa.

- **1960s:** The South African government passes the Children's Act, increasing the legal protection of children. This improves the lives of white children, but it does little to change the lives of black children.

    Today: Although many educational reforms have been instituted since the demolition of the apartheid system, South African president Jacob Zuma acknowledges that many of the programs have failed and black students organize protest marches to demand libraries and access to the Internet.

- **1960s:** Robben Island, off the coast of South Africa, once used as an isolated sanctuary for lepers, is reopened and is used as a prison for anti-apartheid activists.

    Today: Robben Island is declared a national heritage site. The prison on the island has become the Museum of the Freedom Struggle of South Africa.

---

created. By this act, blacks were each assigned to a so-called homeland and could vote only in this small district, thus taking away their rights to vote in countrywide South African elections. In essence, this stripped blacks of citizenship in their own country. To further control blacks, the Public Safety Act and the Criminal Law Amendment were passed in 1953. Through these government actions, the government prevented all forms of political demonstration. Violators could be fined, but they were more often whipped or imprisoned. Thousands were detained in prisons without the right to hearings. Many of these people were tortured and later died while in prison. Even those who were granted trials were often found guilty and sentenced to life in prison.

Although blacks comprised a majority of the population, whites owned most of the land. Schools were segregated and black schools were far inferior to white schools. It was against the law for blacks to socialize with whites. By 1976, black people in South Africa began to riot. The trigger for widespread protesting was the government's attempts to force school children in the township of Soweto to learn Afrikaans, a language specific to the white population. The riots increased and would continue until the laws of apartheid were abolished.

The international community tried different tactics to dissuade apartheid in South Africa. In 1961, former British colonies that were members of the British Commonwealth forced South Africa out of this organization. Almost two decades later, the United States and the United Kingdom joined forces and restricted trade with the apartheid government in South Africa. This combination of international condemnation and the ongoing riots inside the country eventually had an effect. In 1990, the white government repealed the apartheid laws. In the process, Nelson Mandela, who had spent twenty-seven years on Robben Island as a political prisoner, was released. During the next three years, South Africa drafted a new constitution. In 1993, then-president Frederik W. de Klerk and Nelson Mandela were jointly awarded the Nobel Peace Prize for their efforts in abolishing apartheid and stabilizing the country. On April 27, 1994, in an election by all races, Mandela was made the first black president of South Africa. Every year since that historic election, April 27 has been celebrated in South Africa as National Freedom Day.

Retro model automobile (Image copyright Seanelliottphotography, 2009. Used under license from Shutterstock.com)

Coloreds as Defined in South Africa

In South Africa, racial distinction was a large part of the political system of discrimination called apartheid. People were identified partially by the color of their skin. Therefore, there were whites, blacks, Asians (or sometimes referred to as Indians), and coloreds. The group called *coloreds* included people of mixed races.

Though many in the group known as coloreds could trace their ancestry back to black Africans, they did not have a large enough percentage of African blood for them to be called black. Rather, a majority of their ancestors might include people from European or Asian countries as well. Culturally, both blacks and whites considered people in the colored category as a separate racial group. In Paton's short story, Mrs. Maarman considers herself to belong to the colored group. Ha'penny is portrayed as being black, a descendant of one of the original tribes in South Africa. Mrs. Maarman's reluctance to take in Ha'penny as part of her family is based on her feelings that the different races should not live together. This might seem ironic, since Mrs. Maarman is herself of mixed heritage, but Paton's story reflects the cultural protocols of the strict segregation of apartheid.

CRITICAL OVERVIEW

Paton's short story "Ha'penny," as well as the collection in which this short story was published (*Tales from a Troubled Land*), is often overshadowed by his novels. Paton's novel *Cry, the Beloved Country*, for instance, has been called a classic and is the work that first comes to mind when the author's name is mentioned. However, one review is often referenced when *Tales from a Troubled Land* is discussed. John Barkham's essay, "Meekness and Brutality," written for the *New York Times* in 1961, begins by declaring Paton to be "unquestionably the finest novelist to come out of South Africa since Olive Schreiner," (a prolific, early twentieth-century South African writer). Barkham continues by encouraging his readers to pay heed to Paton's other works, such as his short stories. "When, therefore, any fiction from his pen does reach us," Barkham writes, "let us read, mark, learn, and inwardly digest it."

Alfred Kazin, in a 1953 article for the *New York Times*, wrote his review before Paton's short story collection was published. However, his comments about Paton's works reflect on the author's abilities. Kazin comments that Paton "writes as a sensitive liberal, placed in a situation whose ferocious depths plainly alarm him." Kazin is referring to the cruelties of the apartheid system that controlled the South African people of Paton's time. Kazin continues, "With his delicacy, knowledge and tact he can bring out the human values inherent in a social situation, and thus force the subject on our attention."

Also commenting on Paton's most famous novel, Richard Sullivan in a 1948 article for the *New York Times* describes Paton's novel as praiseworthy because "its writing is so fresh, its projection of character so immediate and full, its events so compelling, and its understanding so compassionate." Sullivan concludes that "there is not much current writing that goes deeper than this. There is not much with a lovelier verbal sheen."

In a slightly more recent review of Paton's works, John Romano, also writing for the *New York Times* states that "Paton is relentless in his faith in the moral meaning of individual human experience." Romano also notes, "Paton's faith is not a religious one, but a faith in the function, the usefulness of personal sympathy." He adds that Paton's "place in the literature of social protest has been secured by his steady devotion to the ideal of the empathetic imagination in fiction."

CRITICISM

Joyce Hart

Hart is a published writer and creative writing teacher. In this essay, she explores the character arcs for Paton's three characters in the short story "Ha'penny."

" HE SOUNDS LIKE A VERY SELF-ASSURED MAN, BUT TO A CAREFUL READER, HE MIGHT ALSO SEEM LIKE A CHARACTER WHO IS ABOUT TO LEARN A VERY IMPORTANT LESSON."

In Paton's short story "Ha'penny," the author creates a narrator who shares many of his inner thoughts with the reader. In the beginning, the narrator sounds very confident, especially in his relationships with the young boys in his care at the reformatory. Through his comments about how he performs his role as an authority figure, he assures the reader that his main focus is on improving the lives of the incarcerated boys. If one were to read only the first few pages of this story, this initial impression would remain intact. As the story progresses, though, cracks in the character of the narrator begin to appear. What starts out as a proud and confident man slowly turns into a man full of doubts and remorse. Likewise, the characters of Ha'penny and Mrs. Maarman also are transformed. The progression of these characters' development can be traced. By doing so, readers come to comprehend and to better appreciate the characters' complexities.

The change that the characters go through is referred to, in literary terms, as a character arc. Many authors give their protagonist (the main character of the story) a character arc to create interest. When a character faces events that challenge his or her beliefs, readers relate more closely to that character. When provided with an arc, the fictional character appears more real to the reader because real people go through similar challenges and changes. In some stories, the changes that the character goes through create tension in the story, making the reader wonder what the character will do next or what will happen to him or her. Without an arc, a character appears flat or lifeless and becomes a stereotype of a real person—a formulaic or oversimplified representation. Many stories provide a character arc only for the protagonist. However, in Paton's story "Ha'penny," all three characters are given arcs, and each arc takes a different shape.

The narrator's character arc appears to rise in the beginning of the story and then drops

WHAT DO I READ NEXT?

- Paton wrote an autobiography, *Towards the Mountain* (1980). This work describes his life up to the publication of his most famous work, the novel *Cry, the Beloved Country*. Prior to its publication, Paton worked as the principal of a reformatory, a background that influences parts of his novel.

- Paton is best known as the author of *Cry, the Beloved Country* (1948). The main characters of this story are a black minister and his son from the Zulu territory in South Africa. As the minister attempts to search for his son, who has left home and has become entangled in a misguided life, the themes of apartheid and racial injustice are explored.

- *Tales from a Troubled Land* (1961) is the collection of short stories in which Paton's short story "Ha'penny" appears. All of the stories in this volume deal with the injustices found in South Africa under apartheid.

- Paton put together a collection of his poetry, fiction, and nonfiction essays in the book *Diepkloof: Reflections of Diepkloof Reformatory* (1986). Found in this collection are Paton's thoughts about education, which he attempted to put into practice while he was the principal at this South African reformatory.

- In *Things Fall Apart* (1958), Chinua Achebe, a well-known black African writer, relates the story of a young man living in Nigeria during the late nineteenth century. Achebe's purpose for writing this book was to tell the story of his people through a black African's point of view. Until then, white writers about African life had gained the most attention. The novel focuses on the clash between English colonialists and the traditional culture of black Nigeria in the late 1940s.

- Nadine Gordimer, like Alan Paton, is a white author who focuses on the apartheid system in her writing. In 1991, she was awarded the Nobel Prize for her life's work. Many of her books were banned for long periods of time in South Africa. Gordimer's first novel, *The Lying Days* (1953), is about a young woman who has lived a sheltered life in a white community and whose life changes when she realizes how cruelly black people are treated in South Africa.

- Tsitsi Dangarembga, a black African author from Zimbabwe (formerly Rhodesia), wrote *Nervous Conditions* (2004), a novel that has received very positive reviews in the United States. In this book, Dangarembga tells a partially autobiographical story about a young girl living in Rhodesia. The main themes of this novel are the effects of poverty and lack of education on women living in Rhodesia in the 1960s

- In her young-adult novel *No Turning Back* (1999), Beverley Naidoo tells a compelling story of a young runaway boy, fighting for his survival in the streets of Johannesburg, South Africa. The protagonist, Sipho, can no longer take the abuse of his stepfather, preferring to find his way on his own. The story revolves around the challenges and the people he meets along the way.

- *Handbook for Boys: A Novel* (2002) by award-winning Walter Dean Myers uses barbershop dialogue to help two juvenile delinquents learn some life lessons. Like "Ha'Penny," it examines the impact of positive adult interaction on troubled youth.

---

suddenly near the end, with a hint of recovery before the story closes. As the story opens, the narrator offers a personal glimpse of how he views himself as an authority figure within the reformatory. He is pleased with his powers of observation, as well as with the conclusions he has come to. He feels rather smug about himself as a compassionate man and an authority figure;

he would love to take all the younger boys at the reformatory and place them in a special wing so he could put his behavioral hypotheses to work. The narrator truly believes that he understands these troubled boys. He thinks he has cracked some code that has unlocked the secrets inside their minds. He believes he knows how these boys' minds work and how the boys will react, and he believes he knows how to control the boys. The narrator performs little behavioral experiments, which he shares with the readers, to prove that his theories work. All it takes, he thinks, is an offer of small gestures of affection to these love-starved boys to make them behave. A pat on the head or simple eye contact encourages the boys to do well in their studies, to listen to authority figures, and to work cooperatively. The narrator is proud but not arrogant. He gathers this information and creates his theories not for praise but because he thinks he is helping the boys.

Even this early in the story, though, careful readers might sense the trap that the narrator is heading for. They might find a hint that the narrator is about to trip and fall. The narrator might be walking tall in the first few paragraphs of this story, with his head held high and his thoughts full of self-confidence, but he might also be a little too proud. The narrator seems to believe that he is better than those around him. He insinuates that he knows more about the boys than some of his coworkers do. During times of unrest, "when there was danger of estrangement between authority and boys," the narrator insinuates that he is the only one who knows how to keep the boys calm. If he believes he can control the boys through his glances, he must also believe he knows more than the boys do about themselves. By practicing these "secret relations" with the boys and watching the boys' reactions, the narrator states, "I knew that my authority was thus confirmed and strengthened." In this early portion of the story, the narrator's character arc is artificially high, inflated by his beliefs and apparent successes with the boys' behavior. He sounds like a very self-assured man, but to a careful reader, he might also seem like a character who is about to learn a very important lesson.

The narrator slightly lowers his sense of self-importance when he takes some of the younger boys for weekend drives. During these times, the narrator lessens the distance between himself and the boys, becoming more personal with them. He encourages conversations about their families. Even though he pretends not to know details about the surrounding countryside in order to promote their discussions, he is not otherwise concerned about controlling them. At this point in the story, he is not extolling his knowledge or expertise. Thus, here, his character arc neither rises nor falls. However, the shape of the arc quickly changes when the narrator takes it upon himself to check the validity of Ha'penny's claims.

Ha'penny, the twelve-year-old orphan who creates a family from a mix of fact and imagination, tells the narrator stories of his life before he was incarcerated. Being a keen observer, the narrator notices a flaw in Ha'penny's description of his family. With his curiosity roused, the narrator searches through Ha'penny's personal records. So begins the descent of the narrator's character arc. In his hurry to uncover the truth of Ha'penny's background, the narrator rushes into an investigation. Who is this family that Ha'penny keeps talking about? The narrator must know. He does not go to the boy directly, because Ha'penny has already demonstrated that he has a lively imagination. Instead, the narrator hunts down Mrs. Maarman, the woman Ha'penny has claimed as his mother. Readers might understand this need that the narrator has to uncover the truth, but they might also wonder why the narrator does not think of the consequences of proving that Ha'penny is lying. If the narrator truly does understand the boys in his charge, why does he not think of what harm this might do to the young boy?

Mrs. Maarman reveals the truth: she is not related to Ha'penny in any way. Not only that, she wants nothing to do with the boy. He is a black boy, whereas she is colored. He is a criminal, and her children are not. He is therefore, in her view, a bad influence on her family. Now the narrator knows the truth, and he lets Ha'penny know what he has found. He believes he is doing so obliquely by merely correcting the name of one of Mrs. Maarman's children, but this does not soften the blow. As Ha'penny falls ill and becomes nonresponsive to care, the narrator's opinions of himself disintegrate. For someone who believed he knew what was best for the boys, he has failed miserably. Ha'penny shuts the narrator out of his life, and the narrator must face his part in Ha'penny's death. The narrator's character arc hits the floor. This is not the end, though. The narrator admits his mistakes, learns his lesson, and resolves to do better in the future. Thus, his character arc rises again.

Ha'penny is also given a character arc. He, like the narrator, has an arc that begins artificially high. Ha'penny appears very happy and pleased with himself in the beginning. He has no problem opening up to the narrator as he shares his stories about his family. He writes home every week to his mother, whom he constantly praises. However, his relationship with a family is a sham. Every detail has been fabricated. Though Mrs. Maarman is real, she is not his mother. When the narrator unveils the truth, Ha'penny emotionally and physically crashes. He hits the ground so hard that he cannot get up. His arc in this story actually progresses from bad to worse. He begins a seemingly happy child, despite his circumstances. By the end, he has no strength left to live. Paton has made Ha'penny a tragic figure who was destined for this downward spiral.

In a sense, Mrs. Maarman is the most positive character. Her character arc begins low and continues to rise throughout the story. At the start, she wants nothing to do with Ha'penny. In some ways, she is justified. She has four children of her own and struggles to keep her family together. She sees Ha'penny as a troublemaker and justifies keeping her distance from him. Just before the conclusion of the story, however, Mrs. Maarman has a change of heart. She is transformed in a positive direction as she goes out of her way to try to save Ha'penny when he falls ill. Although she cannot keep him from dying, she attempts to provide him with the family he longed for. She also feels remorse for not having tried to save him earlier. Thus, her arc rises slowly from beginning to end of the story.

Paton could have created the narrator as a rigid but righteous man who truly understood the psychology of the imprisoned boys. He could have also created Ha'penny with enough strength to overcome his challenges. Mrs. Maarman could have remained the woman who did not have the time or energy to love a troubled boy. However, by providing each of these characters with an arc to depict their transformation, no matter what shape the arc eventually takes, Paton created characters with whom his readers can identify. These characters are not stereotypes; they are people who make mistakes. They are fragile, and thus they feel real.

Source: Joyce Hart, Critical Essay on "Ha'penny," in *Short Stories for Students*, Gale, Cengage Learning, 2010.

African street orphan (Image copyright Lloyd Smith, 2009. Used under license from Shutterstock.com)

Christian Science Monitor
In the following article, Paton is credited with using his writing for reconciliation and change through his popular books, such as Cry, the Beloved Country; *however, the country he labored for is further than ever from the ideals he espoused.*

Alan Paton's work touched the lives of millions of people, in his native South Africa and beyond. His first book, *Cry, the Beloved Country*, remains popular and timely 40 years after its publishing. A profound examination of wrenched human relationships in a racially partitioned society, it helped turn world attention toward the cruelty of apartheid and established Mr. Paton, who died yesterday at his home near Durban, as a writer of international stature.

Paton's life and writings span the evolution of modern South Africa, from the building of apartheid to the stirrings of black nationalism. He felt the system's oppression himself at times.

For 11 years he was prevented from traveling abroad. But his renown as a writer shielded him from the kind of direct censure that befell others who held his liberal views.

Paton's voice, appealing for reconciliation and change, was always heard—and will continue to be through his books. The second volume of his autobiography, *The Journey Continued,* is due this July.

This author was, in a sense, much more than a crafter of beautiful prose. His words plumbed the depth of South African experience because he plunged so deeply into that experience. He once remarked that racial matters were of little concern to him as a youth of Scottish background, growing up in Natal Province in a devoutly Christian family. That changed radically in the mid-1930s, when he accepted an appointment as principal of the Diepkloof reformatory for black delinquents in Johannesburg. Paton stayed there 13 years.

That's where his probing insights took shape. As a reform-minded principal, he first felt the sharp attacks of South Africa's white establishment. Always one who believed resolutely that South Africa could change from within, the author later helped found the multiracial South African Liberal Party. The Liberals were harassed and finally outlawed by the ruling National Party, which passed legislation prohibiting the association of whites and blacks.

Ironically, the country Alan Paton labored so valiantly to change seems today further than ever from the ideals he espoused. South Africa's most ardent, right-wing defenders of apartheid appear to be wielding increasing political power. It's a time when all whose thoughts and prayers turn to that agonized country could well remember the words Paton put in the mouth of Stephen Kumalo in *Cry, the Beloved Country*: "These things are not yet at an end. The sun pours down on the earth, on the lovely land that man cannot enjoy."

In those words there's both hope and realism. Key ingredients for anyone who firmly believes, as Paton did, that mankind can improve and wants to work toward that end.

Source: "Alan Paton's Lasting Message," in *Christian Science Monitor*, April 13, 1988, p. 15.

William French

In the following article, French suggests that Paton's age and international status have afforded him protection but he is once again pressing his luck with his new novel about apartheid.

Being a liberal in a police state requires courage and no small amount of luck. Alan Paton has had both; even so, he has survived as a liberal in South Africa partly because of the protection afforded by his international status as a writer. Presumably, at 79, he is also protected by his age, although that detail has not stopped repressive regimes in the past.

Now Paton tests his luck again, with a new novel about apartheid. It's set in the years between 1952 and 1958, when the Nationalist Government was entrenching its position and erecting the legal apparatus to enforce segregation of the races. To do so, it had to limit or eliminate certain freedoms which citizens in democratic countries take for granted. Civil libertarians of all shades rallied to oppose the government measures, but in vain. Their efforts, often heroic, are the main subject of the novel.

Paton is uniquely qualified to write about that period. He was founder and national chairman of the Liberal Party until it was suppressed by the Nationalist Government. His cast of characters includes both real and fictional people and real and imagined events, including a good deal about the Liberal Party. (Paton himself does not appear.) And although Paton avoids direct comment and maintains a neutral authorial presence, there is no mistaking the implicit criticism of current South African race policies.

One of the means he uses to make his point is the introduction of a pro-apartheid character who holds a high position in the department of justice. In a series of letters to his aunt, this man defends and glorifies apartheid as being sanctified by God. He employs the usual doublespeak and doublethink to justify the repressive legislation. He quotes government leaders as predicting that 20 years from then, that is by 1976, the policy will have succeeded and the world will admit that apartheid was right. Blacks will have left the cities and be happily employed in their own areas, and the country will prosper in peace.

Well, we all know that by 1976 South Africa was no closer to its goal than it was in 1956, and is no closer now. And the free world still condemns it, when it is convenient, for a policy that is brutal and inhumane.

As literature, *Ah, But Your Land Is Beautiful* won't win any prizes. It lacks focus and is often disjointed. Too many points of view are presented; characters pop in and out and are never seen again. The narrative is a jumble—there are letters (such as those from the high-ranking bureaucrat to his aunt), editorials, lists of banned books, and disconnected scenes jumping from city to city. In short, Paton's canvas is too vast, and we tend to get lost in the detail.

The weakest part of the plot concerns the attempt of the stern, intellectual deputy minister of justice, a staunch supporter of apartheid, to arrange a liaison with a beautiful black woman, which of course is illegal under the Immorality Act. When he is caught and charged, he commits suicide. Paton is presumably demonstrating the hypocrisy of the regime and man's fallibility, despite harsh laws, but the incident trivializes the plot.

Fortunately, the structural shortcomings don't seriously impair the impact of the novel. It still has the power to outrage us and move us to anguished frustration as the oppressive regime uses police bullies, informers and intimidation to enforce its rules. During a boycott of bus service by blacks in Johannesburg after a fare increase, white drivers who give them a lift are harassed by traffic police. Blacks are prohibited from attending white churches, and clergymen who support the regime refuse to conduct funeral services for whites if blacks are present.

A former cricket star for the South African team resigns as a school principal to devote his time to the Liberal Party; his life and the lives of his family are threatened and after several close calls he decides to move to Australia. We see in numerous similar events a police state in the making.

Paton's main attention is given to the formation of the Liberal Party and its consequences. It was opposed by the African Congress, the Indian Congress (representing the largest single group of colored people) and the Marxist-oriented White Congress, all of which felt it would undermine their own support. But it proved to be a rallying place for both English and Afrikan whites and dissidents of all colors who courageously opposed the regime. Paton doesn't take us to the point where the party was declared illegal, but presumably it was done under the Suppression of Communism Act, which gives the Nationalist Government great power to remove its opponents. The novel ends with the death of Prime Minister Malan and the selection of Dr. Hendrik, the chief architect of apartheid, as his successor. In his acceptance speech he predicts a golden age for South Africa ...

The title, of course, is ironic. It's the phrase used by tourists who don't see or care about the loss of liberty and suppression of the blacks and colored people. Paton also uses it in a positive way, to express the pride felt among the liberals when the blacks defied the bus company. But that optimism is short-lived.

Paton's novel is a powerful reminder that the fight for freedom and justice in South Africa goes on, and we ignore it at our peril.

Source: William French, "Being Liberal in a Police State. A Jumbled Narrative, but One with the Power to Outrage, AH, BUT YOUR LAND IS BEAUTIFUL," in *Globe and Mail* (Canada), October 30, 1982.

SOURCES

Alexander, Peter, *Alan Paton: A Biography*, Oxford University Press, 1996.

Barkham, John, "Meekness and Brutality," in *New York Times*, April 16, 1961, p. BR 4.

Child Justice Project, "A Situational Analysis of Reform Schools and Schools of Industry in South Africa," in *South Africa Department of Education*, http://www.pmg.org.za/docs/2003/appendices/030228situation.htm (accessed on September 11, 2009).

Clark, Nancy L., *South Africa: The Rise and Fall of Apartheid*, Longman, 2004.

Dugger, Celia, "South African Children Push for Better Schools," in *New York Times*, September 25, 2009, p. A4.

Kazin, Alfred, "Downfall of a South African Hero," in *New York Times*, August 23, 1953, p. BR 1.

Paton, Alan, "Ha'penny," in *Tales from a Troubled Land*, Scribner Paperback Fiction, 1961.

Romano, John, "A Novel of Hope and Realism," in *New York Times*, April 4, 1982, p. BR 7.

"South Africa," in *CIA: The World Factbook*, https://www.cia.gov/library/publications/the-world-factbook/geos/sf.html (accessed on September 11, 2009).

Sullivan, Richard, "Fine Novel of a Present-Day Zulu," in *New York Times*, February 1, 1948, p. BR 6.

Thompson, Leonard, *A History of South Africa*, Yale University Press, 2001.

FURTHER READING

Alexander, Peter, *Alan Paton: A Biography*, Oxford University Press Southern Africa, 1996.
    Alexander offers a definitive biography of Paton's life, covering not only his writings but also the background of Paton's involvement in racial issues and his political activism.

Clark, Domini, *South Africa: The Land*, Crabtree, 2008.
    This book offers an easy-to-read overview of

the people, the culture, and the history of South Africa.

Mandela, Nelson, *In His Own Words*, Little, Brown, 2004.
Nelson Mandela, the first black president of South Africa, was largely responsible for bringing an end to the apartheid system. This book offers a collection of Mandela's speeches on topics that range from struggle to education and freedom. After serving twenty-seven years in prison for his political activities, Mandela won the Nobel Peace Prize in 1993.

Meredith, Martin, *Diamonds, Gold, and War: The British, the Boers, and the Making of South Africa*, PublicAffairs, 2008.
Although Meredith goes to great lengths to back up his account with diligent research, this book remains easy to comprehend and interesting to read. The author provides the background of how South Africa was constructed after white people came to the land and discovered diamonds and gold, setting off wars as well as racial discrimination.

Roberts, Martin, *South Africa 1948–1994: The Rise and Fall of Apartheid*, Longman, 2001.
Roberts offers a comprehensive and easily understood history of the harsh segregation system in South African known as apartheid. The book is highlighted with many illustrations and photographs to bring the history to life.

Seidman, David, *Teens in South Africa*, Compass Point Books, 2008.
Contemporary teenagers in South Africa represent the first generation to grow up without apartheid. Though many South African teenagers still must face incredible challenges with poverty and the prominence of AIDS within their communities, this book tells its readers about many of the happier pastimes that the South African teens share with other teens around the world.

The Pit and the Pendulum

EDGAR ALLAN POE

1842

Edgar Allan Poe's short story "The Pit and the Pendulum" was first published in 1842 in *The Gift: A Christmas and New Year's Present for 1843*, edited by Edward L. Carey and Abraham Hart of the publishing company Carey & Hart. A slightly revised version was published in the May 17, 1845, issue of *Broadway Journal*, a literary magazine edited by Poe at the time. The story is included in many anthologies of Poe's work, such as the Modern Library's *Collected Tales and Poems of Edgar Allan Poe*, published in 1992. Poe wrote the story during one of his most prolific periods; he was living in Philadelphia, working as a magazine editor, devising ingenious self-promotion schemes, and lecturing on American poetry.

The story concerns an unnamed protagonist who is condemned to death by a tribunal of the Spanish Inquisition in Toledo, Spain, and the torture he undergoes following his sentencing. He is thrown into a chamber outfitted with several devices designed to kill him: a deep pit filled with water, a slowly descending swinging blade positioned to cut through his heart, and heated, movable iron walls. It is a romantic horror story with gothic overtones, in the vein of "The Tell-Tale Heart" and "The Cask of Amontillado." The difference is that, instead of descending into madness, the protagonist keeps his wits about him and is ultimately rescued just as he is about to be forced to jump into the pit.

Edgar Allan Poe (The Library of Congress)

AUTHOR BIOGRAPHY

Poe was born on January 19, 1809, in Boston, Massachusetts, to traveling actors Eliza and David Poe. David Poe abandoned the family shortly after Edgar's birth and Eliza died in 1811. Poe was taken in by John Allan, a wealthy merchant in Richmond, Virginia, and his wife, Frances, although they never formally adopted the boy. Poe lived in England for several years as a youth. In 1826 he entered the newly founded University of Virginia, where he spent much of his time gambling and became estranged from John Allan. Poe dropped out of the university and enlisted in the U.S. Army under the pseudonym Edgar A. Perry, claiming he was twenty-two years old instead of eighteen. He found success in the army, attaining the rank of sergeant major for artillery and also publishing his first book, *Tamerlane and Other Poems*.

Poe grew tired of the military and revealed his true identity to his commanding officer, who agreed to discharge him only if he reconciled with John Allan. Allan made the reconciliation contingent on Poe's enrolling in the U.S. Military Academy at West Point. Poe's stint there lasted only a few months before he engineered his own court-martial in order to be expelled.

In 1831, Poe moved to New York City to make his living solely as a writer—an unusual and precarious occupation at the time, given the lack of a U.S. copyright law, which made collecting royalties difficult. In 1833, Poe won a contest with his story "Ms. Found in a Bottle," and in 1835 he moved back to Richmond and became the assistant editor of the *Southern Literary Messenger*. That same year he married Virginia Clemm, his thirteen-year-old first cousin.

Poe served as editor for a number of other publications following his departure from the *Southern Literary Messenger* in 1837. He published his own stories in the magazines but became better known as a literary critic. He established the genre of detective fiction in 1841 with "The Murders in the Rue Morgue" and introduced elements of what would later become known as science fiction in many of his other tales. Poe was disgruntled with many of his editorial jobs and dreamed of starting his own magazine, but that dream was never realized.

His greatest success during his lifetime came in 1845, when his poem "The Raven" was published in the *Evening Mirror*. Shortly after that the tragedies began to pile up. Virginia died of tuberculosis in 1847, and Poe increasingly turned to drinking to deal with his grief, depression, and suicidal tendencies. Poe died under mysterious circumstances on October 7, 1849, having been found four days earlier on the streets of Baltimore in a delirious and incapacitated state, wearing someone else's clothes.

After his death, Poe's literary executor, Rufus Wilmot Griswold, deliberately tarnished Poe's reputation by publishing derogatory articles about his unbecoming behavior. Many of Griswold's allegations were untrue, but they remained part of Poe's legacy for generations until his work gained prominence, first in France and later with American readers, who recognized him as a master of suspense and horror.

PLOT SUMMARY

"The Pit and the Pendulum" begins with the narrator sentenced to death by a panel of judges from the Spanish Inquisition. The unnamed narrator is

MEDIA ADAPTATIONS

- The first film adaptation of *The Pit and the Pendulum* was the 1909 French film *Le Puits et le pendule*, by Henri Desfontaines.
- French-born Alice Guy, reputed to be the world's first female film director, directed a version of *The Pit and the Pendulum* at her New Jersey studio in 1913.
- Roger Corman directed a 1961 film version of *The Pit and the Pendulum* loosely based on Poe's story, starring Vincent Price. It was released by American International Pictures.
- Czech animator Jan Švankmajer directed a fifteen-minute animated film titled *The Pit, the Pendulum and the Hope*, released by Krátký Film Praha in 1983.
- Director Stuart Gordon adapted *The Pit and the Pendulum* for a 1991 film that sets the story in 1492 and adds a romance to the plot. Starring Lance Hendriksen, the film was released in the United States by Paramount Home Video.
- The short animated film *Ray Harryhausen Presents: The Pit and the Pendulum*, written by Matt Taylor and directed by Marc Lougee, was released in 2007.
- Many audio versions of *The Pit and the Pendulum* are available on CD and cassette tape and for download, including *The Fall of the House of Usher, The Pit and the Pendulum and Other Tales of Mystery and Imagination*, read by William Roberts and released in 2003 by Naxos Audiobooks.

---

consumed by his fragile mental condition and dreamlike state of consciousness. He does not mention his crime or whether he is really guilty. He does not hear the judges' words, seeing only their black robes and white lips. He compares seven white candles to angels of mercy, but this thought gives way to the anticipatory peace of death. He knows he will be tortured. Suddenly, everything goes black as he falls into a faint.

During a state of semiconsciousness he senses his physical body being transferred downward. He experiences nausea, horror, and stillness all around him. Finally, he hears his heart beating, and his body begins to tingle. He is lying on his back, unshackled, afraid to open his eyes not because of what he will see but because he fears there is nothing to see. Indeed, he opens his eyes to total, oppressive blackness, which feels claustrophobic.

He tries to keep his thoughts together. He knows he is not yet dead, but he feels that it has been a long time since his sentencing. He recognizes that most of those who receive death sentences from the Inquisition are killed at *autos-da-fé* (public religious ceremonies in which convicted heretics are burned at the stake), and he knows there was an *auto-da-fé* on the night of his sentencing. He briefly considers that he is being held until the next *auto-da-fé*, which will take place in several months, and then realizes that such is not the case because leaders of the Inquisition in Toledo, Spain, where is he imprisoned, are killing people just as fast as they can.

He again falls into semiconsciousness. When he recovers, he stands up and waves his arms around to see if he can touch the walls. He is afraid to take a step in case he finds that he has been buried alive in a tomb. He opens his eyes wide, hoping they will adjust to the darkness, and determines his cell is not a tomb. This relieves him somewhat, although he recalls the tortures that supposedly have been committed in the Toledo dungeons. He considers them myths, but he knows he will ultimately die.

He sets about determining the size of the dungeon by counting the steps around the perimeter. He tears a piece of cloth from the hem of his simple, rag-like garment and places it on the ground to mark his starting point. He slowly makes his way around the walls, counting each step. However, the floor is slippery and he falls down. He is overcome with fatigue and falls asleep.

He wakes up and finds a loaf of bread and a pitcher of water next to him, which he consumes eagerly. He continues his trek around the dungeon, counting forty-eight steps until he reaches the strip of fabric, which he adds to the fifty-two steps he counted before he fell. He calculates that the perimeter of the dungeon is fifty yards, but he does not know its shape due to a preponderance of angles. Next, he decides to find out how wide the dungeon is. Ten paces in he trips over the torn hem of his clothing and falls on his face. His head lands on the precipice of a pit, which smells of brackish water. To test the depth of the pit, he pries loose a stone from the wall of the pit and throws it in. It bounces off the sides and finally lands with a splash that echoes loudly. At that moment, a door overhead opens and closes quickly, illuminating him in a flash of light. He congratulates himself for not falling into the pit but realizes that he will simply be subjected to another form of torture. His nerves are frazzled. Though he does not explain why, he fears falling into the pit more than any other form of death. Many hours later he falls asleep again.

He wakes to find more bread and water next to him. He drinks the water quickly, becomes lethargic, and surmises that he has been drugged. The resulting slumber is so deep that he compares it to death. When he wakes up this time, his dungeon is visible thanks to some form of phosphorescent light. He has miscalculated its size. It is only half as large as he thought; that his calculation could be so erroneous puzzles him. Then he realizes he must have nearly made it back to his cloth marker when he fell. Upon waking, he must have reversed his course. He also realizes he misjudged the shape of the cell, which is nearly square. In trying to determine the measurements of his space, he realizes that fatigue and darkness have played tricks on him. The cell is made of metal, not stone. The walls are lined with torture devices, confirming the tales he has heard about the Inquisition.

He is tied to a wooden frame and can move only enough to reach the food left for him, consisting of a plate of spicy meat but no water. Looking upward, he notices that the ceiling of the dungeon is also made of metal and rises roughly thirty or forty feet above him. Father Time is painted on the ceiling, and he is holding a giant pendulum. The pendulum appears to be moving very slowly from side to side. His attention is captured by a multitude of rats climbing out of the well and heading for his meat. A while later—he can no longer estimate time accurately—he notes that the arc of the pendulum is wider and it is swinging faster than before. Even worse, the pendulum has descended closer and he ascertains that it is actually a scythe.

The narrator realizes the hellish punishment he will suffer in return for avoiding the pit. He spends many hours—possibly days—watching the pendulum swing closer and closer until he can smell the steel of the blade as it slices through the air just inches above him. He wishes it would hurry up and kill him already. The waiting drives him to the brink of madness. Eventually he gives up and falls back, calm and happy, like a child staring at a toy. He passes out briefly and wakes up feeling sick. He is about to reach out for his food when he suddenly has an idea that fills him with hope and joy. He struggles to regain a modicum of mental acuity that has been dulled through his relentless suffering. He calculates that the blade is positioned to slice through his heart, but before it does it will slice through his garment. He thinks about what that will feel like; he continues to watch both the pendulum's downward movement and its movement from side to side. He alternately laughs and screams.

When the blade is three inches from his chest, he tries and again fails to free his left arm. Anticipation of death robs him of his sanity. When he has only ten or twelve swings left before the blade slices his skin, he realizes he is tied down by only one long strip of fabric. If he can break it at any point, he will be able to free himself. Hope is restored; his thoughts resolve themselves into a plan. The rats will help him. He smears the remains of the meat on his bonds and hundreds of rats smother his body as they leap toward it, chewing through the cloth. He gently slides off the wooden platform, away from the blade just as it nicks his skin. Immediately the blade retracts to the ceiling. His every move has been observed. Once again he is free but not free, having only postponed his death.

A few minutes later he discerns a sulfurous light streaming from a seam between the iron walls and the stone floor of the cell. The once faint grimacing figures on the walls now have fiery, glowing eyes and sharp outlines. He smells hot iron. The walls are being heated by some external source. He retreats from the walls toward the center of the cell. He thinks that he could jump into the cool well to save himself from the horrific death of being burned alive. The glowing walls light up the well. As he looks down into it, he sees a vision so terrifying that he cannot describe it. He screams and wails.

The dungeon is changing its shape. Its hinged walls are collapsing. He must now decide whether to be crushed to death by the fiery walls or jump into the pit and drown. The walls continue to flatten until he is perched at the edge of the pit. His agony culminates in a final scream as he looks away and prepares to fall into the pit.

At that instant he hears voices and loud crashing noises. The walls retract and an arm reaches out and catches him as he falls. The last three sentences explain everything: the French army has liberated Toledo from the Inquisition and General Lasalle himself has rescued the narrator.

CHARACTERS

Inquisitors

The Inquisitors only appear as black-robed, white-lipped judges in the story's first scene, yet they play an important role as the narrator's nemeses. They represent pure evil, although historically the tribunals of the Inquisition believed they were on God's side. They represent an omniscient force in the story, watching the narrator's every move and counteracting his ability to thwart his death sentence with new punishments.

The Inquisitors leave food and water, which may be drugged, and at first rely on the narrator to fall into the pit himself. When their prisoner discovers the pit and avoids falling into it, they wait until he falls asleep, tie him to a wooden frame, and launch a slowly descending scythe-bladed pendulum above him. The Inquisitors remain as unseen as God himself. They leave food when the narrator is asleep, and when he escapes death by the blade, the pendulum is immediately retracted back to the ceiling—evidence that someone is closely and silently watching his every move. The final torture—the collapsing walls heated by fire—is launched immediately thereafter. Indeed, even when General Lasalle rescues the narrator, the torture immediately ceases without any visible manifestation of the torturers.

Narrator

The unnamed narrator of "The Pit and the Pendulum" is logical, meticulous, and tries to maintain his sanity in the face of certain death. Even while locked in a pitch-black dungeon, he preoccupies himself with determining the size of his cell and the depth of the pit, seemingly inconsequential details that serve to keep his mind active. When he discovers he has erred in calculating the perimeter of the cell, he is troubled by his failure. His preoccupation with logic keeps him from dwelling on the trial, the guilty verdict, or the crime for which he was accused. He relates nothing of his past and is consumed only with how he is feeling at the moment and how to escape from immediate danger.

He thinks well under pressure. The ultimate test of this comes when the pendulum is within a hair's breadth of his heart. He summons up the courage to smear the remains of his meat on his restraining bandages in the hope that the rats will chew through them. The plan works.

Unlike other Poe narrators, such as those in "The Tell-Tale Heart" and the "The Cask of Amontillado," the narrator of "The Pit and the Pendulum" gives every indication of being mentally fit and up to the challenge of thwarting his tormenters even though he knows he will die one way or another. He exhibits an impressive will to live despite his protestations that he welcomes the grave. However, like the narrators of Poe's other stories, he begins to crack under pressure, giggling like a child and screaming like a madman. In the end, he pulls himself together long enough to plan an escape from the pendulum.

The narrator is not religious, as evidenced by his lack of prayer or concern about his soul as he is about to die. He barely mentions God, apart from a brief discussion of the candles appearing to him as angels. His religion is rationality; he believes in himself.

THEMES

Sensory Perception

Poe's goal in "The Pit and the Pendulum" is to create a mood of terror and despair through language. The narrator is condemned to death, and the entire story (save for the last paragraph) focuses on his reaction to this death sentence as it is slowly carried out. The mood is achieved in part by repetition of words such as "death," "dying," "blackness," and "darkness." The darkness requires the narrator to rely on his sense of touch, taste, smell, and hearing. He feels sick and dizzy; the ground is slimy; he hears his heart beating and a stone hit the water in the well; the water smells brackish; he smells the metal of the blade as it slices through the air; the meat tastes spicy; he feels the cold lips of the rats as they climb over his body; his throat is parched. All of these sensory descriptions coalesce into a mood of horror and agony. Poe contrasts these vivid sensory descriptions with descriptions of nothingness—those moments when the narrator is incapacitated or sleeping

TOPICS FOR FURTHER STUDY

- On the surface, "The Pit and the Pendulum" may not appear to have much in common with the Jorge Luis Borges's short story "The Circular Ruins." Borges, a twentieth-century Argentine writer, infused his stories with magic realism and dreamlike imagery. After reading both stories, find three similarities between them in terms of theme, symbolism, and style. Create a Venn diagram or T-chart illustrating how Borges and Poe use these similarities for different effects.

- British comic-book writer Neil Gaiman was influenced early on by Edgar Allan Poe. His award-winning young-adult graphic novel *Coraline* (2002) was criticized by some critics as too frightening for its intended audience. Write an essay in which you argue whether or not the theme of torture and mutilation present in both "The Pit and the Pendulum" and *Coraline* is appropriate for middle and high school audiences.

- In 1997, a group of high school students in Minneapolis calculated that Poe's narrator would have had seventy-one seconds to escape after the rats chewed through his bonds and before the blade sliced through his chest. Using the narrator's description of the dungeon and the measurements he provides, draw a blueprint of the dungeon, including the pit, the walls, and the pendulum. Also theorize about how the moving walls would have worked and how they would have been heated. As an alternative, build a scale model of the dungeon.

- Research the types of torture used during the Spanish Inquisition. Describe the methods in detail and determine whether those methods have been used since and, if so, by whom. Create a PowerPoint presentation to illustrate your findings.

- Poe was a master at using evocative language to heighten the sense of terror in his stories. Write a 500-word original story in the first person, creating a narrator who cannot see either because of blindness or darkness. Use other sensory information to paint a vivid picture of the character's environment.

---

and his cell is plunged into total darkness. The lack of sensory information is as horrifying for the narrator as the stimuli he perceives.

Injustice

The Spanish Inquisition is a real-life historical example of extreme injustice, used nowadays as shorthand for an unwarranted intrusion into a person's privacy. The leaders of the Spanish Inquisition believed they were seeking justice in the name of God, but their trumped-up charges, sham trials, and swift and brutal executions of people they deemed insufficiently pious were regarded then, as now, as a miscarriage of justice. Though Poe is silent on the narrator's crime and whether or not he is guilty, his story represents the triumph of justice (reason) over injustice (intolerance). By foregoing the specifics of the charges against the narrator and by not describing the Inquisitors in detail, Poe keeps politics out of the plot in order to highlight the terror of a man condemned to death.

Sadism

The very title "The Pit and the Pendulum" alludes to torture: a pit into which the prisoner could fall into and drown and a pendulum to slice him in half if he avoids the pit. Both reveal the sadistic side of the Inquisitors. They could easily execute him by quicker means, such as burning him at the stake, which was the most common death for those convicted of heresy during the Spanish Inquisition. Instead they choose to observe him as he slowly descends into madness, prolonging his life by providing food and water. Ostensibly they hope he will fall

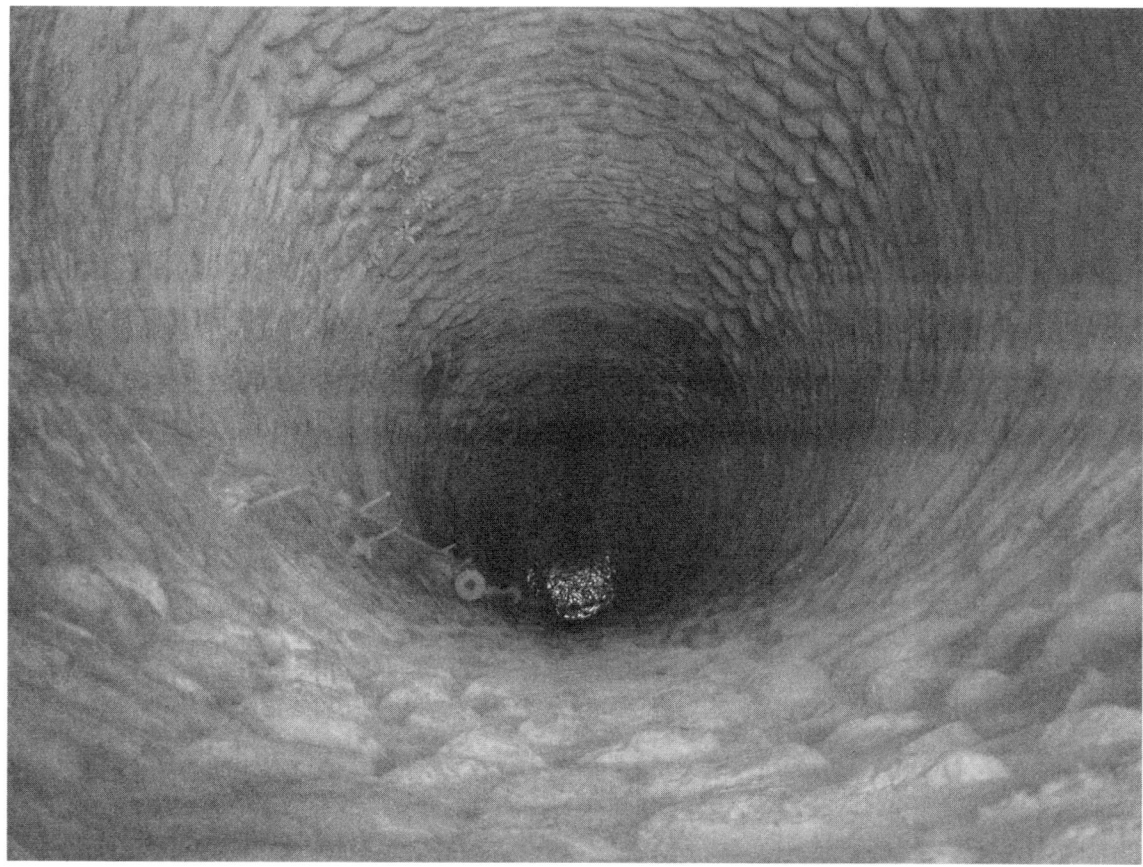

View looking down to the bottom of a pit (Image copyright Iain Frazer, 2009. Used under license from Shutterstock.com)

into the pit. When that does not happen (they verify the fact by opening a door in the ceiling and checking on him), they turn to Plan B, which is the slowly descending pendulum. Once again, they could have killed him quickly, but they make him suffer for many hours while he is tied to a board. They must have concocted their torture with an eye toward enjoying it. Such is the very definition of sadism. Lastly, the fact that their torture chamber is rigged with so many ways to kill a person is evidence that the Inquisitors have invested much time and energy in their pursuit of "justice."

Salvation

"The Pit and the Pendulum" is unusual for Poe in that the narrator is saved from death at the last minute. This salvation is made possible because the narrator has kept his wits about him and has twice thwarted the Inquisitors' plans for his death, long enough for the French army to roll into town and put down the Inquisition. Had the narrator's mind been completely dulled by his ruthless imprisonment, he would have already met his death by falling into the pit or by being sliced through the heart by the pendulum. His mental acuity has saved him. In Poe's world, descent into madness leads to death, whereas reason leads to salvation. Ironically, belief in God—the justification for the Inquisition's persecution—has nothing to do with the narrator's salvation. Indeed, while the narrator spends much time contemplating death and eternal nothingness, he never once mentions God or heaven. He sees death as an eternal rest, not the beginning of eternal life.

STYLE

Gothic Fiction

Gothic fiction is characterized by a preoccupation with death, mystery, decay, madness, and terror. Gothic writers strive to stir the reader's emotions, be it a feeling of the sublime or horror.

The gothic tradition began in England around 1764, when Horace Walpole published his novel *The Castle of Otranto*, which concerns a doomed family cursed by legend and haunted by supernatural events. While gothic fiction often includes elements of romanticism—such as a love of nature, a reverence for beauty, and a rejection of science (which are apparent in Poe's poems "Annabel Lee" and "The Raven,") there are few if any romantic elements in "The Pit and the Pendulum." The story's power is in its ability to evoke horror through the predicament of a protagonist fated to die. The gothic concept of the sublime refers to the psychological state of metaphysical beauty and perfection the narrator describes when the pendulum's blade is within inches of his chest. While gothic literature originated in Europe, American writers of the early nineteenth century—including Washington Irving, Nathaniel Hawthorne, and Henry Wadsworth Longfellow—incorporated many of its elements into their fiction, although none more so than Poe.

The Latin epigraph that precedes the story (which Poe borrowed from the plans for the Jacobin Club House in Paris) lends the tale an added gothic air. Although Poe did not provide the translation, Latin was still commonly read by educated people in the nineteenth century, and many casual readers would have been able to translate the gothic-tinged phrases "wicked mob," "innocent blood," and "grim death." Uncharacteristic of gothic fiction is the last phrase of the translation, "life and health appear," which hints at the story's positive outcome.

Deus ex machina

Deus ex machina literally means "God from the machine." It was a favorite literary device of the ancient Greeks, who often ended their plays by having the hero rescued by a god, who descended to the stage by means of a crane (*machina*), rather than by having the characters work things out for themselves. In more modern literature, *deus ex machina* refers to plots that are solved by a previously unknown, outside force. Many consider it a device that weakens a plot because it is an artificial rather than an organic character-driven solution. In "The Pit and the Pendulum," the narrator's last-minute reprieve by General Lasalle is a classic example of *deus ex machina*. Until the very end, the reader has no clue that anyone is about to put down the Inquisition. Lasalle's outstretched arm reaching for the narrator just as he is about to plummet into the pit is symbolic of the outstretched hand of God descending from the heavens.

First-Person Point of View

Many of Poe's stories are written in the first person. It is an effective way of limiting information and filtering it through one person's perceptions and emotions. Some of Poe's narrators view the action from a distance, such as in "The Fall of the House of Usher," in which a level-headed narrator reports the actions of Roderick Usher as he descends into madness. In other stories, such as "The Tell-Tale Heart," much of the story's power comes from being inside the head of a mentally unbalanced narrator. In all first-person stories, the reader must determine if the narrator is reliable or not in terms of telling the truth and divulging all the information at his or her disposal. In "The Pit and the Pendulum," the narrator seems to give an accurate account of his alternating madness and mental clarity. Because the story is in the first person, the reader feels as helpless as the narrator against the unseen Inquisitors and suffers the same anxiety of not knowing what they are thinking.

Alliteration, Repetition, Metaphor, and Simile

Poe was also a poet, so it is not surprising that he uses techniques commonly found in poetry as a way to establish mood in his stories. He uses repetition of words and phrases multiple times in "The Pit and the Pendulum" to signify the relentlessness of the narrator's torture and to emphasize his unpleasant thoughts. These words sometimes take the form of interjections, such as "oh," "free," "down," and "no." This repetition gives added force to ordinary words and creates a discordant rhythm, adding to the overall tone of the story.

Alliteration abounds in the story as well. This technique involves repeating the same sounds throughout a sentence to achieve a sonorous quality. Poe constructs phrases with repeating "v" sounds and a hissing "s" sound numerous times as a way to heighten the feeling of horror. Other sentences repeat an "f" sound to noticeable effect, evincing a harsh sound on the ears. Like repetition, alliteration used effectively gives additional power to otherwise ordinary words and is yet another tool used to establish the dark tone of the story.

Poe loved similes. A simile compares one thing to another in order to describe it better. In

"The Pit and the Pendulum," Poe states that the Inquisitors' voices sound like a mill wheel. This gives readers an image—the judges' voices are as grinding, harsh, and destructive as a stone wheel that turns wheat into flour. The narrator says the judges' lips are as white as a sheet of paper—a vivid image that denotes their bloodless contempt for their prisoner. Another simile occurs when the narrator compares the seven candles to angels, an example of religious imagery that vanishes in a wave of nausea. Other similes abound: sleep is compared to death; the pit is compared to a set of jaws; the unceasing pendulum is compared to an avalanche. Poe compares otherwise innocuous things to objects weighted with negative connotations as a way to heighten the mood of the story. A metaphor exists when an object is described as something else. The "like" or "as" of the simile is replaced by "is." Although Poe uses metaphor more sparingly than simile, several examples appear in the story. The narrator says the sharp metal smell of the pendulum's blade is sour breath and his torturers are demons.

HISTORICAL CONTEXT

The Spanish Inquisition
By the time Poe wrote "The Pit and the Pendulum," the Spanish Inquisition was over. The Inquisition began in 1478 as a way to punish Jews and Muslims who had converted to Roman Catholicism rather than having been born into it. Thousands of people were put on trial, pronounced guilty, and sentenced to death. Many were burned at the stake. In 1834—eight years before Poe wrote the story—Spain formally abolished the Inquisition, although it had lost much of its power decades earlier.

The Spanish Inquisition was famous for its *autos-da-fé*, in which victims were tried in public, ceremonially paraded through the streets, and burned at the stake following a Catholic Mass. However, over the years, the Inquisition devised many other forms of slow, painful torture designed to elicit a confession rather than to kill someone. The rack involved stretching a person's limbs over movable rollers until they broke free of their sockets. Sometimes a person's face was covered with a cloth and water was poured on it to simulate drowning, a technique known today as waterboarding. The phrase "putting one's feet to the fire" alludes to the Inquisition's practice of literally doing that to the victim. Thumbscrews were used to pinch a heretic's fingers, and sometimes a person's hand was inserted into a metal glove and then heated over a fire. However, the pit, the pendulum, and the collapsing dungeon that appear in Poe's story are products of the author's imagination.

The United States did not have a history of large-scale religious persecution on a par with the Spanish Inquisition, the possible exception being the Salem witch trials in 1692–1693. On the contrary, religious freedom has been a hallmark of the country since its founding, resulting in a climate that fostered many new religions during Poe's lifetime. These included the Church of Jesus Christ of Latter-Day Saints; the Church of Christ, Scientist; and the Adventists, among many others. However, the United States was no stranger to legalized intolerance. As a child growing up in Richmond, Virginia, Poe would have been exposed to the institution of slavery and the harsh conditions under which slaves toiled. Native Americans also suffered under U.S. government policy. In 1831, Native Americans were stripped of their homelands and were forced to march to reservations in Oklahoma in accordance with President Andrew Jackson's Indian Removal Act of 1830. Thousands died along the way.

General Lasalle and Washington Irving
Antoine Lasalle was born into French nobility in 1775 and died in 1809, a generation before Poe wrote "The Pit and the Pendulum." During his lifetime he was known as "The Hussar General" and fought in the French Revolution and the Napoleonic Wars. He joined the army at age eleven and became a lieutenant by age fourteen. He was regarded as a supreme cavalry commander—known for his daring and heroic deeds both on and off the battlefield—dashing good looks, colorful personality, and ability to impress women. His exploits would have been well known to Poe's readers. He fought bravely, drank heavily, and gambled away a fortune. Napoleon looked the other way, forgiving his unbecoming behavior because of his value as a commander.

In 1808, Lasalle arrived in Spain, torched the village of Torquemada, left one thousand Spanish troops dead after a charge at the Pisuerga River, and marched on to Valladolid. Napoleon made Lasalle "Count of the Empire" for his role in capturing Spain for France. However, Lasalle never went to Toledo, and he had nothing at all to do with the Spanish Inquisition. During Poe's time, details of Napoleon's campaign in Spain,

COMPARE & CONTRAST

- **1842:** Although the centuries-long Spanish Inquisition has been abolished for eight years, knowledge of its torture devices remains in the public consciousness through such phrases as "turning the screws" and holding one's "feet to the fire."

    Today: U.S. forces in Iraq are accused of torturing suspected terrorists by submitting them to waterboarding, a technique used in the Spanish Inquisition and approved by the Bush administration in 2001 as an essential tool for eliciting intelligence.

- **1842:** Poe's story "The Pit and the Pendulum" exemplifies the genre of gothic horror, also made popular by Joseph Sheridan Le Fanu in his 1839 story "The Strange Event in the Life of Schalken the Painter," Mary Shelley's 1818 novel *Frankenstein*, and John Polidori's 1819 story "The Vampyre."

    Today: Gothic horror and religious zealotry abound in the best-selling novels of Dan Brown, including *The Da Vinci Code* and *Angels and Demons*.

- **1842:** Some U.S. groups campaign for the elimination of the death penalty, which has been part of the American judicial system since the country's founding. In 1846, Michigan will become the first state to outlaw the execution of prisoners.

    Today: The Innocence Project, a nonprofit legal group, uses DNA evidence to exonerate those wrongly convicted of serious crimes. As of 2009, 240 defendants have been exonerated of the crimes for which they were convicted.

---

including the exploits of General Lasalle, would have been common knowledge among educated readers through the many popular novels that included these historical events in the plot.

In 1842, President Tyler appointed Washington Irving the U.S. minister to Spain. Irving, the author of "The Legend of Sleepy Hollow" and "Rip Van Winkle" was one of Poe's favorite writers; Poe had sought his advice several years earlier on his story "The Fall of the House of Usher." Irving traveled to Spain and found the royal court mired in intrigue during its post-Inquisition turmoil, most of it surrounding the teenaged Isabella II. The Spanish Empire, a relic of a bygone era, was crumbling. Irving found the resulting upheaval exhausting and returned home in 1846 to pursue his writing.

CRITICAL OVERVIEW

Poe was controversial in his day. During his lifetime he was more popular as a literary critic than as a fiction writer and poet. Yet even in the 1840s his stories were published and talked about. He was credited with popularizing the short story as a literary format, and his invention of detective fiction won him many devotees. "He gave to the short story its vogue in America," stated a writer for the 1907 *Cambridge History of English and American Literature*, who believed that his plots suffered from "lack of variety in theme and form." "The Pit and the Pendulum," however, received no specific critical appraisal during Poe's lifetime.

"The Pit and the Pendulum" has never been as popular as some of Poe's other stories, possibly because of its uncharacteristically happy ending. Yet it shares with all of his stories a tonal quality of dread and despair, evoked through the type of language that is the hallmark of gothic and romantic fiction. In *Poe's Fiction: Romantic Irony in the Gothic Tales*, G. R. Thompson writes that "The Pit and the Pendulum" "is one of Poe's clearest dramatizations of the futile efforts of man's will to survive the malevolent perversity of the world and to make order out of chaos."

A bare prison cell (Image copyright Robert Adrian Hillman, 2009. Used under license from Shutterstock.com)

Poe's reputation has grown steadily in the century and a half since his death. Stuart Levine, in his 1972 book *Edgar Poe: Seer and Craftsman*, acknowledges that "The Pit and the Pendulum" "is no doubt sensational... but it will be remembered that sensationalism was one of the tenets of [Poe's] critical theory.... The entire story is designed to produce a single effect [and] the pattern presented is Gothic in its complexity and horror." In the end, Levine states that "the narrator emerges from fear into lucidity, and the lucidity saves him." Other critics have agreed with this assessment. Michael L. Burduck, in *Grim Phantasms: Fear in Poe's Short Fiction*, believes that "The Pit and the Pendulum" "demonstrates the ability of rational thought to transcend the fear produced by intense suffering. Although readers might conclude that Poe is recording the process of disintegration, he actually describes how the speaker in the tale achieves salvation through the complete command of his mental faculties."

Other critics see the story as one of spiritual redemption, with the narrator descending into the equivalent of hell and being saved at the last minute by the Christlike figure of General Lasalle. Scott Peeples, in *Edgar Allan Poe Revisited*, credits luck as much as salvation. "He discovers the pit because he trips at exactly the right moment, and Lasalle similarly arrives in the nick of time," Peeples writes, concluding that, "given the story's apocalyptic imagery, it is logical to read the narrator's deliverance as providential: he helps himself, but ultimately God saves him." However, this explanation rankles some critics, as it appears to violate Poe's own aesthetic dogma. "If the narrator is saved through some providential design," Peeples surmises, "the story itself is flawed, for it violates Poe's theory of internal coherence or single effect." Such absurdity, according to David H. Hirsch, exhibits Poe's belief in the randomness of the narrator's fate in a way that foreshadows the rise of existentialism in the twentieth century. Another event that highlights the meaninglessness of life occurs when the narrator frees himself from his restraints and the pendulum. His freedom is meaningless since he is still in the hands of the Inquisition, and is free only in the sense that he will be able to suffer yet more torture. Peeples concludes that the "rescue's randomness makes it consistent with the purposelessness of his suffering, giving the story its disconcerting 'unity of effect.'"

Jeanne M. Malloy, writing in the journal *Nineteenth-Century Literature*, analyzes the story in terms of its apocalyptic imagery, noting that the seven candles at the start of the story correspond to a verse in the Book of Revelation and set the stage for a tale of biblical proportions. The horrors enumerated in Revelation are detailed, numerous, and gruesome, but they are intended for those who have not been saved. In comparison to the tortures, salvation is so much sweeter, as it is for Poe's narrator. The story would have no power if Lasalle had rescued him at any other moment. In addition, writes Malloy, Lasalle enters "with blaring trumpets, 'fiery walls,' and 'a thousand thunders'... apocalyptic images that describe the narrator's deliverance by General Lasalle as a sort of Second Coming of Christ." That there is no foreshadowing of the event—a condition that bothers many critics—is not a concern for Malloy because Lasalle's entrance mimics Revelation 16:15: "Behold, I come as a thief." Malloy concludes that Poe's use of apocalyptic imagery has less to do with religion than with the influence of the English Romantics, who use similar imagery, as he unfurls a tale of psychic destruction and reconstruction. "Poe, of course, did not have a psychoanalytic vocabulary," Malloy writes. [Sigmund Freud did not begin publishing his ideas of psychoanalysis until fifty years after Poe's death.] "What he did have was an intimate knowledge of the Bible and of English Romantic literature, and he used the biblical apocalypse in a typically Romantic way at the conclusion of the tale: to signal psychological and spiritual redemption achieved through suffering and heightened consciousness."

CRITICISM

Kathy Wilson Peacock

Peacock is a nonfiction writer who specializes in literature and history. In this essay she analyzes Poe's attitude toward religion as depicted through the narrator and the final moment of salvation in "The Pit and the Pendulum."

"The Pit and the Pendulum" is the most unique of Edgar Allan Poe's short stories in

THE MORAL OF THE STORY IS THAT ONE MUST RAGE AGAINST INSANITY, FOR THE REWARD IS EARTHLY SALVATION."

that it has a happy ending. The narrator has been imprisoned in a booby-trapped dungeon and sentenced to death by the Spanish Inquisition. He successfully escapes both the pit and the pendulum, only to be threatened by the superheated walls of his cell, which are closing in on him like a trash compactor. As he teeters on the precipice of oblivion, a thunderous commotion arises and he is snatched from the jaws of death by the semidivine general Antoine Lasalle. A discordant hum of human voices and a trumpet-like blast are heard as Poe grants his narrator salvation after pummeling him with intense gothic despair.

The story violates one of Poe's cardinal storytelling rules outlined in his 1846 essay "The Philosophy of Composition." Unity of effect—establishing a tone and carrying it through to the end of the story—is, according to Poe, a necessary element for a successful story. Yet the deus ex machina ending of "The Pit and the Pendulum" breaks the story's unity of effect by replacing the tone of madness, despair, and death with a joyous celebration. Why would Poe do this? The answer lies in the reason for the disunity, namely, the depiction of salvation. "The Pit and the Pendulum" provides valuable insight into the author's attitude toward religion, a topic on which Poe was mostly silent.

By all accounts, Poe was not a religious man. He was raised by his unofficial foster parents John and Frances Allan of Richmond, Virginia. They had him baptized in the Episcopal Church, and he attended religious services regularly with Frances. A few years later, when the family moved to England, he was enrolled in the Reverend John Bransby's Manor House School, where the curriculum no doubt included a hefty dose of religion. Thus, the youthful Poe was as familiar with Christianity as any other educated individual of his time. However, his scandalous expulsion from West Point Military Academy in 1831 was partly due to his refusal to

WHAT DO I READ NEXT?

- *Midnight Dreary: The Mysterious Death of Edgar Allan Poe* (2000), by John Evangelist Walsh, delves into the strange events of Poe's death in Baltimore in October 1849. Walsh traces Poe's final days and comes up with some plausible scenarios for how the writer came to be bruised, battered, and incoherent before fatally succumbing to his injuries.

- Poe's 1839 short story "The Fall of the House of Usher" is a good example of a gothic horror story concerning a dilapidated manor house, a character who is buried alive, and Poe's favorite theme, namely, the descent into madness. It is widely available in many paperback and short story collections.

- Chilean American Isabel Allende's 1982 novel *The House of the Spirits* is a modern gothic tale featuring magic realism, a crumbling manor house, and supernatural events of a multigenerational Latin American family.

- "The Legend of Sleepy Hollow," Washington Irving's 1820 short story about the school teacher Ichabod Crane and the ghostly Headless Horsemen is an earlier example of an American horror story from one of Poe's favorite writers.

- *The Crucible*, a 1953 play by Arthur Miller, presents the Salem witch trials of 1692–1693 as an allegory for the latter-day witch hunt of the House Un-American Activities Committee, headed by the inquisitor-like senator Joseph McCarthy during the early 1950s, in which many prominent Americans were accused of being members of the Communist Party.

- Enid A. Goldberg and Norman Itzkowitz's biography *Tomas de Torquemada: Architect of Torture During the Spanish Inquisition* (2009), part of the "Wicked History" young-adult series published by Franklin Watts, presents a portrait of one of the most cruel and feared men in history.

- Mary Shelley's 1818 novel *Frankenstein; or The Modern Prometheus* is one of the most famous gothic romantic novels ever written. Victor Frankenstein, a young German physician, creates a murderous monster and suffers extreme mental torment over his misguided attempt at playing God.

---

attend daily chapel services. As a writer, his favorite topic was the death of a beautiful woman—romantic but clearly not religious.

This is not to say that Poe did not believe in God. Poe's copy of the Holy Bible was found in his possession at his death in 1849, and he was known to have attended church in the 1840s with his friend and neighbor Mrs. Marie Louise Shew. As recounted on the Edgar Allan Poe Society of Baltimore Web site, when the topic of religion was broached in a written exchange with fellow poet Thomas Holley Chivers, Poe wrote, "My own faith is indeed my own." He also owned a well-worn copy of *On the Power, Wisdom, and Goodness of God, as Manifested in the Adaptation of External Nature to the Moral and Intellectual Constitution of Man*, by Thomas Chalmers, the leader of the Free Church of Scotland, whose religious philosophy centered on missions and reducing poverty. It seems evident that although Poe did not reject Christianity outright, he did not have much use for the dogma of organized religion.

Poe's rejection of organized religion was in keeping with his antiauthoritarian streak, a trait that caused him a host of problems, not the least of which was keeping a job. His religion could be said to have been English romanticism; he was captivated by the disintegration of the human mind. Such is the foundation of "The Pit and the Pendulum." A man imprisoned by the Spanish Inquisition—his supposed crime is unnamed and irrelevant for Poe's purposes—is sentenced to death and placed in a torture chamber. In the dark, he discovers the pit and is able to avoid it. Then he is strapped to a board and taunted with a guillotine-like pendulum slowly descending over his heart. His predicament results in the unraveling of his mind, but he retains enough sense to escape from his bonds by smearing them with meat and allowing rats to chew through them. This has bought him some time—enough to be rescued by General Lasalle. The moral of the story is that one must rage against insanity, for the reward is earthly salvation.

If this idea were a religion, it would be an amalgam of transcendentalism and humanism, with a bit of English romanticism thrown in for good measure. As a literary man immersed in the culture of nineteenth-century America, Poe would have been familiar with all three. Horror and the sublime are key elements of English romanticism, and both are at the heart of "The Pit and the Pendulum." Romanticism was merely an idea in Poe's day; it did not acquire its formal name until the Victorian writers dubbed it thus. Romanticism was a palpable reaction against the Enlightenment, a craving for beauty and feeling over science and logic. In the United States, romanticism was evident in the tenets of transcendentalism, which espoused a less formal relationship between man and God than earlier religions. Transcendentalism holds that an individual's spiritual intuition is more truthful than religious doctrine. If the Spanish Inquisition represents religious doctrine at its worst, then the narrator of "The Pit and the Pendulum" represents the spiritual intuition that leads to salvation. Humanism, which predates romanticism, is concerned with human dignity and rationality. Trapped within the confines of the dungeon, the narrator suffers from a lack of both—the latter erased by the former—but his salvation at the hands of the swashbuckling romantic hero Lasalle restores them.

Despite his unorthodox view of organized religion, Poe employs several mainstream Christian ideas in "The Pit and the Pendulum." For example, he sets the story at the historical ground zero of religious intolerance—Toledo, Spain, during the Spanish Inquisition. He does, however, blur facts. The ghastly torture of the Inquisition's heyday was long gone by the time General Lasalle rode into Spain in 1808 during the Napoleonic Wars. Despite these inaccuracies, the genesis of the narrator's mental instability is rooted in reality, which represents a departure from many of Poe's tales, in which the horror stems from something more esoteric (a black cat, a talking bird, a diseased eye). This setup allows Poe to depict a rational man descending into madness, clinging to sanity just long enough to savor the victory of divine intervention.

The narrator is unconcerned with determining his guilt or innocence. Rather, he accepts his fate in the manner of a Christian who believes that all God's children are guilty due to original sin. The seven white candles, which at first appear as angels to the narrator, recall the image in the Book of Revelation in which seven white candles appear to represent a white-haired God. The latter, stern and threatening, is suggested by the image of Father Time on the ceiling of the torture chamber. Perhaps the narrator has mistaken God the Father—the most punishing member of the Holy Trinity—for Father Time, just as he initially mistakes the swinging scythe for the pendulum of a grandfather clock.

General Lasalle's outstretched hand calls to mind Michelangelo's *Creation of Adam* from the ceiling frescoes of the Sistine Chapel. More important, it is the *ne plus ultra* of the *deus ex machina*: God from the machine. This is the classic Greek literary device by means of which a character facing certain doom is rescued at the last moment by the outstretched hand of a divine presence, who up to that moment has not been an active participant in the story. That Poe cast a notorious cad and womanizer in the role of God indicates his irreverence for religion. The historical Lasalle was a larger-than-life figure; he was a man with a voracious appetite for vice, yet expert with a horse and a sword, whose only religion was adventure. Surely Lasalle rescues the narrator more for his own personal glory than out of concern for the man's fate. Lasalle is a romantic figure in the classic sense of the word; as such, Poe casts him as God in his romantic, religious vision. His arrival is heralded with the pomp of the Second Coming—with a thunderous clamor that sounds like the trumpets of angels.

The narrator's religion is one in which his worst fear is nothingness. It is the reason he delays opening his eyes near the beginning of the story. He fears what he will *not* see if he is, in fact, dead. This suggests that the man was sentenced to death for insufficient piety; never does he mention heaven or hell. Beyond this mortal existence lies nothingness, he supposes. While he fears this at the beginning of the story, after sustained torture he looks forward to the nothingness of the grave.

Thus, both for Poe and his narrator, salvation is not a heavenly reward but rather earthly freedom. What saves him is hope, not faith—hope, against all odds, that he might be saved. A religious person might have spent those hours in prayer while awaiting death beneath the swinging axe. Poe's narrator uses his rational mind to think of a way to break free from his bonds even as his captors try to undermine his sanity. He holds the key to his own deliverance. Hope is the tool of the humanist, whereas faith is the tool of the Christian. Such is Poe's religious message in this singularly joyous short story.

Source: Kathy Wilson Peacock, Critical Essay on "The Pit and the Pendulum," in *Short Stories for Students*, Gale, Cengage Learning, 2010.

John J. Miller

In the following article, Miller quotes Poe, who said it would be 2,000 years before his work would be properly admired but after only 200 years, Poe is celebrated as a literary legend.

On a snowy night toward the end of his life, Edgar Allan Poe delivered a lecture on the origins of the universe. It was an unusual topic—Poe was always more interested in death than birth—and the reviews were mixed. Frustrated by the response, Poe announced that 2,000 years would pass before his work was properly admired.

His remarks were soon published as "Eureka: A Prose Poem." The book sold a few hundred copies and then slipped into obscurity, forgotten except for the fact that its author went on to become a giant of American literature in something less than two millennia.

It remains to be seen whether anyone will read Poe in the distant future. As we approach the bicentennial of his birth on Jan. 19, however, it's obvious that Poe is far from "nameless here for evermore."

Hardly anyone escapes from high-school English without bumping into at least a little Poe. "The Raven" remains one of the world's most popular poems as well as the inspiration for the name of Baltimore's professional football team. "The Fall of the House of Usher," "The Black Cat," and a number of other short stories are among the most anthologized tales ever written.

An awful lot of Poe looms on the horizon. On Jan. 16, the Postal Service will issue a stamp in his honor. Historic sites in Baltimore, the Bronx, Philadelphia and Richmond, Va., are kicking off year-long celebrations. Publishers plan to take advantage of the bicentennial, too. In October, Doubleday put out *Poe's Children*, a collection of horror stories by the likes of Neil Gaiman and Stephen King. The Mystery Writers of America has just released two additional volumes: *In the Shadow of the Master* includes 16 of Poe's greatest hits, plus commentaries by best-selling novelists such as Michael Connelly and Joseph Wambaugh; *On a Raven's Wing* features original tales by Mary Higgins Clark and others, each inspired by Poe.

Praise for Poe is by no means universal. The reviews always have been mixed, even on large questions about his legacy. "Enthusiasm for Poe is the mark of a decidedly primitive stage of reflection," sniffed Henry James.

Yet there can be no doubt that Poe left a deep mark on literature. He invented both the detective story ("The Murders in the Rue Morgue") and the sequel to the detective story ("The Mystery of Marie Roget" and "The Purloined Letter"). An attraction to new technologies and cutting-edge ideas such as hot-air balloons, mesmerism, and cryptography made him a pioneer of science fiction. He could be a savage critic: "I intend to put up with nothing I can put down," he boasted.

Most important, Poe reshaped the horror story into a tool for probing the darkest corners of human psychology and his own disturbing obsession with death. Early detractors failed to share his vision and accused him of merely aping Gothic thrillers penned by German authors. Poe would have none of it: "I maintain that terror is not of Germany, but of the soul—that I have deduced this terror only from its legitimate sources, and urged it only to its legitimate results," he replied, in a line that neatly sums up his philosophy of fiction.

In the popular imagination, Poe is the dreary, unsmiling, black-clad bard of diabolism. This is the guy, after all, who reveled in themes of torture ("The Pit and the Pendulum"), pestilence ("The Masque of the Red Death"), and premature burial ("Berenice"). Two of his best-known stories are told from the perspective of murderers—one a cold-blooded killer ("The Cask of Amontillado"), the other a madman who dismembers his victim ("The Tell-Tale Heart"). Poe seemed to relish the deaths of beautiful women, especially when he could also describe their morbid resurrections ("Ligeia" and "Morella"). Sometimes it's impossible to know whether he's portraying supernatural events or the ravings of lunatics. His corpse-filled corpus is both engrossing and grotesque.

His biography was a weird tale in its own right. He was born in Boston as Edgar Poe, abandoned by a reckless father at the age of 2, and orphaned by his mother's death when he was 3. The Allans of Richmond took him in, giving their young charge a home and a middle name. As a boy, Poe began his lifelong habit of frequenting cemeteries and concocting elaborate lies. Gambling forced him out of the University of Virginia, defiance drove him from West Point, and the lure of alcohol became a constant curse. He married his 13-year-old cousin when he was more than twice her age. It's not clear whether this odd union was ever consummated.

Just about every biographer has pondered unanswerable questions about Poe's mental health. The latest, Peter Ackroyd in *Poe: A Life Cut Short,* highlights the comment of a young woman Poe courted in his 20s: "He was not well balanced; he had too much brain.... He said often that there was a mystery hanging over him he never could fathom."

His death at 40 is itself shrouded in a fog that only heightens his enigmatic reputation. Poe had planned a business trip from Virginia to New York and promptly vanished. He eventually turned up drunk in a Baltimore tavern, possibly after participating as a pawn in a vote-fraud scheme, and died shortly thereafter. His lost week has become the stuff of literary legend. Whole books have been written about it, both fiction and nonfiction, and his tombstone is now the site of a strange annual ritual. On Poe's birthday, scores of devotees gather in the cold night to watch a shadowy figure known as the "Poe Toaster" leave three red roses and a half-empty bottle of cognac at the author's final resting place. This performance has survived for more than half a century, appears to have been passed on from one generation of visitant to the next, and shows no sign of letting up.

Around the time the original Poe Toaster appeared, Allen Tate made a famous observation: "Everything in Poe is dead." That's true to a point. Much of Poe's fascination with death actually grew from a desire to understand it as a member of the living. In "A Descent Into the Maelstrom," the narrator, a Norwegian fisherman, finds himself sucked into a violent whirlpool and worries that he'll drown in the vortex. "I began to reflect how magnificent a thing it was to die in such a manner, and how foolish it was in me to think of so paltry a consideration as my own individual life in view of so wonderful a manifestation of God's power," he says. "I positively felt a wish to explore its depths, even at the sacrifice I was going to make; and my principal grief was that I should never be able to tell my old companions on shore about the mysteries I should see."

Poe can't reveal what, if anything, he has learned from beyond the grave. But he did leave behind a handful of poems and stories whose eerie splendor continues to haunt us.

Source: John J. Miller, "Poe at 200—Eerie After All These Years," in *Wall Street Journal,* January 15, 2009, p. D7.

Jason Haslam

In the following excerpt, Haslam explores Poe's tale in relation to the debates surrounding prison experiments in the late eighteenth and early nineteenth centuries.

... Even without the architectural strictures of Bentham's panopticon, one can see the outlines of the supposed shift, discussed by Foucault, from an embodied subjectivity that can be rendered "civil" only through violence and the spectacle thereof, to the interiorized, sensible subject who requires surveillance and isolation from negative influence in order to awaken to an embedded sense of propriety. In order to complicate this received genealogical framework, I aim here to sketch some of the particular debates surrounding these practices in the early history of the United States. Closer attention to Rush's foundational statements and to certain reformist criticisms of early penitentiaries reveals an argument for a new kind of publicity and spectacle. This line of argument within the early years of the republic enables us to see both the actual practices and the imagined cultural functions of prisons and punishment in a somewhat different light than that cast by what has become the received history of the penitentiary. As I will further show, this argument about punishment and publicity is thematized—even analyzed—in Poe's "The Pit and the Pendulum." Poe's story helps to refigure our view of early U.S. understandings of the prison and its cultural purpose. In short, although the visual spectacle of punishment might disappear from the public square, the spectacle would (and should, according to

> THIS READING OF THE STORY AS ALLEGORIZING THE MODERN PENITENTIARY CAN ONLY GO SO FAR, HOWEVER. THE INQUISITION MAY HAVE BEEN THEORETICALLY CONCERNED WITH THE REDEMPTION OF SOULS, BUT ITS PRACTICES—AND THE GOTHIC REPRESENTATION THEREOF—FOCUSED MORE ON BODILY TORTURE."

Rush) continue to exist—and have an impact on society—in publicly circulated narrative forms, including literature.

"The Pit and the Pendulum" has often been contextualized within gothic and other literary histories, with scholars pointing to source material and connections from *Blackwood's Magazine* to Edmund Burke. Recent work by Colin (Joan) Dayan and Teresa Goddu, though, has initiated analysis of the story in relation to other cultural contexts, specifically the law, slavery, and race. Building on Dayan's work, I argue that Poe's representation of the Inquisition echoes some key points in contemporary debates surrounding prisons, punishment, and the public sphere. Dayan identifies "The Pit and the Pendulum" as one of Poe's "fictions of containment." She relates these fictions to his life "in Philadelphia from 1838–1844, a city infatuated with prisons and the numerous theories concerning them," especially as manifested in "the utter seclusion" of the "'Philadelphia System.'" Living in Philadelphia, Dayan notes, "Poe had ample evidence of the material apparatus that both guaranteed and maintained the phantasm of criminality essential to the American project" ("Poe, Persons," 406).

Whereas Dayan is interested primarily in analyzing Poe's characters as "legal personalities" (407), I want to explore his tale's relationship to the debates surrounding the prison experiments of the late eighteenth and early nineteenth centuries. These debates frame the prison not just in legal, psychological, and material relation to the prisoner, but also in cultural relation to the larger society—a relation often left out of analyses of the early prison. I will use Rush's and Roscoe's writings to trace particular themes of the debate leading up to Poe's time, including arguments about the public role (and publicity value) of the penitentiary. "The Pit and the Pendulum" serves as a speculative extension of this debate, as it provides a limit case of detention and isolation. Poe's tale helps to highlight telling fractures in the shift in the discourse of punishment from bodily torture and public suffering to narratives of mental and ideological control. Ultimately, the spectacle of punishment remains a central cultural goal and tool of the prison even as the physical punishment itself is hidden behind the prison walls....

II

"The Pit and the Pendulum," at first, seems to allegorize the two aspects of the penitentiary experiment, tying them together into an apparently functional disciplinary and reformative mechanism. The Inquisition's dungeon stands in for both the terror of Rush's unknown punishments and for the possible reformation of the prisoner through isolation (though, as I will argue later, the effects of both these punishment technologies are revised as the story progresses). While Poe's prisoner is sentenced to death, a punishment most early proponents of the penitentiary—including Rush—argued against, the central punishments actually portrayed in the story focus on isolation, bodily pain, and the passage of time, which together form the backbone of Rush's theory of the penitentiary. The threat of death, meanwhile, functions primarily as a limit case for terror, providing the impetus for the narrator's and, given the Inquisition's aims, the whole social fabric's reformation. After nearly falling into the pit, the narrator reflects on the situation:

> The death just avoided was of that very character which I had regarded as fabulous and frivolous in the tales respecting the Inquisition. To the victims of its tyranny, there was the choice of death with its direct physical agonies, or death with its most hideous moral horrors. I had been reserved for the latter. By long suffering my nerves had been unstrung, until I [...] had become in every respect a fitting subject for the species of torture which awaited me.

Poe here narrativizes the shift from "direct, physical agonies," the embodied punishments of the early prison, to the "hideous moral horrors," or internalized punishments of the penitentiary system. The narrator demonstrates the power of cultural terror as outlined by Rush. The limit case of mental terror—the expectation of death—is perpetuated by what Rush calls the "romance" and "fiction" that "encreas[e] the terror of [the penitentiary's] punishments" (11). The Burkean terror of the penitentiary that Rush calls for perfectly renders Poe's narrator into a pliable subject ripe for ideological reformation: a "fitting subject" who is both "fit" for the punishments, and can in turn be "fit" into whatever space is deemed proper by those in control of the punishment narratives.

This newfound pliability is tied not just to the culturally perpetuated terror of the "fabulous and frivolous" stories of the Inquisition that the narrator knows, but also to an isolation that takes on the guise of nearly complete sensory deprivation:

> I felt that my senses were leaving me. [...] Then silence, and stillness, and night were the universe. I had swooned [...] In the return to life from the swoon there are two stages; first, that of the sense of mental or spiritual; secondly, that of the sense of physical existence. [...] After this I call to mind flatness and dampness; and then all is *madness*—the madness of a memory which busies itself among forbidden things. [...] Then, very suddenly, *thought* and shuddering terror, and earnest endeavor to comprehend my true state. [...] Then a rushing revival of soul and a successful effort to move [...] while I strove to imagine where and *what* I could be.

The narrator's swoon follows a linear progression from the destruction to the recreation of his identity, moving from an enforced "silence and stillness," to a "mental or spiritual" reawakening, to a "physical" rebirth, all of which lead to a personal reflection on "*what*" the narrator could be. Thus, Lawrence R. Schehr can write that the story focuses on the space "between the annihilation of the subject at point zero and the completion of the subject at a unitary, integral position" (46). Poe's Inquisition prison allegorizes nearly exactly the logic of the penitentiary's process of punishment, isolation, redemption and re-formation through reflection.

Reading this same passage in light of Rush's larger social project of using tales of the prison to create a docile citizenry, we can see that Poe also places punishment among the "forbidden things" that only literature can scare up, through the "fabulous and frivolous" "tales" that the narrator reads. Poe's tale demonstrates that such a dissemination of horror can virtually paralyze its subjects, bringing about a "flat" and "motionless" citizenry. If "the sentence, the dread sentence of death," is the last that Poe's prisoner hears, then it is also the sentence of promised—though hidden—violence. In the new narratives of punishment, this violence generates national cohesion through fear not of an "unrestrained [...] sovereign" (Foucault, 49), but of an unrestrained punishment, a point to which I will return in the next section. The text's material metaphors for prison technologies continually restrict the narrator's movement: if the pendulum allegorizes the prisoner's "time-served" and other "counted" punishments, then the pit is a literal *mise-en-abyme* of isolation. Constraint here serves to highlight the reduction of cultural possibilities when a narrative or a nation has terror as its governing principle. The narrator and the reader seem left in the position of Rush's terrified—but passive—citizen.

III

This reading of the story as allegorizing the modern penitentiary can only go so far, however. The Inquisition may have been theoretically concerned with the redemption of souls, but its practices—and the gothic representation thereof—focused more on bodily torture. Likewise, the annihilation of the narrator's identity and his reflective recovery from his swoon do not lead to a personal redemption or rehabilitation, but instead render him subject to increasingly horrible punishments and constraint. By the time he is tied beneath the pendulum, it is only "by dint of much exertion" that he can supply himself with food or even see anything. And it is here that we can discern a reflexive gothic critique both of the narrative horror that Rush calls for and of penitentiary isolation itself. Instead of leading, on the one hand, to a responsible, "fit" citizenry and, on the other, to a reformed, "fitting" subjectivity for the prisoner, Poe's tale instead suggests that such narratives lead only to more terror and violence, and that the penitentiary's reform is simply a reinvention of earlier punishments, the newly formed self-surveilling interiority merely a secondary effect of an ever-extant spectacle of torture.

Read through Poe, the underlying concern of Rush's reform tract seems to be the need to replicate, rather than annihilate, earlier forms of respect for the State as sovereign. Note the similarities between Rush's call for the new penitentiaries to effect "terror" and Foucault's analysis of the older forms of spectacular punishment:

Foucault writes, "what had [...] maintained this practice of torture was [...] a policy of terror: to make everyone aware, through the body of [the] criminal, of the unrestrained presence of the sovereign" (49). Reading the origin of the modern prison through Rush rather than Bentham, we can see that this "terror" transmutes the "fictitious relation" of panoptic (self-)surveillance (Foucault, 210) into a fictitious spectacle that places threat (bodily and otherwise) at the fore, rather than as a trace. Read through Rush and his founding role in the U.S. penitentiary movement, the penitentiary itself becomes, at its origin, the "unrestrained [...] sovereign" of the new, supposedly democratic, republic. An undecidable, ultimately indefinable *presence* at the margins of society, the penitentiary dictates, through fear and trembling rather than the subtle dissemination of surveillance, the shape and state of the nation.

Poe's literary critique is prefigured in a political tract by William Roscoe, from which I have already quoted. Roscoe, who is largely forgotten to modern readers, was a significant writer, historian, and public figure at the turn of the nineteenth century. His 1819 pamphlet was entitled *Observations on Penal Jurisprudence, and the Reformation of Criminals, with an Appendix Containing the Latest Reports of the State-Prisons or Penitentiaries of Philadelphia, New-York, and Massachusetts; and Other Documents*. I cite the title at length not only to include that fact that Roscoe examined the penitentiaries in the areas surrounding Poe, but also because of what at first seems to be the slippage in terminology between "state prisons" and "penitentiaries" (penitentiaries being the term used by the institution's proponents to denote a system based on penitence and reform, whereas prisons were seen as sites of corporal punishment). I do not mean to suggest in what follows that Roscoe was a paragon of judicious treatment of prisoners; he defended the penitentiary's practice of absolute isolation, which was tortuous in its own way. However, his critiques of the penitentiary experiment in the U.S., grounded in the very Enlightenment principles out of which the penitentiary itself developed, highlight the debate surrounding punishment in early U.S. history and elsewhere....

Poe's story replicates this philosophical and political debate. Starting with a seeming allegory of the effectiveness of such confining theories as Rush's, Poe's story seamlessly segues into the pointlessness of the "mechanical" terror which Roscoe analyzes. Goddu may read the tale in terms of its relation to slavery, but her argument resonates nicely with Rush and Roscoe's choice of language: "The site of terror and torture is transformed into a marketplace. Terror is turned into a quotation that graces the gates of commerce, consumed now by the mass marketplace rather than enacted by the wicked mob" (107). Rephrased, the public nature of physical punishment is transformed into a physically hidden but culturally publicized terror. The promise of salvation (be it the Inquisition's spiritual salvation, or the sociological salvation of the penitentiary) covers over the reality of a systematized and explicitly mechanized terror and pain.

"The Pit and the Pendulum" suggests—echoing exactly Roscoe's statement that vengeful judgment destroys "our sympathy" with "the frailties of humanity" (7)—that if the reader is supposed to feel a sympathetic terror and to behave to avoid it, then the authors of that terror must themselves be removed from the sympathetic bond of humanity. Poe writes,

> I saw, but with how terrible an exaggeration! I saw the lips of the black-robed judges. They appeared to me white—whiter than the sheet upon which I trace these words—and thin even to grotesqueness; thin with [...] stern contempt of human torture [...] and then my vision fell upon the seven tall candles upon the table. At first they wore the aspect of charity, and seemed white slender angels who would save me: but then all at once there came a most deadly nausea over my spirit, [...] while the angel forms became meaningless spectres, with heads of flame, and I saw that from them there would be no help.

Replicated in the "meaningless spectres" of the horrible candles, the Inquisition's judges—embodiments of both spiritual and secular law—must abandon their sympathetic humanity in the narrative act of perpetuating horror, their lips, from which the "dread sentence" arises, being reflected in the pages of Poe's tale of terror (as others have pointed out, Poe explicitly compares the dreaded judges with the page itself). As Schehr states, the story presents us with a "non recuperative, non-integrated model" of literature and, I would add, of the (non-)reformed subject, within which "the subject can only offer a liquid, intermittent state of non-subjectivity" (59; 63). Poe's gothic tale thus highlights the inhumanity not only of the "Universal Inquisition," but also of the "universal" qualities of sympathy as they are enacted by courts and judges who send the convicted to the penitentiary for reformation. This sympathy may supposedly swing freely back and forth between the fully realized interior lives of Enlightenment individuals but, when used within the hierarchical structures of the foundation of a prison and of a nation, it finds itself halting on the ontological pit of the punished subject and the vengeance enacted upon him.

Such an analysis of the story also re-situates the much debated ending, in which the narrator's rescue appears as either a jarring *deus ex machina* (as opposed to the demonic mechanics of punishment), a phantasmatic inversion of the beginning of the story, or as possibly simply a figment of the narrator's growing insanity. Read in terms of contemporary detention practices, the salvation of the—or any—prisoner cannot be a rational, expected result, but can instead only occur "extra-textually," or from outside of the system of punishment, as a pardon during the prescribed sentence. Rush, in fact, did not want the prisoner to have any idea when the punishment would end: "Let the duration of punishments, for all crimes, be limited, but let this limitation be unknown. I conceive this secret to be of the utmost importance in reforming criminals, and preventing crimes. The imagination, when agitated with uncertainty, will seldom fail of connecting the longest duration of punishment, with the smallest crime" (11). Read in this light, the ending of Poe's story constitutes the exact opposite of what Jeanne M. Malloy calls a "psychological and spiritual redemption achieved through suffering and heightened consciousness" (94). Perhaps Malloy's interpretation would hold true for what Victor Brombert has called the Romantic "happy prison motif," but does not hold true for this gothic tale, in which the narrator is either rescued by an outside force, or loses his mind.

In either case, Poe's story here highlights the arbitrariness of detention, punishment, and their duration in the mid-nineteenth-century prison: it furthers what Dayan refers to, in another context, as Poe's continuing attention to the "artifices of law and the imperatives of fiction" (415). If law is an artifice, Poe's fictional rendering of detention must end with a hyper-extended fiction, an ending that is unbelievable even within the artifice of a gothic tale. Following Judith Butler's analysis of Foucault's statement that "the soul is the prison of the body," it can be argued that the penitentiary only offers a "false stabilization" of the reformed individual and the civic population, and that, further, this is a dangerous falseness and a pernicious stability (Butler, 135). The "unrestrained" sovereignty of a monarch, standing outside the system, is not replaced with a sovereign and grounded civic body, but instead with the supposedly unquestionable and naturalized terror of the prison. If we miss the fact that torture and the narrativized, terrorizing spectacle thereof is actually at the center of the penitentiary experiment and not just as a "trace," then we also risk missing the materiality of that danger and its ongoing existence in modern penal systems. The cultural and material results of the prison experiments in early America neither ceased to exist nor simply devolved into the infamous abuses at Sing Sing later in the nineteenth century, or those at Abu Ghraib early in the twenty-first century, but in fact maintain the possibility of these latter spectacles of punishment.

Source: Jason Haslam, "Pits, Pendulums, and Penitentiaries: Reframing the Detained Subject," in *Texas Studies in Literature and Language*, Vol. 50, No. 3, Fall 2008.

James Southall Wilson

In the following excerpt, Wilson attempts to reconcile the varying perceptions of Poe's personality, providing insight into his macabre writing style.

Years ago I began a pubic address by calling Edgar Allan Poe the Hamlet of American literature and the phrase pleased the fancy of the newspaper headliners at the time. The dark cloak of mystery in which everything about the man and the artist has been wrapped, and the endless and unsatisfactory efforts to pluck out the stops and sound him to his depths have given some almost self-suggesting aptness to the parallel. But it is too obvious a likeness to be a vital one. Poe is rather the epitome of man. In him were gathered as in one microcosm the littleness and the magnanimity, the spleen and the generosity, the heights and the depths of man's nature. To some degree, all that has been said about him was true and nothing that has been said about him was true. He denied the facts of his own life and yet he wrote them plain for all the world to read. He is a contradiction at a hundred points and yet he consistently followed the track of desolating loneliness in fidelity to the cold light of his high north star. This is the strange man of whose personality after a hundred and fifty years

" ELSEWHERE HE WROTE THAT THE GREATEST MISFORTUNE THAT COULD COME TO A MAN WOULD BE TO HAVE AN INTELLIGENCE EVEN A LITTLE SUPERIOR TO ANY OF HIS GENERATION, SINCE THE VERY THINGS WHICH HE SAW BEYOND OTHER MEN WOULD CONVINCE THEM OF HIS INSANITY."

I seek to make a synthesis. What betrayed me into the headstrong task was the sense that for years I had been seeking to realize to myself that strange personality. Out of the innumerable reminiscences of men and women who knew him, I have sought to discount the vagaries of old men whose memories played them fanciful tricks, the vanities of old women whose sentimentality whispered foolish lies, and the falsities of obvious fame-seekers who remembered where no memories were. From all that had been written about him, and out of his own writings, taken with the circumstances of their composition when we knew them, and from the composite face made by considering all his likenesses in relation to the known facts of the sittings, out of these we may try to invoke the manhood of Edgar Poe and to enter through the doorway thus constructed into the inner and spiritual self until we feel that we know the man. But how little we know those of our own household. How then shall I speak with authority of this man whom I have never seen and with whom only three people whom I have known were personally acquainted? Or suppose I have read aright this dark-hued chameleon of genius, how can I make you see as I sometimes think I feel, the baffling contradictions of his life and character?...

I

We are studying the humanity of a great artist. We are concerned only with such facts as we can be convinced are true in our effort to understand and to recreate him imaginatively as a man. Whether he was weak or strong in will or morals, whether he was a drunkard or used opium, whether he was untrustworthy in his use of words or of money, whether he was harsh or jealous in his attitude towards others, whether he was loving and faithful or lustful and variable in his human relations; all these matters are of first importance in reconstructing and in considering intelligently the life of the man from whom issued words sweeter than honey and phrases sharper than edged swords. But we, I hope, are civilized enough to be able to keep our criticism unmixed from our moralities. As critics and seekers for the truth we judge neither the man nor his creator....

These are but a few of the factors that helped make Poe what he was; but of course we will not forget that what he was originally is always the most important explanation of itself and what he became. The most brilliant and variously gifted mind that America had yet produced, sensitive and temperamental, as poets' minds usually are, was born in a body poorly adapted to endure humiliations, privations, and exhausting petty tragedies. His career was marked by accidental misfortunes paralleled only by the disasters produced in vicious circles by the very mental traits that they in part explain.

II

We have constructed sketchily the frame, now let us examine the picture. Physically Poe is recalled to most of us by the late daguerreotypes taken nearly every one of them after the ravages of a long and prostrating spree, near the end of his life when his countenance already showed the disintegration which was so surely taking place in this old man whose age in years was less than forty. I have no doubt that the earlier pictures better reflect the Poe known to those who remembered him before the lonesome latter years. The sharp decline began, I believe, in 1845 when the top of his fame was reached with the popular success of "The Raven." But the catastrophic breaking in health and sanity dates from his wife's death in 1847, two years before his own. As depicted in the earlier portraits and described by those who knew him best, he was a quiet, shy-looking man, nearly always dressed (neatly is the word often used) in well-brushed black; wearing clipped side-whiskers, or clean-shaven, or with a closely trimmed mustache, as fashion suggested; of moderate height—five feet, eight inches, according to the army records—and build, but slight rather than stocky, and with delicately modeled hands and feet; in every detail, his enemies as well as his friends are careful to say, looking the gentleman.

The prominent features of his face were his long but well-formed nose and his large rounded brilliant eyes of hazel-grey. So long and dark were his lashes, so deep-set the eyes under the dark brows, so expansive the pupils of the eyes, that not infrequently those who knew him slightly have described them as dark or brown....

III

It is just as well to remember that there was the young Poe and the older man. There was the reticent Poe among strangers who was also the affable, considerate family man. We cannot imagine the former bursting his gaiters in a contest at leap-frog with a friend at the Fordham cottage. It was the latter who wrote with pathetic gusto of the good things to eat in a cheap New York boarding house. He was encouraging his sick wife's solicitous mother, stranded in Philadelphia for lack of railway fare. There was also the drunk as well as the sober Poe. No study of Poe's personality can proceed far without first a conclusion, or at least an assumption, as to his habits in relation to drugs and intoxicants. I cannot here enter into the arguments or the evidence. I am ready to grant anything that can be proved, but for my own part I think that the assumption that Poe ever used habitually opium in any form is unwarranted by trustworthy evidence....

IV

Poe was by nature and choice an intellectual aristocrat. He was a student at the University of Virginia founded by Thomas Jefferson while that suave revolutionary was yet alive. He might often have met him on its Lawn or been one of the groups that Mr. Jefferson invited to visit him at Monticello. Poe, nonetheless, somewhere in his writings remarked that the greatness of Jefferson ought to cause no man to accept his mistakes. Elsewhere he wrote that the greatest misfortune that could come to a man would be to have an intelligence even a little superior to any of his generation, since the very things which he saw beyond other men would convince them of his insanity....

It little matters now that he offended the moralists of his day till they grew immoral in the bitterness of their denunciation of him. The wonder of his startling genius, the beauty of his melodious and often flawless poetry, the suggestiveness of his criticism, the originality and power of his stories will not be different whatever the man was like. But the significance of his genius gives an interest and importance to the personality of the man that possessed it and to the circumstances that produced or conditioned the manner of its expression. Poe the man was one of millions in the crude America of his day and his behavior as a man was no more important than that of any other one of those millions. But Poe the artist is unique and what affected him concerns all the world of intelligent people.

But should the last of all the Puritans force me to bring moral values to bear where they are irrelevant and find a practical application either in the effort to analyze the man's personality or to evaluate his acts, to my own satisfaction I could do it triumphantly. Over against the pity of his poverty, the mad devastation that drink wrought upon his diseased mind, the liberties that he sometimes took with words, I should place the splendid loyalty of his devotion to those two women who loved him; the courage, the zeal, the uncompromising fidelity with which he served through poverty, drink, and misrepresentation, the life of an artist in a country where his art was not appreciated. Conan Doyle built many tales upon the bare formula of one type of tale that Poe created. Poe scorned to copy himself in his serious work. Each of his tales of analysis has a different theme, though no one would have been quicker than he to see how easily the same tale may be told over with varied incident and changed names. "I could not do that," Poe wrote of a suggestion about his story, "Ligeia," "For I had already written 'Morella.'" For all the pity and irony of his life and personality, to my reading there is more character and as much morality to the story of Poe as may be found in the quiet peace of many good men whose beasts were tamed to an easy yoke.

Source: James Southall Wilson, "Personality of Poe," in *Virginia Magazine of History and Biography*, Vol. 67, No. 2, April 1959, pp. 131–42.

SOURCES

Burduck, Michael L., "A Descent into the Maelstrom," in *Grim Phantasms: Fear in Poe's Short Fiction*, Garland Publishing, 1992, pp. 90–93.

"Edgar Allan Poe," in *The Cambridge History of English and American Literature: An Encyclopedia in Eighteen Volumes*, Vol. 16, edited by A. W. Ward et al., G. P. Putnam's Sons, 1907–1921.

"Edgar Allan Poe and Religion," in *Edgar Allan Poe Society of Baltimore*, January 24, 2009, http://www.eapoe.org (accessed September 18, 2009).

Hirsch, David H., "The Pit and the Apocalypse," in *Sewanee Review*, Vol. 76, Autumn 1968, p. 648.

Levine, Stuart, "The Perception of Beauty," in *Edgar Poe: Seer and Craftsman*, Everett/Edwards, 1972, pp. 19–25.

Ljungquist, Kent, "Burke's *Enquiry* and the Aesthetics of 'The Pit and the Pendulum,'" in *Poe Studies*, Vol. 11, No. 2, December 1978, pp. 26–29.

Lundquist, James, "The Moral of Averted Descent," in *Poe Newsletter*, Vol. 2, No. 2, April 1969, pp. 25–26.

Malloy, Jeanne M., "Apocalyptic Imagery and the Fragmentation of the Psyche: 'The Pit and the Pendulum,'" in *Nineteenth-Century Literature*, Vol. 46, June 1991, pp. 82–95.

Peeples, Scott, "Double Vision and Single Effect: 1839–1944," in *Edgar Allan Poe Revisited*, edited by Nancy A. Walker, Twayne Publishers, 1998, pp. 74–105.

Poe, Edgar Allan, "The Philosophy of Composition," in *The Oxford Book of American Essays*, edited by Brander Matthews, Oxford University Press, 1914, http://www.bartleby.com/109/11.html (accessed September 18, 2009).

———, "The Pit and the Pendulum," in *Tales of Mystery and Imagination*, Portland House Illustrated Classics, 1987, pp. 84–96.

Sova, Dawn B., "The Pit and the Pendulum," in *Edgar Allan Poe A to Z: The Essential Reference to His Life and Work*, Checkmark Books, 2001, pp. 188–90.

Thompson, G. R., *Poe's Fiction: Romantic Irony in the Gothic Tales*, University of Wisconsin Press, 1973, p. 171.

FURTHER READING

Ellis, Markman, *The History of Gothic Fiction*, Edinburgh University Press, 2001.

Markman traces the rise of the gothic novel from Horace Walpole's *Castle of Otranto* to Mary Shelley's *Frankenstein* and Bram Stoker's *Dracula*. He also discusses Matthew Gregory Lewis's 1796 work *The Monk*, considered the first gothic novel, which concerns a priest who is killed at the hands of the Inquisition.

Kamen, Henry, *The Spanish Inquisition: A Historical Revision*, Yale University Press, 1997.

Kamen traces the persecution of various groups during the Inquisition. He feels that much of the rhetoric regarding the horrors of the Inquisition was due to anti-Catholic propaganda and presents a more moderate view of the Inquisition than that of earlier historians.

Kennedy, J. Gerald, ed., *A Historical Guide to Edgar Allan Poe*, Oxford University Press, 2001.

This collection of scholarly essays considers Poe's place in American letters, particularly his penchant for sensationalism, which diverged from the prevailing literary attitude of the day.

Poe, Edgar Allan, *The Portable Edgar Allan Poe*, edited by J. Gerald Kennedy. Penguin Classics, 2006.

This anthology groups Poe's stories and poems thematically. It also includes a generous sampling of his letters, essays, and literary criticism.

Morgan, Jack, *The Biology of Horror: Gothic Literature and Film*, Southern Illinois University Press, 2002.

This scholarly analysis of the concept of horror includes many mentions of Poe, as well as chapters on anxiety in literature, the properties of terror, the gothic hero, and the role of the soul in gothic fiction.

Strychacz, Thomas, "A Note on Willa Cather's Use of Edgar Allan Poe's 'The Pit and the Pendulum,' in *The Professor's House*," in *Modern Fiction Studies*, Vol. 36, No. 1, Spring 1990, pp. 57–60.

Strychacz examines Cather's allusions to Poe's works in her writings, especially the gothic details and the similarity between the characters of Cather's novel and Poe's story.

A Problem

ANTON CHEKHOV
C. 1888

Anton Chekhov's short story "A Problem" is one of his lesser-known works. In a mere ten and a half pages, it tackles such important issues as honor, justice, and the nature of personal responsibility. Questions of youth and free will are also raised over the course of the story. In this sense, "A Problem" is easily comparable to Chekhov's more famous short stories. Aside from its weighty topics, "A Problem" presents an interesting portrait of the men of the Uskov family and the family's overall dynamics. Chekhov also introduces a fascinating character study. The main character, Sasha Uskov, is a young man facing trial due to his bad debts. He awaits his fate as his three uncles decide whether or not to pay off the debt or allow their nephew to face the consequences. The uncles' debates rage on as Sasha eavesdrops in the hall. The young man remains remarkably unaffected by the circumstances, a stark contrast to his distraught family members.

Although the exact publication date of "A Problem" is not known, it was most likely written around 1888, when the bulk of Chekhov's earlier short stories were composed. The story first appeared in English in 1917 in *The Party and Other Stories*. A 2006 BiblioBazaar edition of the volume is also available.

Anton Chekov (International Portrait Gallery / Library of Congress)

AUTHOR BIOGRAPHY

Chekhov was born January 17, 1860, in Taganrog, Russia. He was the third of six children. Chekhov's father, Pavel Egorovich Chekhov, owned a grocery store that went bankrupt when Chekhov was a teenager. Afterward, the family relocated to Moscow, but Chekhov remained behind to complete his studies, finally rejoining his family in 1879. By then, Chekhov's father was working as a laborer, and his mother, Evgeniia Iakovlevna Morozova, was working as a seamstress. That same year, Chekhov began attending the University of Moscow. He graduated five years later with a medical degree and became a doctor. Also in 1884, Chekhov began showing symptoms of the tuberculosis that would eventually kill him.

While Chekhov was a student, he began writing humorous essays and stories to contribute to the family's income. Many such works were published in periodicals under the pseudonym Antosha Chekhonte. Chekhov's first collection of these stories, *Skazki Mel'pomeny* (*The Tales of Melpomene*), was self-published under this pseudonym in 1884. His first collection of a more literary nature, *Pestrye rasskazy* (*Motley Stories*) was published two years later under Chekhov's actual name. The collection was a critical and popular success. Thus, Chekhov's medical career was soon eclipsed by his writing. He was elected to the prominent Literary Fund in 1886 and published his second collection of stories *V sumerkakh* (*In the Twilight*) in 1887. Also in 1887, Chekhov's first play, *Ivanov*, was produced.

The late 1880s were the beginning of Chekhov's prolific output as a playwright and short story writer. His well-known short stories from the time, all later translated into English, include "The Lights," "The Name-Day Party," "The Steppe," and "An Attack of Nerves." All were published in Russian in 1888, the same year Chekhov won the prestigious Pushkin Prize. And although the original publication date of "A Problem" is unknown, it likely appeared at this time. The story was first translated in English in 1917 in *The Party and Other Stories*. In 1890, Chekhov traveled to Sakhalin Island, a penal colony in Siberia. His time there would eventually inspire a series of Sakhalin-based stories. Chekhov also briefly traveled throughout Europe, ultimately settling outside Moscow in 1892, where he purchased a large estate. His siblings settled there with him, and a host of literary and artistic friends visited often. In addition, Chekhov continued to work as a doctor in the surrounding villages.

Also in 1892, Chekhov published one of his best-known short stories, later translated into English as "Ward No. 6." In 1894, Chekhov traveled to Yalta, a warm resort town. The climate soothed his tuberculosis, but Chekhov returned to his estate not long after. In the 1890s, Chekhov's output began to slow; yet, some of his most famous short stories (all later translated into English) were written at this time. These include: "My Life" (1896), "The Lady with the Dog" (1898), and "The Gooseberry" (1898).

Chekhov met the actress Olga Knipper in 1898 and married her in 1901. The couple had no children, though they did have a happy marriage. In 1903, he became editor of the literary section of *Russkaya mysl*. In addition, he spent the late 1890s devoting more time to writing plays. One of his more famous plays, *Chayka*, was produced in 1896. It was later translated as *The Sea Gull* in 1913. His other best-known plays from the time, all later translated into English, include *Uncle Vanya* (1899), *The Cherry Orchard*

(1900), and *Three Sisters* (1901). Chekhov's health continued to deteriorate. In June 1904, he traveled to Badenweiler, Germany, in the hopes of recovering his strength. He died there not long after, on July 2, 1904. His body was interred in Moscow.

Aside from his short stories and plays, Chekhov was a prolific letter writer, and numerous volumes of his correspondence have also been published. He believed in contributing to the community, which is why he continued to practice medicine and educate villagers about basic hygiene and disease prevention throughout his life. In addition, he founded two rural schools. Chekhov's rise to landownership was also remarkable; he was, after all, the grandson of a serf (indentured farmer).

PLOT SUMMARY

In Chekhov's "A Problem," the Uskov family has a secret. As they discuss it, they send their servants away lest they overhear. Half are exiled to the kitchen and the other half are sent away, either to attend the theater or visit the circus. The servants that remain in the house are instructed not to allow any visitors. Some of the family members and servants know the secret, though they pretend not to. Namely, the Colonel's wife, her sister, and the family nanny know what is happening, but they sit silently in the dining room. They avoid the study, where the family meeting is being held.

Twenty-five-year-old Sasha Uskov, "who was the cause of all the commotion," is already waiting in the hall. His maternal uncle, Ivan Markovitch, has instructed him to act contrite and explain himself. Sasha intends to do as he has been told. Ivan will also be present during the impending discussion.

In the study, the family is meeting while Sasha waits. "The subject under discussion was an exceedingly disagreeable and delicate one." Sasha is guilty of having forged a promissory note (similar to forging and then bouncing a check). The promissory note is now past due, which is why Sasha's crime has come to light. Sasha's uncles are debating what to do. They can pay the debt and restore the family's honor, or they can allow Sasha to go to trial and face his crime.

Although the uncles have been discussing these options for a while, they remain undecided. The Colonel, one of Sasha's paternal uncles, speaks nonsensically, and the other uncles say they understand. The Colonel then continues, albeit a little more cogently than before. He argues that by protecting Sasha from the consequences of his actions, they are still doing harm to the family's honor. He uses the army as an example, noting that it retains its honor precisely because it holds its members accountable for any infractions.

Another paternal uncle, who works for the treasury, is mostly quiet. However, he does remark that the family's name will appear in the newspaper if the case goes to trial. Because of this, he is in favor of paying off the debt. Ivan is also in favor of this. He speaks more eloquently than the other men. He talks with compassion of the folly of youth. He indicates that everyone, especially the young, makes mistakes. Even geniuses make mistakes, he says, particularly writers. Ivan also says that Sasha is uneducated and was orphaned at a young age. Sasha was not raised well (through no fault of his own) and some consideration should be granted him because of this. He also says that Sasha's remorseful conscience is punishment enough.

Ivan additionally goes on to argue that it is their Christian duty to show mercy. As Sasha's maternal uncle, Ivan admits that he is not a Uskov, but he still respects the family name. He knows that its history stretches back to the thirteenth century. Ivan says he would hate to see the family name besmirched over a mere fifteen hundred rubles (the equivalent of roughly forty-seven dollars; an amount that would have the purchasing power of approximately one thousand dollars in 2008). Next, he employs philosophy to argue that free will does not exist, therefore implying that Sasha cannot be held responsible for his actions since he does not have free will.

The Colonel remarks that Ivan's dithering has gotten them no closer to a decision. Meanwhile, Sasha sits at the door impassively. He is not afraid of his fate or ashamed of his actions (as Ivan earlier implied). He does not care what happens to him, whether he goes to prison or not. "He was sick of life and found it insufferably hard." This is because he has no money, is drowning in debt, and hates his family. His friends and his girlfriends despise him for constantly mooching from them. The only thing about the current situation that upsets him is overhearing the Colonel call him a criminal.

Sasha believes that criminals are murderers and thieves, people without morals. He is only in debt, which is fairly normal. Even Ivan and the Colonel, the very men deciding his fate, have debt. The only wrong Sasha has committed is forging the promissory note. And even that is relatively common. Sasha's friends, Handrikov and Von Burst, do it all the time. The only difference is that they have managed to pay off the forged notes before they were past due. Even this mistake was not his fault; Handrikov promised to lend him the money before the deadline but then failed to do so.

Sasha admits to himself that it was wrong to forge the Colonel's signature, but he meant no harm. Sasha thinks he cannot be a criminal because it is not in his nature to do harm. He even gives money to the poor when he has it to give.

On the other side of the door, the men continue their debate. The Colonel notes that even if they pay the debt, they have no reason to believe that Sasha will change his degenerate ways. In response, the treasury official mumbles and Ivan equivocates. Eventually, Ivan comes out into the hall. He is clearly distressed and tells Sasha to speak to his uncles "humbly and from the heart."

In the study, looking at his uncles, Sasha feels "suddenly ashamed and uncomfortable." He promises to pay the loan back and explains that he was expecting to be able to pay off the note before things came to a crisis. But then he stops talking and sits down. He does not actually apologize, show remorse, or ask for mercy. Sasha wants to leave, but he also wants to stay and hurt the Colonel, whom he hates.

The Colonel's wife is in the doorway. She begs Sasha to ask his uncles for forgiveness. She is crying and his uncles are distraught. Sasha does not see why his family is upset over so paltry a sum.

An hour has passed and Sasha is back in the hallway. The meeting rages on within the study. Finally, it seems that they have decided not to pay the debt. But following that decision, they are all sad. Even the Colonel, who has gotten his way, is dissatisfied. Ivan sighs for his sister, Sasha's dead mother. He says he can feel her unhappy spirit in the room, begging them to help her son. Ivan is sobbing, and the uncles resume their debate.

It is now past two in the morning, and the meeting is finally over. The Colonel leaves the study via the vestibule to avoid his nephew in the hall. Ivan comes into the hall. He looks ill at ease but happy. Ivan tells Sasha that he can go home and go to sleep. The uncles have decided to pay the debt provided Sasha changes his ways. In fact, Sasha must go to work with Ivan in the country the very next day.

On their way out of the house, Ivan is giving Sasha advice, but Sasha is not listening. He is only relieved that he has escaped punishment. "A gust of joy sprang up within him.... He longed to breathe, to move swiftly, to live!" (This reaction is in stark contrast to Sasha's earlier indifference as to his fate.) Sasha remembers that Von Burst will be at a certain bar tonight, so Sasha decides to join him. Then he remembers that he has no money and that his friends no longer pay his way. He asks Ivan to lend him one hundred rubles.

Ivan is shocked by Sasha's audacity. Clearly desperate, Sasha threatens to turn himself in for the forged note if his uncle does not give him the money. Ivan is horrified, but he gives his nephew the money. Sasha walks away satisfied. He thinks of the liquor and women that await him at the bar. He thinks of the "rights of youth" that Ivan spoke of earlier, and of how he has just exercised his. Yet, Sasha also understands the immorality of his actions. He thinks, "Now I see that I am a criminal; yes, I am a criminal."

CHARACTERS

Colonel

The Colonel is one of Sasha's two paternal uncles. He is a bombastic, haughty, and self-righteous man. When he is first introduced in the story, he speaks loftily but largely nonsensically. His blithering is underscored by the fact that the other uncles profess to understand him. When the Colonel finally begins to make sense, he makes it clear that he is in favor of Sasha facing the consequences of his actions. Though he understands that the honor of the family name is at stake, he implies that the name can have no honor if they allow criminals to go unpunished. The argument is indeed apt, and it is telling that the Colonel uses the army to drive home this point.

The Colonel is unpopular and is portrayed unsympathetically. His voice is twice described as "metallic." He is the only uncle who wishes to see Sasha punished, and as events later show, he is the only uncle who is right. Sasha's demands for money after being given a reprieve prove that, without consequences, he will not change the error of his ways. Still, despite the Colonel's lofty arguments, it is notable that his name was the one forged on the promissory note. This could indicate the Colonel's desire for personal vengeance. This motivation may be hinted at by the Colonel's avoidance of Sasha on his way out of the meeting.

Colonel's Wife

The Colonel's wife knows of Sasha's crime, though she initially pretends not to. She sits in the dining room with her sister and the family nanny as all three keep up a pretense of ignorance. But as the hours pass, she finally grows distraught enough to approach her nephew. She is crying and begging Sasha to lay himself at his uncles' feet and entreat them for mercy. Her displays only cause Sasha to marvel at the upset he has caused. He cannot understand how his relatives can get so worked up over so small a sum.

Handrikov

Handrikov is one of Sasha's so-called friends. He does not actually appear in the narrative, but he is referred to several times by Sasha. Sasha uses Handrikov's bad behavior—being in debt, forging promissory notes—as justification for his own wrongdoing. Indeed, Sasha feels that his current situation is Handrikov's fault. It was he who promised to give Sasha the money to pay off the note before it was due, and it was he who failed to deliver on that promise. Handrikov, however, is hardly Sasha's friend. He abandons his friend in his time of need, and he also despises Sasha because the young man has no money.

Ivan Markovitch

Ivan Markovitch is Sasha's maternal uncle. He is the most eloquent and well-spoken of the three uncles. For instance, he employs philosophical arguments in support of his opinion, cites Sasha's youth, and also discusses Sasha's pitiable upbringing as an uneducated orphan. Ivan employs every argument he can think of in support of his belief that Sasha should be granted clemency. In fact, he even goes so far as to suggest that it is their Christian duty to do so. Following this, he imagines that the spirit of Sasha's dead mother is in the room begging them to help her son. Ivan's loyalty to his nephew may well be connected to his grief for his dead sister.

Ivan clearly cares for and loves his nephew. He is the only uncle who speaks directly to Sasha and advises him on how to behave. He even plans to take Sasha under his wing and take him to work with him in the country. This decision presents Sasha with an opportunity to improve himself. Ivan's efforts are all the more poignant when his nephew cruelly disillusions him at the story's end. Ivan is clearly horrified by Sasha's actions; he sputters incoherently and backs away from his nephew in shock.

Servants

The servants are not important to the overall story, but their presence, or rather their absence, is notable. They represent public opinion, gossip, and the Uskov's family fear of these things. Their dismissal and exile in the kitchen at the beginning of the story set the tone for the action that follows.

Treasury Official

The treasury official is one of Sasha's two paternal uncles. He is in favor of paying off Sasha's debt, but only because he is concerned about seeing the family name appear in a negative light in the newspaper. In fact, this is the only argument that the treasury official sets forth. He says little else and is only further described as mumbling. He is also the only uncle without any debt, and this may be due to his profession (or vice versa). In addition, it is likely that the house in which the meeting is being held belongs to him. The only indication of this is that the other uncles are described leaving, while the treasury official is not.

Sasha Uskov

Sasha Uskov is the story's main character, a twenty-five-year-old man who finds himself facing criminal charges after forging a promissory note. He is unremorseful and unrepentant. In fact, he cannot even bring himself to pretend as much when called upon to explain himself to his uncles. Sasha does not see the error of his ways, nor does he feel that he has committed a wrong. The only mistake he has made, as far as he is concerned, is failing to pay the forged note on time. Further justifications that Sasha sets forth are that his friends forge notes all the time; his friends are all in debt, as are two of his uncles.

Sasha is remarkably stoic throughout most of the story. He is not interested in begging for forgiveness, nor does he care whether or not he goes to jail. To him, his future is bleak since he has no money, is drowning in debt, and has been abandoned by his friends. Sasha's lack of concern demonstrates that he feels that as long as he cannot go to bars with his friends, then he might as well be in jail. The only time he gets upset is at overhearing the Colonel call him a criminal. Sasha does not feel that his actions align him with the likes of thieves and murderers, and he offers numerous self-justifications to this extent. He even gives money to the poor, an act that is somehow meant to prove his moral standing. Yet, while Sasha believes that he did not intend to cause any harm by forging the Colonel's name on the promissory note, it is telling that he later wishes to hurt the Colonel for passing judgment on him. Sasha openly despises the man.

Given that Sasha does not feel he has committed a crime, he cannot understand how his relatives can get so worked up over so small a sum. What he does not understand is that they are upset at the criminality of his actions, a fact that Sasha refuses to recognize. They are also upset at the thought of Sasha going to prison. Sasha's relatives consistently demonstrate that they are more concerned about his well-being than he is.

Sasha remains passionless and emotionless until he learns that his debt will be paid. Only then does he feel "a gust of joy." This feeling seems incongruous when compared with Sasha's earlier stoicism. Sasha gives little thought to his uncle's insistence that he go to work the next day and thinks instead only of partying. Thus, he demands money of his uncle Ivan. He does so despite his uncle's protests and refusals. Sasha even resorts to threats to get the money. Afterward, filled with renewed hope at the thought of the alcohol and women that await him, Sasha finally understands that he is indeed a degenerate and a criminal.

Von Burst

Von Burst is one of Sasha's so-called friends. He does not actually appear in the narrative, but he is referred to several times by Sasha. Sasha uses Von Burst's bad behavior—being in debt, forging promissory notes—as justification for his own malfeasance. Von Burst is hardly Sasha's friend. He abandons his friend in his time of need, and he also despises Sasha because the young man has no money. Nevertheless, this does not stop Sasha from wishing to join Von Burst at the bar at the end of the story.

THEMES

Crime

The question of whether or not Sasha is a criminal takes up a great deal of the narrative of "A Problem." It is clear that the Colonel sees Sasha as such. Aside from the fact that the Colonel's name was the one forged on the promissory note, it is the Colonel who argues forcefully for allowing Sasha's case to go to trial. The Colonel also avoids having any contact with Sasha on his way out of the study. All of Sasha's family members are distraught and concerned by Sasha's criminal actions. Yet Sasha remains unmoved. His friends do the same thing often, and even his uncles are in debt. The only time Sasha shows any emotion is at the idea that his uncle would call him a criminal for doing the same thing his friends do. Sasha refuses to think of himself in such terms. He is not a murderer or a thief, nor did he intend to do anyone any harm. He even gives money to the poor when he can afford to. Thus, how can he be a criminal?

Still, the only thing that Sasha cares about (aside from being called a criminal) is partying with his friends and girlfriends. He is not interested in making an honest living, even when that opportunity is handed to him. These latter circumstances signal the beginning of Sasha's admission that he is a criminal. He is joyful at having escaped the consequences of his actions. But rather than consider how he can avoid making the same mistakes, he immediately thinks of his friend at the bar and his need for money in order to join in the festivities. Sasha then demands money of his uncle, and he continues to do so despite his uncle's protestations. In fact, he succeeds by threatening to turn himself in over the forged promissory note, which would undermine all that Ivan has done for him. It is this act that finally allows Sasha to acknowledge, "Now I see that I am a criminal; yes, I am a criminal."

Honor

Another significant theme in "A Problem" is the question of honor and what it means. It is concern over family honor that exiles the servants to the kitchen or to the theater or circus. The family does not wish its underlings to know the family secret, nor do they want them to gossip about it. In this sense, family honor is maintained via keeping the failures of its members from coming to light. Additionally, honor is ostensibly what

TOPICS FOR FURTHER STUDY

- What do you think is the most important theme in "A Problem?" Write an essay addressing this question and be sure to cite examples from the text to illustrate your choice.
- Use the Internet to research Russia in the late nineteenth century. Be sure to focus your research on politics, history, religion, and culture. Present your findings to the class in a PowerPoint presentation.
- "A Problem" largely revolves around Sasha's chronic debt. How does debt affect people today? Conduct interviews with your relatives and gather their thoughts on debt, both good and bad. Research the opinions of several financial experts on debt. Compile the results into an audio-visual presentation.
- In the story, Ivan implies that Sasha's poor decisions are a result of his being orphaned. Jeff Lemire's *Essex County Volume 1: Tales from the Farm* (2007) is a graphic novel about an orphaned boy, Lester, and the way in which he copes with his loss. (The book has been honored by the American Library Association with an Alex Award for young adults.) In an essay, compare Sasha and Lester's characters.

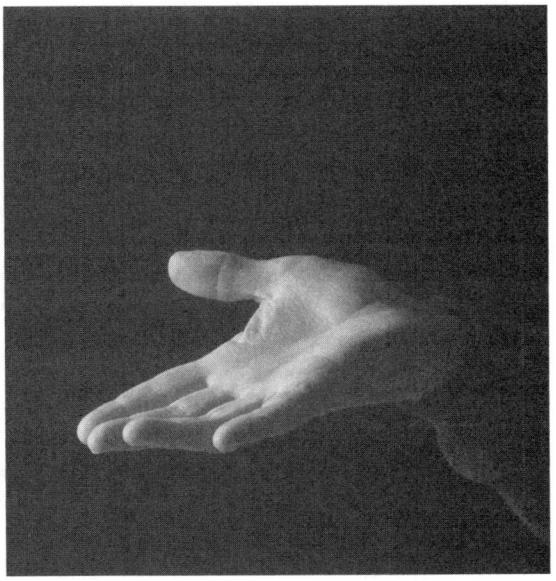

A hand out is a plea for help. (Image copyright John Keith, 2009. Used under license from Shutterstock.com)

brings the uncles together to decide how to proceed. Certainly, that is at the crux of their debate. The uncles do not discuss the morality of Sasha's actions, nor do they concern themselves with his potential prison sentence. Although Ivan speaks of other issues in pursuit of his argument, even he makes mention of the family name and its illustrious history. Yet the other uncles are concerned only with honor. The single intelligible remark that the treasury official makes is to acknowledge that he would hate to see the family's name in the newspaper, especially connected to such a scandal. The bulk of the Colonel's argument is that honor is not about hushing up scandals and forgiving infractions. Instead, honor is about rooting out infractions and ensuring that justice is done. Indeed, he maintains that the army remains an honorable institution precisely because it holds its members accountable for their actions. The Colonel sees no reason why the Uskov family should not uphold the same policy.

Despite the fact that the Colonel is in the minority in his views regarding honor and regarding Sasha's punishment, he persuades both Ivan and the treasury official to agree with him. But as soon as they do so, all three uncles become dejected. Also of note, the concept of honor never occurs to Sasha. It is feasible that his concern at being called a criminal stems from his sense of honor. It is still more likely that it comes from his sense of pride, but given the way in which honor is treated in the story, the two are inextricably intertwined. On the other hand, there is something joyful about Sasha's realization that he is, in fact, a criminal. Perhaps this epiphany, or sudden realization, forever frees him from the obligation of maintaining honor, or even its pretense.

STYLE

Antihero

Sasha is the main character and protagonist of "A Problem." The story is largely told as if he is eavesdropping on the meeting being held on his behalf. Much of the narrative is also concerned with his thoughts on the matter. But Sasha is not the story's hero (that distinction is reserved for Ivan). As a man who is unashamedly drowning in debt and unrepentantly forging promissory notes, he is no hero. He is, in fact, an antihero, a literary figure whose values and or actions are antithetical to heroism. It would be possible for Sasha to be considered a hero were he to change his ways or undergo an epiphany that led to his repentance. Yet, this does not occur. In fact, the exact opposite takes place, as Sasha degenerates further into his bad habits. Over the course of the story, Sasha moves from believing himself to be a law-abiding person to understanding himself to be a criminal. Where a hero's burgeoning understanding of this fact would lead him to take actions to correct this, Sasha only continues. In fact, something in his tone when he embraces his criminality indicates a celebratory note.

Third-Person Limited Point of View

"A Problem" is told from a third-person limited point of view. This point of view is characterized by an unidentified (often objective) narrator who is privy only to the inner thoughts and emotions of one character. The remaining characters in the story can only be referred to on an external level, based on what they are saying or doing. The reader is thus able to scrutinize the thoughts and feelings of Sasha alone. This is appropriate given that he is the protagonist and also the only character who changes over the course of the story. For instance, a great deal of the narrative is devoted to Sasha's thoughts regarding the nature of his infraction and his criminality. Furthermore, given that the uncles can only be understood through their actions, their significance in the story becomes somewhat eclipsed. This is also underscored by the fact that two of Sasha's three uncles are not named; instead, they are referred to only by their professional posts.

HISTORICAL CONTEXT

Reform and Upheaval in Nineteenth-Century Russia

Chekhov was writing during a period of great social, cultural, and political upheaval. The uncertainty of the times can be felt in much of his work, as his characters often struggle to find their place in a social order that they no longer understand. This period of flux began when Tsar Alexander II succeeded Nicholas I in 1855 and immediately began instituting governmental, educational, and economic reforms. The most notable of these was his emancipation of twenty million serfs in 1861. Reforms pertaining to local governments largely took place in 1864, when Russia was divided into districts. Six years later, the formation of elected city councils was established. However, both new organizations isolated their constituents by raising taxes. Judicial reforms were also enacted in 1864, and judicial systems in major cities were modeled after Western courts. Censorship also became more lenient, but after a failed assassination attempt on the tsar in 1866, censorship was again increased. Alexander II additionally oversaw military reforms throughout the 1870s.

Revolutionaries dissatisfied with these sweeping changes finally succeeded in assassinating Alexander II in 1881. He was replaced by his son, Alexander III. The new tsar sought to undo much that his father had done, and he founded a branch of governmental police known as the *Okhrana*. The power of the districts and city councils was greatly reduced as well. Religious censorship was also instituted. Anti-Semitism was encouraged while non-Russian peoples and those worshiping outside the Orthodox Church were all subject to persecution. State universities were subject to increasing restrictions. In the meantime, Russia was falling behind as the rest of Europe pushed into the modern age.

The Age of Realism

Given the political, cultural, and social upheaval in Russia during the nineteenth century, the literature of the day was understandably preoccupied with political and social issues. Because direct political commentary was censored by the government, social critique was largely relegated to the realm of fiction, where it could be discussed indirectly. Realism was a hallmark of this approach, and Russian writers began to increasingly detail the cruder aspects of life in Russia. In addition, literary forms such as the short story and the novel, which had grown increasingly popular in western Europe, began to grow in popularity in Russia as well.

These circumstances all converged to give rise to the Age of Realism, a movement that reached its peak in the 1850s but remained

COMPARE & CONTRAST

- **1880s:** Russia remains a largely rural and agricultural country. While the rest of Europe becomes industrialized at a rapid pace, the rate of industrialization in Russia remains comparatively stagnant. These circumstances leave Russia's economy in a perilous state.

   Today: Following the collapse of the Soviet Union in the 1990s, Russia experiences an economic breakdown far more severe than the Great Depression. However, Russia has begun to recover as it increases its industrial base and moves toward a market economy. An influx of capital investments in the 2000s have also greatly improved the country's growth. However, the global economic downturn in 2008 negatively affects Russia, proving that the country's economic stability remains in flux.

- **1880s:** Russia is in a state of social flux, as roughly 20 million serfs are emancipated by Tsar Alexander II in 1861. This change in the basic social structure of the country plants the seed for a growing middle class and precipitates a loss of power for landholders and the upper class. Many of Chekhov's stories address these changes, and Sasha's insistence on acting more affluent than he is likely derives from a sense of privilege that no longer holds with reality.

   Today: From 2000 to 2006, the middle class grows from 8 million people to 55 million people. Russia also has the world's second largest population of billionaires (following the United States).

- **1880s:** Revolutionaries assassinate Tsar Alexander II in 1881. He is replaced by his son, Alexander III, who rules until 1894. During his reign, Alexander III sets out to undo much of the reform that his father accomplished during the 1860s.

   Today: Russia is now run under a federated government, under a constitution adopted in 1993. In 2000, Vladimir Putin succeeds Boris Yeltsin as president, and he holds the post until 2007. Putin then retains his power by becoming prime minister in 2008.

---

popular into the twentieth century. Early nineteenth-century writers credited with fathering the movement include Alexander Pushkin, Mikhail Lermontov, Vissarion Belinsky, and Nikolai Gogol. The best-known writers of the Age of Realism are Ivan Turgenev, Leo Tolstoy, and Fyodor Dostoyevsky. All three writers have enjoyed continued international fame. Somewhat lesser-known writers of the movement include Nikolai Leskov, Alexander Ostrovsky, and Ivan Goncharov. Without exception, all of these writers' works focus on social critique. Though Chekhov was writing roughly twenty years after these predecessors, his work is nevertheless affiliated with the Age of Realism. Yet, while Chekhov was a realist, his work focuses less on social critique and more on the failures of the individual within society. Like Turgenev, Tolstoy, and Dostoyevsky, Chekhov is considered one of the greatest writers of the nineteenth century.

CRITICAL OVERVIEW

Because "A Problem" is one of Chekhov's more obscure stories, little criticism specific to it remains in print. However, Chekhov's short fiction in general is widely reviewed, and much is directly applicable to the story at hand. For instance, *Writer* contributor Bob Blaisdell notes that

> Chekhov showed... that short fiction could be about characters rather than events, and that stories did not need trick endings. An author

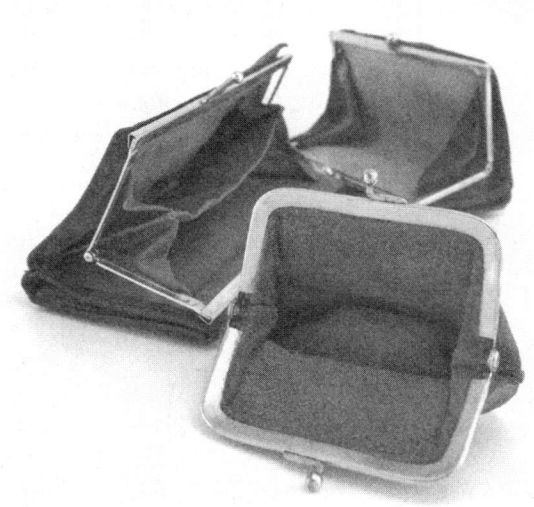

Empty purses indicate debt. (Image copyright Emelyanov, 2009. Used under license from Shutterstock.com)

did not have to be a puppet master or judge and jury; instead, the narrator was, in Chekhov's view, an observer, quiet and deliberately objective, usually with an unstated but sympathetic moral point of view.

Indeed, the bulk of the narrative of "A Problem" is a character study, one that allows Sasha's actions and thoughts to speak for themselves. At no point in the story does the narrator judge the protagonist.

In his *Neophilologus* article, David W. Martin argues that Chekhov is one of the fathers of the modern short story. He finds that a hallmark of contemporary short fiction is that it "describes inner experience, not superficial activities or the logical sequence of events for their own sake." Certainly, this statement applies to the entirety of "A Problem," which is predominantly concerned with Sasha's reflections on the question of his own criminality. Martin is not alone in his assessment. *Studies in Short Fiction* critic Brian Murray declares that Chekhov is "the writer who has most influenced the nature of contemporary American short fiction." Murray then goes on to note,

> At his best Chekhov shows unusual subtlety and sophistication; his fiction is informed not only by his remarkable wide experience in the world, and by a wide variety of human types, but by a degree of empathy that is quite rare in its constancy and intensity.

Offering more praise, Murray continues, "Chekhov was—or at least appeared to be—among the least self-absorbed of writers, and thus his prolific body of work is exceptionally rich and diverse."

CRITICISM

Leah Tieger

Tieger is a freelance writer and editor. In the following essay on Chekhov's "A Problem," she argues that the protagonist, Sasha Uskov, embodies the definition of a sociopath.

Chekhov's "A Problem" is an intensely intimate and detailed character study that also addresses themes of honor and crime. The story obliquely explores justice and the nature of the criminal mind. The story's protagonist, the antihero Sasha Uskov, is certainly a criminal, albeit one who, for the bulk of the story, successfully attempts to convince himself that he is not. Despite this, Sasha exhibits all of the tendencies of a sociopath, an individual suffering from an antisocial personality disorder. There are numerous hallmark traits that define a sociopath, all of which apply to Sasha's character. The first of these is that they do not learn from their experiences and that there is no change in their behavior following a punishment. This can be seen in the story when Sasha continues to amass debt despite being unable to pay the debt he has already accrued. He is determined to "borrow" money from Ivan even after spending hours waiting for his uncles to decide whether he should face punishment for forging the promissory note.

Sociopaths also lack any feelings of responsibility and are absent any moral sensibility. Certainly, Sasha's belief that he has not done anything wrong speaks to both of these traits. Sasha feels that he has committed a victimless offense, that he did not intend anyone any harm, and that what he has done cannot be all that bad since his friends do the very same thing fairly often. These traits directly feed into yet another

WHAT DO I READ NEXT?

- *Crime and Punishment*, by Fyodor Dostoyevsky, was first published in Russian in 1866 and translated into English in 1886. This novel, written at the height of the Age of Realism, remains a classic work of literature today. Furthermore, when compared to "A Problem," the book features many thematic parallels.

- The revised and updated 2004 edition of *Inside the Criminal Mind*, by clinical psychologist Stanton Samenow, presents readers with a nonfiction exploration into criminals and criminality. This classic psychological work debunks myths surrounding the causes and motivations criminal behavior and also discusses effective methods for stopping it.

- *The Cherry Orchard*, one of the last plays Chekhov wrote before his death, was produced in Russian in 1900 and translated into English in 1908. It portrays the downfall of the Ranevskaya family. Drowning in debt, the once wealthy family must sell their estate, including their famous cherry orchard. The orchard will be demolished and the land turned into a housing development. This play is a comment not only on the dying upper class but also on the pitfalls of progress. Grove Press published a paperback edition in 2009.

- Another classic work of Russian literature from the age of realism is Leo Tolstoy's 1875 novel *Anna Karenina*. The book is a powerful examination of the follies of passion, and it follows its eponymous heroine as she carries on an affair and destroys her marriage. Anna's actions also alienate her from her son and her friends.

- For a comprehensive history of Russia from ancient to contemporary times, read *Russia: The Once and Future Empire From Pre-History to Putin* (2006), by Philip Longworth. Aside from a political history, Longworth presents an exploration of Russia's varying climates and terrains. He also describes the expansions and contractions of the Russian empire over several millennia.

- For a young-adult book that explores political uncertainty and issues of class (themes that regularly appear in Chekhov's works), read Ying Chang Compestine's 2007 novel *Revolution Is Not a Dinner Party*. The story is set during China's Cultural Revolution of the 1960s, and it follows Ling and her family as the upheaval forever upsets their lives and demolishes their middle-class lifestyle. The volume was listed as a 2008 Best Book for Young Adults by the American Library Association.

---

aspect of a sociopathic tendency—a distinct lack of guilt. Indeed, if Sasha believes that he is not in the wrong, then how can he even begin to experience guilt? Even more remarkable is Sasha's continued lack of guilt when he finally acknowledges his criminality. At the end of the story, Sasha understands the immorality of his recent actions (bullying Ivan into giving him money), and thus he acknowledges that he is a criminal. But he still shows no traces of guilt. In fact, he experiences quite the opposite—a feeling of exhilaration and exuberance.

Sasha is also typical of a sociopath in that he is unable to form any meaningful human relationships. This trait is shown in several ways throughout the story. One example of this is the absence of character names. For example, the only character aside from Sasha to be named in full is Ivan. But the fact that Sasha is easily able to turn on him shows Sasha's contempt for the relationship. Additionally, while Sasha's friends are given names, they are referred to only by their surname, textually indicating that they are not seen as fully realized individuals. Still, they are afforded more importance than the rest of Sasha's relatives, who barely even register as real people to him. His uncles are merely the Colonel and the treasury official. The Colonel's wife is exactly that, nothing more. Sasha's brief interaction with the Colonel's wife also illustrates another common behavior of the sociopath, that of emotional immaturity. The Colonel's wife is clearly upset, crying and fidgeting with her hands as she implores her nephew to beg for forgiveness. Sasha does not respond to her; he only sits impassively and wonders why everyone around him is so distraught. Sasha's lack of emotional maturity is also felt when he is called upon to explain himself to his uncles. Despite being instructed by Ivan to be apologetic and ask for clemency, Sasha merely explains that he will repay them. While it is clear that he feels no remorse, he cannot even bring himself to pretend to feel it.

Because Sasha's main pursuit in life is partying and gambling with his friends and girlfriends, one could argue that Sasha does not exhibit chronically antisocial behavior (another hallmark of the sociopath). Nevertheless, Sasha still thinks of his friends and girlfriends in terms of the pleasure they provide him. Again, he does not see them as real people, only as forms of entertainment. The feeling, it seems, is mutual, as all of Sasha's associates do not care for him either. They are tired of his debt and his mooching. Handrikov's failure to lend Sasha money despite his promises has led Sasha to the very situation that incites the beginning of the story. Sasha is only able to (partially) name two friends, neither of whom were friend enough to aid him in his time of need. Additionally, it is highly antisocial to proverbially "bite the hand that feeds you," as Sasha does when he accosts Ivan, his only true ally, at the end of the story. This latter act also indicates Sasha's inability to control his impulses, yet another behavior characteristic of the sociopath. While Sasha experiences joy at the realization that he has escaped punishment, he is unable to stop himself from repeating the behaviors that originally led to his nearly being incarcerated. This is yet another factor in Sasha's final realization that he is indeed a criminal.

Still another mannerism typical of sociopaths is self-centeredness, and this trait seems self-evident in the story's protagonist. Sasha does not see others as real people, only as figures moving about the periphery of his life. When he does not understand their emotions, he does not try to. The bulk of the narrative follows Sasha's thought processes regarding his actions and his feelings about them. He gives no thought to how his actions have affected others. Instead, he only acts incredulous at the evidence of their effect.

> THAT TODAY HE IS REGARDED AS A GREAT ARTIST CHEKHOV WOULD CONSIDER AN AMAZING MISTAKE. HE HAD PRIDE IN HIS WORK BUT MODESTY ABOUT ITS EFFECTS."

Additionally, as Sasha leaves the Uskov home with Ivan, he realizes that Ivan is talking to him, but Sasha does not listen. He is too self-absorbed to do so. Sasha is remarkably unaffected by all that goes on around him. Even the prospect of going to jail does not rattle him. His indifferent despair as his fate is being decided is pervasive, drowning out everything else. Sasha's joy at reprieve is similarly all-encompassing. Certainly, it would seem that, given all of these examples, Sasha is inarguably a sociopath. Perhaps that is the very debate at the heart of "A Problem"; the last line ("Now I see that I am a criminal; yes, I am a criminal.") seems to indicate as much. This is the success of Chekhov's character study. Even more remarkable is the acuity of Chekhov's observations of human nature. Indeed, the term sociopath was not coined until 1930, roughly forty years after this story was written.

Source: Leah Tieger, Critical Essay on "A Problem," in *Short Stories for Students*, Gale, Cengage Learning, 2010.

Bob Blaisdell

In the following article, Chekhov is hailed as the master of the short story form for his unique perspective as an author who opened up new ways for the reader to experience the characters.

In his short, productive life, Anton Chekhov (1860–1904), a mild-mannered, hardworking Russian doctor, managed to influence profoundly the development of two branches of world literature, the short story and drama. The stories that you read today in literary journals and magazines and what you see in many plays are something of what they are because of Chekhov. His nearly 600 short stories demonstrate, in Wallace Stegner's view, that he was "the most extraordinary master of that form in literary history." For writers a century later, Chekhov's fiction remains a model of clear-eyed observation and concise expression, and, as we'll see, his many letters also contain a great deal of writing instruction.

Chekhov showed, in such famous stories as "The Lady with the Dog," "The Darling" and "The Kiss," that short fiction could be about characters rather than events, and that stories did not need trick endings. An author did not have to be a puppet master or judge and jury; instead, the narrator was, in Chekhov's view, an observer, quiet and deliberately objective, usually with an unstated but sympathetic moral point of view.

"Measures, judgments, analyses, are foreign to Chekhov's genius," while "impartial observation is basic to it," Stegner wrote in *Atlantic Brief Lives*. "If fiction is a mirror in the roadway, it may also be a mirror in a hallway or drawing room, and in Chekhov often is. It reflects pompous entrances, treacherous kisses, false friendship, agonized self-examination, ridiculous self-deception—reflections of an extraordinary complexity."

Chekhov believed that how characters see themselves is more important, finally, than how an author sees them, and that we as readers can understand characters more deeply if we don't have an author standing between us and them. If we remember the heavy-handedness of most 19th-century short fiction, Chekhov's attitude, coupled with his fine comic and tragic sensibility, was a revelation.

PRACTICE, PRACTICE

Chekhov's first rule of creative writing was to write—a lot. He advised his older but less disciplined brother Alexander: "To have as few failures as possible in fiction writing, or in order not to be so sensitive to failures, you must write more, around one hundred or two hundred stories a year. That is the secret." And to a young but aspiring writer, he wondered, "But can you really have written only fifteen stories?—at this rate you won't learn to write till you are fifty. Write another twenty stories and send them. I shall always read them with pleasure, and practice is essential for you."

In another letter to Alexander, sent in his mid-20s, Chekhov described as succinctly as possible, as translator Simon Karlinsky pointed out, the makeup of his famous stories: 1) An absence of lengthy verbiage of a political-social-economic nature; 2) total objectivity; 3) truthful descriptions of persons and objects; 4) extreme brevity; 5) audacity and originality, avoiding stereotype; 6) compassion.

A related principle for Chekhov was avoiding or curbing egotism. While Alexander managed to publish many stories himself, he embodied the sloth, self-pity and moral lassitude that Anton had determinedly purged himself of. Anton cautioned Alexander about egotism, about intruding and coloring a fictional world with one's own cynical or sentimental views, or what Chekhov calls here and elsewhere simply "subjectivity":

> But even in your writing you lay too much stress upon trivial things. And you were not born a subjective writer.... That kind of writing is not inborn in one; it is acquired.... It is as easy to give up that self-acquired subjectivity as to drink a glass of water. One needs only to be a bit more honest; to throw oneself absolutely overboard, not to push oneself as the hero of one's novel, to deny oneself for even half an hour. There is a story of yours where a young couple sit kissing each other all through dinner, sitting and cooing and talking rubbish. There's not a single sensible word, but thorough sentimentality [or complacency]. And you were not writing for the reader. You wrote because that chatter pleased you. Why don't you describe the dinner—how they ate, what they ate, what the cook was like, how vulgar your hero was, how satisfied with his lazy contentment, how vulgar your heroine, how ridiculous her love for that smug, napkinned, overfed gander? Everyone likes to see well-fed, happy people—that's true. But if you are going to write about them it's not enough to tell what they said and the number of times they kissed. A something else is needed. You must deny yourself the personal impression that honeymoon happiness produces on all embittered persons. Subjectivity is an awful thing—even for the reason that it betrays the poor writer hand over fist.... If only you would give up that subjectivity you would become a most useful writer.

MORAL WRITING

Chekhov was always specific in his criticisms, and they show that his few and rarely stated literary principles were primarily moralistic, holding that a writer's detached, sympathetic observation brought more moral understanding than subjective evaluation. I believe that in regard to his brother (how tactful are siblings, after all?), Chekhov was attempting to apply the same forceful artistic discipline he used on himself. When scolding Alexander's laziness and artistic indifference in 1886, Chekhov makes his feelings clear that thoughtless, unimaginative writing is a moral choice. One might very well write slop, but one shouldn't give up and make such writing the goal:

> Why do you write so little? How disgusting! Sverchok and Boudilnik [editors] have space at your service, and yet you sit with folded arms and whimper, like Hershka [a Russian folk

character] bitten by fleas in his sleep. Why are you idling...? All the stories you sent me for Lakin [an editor] smell strongly of idleness. You have written them in one day? Out of the whole mass I can select only one good, talented story, but all the rest is worthy of the pen of Taganrog Sprightly [a sarcastic reference to the Chekhov boys' backwater hometown's literary journal]. The subjects are impossible.... Only idleness could write for a censored journal about a priest christening a baby in the font—idleness that does not think, that works at one draft, at random.... Respect yourself, for the love of Christ; don't give your hands liberty when your brain is lazy! Write no more than two stories a week, shorten them, polish them. Work should be work. Don't invent sufferings you have not experienced, and don't paint pictures you have not seen—for a lie in a story is much more boring than a lie in conversation.

Anton gets very personal with Alexander, but really only to deliver some general truths:

> The play will be worthless if all the characters resemble you.... Is there no life outside of you? And who is interested in knowing my life or yours, my thoughts or your thoughts? Give people people, and not yourself.
>
> Avoid "choice" diction. The language should be simple and forceful. The lackeys should speak simply, without elegance....

It was in his frustration with his brother, in whom Chekhov recognized greater literary potential than in himself, that he was most severe, blunt and honest:

> My advice is to try to be original in your play and as intelligent as possible; but also, have no fear of appearing stupid. Freethinking is what's needed and only he who is not afraid of writing stupid things is a real freethinker. Don't smooth things over, don't polish them, be clumsy and daring. Brevity is the sister of talent. Keep in mind that declarations of love, infidelities of husbands and wives, the tears of widows and orphans and all other kinds of tears have long since been described. But the main thing: Mom and Dad got to eat. So write.

So, art is a moral act, but let's be practical and remember, first things first, we need to make a living! We sense Chekhov's own struggles to write well and purposefully in his chastising of Alexander about a story:

> "The City of the Future" is a splendid theme, both in novelty and interest. I think that if you are not lazy you will write it well; but, the Devil knows, you are an awfully idle dog! "The City of the Future" will be a work of art only on the following conditions: 1) Absence of long word eruptions of a politico-socio-economic character; 2) thorough objectivity; 3) truthfulness in descriptions of characters and objects; 4) a twofold conciseness; 5) courage and originality (avoid cliches); and 6) sincerity.
>
> ...In descriptions of Nature one has to snatch at small details, grouping them in such a manner that after reading them one can obtain the picture on closing one's eyes.
>
> For instance, you will get a moonlight night if you write that on the dam of the mill a fragment of broken bottle flashed like a small bright star, and there rolled by, like a ball, the black shadow of a dog, or a wolf—and so on. Nature appears animated if you do not disdain to use comparisons of its phenomena with those of human actions, etc.
>
> The same, too, in the sphere of psychology. God defend you from generalizations. Best of all, avoid describing the psychological state of the characters; one should contrive that this is clear from their actions. One should not hunt after an abundance of characters. The center of gravity should be two: he and she.
>
> I am writing you this as a reader with a definite taste. I also write for this reason: that in working you should not feel you are alone. Loneliness in creative activity is a hard lot. Better unfavorable criticism than none. Is that not so?

A SCOLDING FROM TOLSTOY

We can doubt if Alexander agreed with that last statement, but Anton certainly believed it. He never minded criticism of his work for its lack of artistry. In fact, he often seemed to enjoy quoting criticisms of his work. Perhaps the best instance of such enjoyment came in 1900, at the sword of his hero, the great Russian novelist Tolstoy. Chekhov, in his own charming, guileless manner, related to a friend what Tolstoy had told him about his plays: "You know, he does not like my dramas. He swears that I'm not a playwright. There is only one thing that comforts me.... He said to me: 'You know, I cannot abide Shakespeare, but your plays are even worse. Shakespeare, however, grabs the reader by the scruff of his neck and leads him to a definite objective, not permitting him to wander off the road. But where are you going with your heroines? From the divan where they lie to the closet and back.'" At this point in his account, Chekhov laughed so hard that his pince-nez fell off his nose. "But really, Leo Nikolayevich [Tolstoy] is serious," Chekhov continued. "He was ill. I sat with him at his bedside. When I began to get ready to leave, he took my hand, looked me in the eye, and said: 'Anton Pavlovich, you are a fine man.' Then, smiling, he let my hand go and added: 'But your plays are altogether vile.'"

Chekhov's feelings don't seem to have been hurt. He had long been critical of his own work in detail and in general. He defended his work only for its "honesty":

> I am afraid of those who look for a tendency between the lines and who want to see in me either a liberal or a conservative. I am not a liberal, nor a conservative, nor a meliorist, nor a monk, nor an indifferentist. I should like to be a free artist, and nothing more, and I grieve that God has not given me the power to be one. I hate falsehood and violence in all their aspects.... Hypocrisy, stupidity and arbitrariness reign not in shopkeepers' houses and prisons alone. I detect them in science, in literature and in the younger generation.... For these reasons I nurse no particular partiality for gendarmes, or butchers, or savants, or writers, or the younger generation. I look upon trade-marks and labels as prejudices. My Holy of Holies is the human body, health, mind, talent, inspiration, love and the most absolute freedom—freedom from violence and falsehood in whatever they may be manifested. This is the program I would follow if I were a great artist.

That today he is regarded as a great artist Chekhov would consider an amazing mistake. He had pride in his work but modesty about its effects. He saw his place not in the pantheon of world literature with Tolstoy, but as a humble and awestruck teammate of a Hall of Famer:

> I fear Tolstoy's death. If he were to die there would be left in my life a great, empty space. In the first place, I love no man as I do him; I am an unbeliever, but among all faiths, I consider that of Tolstoy nearest my heart.... Secondly, when there is Tolstoy in literature it is easy and pleasant to be a literary worker; even to be aware that you have done and will do nothing is not so terrible, because Tolstoy does enough for all. His activity serves as a justification for those... expectations that are attached to literature. Thirdly, Tolstoy stands unshaken; his authority is tremendous, and while he lives, bad taste in literature, all sorts of vulgarity, insolence, and sentimentality, all kinds of shoddy, irritated ambitions, will remain deep in shadow. His moral authority alone is able to hold to a certain height so-called literary moods and tendencies. Without him, these would be a shepherdless herd or a hodgepodge in which it would be difficult to find anything that rings true.

Chekhov's adherence to modesty serves as a correction to the tendency to vanity and egotism of writers and remains one of his more attractive qualities: "I do not know whether I have ever suffered more than shoemakers, mathematicians, or railway guards do; I do not know who speaks through my lips—God or someone worse." Chekhov's professional expertise as a doctor might be what led him to believe that writers should be modest on principle and leery of presuming moral or intellectual authority.

> It seems to me that the writer of fiction should not try to solve such questions as those of God, pessimism, etc. His business is but to describe those who have been speaking or thinking about God and pessimism, how, and under what circumstances. The artist should be, not the judge of his characters and their conversations, but only an unbiased witness.... My business is merely to be talented, i.e., to be able to distinguish between important and unimportant statements, to be able to illuminate the characters and speak their language.... The time has come for writers, especially those who are artists, to admit that in this world one cannot make anything out, just as Socrates once admitted it, just as Voltaire admitted it. The mob think they know and understand everything; the more stupid they are, the wider, I think, do they conceive their horizon to be. And if an artist in whom the crowd has faith decides to declare that he understands nothing of what he sees,—this in itself constitutes a considerable clarity in the realm of thought, and a great step forward.

Following up the subject of this letter to his friend and editor Aleksey Suvorin, he explained:

> In conversation with my literary colleagues I always insist that it is not the artist's business to solve problems that require a specialist's knowledge. It is a bad thing if a writer tackles a subject he does not understand. We have specialists for dealing with special questions: it is their business to judge of the commune, of the future, of capitalism, of the evils of drunkenness, of boots, of the diseases of women. An artist must judge only of what he understands, his field is just as limited as that of any other specialist—I repeat this and insist on it always. That in his sphere there are no questions, but only answers, can be maintained only by those who have never written and have had no experience of thinking in images....
>
> You are right in demanding that an artist should take an intelligent attitude to his work, but you confuse two things: solving a problem and stating a problem correctly. It is only the second that is obligatory for the artist. In *Anna Karenina* and *Eugene Onegin* [Pushkin's verse novel] not a single problem is solved, but they satisfy you completely because all the problems in these works are correctly stated. It is the

business of the judge to put the right questions, but the answers must be given by the jury according to their own lights.

We have Suvorin to thank for challenging *Chekhov* to continue and clarify his credo (which he would never again reveal so unreservedly):

> You abuse me for objectivity, calling it indifference to good and evil, lack of ideals and ideas, and so on. You would have me, when I describe horse-thieves, say: "Stealing horses is an evil." But that has been known for ages without my saying so. Let the jury judge them; it's my job simply to show what sort of people they are. I write: you are dealing with horse-thieves, so let me tell you that they are not beggars but well-fed people, that they are people of a special cult, and that horse-stealing is not simply theft but a passion. Of course it would be pleasant to combine art with a sermon, but for me personally it is extremely difficult and almost impossible, owing to the conditions of technique. You see, to depict horse-thieves in seven hundred lines I must all the time speak and think in their tone and feel in their spirit, otherwise, if I introduce subjectivity, the image becomes blurred and the story will not be as compact as all short stories ought to be. When I write, I reckon entirely upon the reader to add for himself the subjective elements that are lacking in the story.

So for Chekhov, "objectivity" is the writer's goal, if by subjectivity we mean the judgment that interprets rather than presents, and that squashes or ignores distasteful or disturbing material. His enduring gift to us, through his letters and stories, is a passionate and intense attention to the quiet but resounding details of life's everyday dramas.

Excerpts in this article were drawn from these books: *Anton Chekhov's Life and Thought: Selected Letters and Commentary,* edited by Simon Karlinsky and translated by Michael Henry Helm; *The Life and Letters of Anton Tchekhov,* edited with translation by S. S. Koteliansky and Philip Tomlinson; *Letters on the Short Story, the Drama, and other Literary Topics,* edited by Louis S. Friedland; *The Selected Letters of Anton Chekhov,* edited by Lillian Hellman; and *Leo Tolstoy* by Ernest J. Simmons.

Source: Bob Blaisdell, "A Few Words of Advice from... Anton Chekhov," in *Writer,* Vol. 117, No. 9, September 2004.

David W. Martin

In the following essay, Martin assesses Chekhov's influence on modern English literature and considers his place within the tradition of the short-story genre.

> THE ECONOMY OF STYLE PRESENT HERE, WHERE INVOLVED PSYCHOLOGICAL ANALYSIS GIVES WAY TO VISUAL IMMEDIACY, IS, THEN, CHARACTERISTIC OF THE MODERN SHORT STORY."

The purpose of this essay is to discuss Chekhov's place as a major figure in the art of the short story as it has developed in modern times, with particular regard to his reception and appreciation by people of letters in the English-speaking world. Attention will therefore be paid to some of those comments made on the subject of Chekhov by critics whose background and experience are associated in the main with English literature and whose viewpoint is for this reason different from that of Russian writers on Chekhov and indeed from that of English-speaking slavists.

Apart from this and more importantly there will be an examination of the impact made by Chekhov's stories upon modern writers in English and of his role as an initiator of a new approach to the short story, an approach which was to be developed and broadened by a number of writers of fiction in the West....

First and foremost there arises the question of what exactly is meant by the term "modern short story." Although forms of the story as a genre have existed for centuries, its popularity increased markedly at the beginning of the nineteenth century in response to the requirements of a growing number of literary magazines. The magazine has remained the chief outlet for stories, upon which it has necessarily imposed the stricture of brevity, something of no small importance in the overall composition of a periodical. However, as not infrequently happens, this practical necessity was to become an aesthetic virtue; and even before the first half of the nineteenth century was out, economy of design had come to be regarded as a prime quality of the short story. This we may see from Edgar Allan Poe's writing on the subject.

Allied to the notion of brevity came the concept of singleness of effect. The short story should not digress or involve itself in a multiplicity of plots like the novel, but should rather take for its subject a single occasion or an integral series of occasions, and for its goal an overall effect to which all aspects of action and characterization must be subjugated....

This is not to imply that content became unimportant but rather that writers in more recent years have had less regard for the dramatic, suspenseful, perhaps frightening, certainly unique quality of their themes, and more for the inventiveness and skill with which devices of style and tone are employed to achieve the desired general effect. For this reason it is not impossible nowadays, and has been for some time, for two stories by different writers to be identical in theme but totally dissimilar in the aesthetic impression they create simply because of their individual styles of composition. It is this trait which most clearly distinguishes the specifically modern short story from the genre as a whole.

In the case of Chekhov this feature is strongly felt in a number of statements he made which even go so far as to suggest a total disinterest on his part in the subject of any given composition. To Teleshov he remarked: "You can even write well about the moon, and that's a worn-out theme all right. And it will be interesting. Only you must just the same see something of your own in the moon and not something already seen or exhausted." To Bunin he said: "It is immaterial whether you write about love or not about love, the main thing is that it should be talented." And Avilova records him as saying: "I can write about anything you like. Tell me to write about a bottle and there will be a story entitled "The Bottle." Living images create thought, it is not the thought which creates the image."

Thus, for Chekhov, the image, the literary vehicle, is the living matter of which thought is born; and thought, the supreme act and goal of creativity, is diametrically opposed by him to the initial stage of composition: its basic, often incidental theme or scheme of events. Poe used the term "thought" in a similar sense above. He also referred to this final aim of a work as "effect," "design," "idea"; and from the statements of both writers a certain hierarchy emerges, that of, in ascending order, incident, image, idea.

It is not at all difficult to find stories in Chekhov where the emphasis of the work is placed on the artistic means of expression employed to a certain end, rather than on action, the chain of events, or indeed abstract ideas for their own sake alone. One of the first people to draw attention to this fact in the West was Somerset Maugham, who commented that Chekhov's stories, unlike his own, cannot be recounted after dinner, something which made them inferior; for in Chekhov, Maugham maintained, there is "nothing to tell." Here he alludes to that apparent lack of content which characterizes Chekhov's art, where poetic vision and strength of expression take precedence over outward movement.

We would argue that the unique personality of Chekhov's writing chiefly lies in his formal innovations and characteristics of style, from which come the "idea" and overall effect of a work: yet his stories possess personality not only by dint of the peculiarities of his formal techniques but also because they are essentially lyrical, having a thinking and feeling narrator, rather than syllogistic and removed....

The Chekovian story is a composite of quite deliberately arranged sections and subsections, assembled like the bricks and beams of a house, where every small brick adds to the strength of the whole and every beam carries weight.

J. B. Priestly, discussing a neatly handled scene in "The Bishop," writes:

> Chekhov has a genius—and it *is* genius, not simply an experienced writer's trick—for this power of suggestion, this maximum of effect created by the smallest possible means. (And here his influence on later writers throughout the world has been all to the good). He can do it with people, with situations, with backgrounds. He could do more with fifty words than most of his contemporaries could do with five hundred. He is the master in language of the swift impressionistic sketch or the powerful drawing with most of the lines left out.

What lines, then, are in fact left out of this powerful drawing of Chekhov's, as Priestly puts it? The answer is clear enough: everything that has no bearing on the purpose of the work, and this is to depict the characters' inner life. Thus we shall search in vain in Chekhov for what we take for granted in other fiction—a detailed account of a hero's forbears and family, of his environment, his house, his dress, his education, the less meaningful aspects of conversation, marriage, death—all these things, unless they have radical importance in the revelation of inner life, are either not mentioned by the writer at all or dismissed with a perfunctoriness befitting their actual insignificance.

In short, Chekhov does not dwell on social background or incidental environment, but Beachcroft is right when he comments that

Chekhov's "care for the inner truth of the individual makes the people in his stories points of irradiation which shed light on the conditions of their lives and of other people around them. The discursive background is contained in the truth with which the individual is seen." In other words, depth of vision removes any necessity for superficial narrative scope....

Here, then, then aesthetic effect is encapsulated in the implied concretization of the awaited answer. And in this field we find similarities in the style of Katherine Mansfield. These words occur in her story, "The Daughters of the Late Colonel":

> A perfect fountain of bubbling notes shook from the barrel-organ, round, bright notes, carelessly scattered.
>
> Constantia lifted her big, cold hands as if to catch them....

This device of concretization is also one of visualization; and it is employed in both Chekhov and Mansfield in any number of ways. Nor is it absent from the literary style of more recent practitioners of the art of the short story. The following is from "The Comforts of Home" by F. O'Connor, whose work possesses a number of features of structure and tone which may be traced back to Chekhov. In this passage the reference to Sarah Ham's laugh exemplifies both concrete visualization and personification of an intangible entity: "Thomas... lunged back to the car and sped off. The other door was still hanging open and her laugh, bodiless but real, bounded up the street as if it were about to jump in the open side of the car and ride away with him."

The same visual technique may be used to convey not a simple, single abstraction or emotion but a whole complex of ideas; and again, the vehicle used to convey it may take the form not of a single object or action, but of a more wide-ranging pictorial representation. The morbid imaginings and indeed the whole psychological condition of the dying professor in Chekhov's "A Boring Story" are made immediate and real to us when he comments succinctly that it seems to him that the whole of nature is waiting, its ear cocked, for him to die.

The economy of style present here, where involved psychological analysis gives way to visual immediacy, is, then, characteristic of the modern short story. As Beachcroft concludes, "Not until the stories are really short do the especial insights of the form truly show themselves."...

Chekhov, Woolf and Mansfield's stories are comparatively bereft of incident; for the charge that "nothing happens" can be levelled at the work of all three. Yet the art of the modern story does not require incident or action in time in order to be significant, because it strives to capture what humanity is rather than what it does. There is a story by Virginia Woolf called "The Mark on the Wall." The first sentence reads: "Perhaps it was the middle of January in the present year that I first looked up and saw the mark on the wall." Having seen it, the author begins to wonder what the mark might be, but her imagination takes over and the story branches into a series of philosophic reflections, occasionally returning to the subject of the mark, only to leave it again. There is certainly nothing Chekhovian in these reflections, they have a strangely contrived air, but here is a sample which illustrates the subordination of the incident—the appearance of the mark—to the inner life of the subject.

The modern short story, then, describes inner experience, not superficial activities or the logical sequence of events for their own sake. C. K. Stead in his essay "Katherine Mansfield and the Art of Fiction," writes of Mansfield's realization that:

> fiction did not have to be shaped towards a conclusion, a climax, a dénouement; or... that a fiction [by which Stead means a *modern* short story] is not quite the same thing as a story. A fiction survives, not by leading us anywhere, but by being at every point authentic, a recreation of life, so that we experience it and remember it as we experience and remember actual life itself.

... Narrative linking is absent or reduced to a minimum in Mansfield as in Chekhov again because both writers omit what happens outwardly to their characters, except where it contributes to their characters' life experience. This accent on life experience is particularly evident in passages of description. The eyes and ears of the hero observer or narrator are, we may suppose, open to everything, but we are not presented with this "everything" in the work of fiction, but only with that which reaches the conscious mind and forms part of its experience. On the simplest level this is demonstrated in the especial attention paid by both Chekhov and Mansfield to the recording of salient sensory perceptions: a sudden noise amidst silence, a source of brightness against a dark background....

Chekhov, Mansfield, Joyce and, indeed, Woolf all wrote stories which display the emptiness and aimlessness of the age, its paralysis of spirit. This is in part exemplified in that love of anti-climax and fruitlessness which Chekhov shared with others, from Mansfield to Anderson (see his "A Walk in the Moonlight," for example). Yet the real point to be made here—and with it this essay is concluded—is that it became possible to choose such themes only with the discovery by writers from Chekhov on of those stimulating and incisive techniques of style which have been the subject of discussion above. For how else can one write a viable story depicting banality without being banal? How else can one describe boredom without being boring, or weakness of will without feebleness of expression? The old short story took its strength from the robustness of its theme; the new, from the dynamics of its style, a style which, it might be argued, actually required a certain lack of superficial incident in order to throw its properties into starker relief and by so doing deepen the insight, make keener the vision, more revelatory the epiphany.

Source: David W. Martin, "Chekhov and the Modern Short Story in English," in *Neophilologus*, Vol. 71, No. 2, April 1987, pp. 129–43.

SOURCES

Blaisdell, Bob, "A Few Words of Advice from... Anton Chekhov," in *Writer*, Vol. 117, No. 9, September 2004, p. 26.

Bush, Jason, "Russia: How Long Can the Fun Last?," in *BusinessWeek*, December 7, 2006, http://www.businessweek.com/globalbiz/content/dec2006/gb20061207_520461.htm (accessed September 6, 2009).

Chekhov, Anton, "A Problem," in *The Party and Other Stories*, translated by Constance Garnett, MacMillan, 1917, pp. 159–70.

Curtis, Glenn E., ed., "Literature," in *Russia: A Country Study*, GPO for the Library of Congress, 1996, http://countrystudies.us/russia/43.htm (accessed September 6, 2009).

———, "Transformation of Russia in the Nineteenth Century," in *Russia: A Country Study*, GPO for the Library of Congress, 1996, http://countrystudies.us/russia/6.htm (accessed September 6, 2009).

Finke, Michael, "Anton Chekhov," in *Dictionary of Literary Biography*, Vol. 277, *Russian Literature in the Age of Realism*, edited by Alyssa Dinega Gillespie, Thomson Gale, 2003, pp. 54–79.

Hare, Robert D., *Without Conscience: The Disturbing World of the Psychopaths Among Us*, Guilford Press, 1999.

Hensher, Philip, "Incomparable Naturalism," in *Atlantic Monthly*, Vol. 289, No. 1, January 2002.

Martin, David W., "Chekhov and the Modern Short Story in English," in *Neophilologus*, Vol. 71, No. 2, April 1987, pp. 129–43.

Murray, Brian, "Anton Chekhov: A Study of the Short Fiction," in *Studies in Short Fiction*, Vol. 32, No. 1, Winter 1995, p. 134.

Paxton, Robin, "A Billion Dollars Not Enough for Russian Rich List," in *Reuters*, April 18, 2008, http://www.reuters.com/article/businessNews/idUSL189270520080418?feedType=RSS&feedName;=businessNews (accessed September 6, 2009).

Rayfield, Donald, *Anton Chekhov: A Life*, Northwestern University Press, 2000.

Service, Robert, *A History of Modern Russia: From Nicholas II to Vladimir Putin*, rev. ed., Harvard University Press, 2005.

FURTHER READING

Akhmatova, Anna, *Selected Poems of Anna Akhmatova*, translated by Judith Hemschemeyer, edited and introduced by Roberta Reeder, Zephyr Press, 2000.
> Born almost thirty years after Chekhov, Akhmatova is considered one of the greatest Russian poets of the early twentieth century. This volume provides readers with an overall introduction to her work.

Goldman, Marshall I., *Petrostate: Putin, Power, and the New Russia*, Oxford University Press, 2008.
> For an exploration of contemporary Russia and its politics, this volume is an excellent choice. Goldman's book explores Russia's 1998 economic collapse and its financial ups and downs since. Interviews with Vladimir Putin are also included in the volume.

Pushkin, Alexander, *Eugene Onegin and Other Poems*, translated by Charles Johnston, Everyman's Library, 1999.
> This collection of verse by one of Russia's premier writers includes the classic epic poem *Eugene Onegin* (1833). Pushkin was a predecessor whose writing was likely influential to Chekhov.

Rzhevsky, Nicholas, ed., *An Anthology of Russian Literature from Earliest Writings to Modern Fiction: Introduction to a Culture*, M. E. Sharpe, 2004.
> This comprehensive anthology attempts to distill the common themes and motifs recurrent in Russian literature. An introduction to each work and author is featured, as are annotations and extensive bibliographies.

Suzy and Leah

JANE YOLEN

1993

Jane Yolen's short story "Suzy and Leah" brings the reader into the lives of two oppositional characters living in the United States during World War II. Suzy is an American citizen far removed from the front line terror of the war. Leah is a Jewish refugee living behind a barbed wire fence in a camp near Suzy's home. Leah has witnessed some of the worst horrors of the war. She has lost her mother and young brother. Both died while incarcerated in a German concentration camp.

Neither girl understands the other when they first meet. Their life experiences have little in common. Suzy laughs at Leah's attempts to pronounce English words, unaware that the young German girl speaks three other languages. Leah is leery of Suzy's generosity. She waits for Suzy to turn on her, just as the Nazis have turned on her German Jewish family.

When the girls are pushed together inside the classroom, they become curious about one another, but barriers continue to hinder their strained relationship. Then one day Leah does not show up for class. Suzy wonders what is wrong with her. In the process of searching for her, Suzy discovers Leah's personal journal and learns of Leah's background. Suzy is shocked that the hardships Leah has been through could even exist. The theme of the cruelties of the Holocaust is one that has appeared several times in Yolen's writing. In "Suzy and Leah" the

Jane Yolen (Photograph by Shulamith Oppenheim. Reproduced by permission of Jane Yolen.)

author makes the Holocaust very personal as readers are privy to the private writings of one of the Holocaust's victims.

"Suzy and Leah" was first published in *American Girl* magazine in 1993, which is now out of print. But the short story can be found in the Prentice Hall textbook *Literature: Timeless Voices, Timeless Themes: Bronze Level* (2002).

AUTHOR BIOGRAPHY

Yolen was born on February 11, 1939, in New York City. Her mother, Isabel, was a psychiatric social worker and writer, and her father, Will, was a journalist and movie publicist. Yolen started writing at a young age, and along with her younger brother, Steve, she published a community newspaper before she entered high school. She attended Smith College in Northampton, Massachusetts, where she later became the president of the college's Press Board, won several writing awards, and wrote the lyrics to a class musical.

After graduating from college, she published her first work, the children's book *Pirates in Petticoats* (1963). In 1962, Yolen married David Stemple, a professor of computer science at the University of Massachusetts at Amherst. They had three children. Their marriage lasted forty-four years until Stemple died from cancer in 2006.

In 1976, Yolen received her master's degree in education from the University of Massachusetts. Since then, she has written more than three hundred books in such genres as folklore, fantasy, nonfiction, and science fiction. She was a finalist for the Nebula Award for her books *Sister Light, Sister Dark* (1988), *The Devil's Arithmetic* (1988), *White Jenna* (1989), and *Briar Rose* (1992). In 1993, "Suzy and Leah" was published in *American Girl* magazine. In 1998, she won the Nebula Award for her novelette "Lost Girls."

Yolen's poetry collections include *Dragon Night and Other Lullabies* (1980), *Best Witches* (1989), and *What Rhymes with Moon?* (1993).

Yolen is perhaps best known for the books she has written for children and teens, such as *Hobo Toad and the Motorcycle Gang* (1970), *Wizard's Hall* (1991), *Merlin and the Dragons* (1995), and *Jason and the Gorgon's Blood* (2004).

She has also published a few nonfiction works, including *Guide to Writing for Children* (1989). In 2003, Yolen published *The Radiation Sonnets: For My Love, in Sickness and in Health*, a collection of poems focused on her husband's battle with cancer.

Yolen writes a blog at her Web site and several interviews with the author are available online. She spends her time, when she is not on the road doing readings, at her homes in Massachusetts and in Scotland.

PLOT SUMMARY

Yolen's short story "Suzy and Leah" covers the meeting of two young girls—one is a blonde-haired American student named Suzy; the other is Leah, a dark-haired refugee who has come to the United States from Nazi Germany. At the opening of the story, it is August 1944, approximately one year before the official end of World War II. Readers meet the girls through journal entries they are writing. Suzy addresses her writings to her diary. Leah writes to her mother.

The story begins with Suzy's entry. She writes about her first visit to "*that* place," as she puts it. She is referring to the refugee camp in town, one that everyone has been talking about. She comments that it is "ugly" and looks like ramshackle buildings she has seen on army bases. The camp is surrounded by a high fence, topped with barbed wire. Suzy has brought candy bars with her, as she has been told to do. The children on the other side of the fence flock to her, like animals do "in a zoo." There is one child, though, who does not come to the fence—a young girl with dark hair, who merely stares at Suzy.

The next entry is written by Leah. She writes to her mother though, as Leah puts it, she is "gone from me forever." Leah mentions that she saw Suzy and describes her as yet another girl "with more sweets." Leah does not like the way her friends and all the other children rush to the fence to grab the treats. She writes, "we are no longer prisoners. Even though we are still penned in."

Suzy returns with fruit, and in her diary, she mocks the children on the other side of the fence for not knowing how to peel an orange before eating it. She also comments that the refugee children will soon be attending her school, but she hopes they clean themselves before they do. From the other side of this encounter, Leah writes about the conditions most of the children were in while they struggled through the war and fled from the Nazis. If they were lucky, she writes, they might have eaten bread. So accustomed to the near starvation she experienced, Leah is surprised to find that cereal comes in a box.

In Leah's next entry, she comments on her fears of going to the American school. She says the American adults at her camp have told her she is safe. But she adds that the Germans told her family the same thing when they took them to the camps. It was there that Leah lost her mother and her baby brother, Natan. Leah is also concerned about the language barrier she and her fellow survivors are facing. Leah also mentions a young boy named Avi, who does not speak at all. Avi has not spoken a word since he was hidden in a cupboard to save him from the Nazis. After his grandmother hid him there, she was taken away. Avi was not discovered until three days later. He survived without water or food or "words to comfort him."

When the refugee children appear at Suzy's school, Suzy recognizes one of her old blue dresses. The girl with the dark hair is wearing it. Suzy is a little angry with her mother for not having told her she had given the dress away, but at least the German children are clean, Suzy comments. Leah likes the blue dress she is wearing. But she does not like the name tags that the teachers handed out. She wonders what they might force them to wear next. In Germany, Jewish people were forced to wear yellow stars on their clothes to identify them as being Jewish. This made it easier for Nazi officials to round them up and take them away to the concentration camps. Leah also mentions that she does not like the girl with the yellow hair "who smiles so falsely at me."

Suzy's teacher, Mr. Forest, assigns Suzy to help Leah with her English. He recognizes Leah's language ability and wants her to build up her vocabulary fast so she can help teach the other refugee children. Suzy is reluctant to work with Leah. She refers to her as "Miss Porcupine," adding that Leah is "prickly." Suzy also wishes that Leah would stop wearing the same blue dress. When Leah writes, she mentions the dress and wishes she had another one to wear. She also would prefer to have someone other than Suzy working with her.

Suzy writes that Leah is very grumpy. No matter what Suzy tries to make her smile, Leah refuses. Leah also turns down the gifts that Suzy brings to her, like candy and apples, or even a pretty handkerchief. Suzy's mom suggests that Suzy invite Leah home for dinner. But Suzy is reluctant, claiming that Leah is no fun to be around. She also has witnessed Leah's fear. When Suzy corrects Leah's writing, Suzy says that Leah shrinks back, as if Suzy might strike her.

Leah mentions her fears in her next entry. She is still concerned that Suzy and all the other Americans she has met so far will one day turn on her, just as the Germans turned on her family. One day, Leah writes, "They will remember we are not just refugees but Jews." She continues to refuse the small gifts Suzy brings because she senses Suzy does not really like her. Leah feels that Suzy treats her like a pet, "a pet she does not really like or trust."

By the end of September, Leah's language skills have improved considerably. However, Suzy states that the girl still does not smile. Suzy has noted a peculiar habit that Leah displays. Leah does not eat her lunch. Instead, she wraps the food in a napkin and places it in her pocket. Suzy wonders if Leah is getting enough to eat. In Leah's entry, the young girl writes that she brings her food back to the camp and gives it to Avi. She recognizes that the food she is given at school is not "kosher" (food prepared according to Jewish diet laws), but Avi is too young to know the difference. Leah points out that Avi needs the extra nutrients.

Though Leah's language skills continue to impress the teachers to the point that they have moved her up a grade, Suzy finds it hard to believe that Leah knows so little about the United States. Leah's knowledge of the world is good, Suzy states, but she knows next to nothing about pop culture in America. She does not know the words of songs nor does she know any of the latest dances. Because Leah has little to say to her, Suzy says Leah is "stuck up."

Leah writes about her visit to Suzy's house. Again, while there, she wraps the food she is served and places it in her pocket. She also writes that she was not feeling well, and when she went home, she gave the food to Avi. Leah also notes that she felt very comfortable around Suzy's mother, but she had to hold back her emotions. She is concerned that if she allows her emotions to come out, she will forget her own mother.

Leah does not go to school the next day, and the following day, she is in the hospital because she has to have her appendix taken out. Suzy collects Leah's things from school, including her diary. Suzy's mom packs up some of her daughter's dresses, but Suzy refuses to give away one of her favorites, even though it does not fit her anymore. Suzy later confesses that she read Leah's diary. "I'd kill anyone who did that to me," she writes. After reading Leah's entries, Suzy finds she does not understand everything, so she asks her mom to explain what was going on in Germany. Suzy has trouble believing the horrors Leah has gone through. "How could she live with all that pain?"

The story ends with Leah's entry. She finds out that Suzy has read her journal. Suzy gives Leah her diary to read so they will be even. In the process, both girls learn a little more about one another. Suzy promises that as soon as Leah is out of the hospital, she has one more special dress to give her—the favorite one that Suzy was reluctant to give away earlier. Leah ends her entry happy to have found a new life and a new friend.

CHARACTERS

Avi

Avi is a young boy, a refugee who lives with Leah in the camp. Before being taken to the United States, Avi had lived with his grandmother in Europe. His grandmother hid Avi in a cupboard in her kitchen when Nazi soldiers came to their home. The soldiers did not find him; however, Avi's grandmother never returned, and Avi spent three days without food or water in that cupboard before someone rescued him. When he was found, he would not speak. Even in the refugee camp, Avi continues to be silent except for a few words he says to Leah. Leah takes him into her care and brings him food she was given at school. The food is not kosher, so Leah refuses to eat it. However, she knows that Avi will not know the difference between kosher and non-kosher food. Avi begins to talk more because of Leah's love. Sometimes Leah refers to Avi by her brother's name, Natan, because she misses her dead brother.

Mr. Forest

Mr. Forest is one of the teachers at the school that Suzy and Leah attend. He pairs Suzy with Leah, making Suzy a mentor for Leah in learning English. Mr. Forest recognizes Leah's language skills and wants Suzy to help Leah learn English as quickly as possible. He knows that if Leah can speak English well, she then can help teach the other refugee children.

Leah Shoshana Hershkowitz

Leah is a young Jewish girl who has been rescued from Nazi Germany, where her mother and brother have died in a concentration camp. The details of her rescue are not told. The first time readers meet Leah is at the refugee camp somewhere in the community in which Suzy lives. Leah is more standoffish than the other children in the camp. She refuses to act like an animal in a zoo, as she puts it, and to rush to the fence for treats that the American children bring.

Leah's story is told through her writings to her mother. Leah keeps a journal and though she knows her mother is dead, she writes to her out of loneliness. The horrors of Nazi Germany make her wary of everyone around her. She has trouble understanding people's motives because the Nazis told her and her family so many lies.

Except for her journal, Leah keeps all her feelings to herself. She even hides the pain she feels when her appendix is about to burst. She is afraid that if she opens up and tells anyone how much she hurts, she will be killed. By remaining so closed, the American children around her conclude that Leah is snobbish. They do not understand her fears, because they have no experiences that compare to hers. Leah is also afraid of allowing her positive emotions to come out. For instance, she is afraid to open her heart to Suzy's mother, because she believes this might displace her feelings for her own mother.

Suzy Ann McCarthy

Suzy shares the protagonist role with Leah. The girls are approximately the same age. Suzy is American. It is in Suzy's community that the refugee camp is set up. This allows Suzy to visit the camp and to later build a relationship with some of the refugee children when they attend Suzy's school.

Suzy is only vaguely knowledgeable about the situations and backgrounds of the refugee children. She does not comprehend their fear, their lack of clothes, and their inability to speak English. Suzy mocks the children for not knowing that they should peel an orange before eating it and the strange way they pronounce English words. She does not understand how anyone could not know the words of popular American songs or how to dance.

To some, Suzy could appear selfish in her dealing with Leah. She dislikes that Leah wears her hand-me-down clothes. But Suzy's actions are the result of her ignorance of the horrors these children have been through. Her misinterpretations of Leah's fear and lack of trust are due to Suzy's inability to imagine that so much cruelty could exist in the world. In comparison to Leah, Suzy has lived a very privileged and sheltered life.

As Suzy's world grows wide enough to include the ravages of war and the Nazi persecution of Jews, she becomes more compassionate. Instead of thinking of how the refugee children affect her, she begins to empathize with Leah for the loss of her mother and the torture Leah has endured.

Mutti

Mutti is the name Leah uses to address her mother. The last time Leah saw her mother was in the Nazi concentration camp. Leah knows her mother is dead, but she finds comfort in writing to her as if she were still living. There is little known about Leah's mother, except that Leah misses her badly.

Natan

Natan is Leah's baby brother. Natan was killed in the concentration camp. Sometimes when Leah feels very lonesome, she calls Avi, the young boy at the refugee camp, by Natan's name.

Ruth

Ruth is a refugee in the same camp that Leah is in. Leah mentions that Ruth is a friend. Ruth, unlike Leah, runs to the fence that encloses the refugee camp in attempts to take the treats that the American children bring.

Suzy's Mother

Suzy's mother makes a few brief appearances through Suzy's diary entries. Suzy presents her mother as a kindhearted, compassionate woman. When Suzy is confused by Leah's mannerisms and behavior, Suzy's mom helps clarify the situation, explaining what is happening in Europe during the war. Suzy's mother encourages Suzy's relationship with Leah, suggesting that Suzy invite Leah home for dinner. Leah also writes about Suzy's mother, stating that she could find comfort in the woman, if only Leah were not so afraid of opening her heart. When Leah is taken to the hospital, Suzy's mom goes out of her way to make sure Leah feels emotionally supported.

Yonni

Yonni is another of Leah's acquaintances in the refugee camp. Very little is said about this child.

Zipporah

Zipporah is one of Leah's friends in the refugee camp. Though Leah knows a few words in English, Zipporah is one of the children who knows none, and Leah worries about this.

THEMES

Fear

The character of Leah in Yolen's "Suzy and Leah" is racked with fear. Though she is safe in the present moment of the story, the residue of her experiences in World War II haunts her. In presenting fear as one of the main themes in this story, Yolen emphasizes the effects war has on people even after they have escaped it. No matter how people treat Leah, no matter how nice they

TOPICS FOR FURTHER STUDY

- Research the process by which World War II refugees were allowed into the United States. What was the typical timeline from leaving their country to being granted asylum in the United States? Did these refugees go through Ellis Island? Where were some of the largest refugee camps located? Did the U.S. officials segregate Jewish people from people of other religious beliefs or ethnic backgrounds? What were the statistics of how many people came from the various European countries? Can you also find where these refugees settled in the United States? Were there areas where people of one country might have congregated? Present your findings to your class in a PowerPoint display.

- Find a German language recording, a Web site that teaches German, or a person who speaks German. Bring your language resource to class and inform your classmates that they are going to learn a few key German phrases. Allow ten minutes at the end of class for everyone to respond to the lesson. Did they find the experience difficult? Was it fun? Was anyone able to form a complete sentence at the end of the session? How would they feel if everyone around them were speaking German and they knew only these few words?

- Rather than having Suzy and Leah write diary entries, pretend they are talking to one another face-to-face. Write a scene for the end of this story as if it were a play. Then ask one of your classmates to assist you in reading the scene in front of your class. Stay true to the characters and the story line as Yolen presents them, but give yourself the freedom to create new dialogue. What would these two girls be talking about after they read one another's diaries? What might be their next steps in furthering their relationship?

- What was life like in the Nazi concentration camps? Read about the camps so you know what people went through. Then imagine you are a Jewish teen living in one of the camps. Create a journal that details your days, months, or parts of years spent inside the camp. Choose selections from this journal and read them in front of your class.

- Read the young-adult book *Erika's Story* (2003) by Ruth Vander Zee, in which a girl, when she was just a baby, was thrown off a train that was on its way to a concentration camp. How does this girl's experience differ from Leah's? How are they the same? If you had to chose between being the girl in Zee's story or Leah, which one would you be? Write a book report about this story.

---

are or how good their intentions, she is marred by the hideous conditions in which she lived in Nazi Germany. She is afraid to accept gifts, afraid to expose her emotions, even afraid to notify authorities that she is in physical pain. Her fear consumes her to the point that she is willing to die of appendicitis rather than to die at the hands of some other person whom she imagines will kill her.

Avi is also consumed by fear. After he was abandoned in a cupboard for three days, fear has taken away his voice. Readers can imagine that Avi's grandmother probably told him to not make a sound before she closed the doors of the cupboard. His grandmother did not want the Nazis to find him. That fear continued to control the young boy even after he was rescued and brought to the United States. His grandmother's suggested last words remain in his head, commanding him to be silent for fear he, too, will be taken away to some scary, unknown place as his grandmother was.

Hidden behind some of Suzy's actions are more subtle layers of fear. In Suzy's case, there is fear of strangers or fear of people who speak and act differently than she does. This fear prods Suzy to look at the refugee children as if they belonged to a different species. There are references in the story to the refugee children being seen as if they were animals in a zoo. The refugee children are also dirty, which makes Suzy want to keep her distance for fear she might catch a disease from them. Yolen uses this type of fear to demonstrate how stereotypes of a different ethnic group can be created. It is from Suzy's type of fear that prejudice is often born.

Misunderstanding

Readers are shown, through a comparison between the diary entries that Suzy writes and those Leah composes in her journal, that the two girls constantly misunderstand one another. When Leah is experiencing fear, Suzy thinks that Leah's silence indicates that Leah is uppity, concluding that Leah believes she is better than Suzy. When Suzy offers treats, Leah wonders what the underlying motive of Suzy's gift is. When Leah is sad or feeling lonely and is therefore less responsive to the other children, Suzy misunderstands Leah's withdrawal and refers to her as being grumpy.

Yolen's story points out that misunderstanding can break down relationships, or, even worse, can keep relationships from building in the first place. Because Suzy can only read Leah's expressions, emotions, and needs through her own cultural and psychological experiences, she misunderstands much of what Leah is saying through her body language. Readers can infer that Suzy has never met another child who has suffered as much as Leah has. Things that Suzy worries about, such as pop music and stylish dresses, are superfluous to Leah's recent lifestyle. In the few years before Leah came to the United States, she was existing on the level of survival. To merely find bread crumbs to eat was a reason to rejoice. The misunderstandings between these two girls have the potential of easing once Leah and Suzy open up to one another, but readers can only guess at this conclusion. Suzy might grow to the point of empathizing with Leah once she understands the real pain Leah has endured. But the misunderstanding might continue unless the girls remain as open with one another as they have been in their journal writings.

Jewish Persecution

Though this is not a story of the Holocaust—the imprisonment and murder of millions of Jewish people in Europe during World War II—the

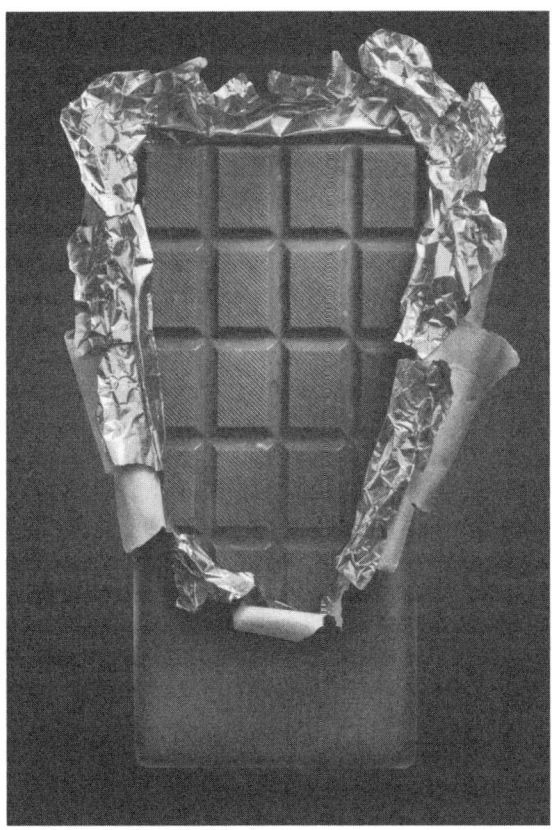

Leah refused to eat the chocolate Suzy passed out. (Image copyright Buruhtan, 2009. Used under license from Shutterstock.com)

theme of Jewish persecution is very much apparent in Leah's journal entries. As Leah reveals her emotional reactions to the new life she is leading in the refugee camp, details of what happened to her and her family in Germany are made known. Her family was taken to a concentration camp, where her mother and brother were killed. The young boy Avi lost his grandmother, and readers can assume he lost his parents as well. The scars of Jewish persecution are fresh and psychologically painful in the refugees' minds.

Also noticeable in this story is the fact that Jewish persecution has followed the refugees to the United States. Though the hints are subtle and the persecution not as severe, Yolen suggests the possibility that segregation and prejudice might continue. Even though the refugees are told they are free, they remain living behind barbed wire fences. Though the children are intelligent, able to speak multiple languages,

Suzy and her American friends laugh at their foreign accents when the Jewish children speak English. They also laugh at their unfamiliarity with nonkosher food. Because the lives of these refugees have very different foundations from those of the children from other backgrounds, the refugees' differences could well continue to make others label them as suspicious and therefore unworthy of others' full trust.

STYLE

Diary Entries

Yolen tells her story "Suzy and Leah" through diary entries. Both protagonists, Suzy and Leah, write separately while they are alone. Their thoughts, therefore, are supposed to be very personal and unfiltered, since both girls assume no one will read them. This provides Yolen with a chance to get inside the girls' heads to some of their deeper, honest thoughts. So rather than narrating a story, telling readers what is happening, Yolen narrates the girls' reactions to what is happening, leaving readers to interpret what is really going on.

Another advantage of using the form of diary entries to tell this story is that Yolen provides the contrasting views of the girls. Readers hear two conflicting interpretations of what is happening. This offers a more fully disclosed narrative since readers hear both sides. By hearing the two distinct points of view, readers are left to ponder that the truth of the events probably lies somewhere in the middle.

One negative effect of hearing the story through the girls' writing is the lack of descriptions. Readers know very little about what each girl (or any other character) looks like, details a more objective and distant narrator might have provided. Therefore, readers are also given only scant descriptions about the details of the setting. Also, the feeling of immediacy is missing. Readers are not privileged to be in the center of the events, confrontations, dialogue, or other moment-to-moment action of this story. Since everything is recorded in diaries, readers are left to figure out the story after everything has already taken place as the girls reflect on what has happened.

Setting

Since very little information about the setting is provided, it is ironic that setting plays an important role in this story. The fact, for example, that part of the story takes place in a refugee camp creates tensions, which helps to create interest. Having the camp as part of the setting also demonstrates the differences between the children who live outside of it and the refugees who live behind the fences. In spite of the significance of the refugee camp, readers know little about how the camp looks, feels, or smells. The buildings are decrepit, readers are told, and the outer grounds are encircled by a barbed wire fence. But those are the only details that are provided. As it turns out, these scant details are all that is necessary to set the environment in which Leah presently lives. All readers need to understand is that Leah's freedom is limited, and the setting in which she lives is impoverished. Further details are unnecessary.

There is another portion of the setting that is never described, never visited, nor explained—the concentration camps in Germany. For many readers, the mere mention of concentration camps brings up images that do not have to be defined. Knowledge of concentration camps and all that happened there, even if the reader is only vaguely familiar with the Holocaust, is a part of history. So Yolen only has to provide allusions to Leah's background, which include the mention of the concentration camps, and most readers are able to fill in the missing blanks. The same is true, for the most part, with the mention of Nazi Germany and the persecution of the Jews. Without providing a detailed narrative about what was going on in Germany during World War II, Yolen creates a setting in readers' minds that is at least loosely recognized. For this story, what is more important than the vivid facts of the setting of the war and the hostilities encountered at the concentration camps are the emotions that come from the experience. The setting in this story, in other words, is less about the physical, concrete details and more about the mental and emotional constructs.

HISTORICAL CONTEXT

Adolf Hitler and Nazi Germany

Germany was defeated in World War I (1914–1918), and in the ensuing years, the politics of this country swung widely between extreme right wing and extreme left wing philosophies. It was during this time that the German Workers' Party was formed. In 1919, Adolf Hitler joined this

COMPARE & CONTRAST

- **1940s:** Adolf Hitler governs Germany through a dictatorship, backed by his Nazi Party.

    Today: Germany is a democratic federal republic with several political parties, including the Christian Democratic Union, Christian Social Union, and the Social Democratic Party.

- **1940s:** Nearly a thousand refugees arrive at Fort Ontario in Oswego, New York, the only refugee camp, at this time, on American soil.

    Today: The Safe Haven Museum and Education Center in Oswego honors the refugees who lived for two years at Fort Ontario.

- **1940s:** Somewhere between five million and nine million Jewish people are killed in Nazi concentration camps in Europe.

    Today: The president of Iran, Mahmoud Ahmadinejad, calls the Holocaust a myth, igniting controversy over Holocaust denial and anti-Semitism.

---

party and quickly rose to power. Hitler changed the name of the party to the National Socialist German Workers' Party, which was, in turn, referred to as the Nazi Party for short. By the end of 1920, the party had about 3,000 members.

As Hitler gained authority, he formulated the belief that Germany would be better off if it rid itself of people who were not of a so-called pure race. In his definition of this pure race, Hitler completely excluded Jewish people. Jews became, in Hitler's way of thinking, the cause of all Germany's ills and must therefore be eliminated.

The Nazis received little attention in the early 1920s until Hitler staged a revolution against authorities in Munich. He failed miserably and was jailed for treason. However, during his trial, he gained the attention of many people in the courtroom as well as the sympathy of the judge. He was given a light sentence of five years, which was later reduced to just one year. While in prison, Hitler wrote the major tenets of his political beliefs in the book *Mein Kampf* (1925, 1926). With his words in print after he was released from prison, Hitler campaigned to increase membership in the Nazi Party. The party grew as Germany's economy faltered. In 1933, Hitler was appointed chancellor of Germany, and under his influence Dachau, Germany's first concentration camp, was created. Dachau provided a place of training for concentration camp guards. Their prisoners, at first, were political dissidents and labor leaders. Later most victims would be Jews. In 1934, President Paul von Hindenburg died, and Hitler proclaimed himself the *Fuhrer*, leader of Germany.

Hitler dominated German politics by this time and quickly followed through on his belief that Germany must be rid of Jews. In 1935, Hitler created the Nuremberg Laws, which stripped Jews of all civil rights. In 1938, hungry for more territory, Hitler ordered his armies into Austria, where they easily took over control. A few months later, Hitler invaded part of Czechoslovakia, and Hitler's anti-Semitism spread. On the night of November 9, Germans went on a destructive spree, burning synagogues, as well as Jewish businesses and homes. In the immediate aftermath, tens of thousands of Jews were sent to concentration camps. Shortly afterward, Jewish children were not allowed to attend school and all Jews were forced to give up all their properties.

In 1939, Hitler's armies invaded Poland. This was the tipping point for the European allies, and World War II began. By the time European forces were engaged in this war, Germany had gained control of Poland. To isolate Jewish people from the rest of the German population, Hitler ordered massive numbers of Jews to be taken to Poland. Special areas called ghettos were set up to house the Jews. In the course of the next few years, these areas were cleared out as Jews were systematically transferred from the

Diary and keys—a gift from Suzy (Image copyright Johanna Goodyear, 2009. Used under license from Shutterstock.com)

ghettos to concentration camps, where they were put to death. By the end of the war, it has been estimated that at least five million Jews, and perhaps as many as nine million, were put to death under the orders established by Hitler.

Fort Ontario, Oswego, New York

On a warm day in August 1944, about one thousand refugees from war-torn Europe were granted asylum in the United States and were transported to an internment camp at Fort Ontario (an old army base) in Oswego, New York. Most of the refugees were Jews who had escaped from Nazi persecution. Though the refugees were safe and well treated, none would be freed from Fort Ontario for two years.

In a symbolic demonstration of humanitarianism in the midst of World War II, President Franklin D. Roosevelt had put aside the normal procedures of immigration and had invited this relatively small group of refugees to come to the United States and to stay until the war ended. Each immigrant had signed an agreement that they would return to their homelands once the war was over. Eleanor Roosevelt worked toward reversing this agreement, but it was not until President Harry Truman took office that the refugees were given the chance to legally apply for American citizenship and were freed.

CRITICAL OVERVIEW

"Suzy and Leah" is among the more obscure stories of Yolen's life's work. Though the story is often found on teachers' syllabi, it is rarely given attention in the press. Therefore, there are no comments from reviewers that express the literary merit of this story. However, Yolen has written other stories on the topic of the Holocaust, to which critics have paid attention.

One such work is Yolen's *The Devil's Arithmetic*. In this novel, the young protagonist,

Hannah, a Jewish teen living in New York, time travels back to the 1940s to Poland. The travel provides Hannah with an eye-opening experience as she witnesses the atrocities committed by the Nazis against Jews. So in many ways, this novel touches on similar themes that are used in Yolen's short story. In her review of this novel in the *New York Times*, Cynthia Samuels states, "Jane Yolen has brought the time travel convention to a new and ambitious level. Instead of fantasy she offers a sober and enriching dose of history." In this novel, though the topic is a gruesome one, Samuels finds that Yolen chose to "omit the sort of graphic descriptions that might overwhelm youngsters." Samuels adds, "Sooner or later all our children must know what happened in the days of the Holocaust." And she recommends Yolen's book to provide the way.

Yolen also wrote *Briar Rose*, another novel on the topic of the Holocaust. In the *Journal of the Fantastic in the Arts*, Ellen R. Weil wrote a critical essay on both of Yolen's Holocaust novels, in which she states why she finds Yolen's writing to be important: "Both novels establish a link between a younger generation and their family histories through emphasizing the importance of memory and storytelling." Weil then adds, "When history itself becomes unimaginable, Yolen seems to suggest, it is only through fantasy and imagination that we can make ourselves part of it, and make it real."

After reviewing one of Yolen's children's books, a reviewer for *PR Newswire* sums up the quality of her lifetime of prize-winning stories, by reminding readers that Yolen has been dubbed "a modern equivalent of Aesop" as well as "the Hans Christian Andersen of America."

CRITICISM

Joyce Hart

Hart is a published writer and creative writing teacher. In this essay, she explores the various forms of prejudice in Yolen's short story "Suzy and Leah."

It is obvious that Yolen was motivated by the horrific acts of World War II to write the short story "Suzy and Leah." The story uses a setting that is based on true events. There really was a refugee camp at Oswego, New York, that matches the description of the camp where Leah

THE IDEA THAT ALL PEOPLE ARE CONNECTED TO ONE ANOTHER BECAUSE THEY SHARE THE COMMON TRAIT OF BEING HUMAN IS OVERLOOKED."

is housed. The stories that Leah recounts about her life before she comes to the United States reflect stories that survivors of the Holocaust have told. Though details about the war and the Holocaust are kept to a minimum and mostly remain in the background, the effects of both linger in the mind and the emotions of the character Leah. So even if the story is not overtly involved with the war and the Holocaust, Yolen has clearly written this story to make a point about what happened in Germany while it was under the control of Hitler's Nazi government. One of the underlying forces that drove Hitler's war against the Jews was his extreme prejudice. And in "Suzy and Leah," Yolen demonstrates how prejudices can form.

In the first sentence of this short story, Yolen has Suzy describe an old army base where a group of refugees have been brought to stay. Suzy refers to it as "*that* place." By emphasizing the word *that*, Yolen creates a negative overtone. Suzy obviously has something to say about the buildings and the place. There is something about the army base that she does not like. Suzy confirms this by writing in her diary that the place is "ugly!" The exclamation point insinuates that this is not a normal "ugly." And in fact it is not. The buildings are run-down, but something else is going on. There is a barbed wire fence going around the place, which makes both those outside the fence as well as those inside the fence realize that a definite line has been drawn between the two groups of people. One group, the barbed wire fence states, is different from the other. These concepts are mirrored in Suzy and Leah's journal entries. Suzy comments that when she offered candy to the children as she stood on the outside of the fence, she felt like she was at the zoo. Leah states that even though they have been told they are no longer prisoners, the fence is visibly keeping her

WHAT DO I READ NEXT?

- Yolen wrote several stories about the plight of Jews during the reign of Nazis in Germany. In her novel *Briar Rose* (1992), Yolen uses the fairy tale "Sleeping Beauty" to help tell the story of one victim of the Holocaust. The story features a grandmother and a granddaughter who is determined to unravel a mystery.

- Another novel written by Yolen that focuses on the atrocities of World War II and Nazi concentration camps is her 1988 book *The Devil's Arithmetic*. Hanna, the protagonist of this story, travels back in time to Poland in the 1940s. She is imprisoned and comes to better appreciate the Jewish customs of her ancestry.

- Julia Alvarez wrote about a different kind of cruelty by a harsh government. In her novel *In the Time of the Butterflies* (1994), Alvarez bases her story on the Mirabal sisters, who were real people living in the Dominican Republic during the corrupt Trujillo dictatorship. These sisters rebel against the system and sacrifice their lives to help lead their people to freedom.

- Ron Koertge's novel *Strays* (2007) follows the challenges of sixteen-year-old Ted, who tells his inner thoughts not to a diary but rather to stray animals. Ted, an orphan, discovers that animals understand him better than people do. Readers follow Ted as he tries to adjust to new foster parents and the other foster kids he must share his bedroom and his life with. His communications with animals are sometimes very funny but can also be painfully sad as Ted struggles with his loneliness.

- For another view of literary diaries, read Sherman Alexie's *The Absolutely True Diary of a Part-Time Indian* (2007). In this story, Junior, a teen living on a Spokane Indian reservation, wants to improve himself by attending a better school off the reservation. This wins him no points with his fellow Native American friends and family and earns him nothing but trouble at the all-white school he wants to attend. Partially based on his life, Alexie creates both incidents readers will laugh at as well as some that will bring tears.

- In *Haven: The Dramatic Story of 1,000 World War II Refugees and How They Came to America* (2000), author Ruth Gruber recounts her story of how she helped the group of refugees who were detained at Fort Ontario, in Oswego, New York, during World War II. This is the camp that Yolen refers to in her short story. Gruber shares her experiences, telling of the dangerous journey the refugees are forced to take to come to the United States and of their adjustment to their new lives in America.

---

freedom at bay. In creating a distinct barrier between two groups of people, one lays the ground for prejudice. The fence implies that the refugees are people who cannot be trusted. This is similar to what Hitler was doing in Europe. He forced Jewish people out of their homes and into ghettos, and at times boarded up the streets so they could not come out at will. So it is little wonder that Suzy subconsciously thinks the refugees are as different from her as animals in a zoo. For Leah, it is easy to associate Suzy, with her blond hair and pretty dresses, with just another variation of the Nazis. The result is that neither girl trusts the other. Leah does not trust Suzy's gifts or smiles. Suzy does not trust Leah's grim expressions.

In Suzy's next entry in her diary, she mocks the refugee children for not knowing how to peel oranges before eating them. In this instance, Suzy practices another elementary form of prejudice.

She assumes everyone should be like her. When they are not, their strangeness increases, which pushes them farther away from what Suzy believes is the norm. Suzy insinuates that the children are stupid not to know that one does not eat the peel of an orange. She also writes that she is afraid to touch the refugees for fear of catching some contagious disease. Suzy implies through her statements about not knowing how to eat a common fruit and being dirty that the refugees are beneath her. Suzy, one can assume, takes baths and dresses neatly each day. Whereas, in her mind, the small boy who touched her might have given her "bugs," she cannot fathom that the conditions in which these refugees live is lacking bathing facilities or that the children do not have clean clothes to wear. It is easier to feel righteous or superior. And this breeds prejudice. A fertile ground in creating prejudices against a group of people exists if one believes those people are of a lower status. People can be led to jump to the conclusion that this group of dirty people does not deserve to live in the same location as those who are better off. So the refugees, Suzy might conclude, deserve to live behind the barbed wire fence.

But Suzy is not the only one who jumps to conclusions. Leah states in her journal that she will not accept any food from "that yellow-haired girl." Granted, Leah is reacting to Suzy's having laughed at her friend for eating the orange peel. But there is something behind Leah's mention of yellow hair that could lead to prejudice. Leah has dark hair. So is Suzy's blond hair enough to make Leah create a barrier between her and Suzy? Has Leah projected her hatred of the Nazis onto Suzy because in her mind Suzy reminds her of light-haired Germans? One form of prejudice that spreads quickly among groups of people is based on appearances, such as the color of one's skin. People with white skin might fear people with dark skin and vice versa because they are concerned that the color makes someone act or think differently. The idea that all people are connected to one another because they share the common trait of being human is overlooked. In Hitler's Germany, anyone with a trace of Jewish blood was rounded up and put to death. What was their crime? They were different from Hitler's definition of the Aryan race—people who originated from a northern European background.

A common language is a good way for people to come to accept one another; however, just because someone speaks a different language, it does not mean that deep down the two people are so foreign to one another that they cannot be considered equals. But Suzy makes a comment about language, part of which is slightly derogatory. She mentions that most of the refugees do not speak English. She is put off by this to the point that she challenges their right to be in this country. She writes, "This is America, after all." With this statement, Suzy dismisses every person who has come to America from a country in which English is not the first language. She insists that anyone who lives in this country needs to speak English. Since the United States is a land of refugees, except for Native Americans (who originally did not speak English, by the way), a large portion of those who are Americans have parents, grandparents, or great-grandparents who did not speak English when they first arrived.

Through her concept that everyone in this country should immediately know how to speak English, Suzy is marginalizing everyone who does not speak English, and subtly insinuating that if they do not, then they should not be in America. Later, Suzy makes fun of the refugee children when they mispronounce words as they struggle to learn English. Suzy demonstrates through her comments that she is clearly not familiar with the study of language. If she had tried to learn German or Chinese or any language other than English, she might empathize with the refugees. She would understand how difficult it is to drop an American accent and pick up the natural tones and sounds of letters in a foreign language. It is too easy to mock someone else when the experience is not shared. Thus, prejudice can develop when one person laughs at another person's language and then uses the differences to call that person strange. Language differences can become very much like the barbed wire fence—an artificial barrier between two groups of people. When Leah ponders the language differences in preparing to attend school, she writes, "There is barbed wire still between us and the world." With this Leah implies language can also keep her cut off from the people who live on the other side of the fence. If language is not common between two groups of people, how can they communicate? There are ways, of course. But those who mock another person's language or accent are erecting a fence, searching for a way to keep so-called foreigners away.

In another incident, Leah states that she dislikes Suzy's name. She says that it is a "silly" name because it means nothing. Then Leah

Leah refused to eat oranges Suzy handed out. (Image copyright Maksim Shmelijov, 2009. Used under license from Shutterstock.com)

claims her name was handed down from her great-grandmother, "who was an important woman in our village." Leah has a right to feel proud of her heritage, but in the process, she puts down Suzy's name. Here is another excuse that people use to diminish the worth of someone from another culture. This is that same trap of putting oneself on a higher level than another person. When people act arrogantly, they are saying they are better than someone else. In Leah's case, she feels above Suzy, but not for anything that Leah accomplished. She did nothing to deserve the honor of her great-grandmother's name except that she was born. And yet she feels superior to Suzy.

Suzy also mentions the differences in culture. She ridicules Leah because Leah does not know how to dance to contemporary American music. Suzy's mind is not open enough to consider that Leah might have dances of her own from her country. Neither does Suzy realize that after experiencing the war and the concentration camps, Leah might not feel like dancing. Nor does Suzy state that she offered to teach Leah words to American songs. It is far too convenient, as well as lazy, to keep the barriers up. Suzy appears determined to stay on her side of the fence, to commit Leah to being incorrigibly different and thus too strange to build a bridge between them. In subtle ways, Suzy has made Leah wear the same yellow star that Hitler made the Jews wear. Here is proof, the yellow star yelled out, that the wearer is different from those who do not need to wear this emblem.

Yolen sets up all these scenes to show how prejudices are formed. Fortunately, she also demonstrates how those prejudices can be deconstructed. When one takes the time to really get to know the other person, to understand where they are coming from and what they are feeling, prejudice can melt away. Yolen ends her story by insinuating that Suzy and Leah were able to do this.

Source: Joyce Hart, Critical Essay on "Suzy and Leah," in *Short Stories for Students*, Gale, Cengage Learning, 2010.

Stephanie Loer

In the following interview, Yolen explains that an idea for a character is what drives her story lines.

Jane Yolen's original story "Disas-Tour Inc." will be published in six weekly chapters in the Living/Arts section beginning next Tuesday. Yolen's stories and poems about fantasy, science fiction, history, and nature are familiar to many young readers. Most of her work reflects a strong sense of family.

Having written more than 200 books for children, young adults, and adults, Yolen has received numerous awards. Her poem "Owl Moon," winner of the 1988 Caldecott Award with John Schoenherr's watercolor illustrations, was inspired by her husband's interest in birding.

Yolen was interviewed recently in her home in Hatfield. More information about her and her books can be found at www.janeyolen.com.

Q. When you begin writing, what drives the story line, the characters, or the plot?

A. Usually an idea or a character begins a story. Then I run after the characters shouting out, "Wait for me!" But in "Disas-Tour Inc.," the actual story of the Titanic certainly gave a timeline and focus to the telling.

Q. Do situations or circumstances from your childhood influence your writing?

A. Only occasionally do I write about something from my own childhood. To be honest, it was a very pleasant and unexciting childhood. It was the best kind to live through, but the worst kind for a writer. I remember little of it.

Q. Was there a certain point in your life when you decided to become a writer?

A. My parents both wrote. My father was a newspaperman and then a publicist who produced a half-dozen books and some movie scripts in his writing career. My mother wrote short stories, though only one was ever published. She also created crossword puzzles and double acrostics, which she sold to magazines and activity books. So I thought all grown-ups were writers. I began writing as a child and have never stopped.

Q. Do you have a special place where you like to do your writing?

A. I have a writing room in my attic, which I call the "aerie."

Q. Why do you think children like your books?

A. Because I love to tell stories.

Q. What advice would you give young people who want to become writers?

A. Be a reader, first. Second, write something every day because the writing muscle needs to be exercised. Third, never let other people tell you, "No! You can't write." Because you can!

Q. When you are not writing, what do you do for recreation?

A. I read, watch movies, travel—especially in Scotland, where we have a second home—go antiquing, visit my grandkids, listen to music, and laugh a lot with my kids.

Q. Are the characters in your books similar to people you know?

A. Sometimes, yes. Commander Toad is my son Adam. He is also Jakkin in "Dragon's Blood." My son Jason is the boy in the novel *The Boy Who Spoke Chimp*. My daughter Heidi is the girl in "Owl Moon." And sometimes, even when I'm not aware of it, maybe bits of the children sneak into a story.

Q. Is writing easy and fun for you, or is it hard work?

A. It is both. It's easy because I love it, and it's hard work because I want to do the very best work I can do.

Q. What new books can your readers anticipate?

A. Several new books are coming out this fall. *Girl in a Cage* is the story of King Robert the Bruce's daughter, who was captured in a Scottish uprising by the wicked King Edward Longshanks and put in a cage on display. How the events of that time changed her from a spoiled princess to a Scottish patriot is told in a novel for readers age 10 and up. And "Harvest Home" is a rhyming picture book that celebrates old-fashioned harvesting of crops in 19th-century America.

Q. How do you feel about having one of your stories in a newspaper?

A. It means a lot of kids get to read it, so I love that. But tomorrow, the story can go on the bottom of the hamster cage, so that hurts.

Source: Stephanie Loer, "Storytelling is a Labor of True Love for Author Yolen," in *Boston Globe*, October 8, 2002, p. E6.

Eileen Beal

In the following article, Beal attests to Yolen's Jewish themes, which were strengthened by her heritage and childhood struggles.

Newsweek Magazine has called grandmotherly Jane Yolen "the Hans Christian Andersen of America." The *New York Times* has called her the "modern equivalent of Aesop." Millions of kids (and growing numbers of adults) have read her 200-plus poetry, fiction, and non-fiction books which respect readers' minds, challenge their imagination, nurture their sense of wonder, and draw deeply on the history and folktales she's been reading and studying all her life. They call her mentor, guide, teacher.

A writer and professional storyteller for 40 years, and a founding member of the Society of Children's Book Writers and Illustrators, Yolen never writes or talks "down" to her audience.

Sometimes, she explained in a late-night phone interview, they share their "ah-ha" moments with her: "A kid wrote me once and said, 'I hope you live to be 99, but who cares, your stories will live forever.'"

All through high school and Smith College she never imagined any career for herself other than writing. "I grew up with parents who read and were writers. All their friends—the people we had over for dinner—were writers."

The daughter of parents who "came out of very religious families and wanted to get as far away from their roots as possible," Yolen has always been proud of her Jewish heritage. But it was often hard to find it, let alone live it, she says, after her parents moved from a very Jewish neighborhood in New York City to "where there were maybe nine other Jewish kids in school."

Moving to Westport "that other world," she called it—actually strengthened Yolen's resolve to retain her heritage. "When I wanted to be confirmed—a surprise to my parents—I was the first girl ever to read out of the Torah...at our Reform congregation...In high school I refused to sing Christmas carols in the school choir unless they also sang Chanukah songs. So they did."

Struggling to live her heritage brought Yolen face-to-face with a cultural disconnect that she says many American Jews experience: "I felt that I was of two worlds and that I wasn't a fit in either."

Walking a path through two worlds—that of the secular Jew and that of the middle-class American shaped Yolen's writing and her career. "I've been writing about themes—especially in my children's books—that I've been wrestling with all my life: the getting of wisdom, taking responsibility for your actions."

Yolen's best-known Jewish book, 10 years in the writing, is *The Devil's Arithmetic* (1988). The National Jewish Book Award novel shows the transformation of a whiney Jewish American brat into a strong young woman who finally comes to understand the meaning *l'chaim* (to life) holds for those who have survived the Holocaust.

Yolen, who has won numerous book awards, stressed that the path she trod to get where she is today was a put-one-foot-in-front-of-the-other-and-just-do-it trail that she almost detoured into the ivory towers of academia.

In the mid-'70s, with about 80 books under her belt, Yolen decided that she wanted to teach children's literature as well as write it, so she enrolled in a Ph.D. program at the University of Massachusetts. Graduate school was an eye-opener, she admitted, and it cured her of her desire to go into the classroom fulltime. "What I found (in graduate school) was that what I really liked was writing," she explained with a wry chuckle.

Not quite. The research papers she did for her M.A. were published as *Touch Magic*, which is a standard text in most children's literature classes today. She also teaches children's literature in college classrooms all over the U.S.—as a guest lecturer. . . .

Source: Eileen Beal, "Teller of Tales of Wonder," in *Cleveland Jewish News*, Vol. 79, No. 14, March 30, 2001, p. 63.

David L. Russell

In the following essay, it is Russell's opinion that Holocaust-focused works are more than just appropriate reading for youth, they are critical as cautionary tales.

A great many books about the Holocaust have been written for young people over the years, and, like all books about the Holocaust, they are unsettling, even painful to read. The Holocaust is among the most difficult topics for a young reader to approach. There are those who deplore any attempt at writing Holocaust literature, claiming, with Michael Wyschogrod, that "art is not appropriate to the holocaust. Art takes the sting out of suffering. Any attempt to transform the holocaust into art demeans the holocaust and must result in poor art" (qtd. in Rosenfeld 14). But the more persuasive argument lies with those who insist that not to speak out is a greater injustice, that it is "blasphemy to remain silent" and give Hitler "one more posthumous victory" (Rosenfeld 14). When we are considering literature for children, we must inevitably confront the question as to whether such a grim topic is at all appropriate for young minds. It reminds us of the age-old argument over the fairy tales—another case in which adults so frequently underestimate children. A great deal of evidence suggests that children from about the ages of ten or twelve and up are fully capable of dealing with the fundamental issues of the Holocaust. (See Deverensky, Minarak, Sherman, and Zack for firsthand accounts of positive classroom experiences with Holocaust literature.) Indeed, the Holocaust should not be viewed as merely a suitable topic for young readers, but an important and necessary topic. And through the literature—diaries, reminiscences, novels—young people not only acquire exposure to the Nazi atrocities, they achieve a measure of perspective on their meaning. Contrary to what Wyschogrod says, art need not remove the sting from suffering and demean its subject—in fact, art, which focuses on the particular, may have greater power to move our emotions than do the numbing statistics of history. We are appalled at the death of millions, but we weep at the death of the one. As Eva Fleischner writes, "we can attain universality only through particularity: there are no shortcuts. The more we come to know about the Holocaust, how it came about, how it was carried out, etc., the greater the possibility that we will become sensitized to inhumanity and suffering whenever they occur" (qtd. in "Preface," *Facing History and Ourselves* xvii). Additionally, it is important to realize that art of the Holocaust is necessarily didactic art—the experience is too sobering for it to be otherwise. Stories of the Holocaust are like cautionary tales, warning us of the danger of complacency, reminding us of the tenuous thread on which human decency is at times suspended.

The Holocaust—its incomprehensible nature aside—is an extraordinarily complex and multifaceted experience. Recognizing that fact many years ago, Eric Kimmel identified various types of Holocaust literature, which he described using the analogy of the concentric rings of Dante's *Inferno*. The outermost ring includes the Resistance novels, depicting the underground movements in which the Jews are typically helpless victims aided by "righteous Gentiles." Refugee novels are stories, largely by Jewish writers, focusing on the flight of Jews and their subsequent struggle for survival. Occupation novels, usually focusing on Jewish characters, describe the exploits of ordinary citizens coping with Nazi rule. At the very center of this Inferno are the harrowing stories of the death camps (Kimmel 85ff.). We cannot grasp the total impact of the

> THE MOST NOTABLY RECURRING WORD IN THE TEXT IS 'REMEMBER.' FROM THE BOOK'S VERY FIRST SENTENCE—'I'M TIRED OF REMEMBERING'—IT IS MEMORY THAT GUIDES THE CHARACTERS THROUGH THIS STORY."

Holocaust without knowledge of all these facets of the experience. An examination of three works of Holocaust fiction—Lois Lowry's *Number the Stars*, Hans Richter's *Friedrich*, and Jane Yolen's *The Devil's Arithmetic*—will reveal how a brutal subject, sensitively handled, can be presented in a fashion appropriate for young readers. These books are testaments to both the very best and the very worst humankind can achieve. Individually, each book is a powerful statement on the Nazi atrocities, and each delivers a distinctive lesson in ethical decision-making and behavior, but taken together they begin to form a cohesive vision of the Holocaust and suggest what may be the ultimate significance of that human experience for us all. The whole becomes greater than the parts....

This brings us to the final work, Jane Yolen's *The Devil's Arithmetic*, the story of a young Jewish girl inside a Nazi concentration camp, and the rarest type of Holocaust literature for younger readers. It is interesting to note how Yolen handles the subject to bring it within the grasp of the teenage audience. *The Devil's Arithmetic* is a time-shift fantasy, employing a story within a story. The protagonist, Hannah, a character based on Yolen herself, is transported from the present back in time to 1942 (how is neither explained nor important to the story), experiences life in Poland as Chaya, an orphaned girl who ends up in a concentration camp, and then, as mysteriously, is transported back to the present, where no perceptible time has elapsed. (Lloyd Alexander uses a similar technique in *The First Two Lives of Lukas-Kasha*.) But aside from the time-shift, the story is closer to historical realism than to fantasy, with its shattering portrayal of the Nazi treatment of the Jews.

The story opens in the present day with Hannah begrudgingly taking part in her family's

Seder dinner at Passover. The very first sentence in the book is Hannah's complaint, "I'm tired of remembering," referring to her impatience with the ritual, which she finds tiresome and repetitious. Hannah, in her early teens, is experiencing the natural rebellion of youth against the family; she is entertaining religious doubts, and traditions seem old-fashioned and irrelevant to her. Among her extended family is her aunt Eva, her grandfather's maiden sister, who is given the honor of lighting the Seder candles. Hannah has always felt a special tie to Eva, who is both wise and gentle. Hannah once thought her aunt's answers to her endless questions were "magical," but "as Hannah got older, the magic disappeared, leaving Aunt Eva a very ordinary person. Hannah hated that it was so, so she pushed the thought away." Aunt Eva becomes a seminal character in the story, which will explain this strange affinity Hannah has felt toward her. When the moment in the Seder ritual is reached that the door is to be opened for the symbolic entrance of Elijah, it is Hannah who is instructed to open it. "Slowly Hannah moved toward the front door, feeling incredibly dumb. She certainly didn't believe that the prophet Elijah would come through the apartment door any more than she believed Darth Vader, or Robin Hood, or...or the Easter Bunny, would." The religious ritual has become foolish superstition for Hannah. She reluctantly moves toward the apartment door, flings it open, and finds herself facing, not the "long, windowless hall with dark green numbered doors leading into other apartments," but "a greening field and a lowering sky." The magical translation back to Poland, 1942, has taken place.

Hannah has been inexplicably incarnated as a recently orphaned Polish girl, recovering from an extended illness in the home of her aunt and uncle, Gitl and Shmuel (who are sister and brother), somewhere in rural Poland. Hannah initially believes that she is dreaming and she accepts the strange circumstances fully expecting to awaken at any time. But the dream will quickly turn into the worst kind of nightmare. As it happens, Hannah's translation has occurred the day before the wedding of Shmuel with the beautiful Fayge, and she joins in the joyous preparations for the event. Understandably perplexed, Hannah nevertheless embraces this new experience with a bit of relish. The name of the Polish girl whose body Hannah inhabits is Chaya—which, Hannah reminds herself is her Hebrew name,

"The one I was given to honor Aunt Eva's dead friend." This presages the story's conclusion, when we learn just who Chaya was. The *badchan,* who is a village entertainer-seer-poet (he reminds Hannah of a jester), says to Hannah: "So, your name is Chaya, which is to say, life. A strong name for a strange time, child. Be good, life and long life to your friends, young-old Chaya." This will become a prophetic remark.

On the wedding day, a procession is formed and heads for the village where Shmuel will meet and marry his bride. Only when the procession reaches the village and Hannah sees army trucks surrounding the synagogue does she realize that she is in the past. She immediately recognizes the Nazi soldiers and knows enough history to realize what is about to happen to all the Jews of the village—including herself. She tries to warn her new-found friends, but to no avail. She foresees the future, but no one will believe her. The villagers are herded into trucks, transported to railway boxcars, and sent on an excruciating journey to a concentration camp. The first death recorded in the book is that of a young child suffocated in the packed railway boxcar—the child was lucky.

The remainder of the novel chronicles the atrocities visited upon the Jews in the camp, the humiliation and degradation (their heads are shaved; their names are exchanged for numbers tattooed on their arms; they are forced to wear the tattered, cast-off garments of the dead) and the savage brutality (the smokestacks of the ovens loom over the camp as a constant reminder of their precarious existence). In the camp, they encounter unspeakably cruel German captors and their day-to-day survival is tenuous at best. There is nothing of human decency; they are treated worse than animals and the German guards seem to relish the torment they inflict. There is a reversal of all human values—the sick, the infirm and the old are, instead of being cared for, destroyed.

The most notably recurring word in the text is "remember." From the book's very first sentence—"I'm tired of remembering"—it is memory that guides the characters through this story. Hannah summons up her memories of her own past experiences—of books she has read and movies she has seen—and they provide her with a wealth of stories she draws upon to entertain the children. As the days, weeks, and months pass, she must also keep alive the memories of her family back in New Rochelle at the Seder, which is somewhere in the future. As Chaya, Shmuel and Gitl naturally expect her to remember a past that she, as Hannah, never had. And, most horrifying of all, she is gifted, like Cassandra of Greek legend, with knowledge of the future (a forward-looking memory of the fate of the Jews) that no one will believe. The memories help to pass the time in the concentration camp where the passing of time itself is a meaningless concept. Every day is the same and carries with it the same expectancy of death. As she witnesses friends and acquaintances, usually the weak and the sick, being taken off to the furnaces, all she really knows is that "each day she remained alive, *she remained alive.* One plus one plus one. The Devil's arithmetic, Gitl called it." There is little else to sustain them. This may be slim hope on which to establish a *raison d'être,* but extraordinary circumstances demand extraordinary determination sustained by vivid memories of a cherished past. In the camp, Hannah befriends Rivka, a girl who has lost both parents, three sisters and a brother to the ovens, who tells Hannah, "As long as we can remember, all those gone before are alive inside us." Hannah/Chaya comes to represent this determination and comes to understand the value of remembering as a part of this strength, of this hope.

At the climax of the story, Hannah/Chaya is "chosen" for the ovens, and, in a final moment of heroism, she makes it possible for Rivka to escape from the camp. Then, summoning all the strength she knows, she walks with two other friends toward the furnaces, and tells them the story of Hannah of New Rochelle as they go and of the wonderful things the future will hold for those who survive. They pause before the door of Lilith's cave, the name the Jews gave to the furnace rooms, and "Then all three of them took deep, ragged breaths and walked in through the door into endless night." It is a profoundly moving passage, depicting the ultimate human dignity and at the same time suggesting the hope that does indeed lie in the future. At this point, the story returns to the present. The doorway to the furnaces is the passage back to the present and Hannah finds herself back in her grandmother's apartment—but a very changed person. The symbolism is profound, for through the ovens of the Third Reich Hannah has been transported into the security of a middle-class apartment in New Rochelle, New York. Chaya's own sacrifice, Hannah learns, made the present possible, for Rivka, who escaped, is Hannah's Aunt Eva. Hannah now grasps the significance of the numbers tattooed on Aunt Eva's arm and comprehends the importance of remembering, which is at once our means of keeping the past alive and ensuring the continuity of our values into the future. Through her extraordinary experience she has achieved an understanding of human suffering, suffering that teaches us what really matters, and her understanding will continue, for another generation at least, the timeless process of renewing the human spirit.

Yolen has presented a frank and sensitive tale of the grimmest aspects of the Holocaust. The time-shift fantasy, Yolen contends, is an ideal vehicle for presenting history to reluctant and skeptical teenagers because it thrusts one of their contemporaries into the past where he or she can ask the very questions that often perplex young readers about history and historical figures. "How can you believe the world is flat when it isn't?" "How can you trust that the people helping you over the mountain will not enslave you? How can you believe these Nazis when they say you are only being resettled?" (Yolen, "An Experiential Act,"*Devil's Arithmetic*). Through the eyes of Hannah, their contemporary, young readers experience one of the most incomprehensible periods of modern history. We see, in the Nazi persecutors, the deplorable depths to which human nature can plummet. We see the phenomenal resilience that is possible in the besieged human spirit. We see the necessity for never forgetting such atrocities. We see the importance of remembering. And so we have descended, to return to Kimmel's analogy, to the Ninth Circle and have stared into the face of evil. Yolen has enabled us to confront directly the most savage of Nazi horrors—even Friedrich's end looks merciful in comparison, and we now know what would have awaited the Rosens had the Johansens' efforts failed.

When I was a high school student in the 1960s, the pastor of our church was a Japanese-American who never lost an opportunity to spark the social conscience of his parish in our small Midwestern town. I still vividly recall one sermon describing a woman who admired what she thought was a beautiful abstract picture hanging above a friend's mantle. But when her friend pointed out to her that it was not an abstract picture at all, but an aerial photograph of a World War II Japanese-American internment camp in the American Southwest, the woman no longer found the picture beautiful. Under close scrutiny, the picture became a haunting reminder of a shameful chapter in American history. From a comfortable distance, we can ignore the atrocities; it is only when we are forced to view them close-up that the ugliness, the horror, the baseness of humanity are revealed. And sooner or later we must realize, along with Yolen's Hannah, that in the face of these horrors, "We are all monsters... because we are letting it happen." Children's books about the Holocaust are unabashedly didactic—they have an overt moral purpose and because of that they are delivered with the same fervor as those Puritan tales of James Janeway or Benjamin Keath that many modern readers find so startling. But the comparison is not so bizarre, for the seventeenth-century Puritan writers conceived the fires of Hell to be every bit as real as the twentieth-century writers know the furnaces of Birkenau to be. And in both cases, the writers have believed it crucial for children to be told their message—and in both cases, the message is a warning and a guide, its ultimate aim being salvation. These are messages that cannot be mollified or sweetened lest they lose their impact.

Because of the complexity of the Holocaust, and because of the scope of the atrocities, it is not possible for any one book to give children a comprehensive understanding of this human tragedy. One critic of adult literature on the subject remarks:

> We have no Milton or Tolstoy of the Holocaust and should not soon await one; in fact, it is wiser to discourage expectation of literature of epic scope and look instead to its opposite, to the shards and fragments that reveal, in their separateness and brokenness, the uncountable small tragedies that together add up to something larger than the tragic sense implies. (Rosenfeld 33)

Holocaust literature for children is always sobering, always enlightening, and it may be some of the most important reading children ever undertake. It reminds us of the appalling truth that of the estimated six million Jews who died as a result of the Holocaust, some one and a half million were children—and so it is a tale that very much involves children. In these novels of the Holocaust we see children telling their story to children, and not to shock or titillate them, but to share their bitter herbs in the hope of securing a happier future. Young readers will emerge from these "shards and fragments" of human experience more serious, more pensive, more wary of humanity. They may also emerge with a deeper sense of the ethical and moral obligations that lie ahead for them—and therein may lie the ultimate value of Holocaust literature. What is appropriate for young readers? The truth, the truth, the truth. The Holocaust leaves no room for deception. It was itself, after all, orchestrated through a grand deception—it would be a cruel irony indeed if we perpetuated its memory with yet more deception. Knowledge of the Holocaust forces us all to confront the fear, ignorance and hatred lurking in the dark recesses of the soul. And in these stories of suffering humanity, we may at times hear above the cries of despair, the faint, persistent murmuring of the compassionate heart that will lead us out of the darkness and toward the light.

Source: David L. Russell, "Reading the Shards and Fragments: Holocaust Literature for Young Readers," in *Lion and the Unicorn*, Vol. 21, No. 2, 1997, pp. 267–80.

Gloria Goodale

In the following article, Goodale discusses the folk story as Yolen's primary and recurring theme.

Life for children's author Jane Yolen is like the proverbial fisherman and the-fish-that-got-away. There's always another story, another question, another book to be conquered.

"If I ever thought I'd written the perfect book, I'd never write again," confesses this award-winning author of nearly 200 fiction and nonfiction books for children as well as adults. Best known for fairy-tale themes, she's also written poetry and a book on the Holocaust—not to mention, songs for her son's rock band, "Boiled in Lead."

What drives this honorary PhD, mother of three, and full-time editor for Harcourt Brace?

While some might say from her prodigious output, that it is nervous energy, Yolen begs to differ. "A nervous sense of wonder," she laughs. She wonders about all sorts of things, from graveyards to magazine articles, not to mention the stalwart questions of childhood: What if toads fell out of your mouth? And what do space-hopping frogs eat? (Croak-a-cola and French flies, of course.)

Ms. Yolen, who started out as a journalist and a poet, says she writes all the time, everywhere she goes, from her farm in Hatfield, Mass., to her home in Scotland. "I never thought I'd end up writing children's books, but I've always loved folk songs, ballads and tales. They're part of my everyday respiration."

These primal story telling forms are a recurring theme in Yolen's work. They are, she says, "what form the basis of human community." A serious student of folklore, Yolen notes, "Human beings are the story animal. With story, we can look at our past, where we are now, and project into the future."

"Jane is completely literate in the history of kid's literature and from the point of view of many cultures," says Lin Oliver, director and co-founder of the Society of Children's Book Writers and Illustrators (SCBWI). "She understands what's common in all our mythologies. Because of this, her writing is very primal, and it feels like it addresses the basic needs of children."

Of Yolen's contribution, Oliver says, "She has an intellectual understanding of our commonality that has created a body of work that really stands alone."

Boyds Mill Press editor Joan O'Donnell, who has worked with Yolen for five years says that beyond being a master storyteller, Yolen has a deep appreciation and recognition of other people's work and talent. Observes O'Donnell, "Jane has edited numerous anthologies and through that, brought new authors to children who might not otherwise know about them."

Indeed, a selflessness and pure love of the form seem to go with the field of children's writing.

"It's certainly not for the money," says SCBWI director Oliver, shaking her head ruefully. She points out that Yolen has taught at SCBWI conferences for the past 25 years,

While Yolen's themes tend toward the mythic, she is very concerned about the *reality* of children's lives today. "I think we're growing them up too quickly. Today they have to deal with death, AIDS, sex, drugs, family disintegration. When I was growing up in New York, nobody ever knew anyone who'd died. Now, my older kids both know someone who's been murdered by the time they were 18. We may have gained something, but we've also lost something."

Says O'Donnell, "[Yolen's] timeless themes and mythologic references leave room for the child's imagination."

"Her books leave room for the child to grow and to think, what if?" O'Donnell adds with a soft laugh. Kids, especially today, need a welcome break from *reality*-based material."

Yolen says, "I don't labor over doing a relevant topic," but she adds that her books still reflect the issues that are on her mind, and mentions her Holocaust-themed book, "*The Devil's Arithmetic*."

"That book, by the way, was burned in a hibachi on the steps of the Kansas City Board of Education just two years ago," Yolen says, by way of noting that some *realities* are too much for some communities.

Which brings up another of Yolen's concerns—the state of children's literature today.

"Publishers are filling us up with what I call bathroom literature—you read it quickly and toss it out," she explains, pointing to wildly successful horror books such as R.L. Stine's Goosebumps series.

Yolen says that she is more of the school of intimation and suggestion, musing that children, like adults, need the challenge of good literature. "Good books demand something back," unlike the disposable, gore-filled horror books that are all the rage today, she adds.

What about the kids who don't like to read? "Read with them," says Yolen, "regardless of their age. All kids love a good story."

Besides, she adds, "It turns out that kids who understand [the concept of a] story, have a better understanding of language systems and consequential actions."

"[Yolen's] work will endure," if for no other reason than that she offers the reader so much, O'Donnell says. "Her work is always fresh because she has her finger in so many pies."

With a net so wide, it's just a matter of time before another fish gets away.

Source: Gloria Goodale, "Kids Need 'A Mix of Myth and Reality,'" in *Christian Science Monitor*, November 4, 1996, p. 13.

Children's Literature Association Quarterly

In the following essay, Yolen is profiled as a champion of "original fairy tales."

Bruno Bettelheim's recently published book, *The Uses of Enchantment*, explains in psychological detail how fairy tales "educate, support, and liberate the emotions of children." But ChLA member Jane Yolen has always known the power of these archetypal stories. In "America's Cinderella," a paper presented at the 1976 Conference, Jane, who has been called "America's leading modern creator of original fairy tales," called for the banishment of the spineless, saccharine Cinderella of American mass-market books and the restoration of the hardy, shrewd prototype who appears in books as early as ninth century China. Like Bettelheim, who analyzes Cinderella at length, she attempted to show how the fairy tale speaks to the child's needs at a sub-conscious and pre-conscious level.

In one of her most recent books, *The Moon Ribbon and Other Tales* (Crowell, 1976), the companion volume to *The Girl Who Cried Flowers* (a National Book Award nominee and winner of the Golden Kite Award), the title story tells of a Cinderella-type heroine named Sylva who escapes the domination of the ubiquitous cruel stepmother and stepdaughter with the magical assistance of a silver ribbon made from the grey hair of her true mother and grandmother. No men are mentioned in the story with its purely matriarchal focus on the development of the young girl from passive to active womanhood. Ms. Yolen explained that the paper she presented at the conference grew along with the book as she attempted to restore Cinderella to her proper characterization.

Concerning fairy tales and fantasy, Jane observes: "The need for deep and literary discussion of this genre especially is so important. Without a symbolic language, a shared symbolic language however, I wonder if children can read them. In other words, if we neglect the classics the Greek, Roman, Celtic, Nordic, Semitic, and Oriental mythologies in our schools, are we dooming young readers, and by extension the adult readers, to a depthless understanding of fiction? *The Grey King* (Susan Cooper, Atheneum) has to be read by young readers without that background as a simple, marvel-filled adventure story. And God knows what they make of Tolkien."

Her personal preference for fantasy covers a wide range of styles. She notes: "LeGuin is my favorite living fantasy (sf) writer at the moment. I also have a passion for Evangeline Walton's *Mabinogion* recreations and *Dune* (Frank Herbert, Chilton). I have reread the Tolkien books a half dozen times and just finished reading *The Hobbit* to my kids. Last year I took a dreambath in Victoriana for children, and got around to rereading *Mowgli* among others."

Jane herself has enriched the field of fantasy literature with the creation of many original fairy tales as well as picture books and nonfiction works. Her picture book, *The Little Spotted Fish*, illustrated by Friso Henstra (Seabury) was selected by the Children's Book Council as part of the 1976 Book Showcase. Her *An Invitation to the Butterfly Ball: A Counting Rhyme* (Parents' Magazine Press) is in its second printing. Besides *The Moon Ribbon*, she has also written *Milkweed Days* (Crowell), a photograph picture book, and a nonfiction work, *Simple Gifts: The Story of the Shakers* (Viking).

A busy lecture schedule has taken her cross-country this Bicentennial year from the University of Maryland, Virginia Polytechnic Institute, and Columbia University to UCLA, Oakland University and Western Washington State. "In between, of course, I am still writing and being a graduate student," says Jane.

In addition to writing and lecturing, this energetic lady is presently engaged in studies for her doctorate in children's literature at the University of Massachusetts. Jane explained that her program includes courses in English Folklore, English Victorian Children's Literature, The Ballad, and Fairy Tales and Writing, as well as Independent Studies. In response to the obvious question of why a successful author feels it necessary to earn a doctorate, Jane responded that she wished to develop in herself a wider and deeper range of knowledge in the field of children's literature. Her dissertation is entitled "Dark Mirrors: Prejudicial Elements in Children's Fantasy Novels," and will examine such prejudices as Charles Kingsley's anti-Irish view-point in *The Water Babies,* the British class system as depicted in P. L. Travers' *Mary Poppins,* and Roald Dahl's *Charlie and the Chocolate Factory.*

Active in all aspects of children's literature, Jane was one of the organizers of the Fourth New England Conference in Children's Literature sponsored by the Society of Children's Writers. Of conference organizing, Jane says: "My dream conference would be one on *Fantasy and Children's Literature,* and would look like this: Joseph Campbell, a keynote speech on "The Mythic Image;" Ursula K. LeGuin, on "Creating a World;" Lloyd Alexander, on "Mining Mythology;" Susan Cooper, on "Good and Evil in Fantasy;" Eleanor Cameron, on "Time

Travel and Time Travelers;" Andre Norton, on "Science Fiction;" Maurice Sendak, on "Capturing Childhood Fantasies;" with Jane herself discussing "Literary Fairy Tales." Remarks Jane thoughtfully: "I would love to set up such a conference... wouldn't it be something!"

Source: "Profile: Jane Yolen," in *Children's Literature Association Quarterly*, Vol. 1, No. 2, Summer 1976.

SOURCES

Bauer, Yehuda, *A History of the Holocaust*, rev. ed., Children's Press, 2002.

"Bestselling Author Jane Yolen Wows with New Novel, Picture Book, and Poetry for Kids," in *PR Newswire*, April 16, 2009.

"The Safe Haven Story," in *Oswego Safe Haven Museum & Education Center*, http://www.oswegohaven.org/story.html (accessed September 18, 2009).

Samuels, Cynthia, "Hannah Learns to Remember," in *New York Times*, November 13, 1988, p. BR 62.

Spielvogel, Jackson J., and David Redles, *Hitler and Nazi Germany: A History*, 6th ed., Prentice Hall, 2009.

Thompson, Raymond H., "Interview with Jane Yolen," in *Interviews with Authors of Modern Arthurian Literature*, August 29, 1988, http://www.lib.rochester.edu/Camelot/intrvws/yolen.htm (accessed September 16, 2009).

Weil, Ellen R., "The Door to Lilith's Cave: Memory and Imagination in Jane Yolen's Holocaust Novels," in *Journal of the Fantastic in the Arts*, Vol. 5, No. 2, 1993, pp. 90–104.

Worth, Robert F., "Despite Warning, Thousands Rally in Iran," in *New York Times*, September 18, 2009, http://www.nytimes.com/2009/09/19/world/middleeast/19iran.html?hp (accessed September 18, 2009).

Yolen, Jane, "Jane Yolen," in *Jane Yolen* Web site, http://janeyolen.com (accessed on September 16, 2009).

———, "Suzy and Leah," in *Literature: Timeless Voices, Timeless Themes: Bronze Level*, Prentice Hall, 2002, pp. 448–56.

FURTHER READING

Friedlander, Saul, *Nazi Germany and the Jews, 1933–1945*, Harper Perennial, 2009.
    This is an abridged version of Friedlander's Pulitzer Prize-winning two-volume history of the Holocaust. The book begins with an overview of the Nazi accession to power in Germany as they moved toward total segregation, humiliation, and impoverishment of German Jews. The second part of this history focuses on the building of the concentration camps and the systematic murder of millions of Jewish people.

Hoobler, Dorothy, and Thomas Hoobler, *The Jewish American Family Album*, Oxford University Press, 1995.
    The history of the Jews, from their beginning to the establishment of the modern state of Israel, is told through personal accounts and reportage. The book follows the lives of Jews both in Europe and in the United States as they are sometimes forced to migrate, as they are persecuted, and as they succeed. Black and white photographs enhance the writing.

Laqueur, Walter, *Generation Exodus: The Fate of Young Jewish Refugees from Nazi Germany*, I. B. Tauris, 2004.
    Laqueur, who was also a refugee, recounts the lives of several young people who escaped Nazi-controlled countries and settled in new places like the United States, Great Britain, India, and Palestine. Not all of these stories end happily, but some refugees, such as Henry Kissinger (secretary of state under President Nixon), proved to be quite successful.

Meltzer, Milton, *Rescue: The Story of How Gentiles Saved Jews in the Holocaust*, HarperCollins, 1991.
    Though many people turned their backs on the plight of Jewish people in Europe as Nazis condemned them to death, many others risked their lives to save their Jewish neighbors and friends. These are their stories, taken from Germany, Poland, Denmark, and other countries that were sympathetic to the rescue of the Jews.

Sender, Ruth Minsky, *The Cage*, Simon Pulse, 1997.
    This is a memoir written by a Jewish woman who spent years in the Lodz ghetto, a segregated part of the city of Lodz, Poland. Her account continues as she is sent to the Auschwitz concentration camp. Though she was saved from Auschwitz, she was still not free. She was forced to serve time in a labor camp in Russia.

Zullo, Allan, and Mara Bovsun, *Survivors: True Stories of Children in the Holocaust*, Scholastic Paperbacks, 2004.
    The true-life stories of nine Jewish boys and girls are covered in this book. Each of these children discovers some way to avoid capture. Some disguised their identities. Others made daring escapes. All of these stories display incredible courage.

Thank You, Ma'm

LANGSTON HUGHES
1963

Poet, short-story writer, novelist, and essayist James Langston Hughes is generally ranked among the greatest black American writers of the first half of the twentieth century, along with Ralph Ellison and Richard Wright. Slightly older than the others, Hughes was an important figure in the Harlem Renaissance, the flourishing of black artistic achievement in Harlem in New York City in the 1920s. Hughes traveled widely, and his aesthetic and political views were informed by the wider perspective of an international black community embracing Paris, Africa, and the Caribbean. Hughes wrote "Thank You, Ma'm" in the mid-1950s and published it in 1963 in *Something in Common and Other Stories* at the end of his career, when the pace of change in the lives of black Americans was accelerating rapidly with the social and political changes of the civil rights movement. In a sense, it is a last look back at the earlier black society of Hughes's youth.

"Thank You, Ma'm" is widely available as one of the most commonly anthologized of Hughes's short stories. The story concerns the decline of Hughes's beloved Harlem neighborhood in the 1950s and 1960s, and serves as an allegory of the need for the black community to resist and reverse that decline.

Langston Hughes (Photo by Gordon Parks. The Library of Congress)

AUTHOR BIOGRAPHY

James Langston Hughes (who wrote as Langston Hughes) was born in Joplin, Missouri, on February 1, 1902. His mother, Caroline (Carrie) Mercer Langston, came from the upper class of the African American community (her uncle was a congressman during Reconstruction, a high-ranking American diplomat, and eventually the president of a college). She was determined to make a career on Broadway, however, and went to New York shortly after graduating from high school. She found no success, and eventually worked as a teacher. She married James Hughes and the family would have had a comfortable middle-class life. After completing correspondence law courses and being denied the opportunity to sit for the bar exam, James Hughes could no longer bear the racial discrimination blacks faced in the United States; the Hugheses moved to Mexico City. Carrie did not like Mexico and she and Langston quickly returned to the United States. Langston went to live with his maternal grandmother, Mary Langston (whose first husband was killed fighting with John Brown during the raid on Harper's Ferry in 1859), in Lawrence, Kansas. He therefore did not face the extreme discrimination experienced by blacks living in the South, but because of the way his family life had been disrupted, he felt all the more keenly the unfair treatment he did experience (for example, his integrated classrooms had a segregated seating chart, and white students praised him for his "rhythm"). Hughes attended high school in Cleveland, Ohio, where he lived with his mother and her second husband after the death of his grandmother. He published in the school newspaper and won honors as a student poet. In 1920, after graduation, crossing the Mississippi by train at St. Louis on the way to visit his father, Hughes wrote "The Negro Speaks of Rivers," often regarded as his best poem. He enrolled in 1921 at Columbia University but completed only one year due to discrimination he faced on campus. He spent the next few years traveling as a ship's crewman, seeing Africa, Europe, and the Caribbean in this way, making important literary contacts wherever he went. He soon began publishing poetry regularly and in 1926 attracted the attention of wealthy black patrons who paid his way to Lincoln University near Philadelphia, Pennsylvania. He spent the summers of his college years on national reading tours for his poetry. His collection *The Weary Blues* was published by Alfred A. Knopf, one of the leading publishers in America, in 1926 while Hughes was an undergraduate at Lincoln University. Once he graduated, Hughes continued a successful writing career, producing new poems, short stories, plays, opera libretti, children's literature, and essays (his popular newspaper columns provided a large part of his income, but were generally thought by contemporary critics to be a squandering of his talent). The majority of his audience was white readers. During his mature period he produced the collection of short stories *The Ways of White Folks* (1934), which is often thought to be his best fiction. He finished what the manuscript identifies as the third draft of the short story "Thank You, Ma'm" as early as May 17, 1954, but it was not published until it was included in his 1963 anthology *Something in Common and Other Stories*. Hughes was also an important editor of anthologies of poems by African as well as by American and Caribbean black writers, such as *Poems from Black Africa, Ethiopia and Other Countries*. He also served as a visiting professor of creative writing at Atlanta University in 1947 and was poet in residence at the Laboratory School of the University of Chicago in 1949.

Hughes lived most of his adult life in Harlem and is considered a leading figure of the black cultural movement of the 1920s known as the Harlem Renaissance. He died in his beloved neighborhood on May 22, 1967, of complications following surgery for prostate cancer.

PLOT SUMMARY

"Thank You, Ma'm" is told in the voice of an impersonal third-person narrator. Hughes begins the story with a description of Mrs. Luella Bates Washington Jones (although her name is not revealed until later in the text). Hughes emphasizes her large physical size and the enormous size of her purse, as though suggesting she is larger than life. As the story begins, she is walking home alone at eleven o'clock at night through dark city streets. Although the urban location is never given a name, it is patently Hughes's own neighborhood of Harlem in the northwestern corner of the New York borough of Manhattan. A comparatively slight boy rushes up behind Mrs. Jones and tries to snatch her purse, but in a bit of slapstick, the strap breaks and the boy falls to the ground together with the purse. Rather than playing the role of the victim, Mrs. Jones is physically overwhelming to her attacker: "She reached down, picked the boy up by his shirt front, and shook him until his teeth rattled." She orders him to pick her purse up off the ground where it had fallen and, not letting go of him, begins to interrogate him in front of a small gathering crowd. The race of the two characters in the story is never mentioned, but it can be inferred that they are black from the matrix of black culture and dialectical speech that they share.

Mrs. Jones sees that the boy's face is dirty and finds out that it is because he has no one at home to take care of him. This leads her to the surprising decision not to simply release him and go about her business, nor to turn him in to the police, but rather to take him home with her to try to help him. Although it would be against the spareness of Hughes's style to say so baldly, it seems that Mrs. Jones is acting out of pity for the boy and the unfortunate circumstances that led him to make his criminal attack against her.

Mrs. Jones physically drags the boy to her apartment, putting him in a half-nelson wrestling hold when he struggles to get away. She tells him that he ought to be her son, because then she could have taught him right from wrong. This is a lesson he must not have properly understood or else he would not have attempted to commit a crime. As it is, she points out to the boy that he is the one who initiated the contact between them, but now she will be the one who determines the extent and nature of that contact and it will be neither brief nor trivial. She proudly announces her full name to the boy, as if that is something to overawe him in addition to her strength and size.

Mrs. Jones brings the boy back to her apartment in a rooming house and finds out his name is Roger. She releases him and instructs him to wash his face at the kitchenette sink. The door of the apartment is open and he could make a run for it, but he surprises himself by instead obeying her. Rather than taking Roger to the police as he fears, Mrs. Jones tells him she is going to make dinner for him since there is no one at his house to cook for him and he must have been hungry if he tried to snatch her purse. Roger responds that he wanted to use the money he might have stolen to buy "blue suede shoes." Mrs. Jones tells him he would have done better to simply ask her for the money to buy "some suede shoes." She herself, Mrs. Jones goes on, has been young and poor and wanted things she could not afford. She adds that he probably expects her to say that she did not steal to get them, but in fact that is not what she is going to tell him. She confesses further to Roger that when she was young she did terrible things that make her ashamed before God. "Everybody's got something in common," she tells Roger, perhaps alluding to the Christian doctrine of original sin.

Mrs. Jones proceeds to cook dinner. Roger again thinks about the possibility of running out the door. But this time it is perfunctory; he has no intention of leaving. He sits where Mrs. Jones can see him and as far as possible from her purse. Roger now wants Mrs. Jones to feel that she can trust him. He even volunteers to help her, though she does not need help. She does trust him. She offers to send him to the store to get milk, trusting that he will return. The shared trust is enough, however, and he does not actually go.

As they eat dinner, Mrs. Jones makes a point of not asking Roger about his home and family. She knows well enough from what he has already said and from the general circumstances of his situation that his answers would do nothing but embarrass him. Instead, she tells him about her job in a hotel beauty shop and all the women who come in and out. When they finish their dinner, Mrs. Jones actually addresses Roger as "son."

When they have finished eating, Mrs. Jones indeed gives Roger ten dollars (comparable to a hundred in today's money) to buy the blue suede shoes. She finally cautions him not to attempt to steal again and to behave himself as she sends him out the door. The title of the story comes from the last paragraph, in which Roger wants to say something more than "Thank you, m'am," but cannot manage to say even that, let alone anything else. The depth of his gratitude is too profound. Whatever Roger does in the future, he has been profoundly influenced by Mrs. Jones's generosity and wisdom.

CHARACTERS

Mrs. Luella Bates Washington Jones

Hughes begins "Thank You, Ma'm" with an evocative description of Jones: "She was a large woman with a large purse that had everything in it but a hammer and nails." This sets the tone for the development of her character. She is powerful and capable. She is overwhelmingly physically superior to the other character, Roger. But at the same time she is maternal, lavishing the attention on Roger that he obviously misses at home: cleaning him, feeding him, giving him money.

The story is set in 1950s Harlem. In that framework, it is possible to deduce a great deal about Mrs. Jones, as Hughes no doubt intended his audience to do. She is substantial in more ways than the physical. She is able to support herself by her own labor. Only limited opportunities were available to women in the 1950s (and still fewer to black women). Mrs. Jones works in a beauty parlor—one of the few jobs open to black women at the time. This also explains why she has to walk home so late: the shop is in a hotel and stays open late. There is not any Mr. Jones in the story so she is probably a widow, or her husband may have abandoned her (a fact that may relate to Hughes's own broken family)—divorce would have been unlikely in the time and culture described in the story.

The fact that Mrs. Jones so readily takes pity on Roger and treats him as she might a son, doing everything she can to give him effective help during their brief acquaintance and overlooking his transgression against her—indeed focusing on that transgression as the point of connection ("But you put yourself in contact with *me*. . . . If you think that that contact is not going to last awhile, you got another thought coming.") demands an explanation. Mrs. Jones tells Roger, "You ought to be my son. I would teach you right from wrong." This leaves no doubt that she is, as it were, transferring maternal feelings onto him. It is possible to go much further is speculating about Mrs. Jones's character, and part of the attractiveness of the story is that Hughes seems to invite the reader to do so. There might be some reason that Mrs. Jones rushes to treat a stranger as if he were her son. It would not be difficult to imagine that she has her own son, perhaps the same age as Roger, and that her contact with him has been forcibly denied by some circumstance. This could have been the death of the child, given the high infant mortality rate before widespread childhood immunization, or she might have been forced to give up a child for adoption at birth, an event more common in the 1940s than today. Mrs. Jones hints that there is some dark secret in her past when she tells Roger, "I have done things, too, which I would not tell you, son—neither tell God, if He didn't already know." This speaks of being driven to commit crimes by the poverty of her own youth. If she blamed herself for whatever misfortune befell any possible child of hers—a perfectly human tendency—she might well speak of it that way in later life.

A curious fact about Mrs. Jones is her name, and the high value she places upon it. When she tells Roger her name she does not say that she is Mrs. Jones, or Luella Jones, and certainly not Luella, but she tells him her full name: "Mrs. Luella Bates Washington Jones." To take such obvious pride in giving this full style and title, as it were, the totality of the name must have some very great personal significance to its bearer that can never be fully known without her explanation, and which, indeed, she might not have been able to put in words as eloquent as merely reciting the full name itself. The title Mrs. speaks of her marriage. Luella is obviously her given name and Bates her middle name—at an informed guess her mother's maiden name. Washington would be her father's family name. Washington speaks of the history of slavery; after the Civil War, many freed slaves, lacking surnames, took prominent patriotic names such as Washington. And that would only be going back to Mrs. Jones's grandfather's time, so well within her living memory. Jones would be her husband's name. In reciting that name, then, she is reciting a family history. That is partly the source of the pride she takes in the name. The last element, Jones, is her married name. If her husband nevertheless died or abandoned her, then whatever position she has now (and it does not seem comparatively to be a bad one) she worked for and achieved by herself, in spite of the loss of her husband, and in spite of all the obstacles to achieving success that stood in the way of women, especially black women, in her lifetime. She might take special pride in using the Mrs. as if to demonstrate to her husband that she could make something of herself even without his help. So the recitation of her full name is a testament to the triumph over adversity of Mrs. Luella Bates Washington Jones and of her family. Raising themselves up from slavery and raising herself up from what past misfortunes we cannot know for certain creates her sense of pride in the name. It is this pride and the determination that underlies it, as well as the wisdom she has acquired through her life, that make her a success in whatever life she has undertaken and give her the confidence and ability to help Roger. Her pride in her identity is the key to understanding Mrs. Jones's character, as well as to unlocking the larger meaning of the story.

Roger

Roger, in contrast to Mrs. Jones, is in many ways a very slight character. To begin with, he is physically small and thin: "He looked as if were fourteen or fifteen, frail and willow-wild." Mrs. Jones is able to drag him around like a doll. Roger is also slight in his fortune. His poverty is obvious from his clothing. If one examines photographs or film footage that were actually taken of everyday scenes in the 1950s, it becomes obvious that only three classes of people wore denim pants and tennis-shoes: those engaged in camping and other strenuous outdoor pursuits, workmen performing manual labor, and poor children. This was as true in Harlem as it was in white communities. Add to this the fact that Roger is ungroomed and unsupervised at home—"There's nobody home at my house," he tells Mrs. Jones—and it is clear that Roger is neglected. But though he has turned to theft, he is not beyond redemption. Roger's age is significant. He is certainly no longer a child, but he is not yet an adult; there is still time for him to become a man in the sense of someone who is an honorable, mature, self-respecting member of the community. Once he sees that Mrs. Jones is going to take care of him, he gives up any idea of running away to save himself. Roger wants her to be able to trust him. He feels real gratitude toward her but is too overwhelmed even to say the title of the story, "Thank you, ma'm."

Roger is again slight in his identity, but it is there that he is built up in the course of the story. He is most likely not entirely lying when he tells Mrs. Jones that he did not "aim to" steal her purse. Rather he seems to have instead strongly desired to buy a pair of blue suede shoes and most likely hit on the idea of purse-snatching quite spontaneously when the opportunity of fulfilling the desire presented itself. This is a kind of adolescent desire that does not have very good or practical reasons behind it but is vaguely connected with status. Although Mrs. Jones does make it possible for him to get the shoes, it is far from certain that he actually does so. He seems instead to have been made happier by having her help build up his self-esteem and becomes more interested in her approval and the help she offers.

THEMES

Negritude

Negritude (properly *négritude* in the original French, but Hughes preferred a more common spelling leaving off the acute accent) was a movement during the 1920s and 1930s among black intellectuals throughout the world: in Africa, the Caribbean, and in the expatriate community of Paris where many blacks from the French colonial empire gathered. Its central idea was that blacks ought to make their own culture for themselves, without reference to the white communities that simultaneously surrounded and rejected them. This motivated the name of the movement, which means "blackness." It did not reject Western culture, since its adherents realized it was neither possible nor desirable to break out of the matrix of Western civilization in which their own education and aesthetic taste were embedded. They believed they should nevertheless create their own black version of that civilization that, if it had to be separate, would not be inherently inferior. Hughes himself coined the slogan "The negro is beautiful" (which became the basis for the 1960s slogan "Black is beautiful"), to express this idea. Hughes developed the aesthetic goals of the movement more fully in a

TOPICS FOR FURTHER STUDY

- What do you think Mrs. Jones means when she says, "I have done things, too, which I would not tell you, son—neither tell God, if He didn't already know"? Write a short story dealing with what in her youth could be behind this statement.

- What happens after "Thank You, Ma'm" is just as intriguing as what happened before. Write a short story that takes place twenty years later, in which Roger, now working in the Peace Corps in Africa, has an encounter with a young man in need of guidance.

- Organize a class discussion around a PowerPoint presentation concerning Mrs. Jones's reaction to Roger. How does she actually respond to him, compared to the range of possible responses? How would you have treated Roger in her place? Could she have turned him in to the police? Asked the crowd of bystanders to help? Continued to be physically aggressive toward him? How might the course of the story have been different in each case?

- Read a book containing moral precepts such as the *Analects* of Confucius, the *Handbook* of Epictetus, or Paul's Epistle to the Romans, and give a presentation to your class describing a few pieces of advice from the book that Mrs. Jones could have given Roger and how they might have helped him.

- Read *Gold Dust*, the 2000 young-adult novel by Chris Lynch about black identity. Write an essay contrasting his themes of self-respect and black identity with similar themes from "Thank You, Ma'm."

---

manifesto he published in the 1920s and recalled in his later essay, "The Twenties: Harlem and its Negritude," "We younger Negro artists who create now intend to express our dark-skinned selves without fear or shame. If white people are pleased, we are glad. If they are not, it doesn't matter." In France, the political dimension of the movement called for French colonies in Africa and the West Indies to become integrated into metropolitan France, so that their inhabitants would be ordinary French citizens (much like the relationship Hawaii bears to the rest of the United States). Although black intellectuals in France looked to the Harlem Renaissance as one of their models, Hughes was the chief bearer of international negritude back to the United States because of his extensive travels and contacts in France. He certainly felt that blacks should have the same rights and status as other Americans, but beyond that, he felt that the black American community should be introspective in many respects. This underlies the ideas of self-help, the building up of internal cohesion within the black community exhibited in "Thank You, Ma'm." It is probably not coincidental that no white character makes even the briefest appearance in the story. Hughes was politically naive, and for a time held a favorable view of the Soviet Union, where he spent most of 1932 on an extended goodwill tour. He was attracted to the claimed lack of racism that played a large role in Soviet propaganda, as were many Western intellectuals, white and black, until Stalin signed a non-aggression pact with Hitler in 1939.

Crime

The action that begins "Thank You, Ma'm" is the petty crime of an attempted purse snatching. The plot of the story develops from the surprising consequences of its failure. Street crime like this was increasingly a fact of life in the Harlem where Hughes lived and set the story as the social cohesion of the community broke down during the 1950s. "Thank You, Ma'm," then, illustrates what is going wrong in the black community, of which crime is at best a symptom or symbol, and suggests how it ought to be corrected. The reaction in the story is not to punish the criminal (Roger), since it would not have served the interests of justice to punish an individual for a social problem. It is instead necessary to repair the broken community structure that seemed to leave the criminal no choice. Hughes is not concerned with crime per se but with the loss of community that makes crime possible. If Harlem had still been acting like a large extended family, as Hughes idealized its past, then this kind of social transgression would not have been an issue. The victim of the crime (Mrs. Jones) therefore responds by nearly adopting the criminal,

Silhouette of a person walking alone (Image copyright Mauro Rodrigues, 2009. Used under license from Shutterstock.com)

reintegrating him into the community from which he had become lost.

STYLE

Black Dialect

The characters in "Thank You, Ma'm" speak in a form of black dialect. This is not standard English but a type of language derived from the history of the black experience in America. It is still frequently spoken by individuals in the black community who have relatively little contact with other groups in American culture, despite standardized and integrated education and the standardizing effect of mass media like radio and television. In fact, black dialect is becoming an increasing powerful influence on the English spoken in American television and films. In part as a result of social isolation, and in part as a badge of community identity, black dialect has been far more resilient than the accents of other immigrant groups. Another factor is that it is not merely an accent but a true distinct variety of English. It is closely related to the speech of white Americans in the southern states, though more archaic. It is descended from the local dialects of the English West Country from which the majority of immigrants to the southern Colonies came in the seventeenth and eighteenth centuries. Once this language was picked up by the slave population, it developed along its own path, though one intertwined with the various dialects spoken by the surrounding white linguistic communities. This dialect is distinct from the standard or northern variety of American English that is more closely related to the dialects of the east coast of England and to the standard English of Oxford and Cambridge Universities, adopted by English aristocrats.

The dialect elements Hughes employs are very slight. He wishes to give his educated black as well as his white readership the flavor of the language without presenting text that might be difficult to read, or might have been considered socially embarrassing in the 1950s. A typical example is in this exchange between Roger and Mrs. Jones from the beginning of the story:

> The boy said, "Yes'm."
>
> The woman said, "What did you want to do it for?"
>
> The boy said, "I didn't aim to."
>
> She said, "You a lie!"

The dialectical elements include the "Yes'm" which is an extreme contraction for "Yes ma'am." This kind of contraction is simply archaic; it is characteristic of Shakespeare's language. The same can be said of the substitution of "What...for" for "why" in Jones's reply. The difference in usage between "aim" and the more standard "intend" is very subtle but probably results from a preference for English roots over words of Latin origin that did not generally enter dialectical speech because Latin learners tended also to adopt more standard forms of English. Standard speakers might think Jones's exclamation is a mistake for "You are a liar!" But dialectical forms are not mistakes. West Country dialects, and hence also the dialects of the American South, frequently prefix *a-* onto present-tense verbs to show continuous or characteristic action (as in "She's a-comin' round the mountain"). That is what is going on here: Jones is distinguishing "You lie!" from "You lie by nature!"

Figurative Language

Language is said to be figurative when it communicates more than its literal meaning. Although figurative language is used in all good writing, it is particularly characteristic of poetry, and Hughes's use of it, even in prose works, reflects his essentially poetic style. For example, at the beginning of "Thank You, Ma'm," Hughes describes Mrs. Jones as carrying "a large purse that had everything in it but a hammer and nails." In point of fact, this statement is not true: there are very many other things Mrs. Jones did not have in her purse. It is hyperbole, suggesting something by giving an exaggerated description in a way that exceeds reality. Just as some women carry little more than a wallet, others carry enormous purses with many compartments containing a wallet, a checkbook, a manicure kit, food, water, keys, pens, pencils, a diary, and numerous other items. The difference goes some way toward defining character. In choosing the evocative, figurative, hyperbolic description of the purse, rather than a ponderous literal description of its fabric and contents, Hughes also sets a comic and playful tone for story.

Allegory

Although "Thank You, Ma'm" is quite readable as a slice of Hughes's beloved Harlem life, it nevertheless seems to contain another message. Of its two characters, Mrs. Jones is large, secure, self-confident, active, while Roger is thin, weak, and desperate. Moreover, Mrs. Jones feeds and cares for Roger and perhaps changes the course of his life by simply by caring about him. It is not hard to see the two characters as representations of the class divisions that existed within the black community in Hughes's day and as the expression of Hughes's belief that the better-off strata of the black community had a responsibility to help their worse-off brethren. Mrs. Jones is able to help Roger not only because of her resources but because she has a sense of pride in her black identity that he lacks, but that she tries to start building in him. Read in this way, the story becomes an allegory of black self-help. It is a tribute to Hughes's style that figures who are so clearly symbolic nevertheless do not lose their humanity.

HISTORICAL CONTEXT

Segregation

Large northern cities like New York or Philadelphia had populations of free blacks going back to Colonial times. Such communities were segregated in certain sections of the city, however. Their members were allowed to own their own homes and other property, or rent living quarters, but only in certain areas, and not in neighborhoods where whites lived. This pattern did not change substantially in the first half of the twentieth century when, between 1914 and 1945, in a movement called the great migration, over a million rural blacks from the South moved to northern cities in the hope of finding social justice and economic opportunity that were denied them in the South. Black neighborhoods like Harlem, where Hughes settled in the 1920s and remained for the rest of his life, retained their traditional social mixture. While all of the residents were black, most were middle-class, based on their work as factory workers, teachers, middle-ranking civil servants, or in other jobs. A proportion remained poor, and a portion became wealthy as entrepreneurs. The social classes lived together because it was not possible for even the most successful members of black society to move into neighborhoods occupied by whites. The shared sense of community between blacks of all classes in a single neighborhood was what chiefly attracted Hughes to Harlem and formed his ideal of black social life. Beginning in the Great Depression of the 1930s, many more blacks fell into poverty because of joblessness, as happened in the rest of the nation. Government relief programs concentrated the poorest unemployed blacks together to make the distribution of social services to them more efficient. Starting in the late 1930s, the policy was to move poor unemployed blacks into specially built large-scale apartment buildings often called "projects," of which the first were the Harlem River Houses, built in 1937. After World War II, just as white city dwellers increasingly moved to new neighborhoods in the suburbs, upper- and middle-class blacks were also finally able to move out of their traditional neighborhoods, albeit to segregated (red-lined) suburbs. In the 1950s and 1960s, this increasingly resulted in ghettos in the inner cities that were occupied exclusively by poor blacks left with the fragments of a broken social structure. So government efforts to help the black community had the unintended effect of destroying the social cohesion that had traditionally sustained the black community in America. This is the social decline that Hughes addressed in "Thank You, Ma'm."

Harlem Renaissance

The Harlem Renaissance, also called the New Negro Movement, was a flourishing of black culture centered on a diverse community of

COMPARE & CONTRAST

- **1950s:** The United States is a heavily segregated society and most blacks, especially in the Jim Crow South, are denied their political and civil rights.

    Today: While discrimination still occurs, it does not exist on the institutional scale it did in the 1950s. The first African American president, Barack Obama, was elected in 2008.

- **1950s:** Harlem is a neighborhood in decline because of rising poverty and crime rates.

    Today: Harlem is still a neighborhood in difficulty but it is recovering as it gains a more economically and racially diverse population.

- **1950s:** Economic opportunity for women, especially black women, is very limited. Work opportunities outside of small family businesses, or as domestic servants, hairdressers, waitresses, or teachers, are rare.

    Today: Following the reforms of the civil rights and feminist movements, black women have a virtually unlimited choice of career paths, as exemplified African American women such as Oprah Winfrey and Condaleezza Rice.

- **1950s:** Mentoring of children from broken homes is often considered the responsibility of the extended family and the community.

    Today: Potential mentors from outside a community are introduced by many organizations such as Big Brothers/Big Sisters and Teach for America.

---

artists who lived in Harlem in the 1920s. Hughes, perhaps its leading voice, preferred to link it to the worldwide aesthetic and cultural movement of negritude. The cultural success of the Harlem Renaissance was fueled by the economic boom of the 1920s and came to an abrupt end with the Great Depression. As Hughes himself put it, looking back on the era at the end of his life, "But by the time the thirties came, the voltage of the Negro Renaissance of the twenties had nearly run its course." One part of the Harlem experience was the creation of a new literature by black authors. Writers like Hughes, Zora Neale Hurston, and Countee Cullen mastered traditional forms of Western literature and became successful poets, novelists, and dramatists. They were successful in gaining acceptance by white publishers and a white reading audience to whom they could speak in their authentic voice. Indeed, their financial success as authors depended upon their white audience. They have often been criticized for creating art in the Western tradition rather than creating a new art valid as some non-Western Other, but however tragic and unjust the black experience had been, it had made them part of Western culture and they wished to proceed in that way rather than succumb to the impulse to rebel against their own tradition and become part of a fantasy that would have been just as Western but less authentic. Indeed, another important feature of the Harlem Renaissance was the penetration of black popular culture into white consciousness. This entailed a constructed perception of blacks as a non-Western Other.

Throughout the nineteenth and early twentieth centuries, blacks had always played an important role in popular American entertainment. By World War I, traditionally black forms of music known as blues and jazz were performed by many musicians, white and black, but a new development was that of groups of all-black musicians performing for all-white audiences (which before had been possible only in the theatrical setting of the minstrel show). Orchestras such as Duke Ellington's became successful, along with famous soloists such as Louis Armstrong. But these kinds of popular performers were lionized by the white public at the time as representing something authentic because their art was seen as primitive. It was patronized in the 1920s specifically because it seemed to represent a non-Western alternative to the culture that had brought about and barely survived the calamity of World War I. Their art was, in the terms of Edward Said's *Orientalism*, a safe fantasy of the anti-Western for Western consumption. Wealthy white audiences traveled to Harlem to see jazz performers at the Cotton Club, which featured all-black performers for an all-white, forcibly segregated audience. While Hughes was able to produce his own plays on Broadway, two other Broadway productions of the period seem more telling of the place of the Harlem Renaissance in the perception of white American culture. In 1920 Eugene O'Neill produced *The Emperor Jones*, which had a black protagonist and a mostly black cast. The main character is a black man of considerable achievement. He amasses a fortune working as a Pullman porter by following the stock tips he overhears his wealthy white charges exchange with each other. But his uncontrolled, primitive, violent nature causes him to commit murder in a bar fight, and he is forced to flee the country. He then manages to become dictator of an island nation in the Caribbean, but is finally destroyed by succumbing to his own superstitious nature. In 1936, Orson Welles staged a Broadway production of Shakespeare's *Macbeth* with an all-black cast and with the popular supposition that this got closer to the primitive, superstitious nature of the play. This version became known as the "Voodoo Macbeth" because its set designs and costume were based on popular conceptions of voodoo religious ceremonies. The overall effect of the Harlem Renaissance was to give blacks a higher profile in American culture, especially American intellectual culture, but at the cost of remaining an isolated Other, a screen for Western fantasy. Many black intellectuals did not reject this identity. Zora Neale Hurston, in her essay, "Characteristics of Negro Expression" (reprinted in Venetria Patton and Maureen Honey's anthology *Double-Take*) embraces it, characterizing ordinary black speech and black artistic writing as powerful because it is primitive and imitative, filled with dramatic uncontrolled emotion, and having greater access to folkloristic roots. Hughes dissented from such views, however.

Hughes lamented that Harlem itself, as a neighborhood that nourished art and intellectualism, did not long survive the renaissance. As economic and social conditions declined, writers moved away: Richard Wright (Hughes's most serious rival as the greatest African American writer) moved to Paris to escape the racism that pervaded American culture. In "Thank You, Ma'm," Hughes depicts this Harlem, a poor place riven with crime, the glory days of the renaissance long past.

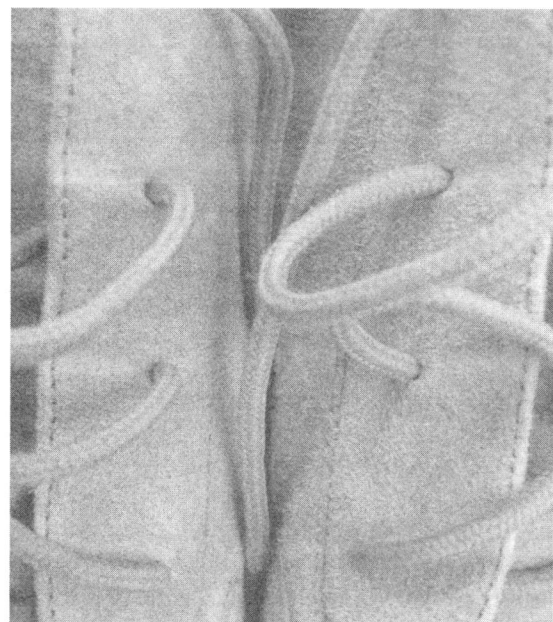

Blue suede shoes (Image copyright Perry Correll, 2009. Used under license from Shutterstock.com)

CRITICAL OVERVIEW

"Thank You, Ma'm" was published in *Something in Common and Other Stories* in 1963. However, most of the stories in this anthology concerned relations between the races, unlike "Thank You, Ma'm," which has a message for the black community alone, so the story received no attention in contemporary reviews of that volume. Nor has it received much attention from critics since then. James A. Emanuel, in the Twayne Author's series volume on Hughes, mentions it only as bringing Harlem directly into Hughes's work and adding to his style a sense of "melodrama...sentiment, and individual pathos." "Thank You, Ma'm" is probably among the least reviewed but most read of Hughes's works.

"Thank You, Ma'm" has received much more attention in the world of secondary education, where its brevity and the simplicity of its language, as well as the age of its character Roger, make it a standard in the secondary language arts curriculum. Mitch Cox, in the *English Journal*, laments that it is all too often the only story not by a white male included in older literature anthologies.

CRITICISM

Bradley A. Skeen

Skeen is a professor of classics. In this essay, he analyzes meanings conveyed by Hughes's use of figurative language in "Thank You, Ma'm," especially his reference to the song "Blue Suede Shoes."

Hughes's story "Thank You, Ma'm" seems straightforward enough on a casual reading and, indeed, its moral message of self-help aimed at the black community could hardly be more blunt. Hughes gives a vivid description of his home in Harlem with its types and characters, lamenting it as a neighborhood in decline. Yet Hughes is a poet and cannot refrain from the figurative use of language that is central to poetry. Some words and phrases in the story that might at first seem prosaic reveal a wealth of symbolic meaning. A trivial example occurs at the very beginning of the story in the physical description of Jones as "a large woman with a large purse that had everything in it but a hammer and nails." Aside from being literally untrue, this evokes in every reader the image of having known, or at least having seen, such a woman, and communicates the idea Hughes wishes to convey much more fully than a far more detailed description could do. In this way Hughes makes his words draw out the experiences and memory of the reader with a far more powerful effect than mere description could do.

There is no getting around the fact that "Thank You, Ma'm" concerns a crime, the kind of petty street crime that was making Harlem an unsafe place to live even when Hughes wrote the story in the 1950s. There is nothing exceptional about a purse snatching, but there is something unusual about Roger's motive in committing it. Mrs. Jones suggests to him that he was driven to the criminal act by hunger and the need to get money to buy something to eat. But that is not the case at all. Roger tells her, "I want a pair of blue suede shoes." Mrs. Jones's reaction has several significances. In the first place, she seems to have heard him as if he had

WHAT DO I READ NEXT?

- *Langston Hughes in the Hispanic World and Haiti*, edited in 1977 by Edward J. Mullen, presents Hughes's writings about Latin America and Spain and his translations from the Spanish, together with a bibliography of the translation of his own works into Spanish, and several essays (some in Spanish) on Hughes's mutual exchange of influence with Spanish-language literature.

- Throughout his career, Hughes wrote for children and young adults and was often active in primary and secondary education. *The Dream Keeper and Other Poems* in 1932 was the first of his many books for the school-age audience.

- Christine Hill's 1997 *Langston Hughes: Poet of the Harlem Renaissance* (part of the African American Biographies series) is one of many biographies of Hughes intended for young adults.

- Hans A. Ostrom's 2002 *A Langston Hughes Encyclopedia* concentrates on Hughes's verse and contains an entry on each of his more than eight hundred published poems.

- The first volume of Hughes's autobiography, *The Big Sea*, published in 1940, concentrates on his life in Harlem in the 1920s.

- The *Encyclopedia of the Harlem Renaissance*, edited in 2004 by Cary D. Wintz and Paul Finkelman, covers the entire cultural spectrum of Hughes's environment, but concentrates on the graphic and performing arts.

said he wanted fancy or nice shoes, and when she mentions them she merely says suede shoes, leaving out the blue. She also suggests that Roger would have done better to ask her for the money to buy them, rather than trying to steal it. She would have gladly given it to him, as she indeed does in the course of the story. She finally tells him, as he departs, not to turn to crime again, "because shoes got by devilish ways will burn

> "HUGHES GIVES A VIVID DESCRIPTION OF HIS HOME IN HARLEM WITH ITS TYPES AND CHARACTERS, LAMENTING IT AS A NEIGHBORHOOD IN DECLINE."

your feet." In one sense, Roger's family ought to have gotten him these shoes, either by buying them for him or by getting him a job so that he could earn the money to buy what he wants, rather than being forced into crime to satisfy his desires. Mrs. Jones indeed steps in and takes the place of Roger's mother.

If the situation Hughes describes is made a little abstract, then a larger meaning emerges from the text. Roger is the part of the black community that is being neglected by the black establishment. He is not given the help he needs to support himself, and the lesson of black history is that no one can go it alone. Whatever misfortunes Mrs. Jones suffered in the past, she was eventually integrated into the community with a job, a place to live, and a respectable life. Roger's desire for the shoes is not frivolous: as Mrs. Jones understands it, they stand for his desire for integration into the community and respectability. If he is not granted that, he will try to advance himself by illegitimate means that will result in failure and damnation, as indicated when she says his feet will potentially be burned by "devilish ways." If the black community failed Roger, or the class of youth that Roger stands for, in the form of his parents, it must, in Hughes's view, make a second effort to help him in the form of Mrs. Jones, or else that class will be responsible for its own disintegration. This simple social allegory is the purpose and message of the story. The black community should help itself in the same way that a family does, or else it will break apart as a neglected family does. Aside from being the practical advice common within many black movements during the period of segregation in which Hughes lived, one may speculate that it deeply appealed to him because of the broken condition of his own family.

This still leaves the matter of the "blue suede shoes." This special significance would be easy to dismiss, because Mrs. Jones does not recognize it, speaking merely of suede shoes. But the reader is bound to recognize that "Blue Suede Shoes" is a song title. In fact the song was a top-selling single for months in 1956. It was written in 1955 by Carl Perkins and was recorded in the following year by the composer as well as by Elvis Presley. It was immensely popular and was well known in the black as well as the white community, and is generally considered by experts in that field as the first "rock'n'roll" song, or at least the first by white songwriters and performers. Mrs. Jones does not pick up on the fact that it is a title because the song was marketed to youth culture, and it would have been out of place for her character to know of it. But Roger's desire for blue suede shoes is undoubtedly meant to be understood by the reader as a reference to the song. By symbolically encoding the song into the story in this way, Hughes gives a much deeper meaning to Roger's statement of what it is that he wants, what it is that he needs, what it is that he is willing to steal for.

In the first place, it is acknowledged that the very type of music that "Blue Suede Shoes" grows out of depends on the youthful desire for freedom and independence. One of the things that Roger is asking for is the freedom and independence that were historically denied to the black community in the United States. But an interrogation of the song can provide much more meaning for Hughes's story than that. The song had its genesis when the songwriter Carl Perkins discussed with his friend Johnny Cash the fact that both had independently heard teen-age boys in the audiences they performed for in dance clubs loudly caution their dance partners not to step on their blue suede shoes. Taking this as his inspiration, Perkins elaborated the theme through hyperbole. In the song the singer invites his partner to do anything to him, to steal from him, to physically assault him, to strip him of his patrimony, but only not to step on his shoes. Modern music critics often relate the song to the vanity about physical appearance then being inculcated into youth culture by popular figures in the mass media such as the flamboyantly dressed Elvis Presley. That is certainly superficially present in Roger's desire for blue suede shoes, but Hughes may have seen a deeper meaning.

Whether called rhythm and blues or rockabilly or the more modern term rock music,

"Blue Suede Shoes" was the first such piece of music to gain popularity that was composed and performed by white songwriters and singers. It was, however, an indisputably black form of music in origin. Perkins, for instance, was familiar with the music that was already being produced by his friend the black songwriter and performer Chuck Berry, and, more to the point, as a youth had leaned how to play the guitar from an elderly black neighbor who was a blues musician. To a reflective, poetic mind like Hughes's, this fact could take on special significance in relation to the song "Blue Suede Shoes." It would be possible to see this form of music, and most twentieth-century popular music in general, as stolen from the black community, and Roger is asking for it back. At the same time, many of the lyrics of the song could easily describe the relationship between the black and white communities that had existed during the time of slavery and continued in Hughes's day during the period of segregation. Hughes described his own encounter with the white majority community in America as one of "power and brutality." This is very well characterized in the physical violence, the destruction of patrimony, and the slander described in the song. In this case, the refusal, after every other loss, to allow anyone to step on the blue suede shoes could be seen as the irreducible pride of the black community in its own identity that has been maintained in the face of every privation the community has suffered.

What Roger wants from Mrs. Luella Bates Washington Jones is her sense of pride, which she has maintained in the face of her life of adversity. That is what the blue suede shoes ultimately symbolize. Roger cannot, as he imagines, steal this sense of pride from her, but she gives it to him freely when she gives him the money to buy the shoes. She has suffered and been humiliated, has been driven to desperate acts herself, but she has triumphed over the obstacles put in her way. Roger wants help to do the same. The generation of black youth that is facing new and unprecedented difficulties—as well as new opportunities in the civil rights movement—needs the support of being integrated into the traditional black community. Hughes saw that this was not happening in the way that it always had, and he wrote the story as a reminder that it needed to happen. The social disintegration and the rising crime rate that were blighting his beloved Harlem were evidence of that failure.

Source: Bradley Skeen, Critical Essay on "Thank You, Ma'm," in *Short Stories for Students*, Gale, Cengage Learning, 2010.

Michigan Chronicle
In the following essay, Hughes is described as a pioneer of the theme of black pride.

The African American has endured many hardships in America. Our story takes us through the dark days of being fettered by the iron chains of slavery to the constraining chains of prejudice. This tragic history has scarred the image of the African American and etched in their hearts a sense of hopelessness and despair. Remarkably, we survived, but still the winds of doubt continued to blow over our existence. Still, we lived in a society that did its best to discredit us. Years passed without an identity, something that would restore pride and give us direction.

It wasn't until the Harlem Renaissance that a symbolic vehicle was nurtured. This period chronicled our journey through the darkness of slavery to the enlightenment of the spiritual identity and the distinctive features that planted the seed to the survival of the African American conscience. Literature played a strong role in the struggle against racial injustice and identity. With the floodgates of oppression stagnating African Americans, it took courageous and insightful writers to confront these social issues and to find a way to quench the thirst for the African identity. The writers who would take a moral stand and to give a sense of dignity where there was none. Plainly said, to give us a voice: a voice that was dripping with the cool taste of hope and promise. That voice was heard through the writing of Langston Hughes.

Today's African American writers, artists, actors, and musicians express a growing sense of Black pride; nowhere was this pride more evident than in the work of Langston Hughes. When I think of the many works of Hughes, I think of not only Black pride, but the Black unity that was expressed during the Harlem Renaissance. Their insight has made it a lot easier to accomplish our dreams because of the pioneering inroads made by people like Langston Hughes.

Langston Hughes celebrated the African American through poetry, fiction and drama. He was able to paint the rich color of their voice and speech inflections and he was sensitive to the

The boys must wash up before dinner. (Image copyright Scott Rothstein, 2009. Used under license from Shutterstock.com)

rhythms of their souls. Through his poetry, I get a better picture of the life our forefathers had to bear. I get an emotional reaction when I read his poem "The Negro Speaks of Rivers." Here he reflects on the significance of the great Mississippi and the fate that this river had on his African brothers and the lamenting for the rivers of Mother Africa. He said, "I've known rivers. I've known rivers ancient as the world and older than the flow of human blood in my veins. My soul has grown deep like the rivers."

These intellects who had an exceptional desire to express the mental and physical experience of the African American race, displayed the courage and heart to take the silent, downtrodden dreams of the disenfranchised and breathe the gift for a promising tomorrow. This is why our journey through the darkness was brightened by his words.

Langston Hughes was deeply impacted by his environment. An environment that was so depressing, and so mournful that they became the sounds of Harlem. An environment that held the Black slave as its statue in the town square. One day that statue would be knocked down through the dreams of Harlem; not what it was then but what it would be. This was Hughes' philosophy. As Langston once said, "Hold fast to dreams for if dreams die life is a broken-winged bird that cannot fly." We are no longer a race. Langston believed, "We have tomorrow before us like a flame."

Close your eyes for a moment and think of a dream that you have, or have had. Did you achieve it, or did you just let it drift away? Was it the logic or the heart that determined whether you would pursue or terminate that dream? These are the questions that Langston Hughes asks us to internalize. In his poem, "Mother to Son," his purpose is to motivate African Americans not to lose hope. It is the struggle itself that forges our character. He writes, "Well son, I'll tell you, life for me ain't been no crystal stair. It's had tacks in it, and splinters, and boards torn up, and places with no carpet on the floor—bare. But all the time I'se been a-climbin' on and reachin' landins and turnin corners, and sometimes goin' in the dark where it ain't been no light. So boy, don't you turn your back, don't you set down on those steps cause you finds it kinder hard, don't you fall now—for I'se still goin honey, I'se still climbin, and life for me ain't been no crystal stair."

Langston Hughes provided me with the key for the journey of any African American: A promise for tomorrow.

Source: "The Journey of my African American Hero," in *Michigan Chronicle*, February 23, 2000, p. B4.

Thomas C. Fleming

In the following article, Fleming reminisces about Hughes and his literary accomplishments.

... Langston Hughes was another famous person whom I met before I became a newsman. Newspeople meet a lot of celebrities; that is a part of the game.

I was attending a dance at Sweet's Ballroom in downtown Oakland; the Jimmy Lunceford band was playing that night. It was one of the nights that was allocated to blacks; the two races never attended the dances on the same night.

I encountered Mason Robeson, who was a colleague of John Pittman, the publisher of the short-lived *Spokesman*, a black weekly in San Francisco. I noted that Mason seemed to be with a short, brown-skinned man. Mason asked me, had I met Lang yet? Then he explained that the man with him was Langston Hughes, whose Simple, the hip cat character that he created, was published in the *Chicago Defender*.

I knew Hughes as a poet and a playwright, from reading the *Pittsburgh Courier*, the *New York Amsterdam News*, and the *Baltimore Afro-American*, all of them powerful black weekly papers that enjoyed national circulations.

I shook hands with Hughes and joined in the conversation. I knew that he and two others from Oakland, William Patterson and Louise Thompson—both graduates of UC Berkeley who, with Hughes and several other big names identified with the Harlem Renaissance—had made a trip to Russia in the late 1920s. I heard that another Oaklander, Matt Crawford, had also gone, and that all of them had met varying degrees of criticism when they returned home.

Hughes received the most publicity because when he took the famed Trans-Siberian train from Moscow to Vladivostok, and took a ship from Siberia to Japan, the Japanese would not let him land, suspecting him of being a Communist spy. At least, that is the story told then to the world. Hughes had to go back to Siberia, and went to neighboring China to take a ship from Shanghai to the U.S.

> HE WAS A SURVIVALIST, WHICH HE SO GRAPHICALLY DISPLAYED IN THE FICTITIOUS CHARACTER HE GAVE THE NAME SIMPLE IN THE COLUMN HE WROTE THAT APPEARED IN THE *CHICAGO DEFENDER* EVERY WEEK."

The Cuban strongman, General Fulgencio Batista, was in complete charge of the island nation. It was a one-man regime, with the dictator looting the nation of all money that the state collected. Hughes enlightened me on this when he informed me that Batista was a black man. He did not say it that way, but stated that Batista was a [black man] which was a surprise to me, since I had always viewed him as being just a Latino, with perhaps a bit of black blood flowing in his veins.

Source: Thomas C. Fleming, "Reflections on Black History: Meetings with Famous Men; Part 1 of 2 Parts," in *Sun Reporter*, Vol. 55, No. 14, April 2, 1998, p. S8.

Thomas C. Fleming

In the following excerpt, Fleming continues to reminisce about meeting Langston Hughes.

Langston Hughes had a very thorough knowledge of people who have no visible source of income, but have learned to do what some people call living by their wits. He was a survivalist, which he so graphically displayed in the fictitious character he gave the name Simple in the column he wrote that appeared in the *Chicago Defender* every week.

Simple was always short on cash, constantly wondering how he would be able to pay rent, or take care of any matters that demanded the use of money.

When I met him at a dance at Sweet's Ballroom in Oakland in the 1930s, I felt drawn to him immediately, for neither of us felt any restraints in talking about the problem, which was race relations, as it is today, and seems like it will continue to be the number one topic of discussion for a long time.

Hughes was staying at the luxurious home of Noel Sullivan, a millionaire patron of the arts who had the urge to be a singer of note, but had an indifferent voice of no recognizable pitch or tone.

But Sullivan had money enough so that he could attract people who shared his interests to attend affairs at his home.

All of the foremost black entertainers or artists found the welcome mat at the Sullivan mansion, located on Telegraph Hill, which he had inherited from his uncle, James Phelan, who had made millions and had served as mayor of San Francisco and later U.S. senator from California.

Noel Sullivan knew of the humiliation that black artists like Paul Robeson, Rolland Hayes and Marian Anderson faced when they had contracts to appear in some music halls in the city to sing in concert.

Most inns and hotels, and some restaurants, including some of the expensive ones in Chinatown, refused to serve blacks, and that included the internationally known artists who have already been identified.

Sullivan made his mansion available. In the case of Langston Hughes, he remained in San Francisco for about six weeks, when he had a suite of rooms in the mansion and a well-trained staff of housekeepers to wait [on] and serve him.

Langston had invited several parties while in residence at the Sullivan home, and his guest list was interracial—blacks and whites of the literary and artistic world. Sullivan always attended these affairs that Hughes held in his home. That is when I told him, on my first visit to a Hughes soiree, that I had fished and hunted on the 12,000-acre ranch [that] was one of the properties that he had inherited from his uncle, and he seemed pleased that I was aware of his inheritance outside of the city.

Another parcel of the inheritance was a great mansion down in Carmel, right off the ocean, staffed with servants, where Hughes spent probably another six weeks before leaving for New York City.

Matt Crawford, Louise Thompson and William Patterson were the three black Californians who had accompanied Hughes, Wallace Thurman and all of the black pioneers who gave birth to the Harlem Renaissance, on a trip to Russia when Lenin was the number one man in the new Communist regime that overthrew the Romanovs' long aristocratic rule in Russia. Crawford also held affairs for Hughes in his Berkeley home. Matt and his wife came to the affairs that Hughes held at the Sullivan home.

Louise Thompson and William Patterson were both graduates from the University of California, in the days when as few as 30 blacks were enrolled at the school, and perhaps one or two at Stanford. Louise and Willie, as everyone in the East Bay called Patterson, married eventually, and stayed over in Moscow for several years. They had one daughter who received her medical training in Russia and now practices medicine in Stockton.

Roy Blackburn was hired by Hughes to be his personal secretary. Hughes, by his own accounts, always suffered from ready cash. He depended on many wealthy people for handouts occasionally. Since there were not too many black writers in any field of endeavor making a lot of money—that is, not like Sinclair Lewis, Ernest Hemingway, and even Carl Van Vechten, the white writer who earned national fame for his best-selling book about the black renaissance....

Hughes also spent some time with Matt Crawford and his family in Berkeley, plus the time he spent at Asilomar. Roy Blackburn spent some time with him on the big estate owned by Noel Sullivan.

Another famous black I met during the early 1930s was Paul Williams, the distinguished black architect who was based in Los Angeles. I met him through Floyd Covington, who was the Urban League's head man in Los Angeles. Los Angeles had an Urban League office as far back as 1928, for that was the year when a friend took me by the Urban League and introduced me to Covington.

I met Charles S. Johnson after we first opened the *Reporter* office and Johnson, who, along with E. Franklin Frazier, were the two most outstanding sociologists in the nation. Johnson came to San Francisco when he received a grant to study the black population explosion that occurred right after Pearl Harbor.

Because the *Reporter* was the only black paper in San Francisco, he came by and sought whatever information I could give. I discovered that he had known Goodlett when Carlton was a student at Howard University. At that time, Goodlett was enrolled at Meharry Medical School, and Johnson was at Fisk University then. The two of us spent many hours talking about the problem, which never gets out of focus whenever people with the same interest in pursuit of equality of opportunity meet.

Frazier had came to Berkeley when Goodlett was a graduate student. They knew one another from Howard days. Goodlett, Frazier and I spent hours talking about many aspects of life, as Frazier had conducted some lectures on the Berkeley campus during summer session.

Langston Hughes' drama *Mulatto* opened at a theater in 1945, after Goodlett came back to San Francisco to practice medicine following his graduation and completion of [an] internship and six months' practice in a small Tennessee town, Columbia.

Ruby Dee was one of the stars, along with Betsy Blair, who was the wife of Gene Kelly, the famous dancer and motion picture star, and James Edwards, a young black actor who was on his way up as a thespian. I don't recall whether Hughes came here for the opening, but all San Francisco blacks attended the presentation at some time during the four or six weeks it ran here.

I recall that Dee, Edwards and Blair came by the Goodletts' home every night after the show ended and stayed, plus many other residents of San Francisco, to play poker, drink booze, and eat whatever food Willette Goodlett prepared. The party would last until about 3 a.m., and of course many of us saw the powerful play more than one time. The play never did go over big anywhere in the nation. I think it ran on Broadway in New York about as long as it did here.

Hughes compiled a play that was too factual for most whites, although the critics gave it lukewarm praise. But the title itself gave the white world many reasons for not flocking to the theaters where it appeared.

Thurgood Marshall used to come to San Francisco every year, sometimes a number of times. He was the chief counsel for the National Association for the Advancement of Colored People, and again, my position as editor of the *Reporter* brought me into frequent contact with him. He asked many questions about the problem—racism—perhaps more intensively than anyone else. I found him to be as much at ease with street blacks as with the so-called talented tenth, a term which W. E. B. Du Bois used to describe the black intellectual world.

Thurgood liked to play poker and eat fried chicken and drink good bourbon whisky: that is what he always told Willette to have ready when he came to town.

Marshall was one of the most learned men that I have ever met. I felt that he knew more about the Constitution of the United States than anyone else. And he startled the white world, with this knowledge, which he used more skillfully than any other lawyer in the country, in his steady fight to convince the white world that the Constitution included black people in defining who is a citizen of this nation.

Source: Thomas C. Fleming, "Reflections on Black History: Meetings with Famous Men; Part 2 of 2 Parts," in *Sun Reporter*, Vol. 55, No. 15, April 9, 1998, pp. 8.

J. Sangirardi-Gray
In the following article, Sangirardi-Gray advises that one of the basic tenets of teaching writing is to encourage children to write about their personal experiences, and she uses Hughes and his work as examples.

One of the basic tenets of process writing in the classroom is to encourage children to write about things from their own life experiences, and because Langston Hughes had a penchant for doing the same, his work has turned into a useful reading/writing connection tool in my classroom. Langston Hughes wrote about what he knew best—his own experiences. The success of his work, which is centered around the experience of the African American, is due to his gift for vivid language that transforms the events of ordinary lives into thought-provoking, evocative creations.

I had worked all year long to bring my student authors to a point in their work where they were writing about their own lives and experimenting with figurative language. Still, what was missing from their thoughtfully crafted tales was richness in language.

By sharing Hughes's short story "Thank You, Ma'm" with my fifth graders, I hoped to illustrate to them the importance of language to a story. After reading the story individually, my students responded in their reading journals. They were intrigued with the unfamiliarity of the language in this short story. Many students noticed that Langston Hughes liked to link words together. My students decided that "blue jeaned sitter" was a clever way to describe the main character's bottom, clothed in dungarees. "Willow-wild," another word they noted, was interpreted as a combination of a description of Roger's looks—thin as a willow—and his behavior. Students agreed that calling him a "being-dragged boy" called up more vivid images in their minds than would a long description of how Mrs. Luella Bates Washington Jones hauled Roger all the way home by his shirt.

In subsequent student writings I began to find some experimentation with this sort of language: "my always-screaming sister"; "at Easter I turn into a chocolate-eating maniac."

Some of the other vocabulary in the story was unfamiliar to them, too. I welcomed questions about words such as icebox and stoop, as they were perfect segues into some personal storytelling, first on my part and later between students and their parents. I loved sharing a personal family story about my grandfather the iceman, and about my childhood memories of playing stickball and eating cool pops on the front steps.

"Why did Roger want to buy a pair of blue suede shoes so badly that he'd steal a woman's pocketbook?" I asked them, and they went home that night and asked their parents why blue suede shoes were so important during the 1950s. The next day my students came to school bursting with stories their parents had told them about Elvis Presley. One child even brought the recording of "Blue Suede Shoes" to class so that we could listen to it. This was something they could relate to, as many of them had experienced in their own lives the desire to follow trends set by celebrities.

They asked me about Hughes's ethnicity, having decided that the characters in the story spoke black English and probably lived in the South. They cited examples of language they felt supported their inference, such as *"you a lie."* I was pleased that they were paying attention to the dialogue. I had assigned the first reading of "Thank You, Ma'm" as silent reading, but we took some time in class to read the story aloud. My students became very aware of the characters' speech patterns as they heard the dialect spoken aloud.

My students began to ask many questions about the author, Langston Hughes, and about the characters, Roger and Mrs. Jones, in the story. The best way to sate their curiosity was to give them an opportunity to explore. I cleaned the library out of Langston Hughes material, including novels, short stories, plays, poetry, songs, and biographies about him. We set up a Langston Hughes Information Center in our classroom. During silent-reading time, my students dove into the books. They were intensely interested in Langston Hughes and how his life was connected to his work. For example, they discovered from some of the biographical materials—including *Langston* (Delacorte), a play about his life by Ossie Davis, and *Black Troubador: Langston Hughes* (Rand) by Charlemae H. Rollins—that he was intensely interested in music and wrote several books about jazz. He had heard the blues played on the streets of Kansas City as a child and tried putting the sound on paper. The students discovered how his poetry was connected with his musical interests through the jazz-like rhythms in *The Dream Keeper and Other Poems* (Knopf), a collection of his poems. They discovered that Langston Hughes did exactly what I had been coaxing them to do all year—he wrote about his own experiences, the things he knew best. Thus he was able to capture the soul of his people in words.

As the year progressed, I began to see more and more an emergence of richness and vivid language in my students' writing. They began to look at literature more closely and with greater appreciation for the craft of the written word. I am convinced that the literature our students read in the classroom strongly influences the way they think about writing.

Source: J. Sangirardi-Gray, "Books in the Classroom: Langston Hughes," in *Horn Book Magazine*, Vol. 67, No. 4, July–August 1991.

SOURCES

Clarke, John Henrik, *Harlem: A Community in Transition*, Citadel Press, 1970.

Cox, Mitch, "Revising the Literature Curriculum for a Pluralist Society," in *English Journal*, Vol. 77, No. 6, October 1988, pp. 30–34.

Dace, Tish, ed., *Langston Hughes: The Contemporary Reviews*, Cambridge University Press, 1997, pp. 675–78.

Emanuel, James A., *Langston Hughes*, Twayne's United States Authors Series, No. 123, Twayne Publishers, 1967, pp. 49, 136.

Hughes, Langston, "The Fascination of Cities," in *Crisis*, Vol. 31, No. 3, January 1926, pp. 138–40; reprinted in *Essays on Art, Race, Politics, and World Affairs*, The Collected Works of Langston Hughes series, Vol. 9, edited by Christopher C. De Santis, University of Missouri Press, 2002, pp. 27–31.

———, "Thank You, Ma'm," in *The Short Stories*, The Collected Works of Langston Hughes series, Vol. 15, edited by R. Baxter Miller, University of Missouri Press, 2002, pp. 299–302.

———, "The Twenties: Harlem and its Negritude," in *African Forum*, Vol. 1, No. 4, 1966, pp. 11–20, reprinted in *Essays on Art, Race, Politics, and World Affairs*, The Collected Works of Langston Hughes series, Vol. 9, edited by Christopher C. De Santis, University of Missouri Press, 2002, pp. 465–74.

Hutchinson, George, *The Harlem Renaissance in Black and White*, Belknap Press, 1995.

McCrum, Robert, William Cran, and Robert MacNeil, *The Story of English*, 3rd ed., Penguin, 2003, pp. 209–50.

Mikolyzk, Thomas A., *Langston Hughes: A Bio-Bibliography*, Greenwood Press, 1990.

Morrison, Craig, *Go Cat Go! Rockabilly Music and its Makers*, University of Illinois Press, 1996.

Said, Edward W., *Orientalism*, Pantheon, 1978.

Patton, Venetia K., and Maureen Honey, eds., *Double-Take: A Revisionist Harlem Renaissance Anthology*, Rutgers University Press, 2006, pp. 61–73.

Wilder, Gary, *The French Imperial Nation-State: Negritude and Colonial Humanism between the Two World Wars*, University of Chicago Press, 2005.

FURTHER READING

De Santis, Christopher C., ed., *Dictionary of Literary Biography*, Vol. 315, *Langston Hughes: A Documentary Volume*, Thomson Gale, 2005.

This volume offers a variety of Langston Hughes items previously available only in archives, including letters and theater posters, and also assembles unreprinted book introductions and public speeches, as well as Hughes's testimony before Joseph McCarthy's Senate committee.

Hughes, Langston, *The Collected Works of Langston Hughes*, University of Missouri Press, 2001.
This series is the standard source for all of Hughes's writings and runs to fifteen volumes as of 2009.

Hughes, Langston, *I Wonder as I Wander*, Rinehart, 1956.
This second volume of Hughes's autobiography focuses on Hughes's travels overseas during the 1930s.

Smith, Katherine Capshaw, ed., *Children's Literature of the Harlem Renaissance*, Indiana University Press, 2004.
The essays in this anthology relate the children's literature produced by black authors to the black experience in America, and consider in particular the aesthetic qualities of Hughes's children's literature written in collaboration with Arna Bontemps.

Where Have You Gone Charming Billy?

TIM O'BRIEN

1975

Tim O'Brien's "Where Have You Gone Charming Billy?" was originally published in *Redbook* magazine in 1975. The story won an O'Henry prize in 1976, and it was published in the *Prize Stories of 1976* and *Prize Stories of the Seventies*. Although it is currently out of print, *Prize Stories of the Seventies* is probably the easiest place to find a copy of the story, although it appears under the chapter title "Night March," which is the title that O'Brien used when he reworked the story in his subsequent novel, *Going After Cacciato*. *Going After Cacciato* was published in 1978, and O'Brien won the National Book Award for it in 1979. *Going After Cacciato* is generally considered one of the best novels about the Vietnam War experience, as well as a book that broke new formal ground by mixing fantastic and realistic styles in a serious war novel.

"Where Have You Gone Charming Billy?" is the story of Private First Class Paul Berlin's attempt to adjust to his first full day of combat in the Vietnam War. Paul Berlin (always referred to by his rank and full name) does not want to be in the war, and he spends much of his first march trying to figure out how he is going to survive the experience. Paul Berlin is terrified, especially after Billy Boy Watkins dies early in the day, and he struggles to contain his terror. The story takes place during a march the platoon takes at night in order to avoid detection. Darkness only amplifies Paul Berlin's terror, since he does not

Tim O'Brien (AP Images)

yet know his fellow soldiers, he is in a hostile foreign country, and he watched a soldier die earlier in the day, ostensibly from fright. The story is an extended meditation on fear and the "tricks" that soldiers use to manage that fear.

AUTHOR BIOGRAPHY

O'Brien was born William Timothy O'Brien on October 1, 1946, in Austin, Minnesota, to William T. O'Brien, an insurance salesman, and Ava E. (Schultz) O'Brien, an elementary school teacher. When he was ten, the family moved from Austin to the small town of Worthington, Minnesota.

O'Brien had a classic midwestern childhood. He played football, golf, and Little League baseball on a team coached by his father. He has admitted, though, that he was not a good athlete, which set him apart from his peers. After high school, O'Brien attended Macalester College in St. Paul, Minnesota, where he majored in political science and was student-body president during his senior year. He graduated Phi Beta Kappa and summa cum laude in 1968.

Two weeks after graduation, he received his draft notice. O'Brien was conflicted about the war. Both of his parents had been active participants in World War II, his father in the Pacific theater and his mother as a WAVE, the women's volunteer arm of the U.S. Navy. When O'Brien was drafted, he considered defecting to Canada, but his parents' service, as well as "the prospect of rejection" by his community, convinced him he had to go. He has, on numerous occasions, referred to this as an act of cowardice. "I committed an act of unpardonable cowardice and evil. I went to a war I believed was wrong and participated in it actively. I pulled the trigger. I was there. And by being there I am guilty."

Tim O'Brien went to Vietnam in 1969 and served in the U.S. Army Fifth Battalion, 46th Infantry, known as the Americal Division. He was sent into the "Pinkville" area, where in the spring of 1968 the United States forces had massacred an estimated five hundred Vietnamese citizens, many of them women and children, in the village of My Lai. When O'Brien arrived, news of the massacre had not yet become public, and he says, "We all wondered why the place was so hostile." O'Brien was promoted to sergeant during his tour, was wounded by shrapnel from a grenade, and returned after thirteen months in Vietnam in 1970.

After the war, O'Brien pursued a Ph.D. in political science at Harvard while writing short stories and articles on the side. In 1973, he left Harvard to work for the *Washington Post* and married Anne Weller (they divorced in 1995). In 1973, his memoir *If I Die in a Combat Zone* was published, and in 1975 he published his first novel, *Northern Lights*. "Where Have You Gone Charming Billy?" appeared in *Redbook* magazine in 1975 and won an O'Henry award that year. In 1978, he published *Going After Cacciato*, which contains a reworked version of "Where Have You Gone Charming Billy?" called "Night March." *Going After Cacciato* was the first big success of O'Brien's career, and he won the National Book Award in 1978 for it. After *Going After Cacciato*, O'Brien was able to write full time, and he published *The Nuclear Age* in 1985, *The Things They Carried* in 1990, *In the Lake of the Woods* in 1994, *Tomcat in Love* in 1998, and *July July* in 2002. He has taught as a distinguished visiting writer at Texas State University.

PLOT SUMMARY

"Where Have You Gone Charming Billy?" takes place during a night march that comes at the end of Paul Berlin's first day in the Vietnam War. The story opens with the platoon moving slowly through the dark and stopping to rest. Paul Berlin brings up the rear, and as they rest, he retreats into his own mind. He is "pretending," trying to will himself to another place, a place that is not Vietnam, a place that is not at war, a place where he did not witness the death of one of his platoon members that afternoon. The soldier who died was Billy Boy Watkins. He stepped on a land mine, which amputated his foot inside his boot. The medic, Doc Peret, tried to calm his panic, but Billy Boy died. While Paul Berlin is pretending not to remember this frightening event, he comes close to falling asleep. The soldier next to him alerts Paul Berlin that they are moving and threatens to shoot him if he is suspected of sleeping.

Paul Berlin follows the soldiers, stumbling to catch up. He is very afraid, and he concentrates on the smells and sounds around him in an effort to allay his fears. His hope is that once they reach the sea, at the end of their night march, they will be safe. As they march, Paul Berlin thinks about the different kinds of fear he felt that day, from the "bundled and tight" fear as Billy Boy Watkins was dying, to the "diffuse and unfocused" fear as they were marching, to his current state, which is "fear of being so terribly afraid again." In order to withstand this fear, Paul Berlin resorts to "tricks" such as counting his steps and thinking of songs. As he marches, counting his steps, Paul Berlin resolves to be a better soldier in the future. He will clean his gun, and remember his training, and learn how to control his "awful fear."

The line of soldiers stops to rest again, and once again, Paul Berlin comes close to falling asleep. The soldier next to him offers him water and a stick of gum and tells him that that "it isn't always so bad." The soldier introduces himself: His real name is Tony, but the soldiers call him Buffalo, or sometimes just Buff. They sit quietly in the dark until Buff starts to laugh a little at the thought of Billy Boy Watkins dying of fright. Paul Berlin imagines the a mock-serious telegram alerting Billy Boy's family that he was "scared to death" in Vietnam. The thought makes Paul Berlin giggle.

Paul Berlin tries to control his giggling, but he cannot. He rolls onto his front, and buries his head in his arms, but he is overcome with hysterical giggling. Buff hisses at him to stop, but he cannot, because in his head he is reliving the events of the afternoon: Billy Boy's death, and how his body fell out of the helicopter and the platoon was forced to search for it in the swampy rice paddy. Buff finally smothers Paul Berlin until he stops giggling and then helps him up, asking if he is all right. "You can get killed, laughing that way," the soldier warns Paul Berlin.

The column of soldiers begins to move again, and Paul Berlin tries to count, but he cannot keep track of the numbers. He tells himself that "he feels better" and that "he would never be so afraid again," but by the end of the story, he has to admit to himself that "he could not stop being afraid."

CHARACTERS

Paul Berlin
Paul Berlin, the protagonist of the story, is a soldier in the U.S. Army in the Vietnam War. Throughout the story, he is identified as "Private First Class Paul Berlin," which emphasizes the way a soldier ceases to be an individual and becomes a member of the platoon.

Paul Berlin's father
Paul Berlin's father is never identified by his own name, but he is a primary character in Paul Berlin's imagination when he thinks about how he will report the war once he returns home.

Paul Berlin's mother
Like Paul Berlin's father, Paul Berlin's mother is never identified by her own name but only by her relationship to Paul Berlin. She is not as central a character to his imagination as his father is, but living long enough to tell her about his experience is one of Paul Berlin's goals for the war.

Buff
See The Soldier

The Soldier
The soldier is not named until late in the story because Private First Class Paul Berlin does not

yet know his name. Eventually the soldier introduces himself as Buff, short for Buffalo. His given name is Toby, but no one calls him that. He tells Paul Berlin that the war is not always as bad as this first day, and then smothers him to help him stop giggling.

Doc Peret
Doc Peret is the unit medic who tends to Billy Boy Watkins after he steps on the land mine. He explains to the soldiers that Billy Boy died of fright.

Billy Boy Watkins
Billy Boy Watkins is the member of the unit who steps on a land mine and then dies of a heart attack brought on by fright. His death, followed as it is by the gruesome spectacle of the body falling from the evacuation helicopter and the subsequent search in the rice paddy for the body, terrifies Paul Berlin.

THEMES

Autobiographical Fiction
Both "Where Have You Gone Charming Billy?" and *Going After Cacciato* are based on O'Brien's experiences in the Vietnam War. O'Brien was drafted right after college, and he has said, "When the draft notice arrived after graduation ... I thought about Canada. I thought about jail. But in the end I could not bear the prospect of rejection: by my family, my country, my friends, my hometown. I would risk conscience and rectitude before risking the loss of love." Like Paul Berlin, O'Brien was a very frightened soldier and one who struggled to make sense of his situation. He has taken Vietnam as the central experience in each one of his books. However, O'Brien is also careful in interviews to distinguish between what he calls the "story-truth" and the "happening-truth" of autobiographical fiction. The former refers to the events in a written story that give it verisimilitude and make a reader believe it, while the latter refers to the truth of the lived experience of authors and characters. Happening-truth "contains the facts of an event, the surface details," while story-truth "presents the pain and passion surrounding the experience: what is felt in your bowels and in your gut and in your heart and in your throat." So while both Paul Berlin and Tim O'Brien served in Vietnam, one cannot surmise that Tim O'Brien necessarily saw a man die of fright, like Billy Boy Watkins. There is not a one-to-one correspondence between story-truth and happening-truth. What an author of autobiographical fiction does, however, is to use the events of his or her life as a starting place for the creation of fictional stories that can fully express the emotional, psychological, and artistic truth of those experiences. In the case of "Where Have You Gone Charming Billy?" we can surmise that O'Brien has used his own experiences as a soldier in Vietnam as the source material for Paul Berlin's terror, as well as his many strategies he uses for managing and overcoming that terror.

Escapism
Escapism is the habit of mind by which a person seeks to escape from reality or routine by diverting the attention to imagination. Paul Berlin does not want to be in the war, and he spends much of his first night in combat trying to mentally escape the situation. On the first page of the story, it is stated that "he was pretending he was not in the war, pretending he had not watched Billy Boy Watkins die of a heart attack that afternoon. He was pretending he was a boy again, camping with his father." Pretending is only one technique by which Paul Berlin seeks to escape the reality of the war. He also uses counting and singing (if only in his head) as ways to avoid experiencing the full reality of his situation. Less successfully, his fit of the giggles is also an attempt to escape the situation. By losing control of his emotions, Paul Berlin momentarily escapes the pressure he feels to not be afraid. Paul Berlin's impulse to escape his circumstances is understandable, and using his imagination as he does to mitigate the horrors of war makes a certain psychological sense, but this tactic also exposes him to danger. Being at war is dangerous and requires attention, and although Paul Berlin's imaginative escapism does not harm him in this story, even he realizes that it could endanger his safety. For Paul Berlin, escapism might be both his best tool for dealing with the war and the very thing that most endangers him.

Fear
Paul Berlin's greatest challenge is learning to handle his fear. On his first day at the war he witnesses another soldier's death, a death that he is told was caused not by his injury but by a heart

TOPICS FOR FURTHER STUDY

- Soldiers return from every war with stories. O'Brien discusses war stories in the documentary *Operation Homecoming: Writing the Wartime Experience*. Watch the documentary (or read the book from which it was derived: *Operation Homecoming: Iraq, Afghanistan and the Home Front*) and interview a soldier from any war about his or her experience of conflict. Videotape the interview if you can, and edit it into a coherent account of that soldier's experience. (If you do not have access to video equipment, write up the interview as a journalistic story.)

- The Vietnam War was famous for many strong photojournalistic images that affected how people in the United States viewed the war. Research photographs of the war and pick three that had an impact. Write up your evaluation of that impact and make a presentation to your class that includes reproductions of the images. Explain the impact of photojournalism on the course of the war and the effect that your specific images had on the domestic audience at home in the United States.

- Before the Vietnam War, there were very few Vietnamese restaurants in America and Vietnamese food was nearly unknown. Find a Vietnamese restaurant in your town and interview the owners. If they are immigrants, how did they come to America? Why did they start a restaurant? Ask them what their favorite dish is and whether they have changed it for an American audience. Then find a recipe for a Vietnamese dish and learn to cook it yourself. Document your interview and cooking experience with photographs or video, and make a presentation to the class about your experience.

- Read *Going After Cacciato* and compare "Where Have You Gone Charming Billy?" to "Night March." Then, examine how "Night March" compares to the fantastical sections concerning the platoon's chase of Cacciato to Paris and the more realistic sections in the Observation Post. Write a paper explaining how the story functions as a part of the novel versus as an independent short story. Which version do you find more effective? Why?

- Read *Fallen Angels* by young-adult author Walter Dean Myers. Choose a character from the novel to either compare or contrast to Paul in "Where Have You Gone Charming Billy?" Write an essay using quotes from both the short story and the novel to support your comparison.

---

attack brought on by his own inability to manage his fear. Doc Peret claims that Billy Boy could have survived the amputation of his foot and blames him for his own death. Billy Boy "got scared and started crying," and despite Doc's morphine injection and consolation, Billy Boy "kept bawling, tightening up, his face going pale and transparent and his veins popping out." Billy Boy's death is a stark warning to Paul Berlin about what will happen to a soldier who cannot control his own emotions. He will cry uncontrollably, just as Paul Berlin succumbs to an uncontrollable fit of the giggles. He will scare himself "stiff." Paul Berlin desperately wants to learn how to control his emotions so that he will survive the war. He resorts to "tricks"—counting, singing, pretending—to distance himself from both the war and his own terror of the war. By the end of the story, he has still not succeeded in this task, no matter how vividly he imagines himself elsewhere; "soon he could even smell the sea, but he could not stop being afraid."

Storytelling

Paul Berlin spends much of this story telling himself stories about what he is experiencing and musing upon the stories he will tell to others when he returns home. At the beginning of the

Dog tags and folded flag on bible (Image copyright Maria Dryfhout, 2009. Used under license from Shutterstock.com)

story, he notes that he will "tell his mother how it smelled... but not how frightened he had been in the afternoon," while at the end of the story he comforts himself by imagining how, in the future, his war experience "would become a funny and sad tale to tell to his father and his friends." O'Brien has said that his intention was to "not write just about the world we live in, but... also write about the world we ought to live in, and could, which is a world of the imagination." Paul Berlin is trapped in a war experience that he finds terrifying and largely incomprehensible. He does not know any of his fellow soldiers, or what the constellations are, or how not to be afraid. In order to make sense of the experience, he tells himself stories. In this he mirrors the task of the writer: to bring order to the chaos of experience by choosing details and putting them in a comprehensible order. Paul Berlin is especially terrified by Billy Boy Watkins's death because he finds it difficult to believe that he died of fright. Paul Berlin saw Billy Boy Watkins step on the mine; he saw Billy Boy's inability to comprehend what had happened to him, and he saw that Billy Boy died, apparently of fright, from a wound which he could have survived. Billy Boy's inability to imagine a story in which he could survive his injury seems to be what has killed him, and subsequently, Paul Berlin spends the remainder of "Where Have You Gone Charming Billy?" trying to tell himself a story in which he himself survives the war, and returns home to tell stories to his parents and his friends. Like counting and singing, storytelling becomes one means by which Paul Berlin seeks to gain some psychological control over his situation, a psychological control he is going to need if he is to survive the war.

STYLE

Metafiction

Metafiction is fiction that takes fiction itself as one of its subjects. That is, metafictional texts not only tell a story but tell a story about the nature of storytelling. Metafictional texts often use this technique to explore the relationship between fiction and reality, as O'Brien does in "Where Have You Gone Charming Billy?" In this story, Paul Berlin spends much of the story thinking about the kinds of war stories he will tell when he gets home and how those stories will be different from the actual experience he is having. Paul Berlin also spends a lot of time pretending to be somewhere else, pretending that events in the story did not happen, pretending in advance what it will be like "when they reached the sea." O'Brien uses Paul Berlin's fantasies to make a metafictional point: he shows that narratives (stories) do not simply arise naturally but are deliberately constructed to produce specific effects. Paul Berlin shapes the stories he tells himself and those he plans to tell when he gets home in much the same way that O'Brien shapes the story of Paul Berlin. One of the central themes of this story is the nature of storytelling itself, and O'Brien's use of narratives within a narrative highlights his belief that the purpose of fiction is, as he has said, "for getting at the truth when the truth isn't sufficient for the truth." Paul Berlin tells himself stories in the hopes that he can shape his experience of Vietnam, and O'Brien writes a story about a character who tells himself stories to show how the stories we tell ourselves shape the people we become. In this way, the story is metafictional—a story about storytelling—as much as it is a story about the Vietnam War.

Third-Person Limited Point of View

A story uses the third-person point of view when the narrator is separate from the protagonist and narrates the events of the story from outside the protagonist's point of view. A third-person story can be identified by its use of the pronouns "he," "she," and "they." The narrative point of view in "Where Have You Gone Charming Billy?" is considered "limited" because the narrator knows only what the protagonist, Paul Berlin, knows. For instance, in the first part of the story, Paul Berlin does not know the name of the soldier next to him, and hence, that character is referred to only as "the soldier." Using the third-person limited narrative allows O'Brien to convey Paul Berlin's confusion about the war to the reader, by only giving the reader as much information as Paul Berlin has. Although the third-person limited point of view remains faithful to the knowledge that the protagonist possesses, it does allow an author to express what a character might be thinking or feeling in language that might be more sophisticated than that which the character might use if describing the situation directly. For instance, when O'Brien describes Paul Berlin's terror during the afternoon as "bundled and tight, and he'd been on his hands and knees, crawling like an insect, an ant escaping a giant's footsteps, thinking nothing, brain flopping like wet cement in a mixer," it is the narrator who is creating those metaphors and ascribing them to Paul Berlin. The metaphors and language are slightly more sophisticated than those a first-person narrator would use, and they describe the inner state of the character in more figurative language than he would probably use if speaking to the reader directly. This is the advantage of the third-person limited narrative. It allows the author to limit the reader's knowledge to what the character actually knows, but it also allows an author to describe the experience that character is having in language the character might not use for himself or herself.

Verisimilitude

Verisimilitude is the term by which we describe how a work of art imitates and represents the known world. Works that rely on verisimilitude suggest a knowable external world that can be accurately described in the text. A verisimilar text is one in which the author has successfully created an illusion of truthfulness or a close approximation of the truth. Even works of fantasy require verisimilitude in order to create a coherent fictional world in which the reader can believe. One of Paul Berlin's chief tasks in "Where Have You Gone Charming Billy?" is to accurately describe to himself the unfamiliar world into which he has been plunged. One aspect of this is Paul Berlin's descriptions of the physical world around him. To Paul Berlin, the world is full of the smells "of mud and algae... of cattle manure and chlorophyll, decay." Paul Berlin cannot always make sense of what things mean (such as the death of Billy Boy Watkins), so he concentrates on describing how they look and smell and sound. When wading through a rice paddy, "his boots made sleepy, sloshing sounds," and when the mine went off, "Billy Boy just stood there with his mouth wide open, looking down, then shaking his head, surprised-looking... finally Billy Boy sat down very casually, not saying a word, his foot lying behind him with most of it still in the boot." These descriptions of the physical world create verisimilitude. The details exist in order to create the illusion that the story happens in the real world, a world of recognizable physical phenomena. Paul Berlin cannot quite comprehend how to be a soldier, and so he concentrates on describing the physical reality in which he finds himself.

HISTORICAL CONTEXT

Vietnam War

The United States' combat involvement in Vietnam began in 1964 with the Gulf of Tonkin Resolution and ended in 1975 with the fall of Saigon. During the Cold War (the period of strained relations between the United States and the Soviet Union following World War II), many in Washington were convinced that there was a vast communist conspiracy to take over the world. South Vietnam was seen as a test of the Domino Theory, the conviction that if communist forces succeeded in South Vietnam, then other south Asian countries would fall like dominoes. Because Vietnam had been divided into two countries after the French-Indochina war, and because North Vietnam's communist government joined the Vietcong rebel forces in their attempt to overthrow the government of South Vietnam, the United States decided it was in the national interest to support the South Vietnamese in repelling communist aggression.

Thus began ten years of war not only in Vietnam but in Laos and Cambodia as well, in which more than fifty-eighty thousand American soldiers were killed, as were millions of Vietnamese, Laotian, and Cambodian citizens. In 1969, to fill a shortfall of soldiers for the war, a draft was instituted, and a lottery was held to determine the order by which young men between the ages of nineteen and twenty-five would be required to serve. This coincided with the peak American involvement in the war, the period of the Tet Offensive. After 1969, domestic opposition to the war, fueled in part by revelations of U.S. war crimes such as the My Lai massacre, slowly forced the United States to withdraw from Vietnam. It was not until 1975, however, when the North Vietnamese forces took over Saigon and the United States was forced to evacuate its embassy, that troops were entirely withdrawn. The Vietnam War is the only war the United States has ever lost.

My Lai Massacre

On March 16, 1968, the men of Charlie Company, Eleventh Brigade, Americal Division, under the command of Lieutenant William Calley, entered the village of My Lai with orders to "search and destroy." Instead of searching out enemy fighters and destroying them, the men rounded up all of the inhabitants of the village—five to seven hundred people—including old people, women, children, and infants, and brutally murdered them. Later accounts by eyewitnesses included horrifying details about old men being bayoneted, infants being shot, and the rape and murder of at least one girl. A few soldiers refused to take part, including Chief Warrant Officer Hugh Thompson, who landed his helicopter and put himself between Calley's men and the remaining survivors of the village in order to rescue them. The U.S. forces attempted to cover up the massacre, and it was nearly a year before freelance reporter Seymour Hersh broke the story. He was aided by Ronald Ridenhour, who heard eyewitness reports of the massacre from soldiers who had taken part. Ridenhour tried unsuccessfully to alert the authorities to what had taken place. When news of the massacre became public, Lieutenant Calley was charged with murder. He was sentenced to life in prison but was released on appeal in 1974. In 2009, William Calley finally apologized for the massacre, saying, "There is not a day that goes by that I do not feel remorse for what happened that day in My Lai." In 1994, O'Brien visited the area and wrote, "I more or less understand what happened that day in March 1968, how it happened, the wickedness that soaks into your blood and heats up and starts to sizzle. I know the boil that precedes butchery. At the same time, however, the men in Alpha Company did not commit murder. We did not turn our machine guns on civilians; we did not cross that conspicuous line between rage and homicide."

Visual Media and Antiwar Sentiment

The Vietnam War never had the sort of clear purpose that previous wars had, but to most of middle America, the idea of opposing the government was antithetical to their values. However, Vietnam was also the first war to be covered extensively by television news, as well as by print media that were willing to publish graphic photographs that were unflattering to the U.S. war effort. Walter Cronkite was the anchor for the *CBS Evening News*, where his authoritative delivery and reputation for integrity earned him the title "the most trusted man in America." In 1968, Cronkite traveled to Vietnam to report on the aftermath of the Tet Offensive. When he returned, he did a special report for the network, and asked to close with a three-minute editorial opinion in which he said, "For it seems more certain than ever that the bloody experience of Vietnam is to end in a stalemate. To say that we are closer to victory today is to believe, in the face of the evidence, the optimists who have been

COMPARE & CONTRAST

- **1969:** This is the heyday of the hippie movement, which has its zenith the weekend of August 15–18, when more than 500,000 people converge on Bethel, New York, for the Woodstock music festival. Huge crowds gather in the rain-soaked fields to watch thirty-two acts, including Richie Havens, Janis Joplin, The Grateful Dead, and Jimi Hendrix. The event is famous as a central "happening" that celebrates hippie ideals of peace, free love, and expanding human consciousness, although it is criticized by those who disapprove of drug use, casual sex, and gathering in the mud.

- **1975:** By 1975, the hippie movement has been largely incorporated into mainstream culture; love beads, mustaches, and tie dye have become fashion items rather than emblems of political belief. The mid-1970s are characterized by a general malaise in American culture, and the idealism of the hippie music scene gradually gives way to the hypnotic dance rhythms of disco and the pounding rebellion of the punk movement.

    Today: The legacy of the hippie movement on music is most evident in the tradition of annual music festivals such as South by Southwest in Austin, Texas; the Telluride Bluegrass Festival in Colorado; and the New Orleans Jazz Festival. These festivals have strong identities, and many repeat visitors come as much for the hippie values of peace, joy, and human fellowship as for the individual musical acts.

- **1969:** Domestic opposition to the Vietnam War grows as the fighting escalates. On November 15, 1969, the biggest antiwar demonstration of the Vietnam era takes place in Washington, D.C. Half a million people gather on the Mall in Washington, where speakers including Senator Edward Kennedy and Dr. Benjamin Spock address the crowd, urging an end to the war.

- **1975:** After the Paris Peace Accords of 1973, the United States pulls nearly all of its troops from South Vietnam and the antiwar protest movement loses its momentum, particularly after the fall of Saigon in April of 1975.

    Today: The antiwar movement of the Vietnam era sets the template for subsequent protest movements. Techniques used by protesters of the Vietnam era, including sit-ins, huge public marches, and boycotting corporations that support the war effort, are used by those who object to the current wars in Iraq and Afghanistan.

- **1969:** The "Vietnamization" of the war begins as the newly elected president Richard Nixon orders the U.S. forces to begin handing over prosecution of the war to the South Vietnamese army. The failure of the South Vietnamese forces to cut off the supply routes at the Ho Chi Minh trail was seen as a serious blow to this early attempt to withdraw. The United States continues to send troops to Vietnam for the next four years, although the troop levels continually drop after 1969.

- **1975:** In late April of 1975, the North Vietnamese capture Saigon, the capitol of South Vietnam. Americans watch on television as Marines evacuate Americans and Vietnamese from the roof of the U.S. embassy by helicopter. Thousands of Vietnamese evacuate along with American citizens to Navy ships waiting offshore, but thousands more ultimately have to be left behind.

    Today: In 1995, the United States formally establishes diplomatic relations with Vietnam, and in 1999, ownership of the U.S. embassy is returned to the United States. In the years after that, a vital tourist and commercial relationship develops between the two nations. In 2006, President George W. Bush makes a formal diplomatic visit to the nation.

Soldier kneeling for fallen comrade (Image copyright Robert F. Balazik, 2009. Used under license from Shutterstock.com)

wrong in the past." When President Lyndon Johnson heard this, he reportedly said, "If I've lost Cronkite, I've lost America." It was not only television reporting that brought the war home to Americans to whom Southeast Asia was a remote and frightening place. A number of iconic photographs hold a place in the nation's collective memory and have come to stand for the Vietnam experience. In particular, three stand out: Nick Ut's photograph of nine-year old Phan Thi Kim Phuc screaming in pain after being burned with napalm, Eddie Adam's graphic photo of the moment the bullet shot by Brigadier General Nguyen Ngoc Loan enters the skull of a captured Vietcong officer, and Ronald Haeberle's photograph of the murdered victims of My Lai lying in the drainage ditch. These photos and others like them brought the reality of the war home to the American public. The growing antiwar movement, an unpopular military draft, and the high rate of U.S. casualties, combined with a declining economy and the growing realization that the best we could hope for in Vietnam was, as Walter Cronkite said, a "stalemate," all contributed to the strong sense by the early 1970s that we had to get out of Vietnam.

CRITICAL OVERVIEW

"Where Have You Gone Charming Billy?" was originally published in *Redbook* magazine in 1975. It won an O'Henry Prize, an annual award given to the twenty best short stories published in U.S. and Canadian magazines, and was published in *Prize Stories 1976: The O'Henry Awards* and in the subsequent collection, *Prize Stories of the Seventies*. Although *Prize Stories of the Seventies* is out of print, it is still in many library collections and readily available online, so it is probably the easiest source in which to find the original version of "Where Have You Gone Charming Billy?"

"Where Have You Gone Charming Billy?" is one of six previously published short stories that O'Brien subsequently reworked as chapters in *Going After Cacciato*. In that novel, "Where Have You Gone Charming Billy?" appears as "Night March." Although there is little independent scholarship about "Where Have You Gone Charming Billy?" the novel in which "Night March" appears has come to be considered one of the finest fictional works about the Vietnam War.

Going After Cacciato was published in 1978 to both critical and popular acclaim. It won the National Book Award for Fiction in 1979 and is considered one of the classics of Vietnam War literature. Mark A. Heberle notes that it "has provoked more critical articles and studies than any other literary representation of Vietnam and has probably been more widely read and more frequently taught in schools and universities." Of particular note is the way that O'Brien uses fantasy, surrealism, and metafiction to highlight the unreal qualities of that conflict. Of the novel, Richard Freedman said in the *New York Times*, "To call *Going After Cacciato* a novel about war is like calling *Moby Dick* a novel about whales."

CRITICISM

Charlotte M. Freeman

Freeman is a freelance writer and editor who holds a Ph.D. in English. In this essay, she examines how O'Brien portrays the essential task of any soldier, learning to accommodate his own terror, in "Where Have You Gone Charming Billy?"

WHAT DO I READ NEXT?

- *Going After Cacciato* (1978) is the novel in which Tim O'Brien reworked "Where Have You Gone Charming Billy?" as "Night March," O'Brien won the National Book Award for this novel, and critical acclaim abounds for the way he mixes techniques of fantasy and realism to portray Paul Berlin's quest to survive the war with some measure of sanity.

- *A Rumor of War* (1976) is Philip Caputo's memoir of his three years serving as a U.S. Marine in Vietnam, with a postscript that incorporates his experience nearly ten years later covering the fall of Saigon as a reporter for the *Chicago Tribune*. One of the most highly acclaimed memoirs of the Vietnam experience, the book is intensely personal. Caputo describes his journey from an idealistic twenty-year-old to a veteran of one of America's most ambiguous wars.

- Philip Caputo follows up his adult memoir and report on the Vietnam War with *10,000 Days of Thunder, A History of the Vietnam War* (2005), a book he wrote especially for young-adult readers. The book covers the history of the war and how the United States became involved, and it also focuses on the many groups affected by the war: U.S. soldiers, the Vietcong, nurses, villagers, and journalists. The book contains many photographs to humanize the conflict. Although the book is written by a journalist known for his adult work, this book manages to simplify the issues without talking down to its audience.

- Often considered the best account of the Vietnam War, Michael Herr's *Dispatches* (1977) is a memoir of his experience covering the Vietnam War for *Esquire* magazine. Herr garnered acclaim not only for the literary qualities of his prose but for the access he gave to soldiers and veterans whose voices had not been heard before. The book is a brutally honest depiction of a war that was often murky to both the combatants in the field and those at home who wondered what the United States was doing there at all.

- Jana Laiz has received critical acclaim for her young-adult novel *Weeping Under This Same Moon*. In this story, two teenage girls, one American, one a Vietnamese refugee, become friends. Hannah is an angry and rebellious American teenager who does not fit in at her high school. When she hears of the plight of the "Boat People," she is moved to act. She becomes friends with Mei, a young artist who has been sent to America with her younger siblings, and both girls overcome their isolation and despair through their developing friendship.

- *Escape from Saigon: How a Vietnam War Orphan Became an American Boy* (2004) by Andrea Warren is a young-adult account that provides a true-life picture of the journey of an eight-year-old Amerasian boy airlifted from Saigon in 1975 through his return to Vietnam twenty years later.

"Where Have You Gone Charming Billy?" is the story of Paul Berlin's first night in the Vietnam War. Paul Berlin is terrified. He is in a strange, dark landscape. Earlier that day, he witnessed the death of one of his fellow soldiers, a death made even more terrifying by the medic Doc Peret's assertion that Billy Boy Watkins died not from the grenade wound but as a result of his own fear. Subsequently, Paul Berlin's understandable fear of this new and life-threatening situation takes on an even darker hue, for if fear alone can kill a soldier, and if Paul Berlin is afraid, then his fear must be putting him at an even greater risk. As a result, Paul Berlin spends his entire first night of the war trying to avoid not only the sort of physical

> TRY AS HE MIGHT, PAUL BERLIN CANNOT BREAK OUT OF THE ISOLATION OF HIS OWN TERROR, JUST AS HE CANNOT TRULY ADMIT TO HIMSELF HOW CRIPPLED HE IS BY HIS FEAR."

exposure that would allow the enemy to shoot at him but the sort of emotional exposure which might humiliate him in front of his fellow soldiers. Because he will depend on these men he does not yet know, he must somehow ensure that they do not think he has been made unreliable by his fear. Finally, he is trying very hard to avoid exposing the true depths of his fear to himself, for as he saw in the afternoon, a soldier's own fear is capable of killing him. Just as Paul Berlin must navigate the frightening external landscape of the Vietnamese jungle in order to reach the safety of the sea, so must he navigate his own interior landscape of frozen terror in order to reach some position of emotional safety from which he can continue as a soldier.

The story opens with a line of men moving slowly, "like sheep in a dream," through a dark landscape. Although Paul Berlin understands that they are marching at night so that the darkness will protect them, the darkness adds another level of confusion to his experience. He quite literally cannot see what is happening most of the time. He is in the Southern Hemisphere, so even the stars are foreign to him. He recognizes the Southern Cross but cannot yet name the other stars. He can, however, recognize the moon, and throughout the story he keeps a close eye on its progress across the sky. On the one hand, it is the only thing he recognizes, and so bears the comfort of the familiar. On the other hand, the moonlight will expose the soldiers to the enemy, and so the one thing that is familiar to him is also the thing that could get him killed. The progress of the moon is symbolic of Paul Berlin's emotional state. At the beginning of the story, when he is still hiding from the reality of his situation by pretending that he is camping, the moon has not yet risen and so cannot expose this pretense. Later, when he first sees the moon, it is "pale and shrunken to the size of a dime."

This appearance of a small and weak moon coincides with Paul Berlin's nearly stifled memory of being "unable" to fire his gun that afternoon. Although he can admit that he was unable to fire, and although it is safe to assume from his resolution "that next time he would be ready and not so afraid" that he failed to fire during a moment of fighting, his ability to tell himself the truth about what happened is still pale and small, like the moon. He cannot fully admit to himself that he failed in his first real moment of fighting. Finally, the moon appears "very high now, and very bright," bright enough that the platoon must stop and wait for cloud cover before continuing their march. It is at this point, when the moon threatens to physically expose the soldiers, that Paul Berlin succumbs to a fit of giggles. The moon is bright, and he is making unnecessary noise; both circumstances threaten not only his safety but that of the soldiers around him. It is not until the moon goes back behind the clouds that Paul Berlin manages to regain control over himself. His terror at Billy Boy Watkins's death cannot survive the bright light of emotional exposure, and he retreats into a state of semihysteria.

In another story, "The Things They Carried," O'Brien makes an observation that applies as well to Paul Berlin. He says that all soldiers carry their "greatest fear, which was the fear of blushing. Men killed, and died, because they were embarrassed not to.... They died so as not to die of embarrassment." Paul Berlin spends the bulk of this story trying very hard to avoid being embarrassed by having his own terror exposed to his fellow soldiers. Early in the story, when Paul Berlin is pretending "he [is] not a soldier," he is awakened from his reverie by the soldier next in line, who accuses him of sleeping. "I'd shoot you if I thought you was sleeping," the soldier says, expressing the danger Paul fears from his fellow soldiers. He does not yet know the men in his platoon. The soldier next to him is a "shadow," and even later, when they share water and a stick of gum, Paul cannot "find" the soldier's face in the darkness. The soldiers are indistinguishable to Paul at that point, although he resolves to "learn their names and laugh at their jokes," so that afterward he would have "war buddies." But for the duration of this story, all the other soldiers, even Buff after he introduces himself, remain indistinct and frightening to Paul. It is upon these indistinct and frightening others that Paul will depend for his survival. Just as he resolves not to tell either of his parents how frightened he had been, Paul must also hide his fear from his fellow soldiers.

Try as he might, Paul Berlin cannot break out of the isolation of his own terror, just as he cannot truly admit to himself how crippled he is by his fear. Early in the story, Paul Berlin tells himself they will be safe when they reach the sea because "their rear would be guarded by five thousand miles of open ocean," ocean across which lies home, the United States, a safe harbor. He cannot go home, but he can get to the sea, across which lies home. However, Paul succumbs to the fanciful belief that, when the platoon reaches the sea, they will "swim and dive into the breakers and hunt crayfish." These are the actions of boys at play, not soldiers at war, and this reverie, coming on the heels of Paul Berlin's pretense that he is not at war but camping "along the Des Moines river" with his father, indicates that he is clinging to false hopes that the war will somehow change into a situation not of continual danger but of adventure and play. Paul spends much of the story attempting to escape the actual experience of war, whether by pretending to be someplace else, or by counting, or by singing songs inside his head. He also seeks to control his terror by making up stories, stories in which he "would never let on how frightened he had been." "A good war story" is what he seeks, one that contains the experience and covers up how terrified he had been.

What Paul Berlin learned that afternoon when Billy Boy Watkins was "scared to death" was that fear can kill. It is not enough to stay in the darkness, to wait for the moon to go back behind the clouds. It is not enough even to remember his training, to remember to stay off the center of the paths, or to remain "ag-ile, mo-bile, hos-tile"; he would somehow have to learn how to stop the fear that left his "brain flopping like wet cement in a mixer." It is that fear, the fear that Paul Berlin expends so much effort hiding even from himself, that can kill a person. That is what killed Billy Boy Watkins, after all: his own fear. If Billy Boy Watkins, who was "tough as nails," could die of fright, then what hope does Paul Berlin have, a boy so frightened he was unable to discharge his weapon in the afternoon, a boy so terrified he succumbs to a hysterical fit of the giggles while on a night march to the sea?

Despite his terror of being exposed as a coward, Paul Berlin learns during the course of the story that he can depend on his fellow soldiers to save him, even if being saved means being "smothered." Buff does not shoot Paul Berlin for his terror; instead, he does what he can to help him get past the crippling fit of giggles that endangers them all. The trick, Buff tells him, is "to stay calm." Paul Berlin spends the whole first half of the story attempting to calm himself with counting, with songs, and with stories he makes up in his head about what he will tell his parents when he gets home. At the story's end, he returns to these "tricks," but they do not work for him anymore. The numbers come "without sequence, randomly, a jumbled and tumbling and chaotic rush of numbers that [runs] like fluid through his head." Once again he tells himself the kind of story that helped earlier in the night, but he finds that no matter how much he tries to convince himself that "he would never be so afraid again" it is not true. The last words of the story sum up Paul Berlin's truth, the truth he can finally admit to himself: "He could not stop being afraid."

By the end of the story, Paul Berlin has not been able to conquer his fear, in part because any sensible person should be deeply afraid in a war. The only soldiers who are not afraid in war are psychopaths and characters in propaganda movies. What Paul Berlin has managed to accomplish is to make real contact with another person in his platoon. He has been exposed to Buff as terrified and not in control of his own emotions, but rather than being shot, as threatened at the beginning of the story, he has learned that he can count on a fellow soldier, even in a moment of humiliation. He also manages, by the end of the story, to admit his own fear to himself, and to begin to learn how to carry it. He might never stop being afraid, but he might just survive the war, might just survive long enough to go home and tell "war stories."

Source: Charlotte M. Freeman, Critical Essay on "Where Have You Gone Charming Billy?," in *Short Stories for Students*, Gale, Cengage Learning, 2010.

Jonathan D'Amore

In the following interview, Tim O'Brien spends an afternoon with D'Amore discussing his life in writing and how he writes about life.

Tim O'Brien, author of *The Things They Carried, Going After Cacciato,* and *In the Lake of the Woods,* among other critically lauded

A helicopter fails to rescue a soldier. (Image copyright Elanur Us, 2009. Used under license from Shutterstock.com)

works of fiction and memoir, visited the University of North Carolina as the Morgan Family Writer-in-Residence during the Spring 2007 semester. O'Brien spent part of an afternoon with me discussing his life in writing and how he writes about life. This author, who claims to feel most compelled to pursue in his books the questions that don't have definitive answers, graciously provided thoughtful and provocative—and occasionally definitive—answers to my many questions. We talked in Chapel Hill on February 27, 2007.

D'Amore: Vietnam, unsurprisingly, had a major impact on your life, and it's not too much of a stretch to say that the war is at the center of your writing life. I know I don't do more than invite speculation with this question, but I'll ask anyway: If you hadn't been drafted into Vietnam, if you'd crossed your metaphorical Rainy River, or if you'd been born five or ten years later, would you have become a writer anyway? Are you a writer by nature or by necessity?

O'Brien: Well, the short answer is: I don't know. A somewhat longer answer is that I think I'd still be a writer, but most likely writer in exile. Someone writing about leaving one's country, and the horrors of that: the dislocations, the lingering sense of moral failure, or moral rectitude, which can also haunt you. But I do guess that I would be writing. I'd be writing about

> "THAT IS MY DREAM. A DREAM OF AMBIGUITY, OF ETERNAL AND LASTING UNCERTAINTY, WHICH IS AN IDEA A GOOD MANY AMERICANS FIND LESS THAN PALATABLE."

those things, which I think would haunt me as much as Vietnam does.

JD: Writing about your experience in Vietnam in If I Die in a Combat Zone *made you fairly well-known when you were relatively young, just twenty-seven, and you became a National Book Award winner in your early thirties. You're often held up as one of your generation's best writers and certainly thought to be the preeminent literary chronicler of the Vietnam War. Now* The Things They Carried *is a core text in many classrooms. How has this literary fame affected you, personally; professionally, artistically?*

TO: Again, the answer is that I don't know, because I don't know the alternative. It may have been otherwise, or it may have turned out that had the books not succeeded, my life would have been, in most meaningful ways, identical. And that's because my objective as a writer was never fame or money or awards; it was that story to be told as I'm sitting alone and staring at that blank page, writing about material that didn't just interest me but really inflamed me, made my stomach burn at night and kept me awake. And not just the horrors of Vietnam: I'm speaking about lost love, about childhood, about aspiration. The same types of things kept me awake when no one knew my name that keep me awake now that some people do know my name.

Some things are easier when you're well-known. Certainly financially: you don't have to rely on a single success; you know that your next book doesn't have to sell a billion copies because you're secure already, so you can kind of do and try what you want. But you feel expectations, also. At least it feels as though there are expectations placed upon me. An expectation to revisit certain ground, for example, but to revisit it in a different way, and there are times when to me that ground is finally barren and dusty; when I see no promise there, and I don't want to revisit it, in a new way or not. And I fight that psychologically. I have to tell myself, "Tim, you've got one life to lead; you're sixty years old, you can probably write one more good book, so write the book you want to write." That's basically what I've told myself with every book.

JD: Well, from book to book, can you see how you've changed or matured? At this point, has writing gotten easier for you? More challenging?

TO: Writing is not easier. I can flatly say that. I'm glad it's not easy though. I doubt I would do it if I weren't struggling over the language and the flow of stories. Because deciding how to tell a story that you think is extraordinary, with language that's appropriate to it, is a challenging enterprise that I find fun. It's a frustrating sort of fun, I must add in a hurry, like doing a difficult jigsaw puzzle when you lose focus on the whole scope of the picture you're trying to put together, because you're locked in on these individual little pieces of cardboard; then it can be frustrating, when you're locked on one sentence or just a noun. That locking sensation can be difficult because you've lost sight of the whole puzzle, you ought to just drop that piece and move on to the next. So as a general statement: writing is hard for me and yet really, really fun, simultaneously.

JD: Are there other particular authors you think make the pieces fit well? Whose texts might show you a way to grapple with your own, or inspire you to try something different?

TO: Of course. I have a whole slew of them, that at different stages of my life have had different degrees of influence. I choose to follow the influence of life over the influence of literature, but you do carry with you as a writer all the books you've read—good and bad, and even the bad ones are of influence in the sense of "avoid this" or "I don't want to sound like that terrible book"; then books you've loved or liked or admired will beckon, will say, "be more like me." But I don't ever make a conscious effort to model prose after the heroes of my past, Conrad being chief among them in my personal pantheon, which includes Borges and Marquez, Hemingway and Faulkner and Dos Passos.

JD: What about writers working today? Can you think of any who fit your way of looking at the world? Do you read any of your contemporaries with an appreciation that they're doing something you feel in concert with?

TO: Oh constantly. There are people whom I admire immensely who do things that not only I couldn't do, but that I wouldn't do. John Updike, for example: I could no more write like John Updike than I could fly up to Mars and back, and I admire the beauty, of his similes, the agility, and fluidity, of his prose—a fluidity and agility that would not come naturally to me. I'm a Midwesterner and I don't have or necessarily want that kind of diction, yet I admire immensely the intricate beauty of Updike's sentences. And many other writers, such as Robert Stone, who is a writer I admire for wholly different reasons—though he's a beautiful stylist in all kinds of ways—he has a knack for going after literary and philosophical big game. He's not hunting pigeons and squirrels, he's a big game hunter. He's hunting God and the dark curtain of life with an edginess of prose that I find fully admirable but wouldn't try to duplicate in a million years, because I'd only fail dismally.

JD: You teach writing—

TO: I try to teach.

JD: Fair enough: you try to teach writing, so you provide guidance to students in that way, and you're almost certainly a model for many aspiring writers, most likely for men and women of my generation who have done military service in one of our recent wars. For them, though they've not had the same experience you did, theirs is related. How would you advise someone who wanted to write about their experience in Iraq or Afghanistan or one of the conflicts in the 1990s? How should they approach that task?

TO: I think how and what you write is largely dependent on the temperament and baggage you bring to a war with you. What you're going to bring home and write about; what you're going to notice in the war. For example, if your politics are conservative and you've been deeply influenced by recent events, you're for the war, you're going to be writing a different kind of book than someone that brings a different temperament to it. And by different I don't necessarily mean opposed to the war: one might be indifferent to it, or scared out of one's mind. Or some people bring to war an adventuristic, I-want-to-find-out-about-death-and-myself attitude. Others bring a piety to it, see a kind of godliness in the proximity to death. So the literature that will ultimately come from social phenomenon [sic] like the war in Iraq or Vietnam or the Civil Rights struggle will finally bear the indelible stamp of individual temperaments or personalities.

JD: Soldiers, you say, are storytellers. And you identify yourself as a storyteller. In The Things They Carried, *you wrote, "The thing about a story is that you dream it as you tell it, hoping that others might then dream along with you, and in this way memory and imagination and language combine to make spirits in the head." I wonder, do you feel a distinction between telling a story—that is, speaking it—and writing one? Do you feel differently telling a story to an audience—to an individual or group of people—as opposed to writing it down?*

TO: For me there's a difference between storytelling and writing a story, though if I were to try to articulate it exactly, I'd probably fail. I can try inexactly though, and say that it has much to do with practical things such as revision.

Oftentimes, when I'm orally telling a story or an anecdote, say, about what might have happened to me last night in a bar, because of the pressures that are on your tongue as a result of your speaking to someone and looking them in the face and trying to get it done briskly and quickly, you're not going to have the time to find that right adjective or the right noun, and you'll sacrifice it in the interest of moving the story along. As a writer you don't make that sacrifice. At least I don't: I pause, and I try alternative bits of dialogue, with the hope of getting it right, telling the story right. And even knowing I'll probably fail anyway it will be more right then the oral version.

There's a beauty to both, to telling that story orally about what happened last night to that human being sitting across from you and to meticulously going over and over and over. They both have virtues. One may have more energy, may have a sense of spontaneity as you're listening to the teller tell it, but the other has the somewhat greater virtue of precision and harmony and beauty that the first didn't. To combine the energy of a tale or anecdote with the craft of applying language to event, to blend those two seems to me what art tries to be—what it should be.

JD: And when a story, spoken aloud or written down, becomes more like the dreaming and less like the actual happening, you don't feel troubled by it. You've said often that what you call "story-truth" can be more "true" than the happening truth.

TO: I think a story may contain nothing from the actual world or events that happened but may be nonetheless faithful to the world we live in, to the fears we all fear, and the joys we experience. As far as I know, no one has actually gone to Tralfamadore or played croquet with a flamingo for a mallet, and yet when you read *Slaughterhouse Five* or *Alice in Wonderland,* even knowing that the events could not have happened in the world we live in, they still occur in a world of truth that is the world of the story, in which you suspend disbelief and you're dreaming along with the dreamer of that story. The relevance of the actual world that we've lived in to the story is, in some cases, non-existent and, in other cases, marginal. And in other cases, like naturalistic fiction, it's very important. But nonetheless, when listening to a story or reading a story, if your effort is to connect literally the story to the world beyond the book, you're really beyond the intent of the storyteller.

JD: So that's a good writer: someone who can make the story true, make the story relevant, whether or not it's a representation in factual terms of the world. Making the story relevant, both to the author and hopefully a larger audience—would you say that's the skill of the writer?

TO: It's part of the skill of the writer, to have the details of the story activate the soul of the reader to feel pain and to feel joy and to feel terror, to wince and to wonder, to feel awe at the unfolding of the extents within the story, to feel suspense and ask, "what next?" The writer has to activate those senses of the spirit, direct all those senses at the ongoing story as it unfolds. That's my primary mission as a writer: to have a reader join the dream of the story, and want to be part of it, and not to be distracted by bad sentences and mistakes and infelicities and melodrama, by all the blunders that can be made in writing I don't like. I aim not to detract from the dreaming of the dream, so that it feels whole and continuous, uninterrupted by error or misjudgment. It also has to do with the sound of the prose, with the music beneath of the story. In the case of John Updike it's one kind of music; with Toni Morrison, it's another; with Raymond Carver, another—and there are recognizable musics or melodies beneath these tales being told by these people. And to be faithful to the voice one chooses to tell a story, and not just be faithful to but to exploit the voice in as many ways as you can and make the voice part of the story, even if it's a purely narrative voice, if it has no origin in the story, if it's just the voice of the author himself or herself. All those elements go into a single purpose for me, which is, academically, suspending disbelief, but which to me is much more little-boyish. There's a little-boyish feel to it. I don't want anything getting in the way of the dream of the dream.

JD: Well, the dream of the dream in your books often strikes a very ambiguous note.

TO: Yeah, I'd say.

JD: I think a big part of what your writing conveys is a sense of ambiguity about the world in your books and in the world outside them.

TO: That is my dream. A dream of ambiguity, of eternal and lasting uncertainty, which is an idea a good many Americans find less than palatable. I think Americans search for certainty and for hard edges to things, and part of the reason I'll never sell like, say, Elmore Leonard or James Patterson is because I admit of ambiguity. I like it. I'm tantalized onward by it. I wallow in it. I actually enjoy it.

JD: Have you come to appreciate that more and more as life has gone on? Or have you always been someone who's seen ambiguity in the world?

TO: For my whole life, I remember being tantalized by the Alamo, because there's such an absence of much record of what occurred there in the final hours. Even from the Mexican side, there's very little testimony, some, but not a lot. I'm tantalized by what happened in those final hours of Custer's last Stand or what happened to Amelia Earhart. I'm tantalized by the Kennedy assassination—not so much asking "did Oswald act alone?" but "what were Kennedy's last thoughts as he was cruising down that street in Dallas? What was in his mind? Dinner that night? Nothing?" These things are unknown and probably unknowable, and for many of us they're frustrating. We build religions to explain the unknowable, sometimes very odd religions, as a way of firming up the boundaries and saying, "Ah, I do know. Even if it's known only through faith, it's "known."

I don't go for that. Maybe it's a temperamental thing, I suppose, but I'd prefer to have the mystery expanded as opposed than [sic] firmed up. That is to say, I want the mystery to get bigger and deeper and deeper. Hence, in all of my books, the character's problem, whatever it may be early on is not resolved in the end, it's compounded. By the end of the book, the mystery is only deeper. *In the Lake of the Woods* is the best example, but it's true also of [*Going After*] *Cacciato* and it's true of *The Things They Carried*. It's probably true of all my books, because that's the human being I am: I'm not an explainer or a tidier-upper, I'm a messer-upper, and by temperament I look for complication maybe where others probably don't.

JD: For you, asking questions is not about finding definitive answers? Maybe just more questions?

TO: Every question leads to the next.

JD: So ambiguity is reassuring to you.

TO: I love it. I love the feel of it because it has a hopeful sense of discovery at the end. It hasn't been discovered, but it might come around tomorrow, or the next day. It gives me a reason to draw the next breath, and light the next cigarette, and take the next step through life. I like that things haven't been neatly tidied up two decades ago or two centuries ago, but still remain open to us. There is something about the unknown that—even though it's frustrating to all of us—that's incredibly fascinating. All you need to do is turn on the History Channel for evidence of my proposition, in the latest show on Lizzie Borden or Amelia Earhart. We're fascinated by what's just beyond our grasp. We're always going after it like we're chasing a butterfly with a net, and the butterfly is just a little too small and fits right through the little spaces in the net, and we can't quite catch it, but by God we love chasing it. What we're chasing—at least, what I'm chasing—is that mutating thing we call the human spirit.

Source: Jonathan D'Amore, "'Every Question Leads to the Next:' An Interview with Tim O'Brien," in *Carolina Quarterly*, Vol. 58, No. 2, Spring 2007, pp. 31–40.

Rosemary King

In the following review, King discusses O'Brien's attempt to lure readers into debate over fact and fiction in war story narratives.

The title of Tim O'Brien's short story "How to Tell a True War Story" is a pun. On one hand, O'Brien is asking how a listener can distinguish whether a story is a factual retelling of events; on the other he outlines "how to tell" a war story. The meaning of the title depends on the reader's position: If listening to a war story, the title suggests, O'Brien will help you to discern whether the story is real; if telling a war story, the title implies that O'Brien will show you how to narrate a story well. The title, however, defies paradigmatic balance. In other words, the reader is drawn into the role of storyteller as O'Brien works to untangle the relationship between fact and fiction.

O'Brien's word play in the title hinges on the definition of "true," a word he uses alternately throughout the story to mean either factually accurate, or something higher and nobler. He does this through three embedded narratives: Mitchell Sanders's narration of Curt Lemon's death; the narrator's description of hearing Sanders's story; and Tim O'Brien's commentary on how to tell a true war story. Each narrator claims his story is an authentic retelling of events as they occurred in Vietnam, asserting the historicity of their narratives. For example, Sanders introduces his story by claiming it is "God's truth" (O'Brien 79). Then he periodically interrupts the story exclaiming its veracity: "This next part [...] you won't believe [...]. You won't. And you know why? [...] Because it happened. Because every word is absolutely dead-on true" (81). Similarly, in the second embedded narration, the narrator tries to convince the reader that he was in Vietnam listening to Sanders's story firsthand when he blatantly states, "I heard this one, for example, from Mitchell Sanders" (79). He continues by recalling where he heard the story, how night slowly fell, the confines of a muddy foxhole, and the garbling of a nearby river, and concludes, "The occasion was right for a good story" (79). The narrator repeatedly says "I remember" throughout the passage to suggest further that he actually remembers Sanders telling the story. In the third narrative, Tim O'Brien recalls how he narrates the episode to an audience. He says, "I'll picture Rat Kiley's face, his grief," for instance, hinting that he was present at Lemon's death (90). In addition, he states that although he may have warped the details slightly, "it happened in this little village on the Batangan Peninsula [...]" (91). Tim O'Brien suggests here that he may have fictionalized past events; even as an eyewitness to Lemon's death, however, the "facts" of the event are unclear at best.

At the same time that O'Brien's characters privilege factual accuracy, they undercut it as well. Sanders, for instance, completes his description of Lemon's death only to add, "I got a confession to make [...]. Last night, man, I had to make up a few things" (83). He then tries to recapture his credibility with the listener by pleading, "Yeah, but listen, it's still true" (84). In a sense, Sanders constructs his story (a "way of knowing" in the present) based on what he believes to have happened (a "way of knowing" in the past). As in Sanders's narrative, Tim O'Brien admits fictionalizing "true" war stories as well: "In war you lose your sense of the definite, hence your sense of truth itself, and therefore it's safe to say that in a true war story nothing is ever absolutely true" (88, emphasis added). At the end, Tim O'Brien admits that his narration is fictional: "Beginning to end [...] it's all made up. Every goddamn detail [...]. None of it happened. None of it. And even if it did happen [...]" (91). The line between fact and fiction in a true war story is more than merely blurred—the line is erased altogether, and fact becomes fiction.

O'Brien's title delivers punch not only through the conflated definition of true but also through the distinction of what makes a war story "true." He underscores the importance of manipulating what actually happened to get at the essence of truth.

> Yet even if it did happen—and maybe it did, anything's possible—even then you know it can't be true, because a true war story does not depend upon that kind of truth. Absolute occurrence is irrelevant. A thing may happen and be a total lie; another thing may not happen and be truer than the truth. (O'Brien 89, emphasis added)

"True war stories," then, capture the genuine experience of war because truth registers only through "gut instinct" (84). Again, O'Brien submits that factual events should not be given a degree of authority simply because they occurred in the past; more important than the historical artifact of what actually occurred is the significance, or truth, of the experience. O'Brien's concept has deep implications for story telling because he suggests that altering facts may be more significant than clinging to the story of what actually transpired. Several critics have commented on O'Brien's unique blend of fact and fiction. For example, in *Understanding Tim O'Brien*, Steven Kaplan summarizes: "O'Brien destroys the line dividing fact from fiction, and tries to show [...] that fiction (or the imagined world) can often be truer than fact" (171). What is more significant than the "dividing line," however, is the reader's position in this debate as storyteller.

In "How to Tell a True War Story," O'Brien lures readers into a debate over fact and fiction that ultimately privileges the latter. Paradoxically, this debate situates readers as storytellers—even as they read or "listen" to the story—with O'Brien giving advice on "how to tell" a "true war story" by revising factual events. Further, once readers have finished O'Brien's story, they are no longer storytellers but are now listeners—even though they are finished reading or "listening" to the story. The pun of the title thus plays out when the reader tells the story while reading it and listens to the story when finished.

Source: Rosemary King, "O'Brien's 'How to Tell a True War Story,'" in *Explicator*, Vol. 57, No. 3, Spring 1999, pp. 182–185.

Don Lee

In the following article, Lee states that the best thing about O'Brien surviving his war experience was that he could write about it.

The good news is that Tim O'Brien is writing fiction again. In 1994, after his sixth book, *In the Lake of the Woods,* was released, he distressed his many fans by vowing to stop writing fiction "for the foreseeable future." Then, a few months later, he published a now famous essay in the *New York Times Magazine* that described his return to Vietnam. With his girlfriend at the time, he visited My Lai, where on March 16, 1968, a company of American soldiers massacred an entire village in a matter of four hours—women, children, old men, chickens, dogs. The body count ranged from two to five hundred.

From 1969–70, O'Brien had been an infantryman in the Quang Ngai province, and his platoon had been stationed in My Lai a year after the massacre. Then and now, he could feel the evil in the place, "the wickedness that soaks into your blood and heats up and starts to sizzle." In the *Times* cover story, O'Brien elaborated on the complex associations of love and insanity that can boil over during a war, almost inevitably exploding into atrocity. But he went a step further, drawing parallels between the "guilt, depression, terror, shame" that infected both his Vietnam experience and his present life, especially now that his girlfriend had left him. Chillingly, he admitted, "Last night suicide was on my mind. Not whether, but how." This time, his fans were not the only ones concerned. Friends and strangers alike called him: shrinks to sign him up, clergymen to save his soul, people who thought he had disclosed way too much, others who thought he had disclosed too little.

> HE IS A METICULOUS, SOME WOULD SAY FANATICAL, CRAFTSMAN. IN GENERAL, HE WRITES EVERY DAY, ALL DAY. HE DOES PRACTICALLY NOTHING ELSE."

Today, O'Brien has no regrets about publishing the article. He considers it one of the best things he has ever written. "I reread it maybe once every two months," he says, "just to remind myself what writing's for. I don't mean catharsis. I mean communication. It was a hard thing to do. It saved my life, but it was a... of a thing to print." After taking nine months off and pulling his life back together, O'Brien started another novel, intrigued enough by the first page to write a second, propelled, as always, by his fundamental faith in the power of storytelling.

Born in 1946, O'Brien was raised in small-town Minnesota, his father an insurance salesman, his mother an elementary school teacher. As a child, O'Brien was lonely, overweight, and a professed "dreamer," and he occupied himself by practicing magic tricks. For a brief time, he contemplated being a writer, inspired by some old clippings he'd found of his father's—personal accounts about fighting in Iwo Jima and Okinawa that had been published in *The New York Times* during World War II. When O'Brien entered college, however, his aspirations turned political. He was a political science major at Macalester, attended peace vigils and war protests, and planned to join the State Department to reform its policies. "I thought we needed people who were progressive and had the patience to try diplomacy instead of dropping bombs on people."

He never imagined he would be drafted upon graduation and actually sent to Vietnam. "I was walking around in a dream and repressing it all," he says, "thinking something would save my ass. Even getting on the plane for boot camp, I couldn't believe any of it was happening to me, someone who hated Boy Scouts and bugs and rifles." When he received his classification—not as a clerk, or a driver, or a cook, but as an infantryman—he seriously considered deserting to Canada. He now thinks it was an act of cowardice not to, particularly since he was against the war, but in 1969, as a twenty-two-year-old, he had feared the disapproval of his family and friends, his townspeople and country. He went to Vietnam and hated every minute of it, from beginning to end.

When he came back to the States, he had a Purple Heart (he was wounded by shrapnel from a hand grenade) and several publishing credits. Much like his father, he had written personal reports about the war that had made their way into Minnesota newspapers, and while pursuing a doctorate at the Harvard School of Government, O'Brien expanded on the vignettes to form a book, *If I Die in Combat, Box Me Up and Ship Me Home.* He sent it first to Knopf, whose editors had high praise for the book. Yet they were already publishing a book about Vietnam, *Dispatches* by Michael Herr, and suggested that O'Brien try the editor Seymour Lawrence, who was in Boston. "He called me at my dormitory at Harvard," O'Brien recalls. "He said, 'Well, we're taking your book. Why don't you come over, I'll take you to lunch.' It was a big, drunken lunch at Trader Vic's in the old Statler Hilton, during the course of which we decided to fire my agent. Sam said, 'Look, you're not going to get much money, there's no way, might as well fire the guy. Why give him ten percent?'"

If I Die in Combat was published in 1973, just as O'Brien was being hired as a national affairs reporter for the *Washington Post,* where he'd been an intern for two summers. "I didn't know the first thing about writing for a newspaper, but I learned fast," says O'Brien, who never took a writing workshop. The job helped tremendously in terms of discipline, which, O'Brien confesses, was a problem for him until then. "I learned the virtue of tenacity."

After his one-year stint at the *Post,* O'Brien simply wrote books. In 1975, he published *Northern Lights,* about two brothers—one a war hero, the other a farm agent who stayed home in Minnesota—who struggle to survive during a cross-country ski trip. *Going After Cacciato* came out in 1978. In the novel, an infantryman named Cacciato deserts, deciding to walk from Southeast Asia to Paris for the peace talks. Paul Berlin is ordered to capture Cacciato, and narrates an extended meditation on what might have happened if Cacciato had made it all the way to Paris. The novel won the National Book Award over John Irving's *The World According to Garp* and John Cheever's *Stories.*

The Nuclear Age, about a draft dodger turned uranium speculator who is obsessed with the threat of nuclear holocaust, was released in 1985, and then, in 1990, came *The Things They Carried,* which was a finalist for both the Pulitzer Prize and the National Book Critics Circle Award. The collection of interrelated stories revolves around the men of Alpha Company, an infantry platoon in Vietnam. The title story is a recitation of the soldiers' weapons and gear, the metaphorical mixing with the mundane: they carried M-60's and C rations and Claymores, and "the common scent of cowardice barely restrained, the instinct to run or freeze or hide, and in many respects this was the heaviest burden of all, for it could never be put down, it required perfect balance and perfect posture." A central motif in the book is the process of storytelling itself, the way imagination and language and memory can blur fact, and why "story-truth is truer sometimes than happening-truth."

In his latest novel, *In the Lake of the Woods,* which is now in paperback, O'Brien takes this question of how much we can know about an event or a person one step further. John and Kathy Wade are staying at a secluded lakeside cottage in northern Minnesota. He has just lost a senatorial election by a landslide, after the revelation that he was among the soldiers at My Lai, a fact he has tried to conceal from everyone—including his wife; even, pathologically, himself—for twenty years. A week after their arrival at the lake, Wade's wife disappears. Perhaps she drowned, perhaps she ran away, perhaps Wade murdered her. The mystery is never solved, and the lack of a traditional ending has produced surprisingly vocal reactions from readers.

"I get calls from people" O'Brien says. They ask questions, they offer their own opinions about what happened, they want to know, missing the point of the novel, that life often does not offer solutions or resolutions, that it is impossible to know completely what secrets lurk within people. As the anonymous narrator, who has conducted a four-year investigation into the case, comments in a footnote: "It's human nature. We are fascinated, all of us, by the implacable otherness of others. And we wish to penetrate by hypothesis, by daydream, by scientific investigation those leaden walls that encase the human spirit, that define it and guard it and hold it forever inaccessible. ('I love you' someone says, and instantly we begin to wonder—'Well, how much?'—and when the answer comes—'With my whole heart'—we then wonder about the wholeness of a fickle heart.) Our lovers, our husbands, our wives, our fathers, our gods—they are all beyond us."

O'Brien feels strongly that *In the Lake of the Woods* is his best book to date, but it took its toll on him. He is a meticulous, some would say fanatical, craftsman. In general, he writes every day, all day. He does practically nothing else. He lifts weights, watches baseball, occasionally plays golf, and reads at night, but rarely ventures from his two-bedroom apartment near Harvard Square. He'll eke out the words, then discard them. It took him an entire year to finish nine pages of *The Nuclear Age,* although he tossed out thousands.

Always, it will begin with an image, "a picture of a human being doing something." With *Going After Cacciato,* it was the image of a guy walking to Paris: "I could see his back." With *The Things They Carried,* it was "remembering all this crap I had on me and inside me, the physical and spiritual burdens." With *In the Lake of the Woods,* it was a man and a woman lying on a porch in the fog along a lake: "I didn't know where the lake was at the time. I knew they were unhappy. I could feel the unhappiness in the fog. I didn't know what the unhappiness was about. It required me to write the next page. A lost election. Why was the election lost? My Lai. All of this was discovered after two years of writing."

But when O'Brien finished *In the Lake of the Woods,* he stopped writing for the first time in over twenty years. "I was burned out" he says. "The novel went to the bottom of the well for me. I felt emotionally drained. I didn't see the point of writing anymore." In retrospect, the respite was good for him. He likens the hiatus to Michael Jordan's brief leave from basketball: "He may not be a better basketball player when he comes back, but he's going to be a better person."

Of course, the road back has not been easy, particularly with the loss of his editor and good friend, Sam Lawrence, who died in 1993. "Through the ups and downs of any writer's career, he was always there, with a new contract, and optimism. Another of his virtues was that he didn't push. Sam didn't give a shit if you missed a deadline. He wanted a good book, no matter how long it took." For the moment, O'Brien has yet to sign up with another publisher for his novel in progress, which opens with two boys building an airplane in their backyard. He prefers to avoid the pressure. "Maybe it's Midwestern" he says. "When I sign a contract, I think I owe them X dollars of literature."

And in defiance of some editors and critics, who suggest he should move on from Vietnam, he will in all likelihood continue to write about the war. "All writers revisit terrain. Shakespeare did it with kings, and Conrad did it with the ocean, and Faulkner did it with the South. It's an emotional and geographical terrain that's given to us by life. Vietnam is there the way childhood is for me. There's a line from Michael Herr: 'Vietnam's what we had instead of happy childhoods.' A funny, weird line, but there's some truth in it."

Yet to categorize O'Brien as merely a Vietnam War writer would be ludicrously unfair and simplistic. Any close examination of his books reveals there is something much more universal about them. As much as they are war stories, they are also love stories. That is why his readers are as apt to be female as male. "I think in every book I've written," O'Brien says, "I've had the twins of love and evil. They intertwine and intermix. They'll separate, sometimes, yet they're hooked the way valances are hooked together. The emotions in war and in our ordinary lives are, if not identical, damn similar."

Source: Don Lee, "About Tim O'Brien," in *Ploughshares,* Vol. 21, No. 4, Winter 1995, pp. 196–202.

Albert E. Wilhelm

In the following review, Wilhelm explains the purpose of the allusions to the song "Billy Boy" in emphasizing the theme of initiation in the short story.

Before being joined and published as a novel, several chapters of Tim O'Brien's *Going After Cacciato* appeared as individual short stories. Frequently these stories were much shorter than the corresponding chapters in O'Brien's novel, and they usually bore different titles. For example, in the October 1977 issue of *Esquire,* O'Brien published a story entitled "Fisherman." Subsequently he expanded this piece to form two separate chapters in *Going After Cacciato,* and he renamed these chapters "Lake Country" and "World's Greatest Lake Country."

> **THE COMMON ELEMENT IN ALL THESE CASES IS A DECEPTIVE WHOLESOMENESS. WHAT APPEARS HEALTHFUL AND NUTRITIOUS IS IN FACT DEADLY. SUCH ARE THE LESSONS THAT PAUL MUST RAPIDLY LEARN IN 'WHERE HAVE YOU GONE, CHARMING BILLY?'"**

Critical commentary on *Going After Cacciato* is, of course, both extensive and illuminating, but O'Brien's early short stories have been largely ignored. Even though many of these stories were absorbed into a longer work, the individual stories are significantly different both in text and in context from corresponding chapters of the completed novel. Indeed, several of the stories won prizes as pieces of short fiction and thus deserve attention as examples of that genre. In order to illustrate the distinctive features of O'Brien's short stories, this note will focus on a story entitled "Where Have You Gone, Charming Billy?," which was first published in the May 1975 issue of *Redbook*. After much revision it reappeared with the title "Night March" as Chapter 31 of *Going After Cacciato*. In its original version, O'Brien's story contains persistent allusions to folk ballads, and these allusions provide significant clues for interpretation.

With his change of title to "Night March," O'Brien shifts his focus from the plight of an individual to the joint activities of a military unit. In its original form, however, the piece is a very moving initiation story, and its allusive title works nicely to reinforce important themes. This title refers, of course, to the old folk song "Billie Boy," and lines from the song appear at several points in the account of Paul Berlin's "first day at the war." Even though O'Brien's title alludes to the second line of the folk song, his phrasing is distinctive. Bertrand Bronson has identified twenty-nine variants of "Billie Boy," but none of them exactly matches the wording of O'Brien's question. Numerous versions of the song ask, "Where have you been, Billie Boy," and five versions ask, "Where are you going?" (Bronson 226–36). O'Brien's use of the verb *go* with a shift in tense may appear insignificant, but it establishes an elegiac tone not present in the lighthearted song. On his first day in battle, Paul has witnessed the bizarre death of Billy Boy Watkins. As he reflects on the death of his fellow soldier, he also mourns the loss of his own innocence—especially that sense of himself "when he was a boy... camping with his father in the midnight summer along the Des Moines River." In O'Brien's story, then, the question from a comic folk song becomes a plaintive reiteration of the *ubi sunt* motif.

The text of the *Redbook* story (but not that of the novel) quotes part of the folk song's description of Billie Boy's girl. Each stanza of the song typically ends with a line affirming that she is "a young thing and cannot leave her mother." This "young" girl's actual age remains indefinite, but in various versions of the song she is said to be "twice forty-five eleven" and "a hundred like and nine" (Bronson 230, 234). Even though these ages may be difficult to calculate precisely, it seems clear that the girl is far from young. Indeed, the folk song's outrageous math may imply a triple-digit age. If, at this stage, she is still too young to leave her mother, what can be said of the confused adolescents who populate O'Brien's story? The reader is invited to transfer the song's comic assertion about a young girl and see its more painful relevance in describing the dead Billy Boy, Paul Berlin, and all the youthful soldiers who are suffering the shock of separation from mothers and motherland.

O'Brien's *Redbook* story depicts Paul's painful initiation, but it also shows his attempt to deal with that pain by means of an imaginative transformation. During the march Paul "pretended he was not a soldier" and "that Billy Boy Watkins had not died of a heart attack that afternoon." By the end of the march he has transformed tragedy into comedy by creating a parody of a death notification:

> He imagined Billy's father opening the telegram: SORRY TO INFORM YOU THAT YOUR SON BILLY BOY WAS YESTERDAY SCARED TO DEATH IN ACTION IN THE REPUBLIC OF VIETNAM, VALIANTLY SUCCUMBING TO A HEART ATTACK SUFFERED WHILE UNDER ENORMOUS STRESS, AND IT IS WITH GREATEST SYMPATHY THAT... He giggled again. He rolled onto his belly and pressed his face into his arms. His body was shaking with giggles.

In the last paragraph of the story, Paul copes with his immediate pain by projecting into the future. The horror of Billy's death is reduced to "a funny war story that he would tell to his father." The bizarre episode will become the basis for "a good joke."

If allusions to the song "Billie Boy" are useful in emphasizing the theme of initiation, they are equally apt in reinforcing this idea of imaginative transformation. According to Bronson, "Billie Boy" is a "spirited parody" of the tragic ballad "Lord Randal" (226). Just as Paul Berlin takes the horrors of war and recreates them in a ludicrous and hence more tolerable form, this song takes a tragic episode of courtship and transforms it into a comic series of questions and answers.

To understand how "Billie Boy" functions as a parody, one must examine the grim materials on which it is apparently based. Like O'Brien's story and the song "Billie Boy," the ballad "Lord Randal" begins with a question addressed to a young man: "O where have you been, Lord Randal, my son?" Later stanzas of the song focus on the source of the poison Lord Randal has consumed and the various legacies he will leave his survivors. These narrative elements, although they have been radically altered in "Billie Boy," provide an additional subtext for O'Brien's story about the war in Vietnam. "Lord Randal" emphasizes betrayal by one who should be worthy of trust, and O'Brien's soldiers in Vietnam feel equally betrayed and abandoned. The murderer of Lord Randal is identified differently in various versions of the ballad. Typically the villain is Randal's sweetheart, but some of the 103 variants collected by Bronson place the blame on his wife, sister, grandmother, and even his father. In all cases, however, the betrayal is even more devastating because it is executed by one who is presumably so close and loving. Still another detail that suggests misplaced confidence is the specific source of the poison consumed by Lord Randall. Here again the many versions of the ballad differ greatly. Most of the variants printed by Bronson identify the poison source as eels or fishes, but some versions specify "dill and dill broth," "sweet milk and parsnips," "eggs fried in butter," and bread with mutton (Bronson 211–214). The common element in all these cases is a deceptive wholesomeness. What appears healthful and nutritious is in fact deadly. Such are the lessons that Paul must rapidly learn in "Where Have You Gone, Charming Billy?" A path that looks safe may be planted with "land mines and booby traps." His fellow soldier Watkins may seem "tough as nails," but he suffers a fatal attack of fear. The mission in Vietnam may at first appear grand and glorious, but soon Paul will see only hollowness and horror.

Among the legacies that Lord Randal will leave his survivors, the most notable are those intended for the one who betrayed him. In various versions of the ballad, these bequests include "the rope and the gallows," the "keys of hell's gates," "hell fire and brimstone," and a "barrel of powder, to blow her up high" (Bronson 201, 196, 207, 215). If the prevailing tone of "Lord Randal" is bitter and vengeful, that of "Billie Boy" is outrageously comic. Instead of brutal legacies left to a false lover, we find in the later song a list of singular achievements attributed to one who will apparently remain endlessly faithful. For example, in the version of the song that Bronson identifies as number 26, Billie's sweetheart "can bake a cherry pie / As quick as a cat can wink her eye." She can "sweep up a house / As quick as a cat can catch a mouse" and even "make up a bed / Seven feet above her head" (235). In "Billie Boy" then, hyperbolic comedy displaces the cynicism and bitterness of "Lord Randal." In a similar fashion Paul Berlin's comic telegram uses hyperbole to keep the horrors of war at bay.

Other differences between "Where Have You Gone, Charming Billy?" and "Night March" could be noted, but this difference in use of ballad allusions is central. While some ballad allusions are retained in the novel, such references are more persistent and more significant in the Redbook story. Throughout O'Brien's story the ballad subtexts provide ironic resonance. With its references to cherry pies and protective mothers, the song "Billie Boy" conjures up an image of home and family that contrasts sharply with the dangerous world into which Paul is initiated. Descriptions of Billie Boy's sweetheart and her remarkable domestic skills suggest fidelity and invincibility—qualities prominent in the rhetoric but seldom in the reality of Vietnam. The ballad "Lord Randal" offers a subtext that is more deeply submerged but equally important in O'Brien's story. Most versions of the song focus on the last words of a young man who courted unwisely and suffered death at the hands of his treacherous lover.

Such materials echo the American dilemma in Southeast Asia where idealistic commitments turned bad and left behind a bitter legacy.

Source: Albert E. Wilhelm, "Ballad Allusions in Tim O'Brien's 'Where Have you Gone, Charming Billy?,'" in *Studies in Short Fiction*, Vol. 28, No. 2, Spring 1991.

SOURCES

Abrahams, William, ed., *Prize Stories of the Seventies: From the O. Henry Awards*, Doubleday, 1981, pp. 258–65.

"Background Note: Vietnam," in *U.S. Department of State: Diplomacy in Action*, http://www.state.gov/r/pa/ei/bgn/4130.htm (accessed September 17, 2009).

Baldick, Chris, "Metafiction," "Third-Person Narrative," and "Verisimilitude," in *The Oxford Dictionary of Literary Terms*, Oxford University Press, 2009, pp. 203, 335, 349.

Brogan, Hugh, *The Penguin History of the USA: New Edition*, Penguin Books, 2001, pp. 645–49, 668.

Childs, Peter, "Realism," in *The Routledge Dictionary of Literary Terms*, Routledge, 2005, pp. 198–200.

Cuddon, J. A., "Realism" and "Verisimilitude," in *The Penguin Dictionary of Literary Terms and Literary Theory*, Penguin, 2000, pp. 729–33, 963–64.

Dowswell, Paul, *The Vietnam War*, Cold War series, World Almanac Library, 2002, pp. 40–41.

Engler, Bernd, "Metafiction (1960)," in *The Literary Encyclopedia*, http://www.litencyc.com/php/stopics.php?rec=true&UID=715 (accessed September 17, 2009).

"Ex-Officer Apologizes for Killings at My Lai," in *New York Times*, August 22, 2009, http://www.nytimes.com/2009/08/23/us/23mylai.html?scp=1&sq=Calley%20apologizes&st=cse (accessed September 17, 2009).

Freedman, Richard, "A Separate Peace," in *New York Times*, http://www.nytimes.com/books/98/09/20/specials/obrien-cacciato.html (accessed September 17, 2009).

"Final Words: Cronkite's Vietnam Commentary," in *National Public Radio*, http://www.npr.org/templates/story/story.php?storyId=106775685 (accessed September 17, 2009).

Heberle, Mark A., *A Trauma Artist: Tim O'Brien and the Fiction of Vietnam*, University of Iowa Press, 2001, p. 109.

Herr, Michael, *Dispatches*, Knopf, 1977.

Herzog, Tony C., *Tim O'Brien*, Twayne's United States Author series, No. 691, Twayne Publishers, 1997, pp. 1–37.

Levy, Debbie, *The Vietnam War*, Chronicle of America's Wars series, Lerner Publications, 2004, pp. 48.

Linder, Douglas, "An Introduction to the My Lai Courts-Martial," in *Famous American Trials: The My Lai Courts-Martial 1970*, University of Missouri-Kansas City School of Law, http://www.law.umkc.edu/faculty/projects/ftrials/mylai/Myl_intro.html (accessed September 17, 2009).

O'Brien, Tim, "The Vietnam in Me," in *New York Times*, http://www.nytimes.com/books/98/09/20/specials/obrien-vietnam.html (accessed September 17, 2009).

———, "Telling Tails," in *Atlantic*, http://www.theatlantic.com/doc/print/200908/tim-obrien-essay (accessed September 17, 2009).

———, "Tim O'Brien Lecture Transcript, in *Writing Vietnam*, http://www.stg.brown.edu/projects/WritingVietnam/obrien.html (accessed September 17, 2009).

———, *Going After Cacciato*, Broadway, 1999, pp. 209–219.

———, *The Things They Carried*, Broadway, 1998, pp. 21.

———, "Where Have You Gone, Charming Billy?" in *Redbook*, Vol. 145, May 1975, pp. 81, 127–32.

Solotaroff, Theodore, "Memoirs for Memorial Day," in *New York Times*, http://www.nytimes.com/books/97/08/10/reviews/caputo-rumor.html (accessed September 17, 2009).

Smith, Patrick A., *Tim O'Brien: A Critical Companion*, Critical Companions to Popular Contemporary Writers series, Greenwood Press, 2005, pp. 1–9, 61–80.

"Vietnam Online," in *American Experience*, Public Broadcasting System, http://www.pbs.org/wgbh/amex/vietnam/trenches/my_lai.html (accessed September 17, 2009).

"Walter Cronkite Dies," in *CBS Evening News with Katie Couric*, July 17, 2009, http://www.cbsnews.com/stories/2009/07/17/eveningnews/main5170556.shtml (accessed September 17, 2009).

"Cold War" and "Vietnam War," in *A Dictionary of World History*, Oxford University Press, 2007, pp. 139–40, 674–75.

FURTHER READING

Heberle, Mark A., *A Trauma Artist: Tim O'Brien and the Fiction of Vietnam*, University of Iowa Press, 2001.
    This book is a critical examination of O'Brien's work that takes trauma and post-traumatic reaction as the core topics of his short stories and novels.

Herr, Michael, *Dispatches*, Cassell, 2002.
    The *New York Times Book Review* called *Dispatches* the finest nonfiction account of the Vietnam War. Herr used the techniques of what was to become the "new journalism," a literary style that combined the narrative qualities of fiction while remaining true to the verifiable facts upon which journalism depends.

Herzog, Tony C., *Tim O'Brien*, Twayne's United States Author Series, No. 691, Twayne Publishers, 1997.
    In this volume, which is part of a larger series of literary critiques of American authors, Herzog reports on extensive interviews with O'Brien

and also brings his own experience in Vietnam into consideration. It provides a good critical overview of O'Brien's work and a fine source of secondary materials.

O'Brien, Tim, *The Things They Carried*, Houghton Mifflin, 1990.

The Things They Carried is a collection of related autobiographical short stories. Although each of them stands separately, in the aggregate they function much like the chapters of a novel. As in the rest of O'Brien's work, many of the incidents are taken from his life; however, he insists that they are fiction and not memoir. In recent years, O'Brien has used one story "On the Rainy River" as an example of the fictionality of his work. At readings, O'Brien will tell audiences the story as though it happened to him, and then reveal that "none of it's true.... It's invented.... I've never been to the Rainy River in my life." He uses this example to impress upon interviewers and readers that "the story is still true, even though...it's made up."

O'Brien, Tim, *In the Lake of the Woods*, Penguin Books, 1994.

In the Lake of the Woods is the story of John Wade, a Vietnam veteran who has moved to a small cabin in northern Minnesota to recover after a losing campaign for the U.S. Senate following revelations that he had been involved in a massacre like the one at My Lai. He awakes one morning to discover that his wife Kathy is missing. The novel mixes genres, incorporating "interviews" with John and Kathy's friends, news reports of the incident, and John's flashbacks in order to raise questions about what happened to Kathy. The novel posits several possibilities but never directly answers the question.

Peacock, Doug, *Grizzly Years*, Holt, 1996.

Doug Peacock returned from two tours of duty as a medic in Vietnam shattered by the experience. What saved him was a map of Wyoming and Montana, a map he studied while in Vietnam, memorizing the places without roads. When he returned, he headed into these areas, seeking solitude and the chance to recover from his experience. What he found was grizzly bears, and over the course of the next decade he studied them denning, feeding, playing, and raising their young. While learning to coexist with these dangerous animals, Peacock began to heal from his Vietnam experience. Despite his lack of formal biology training, Peacock is considered one of the foremost authorities on grizzly behavior, and he has become one of America's most dedicated defenders of wild spaces and wild animals.

Smith, Patrick A., *Tim O'Brien: A Critical Companion*, Critical Companions to Popular Contemporary Writers Series, Greenwood Press, 2005.

Smith provides a collection of essays critiquing each of O'Brien's works, as well as a biographical essay.

Glossary of Literary Terms

A

Aestheticism: A literary and artistic movement of the nineteenth century. Followers of the movement believed that art should not be mixed with social, political, or moral teaching. The statement "art for art's sake" is a good summary of aestheticism. The movement had its roots in France, but it gained widespread importance in England in the last half of the nineteenth century, where it helped change the Victorian practice of including moral lessons in literature. Oscar Wilde and Edgar Allan Poe are two of the best-known "aesthetes" of the late nineteenth century.

Allegory: A narrative technique in which characters representing things or abstract ideas are used to convey a message or teach a lesson. Allegory is typically used to teach moral, ethical, or religious lessons but is sometimes used for satiric or political purposes. Many fairy tales are allegories.

Allusion: A reference to a familiar literary or historical person or event, used to make an idea more easily understood. Joyce Carol Oates's story "Where Are You Going, Where Have You Been?" exhibits several allusions to popular music.

Analogy: A comparison of two things made to explain something unfamiliar through its similarities to something familiar, or to prove one point based on the acceptance of another. Similes and metaphors are types of analogies.

Antagonist: The major character in a narrative or drama who works against the hero or protagonist. The Misfit in Flannery O'Connor's story "A Good Man Is Hard to Find" serves as the antagonist for the Grandmother.

Anthology: A collection of similar works of literature, art, or music. Zora Neale Hurston's "The Eatonville Anthology" is a collection of stories that take place in the same town.

Anthropomorphism: The presentation of animals or objects in human shape or with human characteristics. The term is derived from the Greek word for "human form." The fur necklet in Katherine Mansfield's story "Miss Brill" has anthropomorphic characteristics.

Anti-hero: A central character in a work of literature who lacks traditional heroic qualities such as courage, physical prowess, and fortitude. Anti-heroes typically distrust conventional values and are unable to commit themselves to any ideals. They generally feel helpless in a world over which they have no control. Anti-heroes usually accept, and often celebrate, their positions as social outcasts. A well-known anti-hero is Walter Mitty in James Thurber's story "The Secret Life of Walter Mitty."

Archetype: The word archetype is commonly used to describe an original pattern or model from which all other things of the same kind are made. Archetypes are the literary images that grow out of the "collective unconscious," a theory proposed by psychologist Carl Jung. They appear in literature as incidents and plots that repeat basic patterns of life. They may also appear as stereotyped characters. The "schlemiel" of Yiddish literature is an archetype.

Autobiography: A narrative in which an individual tells his or her life story. Examples include Benjamin Franklin's *Autobiography* and Amy Hempel's story "In the Cemetery Where Al Jolson Is Buried," which has autobiographical characteristics even though it is a work of fiction.

Avant-garde: A literary term that describes new writing that rejects traditional approaches to literature in favor of innovations in style or content. Twentieth-century examples of the literary avant-garde include the modernists and the minimalists.

B

Belles-lettres: A French term meaning "fine letters" or "beautiful writing." It is often used as a synonym for literature, typically referring to imaginative and artistic rather than scientific or expository writing. Current usage sometimes restricts the meaning to light or humorous writing and appreciative essays about literature. Lewis Carroll's *Alice in Wonderland* epitomizes the realm of belles-lettres.

Bildungsroman: A German word meaning "novel of development." The *bildungsroman* is a study of the maturation of a youthful character, typically brought about through a series of social or sexual encounters that lead to self-awareness. J. D. Salinger's *Catcher in the Rye* is a *bildungsroman*, and Doris Lessing's story "Through the Tunnel" exhibits characteristics of a *bildungsroman* as well.

Black Aesthetic Movement: A period of artistic and literary development among African Americans in the 1960s and early 1970s. This was the first major African-American artistic movement since the Harlem Renaissance and was closely paralleled by the civil rights and black power movements. The black aesthetic writers attempted to produce works of art that would be meaningful to the black masses. Key figures in black aesthetics included one of its founders, poet and playwright Amiri Baraka, formerly known as Le Roi Jones; poet and essayist Haki R. Madhubuti, formerly Don L. Lee; poet and playwright Sonia Sanchez; and dramatist Ed Bullins. Works representative of the Black Aesthetic Movement include Amiri Baraka's play *Dutchman,* a 1964 Obie award-winner.

Black Humor: Writing that places grotesque elements side by side with humorous ones in an attempt to shock the reader, forcing him or her to laugh at the horrifying reality of a disordered world. "Lamb to the Slaughter," by Roald Dahl, in which a placid housewife murders her husband and serves the murder weapon to the investigating policemen, is an example of black humor.

C

Catharsis: The release or purging of unwanted emotions—specifically fear and pity—brought about by exposure to art. The term was first used by the Greek philosopher Aristotle in his *Poetics* to refer to the desired effect of tragedy on spectators.

Character: Broadly speaking, a person in a literary work. The actions of characters are what constitute the plot of a story, novel, or poem. There are numerous types of characters, ranging from simple, stereotypical figures to intricate, multifaceted ones. "Characterization" is the process by which an author creates vivid, believable characters in a work of art. This may be done in a variety of ways, including (1) direct description of the character by the narrator; (2) the direct presentation of the speech, thoughts, or actions of the character; and (3) the responses of other characters to the character. The term "character" also refers to a form originated by the ancient Greek writer Theophrastus that later became popular in the seventeenth and eighteenth centuries. It is a short essay or sketch of a person who prominently displays a specific attribute or quality, such as miserliness or ambition. "Miss Brill," a story by Katherine Mansfield, is an example of a character sketch.

Classical: In its strictest definition in literary criticism, classicism refers to works of ancient Greek or Roman literature. The term may also be used to describe a literary work of recognized importance (a "classic") from any time period or literature that exhibits the traits of classicism. Examples of later works and authors now described as classical include French literature of the seventeenth century, Western novels of the nineteenth century, and American fiction of the mid-nineteenth century such as that written by James Fenimore Cooper and Mark Twain.

Climax: The turning point in a narrative, the moment when the conflict is at its most intense. Typically, the structure of stories, novels, and plays is one of rising action, in which tension builds to the climax, followed by falling action, in which tension lessens as the story moves to its conclusion.

Comedy: One of two major types of drama, the other being tragedy. Its aim is to amuse, and it typically ends happily. Comedy assumes many forms, such as farce and burlesque, and uses a variety of techniques, from parody to satire. In a restricted sense the term comedy refers only to dramatic presentations, but in general usage it is commonly applied to nondramatic works as well.

Comic Relief: The use of humor to lighten the mood of a serious or tragic story, especially in plays. The technique is very common in Elizabethan works, and can be an integral part of the plot or simply a brief event designed to break the tension of the scene.

Conflict: The conflict in a work of fiction is the issue to be resolved in the story. It usually occurs between two characters, the protagonist and the antagonist, or between the protagonist and society or the protagonist and himself or herself. The conflict in Washington Irving's story "The Devil and Tom Walker" is that the Devil wants Tom Walker's soul but Tom does not want to go to hell.

Criticism: The systematic study and evaluation of literary works, usually based on a specific method or set of principles. An important part of literary studies since ancient times, the practice of criticism has given rise to numerous theories, methods, and "schools," sometimes producing conflicting, even contradictory, interpretations of literature in general as well as of individual works. Even such basic issues as what constitutes a poem or a novel have been the subject of much criticism over the centuries. Seminal texts of literary criticism include Plato's *Republic*, Aristotle's *Poetics*, Sir Philip Sidney's *The Defence of Poesie*, and John Dryden's *Of Dramatic Poesie*. Contemporary schools of criticism include deconstruction, feminist, psychoanalytic, poststructuralist, new historicist, postcolonialist, and reader-response.

D

Deconstruction: A method of literary criticism characterized by multiple conflicting interpretations of a given work. Deconstructionists consider the impact of the language of a work and suggest that the true meaning of the work is not necessarily the meaning that the author intended.

Deduction: The process of reaching a conclusion through reasoning from general premises to a specific premise. Arthur Conan Doyle's character Sherlock Holmes often used deductive reasoning to solve mysteries.

Denotation: The definition of a word, apart from the impressions or feelings it creates in the reader. The word "apartheid" denotes a political and economic policy of segregation by race, but its connotations—oppression, slavery, inequality—are numerous.

Denouement: A French word meaning "the unknotting." In literature, it denotes the resolution of conflict in fiction or drama. The *denouement* follows the climax and provides an outcome to the primary plot situation as well as an explanation of secondary plot complications. A well-known example of *denouement* is the last scene of the play *As You Like It* by William Shakespeare, in which couples are married, an evildoer repents, the identities of two disguised characters are revealed, and a ruler is restored to power. Also known as "falling action."

Detective Story: A narrative about the solution of a mystery or the identification of a criminal. The conventions of the detective story include the detective's scrupulous use of logic in solving the mystery; incompetent or ineffectual police; a suspect who appears guilty at first but is later proved innocent; and the detective's friend or confidant—often the narrator—whose slowness in interpreting clues emphasizes by contrast the detective's brilliance. Edgar Allan Poe's "Murders in the Rue Morgue" is commonly regarded as the earliest example of this type of story. Other practitioners are Arthur Conan Doyle, Dashiell Hammett, and Agatha Christie.

Dialogue: Dialogue is conversation between people in a literary work. In its most restricted sense, it refers specifically to the speech of characters in a drama. As a specific literary genre, a "dialogue" is a composition in which characters debate an issue or idea.

Didactic: A term used to describe works of literature that aim to teach a moral, religious, political, or practical lesson. Although didactic elements are often found inartistically pleasing works, the term "didactic" usually refers to literature in which the message is more important than the form. The term may also be used to criticize a work that the critic finds "overly didactic," that is, heavy-handed in its delivery of a lesson. An example of didactic literature is John Bunyan's *Pilgrim's Progress*.

Dramatic Irony: Occurs when the reader of a work of literature knows something that a character in the work itself does not know. The irony is in the contrast between the intended meaning of the statements or actions of a character and the additional information understood by the audience.

Dystopia: An imaginary place in a work of fiction where the characters lead dehumanized, fearful lives. George Orwell's *Nineteen Eighty-four*, and Margaret Atwood's *Handmaid's Tale* portray versions of dystopia.

E

Edwardian: Describes cultural conventions identified with the period of the reign of Edward VII of England (1901–1910). Writers of the Edwardian Age typically displayed a strong reaction against the propriety and conservatism of the Victorian Age. Their work often exhibits distrust of authority in religion, politics, and art and expresses strong doubts about the soundness of conventional values. Writers of this era include E. M. Forster, H. G. Wells, and Joseph Conrad.

Empathy: A sense of shared experience, including emotional and physical feelings, with someone or something other than oneself. Empathy is often used to describe the response of a reader to a literary character.

Epilogue: A concluding statement or section of a literary work. In dramas, particularly those of the seventeenth and eighteenth centuries, the epilogue is a closing speech, often in verse, delivered by an actor at the end of a play and spoken directly to the audience.

Epiphany: A sudden revelation of truth inspired by a seemingly trivial incident. The term was widely used by James Joyce in his critical writings, and the stories in Joyce's *Dubliners* are commonly called "epiphanies."

Epistolary Novel: A novel in the form of letters. The form was particularly popular in the eighteenth century. The form can also be applied to short stories, as in Edwidge Danticat's "Children of the Sea."

Epithet: A word or phrase, often disparaging or abusive, that expresses a character trait of someone or something. "The Napoleon of crime" is an epithet applied to Professor Moriarty, arch-rival of Sherlock Holmes in Arthur Conan Doyle's series of detective stories.

Existentialism: A predominantly twentieth-century philosophy concerned with the nature and perception of human existence. There are two major strains of existentialist thought: atheistic and Christian. Followers of atheistic existentialism believe that the individual is alone in a godless universe and that the basic human condition is one of suffering and loneliness. Nevertheless, because there are no fixed values, individuals can create their own characters—indeed, they can shape themselves—through the exercise of free will. The atheistic strain culminates in and is popularly associated with the works of Jean-Paul Sartre. The Christian existentialists, on the other hand, believe that only in God may people find freedom from life's anguish. The two strains hold certain beliefs in common: that existence cannot be fully understood or described through empirical effort; that anguish is a universal element of life; that individuals must bear responsibility for their actions; and that there is no common standard of behavior or perception for religious and ethical matters. Existentialist thought figures prominently in the works of such authors as Franz Kafka, Fyodor Dostoyevsky, and Albert Camus.

Expatriatism: The practice of leaving one's country to live for an extended period in another country. Literary expatriates include Irish author James Joyce who moved to Italy and France, American writers James Baldwin, Ernest Hemingway, Gertrude Stein, and F. Scott Fitzgerald who lived and wrote in

Paris, and Polish novelist Joseph Conrad in England.

Exposition: Writing intended to explain the nature of an idea, thing, or theme. Expository writing is often combined with description, narration, or argument.

Expressionism: An indistinct literary term, originally used to describe an early twentieth-century school of German painting. The term applies to almost any mode of unconventional, highly subjective writing that distorts reality in some way. Advocates of Expressionism include Federico Garcia Lorca, Eugene O'Neill, Franz Kafka, and James Joyce.

F

Fable: A prose or verse narrative intended to convey amoral. Animals or inanimate objects with human characteristics often serve as characters in fables. A famous fable is Aesop's "The Tortoise and the Hare."

Fantasy: A literary form related to mythology and folklore. Fantasy literature is typically set in non-existent realms and features supernatural beings. Notable examples of literature with elements of fantasy are Gabriel Gárcia Márquez's story "The Handsomest Drowned Man in the World" and Ursula K. Le Guin's "The Ones Who Walk Away from Omelas."

Farce: A type of comedy characterized by broad humor, outlandish incidents, and often vulgar subject matter. Much of the comedy in film and television could more accurately be described as farce.

Fiction: Any story that is the product of imagination rather than a documentation of fact. Characters and events in such narratives may be based in real life but their ultimate form and configuration is a creation of the author.

Figurative Language: A technique in which an author uses figures of speech such as hyperbole, irony, metaphor, or simile for a particular effect. Figurative language is the opposite of literal language, in which every word is truthful, accurate, and free of exaggeration or embellishment.

Flashback: A device used in literature to present action that occurred before the beginning of the story. Flashbacks are often introduced as the dreams or recollections of one or more characters.

Foil: A character in a work of literature whose physical or psychological qualities contrast strongly with, and therefore highlight, the corresponding qualities of another character. In his Sherlock Holmes stories, Arthur Conan Doyle portrayed Dr. Watson as a man of normal habits and intelligence, making him a foil for the eccentric and unusually perceptive Sherlock Holmes.

Folklore: Traditions and myths preserved in a culture or group of people. Typically, these are passed on by word of mouth in various forms—such as legends, songs, and proverbs—or preserved in customs and ceremonies. Washington Irving, in "The Devil and Tom Walker" and many of his other stories, incorporates many elements of the folklore of New England and Germany.

Folktale: A story originating in oral tradition. Folk tales fall into a variety of categories, including legends, ghost stories, fairy tales, fables, and anecdotes based on historical figures and events.

Foreshadowing: A device used in literature to create expectation or to set up an explanation of later developments. Edgar Allan Poe uses foreshadowing to create suspense in "The Fall of the House of Usher" when the narrator comments on the crumbling state of disrepair in which he finds the house.

G

Genre: A category of literary work. Genre may refer to both the content of a given work—tragedy, comedy, horror, science fiction—and to its form, such as poetry, novel, or drama.

Gilded Age: A period in American history during the 1870s and after characterized by political corruption and materialism. A number of important novels of social and political criticism were written during this time. Henry James and Kate Chopin are two writers who were prominent during the Gilded Age.

Gothicism: In literature, works characterized by a taste for medieval or morbid characters and situations. A gothic novel prominently features elements of horror, the supernatural, gloom, and violence: clanking chains, terror, ghosts, medieval castles, and unexplained phenomena. The term "gothic novel" is also applied to novels that lack elements of the traditional Gothic setting but that create a similar atmosphere of terror or dread. The term can also be applied to stories, plays, and poems. Mary Shelley's *Frankenstein* and Joyce Carol Oates's *Bellefleur* are both gothic novels.

Grotesque: In literature, a work that is characterized by exaggeration, deformity, freakishness, and disorder. The grotesque often includes an element of comic absurdity. Examples of the grotesque can be found in the works of Edgar Allan Poe, Flannery O'Connor, Joseph Heller, and Shirley Jackson.

H

Harlem Renaissance: The Harlem Renaissance of the 1920s is generally considered the first significant movement of black writers and artists in the United States. During this period, new and established black writers, many of whom lived in the region of New York City known as Harlem, published more fiction and poetry than ever before, the first influential black literary journals were established, and black authors and artists received their first widespread recognition and serious critical appraisal. Among the major writers associated with this period are Countee Cullen, Langston Hughes, Arna Bontemps, and Zora Neale Hurston.

Hero/Heroine: The principal sympathetic character in a literary work. Heroes and heroines typically exhibit admirable traits: idealism, courage, and integrity, for example. Famous heroes and heroines of literature include Charles Dickens's Oliver Twist, Margaret Mitchell's Scarlett O'Hara, and the anonymous narrator in Ralph Ellison's *Invisible Man*.

Hyperbole: Deliberate exaggeration used to achieve an effect. In William Shakespeare's *Macbeth,* Lady Macbeth hyperbolizes when she says, "All the perfumes of Arabia could not sweeten this little hand."

I

Image: A concrete representation of an object or sensory experience. Typically, such a representation helps evoke the feelings associated with the object or experience itself. Images are either "literal" or "figurative." Literal images are especially concrete and involve little or no extension of the obvious meaning of the words used to express them. Figurative images do not follow the literal meaning of the words exactly. Images in literature are usually visual, but the term "image" can also refer to the representation of any sensory experience.

Imagery: The array of images in a literary work. Also used to convey the author's overall use of figurative language in a work.

In medias res: A Latin term meaning "in the middle of things." It refers to the technique of beginning a story at its midpoint and then using various flashback devices to reveal previous action. This technique originated in such epics as Virgil's *Aeneid*.

Interior Monologue: A narrative technique in which characters' thoughts are revealed in a way that appears to be uncontrolled by the author. The interior monologue typically aims to reveal the inner self of a character. It portrays emotional experiences as they occur at both a conscious and unconscious level. One of the best-known interior monologues in English is the Molly Bloom section at the close of James Joyce's *Ulysses*. Katherine Anne Porter's "The Jilting of Granny Weatherall" is also told in the form of an interior monologue.

Irony: In literary criticism, the effect of language in which the intended meaning is the opposite of what is stated. The title of Jonathan Swift's "A Modest Proposal" is ironic because what Swift proposes in this essay is cannibalism—hardly "modest."

J

Jargon: Language that is used or understood only by a select group of people. Jargon may refer to terminology used in a certain profession, such as computer jargon, or it may refer to any nonsensical language that is not understood by most people. Anthony Burgess's *A Clockwork Orange* and James Thurber's "The Secret Life of Walter Mitty" both use jargon.

K

Knickerbocker Group: An indistinct group of New York writers of the first half of the nineteenth century. Members of the group were linked only by location and a common theme: New York life. Two famous members of the Knickerbocker Group were Washington Irving and William Cullen

Bryant. The group's name derives from Irving's *Knickerbocker's History of New York*.

L

Literal Language: An author uses literal language when he or she writes without exaggerating or embellishing the subject matter and without any tools of figurative language. To say "He ran very quickly down the street" is to use literal language, whereas to say "He ran like a hare down the street" would be using figurative language.

Literature: Literature is broadly defined as any written or spoken material, but the term most often refers to creative works. Literature includes poetry, drama, fiction, and many kinds of nonfiction writing, as well as oral, dramatic, and broadcast compositions not necessarily preserved in a written format, such as films and television programs.

Lost Generation: A term first used by Gertrude Stein to describe the post-World War I generation of American writers: men and women haunted by a sense of betrayal and emptiness brought about by the destructiveness of the war. The term is commonly applied to Hart Crane, Ernest Hemingway, F. Scott Fitzgerald, and others.

M

Magic Realism: A form of literature that incorporates fantasy elements or supernatural occurrences into the narrative and accepts them as truth. Gabriel Gárcia Márquez and Laura Esquivel are two writers known for their works of magic realism.

Metaphor: A figure of speech that expresses an idea through the image of another object. Metaphors suggest the essence of the first object by identifying it with certain qualities of the second object. An example is "But soft, what light through yonder window breaks? / It is the east, and Juliet is the sun" in William Shakespeare's *Romeo and Juliet*. Here, Juliet, the first object, is identified with qualities of the second object, the sun.

Minimalism: A literary style characterized by spare, simple prose with few elaborations. In minimalism, the main theme of the work is often never discussed directly. Amy Hempel and Ernest Hemingway are two writers known for their works of minimalism.

Modernism: Modern literary practices. Also, the principles of a literary school that lasted from roughly the beginning of the twentieth century until the end of World War II. Modernism is defined by its rejection of the literary conventions of the nineteenth century and by its opposition to conventional morality, taste, traditions, and economic values. Many writers are associated with the concepts of modernism, including Albert Camus, D. H. Lawrence, Ernest Hemingway, William Faulkner, Eugene O'Neill, and James Joyce.

Monologue: A composition, written or oral, by a single individual. More specifically, a speech given by a single individual in a drama or other public entertainment. It has no set length, although it is usually several or more lines long. "I Stand Here Ironing" by Tillie Olsen is an example of a story written in the form of a monologue.

Mood: The prevailing emotions of a work or of the author in his or her creation of the work. The mood of a work is not always what might be expected based on its subject matter.

Motif: A theme, character type, image, metaphor, or other verbal element that recurs throughout a single work of literature or occurs in a number of different works over a period of time. For example, the color white in Herman Melville's *Moby Dick* is a "specific" motif, while the trials of star-crossed lovers is a "conventional" motif from the literature of all periods.

N

Narration: The telling of a series of events, real or invented. A narration may be either a simple narrative, in which the events are recounted chronologically, or a narrative with a plot, in which the account is given in a style reflecting the author's artistic concept of the story. Narration is sometimes used as a synonym for "storyline."

Narrative: A verse or prose accounting of an event or sequence of events, real or invented. The term is also used as an adjective in the sense "method of narration." For example, in literary criticism, the expression "narrative technique" usually refers to the way the author structures and presents his or her story. Different narrative forms include diaries, travelogues, novels, ballads, epics, short stories, and other fictional forms.

Narrator: The teller of a story. The narrator may be the author or a character in the story through whom the author speaks. Huckleberry Finn is the narrator of Mark Twain's *The Adventures of Huckleberry Finn*.

Novella: An Italian term meaning "story." This term has been especially used to describe fourteenth-century Italian tales, but it also refers to modern short novels. Modern novellas include Leo Tolstoy's *The Death of Ivan Ilich*, Fyodor Dostoyevsky's *Notes from the Underground*, and Joseph Conrad's *Heart of Darkness*.

O

Oedipus Complex: A son's romantic obsession with his mother. The phrase is derived from the story of the ancient Theban hero Oedipus, who unknowingly killed his father and married his mother, and was popularized by Sigmund Freud's theory of psychoanalysis. Literary occurrences of the Oedipus complex include Sophocles' *Oedipus Rex* and D. H. Lawrence's "The Rocking-Horse Winner."

Onomatopoeia: The use of words whose sounds express or suggest their meaning. In its simplest sense, onomatopoeia may be represented by words that mimic the sounds they denote such as "hiss" or "meow." At a more subtle level, the pattern and rhythm of sounds and rhymes of a line or poem may be onomatopoeic.

Oral Tradition: A process by which songs, ballads, folklore, and other material are transmitted by word of mouth. The tradition of oral transmission predates the written record systems of literate society. Oral transmission preserves material sometimes over generations, although often with variations. Memory plays a large part in the recitation and preservation of orally transmitted material. Native American myths and legends, and African folktales told by plantation slaves are examples of orally transmitted literature.

P

Parable: A story intended to teach a moral lesson or answer an ethical question. Examples of parables are the stories told by Jesus Christ in the New Testament, notably "The Prodigal Son," but parables also are used in Sufism, rabbinic literature, Hasidism, and Zen Buddhism. Isaac Bashevis Singer's story "Gimpel the Fool" exhibits characteristics of a parable.

Paradox: A statement that appears illogical or contradictory at first, but may actually point to an underlying truth. A literary example of a paradox is George Orwell's statement "All animals are equal, but some animals are more equal than others" in *Animal Farm*.

Parody: In literature, this term refers to an imitation of a serious literary work or the signature style of a particular author in a ridiculous manner. A typical parody adopts the style of the original and applies it to an inappropriate subject for humorous effect. Parody is a form of satire and could be considered the literary equivalent of a caricature or cartoon. Henry Fielding's *Shamela* is a parody of Samuel Richardson's *Pamela*.

Persona: A Latin term meaning "mask." Personae are the characters in a fictional work of literature. The persona generally functions as a mask through which the author tells a story in a voice other than his or her own. A persona is usually either a character in a story who acts as a narrator or an "implied author," a voice created by the author to act as the narrator for himself or herself. The persona in Charlotte Perkins Gilman's story "The Yellow Wallpaper" is the unnamed young mother experiencing a mental breakdown.

Personification: A figure of speech that gives human qualities to abstract ideas, animals, and inanimate objects. To say that "the sun is smiling" is to personify the sun.

Plot: The pattern of events in a narrative or drama. In its simplest sense, the plot guides the author in composing the work and helps the reader follow the work. Typically, plots exhibit causality and unity and have a beginning, a middle, and an end. Sometimes, however, a plot may consist of a series of disconnected events, in which case it is known as an "episodic plot."

Poetic Justice: An outcome in a literary work, not necessarily a poem, in which the good are rewarded and the evil are punished, especially in ways that particularly fit their virtues or crimes. For example, a murderer may himself be murdered, or a thief will find himself penniless.

Poetic License: Distortions of fact and literary convention made by a writer—not always a poet—for the sake of the effect gained. Poetic license is closely related to the concept of "artistic freedom." An author exercises poetic license by saying that a pile of money "reaches as high as a mountain" when the pile is actually only a foot or two high.

Point of View: The narrative perspective from which a literary work is presented to the reader. There are four traditional points of view. The "third person omniscient" gives the reader a "godlike" perspective, unrestricted by time or place, from which to see actions and look into the minds of characters. This allows the author to comment openly on characters and events in the work. The "third person" point of view presents the events of the story from outside of any single character's perception, much like the omniscient point of view, but the reader must understand the action as it takes place and without any special insight into characters' minds or motivations. The "first person" or "personal" point of view relates events as they are perceived by a single character. The main character "tells" the story and may offer opinions about the action and characters which differ from those of the author. Much less common than omniscient, third person, and first person is the "second person" point of view, wherein the author tells the story as if it is happening to the reader. James Thurber employs the omniscient point of view in his short story "The Secret Life of Walter Mitty." Ernest Hemingway's "A Clean, Well-Lighted Place" is a short story told from the third person point of view. Mark Twain's novel *Huckleberry Finn* is presented from the first person viewpoint. Jay McInerney's *Bright Lights, Big City* is an example of a novel which uses the second person point of view.

Pornography: Writing intended to provoke feelings of lust in the reader. Such works are often condemned by critics and teachers, but those which can be shown to have literary value are viewed less harshly. Literary works that have been described as pornographic include D. H. Lawrence's *Lady Chatterley's Lover* and James Joyce's *Ulysses*.

Post-Aesthetic Movement: An artistic response made by African Americans to the black aesthetic movement of the 1960s and early 1970s. Writers since that time have adopted a somewhat different tone in their work, with less emphasis placed on the disparity between black and white in the United States. In the words of post-aesthetic authors such as Toni Morrison, John Edgar Wideman, and Kristin Hunter, African Americans are portrayed as looking inward for answers to their own questions, rather than always looking to the outside world. Two well-known examples of works produced as part of the post-aesthetic movement are the Pulitzer Prize–winning novels *The Color Purple* by Alice Walker and *Beloved* by Toni Morrison.

Postmodernism: Writing from the 1960s forward characterized by experimentation and application of modernist elements, which include existentialism and alienation. Postmodernists have gone a step further in the rejection of tradition begun with the modernists by also rejecting traditional forms, preferring the anti-novel over the novel and the anti-hero over the hero. Postmodern writers include Thomas Pynchon, Margaret Drabble, and Gabriel Gárcia Márquez.

Prologue: An introductory section of a literary work. It often contains information establishing the situation of the characters or presents information about the setting, time period, or action. In drama, the prologue is spoken by a chorus or by one of the principal characters.

Prose: A literary medium that attempts to mirror the language of everyday speech. It is distinguished from poetry by its use of unmetered, unrhymed language consisting of logically related sentences. Prose is usually grouped into paragraphs that form a cohesive whole such as an essay or a novel. The term is sometimes used to mean an author's general writing.

Protagonist: The central character of a story who serves as a focus for its themes and incidents and as the principal rationale for its development. The protagonist is sometimes referred to in discussions of modern literature as the hero or anti-hero. Well-known protagonists are Hamlet in William Shakespeare's *Hamlet* and Jay Gatsby in F. Scott Fitzgerald's *The Great Gatsby*.

R

Realism: A nineteenth-century European literary movement that sought to portray familiar characters, situations, and settings in a realistic manner. This was done primarily by using an objective narrative point of view and through the buildup of accurate detail. The standard for success of any realistic work depends on how faithfully it transfers common experience into fictional forms. The realistic method may be altered or extended, as in stream of consciousness writing, to record highly subjective experience. Contemporary authors who often write in a realistic way include Nadine Gordimer and Grace Paley.

Resolution: The portion of a story following the climax, in which the conflict is resolved. The resolution of Jane Austen's *Northanger Abbey* is neatly summed up in the following sentence: "Henry and Catherine were married, the bells rang and every body smiled."

Rising Action: The part of a drama where the plot becomes increasingly complicated. Rising action leads up to the climax, or turning point, of a drama. The final "chase scene" of an action film is generally the rising action which culminates in the film's climax.

Roman a clef: A French phrase meaning "novel with a key." It refers to a narrative in which real persons are portrayed under fictitious names. Jack Kerouac, for example, portrayed various friends under fictitious names in the novel *On the Road*. D. H. Lawrence based "The Rocking-Horse Winner" on a family he knew.

Romanticism: This term has two widely accepted meanings. In historical criticism, it refers to a European intellectual and artistic movement of the late eighteenth and early nineteenth centuries that sought greater freedom of personal expression than that allowed by the strict rules of literary form and logic of the eighteenth-century neoclassicists. The Romantics preferred emotional and imaginative expression to rational analysis. They considered the individual to be at the center of all experience and so placed him or her at the center of their art. The Romantics believed that the creative imagination reveals nobler truths—unique feelings and attitudes—than those that could be discovered by logic or by scientific examination. "Romanticism" is also used as a general term to refer to a type of sensibility found in all periods of literary history and usually considered to be in opposition to the principles of classicism. In this sense, Romanticism signifies any work or philosophy in which the exotic or dreamlike figure strongly, or that is devoted to individualistic expression, self-analysis, or a pursuit of a higher realm of knowledge than can be discovered by human reason. Prominent Romantics include Jean-Jacques Rousseau, William Wordsworth, John Keats, Lord Byron, and Johann Wolfgang von Goethe.

S

Satire: A work that uses ridicule, humor, and wit to criticize and provoke change in human nature and institutions. Voltaire's novella *Candide* and Jonathan Swift's essay "A Modest Proposal" are both satires. Flannery O'Connor's portrayal of the family in "A Good Man Is Hard to Find" is a satire of a modern, Southern, American family.

Science Fiction: A type of narrative based upon real or imagined scientific theories and technology. Science fiction is often peopled with alien creatures and set on other planets or in different dimensions. Popular writers of science fiction are Isaac Asimov, Karel Capek, Ray Bradbury, and Ursula K. Le Guin.

Setting: The time, place, and culture in which the action of a narrative takes place. The elements of setting may include geographic location, characters's physical and mental environments, prevailing cultural attitudes, or the historical time in which the action takes place.

Short Story: A fictional prose narrative shorter and more focused than a novella. The short story usually deals with a single episode and often a single character. The "tone," the author's attitude toward his or her subject and audience, is uniform throughout. The short story frequently also lacks *denouement*, ending instead at its climax.

Signifying Monkey: A popular trickster figure in black folklore, with hundreds of tales about this character documented since the 19th century. Henry Louis Gates Jr. examines the history of the signifying monkey in *The Signifying Monkey: Towards a Theory of Afro-American Literary Criticism*, published in 1988.

Simile: A comparison, usually using "like" or "as," of two essentially dissimilar things, as in "coffee as cold as ice" or "He sounded like a broken record." The title of Ernest Hemingway's "Hills Like White Elephants" contains a simile.

Socialist Realism: The Socialist Realism school of literary theory was proposed by Maxim Gorky and established as a dogma by the first Soviet Congress of Writers. It demanded adherence to a communist worldview in works of literature. Its doctrines required an objective viewpoint comprehensible to the working classes and themes of social struggle featuring strong proletarian heroes. Gabriel Gárcia Márquez's stories exhibit some characteristics of Socialist Realism.

Stereotype: A stereotype was originally the name for a duplication made during the printing process; this led to its modern definition as a person or thing that is (or is assumed to be) the same as all others of its type. Common stereotypical characters include the absent-minded professor, the nagging wife, the troublemaking teenager, and the kindhearted grandmother.

Stream of Consciousness: A narrative technique for rendering the inward experience of a character. This technique is designed to give the impression of an ever-changing series of thoughts, emotions, images, and memories in the spontaneous and seemingly illogical order that they occur in life. The textbook example of stream of consciousness is the last section of James Joyce's *Ulysses*.

Structure: The form taken by a piece of literature. The structure may be made obvious for ease of understanding, as in nonfiction works, or may obscured for artistic purposes, as in some poetry or seemingly "unstructured" prose.

Style: A writer's distinctive manner of arranging words to suit his or her ideas and purpose in writing. The unique imprint of the author's personality upon his or her writing, style is the product of an author's way of arranging ideas and his or her use of diction, different sentence structures, rhythm, figures of speech, rhetorical principles, and other elements of composition.

Suspense: A literary device in which the author maintains the audience's attention through the buildup of events, the outcome of which will soon be revealed. Suspense in William Shakespeare's *Hamlet* is sustained throughout by the question of whether or not the Prince will achieve what he has been instructed to do and of what he intends to do.

Symbol: Something that suggests or stands for something else without losing its original identity. In literature, symbols combine their literal meaning with the suggestion of an abstract concept. Literary symbols are of two types: those that carry complex associations of meaning no matter what their contexts, and those that derive their suggestive meaning from their functions in specific literary works. Examples of symbols are sunshine suggesting happiness, rain suggesting sorrow, and storm clouds suggesting despair.

T

Tale: A story told by a narrator with a simple plot and little character development. Tales are usually relatively short and often carry a simple message. Examples of tales can be found in the works of Saki, Anton Chekhov, Guy de Maupassant, and O. Henry.

Tall Tale: A humorous tale told in a straightforward, credible tone but relating absolutely impossible events or feats of the characters. Such tales were commonly told of frontier adventures during the settlement of the west in the United States. Literary use of tall tales can be found in Washington Irving's *History of New York,* Mark Twain's *Life on the Mississippi,* and in the German R. F. Raspe's *Baron Munchausen's Narratives of His Marvellous Travels and Campaigns in Russia.*

Theme: The main point of a work of literature. The term is used interchangeably with thesis. Many works have multiple themes. One of the themes of Nathaniel Hawthorne's "Young Goodman Brown" is loss of faith.

Tone: The author's attitude toward his or her audience maybe deduced from the tone of the work. A formal tone may create distance or convey politeness, while an informal tone may encourage a friendly, intimate, or intrusive feeling in the reader. The author's attitude toward his or her subject matter may also be deduced from the tone of the words he or she uses in discussing it. The tone of John F. Kennedy's speech which included the appeal to "ask not what your country can do for you" was intended to instill feelings of camaraderie and national pride in listeners.

Tragedy: A drama in prose or poetry about a noble, courageous hero of excellent character who, because of some tragic character flaw, brings ruin upon him- or herself. Tragedy treats its subjects in a dignified and serious manner, using poetic language to help evoke pity and fear and bring about catharsis, a purging of these emotions. The tragic form was practiced extensively by the ancient Greeks. The classical form of tragedy was revived in the sixteenth century; it flourished especially on the Elizabethan stage. In modern times, dramatists have attempted to adapt the form to the needs of modern society by drawing their heroes from the ranks of ordinary men and women and defining the nobility of these heroes in terms of spirit rather than exalted social standing. Some contemporary works that are thought of as tragedies include *The Great Gatsby* by F. Scott Fitzgerald, and *The Sound and the Fury* by William Faulkner.

Tragic Flaw: In a tragedy, the quality within the hero or heroine which leads to his or her downfall. Examples of the tragic flaw include Othello's jealousy and Hamlet's indecisiveness, although most great tragedies defy such simple interpretation.

U

Utopia: A fictional perfect place, such as "paradise" or "heaven." An early literary utopia was described in Plato's *Republic,* and in modern literature, Ursula K. Le Guin depicts a utopia in "The Ones Who Walk Away from Omelas."

V

Victorian: Refers broadly to the reign of Queen Victoria of England (1837-1901) and to anything with qualities typical of that era. For example, the qualities of smug narrow-mindedness, bourgeois materialism, faith in social progress, and priggish morality are often considered Victorian. In literature, the Victorian Period was the great age of the English novel, and the latter part of the era saw the rise of movements such as decadence and symbolism.

Cumulative Author/Title Index

A

A & P (Updike): V3
Achebe, Chinua
   Civil Peace: V13
   Vengeful Creditor: V3
Adams, Alice
   Greyhound People: V21
   The Last Lovely City: V14
African Passions (Rivera): V15
Africans (Kohler): V18
Aftermath (Waters): V22
After Twenty Years (Henry): V27
Agüeros, Jack
   Dominoes: V13
Aiken, Conrad
   Silent Snow, Secret Snow: V8
The Aleph (Borges): V17
Alexie, Sherman
   Because My Father Always Said He Was the Only Indian Who Saw Jimi Hendrix Play "The Star-Spangled Banner" at Woodstock: V18
All the Years of Her Life (Callaghan): V19
Allen, Woody
   The Kugelmass Episode: V21
Allende, Isabel
   And of Clay Are We Created: V11
   The Gold of Tomás Vargas: V16
Alvarez, Julia
   Liberty: V27
America and I (Yezierska): V15
American History (Cofer): V27
Amigo Brothers (Thomas): V28
And of Clay Are We Created (Allende): V11

Anderson, Sherwood
   Death in the Woods: V10
   Hands: V11
   Sophistication: V4
Animal Stories (Brown): V14
Anxiety (Paley): V27
The Arabian Nights (Burton): V21
Araby (Joyce): V1
Art Work (Byatt): V26
Asimov, Isaac
   Nightfall: V17
Astronomer's Wife (Boyle): V13
Atwood, Margaret
   Happy Endings: V13
   Rape Fantasies: V3
Aunty Misery (Cofer): V29
Average Waves in Unprotected Waters (Tyler): V17
Axolotl (Cortázar): V3

B

Babel, Isaac
   My First Goose: V10
Babette's Feast (Dinesen): V20
Babylon Revisited (Fitzgerald): V4
Baida, Peter
   A Nurse's Story: V25
Baldwin, James
   The Rockpile: V18
   Sonny's Blues: V2
Balzac, Honore de
   La Grande Bretèche: V10
Bambara, Toni Cade
   Blues Ain't No Mockin Bird: V4
   Gorilla, My Love: V21
   The Lesson: V12
   Raymond's Run: V7

Barn Burning (Faulkner): V5
Barnes, Julian
   Melon: V24
Barrett, Andrea
   The English Pupil: V24
Barth, John
   Lost in the Funhouse: V6
Barthelme, Donald
   The Indian Uprising: V17
   Robert Kennedy Saved from Drowning: V3
Bartleby the Scrivener, A Tale of Wall Street (Melville): V3
The Bass, the River, and Sheila Mant (Wetherell): V28
Bates, H. E.
   The Daffodil Sky: V7
The Bear (Faulkner): V2
The Beast in the Jungle (James): V6
Beattie, Ann
   Imagined Scenes: V20
   Janus: V9
Because My Father Always Said He Was the Only Indian Who Saw Jimi Hendrix Play "The Star-Spangled Banner" at Woodstock (Alexie): V18
Beckett, Samuel
   Dante and the Lobster: V15
The Beginning of Homewood (Wideman): V12
Bellow, Saul
   Leaving the Yellow House: V12
   A Silver Dish: V22
Bender, Aimee
   The Rememberer: V25
Benet, Stephen Vincent
   An End to Dreams: V22

Berriault, Gina
   The Stone Boy: V7
   Women in Their Beds: V11
The Best Girlfriend You Never Had (Houston): V17
Bierce, Ambrose
   The Boarded Window: V9
   A Horseman in the Sky: V27
   An Occurrence at Owl Creek Bridge: V2
Big Black Good Man (Wright): V20
Big Blonde (Parker): V5
The Birds (du Maurier): V16
Bisson, Terry
   The Toxic Donut: V18
Black Boy (Boyle): V14
The Black Cat (Poe): V26
Black Is My Favorite Color (Malamud): V16
Blackberry Winter (Warren): V8
Bliss (Mansfield): V10
Blood-Burning Moon (Toomer): V5
Bloodchild (Butler): V6
The Bloody Chamber (Carter): V4
Bloom, Amy
   Silver Water: V11
Blues Ain't No Mockin Bird (Bambara): V4
The Blues I'm Playing (Hughes): V7
The Boarded Window (Bierce): V9
Boccaccio, Giovanni
   Federigo's Falcon: V28
Boll, Heinrich
   Christmas Not Just Once a Year: V20
Borges, Jorge Luis
   The Aleph: V17
   The Circular Ruins: V26
   The Garden of Forking Paths: V9
   Pierre Menard, Author of the Quixote: V4
Borowski, Tadeusz
   This Way for the Gas, Ladies and Gentlemen: V13
Boule de Suif (Maupassant): V21
Bowen, Elizabeth
   A Day in the Dark: V22
   The Demon Lover: V5
Bowles, Paul
   The Eye: V17
A Boy and His Dog (Ellison): V14
Boyle, Kay
   Astronomer's Wife: V13
   Black Boy: V14
   The White Horses of Vienna: V10
Boyle, T. Coraghessan
   Stones in My Passway, Hellhound on My Trail: V13
   The Underground Gardens: V19
Boys and Girls (Munro): V5
Bradbury, Ray
   The Golden Kite, the Silver Wind: V28

There Will Come Soft Rains: V1
The Veldt: V20
Brazzaville Teen-ager (Friedman): V18
Bright and Morning Star (Wright): V15
Brokeback Mountain (Proulx): V23
Brown, Jason
   Animal Stories: V14
Brownies (Packer): V25
Burton, Richard
   The Arabian Nights: V21
Butler, Octavia
   Bloodchild: V6
Butler, Robert Olen
   A Good Scent from a Strange Mountain: V11
   Titanic Survivors Found in Bermuda Triangle: V22
B. Wordsworth (Naipaul): V29
Byatt, A. S.
   Art Work: V26

C

Callaghan, Morley
   All the Years of Her Life: V19
Calvino, Italo
   The Feathered Ogre: V12
Camus, Albert
   The Guest: V4
The Canal (Yates): V24
The Canterville Ghost (Wilde): V7
Capote, Truman
   A Christmas Memory: V2
Caroline's Wedding (Danticat): V25
Carter, Angela
   The Bloody Chamber: V4
   The Erlking: V12
Carver, Raymond
   Cathedral: V6
   Errand: V13
   A Small, Good Thing: V23
   What We Talk About When We Talk About Love: V12
   Where I'm Calling From: V3
The Cask of Amontillado (Poe): V7
The Catbird Seat (Thurber): V10
Cathedral (Carver): V6
Cather, Willa
   The Diamond Mine: V16
   Neighbour Rosicky: V7
   Paul's Case: V2
   A Wagner Matinee: V27
The Celebrated Jumping Frog of Calaveras County (Twain): V1
The Censors (Valenzuela): V29
The Centaur (Saramago): V23
The Challenge (Vargas Llosa): V14
Chandra, Vikram
   Dharma: V16
Charles (Jackson): V27

Cheever, John
   The Country Husband: V14
   The Swimmer: V2
Chekhov, Anton
   The Darling: V13
   Gooseberries: V14
   Gusev: V26
   The Lady with the Pet Dog: V5
   A Problem: V29
Chesnutt, Charles Waddell
   The Goophered Grapevine: V26
   The Sheriff's Children: V11
Children of the Sea (Danticat): V1
Chopin, Kate
   Désirée's Baby: V13
   A Point at Issue!: V17
   The Storm: V26
   The Story of an Hour: V2
A Christmas Memory (Capote): V2
Christmas Not Just Once a Year (Böll): V20
The Chrysanthemums (Steinbeck): V6
A Circle in the Fire (O'Connor): V19
The Circular Ruins (Borges): V26
Cisneros, Sandra
   Eleven: V27
   Little Miracles, Kept Promises: V13
   Woman Hollering Creek: V3
Civil Peace (Achebe): V13
Clarke, Arthur C.
   Dog Star: V29
   "If I Forget Thee, O Earth...": V18
   The Star: V4
A Clean, Well-Lighted Place (Hemingway): V9
Cofer, Judith Ortiz
   American History: V27
   Aunty Misery: V29
Collier, Eugenia W.
   Marigolds: V28
Connell, Richard
   The Most Dangerous Game: V1
Conrad, Joseph
   Heart of Darkness: V12
   The Secret Sharer: V1
Conscience of the Court (Hurston): V21
Contents of a Dead Man's Pockets (Finney): V29
A Conversation from the Third Floor (El-Bisatie): V17
A Conversation with My Father (Paley): V3
The Conversion of the Jews (Roth): V18
Cortázar, Julio
   Axolotl: V3
   House Taken Over: V28
   The Pursuer: V20
The Country Husband (Cheever): V14

Crane, Stephen
    A Mystery of Heroism: V28
    The Open Boat: V4
Crazy Sunday (Fitzgerald): V21
The Curing Woman (Morales): V19

D

The Daffodil Sky (Bates): V7
Dahl, Roald
    Lamb to the Slaughter: V4
Dante and the Lobster (Beckett): V15
Danticat, Edwidge
    Caroline's Wedding: V25
    Children of the Sea: V1
The Darling (Chekhov): V13
Davies, Peter Ho
    Think of England: V21
Davis, Rebecca Harding
    Life in the Iron Mills: V26
A Day in the Dark (Bowen): V22
Day of the Butterfly (Munro): V28
de Balzac, Honore
    La Grande Bretèche: V10
de Maupassant, Guy
    Boule de Suif: V21
    The Necklace: V4
    Two Friends: V28
de Unamuno, Miguel
    Saint Emmanuel the Good, Martyr: V20
The Dead (Joyce): V6
Death in the Woods (Anderson): V10
Death in Venice (Mann): V9
The Death of Ivan Ilych (Tolstoy): V5
Debbie and Julie (Lessing): V12
The Deep (Swan): V23
The Demon Lover (Bowen): V5
Desai, Anita
    Games at Twilight: V28
Desiree's Baby (Chopin): V13
The Destructors (Greene): V14
The Devil and Tom Walker (Irving): V1
Devlin, Anne
    Naming the Names: V17
Dharma (Chandra): V16
The Diamond as Big as the Ritz (Fitzgerald): V25
The Diamond Mine (Cather): V16
Diaz, Junot
    The Sun, the Moon, the Stars: V20
The Difference (Glasgow): V9
Dinesen, Isak
    Babette's Feast: V20
    The Ring: V6
    The Sailor-Boy's Tale: V13
    Sorrow-Acre: V3
Disorder and Early Sorrow (Mann): V4
Divakaruni, Chitra Banerjee
    Meeting Mrinal: V24
    Mrs. Dutta Writes a Letter: V18

Doctorow, E. L.
    The Writer in the Family: V27
Doerr, Anthony
    The Shell Collector: V25
The Dog of Tithwal (Manto): V15
Dog Star (Clarke): V29
The Doll's House (Mansfield): V29
Dominoes (Agüeros): V13
Don't Look Now (du Maurier): V14
The Door in the Wall (Wells): V3
Dostoevsky, Fyodor
    The Grand Inquisitor: V8
Doyle, Arthur Conan
    The Red-Headed League: V2
du Maurier, Daphne
    The Birds: V16
    Don't Look Now: V14
Dubus, Andre
    The Fat Girl: V10
Dybek, Stuart
    Hot Ice: V23

E

The Eatonville Anthology (Hurston): V1
Edwards, Kim
    The Way It Felt to Be Falling: V18
Eisenberg, Deborah
    Someone to Talk To: V24
El-Bisatie, Mohamed
    A Conversation from the Third Floor: V17
Elbow Room (McPherson): V23
The Elephant Vanishes (Murakami): V23
Eleven (Cisneros): V27
Eliot, George
    The Lifted Veil: V8
Ellison, Harlan
    A Boy and His Dog: V14
    I Have No Mouth, and I Must Scream: V15
    Jeffty Is Five: V13
    "Repent, Harlequin!" Said the Ticktockman: V21
Ellison, Ralph
    The Invisible Man, or Battle Royal: V11
    King of the Bingo Game: V1
The End of Old Horse (Ortiz): V22
An End to Dreams (Benét): V22
The English Pupil (Barrett): V24
Erdrich, Louise
    Fleur: V22
    The Red Convertible: V14
The Erlking (Carter): V12
Errand (Carver): V13
The Eskimo Connection (Yamamoto): V14
Eveline (Joyce): V19
Everyday Use (Walker): V2

Everything That Rises Must Converge (O'Connor): V10
Exchanging Glances (Wolf): V14
The Eye (Bowles): V17
Eyes of a Blue Dog (García Márquez): V21

F

The Fall of Edward Barnard (Maugham): V17
The Fall of the House of Usher (Poe): V2
The Far and the Near (Wolfe): V18
Far, Sui Sin
    Mrs. Spring Fragrance: V4
The Fat Girl (Dubus): V10
Faulkner, William
    Barn Burning: V5
    The Bear: V2
    Race at Morning: V27
    A Rose for Emily: V6
    That Evening Sun: V12
The Feathered Ogre (Calvino): V12
Federigo's Falcon (Boccaccio) V28
Ferrell, Carolyn
    Proper Library: V23
Fever (Wideman): V6
Finney, Jack
    Contents of a Dead Man's Pockets: V29
The First Seven Years (Malamud): V13
The First Year of My Life (Spark): V28
Fish (McCorkle): V24
Fitzgerald, F. Scott
    Babylon Revisited: V4
    Crazy Sunday: V21
    The Diamond as Big as the Ritz: V25
    Winter Dreams: V15
Flaubert, Gustave
    A Simple Heart: V6
Fleur (Erdrich): V22
Flight (Steinbeck): V3
Flowering Judas (Porter): V8
Forty-Five a Month (Narayan): V29
Fountains in the Rain (Mishima): V12
Four Summers (Oates): V17
Freeman, Mary E. Wilkins
    A New England Nun: V8
    Old Woman Magoun: V26
    The Revolt of 'Mother': V4
Friedman, Bruce Jay
    Brazzaville Teen-ager: V18

G

Gaines, Ernest
    The Sky is Gray: V5
Galsworthy, John
    The Japanese Quince: V3

Games at Twilight (Desai): V28
García Márquez, Gabriel
   Eyes of a Blue Dog: V21
   The Handsomest Drowned Man in the World: V1
   A Very Old Man with Enormous Wings: V6
   The Woman Who Came at Six O'Clock: V16
The Garden of Forking Paths (Borges): V9
The Garden Party (Mansfield): V8
Gardner, John
   Redemption: V8
Gibson, William
   Johnny Mnemonic: V26
The Gift of the Magi (Henry): V2
Gilchrist, Ellen
   Victory Over Japan: V9
The Gilded Six-Bits (Hurston): V11
Gilman, Charlotte Perkins
   Three Thanksgivings: V18
   The Yellow Wallpaper: V1
Gimpel the Fool (Singer): V2
Girl (Kincaid): V7
A Girl like Phyl (Highsmith): V25
The Girls (Williams): V25
Glasgow, Ellen
   The Difference: V9
Glaspell, Susan
   A Jury of Her Peers: V3
Gogol, Nikolai
   The Overcoat: V7
The Golden Kite, the Silver Wind (Bradbury): V28
The Gold of Tomás Vargas (Allende): V16
The Good Doctor (Haslett): V24
A Good Man Is Hard to Find (O'Connor): V2
A Good Scent from a Strange Mountain (Butler): V11
The Good Shopkeeper (Upadhyay): V22
Goodbye, Columbus (Roth): V12
The Goophered Grapevine (Chesnutt): V26
Gooseberries (Chekhov): V14
Gordimer, Nadine
   Once Upon a Time: V28
   Town and Country Lovers: V14
   The Train from Rhodesia: V2
   The Ultimate Safari: V19
Gorilla, My Love (Bambara): V21
The Grand Inquisitor (Dostoevsky): V8
The Grasshopper and the Bell Cricket (Kawabata): V29
The Grave (Porter): V11
A Great Day (Sargeson): V20
Great Day (Malouf): V24
Greatness Strikes Where It Pleases (Gustafsson): V22

The Green Leaves (Ogot): V15
Greene, Graham
   The Destructors: V14
Greyhound People (Adams): V21
The Guest (Camus): V4
Guests of the Nation (O'Connor): V5
A Guide to Berlin (Nabokov): V6
Gusev (Chekhov): V26
Gustafsson, Lars
   Greatness Strikes Where It Pleases: V22

H

Half a Day (Mahfouz): V9
The Half-Skinned Steer (Proulx): V18
Han's Crime (Naoya): V5
Hands (Anderson): V11
The Handsomest Drowned Man in the World (García Márquez): V1
Ha'Penny (Paton): V29
Happy Endings (Atwood): V13
Harrison Bergeron (Vonnegut): V5
Harte, Bret
   The Outcasts of Poker Flat: V3
The Harvest (Rivera): V15
Haslett, Adam
   The Good Doctor: V24
Hawthorne, Nathaniel
   The Minister's Black Veil: A Parable: V7
   My Kinsman, Major Molineux: V11
   The Wives of the Dead: V15
   Young Goodman Brown: V1
He (Porter): V16
Head, Bessie
   Life: V13
   Snapshots of a Wedding: V5
Heart of Darkness (Conrad): V12
Heinlein, Robert A.
   Waldo: V7
Helprin, Mark
   Perfection: V25
Hemingway, Ernest
   A Clean, Well-Lighted Place: V9
   Hills Like White Elephants: V6
   In Another Country: V8
   The Killers: V17
   The Short Happy Life of Francis Macomber: V1
   The Snows of Kilimanjaro: V11
   Soldier's Home: V26
Hemon, Aleksandar
   Islands: V22
Hempel, Amy
   In the Cemetery Where Al Jolson Is Buried: V2
Hendel, Yehudit
   Small Change: V14
Henne Fire (Singer): V16
Henry, O.
   After Twenty Years: V27

   The Gift of the Magi: V2
   Mammon and the Archer: V18
Here's Your Hat What's Your Hurry (McCracken): V25
Highsmith, Patricia
   A Girl like Phyl: V25
Hills Like White Elephants (Hemingway): V6
The Hitchhiking Game (Kundera): V10
Hoeg, Peter
   Journey into a Dark Heart: V18
Holiday (Porter): V23
A Horse and Two Goats (Narayan): V5
A Horseman in the Sky (Bierce): V27
Hot Ice (Dybek): V23
House Taken Over (Cortázar): V28
Houston, Pam
   The Best Girlfriend You Never Had: V17
How I Contemplated the World from the Detroit House of Correction and Began My Life Over Again (Oates): V8
How Much Land Does a Man Need? (Tolstoy): V28
How to Tell a True War Story (O'Brien): V15
Hughes, Langston
   The Blues I'm Playing: V7
   Slave on the Block: V4
   Thank You Ma'm: V29
A Hunger Artist (Kafka): V7
Hurst, James
   The Scarlet Ibis: V23
Hurston, Zora Neale
   Conscience of the Court: V21
   The Eatonville Anthology: V1
   The Gilded Six-Bits: V11
   Spunk: V6
   Sweat: V19

I

I Have No Mouth, and I Must Scream (Ellison): V15
I Stand Here Ironing (Olsen): V1
If I Forget Thee, O Earth . . ." (Clarke): V18
If You Sing like That for Me (Sharma): V21
Imagined Scenes (Beattie): V20
Immigration Blues (Santos): V19
Immortality (Yiyun Li): V24
In Another Country (Hemingway): V8
In the Cemetery Where Al Jolson Is Buried (Hempel): V2
In the Garden of the North American Martyrs (Wolff): V4
In the Kindergarten (Jin): V17

In the Middle of the Fields (Lavin): V23
In the Penal Colony (Kafka): V3
In the Shadow of War (Okri): V20
In the Zoo (Stafford): V21
The Indian Uprising (Barthelme): V17
The Interlopers (Saki): V15
The Invalid's Story (Twain): V16
The Invisible Man, or Battle Royal (Ellison): V11
Irving, Washington
   The Devil and Tom Walker: V1
   The Legend of Sleepy Hollow: V8
   Rip Van Winkle: V16
Islands (Hemon): V22

J

Jackson, Shirley
   Charles: V27
   The Lottery: V1
Jacobs, W. W.
   The Monkey's Paw: V2
James, Henry
   The Beast in the Jungle: V6
   The Jolly Corner: V9
Janus (Beattie): V9
The Japanese Quince (Galsworthy): V3
Jeeves Takes Charge (Wodehouse): V10
Jeffty Is Five (Ellison): V13
Jewett, Sarah Orne
   A White Heron: V4
The Jilting of Granny Weatherall (Porter): V1
Jim Baker's Blue Jay Yarn (Twain): V27
Jin, Ha
   In the Kindergarten: V17
Johnny Mnemonic (Gibson): V26
Johnson, Charles
   Menagerie, a Child's Fable: V16
The Jolly Corner (James): V9
Jones, Thom
   The Pugilist at Rest: V23
Journey into a Dark Heart (Høeg): V18
Joyce, James
   Araby: V1
   The Dead: V6
   Eveline: V19
Julavits, Heidi
   Marry the One Who Gets There First: V23
A Jury of Her Peers (Glaspell): V3

K

Kafka, Franz
   A Hunger Artist: V7
   In the Penal Colony: V3
   The Metamorphosis: V12

Kawabata, Yasunari
   The Grasshopper and the Bell Cricket: V29
Kew Gardens (Woolf): V12
The Killers (Hemingway): V17
Kincaid, Jamaica
   Girl: V7
   What I Have Been Doing Lately: V5
King of the Bingo Game (Ellison): V1
Kingston, Maxine Hong
   On Discovery: V3
Kipling, Rudyard
   Mowgli's Brothers: V22
   Mrs. Bathurst: V8
   Rikki-Tikki-Tavi: V21
Kitchen (Yoshimoto): V16
Kohler, Sheila
   Africans: V18
The Kugelmass Episode (Allen): V21
Kundera, Milan
   The Hitchhiking Game: V10

L

La Grande Bretèche (Balzac/de Balzac): V10
The Lady with the Pet Dog (Chekhov): V5
The Lady, or the Tiger? (Stockton): V3
Lagerlöf, Selma
   The Legend of the Christmas Rose: V18
Lahiri, Jhumpa
   A Temporary Matter: V19
   This Blessed House: V27
Lamb to the Slaughter (Dahl): V4
Last Courtesies (Leffland): V24
The Last Lovely City (Adams): V14
Last Night (Salter): V25
Lavin, Mary
   In the Middle of the Fields: V23
Lawrence, D. H.
   Odour of Chrysanthemums: V6
   The Rocking-Horse Winner: V2
Le Guin, Ursula K.
   The Ones Who Walk Away from Omelas: V2
Leaving the Yellow House (Bellow): V12
Lee, Don
   The Price of Eggs in China: V25
Leffland, Ella
   Last Courtesies: V24
The Legend of Sleepy Hollow (Irving): V8
The Legend of the Christmas Rose (Lagerlöf): V18
Lessing, Doris
   Debbie and Julie: V12
   A Mild Attack of Locusts: V26
   Through the Tunnel: V1
   To Room Nineteen: V20

The Lesson (Bambara): V12
Li, Yiyun
   Immortality: V24
Liberty (Alvarez): V27
Life (Head): V13
Life in the Iron Mills (Davis): V26
The Life You Save May Be Your Own (O'Connor): V7
The Lifted Veil (Eliot): V8
Little Miracles, Kept Promises (Cisneros): V13
London, Jack
   To Build a Fire: V7
Long Distance (Smiley): V19
The Long-Distance Runner (Paley): V20
Lost in the Funhouse (Barth): V6
The Lottery (Jackson): V1
Lullaby (Silko): V10

M

The Magic Barrel (Malamud): V8
Mahfouz, Naguib
   Half a Day: V9
Malamud, Bernard
   Black Is My Favorite Color: V16
   The First Seven Years: V13
   The Magic Barrel: V8
Malouf, David
   Great Day: V24
Mammon and the Archer (Henry): V18
The Man That Corrupted Hadleyburg (Twain): V7
The Man to Send Rain Clouds (Silko): V8
The Man Who Lived Underground (Wright): V3
The Man Who Was Almost a Man (Wright): V9
The Management of Grief (Mukherjee): V7
Mann, Thomas
   Death in Venice: V9
   Disorder and Early Sorrow: V4
Mansfield, Katherine
   Bliss: V10
   The Doll's House: V29
   The Garden Party: V8
   Marriage à la Mode: V11
   Miss Brill: V2
Manto, Saadat Hasan
   The Dog of Tithwal: V15
A Map of Tripoli, 1967 (Wetzel): V17
Marigolds (Collier): V28
Marriage à la Mode (Mansfield): V11
Marry the One Who Gets There First (Julavits): V23
Marshall, Paule
   To Da-duh, in Memoriam: V15

Mason, Bobbie Ann
   Private Lies: V20
   Residents and Transients: V8
   Shiloh: V3
The Masque of the Red Death (Poe): V8
Mateo Falcone (Merimee): V8
Maugham, W. Somerset
   The Fall of Edward Barnard: V17
McCorkle, Jill
   Fish: V24
McCracken, Elizabeth
   Here's Your Hat What's Your Hurry: V25
McCullers, Carson
   Wunderkind: V5
McPherson, James Alan
   Elbow Room: V23
The Medicine Bag (Sneve): V28
Meeting Mrinal (Divakaruni): V24
Melanctha (Stein): V5
Melon (Barnes): V24
Melville, Herman
   Bartleby the Scrivener, A Tale of Wall Street: V3
Menagerie, a Child's Fable (Johnson): V16
Meneseteung (Munro): V19
Merimee, Prosper
   Mateo Falcone: V8
The Metamorphosis (Kafka): V12
The Middleman (Mukherjee): V24
A Mild Attack of Locusts (Lessing): V26
The Minister's Black Veil: A Parable (Hawthorne): V7
Mishima, Yukio
   Fountains in the Rain: V12
   Swaddling Clothes: V5
Miss Brill (Mansfield): V2
Mistry, Rohinton
   Swimming Lessons: V6
The Monkey's Paw (Jacobs): V2
Moon Lake (Welty): V26
Moore, Lorrie
   You're Ugly, Too: V19
Morales, Alejandro
   The Curing Woman: V19
Morrison, Toni
   Recitatif: V5
The Most Dangerous Game (Connell): V1
Mowgli's Brothers (Kipling): V22
Mphahlele, Es'kia (Ezekiel)
   Mrs. Plum: V11
Mrs. Bathurst (Kipling): V8
Mrs. Dutta Writes a Letter (Divakaruni): V18
Mrs. Plum (Mphahlele): V11
Mrs. Spring Fragrance (Far): V4
Mukherjee, Bharati
   The Management of Grief: V7
   The Middleman: V24

Munro, Alice
   Boys and Girls: V5
   Day of the Butterfly: V28
   Meneseteung: V19
   Walker Brothers Cowboy: V13
Murakami, Haruki
   The Elephant Vanishes: V23
My First Goose (Babel): V10
My Kinsman, Major Molineux (Hawthorne): V11
My Life with the Wave (Paz): V13
A Mystery of Heroism (Crane): V28

N

Nabokov, Vladimir
   A Guide to Berlin: V6
   That in Aleppo Once....: V15
Naipaul, V. S.
   B. Wordsworth: V29
Naming the Names (Devlin): V17
Naoya, Shiga
   Han's Crime: V5
Narayan, R. K.
   Forty-Five a Month: V29
   A Horse and Two Goats: V5
The Necessary Grace to Fall (Ochsner): V24
The Necklace (Maupassant): V4
Neighbour Rosicky (Cather): V7
The New Dress (Woolf): V4
A New England Nun (Freeman): V8
The News from Ireland (Trevor): V10
The Night the Ghost Got In (Thurber): V19
Night (Tolstaya): V14
Nightfall (Asimov): V17
No. 44, The Mysterious Stranger (Twain): V21
A Nurse's Story (Baida): V25

O

O'Brien, Tim
   How to Tell a True War Story: V15
   The Things They Carried: V5
   Where Have You Gone Charming Billy?: V29
O'Connor, Flannery
   A Circle in the Fire: V19
   Everything That Rises Must Converge: V10
   A Good Man Is Hard to Find: V2
   The Life You Save May Be Your Own: V7
O'Connor, Frank
   Guests of the Nation: V5
O'Flaherty, Liam
   The Sniper: V20
   The Wave: V5
Oates, Joyce Carol
   Four Summers: V17

   How I Contemplated the World from the Detroit House of Correction and Began My Life Over Again: V8
   Where Are You Going, Where Have You Been?: V1
An Occurrence at Owl Creek Bridge (Bierce): V2
Ochsner, Gina
   The Necessary Grace to Fall: V24
Odour of Chrysanthemums (Lawrence): V6
Ogot, Grace
   The Green Leaves: V15
Okri, Ben
   In the Shadow of War: V20
Old Woman Magoun (Freeman): V26
Olsen, Tillie
   I Stand Here Ironing: V1
Once Upon a Time (Gordimer): V28
On Discovery (Kingston): V3
One Day in the Life of Ivan Denisovich (Solzhenitsyn): V9
The Ones Who Walk Away from Omelas (Le Guin): V2
The Open Boat (Crane): V4
The Open Window (Saki): V1
Orringer, Julie
   The Smoothest Way Is Full of Stones: V23
Ortiz, Simon J.
   The End of Old Horse: V22
Orwell, George
   Shooting an Elephant: V4
The Outcasts of Poker Flat (Harte): V3
The Overcoat (Gogol): V7
Ozick, Cynthia
   The Pagan Rabbi: V12
   Rosa: V22
   The Shawl: V3

P

Packer, ZZ
   Brownies: V25
The Pagan Rabbi (Ozick): V12
Paley, Grace
   Anxiety: V27
   A Conversation with My Father: V3
   The Long-Distance Runner: V20
Paris 1991 (Walbert): V24
Parker, Dorothy
   Big Blonde: V5
Paton, Alan
   Ha'Penny: V29
Paul's Case (Cather): V2
Paz, Octavio
   My Life with the Wave: V13
The Pearl (Steinbeck): V22
A Perfect Day for Bananafish (Salinger): V17

Perfection (Helprin): V25
Phillips, Jayne Anne
   Souvenir: V4
Pierre Menard, Author of the Quixote (Borges): V4
The Pit and the Pendulum (Poe): V29
Poe, Edgar Allan
   The Black Cat: V26
   The Cask of Amontillado: V7
   The Fall of the House of Usher: V2
   The Masque of the Red Death: V8
   The Pit and the Pendulum: V29
   The Purloined Letter: V16
   The Tell-Tale Heart: V4
A Point at Issue! (Chopin): V17
Pomegranate Seed (Wharton): V6
Porter, Katherine Anne
   Flowering Judas: V8
   The Grave: V11
   He: V16
   Holiday: V23
   The Jilting of Granny Weatherall: V1
Powell, Padgett
   Trick or Treat: V25
The Price of Eggs in China (Lee): V25
Private Lies (Mason): V20
A Problem (Chekhov): V29
Proper Library (Ferrell): V23
Proulx, E. Annie
   Brokeback Mountain: V23
   The Half-Skinned Steer: V18
The Pugilist at Rest (Jones): V23
The Purloined Letter (Poe): V16
The Pursuer (Cortázar): V20
Pushkin, Alexander
   The Stationmaster: V9

R

Race at Morning (Faulkner): V27
Rape Fantasies (Atwood): V3
Raymond's Run (Bambara): V7
Recitatif (Morrison): V5
The Red Convertible (Erdrich): V14
The Red-Headed League (Doyle): V2
Redemption (Gardner): V8
The Rememberer (Bender): V25
Repent, Harlequin!" Said the Ticktockman (Ellison): V21
The Replacement (Robbe-Grillet): V15
Residents and Transients (Mason): V8
Resurrection of a Life (Saroyan): V14
The Revolt of 'Mother' (Freeman): V4
Rikki-Tikki-Tavi (Kipling): V21
The Ring (Dinesen): V6
Rip Van Winkle (Irving): V16
Rivera, Beatriz
   African Passions: V15
Rivera, Tomás
   The Harvest: V15
Robbe-Grillet, Alain
   The Replacement: V15
Robert Kennedy Saved from Drowning (Barthelme): V3
The Rocking-Horse Winner (Lawrence): V2
The Rockpile (Baldwin): V18
Roman Fever (Wharton): V7
Rosa (Ozick): V22
A Rose for Emily (Faulkner): V6
Roselily (Walker): V11
Roth, Philip
   The Conversion of the Jews: V18
   Goodbye, Columbus: V12
Rules of the Game (Tan): V16

S

The Sailor-Boy's Tale (Dinesen): V13
Saint Emmanuel the Good, Martyr (Unamuno/de Unamuno): V20
Saki
   The Interlopers: V15
   The Open Window: V1
Salinger, J. D.
   A Perfect Day for Bananafish: V17
Salter, James
   Last Night: V25
Santos, Bienvenido
   Immigration Blues: V19
Saramago, José
   The Centaur: V23
Sargeson, Frank
   A Great Day: V20
Saroyan, William
   Resurrection of a Life: V14
Sartre, Jean-Paul
   The Wall: V9
Say Yes (Wolff): V11
Sayers, Dorothy L.
   Suspicion: V12
The Scarlet Ibis (Hurst): V23
Scott, Sir Walter
   Wandering Willie's Tale: V10
The Secret Life of Walter Mitty (Thurber): V1
The Secret Sharer (Conrad): V1
Sharma, Akhil
   If You Sing like That for Me: V21
The Shawl (Ozick): V3
The Shell Collector (Doerr): V25
The Sheriff's Children (Chesnutt): V11
Shiloh (Mason): V3
Shooting an Elephant (Orwell): V4
The Short Happy Life of Francis Macomber (Hemingway): V1
Silent Snow, Secret Snow (Aiken): V8
Silko, Leslie Marmon
   Lullaby: V10
   The Man to Send Rain Clouds: V8
   Storyteller: V11
   Yellow Woman: V4
Silver, Marisa
   What I Saw from Where I Stood: V25
A Silver Dish (Bellow): V22
Silver Water (Bloom): V11
A Simple Heart (Flaubert): V6
Singer, Isaac Bashevis
   Gimpel the Fool: V2
   Henne Fire: V16
   The Spinoza of Market Street: V12
   Zlateh the Goat: V27
The Sky is Gray (Gaines): V5
Slave on the Block (Hughes): V4
The Slump (Updike): V19
Small Change (Hendel): V14
A Small, Good Thing (Carver): V23
Smiley, Jane
   Long Distance: V19
The Smoothest Way Is Full of Stones (Orringer): V23
Snapshots of a Wedding (Head): V5
Sneve, Virginia Driving Hawk
   The Medicine Bag: V28
The Sniper (O'Flaherty): V20
The Snows of Kilimanjaro (Hemingway): V11
Soldier's Home (Hemingway): V26
Solzhenitsyn, Alexandr
   One Day in the Life of Ivan Denisovich: V9
Someone to Talk To (Eisenberg): V24
Sonny's Blues (Baldwin): V2
Sontag, Susan
   The Way We Live Now: V10
Sophistication (Anderson): V4
Sorrow-Acre (Dinesen): V3
Souvenir (Phillips): V4
Sparks, Muriel
   The First Year of My Life: V28
The Spinoza of Market Street (Singer): V12
A Spinster's Tale (Taylor): V9
Spunk (Hurston): V6
Stafford, Jean
   In the Zoo: V21
The Star (Clarke): V4
The Stationmaster (Pushkin): V9
Stein, Gertrude
   Melanctha: V5
Steinbeck, John
   The Chrysanthemums: V6
   Flight: V3
   The Pearl: V22
Stockton, Frank R.
   The Lady, or the Tiger?: V3
The Stone Boy (Berriault): V7
Stones in My Passway, Hellhound on My Trail (Boyle): V13
The Storm (Chopin): V26

The Story of an Hour (Chopin): V2
Storyteller (Silko): V11
The Sun, the Moon, the Stars (Díaz): V20
Suspicion (Sayers): V12
Suzy and Leah (Yolen): V29
Swaddling Clothes (Mishima): V5
Swan, Mary
  The Deep: V23
Sweat (Hurston): V19
The Swimmer (Cheever): V2
Swimming Lessons (Mistry): V6

T
Tan, Amy
  Rules of the Game: V16
  Two Kinds: V9
Taylor, Peter
  A Spinster's Tale: V9
The Tell-Tale Heart (Poe): V4
A Temporary Matter (Lahiri): V19
Thank You Ma'm (Hughes): V29
That Evening Sun (Faulkner): V12
That in Aleppo Once . . . (Nabokov): V15
There Will Come Soft Rains (Bradbury): V1
The Things They Carried (O'Brien): V5
Think of England (Davies): V21
This Blessed House (Lahiri): V27
This Way for the Gas, Ladies and Gentlemen (Borowski): V13
Thomas, Piri
  Amigo Brothers: V28
Three Thanksgivings (Gilman): V18
Through the Tunnel (Lessing): V1
Thurber, James
  The Catbird Seat: V10
  The Night the Ghost Got In: V19
  The Secret Life of Walter Mitty: V1
Titanic *Survivors Found in Bermuda Triangle* (Butler): V22
To Build a Fire (London): V7
To Da-duh, in Memoriam (Marshall): V15
To Room Nineteen (Lessing): V20
Tolstaya, Tatyana
  Night: V14
Tolstoy, Leo
  The Death of Ivan Ilych: V5
  How Much Land Does a Man Need: V28
Toomer, Jean
  Blood-Burning Moon: V5
Town and Country Lovers (Gordimer): V14
The Toxic Donut (Bisson): V18
The Train from Rhodesia (Gordimer): V2

Trevor, William
  The News from Ireland: V10
Trick or Treat (Powell): V25
Twain, Mark
  The Celebrated Jumping Frog of Calaveras County: V1
  The Invalid's Story: V16
  Jim Baker's Blue Jay Yarn: V27
  The Man That Corrupted Hadleyburg: V7
  No. 44, The Mysterious Stranger: V21
Two Friends (de Maupassant): V28
Two Kinds (Tan): V9
Tyler, Anne
  Average Waves in Unprotected Waters: V17

U
The Ultimate Safari (Gordimer): V19
Unamuno, Miguel de
  Saint Emmanuel the Good, Martyr: V20
The Underground Gardens (Boyle): V19
Upadhyay, Samrat
  The Good Shopkeeper: V22
Updike, John
  A & P: V3
  The Slump: V19
The Use of Force (Williams): V27

V
Valenzuela, Luisa
  The Censors: V29
Vargas Llosa, Mario
  The Challenge: V14
The Veldt (Bradbury): V20
Vengeful Creditor (Achebe): V3
A Very Old Man with Enormous Wings (García Márquez): V6
Victory Over Japan (Gilchrist): V9
Vonnegut, Kurt
  Harrison Bergeron: V5

W
A Wagner Matinee (Cather): V27
Walbert, Kate
  Paris 1991: V24
Waldo (Heinlein): V7
Walker Brothers Cowboy (Munro): V13
Walker, Alice
  Everyday Use: V2
  Roselily: V11
The Wall (Sartre): V9
Wandering Willie's Tale (Scott): V10
Warren, Robert Penn
  Blackberry Winter: V8
Waters, Mary Yukari
  Aftermath: V22

The Wave (O'Flaherty): V5
The Way It Felt to Be Falling (Edwards): V18
The Way We Live Now (Sontag): V10
Wells, H. G.
  The Door in the Wall: V3
Welty, Eudora
  Moon Lake: V26
  Why I Live at the P.O.: V10
  A Worn Path: V2
Wetherell, W. D.
  The Bass, the River, and Sheila Mant: V28
Wetzel, Marlene Reed
  A Map of Tripoli, 1967: V17
Wharton, Edith
  Pomegranate Seed: V6
  Roman Fever: V7
What I Have Been Doing Lately (Kincaid): V5
What I Saw from Where I Stood (Silver): V25
What We Cannot Speak About We Must Pass Over in Silence (Wideman): V24
What We Talk About When We Talk About Love (Carver): V12
Where Are You Going, Where Have You Been? (Oates): V1
Where Have You Gone Charming Billy? (O'Brien): V29
Where I'm Calling From (Carver): V3
A White Heron (Jewett): V4
The White Horses of Vienna (Boyle): V10
Why I Live at the P.O. (Welty): V10
Wideman, John Edgar
  The Beginning of Homewood: V12
  Fever: V6
  What We Cannot Speak About We Must Pass Over in Silence: V24
Wilde, Oscar
  The Canterville Ghost: V7
Williams, Joy
  The Girls: V25
Williams, William Carlos
  The Use of Force: V27
Winter Dreams (Fitzgerald): V15
The Wives of the Dead (Hawthorne): V15
Wodehouse, Pelham Grenville
  Jeeves Takes Charge: V10
Wolf, Christa
  Exchanging Glances: V14
Wolfe, Thomas
  The Far and the Near: V18
Wolff, Tobias
  In the Garden of the North American Martyrs: V4
  Say Yes: V11
Woman Hollering Creek (Cisneros): V3

*The Woman Who Came at Six
    O'Clock* (García Márquez):
    V16
Women in Their Beds (Berriault):
    V11
Woolf, Virginia
    Kew Gardens: V12
    The New Dress: V4
A Worn Path (Welty): V2
Wright, Richard
    Big Black Good Man: V20
    Bright and Morning Star: V15
    The Man Who Lived Underground:
        V3
The Man Who Was Almost a Man:
    V9
The Writer in the Family
    (Doctorow): V27
Wunderkind (McCullers): V5

Y

Yamamoto, Hisaye
    The Eskimo Connection: V14
Yates, Richard
    The Canal: V24
The Yellow Wallpaper (Gilman): V1
Yellow Woman (Silko): V4

Yezierska, Anzia
    America and I: V15
Yiyun Li
    Immortality: V24
Yolen, Jane
    Suzy and Leah: V29
Yoshimoto, Banana
    Kitchen: V16
You're Ugly, Too (Moore): V19
Young Goodman Brown
    (Hawthorne): V1

Z

Zlateh the Goat (Singer): V27

Cumulative Nationality/Ethnicity Index

African American
Baldwin, James
   The Rockpile: V18
   Sonny's Blues: V2
Bambara, Toni Cade
   Blues Ain't No Mockin Bird: V4
   Gorilla, My Love: V21
   The Lesson: V12
   Raymond's Run: V7
Butler, Octavia
   Bloodchild: V6
Chesnutt, Charles Waddell
   The Goophered Grapevine: V26
   The Sheriff's Children: V11
Collier, Eugenia W.
   Marigolds: V28
Ellison, Ralph
   King of the Bingo Game: V1
Hughes, Langston
   The Blues I'm Playing: V7
   Slave on the Block: V4
   Thank You Ma'm: V29
Hurston, Zora Neale
   Conscience of the Court: V21
   The Eatonville Anthology: V1
   The Gilded Six-Bits: V11
   Spunk: V6
   Sweat: V19
Marshall, Paule
   To Da-duh, in Memoriam: V15
McPherson, James Alan
   Elbow Room: V23
Toomer, Jean
   Blood-Burning Moon: V5
Walker, Alice
   Everyday Use: V2
   Roselily: V11
Wideman, John Edgar
   The Beginning of Homewood: V12
   Fever: V6
   What We Cannot Speak About We Must Pass Over in Silence: V24
Wright, Richard
   Big Black Good Man: V20
   Bright and Morning Star: V15
   The Man Who Lived Underground: V3
   The Man Who Was Almost a Man: V9

American
Adams, Alice
   Greyhound People: V21
   The Last Lovely City: V14
Agüeros, Jack
   Dominoes: V13
Aiken, Conrad
   Silent Snow, Secret Snow: V8
Alexie, Sherman
   Because My Father Always Said He Was the Only Indian Who Saw Jimi Hendrix Play "The Star-Spangled Banner" at Woodstock: V18
Allen, Woody
   The Kugelmass Episode: V21
Alvarez, Julia
   Liberty: V27
Anderson, Sherwood
   Death in the Woods: V10
   Hands: V11
   Sophistication: V4
Asimov, Isaac
   Nightfall: V17
Baida, Peter
   A Nurse's Story: V25
Baldwin, James
   The Rockpile: V18
   Sonny's Blues: V2
Bambara, Toni Cade
   Blues Ain't No Mockin Bird: V4
   Gorilla, My Love: V21
   The Lesson: V12
   Raymond's Run: V7
Barrett, Andrea
   The English Pupil: V24
Barth, John
   Lost in the Funhouse: V6
Barthelme, Donald
   The Indian Uprising: V17
   Robert Kennedy Saved from Drowning: V3
Beattie, Ann
   Imagined Scenes: V20
   Janus: V9
Bellow, Saul
   Leaving the Yellow House: V12
   A Silver Dish: V22
Bender, Aimee
   The Rememberer: V25
Benet, Stephen Vincent
   An End to Dreams: V22
Berriault, Gina
   The Stone Boy: V7
   Women in Their Beds: V11
Bierce, Ambrose
   The Boarded Window: V9
   A Horseman in the Sky: V27
   An Occurrence at Owl Creek Bridge: V2

Cumulative Nationality/Ethnicity Index

Bisson, Terry
The Toxic Donut: V18
Bloom, Amy
Silver Water: V11
Bowles, Paul
The Eye: V17
Boyle, Kay
Astronomer's Wife: V13
Black Boy: V14
The White Horses of Vienna: V10
Boyle, T. Coraghessan
Stones in My Passway, Hellhound on My Trail: V13
The Underground Gardens: V19
Bradbury, Ray
The Golden Kite, the Silver Wind: V28
There Will Come Soft Rains: V1
The Veldt: V20
Brown, Jason
Animal Stories: V14
Butler, Octavia
Bloodchild: V6
Butler, Robert Olen
A Good Scent from a Strange Mountain: V11
Titanic *Survivors Found in Bermuda Triangle:* V22
Capote, Truman
A Christmas Memory: V2
Carver, Raymond
Cathedral: V6
Errand: V13
A Small, Good Thing: V23
What We Talk About When We Talk About Love: V12
Where I'm Calling From: V3
Cather, Willa
The Diamond Mine: V16
Neighbour Rosicky: V7
Paul's Case: V2
A Wagner Matinee: V27
Cheever, John
The Country Husband: V14
The Swimmer: V2
Chesnutt, Charles Waddell
The Goophered Grapevine: V26
The Sheriff's Children: V11
Chopin, Kate
Désirée's Baby: V13
A Point at Issue!: V17
The Storm: V26
The Story of an Hour: V2
Cisneros, Sandra
Eleven: V27
Little Miracles, Kept Promises: V13
Woman Hollering Creek: V3
Cofer, Judith Ortiz
American History: V27
Aunty Misery: V29
Collier, Eugenia W.
Marigolds: V28

Connell, Richard
The Most Dangerous Game: V1
Crane, Stephen
A Mystery of Heroism: V28
The Open Boat: V4
Davies, Peter Ho
Think of England: V21
Davis, Rebecca Harding
Life in the Iron Mills: V26
Diaz, Junot
The Sun, the Moon, the Stars: V20
Doctorow, E. L.
The Writer in the Family: V27
Doerr, Anthony
The Shell Collector: V25
Dubus, Andre
The Fat Girl: V10
Dybek, Stuart
Hot Ice: V23
Edwards, Kim
The Way It Felt to Be Falling: V18
Eisenberg, Deborah
Someone to Talk To: V24
Ellison, Harlan
A Boy and His Dog: V14
I Have No Mouth, and I Must Scream: V15
Jeffty Is Five: V13
"Repent, Harlequin!" Said the Ticktockman: V21
Ellison, Ralph
The Invisible Man, or Battle Royal: V11
King of the Bingo Game: V1
Erdrich, Louise
Fleur: V22
The Red Convertible: V14
Faulkner, William
Barn Burning: V5
The Bear: V2
Race at Morning: V27
A Rose for Emily: V6
That Evening Sun: V12
Ferrell, Carolyn
Proper Library: V23
Finney, Jack
Contents of a Dead Man's Pockets: V29
Fitzgerald, F. Scott
Babylon Revisited: V4
Crazy Sunday: V21
The Diamond as Big as the Ritz: V25
Winter Dreams: V15
Freeman, Mary E. Wilkins
A New England Nun: V8
Old Woman Magoun: V26
The Revolt of 'Mother': V4
Friedman, Bruce Jay
Brazzaville Teen-ager: V18
Gaines, Ernest
The Sky is Gray: V5

Gardner, John
Redemption: V8
Gibson, William
Johnny Mnemonic: V26
Gilchrist, Ellen
Victory Over Japan: V9
Gilman, Charlotte Perkins
Three Thanksgivings: V18
The Yellow Wallpaper: V1
Glasgow, Ellen
The Difference: V9
Glaspell, Susan
A Jury of Her Peers: V3
Harte, Bret
The Outcasts of Poker Flat: V3
Haslett, Adam
The Good Doctor: V24
Hawthorne, Nathaniel
The Minister's Black Veil: A Parable: V7
My Kinsman, Major Molineux: V11
The Wives of the Dead: V15
Young Goodman Brown: V1
Heinlein, Robert A.
Waldo: V7
Helprin, Mark
Perfection: V25
Hemingway, Ernest
A Clean, Well-Lighted Place: V9
Hills Like White Elephants: V6
In Another Country: V8
The Killers: V17
The Short Happy Life of Francis Macomber: V1
The Snows of Kilimanjaro: V11
Soldier's Home: V26
Hempel, Amy
In the Cemetery Where Al Jolson Is Buried: V2
Henry, O.
After Twenty Years: V27
The Gift of the Magi: V2
Mammon and the Archer: V18
Highsmith, Patricia
A Girl like Phyl: V25
Houston, Pam
The Best Girlfriend You Never Had: V17
Hughes, Langston
The Blues I'm Playing: V7
Slave on the Block: V4
Thank You Ma'm: V29
Hurst, James
The Scarlet Ibis: V23
Hurston, Zora Neale
Conscience of the Court: V21
The Eatonville Anthology: V1
The Gilded Six-Bits: V11
Spunk: V6
Sweat: V19

Irving, Washington
    The Devil and Tom Walker: V1
    The Legend of Sleepy Hollow: V8
    Rip Van Winkle: V16
Jackson, Shirley
    Charles: V27
    The Lottery: V1
James, Henry
    The Beast in the Jungle: V6
    The Jolly Corner: V9
Jewett, Sarah Orne
    A White Heron: V4
Johnson, Charles
    Menagerie, a Child's Fable: V16
Jones, Thom
    The Pugilist at Rest: V23
Julavits, Heidi
    Marry the One Who Gets There First: V23
Kincaid, Jamaica
    Girl: V7
    What I Have Been Doing Lately: V5
Kingston, Maxine Hong
    On Discovery: V3
Lahiri, Jhumpa
    A Temporary Matter: V19
    This Blessed House: V27
Lavin, Mary
    In the Middle of the Fields: V23
Le Guin, Ursula K.
    The Ones Who Walk Away from Omelas: V2
Lee, Don
    The Price of Eggs in China: V25
Leffland, Ella
    Last Courtesies: V24
London, Jack
    To Build a Fire: V7
Malamud, Bernard
    Black Is My Favorite Color: V16
    The First Seven Years: V13
    The Magic Barrel: V8
Marshall, Paule
    To Da-duh, in Memoriam: V15
Mason, Bobbie Ann
    Private Lies: V20
    Residents and Transients: V8
    Shiloh: V3
McCorkle, Jill
    Fish: V24
McCracken, Elizabeth
    Here's Your Hat What's Your Hurry: V25
McCullers, Carson
    Wunderkind: V5
McPherson, James Alan
    Elbow Room: V23
Melville, Herman
    Bartleby the Scrivener, A Tale of Wall Street: V3
Moore, Lorrie
    You're Ugly, Too: V19

Morales, Alejandro
    The Curing Woman: V19
Morrison, Toni
    Recitatif: V5
Mukherjee, Bharati
    The Management of Grief: V7
    The Middleman: V24
Nabokov, Vladimir
    A Guide to Berlin: V6
    That in Aleppo Once....: V15
O'Brien, Tim
    How to Tell a True War Story: V15
    The Things They Carried: V5
    Where Have You Gone Charming Billy?: V29
O'Connor, Flannery
    A Circle in the Fire: V19
    Everything That Rises Must Converge: V10
    A Good Man Is Hard to Find: V2
    The Life You Save May Be Your Own: V7
Oates, Joyce Carol
    Four Summers: V17
    How I Contemplated the World from the Detroit House of Correction and Began My Life Over Again: V8
    Where Are You Going, Where Have You Been?: V1
Ochsner, Gina
    The Necessary Grace to Fall: V24
Olsen, Tillie
    I Stand Here Ironing: V1
Orringer, Julie
    The Smoothest Way Is Full of Stones: V23
Ortiz, Simon J.
    The End of Old Horse: V22
Ozick, Cynthia
    The Pagan Rabbi: V12
    Rosa: V22
    The Shawl: V3
Packer, ZZ
    Brownies: V25
Paley, Grace
    Anxiety: V27
    A Conversation with My Father: V3
    The Long-Distance Runner: V20
Parker, Dortothy
    Big Blonde: V5
Phillips, Jayne Anne
    Souvenir: V4
Poe, Edgar Allan
    The Black Cat: V26
    The Cask of Amontillado: V7
    The Fall of the House of Usher: V2
    The Masque of the Red Death: V8
    The Pit and the Pendulum: V29
    The Purloined Letter: V16
    The Tell-Tale Heart: V4

Porter, Katherine Anne
    Flowering Judas: V8
    The Grave: V11
    He: V16
    Holiday: V23
    The Jilting of Granny Weatherall: V1
Powell, Padgett
    Trick or Treat: V25
Proulx, E. Annie
    Brokeback Mountain: V23
    The Half-Skinned Steer: V18
Rivera, Beatriz
    African Passions: V15
Rivera, Tomás
    The Harvest: V15
Roth, Philip
    The Conversion of the Jews: V18
    Goodbye, Columbus: V12
Salinger, J. D.
    A Perfect Day for Bananafish: V17
Salter, James
    Last Night: V25
Santos, Bienvenido
    Immigration Blues: V19
Saroyan, William
    Resurrection of a Life: V14
Sharma, Akhil
    If You Sing like That for Me: V21
Silko, Leslie Marmon
    Lullaby: V10
    The Man to Send Rain Clouds: V8
    Storyteller: V11
    Yellow Woman: V4
Silver, Marisa
    What I Saw from Where I Stood: V25
Singer, Isaac Bashevis
    Gimpel the Fool: V2
    Henne Fire: V16
    The Spinoza of Market Street: V12
    Zlateh the Goat: V27
Smiley, Jane
    Long Distance: V19
Sneve, Virginia Driving Hawk
    The Medicine Bag: V28
Sontag, Susan
    The Way We Live Now: V10
Stafford, Jean
    In the Zoo: V21
Stein, Gertrude
    Melanctha: V5
Steinbeck, John
    The Chrysanthemums: V6
    Flight: V3
    The Pearl: V22
Stockton, Frank R.
    The Lady, or the Tiger?: V3
Tan, Amy
    Rules of the Game: V16
    Two Kinds: V9
Taylor, Peter
    A Spinster's Tale: V9

Thomas, Piri
   Amigo Brothers: V28
Thurber, James
   The Catbird Seat: V10
   The Night the Ghost Got In: V19
   The Secret Life of Walter Mitty: V1
Toomer, Jean
   Blood-Burning Moon: V5
Twain, Mark
   The Celebrated Jumping Frog of Calaveras County: V1
   The Invalid's Story: V16
   Jim Baker's Blue Jay Yarn: V27
   The Man That Corrupted Hadleyburg: V7
   No. 44, The Mysterious Stranger: V21
Tyler, Anne
   Average Waves in Unprotected Waters: V17
Updike, John
   A & P: V3
   The Slump: V19
Vonnegut, Kurt
   Harrison Bergeron: V5
Walbert, Kate
   Paris 1991: V24
Walker, Alice
   Everyday Use: V2
   Roselily: V11
Warren, Robert Penn
   Blackberry Winter: V8
Waters, Mary Yukari
   Aftermath: V22
Welty, Eudora
   Moon Lake: V26
   Why I Live at the P.O.: V10
   A Worn Path: V2
Wetherell, W. D.
   The Bass, the River, and Sheila Mant: V28
Wetzel, Marlene Reed
   A Map of Tripoli, 1967: V17
Wharton, Edith
   Pomegranate Seed: V6
   Roman Fever: V7
Wideman, John Edgar
   The Beginning of Homewood: V12
   Fever: V6
   What We Cannot Speak About We Must Pass Over in Silence: V24
Williams, Joy
   The Girls: V25
Williams, William Carlos
   The Use of Force: V27
Wolfe, Thomas
   The Far and the Near: V18
Wolff, Tobias
   In the Garden of the North American Martyrs: V4
   Say Yes: V11
Wright, Richard
   Big Black Good Man: V20
   Bright and Morning Star: V15
   The Man Who Lived Underground: V3
   The Man Who Was Almost a Man: V9
Yamamoto, Hisaye
   The Eskimo Connection: V14
Yates, Richard
   The Canal: V24
Yezierska, Anzia
   America and I: V15
Yolen, Jane
   Suzy and Leah: V29

Antiguan
Kincaid, Jamaica
   Girl: V7
   What I Have Been Doing Lately: V5

Argentinian
Borges, Jorge Luis
   The Aleph: V17
   The Circular Ruins: V26
   The Garden of Forking Paths: V9
   Pierre Menard, Author of the Quixote: V4
Cortázar, Julio
   Axolotl: V3
   House Taken Over: V28
   The Pursuer: V20
Valenzuela, Luisa
   The Censors: V29

Asian American
Kingston, Maxine Hong
   On Discovery: V3
Lee, Don
   The Price of Eggs in China: V25
Tan, Amy
   Rules of the Game: V16
   Two Kinds: V9
Yamamoto, Hisaye
   The Eskimo Connection: V14

Australian
Malouf, David
   Great Day: V24

Austrian
Kafka, Franz
   A Hunger Artist: V7
   In the Penal Colony: V3
   The Metamorphosis: V12

Bosnian
Hemon, Aleksandar
   Islands: V22

Canadian
Atwood, Margaret
   Happy Endings: V13
   Rape Fantasies: V3
Bellow, Saul
   A Silver Dish: V22
Callaghan, Morley
   All the Years of Her Life: V19
Mistry, Rohinton
   Swimming Lessons: V6
Mukherjee, Bharati
   The Management of Grief: V7
   The Middleman: V24
Munro, Alice
   Boys and Girls: V5
   Day of the Butterfly: V28
   Meneseteung: V19
   Walker Brothers Cowboy: V13
Swan, Mary
   The Deep: V23

Chilean
Allende, Isabel
   And of Clay Are We Created: V11
   The Gold of Tomás Vargas: V16

Chinese
Jin, Ha
   In the Kindergarten: V17
Yiyun Li
   Immortality: V24

Colombian
García Márquez, Gabriel
   Eyes of a Blue Dog: V21
   The Handsomest Drowned Man in the World: V1
   A Very Old Man with Enormous Wings: V6
   The Woman Who Came at Six O'Clock: V16

Cuban
Calvino, Italo
   The Feathered Ogre: V12
Rivera, Beatriz
   African Passions: V15

Czech
Kafka, Franz
   A Hunger Artist: V7
   In the Penal Colony: V3
   The Metamorphosis: V12
Kundera, Milan
   The Hitchhiking Game: V10

Danish
Dinesen, Isak
   Babette's Feast: V20
   The Ring: V6

The Sailor-Boy's Tale: V13
Sorrow-Acre: V3
Høeg, Peter
   Journey into a Dark Heart: V18

Dominican

Alvarez, Julia
   Liberty: V27
Díaz, Junot
   The Sun, the Moon, the Stars: V20

Egyptian

El-Bisatie, Mohamed
   A Conversation from the Third Floor: V17
Mahfouz, Naguib
   Half a Day: V9

English

Barnes, Julian
   Melon: V24
Bates, H. E.
   The Daffodil Sky: V7
Bowen, Elizabeth
   The Demon Lover: V5
Burton, Richard
   The Arabian Nights: V21
Byatt, A. S.
   Art Work: V26
Carter, Angela
   The Bloody Chamber: V4
   The Erlking: V12
Clarke, Arthur C.
   Dog Star: V29
   "If I Forget Thee, O Earth…": V18
   The Star: V4
Conrad, Joseph
   Heart of Darkness: V12
   The Secret Sharer: V1
Davies, Peter Ho
   Think of England: V21
du Maurier, Daphne
   The Birds: V16
   Don't Look Now: V14
Eliot, George
   The Lifted Veil: V8
Far, Sui Sin
   Mrs. Spring Fragrance: V4
Galsworthy, John
   The Japanese Quince: V3
Greene, Graham
   The Destructors: V14
Jacobs, W. W.
   The Monkey's Paw: V2
Kipling, Rudyard
   Mowgli's Brothers: V22
   Mrs. Bathurst: V8
   Rikki-Tikki-Tavi: V21
Lahiri, Jhumpa
   A Temporary Matter: V19
   This Blessed House: V27
Lawrence, D. H.
   Odour of Chrysanthemums: V6
   The Rocking-Horse Winner: V2
Lessing, Doris
   Debbie and Julie: V12
   A Mild Attack of Locusts: V26
   Through the Tunnel: V1
   To Room Nineteen: V20
Maugham, W. Somerset
   The Fall of Edward Barnard: V17
Okri, Ben
   In the Shadow of War: V20
Orwell, George
   Shooting an Elephant: V4
Saki
   The Interlopers: V15
   The Open Window: V1
Sayers, Dorothy L.
   Suspicion: V12
Wells, H. G.
   The Door in the Wall: V3
Williams, William Carlos
   The Use of Force: V27
Wodehouse, Pelham Grenville
   Jeeves Takes Charge: V10
Woolf, Virginia
   Kew Gardens: V12
   The New Dress: V4

Eurasian

Far, Sui Sin
   Mrs. Spring Fragrance: V4

French

Balzac, Honore de
   La Grande Bretèche: V10
Beckett, Samuel
   Dante and the Lobster: V15
Camus, Albert
   The Guest: V4
Cortázar, Julio
   Axolotl: V3
   The Pursuer: V20
de Maupassant, Guy
   Boule de Suif: V21
   The Necklace: V4
   Two Friends: V28
Flaubert, Gustave
   A Simple Heart: V6
Merimee, Prosper
   Mateo Falcone: V8
Robbe-Grillet, Alain
   The Replacement: V15
Sartre, Jean-Paul
   The Wall: V9

German

Böll, Heinrich
   Christmas Not Just Once a Year: V20
Mann, Thomas
   Death in Venice: V9
   Disorder and Early Sorrow: V4
Wolf, Christa
   Exchanging Glances: V14

Haitian

Danticat, Edwidge
   Caroline's Wedding: V25
   Children of the Sea: V1

Hispanic American

Allende, Isabel
   And of Clay Are We Created: V11
   The Gold of Tomás Vargas: V16
Alvarez, Julia
   Liberty: V27
Cisneros, Sandra
   Eleven: V27
   Little Miracles, Kept Promises: V13
   Woman Hollering Creek: V3
Cofer, Judith Ortiz
   American History: V27
   Aunty Misery: V29
García Márquez, Gabriel
   Eyes of a Blue Dog: V21
   The Handsomest Drowned Man in the World: V1
   A Very Old Man with Enormous Wings: V6
   The Woman Who Came at Six O'Clock: V16
Morales, Alejandro
   The Curing Woman: V19
Rivera, Beatriz
   African Passions: V15
Rivera, Tomás
   The Harvest: V15
Thomas, Piri
   Amigo Brothers: V28

Indian

Chandra, Vikram
   Dharma: V16
Desai, Anita
   Games at Twilight: V28
Divakaruni, Chitra Banerjee
   Meeting Mrinal: V24
   Mrs. Dutta Writes a Letter: V18
Lahiri, Jhumpa
   A Temporary Matter: V19
   This Blessed House: V27
Manto, Saadat Hasan
   The Dog of Tithwal: V15
Mistry, Rohinton
   Swimming Lessons: V6
Mukherjee, Bharati
   The Management of Grief: V7
   The Middleman: V24

Naipaul, V. S.
   B. Wordsworth: V29
Narayan, R. K.
   Forty-Five a Month: V29
   A Horse and Two Goats: V5
Sharma, Akhil
   If You Sing like That for Me: V21

Irish
Beckett, Samuel
   Dante and the Lobster: V15
Bowen, Elizabeth
   A Day in the Dark: V22
   The Demon Lover: V5
Devlin, Anne
   Naming the Names: V17
Joyce, James
   Araby: V1
   The Dead: V6
   Eveline: V19
Lavin, Mary
   In the Middle of the Fields: V23
O'Connor, Frank
   Guests of the Nation: V5
O'Flaherty, Liam
   The Sniper: V20
   The Wave: V5
Trevor, William
   The News from Ireland: V10
Wilde, Oscar
   The Canterville Ghost: V7

Israeli
Hendel, Yehudit
   Small Change: V14

Italian
Boccaccio, Giovanni
   Federigo's Falcon: V28
Calvino, Italo
   The Feathered Ogre: V12

Japanese
Kawabata, Yasunari
   The Grasshopper and the Bell Cricket: V29
Mishima, Yukio
   Fountains in the Rain: V12
   Swaddling Clothes: V5
Murakami, Haruki
   The Elephant Vanishes: V23
Naoya, Shiga
   Han's Crime: V5
Waters, Mary Yukari
   Aftermath: V22
Yoshimoto, Banana
   Kitchen: V16

Jewish
Asimov, Isaac
   Nightfall: V17
Babel, Isaac
   My First Goose: V10
Bellow, Saul
   Leaving the Yellow House: V12
   A Silver Dish: V22
Berriault, Gina
   The Stone Boy: V7
   Women in Their Beds: V11
Doctorow, E. L.
   The Writer in the Family: V27
Eisenberg, Deborah
   Someone to Talk To: V24
Friedman, Bruce Jay
   Brazzaville Teen-ager: V18
Helprin, Mark
   Perfection: V25
Kafka, Franz
   A Hunger Artist: V7
   In the Penal Colony: V3
   The Metamorphosis: V12
Malamud, Bernard
   Black Is My Favorite Color: V16
   The First Seven Years: V13
   The Magic Barrel: V8
Orringer, Julie
   The Smoothest Way Is Full of Stones: V23
Ozick, Cynthia
   The Pagan Rabbi: V12
   Rosa: V22
   The Shawl: V3
Paley, Grace
   Anxiety: V27
   A Conversation with My Father: V3
   The Long-Distance Runner: V20
Roth, Philip
   The Conversion of the Jews: V18
   Goodbye, Columbus: V12
Salinger, J. D.
   A Perfect Day for Bananafish: V17
Singer, Isaac Bashevis
   Gimpel the Fool: V2
   Henne Fire: V16
   The Spinoza of Market Street: V12
   Zlateh the Goat: V27
Stein, Gertrude
   Melanctha: V5
Yolen, Jane
   Suzy and Leah: V29

Kenyan
Ogot, Grace
   The Green Leaves: V15

Mexican
Paz, Octavio
   My Life with the Wave: V13

Native American
Alexie, Sherman
   Because My Father Always Said He Was the Only Indian Who Saw Jimi Hendrix Play "The Star-Spangled Banner" at Woodstock: V18
Erdrich, Louise
   Fleur: V22
   The Red Convertible: V14
Ortiz, Simon J.
   The End of Old Horse: V22
Silko, Leslie Marmon
   Lullaby: V10
   The Man to Send Rain Clouds: V8
   Storyteller: V11
   Yellow Woman: V4
Sneve, Virginia Driving Hawk
   The Medicine Bag: V28

Nepalese
Upadhyay, Samrat
   The Good Shopkeeper: V22

New Zealander
Mansfield, Katherine
   Bliss: V10
   The Doll's House: V29
   The Garden Party: V8
   Marriage à la Mode: V11
   Miss Brill: V2
Sargeson, Frank
   A Great Day: V20

Nigerian
Achebe, Chinua
   Civil Peace: V13
   Vengeful Creditor: V3
Okri, Ben
   In the Shadow of War: V20

Peruvian
Vargas Llosa, Mario
   The Challenge: V14

Philippine
Santos, Bienvenido
   Immigration Blues: V19

Polish
Borowski, Tadeusz
   This Way for the Gas, Ladies and Gentlemen: V13
Conrad, Joseph
   Heart of Darkness: V12
   The Secret Sharer: V1
Singer, Isaac Bashevis
   Gimpel the Fool: V2
   Henne Fire: V16

The Spinoza of Market Street: V12
Zlateh the Goat: V27

Portuguese
Saramago, José
The Centaur: V23

Puerto Rican
Cofer, Judith Ortiz
American History: V27
Aunty Misery: V29
Williams, William Carlos
The Use of Force: V27

Russian
Asimov, Isaac
Nightfall: V17
Babel, Isaac
My First Goose: V10
Chekhov, Anton
The Darling: V13
Gooseberries: V14
Gusev: V26
The Lady with the Pet Dog: V5
A Problem: V29
Dostoevsky, Fyodor
The Grand Inquisitor: V8
Gogol, Nikolai
The Overcoat: V7
Nabokov, Vladimir
A Guide to Berlin: V6
That in Aleppo Once....: V15
Pushkin, Alexander
The Stationmaster: V9
Solzhenitsyn, Alexandr
One Day in the Life of Ivan Denisovich: V9
Tolstaya, Tatyana
Night: V14
Tolstoy, Leo
The Death of Ivan Ilych: V5
How Much Land Does a Man Need: V28
Yezierska, Anzia
America and I: V15

Scottish
Doyle, Arthur Conan
The Red-Headed League: V2
Scott, Sir Walter
Wandering Willie's Tale: V10
Spark, Muriel
The First Year of My Life: V28

South African
Gordimer, Nadine
Once Upon a Time: V28
Town and Country Lovers: V14
The Train from Rhodesia: V2
The Ultimate Safari: V19
Head, Bessie
Life: V13
Snapshots of a Wedding: V5
Kohler, Sheila
Africans: V18
Mphahlele, Es'kia (Ezekiel)
Mrs. Plum: V11
Paton, Alan
Ha'Penny: V29

Spanish
Unamuno, Miguel de
Saint Emmanuel the Good, Martyr: V20
Vargas Llosa, Mario
The Challenge: V14

Swedish
Gustafsson, Lars
Greatness Strikes Where It Pleases: V22
Lagerlöf, Selma
The Legend of the Christmas Rose: V18

Trinidadan
Naipaul, V. S.
B. Wordsworth: V29

Welsh
Dahl, Roald
Lamb to the Slaughter: V4

West Indian
Kincaid, Jamaica
Girl: V7
What I Have Been Doing Lately: V5

Subject/Theme Index

Numerical

1930s (Decade)
  B. Wordsworth: 28–29
1940s (Decade)
  B. Wordsworth: 28–29
1970s (Decade)
  The Censors: 51–52, 54, 56–57

A

Abandonment
  Dog Star: 85, 87
Acceptance
  Forty-Five a Month: 139
  Ha'penny: 176
Activism
  The Censors: 57
Adolescents
  Ha'penny: 173–174
Aesthetic values
  The Grasshopper and the Bell Cricket: 157–159, 159–165
Aesthetics
  The Doll's House: 113, 116
Affection
  Ha'penny: 173
African American culture
  Thank You, Ma'm: 253, 255, 257–258, 260–262, 264, 265–267
African American history
  Thank You, Ma'm: 260–262, 264
African American literature
  Thank You, Ma'm: 254, 260–262
Aggression (Psychology)
  The Doll's House: 105, 106
Alienation
  Contents of the Dead Man's Pocket: 71–73, 78
  The Grasshopper and the Bell Cricket: 167
Allegories
  Thank You, Ma'm: 253, 260, 264
Alliteration
  The Pit and the Pendulum: 195
Allusions
  The Grasshopper and the Bell Cricket: 158
  Where Have You Gone Charming Billy?: 292–294
Ambiguity
  Dog Star: 92
  Where Have You Gone Charming Billy?: 288
Ambition
  Contents of the Dead Man's Pocket: 67, 70, 73, 78
American culture
  Aunty Misery: 14–18
Anger
  The Doll's House: 104
  Forty-Five a Month: 126, 127, 135
Anguish. *See* Suffering
Animals
  Dog Star: 84–85, 88
Antiheroes
  Aunty Misery: 8
  A Problem: 217–218, 220
Antiwar sentiment. *See* Pacifism
Anxiety
  The Censors: 54, 64, 65
  Contents of the Dead Man's Pocket: 73
  The Doll's House: 121
Apartheid
  Ha'penny: 178–180, 181, 184–185, 185–186

Apocalypse
  The Pit and the Pendulum: 199
Arrogance
  Ha'penny: 178
  A Problem: 214
  Suzy and Leah: 243
Art
  The Grasshopper and the Bell Cricket: 159–165
Astronomy
  Dog Star: 90
Authority
  Ha'penny: 182
Autobiographical fiction
  Aunty Misery: 19–20
  Where Have You Gone Charming Billy?: 275
Autonomy
  The Doll's House: 116–117

B

Beauty
  B. Wordsworth: 33
  Contents of the Dead Man's Pocket: 70
  The Doll's House: 120
  The Grasshopper and the Bell Cricket: 157, 166
Belonging
  The Doll's House: 109
  Ha'penny: 175, 176

C

Caribbean culture
  B. Wordsworth: 22, 28–30, 34–35, 36–38

Subject/Theme Index

Censorship
    The Censors: 44, 45, 47, 53–56, 57–59
Change (Philosophy)
    Dog Star: 93
Characterization
    B. Wordsworth: 42
    The Doll's House: 111–113
    Forty-Five a Month: 133–136, 138
    The Grasshopper and the Bell Cricket: 168–169
    Ha'penny: 181–184
    A Problem: 211, 220, 227–228
    Suzy and Leah: 244
Charity
    Aunty Misery: 1, 3, 7, 12
Childhood
    The Doll's House: 121–123
Class conflict
    The Doll's House: 106, 108
Cold War
    Contents of the Dead Man's Pocket: 74, 77–78
Colonialism
    B. Wordsworth: 34, 35, 37, 38, 39–40, 41
Communications
    Ha'penny: 173–174
Community
    Forty-Five a Month: 139, 141
    Thank You, Ma'm: 253, 260, 263, 264
Compassion
    B. Wordsworth: 25, 33
    The Doll's House: 118
    Ha'penny: 171, 175, 176, 182
    Suzy and Leah: 234
Competition
    The Doll's House: 101, 103, 104, 106
Confidence
    Ha'penny: 181
Confinement
    Forty-Five a Month: 144
Conflict
    Contents of the Dead Man's Pocket: 73
Conformity
    The Doll's House: 106–107, 118
    The Grasshopper and the Bell Cricket: 151
Connectedness
    Contents of the Dead Man's Pocket: 71, 72, 73
    The Doll's House: 108, 112, 119
Consciousness
    The Doll's House: 118
    Forty-Five a Month: 140
Consolation
    B. Wordsworth: 33
Control (Psychology)
    The Censors: 65

Courage
    Contents of the Dead Man's Pocket: 71
    Ha'penny: 175
Creativity
    B. Wordsworth: 39–40
Crime
    A Problem: 216, 218, 220, 221
    Thank You, Ma'm: 256, 258–259, 263–264
Cruelty
    The Doll's House: 101, 103–104, 105, 106, 112
    The Pit and the Pendulum: 188, 192, 201, 202, 205–206
    Suzy and Leah: 230
Cultural identity
    B. Wordsworth: 39–40
    Suzy and Leah: 245
Culture
    B. Wordsworth: 34, 40–41
    Ha'penny: 174
    Suzy and Leah: 243

D

Danger
    The Censors: 45, 64, 65
    Contents of the Dead Man's Pocket: 69
    Where Have You Gone Charming Billy?: 284
Death
    Aunty Misery: 1, 3, 4, 5, 7, 10, 12
    The Doll's House: 116
    The Grasshopper and the Bell Cricket: 166–167
    Ha'penny: 176, 178
    The Pit and the Pendulum: 191, 194, 195, 202–203
    Where Have You Gone Charming Billy?: 284, 293
Deception
    Ha'penny: 184
Denial
    The Censors: 56
Despair
    The Pit and the Pendulum: 197
Desperation
    Dog Star: 92
    Forty-Five a Month: 135
Detachment
    Dog Star: 86
Deus ex machina
    The Pit and the Pendulum: 195, 199, 201, 207
Disapproval
    The Doll's House: 113
Disillusionment
    The Grasshopper and the Bell Cricket: 150

Domesticity
    The Doll's House: 118
Dreams
    Dog Star: 83, 84, 86, 87, 88
Dualism (Philosophy)
    The Doll's House: 122
Duty
    Forty-Five a Month: 127, 130
    A Problem: 215

E

Embarrassment
    Where Have You Gone Charming Billy?: 283
Emotions
    B. Wordsworth: 33
    The Censors: 64
    Dog Star: 85, 86
    Where Have You Gone Charming Billy?: 277, 283
Empathy
    The Doll's House: 104
    Ha'penny: 181
    Suzy and Leah: 234
Emptiness
    A Problem: 229
Epiphanies
    Contents of the Dead Man's Pocket: 67, 74, 78
    The Grasshopper and the Bell Cricket: 166
    Ha'penny: 177–178
Escapism
    Where Have You Gone Charming Billy?: 275
Exclusion
    The Doll's House: 101, 103, 107, 108, 118–119, 120
Exploration
    Dog Star: 88–89

F

Failure (Psychology)
    B. Wordsworth: 26, 35
    Ha'penny: 183
    Thank You, Ma'm: 263
    Where Have You Gone Charming Billy?: 283
Fairy tales
    Suzy and Leah: 250–252
Faith
    Ha'penny: 181
Familial love
    Forty-Five a Month: 124
    Ha'penny: 171, 176
    A Problem: 215
Family
    Forty-Five a Month: 139
    Ha'penny: 173, 174–175, 176
Family relationships
    Forty-Five a Month: 129–130

Fatalism
  The Doll's House: 113
Fate
  The Grasshopper and the Bell Cricket: 150
Father-child relationships
  Forty-Five a Month: 124, 126, 127, 130, 132–134, 135–136
Fatherhood
  Forty-Five a Month: 133
Fear
  The Censors: 62–65
  Contents of the Dead Man's Pocket: 69, 71, 79
  Dog Star: 85
  The Pit and the Pendulum: 198
  Suzy and Leah: 232, 234–236, 242
  Where Have You Gone Charming Billy?: 272–273, 274, 275–276, 282–283
Fear of death
  The Censors: 64
Figurative literature
  Thank You, Ma'm: 259–260, 263
Folk culture
  Aunty Misery: 1, 8–9, 10, 12
  Suzy and Leah: 249–250
Forgiveness
  Ha'penny: 175
Free will
  A Problem: 211, 213
Freedom
  The Pit and the Pendulum: 202
Friendship
  B. Wordsworth: 22, 24, 25
  Suzy and Leah: 233
Frustration
  Forty-Five a Month: 135, 144
Future
  Dog Star: 93–96, 97–98, 99
  The Grasshopper and the Bell Cricket: 158–159, 168
  Where Have You Gone Charming Billy?: 294

G

Generosity
  The Doll's House: 122
  Suzy and Leah: 230
German history
  Suzy and Leah: 237–239
Goodness
  The Grasshopper and the Bell Cricket: 150
Gothicism
  The Pit and the Pendulum: 188, 194–195, 197, 199
Gratitude
  Thank You, Ma'm: 256, 257
Greed
  Aunty Misery: 4

Grief
  Forty-Five a Month: 130
Guilt
  Contents of the Dead Man's Pocket: 69, 70
  Forty-Five a Month: 130

H

Happiness
  Forty-Five a Month: 136
  The Grasshopper and the Bell Cricket: 153
  Thank You, Ma'm: 257
Harlem Renaissance
  Thank You, Ma'm: 253, 260–262, 265
Hate
  The Doll's House: 118
  Suzy and Leah: 242
Helpfulness
  Thank You, Ma'm: 260, 263, 264
Heritage
  Suzy and Leah: 245
Heroes
  Aunty Misery: 8
Hispanic American literature
  Aunty Misery: 14–18
Hispanic Americans
  Aunty Misery: 14–18
Holocaust
  Suzy and Leah: 230, 238–239, 239–240, 245–249
Honesty
  A Problem: 225
Honor
  Aunty Misery: 4
  A Problem: 211, 213, 214, 216–217, 220
Hope
  The Doll's House: 112
  Forty-Five a Month: 136
  The Pit and the Pendulum: 191
  Where Have You Gone Charming Billy?: 284
Horror fiction
  The Pit and the Pendulum: 188, 202–203
Hostility
  The Doll's House: 112
Human condition
  Forty-Five a Month: 133, 137
  Ha'penny: 181
Human nature
  The Censors: 56–59
  The Pit and the Pendulum: 207
  A Problem: 222
Human potential
  Dog Star: 98
Humanism
  The Pit and the Pendulum: 201, 202

Humanity
  B. Wordsworth: 38
  The Pit and the Pendulum: 206
  Thank You, Ma'm: 260
Humiliation
  The Doll's House: 101, 104, 105, 112
Humor
  B. Wordsworth: 41
  Forty-Five a Month: 134–135, 138–139, 142

I

Identity
  Thank You, Ma'm: 257, 260, 265–267
Ignorance (Theory of knowledge)
  Suzy and Leah: 234
Illusion (Philosophy)
  B. Wordsworth: 25, 26
Imagery (Literature)
  The Grasshopper and the Bell Cricket: 146, 149, 151–152, 168
  The Pit and the Pendulum: 199, 201
  Thank You, Ma'm: 269
Imagination
  The Doll's House: 104, 107, 119, 121
  The Grasshopper and the Bell Cricket: 159
  Ha'penny: 174
  The Pit and the Pendulum: 207
  Where Have You Gone Charming Billy?: 293–294
Immigrant life
  Aunty Misery: 9
Immortality
  Aunty Misery: 1, 3, 6, 12
Imperialism
  Dog Star: 98–99
Imprisonment
  The Pit and the Pendulum: 203–207
Indian culture
  Forty-Five a Month: 133, 137, 144
Indian history
  Forty-Five a Month: 131
Individual responsibility
  A Problem: 211
Individualism
  The Grasshopper and the Bell Cricket: 150, 152
Inhumanity
  The Pit and the Pendulum: 206–207
Injustice
  The Doll's House: 120
  Forty-Five a Month: 132
  The Pit and the Pendulum: 193
Innocence
  B. Wordsworth: 41
  The Grasshopper and the Bell Cricket: 153, 168

Insanity. *See* Madness
Insensitivity
  The Doll's House: 104
Intelligence
  Contents of the Dead Man's Pocket: 71
  Dog Star: 86
Intuition
  The Grasshopper and the Bell Cricket: 169
Irony
  B. Wordsworth: 41
  The Censors: 50, 65
  Contents of the Dead Man's Pocket: 68
  Forty-Five a Month: 140–141
  Where Have You Gone Charming Billy?: 294
Isolation
  Contents of the Dead Man's Pocket: 73, 78
  The Pit and the Pendulum: 204, 205
  Where Have You Gone Charming Billy?: 284

J

Japanese culture
  The Grasshopper and the Bell Cricket: 146, 153–155, 157–159, 159–165
Jealousy
  The Doll's House: 101
  The Grasshopper and the Bell Cricket: 149
Jewish identity
  Suzy and Leah: 245
Jewish persecution
  Suzy and Leah: 230, 236–237
Joy
  The Doll's House: 112
  Forty-Five a Month: 135
  The Pit and the Pendulum: 191
  A Problem: 214, 216, 221
Justice
  A Problem: 211, 220

K

Kindness
  Aunty Misery: 3, 5, 12
  Contents of the Dead Man's Pocket: 70
  Suzy and Leah: 234
Knowledge
  The Doll's House: 119

L

Language and languages
  Aunty Misery: 8, 16–17, 19–21
  B. Wordsworth: 27
  Suzy and Leah: 242
  Thank You, Ma'm: 259, 263, 269

Latin American culture
  Aunty Misery: 8–9
  The Censors: 52–53
Latin American history
  The Censors: 44, 50–52, 54, 56–57, 59–62, 65–66
Life and death
  Contents of the Dead Man's Pocket: 71
Logic. *See* Rationality
Loneliness
  Aunty Misery: 1, 7
  Contents of the Dead Man's Pocket: 73, 78
  Ha'penny: 174, 176
Loss
  Dog Star: 92
  The Grasshopper and the Bell Cricket: 167
Love
  The Censors: 49–50
  Contents of the Dead Man's Pocket: 70, 71
  Dog Star: 87
  The Doll's House: 118
  The Grasshopper and the Bell Cricket: 149, 150–151, 168
  Ha'penny: 175
  Suzy and Leah: 233
Lower class
  The Doll's House: 101, 103, 106, 113
Lyricism
  The Grasshopper and the Bell Cricket: 156

M

Madness
  The Pit and the Pendulum: 193, 194, 201
Meaninglessness
  B. Wordsworth: 25
  Contents of the Dead Man's Pocket: 71, 78
  The Pit and the Pendulum: 198–199
Memory
  The Doll's House: 119–120
  Suzy and Leah: 247–248
Mental disorders
  A Problem: 220–222
Mercy
  A Problem: 213
Misery
  Aunty Misery: 3, 4, 6, 8, 12
Mistakes
  Ha'penny: 175, 176, 178, 183
  A Problem: 213, 214
Misunderstanding
  Suzy and Leah: 236
Modern life
  Contents of the Dead Man's Pocket: 71, 73, 78
Modernism (Literature)
  The Doll's House: 109–110

Moral ambiguity
  The Doll's House: 107–108
Morality
  Aunty Misery: 1
  The Doll's House: 120
  Ha'penny: 181
  A Problem: 223–224
Mortality
  Aunty Misery: 1, 5–6
Mortification. *See* Humiliation
Mother-child relationships
  Forty-Five a Month: 129–130
  Thank You, Ma'm: 256
Music
  B. Wordsworth: 37
  Thank You, Ma'm: 264–265
Mysticism
  Dog Star: 92

N

Narrators
  Aunty Misery: 4
  The Censors: 47, 50
  Dog Star: 85, 90
  The Doll's House: 108
  Ha'penny: 175, 178–180
Nature
  B. Wordsworth: 25, 28, 31–33
  The Grasshopper and the Bell Cricket: 159, 166
New Zealand history
  The Doll's House: 109
Northeastern United States
  Thank You, Ma'm: 253, 255, 257, 258, 260, 261, 262, 263
Northingness
  The Pit and the Pendulum: 201

O

Observation
  B. Wordsworth: 25–26, 32–33
  Ha'penny: 182, 183
Old age
  Aunty Misery: 1, 2, 4
Omniscience
  The Censors: 50
  The Doll's House: 108
Oppression (Politics)
  The Censors: 44, 50–52, 54, 56–57, 61, 65–66
  Ha'penny: 184–185
Outsiders
  The Doll's House: 112, 122

P

Pacifism
  Where Have You Gone Charming Billy?: 279, 281
Pain
  Where Have You Gone Charming Billy?: 294

Paradoxes
　Dog Star: 88
　Forty-Five a Month: 142
　The Grasshopper and the Bell Cricket: 169
Paranoia
　The Censors: 47–49, 55
Parapsychology
　Dog Star: 87–88
Parent-child relationships
　Forty-Five a Month: 129–130
Parody
　Where Have You Gone Charming Billy?: 294
Past
　The Grasshopper and the Bell Cricket: 168
Persecution
　The Censors: 65
　The Doll's House: 119
　The Pit and the Pendulum: 196–197, 201
Personal responsibility. *See* Individual responsibility
Personification
　Aunty Misery: 7–8
Perversity
　The Pit and the Pendulum: 197
Pessimism
　Forty-Five a Month: 134
Plots
　Contents of the Dead Man's Pocket: 73
Point of view (Literature)
　Aunty Misery: 8
　Forty-Five a Month: 130
　The Grasshopper and the Bell Cricket: 152
　The Pit and the Pendulum: 195–196
　A Problem: 218
　Where Have You Gone Charming Billy?: 278
Pointlessness. *See* Meaninglessness
Politics
　The Censors: 44, 65
Poverty
　B. Wordsworth: 24
　Ha'penny: 175
Power (Philosophy)
　The Censors: 65–66
Pragmatism
　Dog Star: 86
Prediction (Psychology)
　Dog Star: 93–96
　The Grasshopper and the Bell Cricket: 159
Prejudice
　Suzy and Leah: 240–243
Pretension
　B. Wordsworth: 35

Pride
　The Doll's House: 104, 108, 109
　Ha'penny: 174, 181, 183
　A Problem: 217
　Thank You, Ma'm: 256–257, 260, 265–267
Profundity
　The Grasshopper and the Bell Cricket: 158, 169
Progress
　B. Wordsworth: 28
　Dog Star: 94
Psychology
　The Pit and the Pendulum: 202
Punishment
　Aunty Misery: 4, 12
　The Pit and the Pendulum: 189–191, 192, 201, 203–207
　A Problem: 217
Purity
　The Grasshopper and the Bell Cricket: 150, 168

R

Race relations
　Ha'penny: 174, 180, 184–185
Rationality
　The Pit and the Pendulum: 192, 198
Realism (Cultural movement)
　Forty-Five a Month: 130–131
　A Problem: 218–219
Reality
　B. Wordsworth: 34, 35
　The Doll's House: 113, 117, 121
Reason
　The Pit and the Pendulum: 194
Rebellion
　The Doll's House: 107–108, 119, 120
Rebirth
　The Pit and the Pendulum: 205
Redemption
　The Pit and the Pendulum: 198, 205
Reflection
　The Pit and the Pendulum: 205
Reform
　The Pit and the Pendulum: 204–206
Refugees
　Suzy and Leah: 232, 233, 239, 240–242
Regret
　Ha'penny: 174, 175
Rehabilitation. *See* Reform
Rejection. *See* Exclusion
Religion
　Forty-Five a Month: 139
　The Pit and the Pendulum: 199–202

Remorse
　Ha'penny: 184
Repetition
　The Pit and the Pendulum: 195
Rescue
　The Pit and the Pendulum: 188, 192, 199, 201
Resentment
　The Doll's House: 120
Responsibility
　Ha'penny: 176
　Thank You, Ma'm: 260
Rest
　Aunty Misery: 12
Revelation
　Contents of the Dead Man's Pocket: 70
Reverence for life
　B. Wordsworth: 26
Rivalry
　The Doll's House: 101, 103, 120
Romanticism
　The Pit and the Pendulum: 199, 200–201
Russian history
　A Problem: 218

S

Sadism
　The Pit and the Pendulum: 193–194
Sadness
　Dog Star: 85
　Forty-Five a Month: 126, 127, 136
Salvation
　The Pit and the Pendulum: 194, 199, 202, 207
Scapegoating
　The Doll's House: 117
Science
　Dog Star: 88–89, 93, 96–97, 97–98
Science fiction
　Contents of the Dead Man's Pocket: 80
　Dog Star: 82, 89–90, 97–98, 98–99
Self confidence
　Ha'penny: 183
　Thank You, Ma'm: 260
Self control
　Where Have You Gone Charming Billy?: 276, 284
Self identity
　B. Wordsworth: 34
Self image
　B. Wordsworth: 31
　Ha'penny: 183
Self knowledge
　Forty-Five a Month: 137, 139
Self righteousness. *See* Arrogance

Subject/Theme Index

Self worth
   Thank You, Ma'm: 257
Selfishness
   Aunty Misery: 4
   The Doll's House: 104
   A Problem: 222
Selflessness
   Dog Star: 87
Sensory perception
   The Pit and the Pendulum: 192–193, 205
   A Problem: 228–229
Sentimentality
   B. Wordsworth: 39, 41
Setting (Literature)
   B. Wordsworth: 42
   Suzy and Leah: 237
Sex roles
   The Doll's House: 118–119
Shame
   The Doll's House: 105
   Ha'penny: 174
   A Problem: 214
Similes
   The Pit and the Pendulum: 195–196
Simplicity
   The Grasshopper and the Bell Cricket: 158, 169
Sincerity
   Forty-Five a Month: 137
Skepticism
   Dog Star: 90
Social class
   The Doll's House: 101, 103, 105–107, 112, 113, 117–121
   Forty-Five a Month: 131
Social identity
   The Doll's House: 119
Social values
   The Doll's House: 101
Sociopathy. *See* Mental disorders
Sorrow
   Forty-Five a Month: 127
South African culture
   Ha'penny: 178–180
Space exploration
   Dog Star: 90–91, 93–96, 98–99
Spanish history
   The Pit and the Pendulum: 193, 196–197
Stereotypes (Psychology)
   The Doll's House: 118
Stoicism
   A Problem: 215–216
Storytelling
   Forty-Five a Month: 142
   Where Have You Gone Charming Billy?: 276–277, 287, 288–290
Strength
   Ha'penny: 175
   Thank You, Ma'm: 256, 260
Struggle
   Forty-Five a Month: 124
Success
   Contents of the Dead Man's Pocket: 71, 75
Suffering
   Aunty Misery: 3
   Forty-Five a Month: 127, 136
   The Pit and the Pendulum: 198
Superiority
   Suzy and Leah: 243
Supernatural
   Dog Star: 85
Surrealism
   Where Have You Gone Charming Billy?: 281
Survival
   Ha'penny: 176
   The Pit and the Pendulum: 192, 197
   Where Have You Gone Charming Billy?: 284
Suspense
   Contents of the Dead Man's Pocket: 67, 73, 79
Suspicion
   The Censors: 47
Symbolism
   B. Wordsworth: 28
   The Doll's House: 108, 113–116, 119, 120
   The Grasshopper and the Bell Cricket: 146, 152–153, 158, 159–165, 168
   Ha'penny: 173
   Thank You, Ma'm: 263, 265
   Where Have You Gone Charming Billy?: 283
Sympathy
   Aunty Misery: 12
   The Doll's House: 118–119
   Ha'penny: 176, 181
   The Pit and the Pendulum: 206–207

T

Technology
   Dog Star: 93, 97–98
Technology and civilization
   Dog Star: 82, 93–95
Terror
   The Pit and the Pendulum: 193, 195, 204–205
Time
   Contents of the Dead Man's Pocket: 76–78
   Dog Star: 93–94
Time travel
   Contents of the Dead Man's Pocket: 80
Torture. *See* Cruelty; Sadism
Totalitarianism
   The Censors: 58–59
Tradition
   Forty-Five a Month: 139
   The Grasshopper and the Bell Cricket: 168
Tranquility
   The Grasshopper and the Bell Cricket: 158
Transcendence
   The Doll's House: 121
Transcendentalism
   The Pit and the Pendulum: 201
Transformation
   Aunty Misery: 5
   The Censors: 44, 46–47, 50, 55
   The Doll's House: 112, 121
   Ha'penny: 181–184
   Where Have You Gone Charming Billy?: 293–294
Translation
   The Grasshopper and the Bell Cricket: 152–153, 167
Triumph
   The Doll's House: 105, 113
   Thank You, Ma'm: 257, 265
Trust
   Forty-Five a Month: 136
   Suzy and Leah: 230, 241
   Thank You, Ma'm: 257
Truth
   The Censors: 65
   The Grasshopper and the Bell Cricket: 166
   Where Have You Gone Charming Billy?: 278, 289

U

Understanding
   The Doll's House: 118
   Ha'penny: 175, 183
   Suzy and Leah: 243
Unity
   The Grasshopper and the Bell Cricket: 159–165
Universality
   The Grasshopper and the Bell Cricket: 165
Upper class
   The Doll's House: 106
Urban life
   Thank You, Ma'm: 255, 263

V

Values (Philosophy)
   Contents of the Dead Man's Pocket: 67, 69, 70, 71, 78
Vietnam War, 1959-1975
   Where Have You Gone Charming Billy?: 272, 274, 275, 279–281, 282–284, 285, 290–292, 293–295
Violence
   The Censors: 59–62
   The Pit and the Pendulum: 205

Vision
The Doll's House: 121

W

Wars
The Censors: 59–62
Suzy and Leah: 230, 232, 234
Where Have You Gone Charming Billy?: 272, 275, 284, 288–289, 290–292

Weakness
Thank You, Ma'm: 260

Wealth
Forty-Five a Month: 142

Will to live. *See* Survival

Work
Contents of the Dead Man's Pocket: 69, 70
Forty-Five a Month: 124, 126, 127, 129, 135

Working class
Forty-Five a Month: 124, 127, 129, 130, 131, 144

World War II, 1939-1945
Forty-Five a Month: 131
Suzy and Leah: 230, 231, 236–237, 238–239

Y

Youth
A Problem: 211